GLENIN—

initiated by her father into the secrets of Malerrisi magic, she craves the power and position she believes are her rightful heritage—and she will do anything and use anyo...

fostered u... ... a treacherous attack des... ...devote herself to championing the underground resistance force known as the Rising—and to protecting the younger sister whose very existence is the most closely guarded secret in their world.

CAILET—

destined from birth to become the Mage Guardians' last, best hope, she will grow to young womanhood ignorant of her abilities and her destiny—and will prevail only if she can overcome the spell barriers long ago imposed upon her magic.

Bound together by ties of their ancient Blood Line, torn asunder by the magical intrigues and political ambitions of their elders, these three Mageborn sisters will fight their own private war, and the victors will determine whether or not the Wild Magic and the Wraithenbeasts are once again loosed to wreak havoc upon their world.

EXILES

VOLUME 1:
The Ruins of Ambrai

MELANIE RAWN

DAW BOOKS, INC.
DONALD A. WOLLHEIM, FOUNDER
375 Hudson Street, New York, NY 10014

ELIZABETH R. WOLLHEIM
SHEILA E. GILBERT
PUBLISHERS

First Paperback Printing, November 1995

18   17   16

DAW TRADEMARK REGISTERED
U.S. PAT. OFF. AND FOREIGN COUNTRIES
—MARCA REGISTRADA.
HECHO EN U.S.A.

PRINTED IN THE U.S.A.

For my grandmother,
Stella Alderson
1885–1976

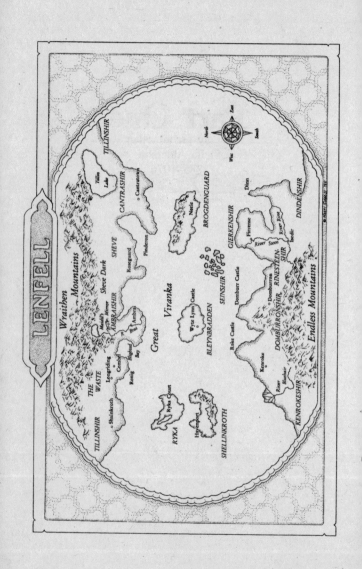

Part One

942–967

Collan

1

He remembered the wind.

Skittering in the far reaches of his mind were other memories: warmth, and light, and snug belonging in some cheerful firelit room where a woman sang. Had these images been useful, he would have remembered them more clearly. What he knew in this life, he knew because it helped him survive.

Thus the wind. Sudden and brutal, it shoved him down an embankment into a muddy ditch, where he lay bruised and stunned while it howled down the gorge like a wounded wild animal. He tried to move, to get up and run, but was helplessly pinned. When the wind died as quickly as it had been born, he crawled out of the ditch bleeding.

Years after, he learned that while he sprawled in the mud, flattened by the wind, brigands set fire to his mother's house. She died along with whoever else had been within—his sisters and brothers, perhaps. He didn't remember.

More years passed before he learned that no one else had felt the wind.

He went back a long time later, and saw how it might have happened. Maslach Gorge formed a natural funnel and some freakish shift in pressure could have forced air down it. As he walked back to where another house was built around the stern chimney and another woman lived with her children, he wondered why he remembered no root-torn trees, no leaf-stripped bushes. Surely so amazingly powerful a wind had felled other things besides him.

Well, a child that age would not have noticed. He could not have said exactly how old he was when it happened. Four, he guessed—perhaps a little less, certainly no more. Eventually he chose the Feast of St. Lirance, first day and first full moon of the year, as his Birthingday. The Lady of the Winds had saved his life.

He didn't remember why he'd wandered so far from the house. Neither did he remember the winter cold that must have been, or the time he certainly spent stumbling across ice-crusted grainfields into the forest. He had a clear memory of the cartroad, however, for it, too, had been of use to him. The rutted track had led him to where people were: people who fed him, warmed him, kept him alive, and at length sold him as a slave.

Groggy with cold and exposure, he went to the people willingly. One of them picked him up from the dirt road and settled him on her hip. She wore a plain silver bracelet set with blue onyx. If he squinted through his lashes, the pale gold sliver in the stone looked like a candle flame. He trusted the wearer because he recognized the bracelet: it had been worn by the singer beside the fire. He snuggled against the woman wearing silver and onyx, and fell asleep. It was only when he woke the next morning inside an iron cage within a dark wagon that he began to be afraid.

They fed him, tended his cuts and bruises and frostbitten toes, and kept him in the cage as they traveled. He was given clean if threadbare clothes, woolen socks too big for his feet, and a chipped clay jug to relieve himself in. The outside world vanished for him. He knew only the wooden slats of the rocking wagon, the crates and carpets piled within, and the cold iron cage.

It had been made for an animal—barely big enough to crouch in, or sit in with knees to chin. Tufts of fur snarled in the hinges. He plucked them out carefully and rolled them into a ball to feel the softness. The bronze fur smelled of cat, and for some reason that comforted him. A shred of silvery claw had been left behind as well, torn on a hinge. He remembered the fur and the claw because they'd told him something important. No feline, for all its strength and cunning, could reason even as simply as a four-year-old child. Hinges went with doors. Doors had latches that made them open. The cage had hinges, so there must be a door with a latch—and he could open it.

So he did.

The hinges squealed betrayal. The wagon jerked to a stop. He tumbled through the cage door just as the woman wearing the armlet appeared in a sudden sun-blaze rectangle at the back of the wagon. She slapped him hard enough to split his lip, stuffed him back into the cage, and tied his ankles to the iron with thick, prickly twine.

The people never talked to him. To each other, yes, and they even sang sometimes after the wagon had stopped and it got colder and darker. But they never talked to him. He wondered, years later, why they'd been so circumspect around so small a child. Surely they couldn't have feared he would identify them to the authorities. There *were* no authorities in the Tillinshir backlands where brigand wagons rolled. He didn't understand about the cage, either. How far could a little boy run before they caught him?

He was halfway through his life before he knew the reason for the cage was the armlet, and what it had told the brigands about the woman they'd killed, the woman who had been his mother.

He never knew how many days he spent in the cage. Forty, perhaps fifty, to judge by the distance from Maslach Gorge to Scraller's Fief. One day he was dragged out by the scruff to stand on shaky legs before a tall, skeletal man whose black eyes were the coldest he had ever seen—but not the coldest he would ever see in his life.

He remembered how Flornat the Slavemaster had looked him over with those eyes like chips of ice-sheened obsidian, and paid for his new acquisition in real gold. This memory had nothing to do with survival; it burned with shame in his mind. Even at four years old, he understood that the man had traded a shiny yellow circle for him, the way he'd once seen someone—he didn't know who—trade a brass cutpiece for a copper kettle. A price had been put on him: a cost for a commodity, a statement of his worth, a definition of his value by someone who saw him only as a live, healthy, usable item for sale.

He told her about it once, about how it had made him feel like a thing instead of a person. The revelation came after a shouting match caused by the innocent gift of a silver earring. She hadn't been trying to buy him—but she hadn't understood his revulsion, either. After he calmed to rationality, he realized it was probably the blue onyx dangling from the silver circle that had ignited memory and temper. She'd done her best to make it up to him, but how could a Lady of Blood, born to pride and privilege, understand the unique humiliation of knowing you had been sold?

His owner was Scraller Pelleris. Scraller was that vanishing rarity, a man in complete charge of his family's estate. He had inherited by virtue of having outlived every single one of his relations. Virtue, of course, had nothing to do with it. By the time Scraller acquired a certain very young copper-haired slave, talk had long since died down about the fortuitous (for Scraller) deaths of three sisters, four aunts, and five cousins. His mother had drawn her final breath approximately one minute after Scraller drew his first. It was said she had a premonition of what her son would become and, as she died, muttered, "I choose to join the Wraiths." Presumably this was preferable to staying around to watch her lastborn's career. Before Scraller was twenty, she had welcomed all her relatives into the Wraithenwood, probably with an *I told you so.*

Pelleris Fief became known by Scraller's nickname. In the local parlance of The Waste, a "scrall" was the clever and invariably criminal act of making something out of nothing. Despite its connotation, Scraller used it with pride. Many people—including his own late, unlamented family—had called him worse.

Scraller's Fief was a massive stone warren built atop a substantial pile of rock in The Waste. A climb of three hundred and eighty-six steps—one for each day of the year—past two barbicans bristling with guards led through iron gates to a courtyard scarcely wide enough to circle a wagon in. The main tower was a gigantic construction of gray granite roofed in blue tile. From the courtyard, the effect was that of a face topped by a thatch of blue hair. A broad balcony and overhanging stone canopy, both studded with iron spikes, formed toothy half-open jaws. Above were two tall windows like great pale eyes reflecting the sun. The nose was the banner dangling between the windows, crimson edged in brown and lacking a device. The First Tier Pelleris family had neither money nor influence to purchase their way into Blood status. They owned much of The Waste, but as the name implied, that wasn't saying much. Scraller's ambition was to swell his coffers and create a court worthy of notice by First Councillor Avira Anniyas, so he could ride through his gates into his courtyard and behold his castle grinning down at him with a golden galazhi galloping across its crimson nose like a wart on the nose of a drunkard.

When Scraller was twenty-eight, the death of the last notable opponent of the First Councillor's power gave him the opportunity he needed. In exchange for a percentage off the top, Scraller was given complete control over all economic activities in The Waste. Again, this wasn't saying much. But Scraller hadn't earned his nickname in vain. He undertook a massive drainage project—never mind that the noxious siphoning of The Waste Water polluted the sea into which it spilled for five years afterward. Dried salts scraped off sun-baked land revealed soil perfect for concrete—never mind that half of it was adulterated with those same salts, and tended to crumble after ten years. Scraller made a luscious profit, even after Avira Anniyas took her share.

So it was that Scraller was elevated to the status of Blood. Golden galazhi minced not only across the courtyard banner but on every door, carpet, chair, fireplace hood, pillow slip, and napkin in the castle. (The launderers said that its execution in gold embroidery on Scraller's crimson underdrawers was especially fine.) The First Councillor was generous to those who served her well. Besides, The Waste was so far from Ryka Court that she didn't much care what happened there so long as her percentage kept rolling in, the concrete for her own building projects was top grade, and the rebellious Mage Guardians found no succor at the Fief.

In the Council Year 942, Scraller's latest acquisition had no knowledge of economic or political matters. He knew that he had been safe, and now was not; that he'd been sold, and did not like it. And when Scraller's mark—the inevitable galazhi—was painfully etched in yellow ink on his right shoulder, he knew it was all real. The warm hearth and the woman's soft singing were gone forever.

Eventually he was found to be quick of mind, so he was given the rudiments of an education—just enough to make him a more useful servant to his master. He was taught to read and write, and showed an aptitude for mathematics. But it was several years before his real value became apparent.

He was a musician born. To him, notes on a page were like numbers in a column that added up to a sum—or a song.

Cool, precise, with only one right answer, music and mathematics were the same to him.

It took a Bard silenced forever and a Lady of ancient Blood to teach him that they weren't the same at all.

Scraller had no need of another steward to count his wealth, his slaves, or his crimes. What he did require, for the elevation of his court to elegance, was a truly gifted musician. And this was what became of the boy spared from death by the wind.

He retained precisely one possession from the time before the wind and the brigands: his name. Though he was given a new one, he stubbornly clung to the only thing he owned. So, after a few weeks of slaps when he did not answer to the new name, they shrugged and gave in. He was only a little boy, after all. He couldn't be expected to learn as swiftly as an older child. And what did it matter what he was called, as long as he caused no trouble?

It was the first of Collan's victories, and for many years was his last.

2

His first summer at Scraller's Fief, Collan was judged deft enough with his big, long-fingered hands to leave Cradle Quarters and start justifying the gold the Slavemaster had paid for him. At first he was assigned to the kitchens. Simple tasks: shelling nuts, washing vegetables, plucking fowl. Scraller's household numbered well over three thousand, and feeding so many was a lot of work. Col also spent many hours on the hearth treadmills, walking or running as the cooks demanded to turn spits over the fire. He remembered little of that time except exhaustion and heat. But never in his adult life would he enter a kitchen in castle or cottage without feeling slightly nauseated.

Although he couldn't have spent more than a few hours each day at this exhausting task, it seemed his life consisted solely of treadmill and pallet for years. The work toughened him at an early age—which was part of the process. Toughening the body while breaking the spirit was the rule.

They underestimated Collan badly.

One morning—he must have been about six—he was liberated forever from the kitchen. For reasons he neither knew nor cared about, the galazhi had fawned early that year. He and many others were sent to the high pastures to help the herders. It was new spring and incredibly cold, the crusty snow patched with blood like a gory quilt. He learned swiftly that by reaching into a doe's body, first to tug the fawn out and then for the afterbirth, he could keep his hands warm. Twins were best; he could plunge his fingers thrice into hot slick blood and mucus, and keep from freezing just that much longer. He gave thanks whenever the Chief Herdsman announced that a doe he tended bore twins.

The rest of him didn't fare as well. His socks were more holes than knitting; nothing but his thick hair protected his head from cold, acidic rain. By the third day his nose was streaming, his hair was falling out in clumps, his scalp was burned, and he reeled with fever. He was returned to the Fief and banished to the infirmary. When the fever broke he pretended a slow recovery. This deception led to his being taught to read and write.

It happened because Flornat the Slavemaster had whipped Taguare the Bookmaster to within a sliver of his life, for what offense Collan never learned. Taguare occupied the other sickbed before the hearth, and as they recuperated together, the Bookmaster discovered a mind worth training.

Not that Col *knew* anything. But to distract himself from his pain, Taguare told his own favorite stories, and found an appreciative, perceptive audience. He encouraged questions, trying to get a feel for Col's wits. They were promising. Taguare asked for and received permission to add him to the small class of slave children deemed teachable. Now the boy spent his mornings running errands for various functionaries, his afternoons in the animal pens, and the time between dinner and bed in a tiny schoolroom with four other boys and six girls under Taguare's tutelage. All were older than he, and far ahead of him in learning. But Collan rewarded the Bookmaster's instincts. A talent for words and numbers was revealed. And he was always hungry for more.

He learned reading, writing, and ciphering; basic geography (limited to The Waste, which no slave of Scraller's ever left); what botany was applicable to a notoriously barren land; more than he ever wanted to know about galazhi; and multitudes of tales about Wraithenbeasts. These included no practical advice for escape—no one lived past a Sighting—and were intended solely as a warning; the threat of Wraithenbeasts kept slaves pent better than guarded walls.

There were two other subjects to the curriculum: religion and music. Had this been brought to Scraller's notice, he would have pronounced both a total waste of time for slaves. But Taguare taught his pupils the Saintly Calendar because he was a sincerely religious man, and he taught them to sing because he loved music. Collan was an indifferent student of religion (except for selecting his Birthingday in tribute to the only Saint who'd ever helped him; the others seemed pretty useless), but he soaked up music like a garden drinks clean spring rain.

When his gift became evident, his morning duties were halved so he could be taught by Carlon the Lutenist—an average talent, but a kindly man. This worthy begged Flornat to add study with him to Col's day, and after a demonstration of the boy's raw talent, the Slavemaster heeded his request. Scraller was informed, and approved the plan. He kept Bookmaster and Lutenist as proof of the elegance of his court. He was, of course, both illiterate and tone-deaf.

Collan's life settled into a different routine. He still worked ten hours of the day's fifteen, but at least he was liberated from the kitchen. Rising by torchlight at Fourth, he ate in the quarters, then washed and presented himself for three hours of delivering messages among Scraller's stewards, who had not deigned to address each other in person anytime during the last fifteen years. Their universal illhumor was expressed in various ways on Collan's person until Taguare reminded them that the boy—particularly his hands—was Scraller's property. They didn't hit him after that, though they often looked as if they'd like to.

From Half-Seventh to Ninth, he had music lessons with Carlon. Half an hour for another meal and a brief rest—Scraller was solicitous of his property—and a long afternoon of tending animals was followed by dinner at Twelfth and study with Taguare. Then, at Fourteenth, he would curl into a blanket and sleep like the dead until the bell clamored its demand five hours later. He never dreamed.

It bothered him to come to his lessons with the Bookmaster stinking of the sty. Only Scraller's personal servants were allowed to bathe more than once a week; in The

Waste, water was rationed at the best of times. Along with an aversion to kitchens, Collan took with him from Scraller's a lifelong hatred of being dirty. And he could never bear to eat pork—not because he'd conceived any fondness for pigs, but because he could never forget their stench.

As his time with Carlon the Lutenist came in the morning, his hands and clothes were always clean for his music lessons—his escape into the cool, pure world of notes that summed into songs. He learned ballads and rounds, hymns and chanteys and lays, and as the strings obeyed the growing mastery of his fingers the words made strange and delightful pictures in his mind. Though he was unsure what *love* and *desire* and other odd words meant, any sound that accompanied music must by mere association tell of wondrous things.

Taguare didn't reveal, and Carlon never mentioned, what awaited him if Scraller found his performance pleasing—or, more to the point, if Scraller's guests found him so. His voice was clear and fine. To keep it intact, at the first sign of maturity Collan would be castrated.

Taguare said nothing because of his guilt; if he hadn't discovered the boy's quickness of mind, the gift for music would have gone unnoticed as well. But Collan's only real joy came from the very thing that would unman him. One day, before it was too late, Taguare promised himself he would warn the boy to "lose" his voice.

Carlon said nothing because it was to him a perfectly natural state. What was the loss, compared to privileged position? He himself had never minded.

In Collan's ninth year—more or less—he first sang before Scraller's Court. For the occasion he was washed by bath attendants for the first time in his life. The scrubbing left his dark skin an angry red, but not a single flea or louse survived. He was then dressed in a motley of cast-off clothing. The plain brown shirt, from a page recently promoted to footman's crimson, billowed around Collan's skinny chest and arms. The shortness of the same page's brown trousers had been disguised by sewing a row of slightly snagged crimson silk ribbon at the hems, thus decently covering his ankles. (In fact, Scraller liked the effect so much he ordered the same addition to the livery of all his pages. It was the first time Collan set a fashion, but not the last.)

The longvest, hemmed to proper knee-length, belonged to Carlon, unworn since his girth had expanded beyond the seemly closure of the buttons. A gaudy creation of turquoise flame-stitching on thick yellow tapestry silk, the padded shoulders extended a full five inches beyond the boy's arms. Stiff, heavy, and so big on him that one glance in a mirror told him he looked ridiculous, the longvest's effect on his appearance irked him mightily—so much so that he forgot to be nervous about his performance.

At least the slippers fit. They were soft new doeskin, and Taguare's gift, made by his friend, the cobbler. "You're like a Senison puppy," the Bookmaster told Collan, smiling. "You'll grow into those hands and feet of yours, Col—and top me by at least a head when you're finished!"

The slippers were the latest absurdity in style, with elongated, pointed toes. But they were new, and his, and so comfortable that he didn't mind too much that they made his feet look even bigger than they were.

He would remember the slippers and the longvest for reasons having nothing to do with survival. Cobblers and tailors would moan in later years when they saw Col coming, for his insistence on perfect fit took hours. After he began his infamous and highly lucrative career, he would never again wear any garment that had belonged to another man. His clothing from head to foot was his and his alone. And he never wore a coif if he could possibly avoid it.

They had virulent arguments about that, he and she. It completely escaped him how a woman who could exert every particle of her formidable powers to the overthrow of the existing government—and the social order that nurtured it—could be so utterly dedicated to the preservation of some of its customs. *"Bred in the bone,"* the old man told him once, with a mild shrug. *"You must remember Who She is, my lad."*

The hated coif was a woven hood that fit tightly to the skull and fastened at the throat with buttons or, in the case of Bloods and the First and Second Tiers, sigil pins. Modesty dictated that every male's head be hidden from brow to nape. Not a single hair could show. Saints knew how many ladies would be scandalized—not to mention Scraller, who according to rumor was balding—if even a slave-child appeared with his head uncovered.

So when they dressed him before his first appearance at

court, he submitted to a garish crimson coif. After strict inspection, Flornat the Slavemaster pronounced him fit to be seen by polite company. Collan was taken to a dark hallway off the banquet room to await summons.

Carlon had lent his own second-best lute for the occasion. Col clutched it by the neck as if strangling a snake. He was sweating in the heavy longvest and his scalp itched even though he knew there wasn't a live bug on him anywhere. This alone was an odd enough sensation to start his nerves twanging. But worse was the coif: a bad fit around his abundance of curling coppery hair, the throat strap made it difficult to breathe.

So he took the fool thing off.

No one came to fetch him; a door simply opened and a hand waved him into the banquet hall. He'd never been inside it in his life—indeed, never been in any of the public rooms, only the kitchen and work chambers and the warren of halls. Collan was as startled by the place as the people within were by him.

Not a hall; a cavern, cut into living rock and festooned with the banners of Scraller's guests—and dozens of inevitable galazhi. Long tables formed a hollow square around a blazing bonfire. Dogs and cats slunk and scrabbled underfoot, their yowls underscoring the babble of three hundred diners. All the ladies wore bright gowns and elaborate headpieces, some so fantastically antennaed as to imperil their neighbors' eyesight. All the men were formally robed and coifed, though some dared to leave their top shirt buttons undone to hint at a furred chest.

Scraller himself was one of these. His crimson coif was embroidered with his cherished sigil and decorated with jewels, and his robes were properly concealing as befitted a modest male, but his shirt was open to the breastbone. The wiry black hair thus revealed had bits of dinner clinging to it.

Collan strode forward and made his bows to the ladies and then to Scraller, as instructed. He ran a nervous hand through his hair as he straightened up. This unconscious emphasis on his uncovered state did not amuse Scraller. He drew breath to condemn the boy—then noted that all but the stuffiest of his female guests had begun to smile.

He scrutinized his possession. A handsome child, no doubt of it: manly, despite his scant years; well-formed, for all his scrawniness. The ladies were imagining him fifteen inches of height, ten years of age, and eighty pounds of solid muscle into the future. And Scraller saw not just their admiration but his own profit gleaming in their gazes.

"Sing, boy," he commanded, and eased his spindly form back in a chair with galazhi-horn finials.

Anyone less proud—or more perceptive—would have sought to please his audience. Collan never made music except to please himself. Carlon deplored this fault in presentation ("Sing to *me,* not the empty air! Look in my eyes!"), but had to admit that the boy's aloofness was intriguing. Collan never sang *for* anyone; he merely allowed others to listen, not much caring if they did or not. In his whole life he found only two people he truly wanted to sing for—and when he did, the music was such to win and break hearts.

But because those two persons did not yet exist in his life—indeed, one of them was not yet born—Col played and sang for his own satisfaction. His very indifference to audience reaction made him a triumph that night and at every banquet thereafter for the next four years. Word spread that Scraller possessed a slave with a voice and fingers inspired by St. Velenne herself. Offers were made, all of which Scraller turned down. Col was excused from running errands, tending animals, and any work that might damage his hands or expose his voice to dangerous weather. His sole daily occupations were music practice with Carlon, lessons with Taguare, and acting as Scraller's personal page.

Oddly, he missed the animals, even though it was nice not to stink anymore. Pigs and galazhi and horses demanded nothing of him but friendly care. He definitely did not miss scurrying around the maze of the fief at the whim of ill-tempered stewards.

He purely loathed the hours he spent with Scraller.

There was no physical abuse. He was much too precious a commodity. Scraller's taste didn't run to boys, anyway. But his very praise and attention, growing more lavish as Col's worth grew, became emotional abuse. When it was found that the boy spoke as pleasingly as he sang, the abuse became intellectual as well. In those four years, he read aloud more excruciatingly bad poetry, more blazingly false history, and more disgustingly turgid pornography than anyone should have to endure in four lifetimes.

Collan knew the poems were dreadful because Minstrel's

instinct told him so. He knew the history was untrue because Taguare had let him read secret copies of treatises from the time before the First Councillor. (Besides, one of Scraller's own books had Avira Anniyas winning the Battle of Domburron *and* killing Warrior Mage Lirsa Bekke with her own hands, and everyone knew the two events had occurred on the same day a thousand miles apart.)

The pornography simply nauseated him. Scraller, however, found it vastly romantic. He would slump back in his chair, tears of enjoyment trickling fat and slow down his cheeks as the Humble Whomever yielded his tense and trembling virginity to the erotic mastery of the Blooded Lady Thus-and-so, who then proceeded to fuck him blind. Such forthright terms were never used, however; Scraller preferred his titillations couched in coy and cloying euphemisms. He savored descriptive metaphor: "burning monolith of manhood" and "fierce craving cavern of womanly desire" brought gusting sighs of sensuous delight. He adored scenes of bondage, but only if silken cords were specified. The word "rape" made him scowl horribly—even if it was obvious that rape was precisely what the story was about. By the fifth night of reading this offal, Col knew that if he vocalized the Humble Whomever's impassioned grunts and the Blooded Lady Thus-and-so's litany of You'll-love-what-I'm-going-to-do-to-you-you-handsome-peasant-brute one more time, he'd vomit.

But he learned how to keep saying the words with the feeling Scraller deemed appropriate, while his mind disconnected and roamed elsewhere.

Scraller's evening entertainment might have given him a warped view of sex. That it did not was due to his own good sense and his observations in Quarters. Slaves were forbidden marriage, but they could bedshare with whomever they pleased. Collan learned that such activities sometimes occasioned soft laughter, sometimes muffled weeping, and occasionally bruises. But the persons he liked and respected, whichever sex they bedded, were always attended to their blankets by laughter. Nobody in Scraller's books ever laughed, except in virile triumph or cruel mockery—or perhaps it was cruel triumph and virile mockery, he'd stopped paying attention long since.

Truly told, he came to feel rather sorry for Scraller. Forbidden by a sense of his own exalted worth from besmirching himself with slave women, adamantly refusing to marry and thus put his wealth into a woman's hands, he had two choices: his female guests, if they felt so inclined, and his books.

It was years before Col actually tagged those books with the term *pornography,* and others would have blinked in surprise at what he considered obscene—mild indeed by some standards. But Col never reversed his opinion of Scraller's bedtime stories, for later experience taught him that bedding *was* obscene unless he lay down with a woman's glad laughter as well as the woman herself.

Love was something he wouldn't understand until he was past thirty years old, and the irony of it was that he *was* the Humble Whomever, and she *was* the Blooded Lady Thus-and-So. But oh, how they laughed. . . .

Once she stopped wanting to murder him.

3

During his fourth summer as Scraller's page, the old man came for him.

Col was dawdling on his way up the privy stair, hoping Scraller was in a mood for a few songs tonight. Anything but another Humble Whomever.

"Well? Hurry up, boy!" Flornat ordered from the upper landing. "You can't mean to keep him waiting!"

Sighing, Col trudged up the steps and down the hall to the bedchambers. There were three, in use as Scraller's temper of the evening dictated. One was painted as an evocation of the tangled swamps of Rokemarsh, all wild green shapes and fantastical flowers, with nudes of all descriptions cavorting in the mud. Another room mimicked the stark landscape of Caitiri's Hearth, glittering black mountains topped by silvery snow; Collan always felt rather sorry for the nudes on these walls, coupling on sharp obsidian and hard white ice. He hadn't been inside the third bedchamber in quite some time, for it had been redecorated. It was to this room that Flornat led him now.

Col's jaw dropped open. He'd seen woodcuts of Firrense

in some of Taguare's books, and the new decor was obviously intended to recreate the most famous walls of the Painted City. All the Saints were here, all right, just as in the picture that ran all the way down the walls of one of Firrense's streets. But as casual as Collan was about religion, he saw this room as blasphemy. The sight of hundreds of Saints disporting themselves in giggling ecstacy was designed to shock, and succeeded.

Scraller lounged on a massive pile of silk and velvet cushions, his head moving slowly on his skinny neck like a lizard's as he regarded his latest triumph. Every so often he brought a tankard of wine to his lips, drank, and let his arm sink languidly back to the pillows. Flornat whispered an announcement of Col's arrival from the door, then beat a retreat.

There was a wooden lectern over in the corner, where St. Venkelos the Judge was wrapping himself in St. Lirance Cloudchaser's long, wild black hair. Col turned away before he could discern what else the pair were doing, and fixed his gaze on the open book of erotic poems.

He read in his usual style, detaching himself from the words while giving each one salacious emphasis. So remote was his mind from the text that it took him twenty minutes to realize that each poem was an obscene parody of a hymn to a specific Saint. Quick glances at Scraller showed him that the man turned to the appropriate portrait with each title. Col read on, and stopped looking, stopped thinking, stopped hearing the sound of his own voice.

All at once he heard a drawn-out moan. His tongue tripped over a rhyme as his eyes shifted involuntarily to where Scraller sprawled on the cushions. His robes were parted, his naked body exposed to the lamplight, and his hands were very, very busy.

"Come—here—"

Collan sidled away from the lectern, his foot catching on its legs. It and he and the book toppled to the floor. Scrambling to his feet, he made for the door. Locked.

"*Here*, boy," Scraller panted, as if ordering one of his hunting hounds.

Col pounded at the face of St. Gelenis First Daughter painted on the wooden door, fought with the gilded galazhi-horn handle the Saint smirked at: it was St. Chevasto's cock.

"Not that one—mine," Scraller said from just behind him.

His shoulder was seized, he was spun around to face his owner. "I'll kill you first," he snarled.

The door slammed into his back, knocking him into Scraller. They both went down in a sprawl. Collan rolled off him at once and leaped to his feet.

"Time to go, I think," the old man said, appearing like a Wraith—or at least what Col had heard about Wraiths, for he'd never seen one and hoped he never would. The old man was old even then, his face as wrinkled as the shell of a black walnut and approximately the same color, his shoulder-length white hair uncovered by a coif and as startling as the intense green of his eyes. These were very large and fine, shaded by a bristle of black lashes and formidable snowy eyebrows. Col stared at him, unable to move, not knowing whether to be more astonished by his sudden appearance, his black face, or his words.

"Well? Come on, then. Or are you deaf?" The old man's voice was deep and rich with sarcasm. "A deaf musician— what a prodigy. But I'm convinced you heard me. Come along now, we'll pack your things. In case you hadn't noticed, I'm taking you out of here for good and all."

"Huh?" Col managed.

"Nothing to pack, I suppose. Well, that's the way of things, isn't it? You don't even own your own skin. Filthy institution, slavery. Come along, then, just as you are. I don't have much time to waste on you."

And with that, he turned and left the room.

Scraller moaned once, stirred, and went limp again on the carpet. Col glanced down at him, then delivered a hard kick to his scrawny chest before galloping through the door after the old man.

"Hurry up!" The black-cloaked apparition was striding down the hallway. "Spells of Silence and Invisibility aren't easy, even for me."

"Invis—" Col caught up with him. "You're a *Mage!*"

"Warrior Mage Guardian and First Sword Gorynel Desse, at your service—at least until we're out of this sewer. I've only an hour's lease on this spell and it has to get us nearly to Combel." He didn't look at Col during this speech, not even when the boy blurted in surprise at the notion of riding to Combel in an hour.

"Are you crazy?"

"It's been so speculated," Gorynel Desse admitted. "If you ever get to know me, you can judge for yourself."

"There aren't any more Mages. They all died at Ambrai."

"Just because Avira Anniyas says so?" He snorted. "Walk your shoes a little faster, please. I don't have all night and escapes are tricky at best."

Collan balked, planting his shoes firmly on the stone floor. A slave had tried to escape last autumn. His head, carefully preserved in a glass jar, still adorned the entrance to Quarters.

The Mage stopped and swung around, white hair and black cloak swirling. "To address your self-evident objections in order—I spelled Scraller just now. He won't wake up until Seventh tomorrow. Secondly, we won't be caught unless you persist in your present imitation of a potted plum tree. Thirdly, my reason for doing this is irrelevant at the moment, but your reason for accompanying me is quite urgent. An ongoing argument between Taguare the Bookmaster and Flornat the Slavemaster was resolved this morning. The latter won. You are officially thirteen years old, and if you want to get any older with all parts intact, hurry up."

Collan approached, still suspicious but with a cold knot tightening in his stomach. "What d'you mean?"

"I mean," said Gorynel Desse, "that tomorrow you're scheduled for the gelder's knife to preserve that charming voice of yours, and unless you want to spend the rest of your life as a eunuch, *move!*"

Col moved.

A little over an hour later they were indeed at the outskirts of Combel, taken there by their own feet and Gorynel Desse's magic.

"It's a difficult spell," the old man said as they tramped through the dark, moonless night. "Curiously, it won't work on horses. Something about them absolutely refuses to believe that a mile isn't really a mile. They're very stupid or very clever, I can't decide which. Folding isn't something just any Mage can do, either, and it's doubly difficult on top of Invisibility. But it so happens that I—"

"I thought you said there was a spell of silence, too."

"Oh, I got rid of that one at the bottom of all those tedious steps. Now, what was I saying before you so rudely interrupted? Ah, yes. I was bragging about my Folding spell. A fortunate thing I'm so good at it, too, for it's saved my moderately useful life several times."

"How?" Collan asked.

"Stories best saved for another occasion. As for the spell . . . there's a simpler version whereby a Mage compresses objects for easy transport—or concealment. It's something like folding a napkin. This particular application takes more power and concentration. I'm Folding pieces of land, you see."

Oddly enough, Collan did. Sort of. "So one step equals two or three?"

"More like ten or twelve. I've never worked out the exact ratio. But I understand you're mathematically inclined. Why don't you puzzle it out for me?"

He knew how far it was from the castle to Combel. He'd been there with Carlon this spring, buying strings and songbooks at St. Sirrala's Fair. By the time they arrived at the outlying mansions of the (relatively) wealthy, he reported his calculations.

"One to eight-point-six-five-two?" the Mage repeated. "Only that? Hmm. Well, I'm getting old, I suppose. Wish I'd been able to find the Ladder rumored to be at Scraller's." Not pausing to explain this latest incomprehensibility, he strode down a cobbled lane lined with columned and tiled homes. "She'll be waiting for us, I hope," he muttered. "I do hate having to talk my way in past the servants. One tends to look so disreputable on these occasions, and now that Warrior Regimentals are dangerous—"

"I thought we were invisible."

"Do I look like a Mage Captal to you, boy?" Desse responded sharply. "Five spells simultaneously while juggling three daggers and an onion—" He snorted. "How our Leninor loved to show off! But every use of power is paid for. And I'm going to be paying for this night until spring thaw!"

"Who's waiting for us?" Suddenly Collan grabbed the old man's sleeve. "Did you buy me from Scraller for somebody else?"

"Great Saints, no!" He pulled Col out from under the jittery luminescence of a street lamp. "You listen to me, boy. You're free now. The only person who can sell you is yourself, because the only person who can place a value on your worth is *you*. Now, some sell themselves for money, or wine, or an advantageous marriage. Others count their coin in power of various sorts. But people who are truly worth something can't be bought. Do you understand?"

He understood one thing perfectly. "If you didn't buy me, and I'm free, then I'm gone."

"And how far do you think you'd get?"

"Pretty far by morning," Col retorted.

"Which is when they'll miss you—and a whole night is quite sufficient for the trip to Combel on foot." He eyed the boy narrowly. "There are no horses missing at the castle. This is the only logical destination—not even an idiot ignorant lute player would head out into The Waste, especially unmounted. Therefore this is the first place they'll look. You have no identification disk, no horse, no refuge, and no friends. How does that all add up in the mathematics of survival?"

Collan was silent.

"All right, then. Come on. It's just down this lane. You'll like Lady Lilen. She's an old friend of mine. She's not a Mage, but her grandmother was, and—well, I daresay you'll hear the family history sometime or other."

The Lady herself met them at the back door of her mansion. She was small, comfortably plump, and only a few years younger than Gorynel Desse as far as Collan could judge. She ushered them through a short hallway to the kitchen, where steaming stew and thick slices of crusty bread smeared with soft cheese waited. Collan pounced. Folded road or not, it had been a long walk.

"The itinerant herbalist again?" Lady Lilen inquired teasingly of the Mage, twitching his robe with dainty, well-kept fingers. "Gorsha, dearest, you're *so* much more impressive as the Unnamed Lady's Questing Father!"

"Which requires baggage suitable to a Blooded's comforts, and I travel fast and light these days. Is that a Cantrashir red I smell mulling on the hearth?"

They conferred quietly beside the fire, sipping hot spiced wine. Col ignored them for the most part, seated on a tall stool at the butcher block, devouring the stew. He was pleasantly drowsy by the time he finished, but now that his belly wasn't rumbling he was curious enough to look and listen again.

Copper pots and iron skillets hung from hooks on the hearth's stone hood and around the massive stove. The smoke-stained yellow bricks of the oven were accented by inset blue and green tiles, which repeated above the two sinks and across the spotless floor. This was a *nice* kitchen. Collan felt strangely safe here, and attributed it to the lack of a treadmill near the hearth.

"He can't stay," he heard Lady Lilen say, and the sensation of security vanished. "I would've sent you a message if I'd known where you were—and if you'd given me a little more time. Yes, I know these things are always sudden, but you have a positive gift for last-instant arrangements, Gorsha!"

"What's the trouble?"

"What it always is these days. Ostinhold isn't living up to Scraller's expectations. His agents have been by almost every day for a week, going over my account books. I keep telling them it's impossible to produce the herds he envisions, but he seems to think galazhi breed—"

"—like Ostins!" the old man teased, and Lady Lilen blushed. "Sorry, my lovely, but you walked right into that one! I understand your difficulty with Scraller, but what better place for the boy than in a house already being investigated? Hide in plain sight is a Mage Guardian's best—"

"You *don't* understand. Scraller himself is coming tomorrow. And I've learned that Anniyas is encouraging him."

Collan slid off the stool.

"Stay where you are," said the Mage without looking at him.

"You *are* crazy!" he burst out. "I'm getting out of here! Now! Tonight!"

Desse relaxed back in his chair. "Go right ahead."

Collan started for the hall. Each step brought him approximately a quarter of an inch nearer the doorway. He kept at it, stubbornly staring at the opening that seemed to mock him. It didn't retreat into the distance or anything so obvious. He just couldn't get to it.

"Spells," said the Mage, sipping wine, "can be reversed."

Glowering, Col returned to his stool.

"If you're quite finished, Guardian Desse," sniffed Lady Lilen, "let me tell you what I've worked out."

At dawn, after a restless night in a real bed with feather pillows and soft scented sheets—the first ever in his life—Collan was put on a horse. This animal was attached to a cart, one of many going to Renig with four of the Ostin daughters. They were to stay with an aunt during the Shir capital's autumn social season, a journey planned for months. The bored inspector who scrawled his signature on travel documents yawned as he waved them on their way.

The addition of one copper-haired boy to the entourage was not remarked upon. By Half-Seventh the alarm regarding an escaped slave reached Combel from Scraller's Fief, but no one connected the extra child with the runaway. Lady Lilen, already under scrutiny, certainly would never be so foolish as to assist the escapee and bring Scraller's wrath down on her head.

As it happened, Collan himself removed all danger from the Ostin Blood. He was not with the young ladies when they arrived at Renig. The second night of the trip, he stole a horse—a feisty little mare, not the druge gelding that pulled the cart—and galloped away.

Desse was furious when he heard of it. But by that time his attention was engaged by other matters and he was too busy hiding himself to worry about finding someone else. And if the boy was too stupid to know when people were trying to help him—well, so much for him.

For the time being.

4

Collan was on his own from Applefall to Snow Sparrow: six long, scary weeks. He worked for food and lodging when he could, stole when he had to, and nearly got caught a hundred times. Taguare had called him not yet thirteen; truly told, early the next year he would be fourteen, and in the manner of boys that age grew over an inch in those six weeks alone. Scanty, irregular meals melted what flesh he had right off him and by the first of Candleweek Col could have believably claimed close kinship with any scarecrow in the fields around Cantrashir, except that the scarecrows looked better fed.

How he made it as far as Cantrashir was a tale he decided to save for his grandchildren—after some judicious editing. He did compose a ballad about the journey through the Dead

White Forest and the Wraithenwood, but the song was only in his head. As identifiable by his musical skills as he was by the mark inked into his shoulder, he hid all his schooling. A pity, too, for there was plenty of money to be made as a roving singer, or assisting semi-literate merchants with their account books, or reading to wealthy ladies. But he would have had to explain how such learning had ever come to an orphaned peasant boy, and instinct told him the best disguise was to appear half-witted. He became rather good at it.

She teased him about it, of course. "Do the Village Idiot, darling," she'd say in a coaxing sweet voice that made him gnash his teeth. But he taught her—sometimes by main force—the art of dissembling behind one mask or another, and several times it kept her stubborn head firmly attached to her lovely neck. Her lovely *stiff* neck.

Impossible woman.

By the time Gorynel Desse appeared again, several important events had occurred. None of them impressed Collan when the old man finally found him, wearing his fool's face and juggling whatever the crowd tossed at him in the middle of the Lesser Cantratown Market. The deal was that if he could keep up to seven items aloft for five whole minutes, they were his. And wasn't it kind of the Saints, people murmured—while three plums, a small wine bottle, and two leaf-wrapped pasties orbited the imbecile face—to give the child such quickness of hand and eye to make up for an obviously deficient set of wits?

The shabby old Warrior Mage stepped to the front of the crowd and threw a box of matches into the succession. Col reacted as if the things had lit spontaneously. Bottle shattered, fruit went *splat,* and thick yellow leaves parted to send pasties flying into the ample chest of a matron who strenuously objected to having her gown besmirched. Col proved his feet were as fast as his hands, and ran like hell.

Desse caught up with him on the edge of town and bought him dinner—the least the old man could do after ruining his prospective meal—and Col nodded complete disinterest in whatever the Mage said.

"If you'd bothered to stick around this autumn, you would've learned a few things. For instance—Lady Maichen Ambrai divorced her husband, left her home, and took her younger daughter with her. No one knows where they've gone."

"Uh-huh," said Col, and kept eating.

"The elder daughter took her father's name of Feiran and is with him at Ryka Court."

"Mmm," said Col, taking a swig of ale.

"Auvry Feiran is high in Anniyas' favor nowadays, recently promoted to Commandant of the Council Guard."

"Pass the green pepper," said Col.

"He's efficient, too. Ambrai was destroyed, as you heard at Scraller's."

"Too bad."

"And you're going to go live with a friend of mine."

Col stuffed the last of the bread into his pocket and drained ale down his throat. "Nice talking to you, old man."

"Sit down," the Mage said.

He pulled a bored face. "Are you going to Fold the floor again?"

"No." Desse calmly buttered a slice of bread. "I didn't Fold it the last time. You really must learn a little something about magic—at least enough to call a spell by its right name."

And in spite of Col's infuriated efforts to the contrary, his knees bent and his rump connected with the bench once more.

"That one, for instance," the Mage went on, "is commonly called Stay Put."

Collan capitulated with poor grace. "Look, what's all this to do with me? I don't know any of these people and I don't want to. I'm doing fine as I am."

Eloquent green eyes below wildly tufted brows took in every detail of his patched clothes, skinny frame, and lank, dirty, uncoifed hair.

"It'll get better once the big merchant fairs start," Collan defended. "St. Tirreiz's Day I made so many cutpieces I jingled!"

"Congratulations. Did I mention yet that my friend's name is Falundir?"

Wild wolves couldn't have parted Col from his seat now. Falundir was a name pronounced with deepest reverence by Carlon the Lutenist. The last true Bard, Falundir scorned to perform anyone's work but his own. His were the most glorious songs Col had ever learned. He had never played them for Scraller's guests; they were too pure to be sullied by such an audience.

"I heard he was dead," Collan whispered.

"You think *everyone* is dead. Geridon's Golden Stones, you're as gullible as Anniyas. Falundir is as much alive as I am, and marginally more willing to tolerate your company."

"Me?" It came out as a squeak; his voice was changing apace, mouse one minute and lion the next. He cherished his vocal insecurities devotedly—for obvious reasons. Reminded of the debt he owed the old man, aware of the incredible favor about to be done him, Collan drew a steadying breath and placed his hands flat on the table. He was shocked at how rough and raggedy they'd become: the dirty, awkward hands of a laborer, not a musician. It seemed forever since he'd picked up a lute. Fear clotted in his throat.

"You'll remember how to play," Desse assured him, correctly reading his panicky face. "Do you accept?"

"Yes!"

The old man grunted. "First intelligent thing you've ever said."

Col wasn't listening. "But why would he want—?"

"Because he needs your help. And don't ever tell him I said so."

"I don't understand."

"The First Councillor is a rather demanding critic."

"What the hell does *that* mean?"

Flatly: "The sentiments expressed in one of Falundir's songs were judged inappropriate. Avira Anniyas personally sliced the tendons at the base of each finger, then cut out his tongue."

The ale soured in Col's stomach and he thought he was going to be sick. "Blessed St. Velenne," he breathed.

"Make yourself useful, and Falundir might consider keeping you past winter. I assured him you'd work your stones off—stones you still have, thanks to me."

"I remember," Collan grated.

"Good." The old man stretched and stood up. "Remember it as well the next time you consider a midnight flit from people who're trying to help you."

But he never even considered leaving Falundir.

The house in the depths of Sheve Dark was simple bordering on primitive: a roof and a hearth and a room. Much of Col's time and energy was expended in hunting, fishing, tending vegetables, and otherwise keeping them both fed. There was no society but their own. Gorynel Desse's annual visits were brief. The winters were green ice, the summers green fire. But work was familiar and solitude soothing. The hearth warmed him in winter and forest ponds cooled him in summer. And the finest Bard who ever lived made of Collan his hands and eventually his voice.

It made him dizzy whenever he thought about it.

Falundir was a small, frail, testy man of forty or so, blue-eyed, beak-nosed, and nearly as black-skinned as Gorynel Desse. Most folk, Col had learned on his travels, were pretty much brown; some fairer, some darker, some blondish, some reddish like himself. The Mage and the Bard were two of only ten people he'd ever seen whose skin was distinctively black. Blood, Tier, or slave, extremes of coloring were unusual.

Unlike Carlon, with his taste for elaborate clothing, Falundir wore whatever Col washed and set out for him. But, like Carlon, he was a castrate. His voice as a youth had been the purest in all Lenfell; Col heard its remnants whenever the Bard thought himself alone in the cottage. At those times Falundir hummed melodies he could no longer put words to, piercing the dank forest air with crystalline sweetness. Col learned to keep completely still outside the window so the Bard wouldn't remember his presence—and committed every fragment to memory in the personal number-code that was music to him.

Communication was naturally a problem after Gorynel Desse's departure. Having spent his life expressing himself in perfect phrases of his own creation, Falundir refused even to attempt speech now. The boy did a lot of guessing and questioning; the Bard did a lot of grimacing and gesturing. Eventually they worked out a language of their own.

It frustrated Col unbearably that there was no way for Falundir to share the details of his life. Desse had told him a little. Born a slave in Shellinkroth, music had won Falundir his freedom at eighteen. He'd performed before everyone worth mentioning, traveled the length and breadth of Lenfell, known Mage Guardians and Lords of Malerris and notables of every Name, witnessed and written about great events. But his life was locked away now: the poet's eloquence muted, the minstrel's fingers useless.

The crippling was recent. Desse had taken him to stay

with friends while his wounds healed, then installed him in a cottage ten miles into Sheve Dark and set out to find Collan.

"I didn't like leaving him alone from Harvest to Candleweek," the old man had admitted. "And bringing you to him is a risk. You still have your hands and voice. Don't be surprised if he's hostile at first. Have patience. You can understand what he's lost."

After a few days, Collan began to think the winter silence of Sheve Dark was the biggest risk of all. The snowy forest was unnervingly quiet, not even a bird to twitter or a squirrel to rustle the undergrowth. After such glorious music as Falundir had made—this?

Intimidated by the forest silence—not to mention Falundir's renown—Col didn't say much at first. After a couple of weeks, he began talking just to hear the noise. Falundir endured this rambling babble for an hour one morning, then snorted and left the cottage. Col took the hint and shut up for several days. Then one evening the Bard settled before the hearth, pointed at Collan, then at his own lips, and nodded.

"You want me to—what should I talk about?"

A shrug. A graceful circle described in the air by a useless hand.

He found himself telling the Bard everything. His early memory of wind; slavery at Scraller's Fief; wanderings as a street entertainer and thief. He talked until his throat was raw and the Ladymoon set. Falundir mulled homemade mead for him, and he talked on until midnight.

That was how they spent most evenings that winter. Col remembered much he'd thought forgotten. If he paused, Falundir would scowl and fix him with a stern look from bright blue eyes, and Col would strive to recall a scene down to the smallest mote of remembrance. He learned how to let a memory flow out of him in words that made precise pictures. Too many words, he knew; he hadn't the Bard's gift for summing emotion or sensory detail in a few choice syllables. But memories led to more memories, and after a time he understood that together the notes formed the music of his life. Some tones rang clear and strong; others were sweetly delicate as whispered grace notes—and many were raucous, painfully out of tune. But they were all him, and all his, played to the drumbeat of his own heart.

It was nearly spring before he felt brave enough to discuss music or poetry with the great Bard. Part of it was shyness; part of it was his certainty that his frustration would grow even more acute. Falundir could not contribute to the conversation. But their communication system took some of the edge off Col's need. He would make a statement or ask a question, and the Bard would indicate *yes* or *no* and either encourage further talk on the subject or hold one hand up to end it.

It was better than nothing, but it drove Collan crazy just the same.

One evening as they fortified themselves against the cold by liberally sampling Falundir's mead, Col gave a cloying recital of one of Scraller's bedtime stories. And sound issued from the Bard: laughter. Rich, carefree, even musical, showing Collan how fine a voice it had once been. The twinkle in blue eyes lasted into the next day. How long had it been since Falundir had found anything even remotely funny, let alone laughed?

The days lengthened and grew warmer, hunting improved, and the vegetable beds sprouted weed bouquets. One afternoon Col knelt beside the cabbages, ripping up dragoneye and spike bloom while Falundir grappled with the hoe, preparatory to planting the corn. All at once the Bard let out a soft groan. Collan turned, alarmed. The fierceness of the blue eyes in the dark face toppled him back on his heels as surely as the long-ago wind had flattened him into a muddy ditch. The look was one of bitter grief and terrible hatred. And it was directed at him.

What have I done? he tried to say, but his lips wouldn't form the words. He was as mute as Anniyas had made Falundir.

And then he realized. He'd been singing—softly, under his breath, but singing. And the song had been one of Falundir's.

"I—I'm sorry—" he stammered. "I didn't mean—"

The Bard flung the hoe onto the new earth, and disappeared into the forest as silently as a Wraith.

It was well after dark before he returned. Col huddled miserably before the fire, dinner ready but uneaten. He served Falundir, then himself, but still had no appetite. After a time, Falundir set aside his bowl and rose. Collan didn't dare look at him. When one lax hand fell onto his shoulder, he flinched.

A small silver key dropped into Col's lap. He knew at once what it opened: the cupboard over Falundir's bed was closed with the only lock in the cottage. His knees shook as he approached and opened it, certain there would be incredible treasure within. He was right.

Songbooks. Great leather-bound folios of music and words, glossed in Falundir's own hand, were stacked ten deep. Behind them, wrapped in Bardic blue silk inside an unmistakable bronzewood case, was a lute.

Falundir's songs. Falundir's lute.

"I can't," Col blurted, taking a step back.

A gentle hand pushed him forward. He looked over his shoulder. The thin dark face smiled, bright eyes glittery with tears. Col ached with empathetic anguish. Surely the books and lute had not been unlocked since the Bard began his exile here. To see them again, to hear the words sung and the instrument coaxed into tune and played—and by so giftless a lout as Col—

Falundir extended both hands. Slowly, he drew the fingers in to the palms. They curled only a little; tendons meant to bend knuckles had long since atrophied. His thumbs could hold objects by pressing into his palms, but that was all. His fingers would never dance across the strings again.

It was the first time Collan had felt anyone's pain but his own, and the onslaught unnerved him. He cast a single desperate glance at Falundir's liquid blue eyes, and fled the cottage.

As with all his most vivid memories, that evening was imprinted on his mind for survival's sake. More surely than changes in voice or height, it signaled approaching adulthood. A gift from his mother—meager though it eventually proved when compared with others—made itself felt that night. And Col rejected it utterly.

5

He wasn't fool enough to reject the Bard's gift of music.

At first he practiced alone, deep in Sheve Dark, with only the summer denizens of gargantuan trees as his audience. But as summer turned to autumn, it grew too cold and his fingers lost the suppleness they'd regained. So for the first weeks of winter, he neither played nor sang.

Falundir never touched the books or the lute. Gradually he was able to look at them without tears springing to his eyes. One night he simply pointed to the cupboard, and Collan helplessly brought out the instrument and began to play.

Now that he had an audience whose opinion he valued—unlike Scraller and his moronic guests—he found he could neither sing a note nor move his fingers in the simplest of chordings. The humiliation was worse than being sold.

Falundir's reaction was a total lack of reaction. Col put the lute away.

The next night it was waiting for him by his chair at the hearth. The implication stunned him. Falundir simply watched his eyes, no expression on his face at all. Collan sat, tuned the lute, and once more tried to play.

He was a little better this time. He still winced at every mistake, and cast anxious glances at the Bard. At length Falundir pointed to himself and shook his head. Then he gestured expansively to Collan and nodded.

Not for me; for yourself. That was what Falundir meant. What Col had always known instinctively was confirmed by a Bard who had refused to compromise his music for the First Councillor's political peace.

It never became exactly *easy* to play for Falundir. Collan never forgot who was with him, listening with exquisitely sensitive ears, crippled hands twitching every so often as rippling notes stirred his fingers' memory. But as they worked out a teaching system, the Bard humming the notes he wished to hear, Col's confidence increased and he wasn't so much mortified by mistakes as irritated by them.

From the folios, he learned every song Falundir had ever

written down. He wondered sometimes what it must do to his teacher, hearing compositions he could never again perform the way he'd intended. Col clung to something Carlon had told him once—that the best songs lived on their own. "Even an indifferent Minstrel can't ruin its essence, and a superior talent both draws on and adds to it. It's the mediocre piece that needs a really good player to make it come alive—and at the hands and voice of an idiot, such songs are exposed for the disasters they truly are." Collan doubted there was anything he could add to the lives of Falundir's works—and he knew they made him sound a much finer talent than he really was.

When he knew every piece in the folios, he yearned for more. But more there would never be. Falundir could hum new tunes for him to pick out on the lute, but of words there could be nothing. Speech and pen had been gateways for the Bard's soul, and were now locked tight. Still, Collan carefully wrote down the new melodies, hoping that someday a poet worthy of the music would hear it and do it justice.

Seasons passed, the green chill of winter following the suffocating green heat of summer in Sheve Dark. Gorynel Desse arrived every spring, and at those times Falundir would send Collan out to hunt extra meat. What the Warrior Mage told his old friend during these private times remained a mystery to Col. At first, he lingered outside the cottage, trying to overhear. But Desse must have used a Silence spell, for even crouched beneath an open window with a snatched glance inside showing him the Mage's moving lips, Col heard nothing. He shrugged and went hunting.

Sheve Dark was so luxuriant that anyone unaccustomed to threading through the maze of Scraller's Fief would have been hopelessly lost in a hundred paces. Collan never was. Though all trees looked pretty much the same to him, he soon mapped out the forest in his head with mathematical precision.

For hundreds of miles, gigantic redwood pillars rose two hundred feet before spreading needle-thick arms toward each other, a canopy that shut out all but the fiercest sunlight. Birds of flamboyant colors and raucous voices lived in the upper branches. Lesser trees, underbrush, and the heavy cushion of needles provided homes for other creatures: slow, shy pricklebacks, squirrels and other rodents, and deer with racks ten feet across. At the forest's edge was Sleginhold, the largest town and only manor house in more than a hundred miles. Its inhabitants ventured into the Dark sometimes to hunt, fish, or gather medicinal plants, but Collan avoided them and they never seemed to find the cottage. He didn't understand that until one of Desse's visits, when the old man let him watch while he renewed the Wards.

"They're all different," the Mage explained as they trod a barely visible trail. "Identical spells attract suspicion."

Collan nodded. "If you put too many Look That Way Wards—"

"Exactly. I vary them with I'm Thirsty, Deer In The Thicket, Is My Horse Lame, and so on. My favorite is What Did I Leave Behind." He grinned, white teeth flashing in his dark face. "I've seen folk hurry halfway home, convinced that the bow in their hands is in fact propped against the front door."

"But that's not real protection," Col argued. "It's just distraction. People could get through if they wanted to."

"Why would they want to? And why should I waste my energies building a Keep Out, and then spend a day recovering from it, when it would only advertise that there's something here I don't want people to see? Distraction does just fine. Second rule of magic, my lad: be subtle. Don't overdo it."

"Why tell me about it?" Col grumbled. "It's not as if I have any magic."

"Not a whisper," was the blithe reply. "Be grateful. You never know what exhaustion is until you've Folded a hundred miles of road in a single day, or Warded a whole castle in a single night, or helped a dozen fumble-witted Novices make their first Mage Globes." He sighed. "Still, as I told you once, everyone ought to know about magic and how we Mage Guardians work."

"If these Wards are so good, why don't I feel them?"

"Do you think I'm an amateur, boy?" Desse growled.

"What about the Lords of Malerris? Do they believe in subtlety, too?"

This earned him a curious look from intense green eyes. "You didn't ask if we're the same as they."

Col snorted and drew aside a heavy branch so the old man could pass.

"Collan, lad, their subtleties are so unfathomable that no two of them understand the ploys of a third. What they do believe is that the first rule of magic does not apply to them."

"Which is?"

"Harm nothing."

Collan stopped walking and gave the Warrior Mage's sword a skeptical look.

"Oh, I've killed—to my shame," Gorynel Desse admitted. "But the one time I should have killed, my resolve failed. Here's the first Ward," he continued, striding forward to a brambleberry bush. "Damned inconvenient, having to renew this one every year when it leafs out. The branches don't take, you see. Truly told, I often wonder why I didn't use stones for all of them. Rock soaks up magic better than anything but silk and pure metal."

He continued explaining after the Ward was reset. Whereas stones were more readily spelled than living things, a covering of dirt or leaves obscured the Ward. Unless the rock was really massive, it could be moved. Then again, large outcrops invited hammer and chisel.

"It's a pretty problem, deciding on the substance of a Ward," he concluded. "And a good thing I can manage to travel through Sheve every year."

Those years were tallied infrequently in Collan's mind. He recognized the passage of seasons, but they seemed to have little to do with his life but for the cycle of plant, harvest, hunt. He learned music, refined his technique, wrote down Falundir's new melodies, and read the books Gorynel Desse brought.

The Mage also provided a sword. Battling a swaying branch and practicing stab-thrusts on a melon were poor substitutes for sparring with a living opponent, but Desse explained that all he need do was *look* as if he knew what he was doing with a sword, and most people would back off. If they didn't—well, the boy could still run like blazes.

"Besides," the Mage added, "your imagination can provide opponents for practice when I'm not here. And, truly told, you're a natural at swordplay."

One spring day he found himself at the edge of the Dark, looking past the rolling farmland of Sleginhold at the annual St. Sirrala's Fair. Village, manor, and hillsides were aglow with flowers to honor the gentle Virgin Saint. The display was enchanting even at several miles. He hadn't seen a St. Sirrala's Fair since Carlon had taken him to Combel the spring before Desse had come for him. Four years ago? That made him seventeen years old. The realization was a shock.

He'd noticed he'd been growing, of course. Desse brought clothes and boots each year, too big at first but always too small by the next visit. His voice had settled into supple maturity, lacking the purity of his childish treble but richer in tone and expression under Falundir's tutelage. It seemed, however, that he'd attained manhood unawares.

Well, almost unawares. For several years he'd been having highly embarrassing dreams with even more embarrassing results. The past two autumns he'd risked the main road during Hunt Week in hope of seeing the beauteous Lady Agatine Slegin and her ladies. Their wild rides through Sheve Dark were attended by much merriment, sending every deer and rabbit in ten miles scurrying for cover. The object was not the kill but celebration of St. Fielto's Chase. Collan had been rewarded with many interesting views of the ladies. Deciding which was the most appealing was an exquisite frustration.

But even the humblest was far above his reach. He knew the name his mother had given him, but whether he was Blood or Tier, he had no idea. Without an identity disk, no woman above the rank of slave would permit him to touch her.

Life would've been much easier, he reflected as he watched the faraway fair, if he'd been born like Taguare the Bookmaster and preferred men.

He wasn't really aware of stashing bow and quiver in the undergrowth, or of descending the grassy hillside, or of kneeling before the stream that chattered down a rocky cleft. The next thing he knew for certain was a cold splash of water on his face, delivered by his own cupped palms. He woke up—sort of—and saw where he was, but didn't ask himself how he'd gotten there. Neither did he question why he was about to join the village revel. He wanted to hear voices— somebody other than himself or Gorynel Desse or the two elderly women who lived near Deertrack Pond, with whom he traded meat for candles and honey for Falundir's mead. He wanted to *talk* with someone.

Preferably female.

And young.

And pretty.

Had he planned all winter, he could have chosen no better time or place for it than St. Siralla's Fair. Dozens of girls wearing spring gowns and crowns of fresh flowers drifted like bright butterflies along the booth-lined road between village and manor house. The girls were supervised by mothers, aunts, or sisters, the older ladies attended by husbands in snug coifs who delved into jingling purses to pay for ribbons, trinkets, snacks, and games. Young men strutted along daringly bareheaded, wearing shirts as brightly colored as the girls' dresses. The whole laughing, carefree scene made Col yearn to join in. He hung back, though, the years in Sheve Dark making him shy.

Still ... he wanted to hear voices close to, not at a halfmile remove. So he strode toward the flowered arch that marked the entrance to the Fair.

From either side of the arch tubs of climbing roses soared ten feet overhead in a sun-warmed display of yellow and orange. Tucked in at intervals were clusters of blue daisies, white Miramili's Bells, and purple lilies. Collan passed beneath the arch with dazzled eyes and itchy nose—predictable in one accustomed to the moist, earthy scents of a greenbrown forest.

He sneezed in earnest when someone handed him a sprig of Miramili's Bells and bade him welcome. A sympathetic chuckle greeted his explosion.

"Try the booth with the beehive sign," the young man suggested as Col wiped his streaming eyes. "Nothing better for a touchy nose than a big slice of bread dripping with local honey."

"Personal experience?" Col asked.

The young man laughed. He was about Collan's age, dressed in the Slegin Blood's blue and yellow livery that complimented his wood-brown skin. "Shameful in a son of Roseguard's Groundskeeper, isn't it! Wish I could inherit Fa's nose along with his position! Haven't seen you around before—though we don't make it to the Hold often. Fa hates to leave his roses. Name's Verald, by the way."

"Collan. Thanks for the advice." He tried to hand the flowers back, but Verald shook his head.

"Slegin Blood custom. You give the Bells to the first pretty girl you see—they cluster around the gate until midmorning, trying to collect as many as they can. They've all gone on to the Fair by now, so you won't be mobbed." He paused, silver-gray eyes alight with speculation. "Do me a favor in exchange for the advice?"

"Sure." Col repressed another sneeze, rubbing his nose.

"If you've no other preference, give them to a little girl in green with a pink sash. She'll have a coronet of pink rosebuds—too young for the full crown, y'see."

Col didn't, but nodded anyway.

"She just turned ten, and it'd be the thrill of her life to be gifted with First Flowers."

"You're her brother?" he guessed.

Verald laughed again. "I'm her intended husband! It's not as shocking as it sounds. Our families approve. It's not as if she's Blood—neither am I, truly told—although I'm six years older than she, so there's *that* prejudice to deal with."

Not knowing enough about the marriage customs of Bloods or Tiers to be shocked, he replied politely, "She sounds charming. What's her name?"

"Sela." He spotted more late arrivals and snatched up sprigs of Bells. Turning to give welcome, he called back over his shoulder, "Remember—green dress, pink sash!"

Col wandered away, resolving to find the child as soon as possible and get rid of the flowers. His nose felt as if it were swelling right into his brain.

But there were so many blooms decorating the booths that abandoning a single sprig would do him no good. He couldn't avail himself of Verald's advice about the honey, for his pockets were empty of cutpieces. Honor demanded, however, that he find this Sela. Happily, she was at one of the first booths he encountered, where children were flinging soft cloth bags at cowbells. Every score was rewarded with a sweet. The clamor of bells, shrieks, and giggles was nearly deafening after the silence of Sheve Dark.

Sela was pleading more cutpieces from a tall, sternly lovely woman who could only be her mother. The cant of green eyes and the delicate arch of cheekbones proclaimed it as surely as the woman's words about spoiling her appetite. Col stepped around two boys arguing over a fistful of sweets and offered the tiny white Bells with a deep bow and a smile.

Sela gasped. "For me?"

Her mother fixed a long, long look on Collan. Over Sela's head he mouthed, *From Verald,* and she relaxed.

"Mama! Look! First Flowers!"

"How pretty they are! Now, Sela, you must thank the kind young man."

Col had no idea what thanks might entail. When Sela tugged at his hand, he bent down and received a slightly sticky kiss tasting of candied violets.

She blushed hotly and darted away, calling for her friends to come see her First Flowers. Her mother nodded pleasantly to Collan and followed, leaving him to contemplate his first kiss.

From a ten-year-old.

Grinning ruefully, he set out to enjoy the Fair.

The most popular booth featured young men dressed in nothing more than trousers and grins. One by one they stood on a ladder above a huge vat of cold water, each new arrival greeted with cheers and teasing laughter, while girls lined up to buy painted wooden rings. These were tossed at full winebottles. If the girl failed to score two rings on the same bottle, the next got her chance. When someone succeeded, the youth let out a yell and jumped into the water. Later, after he dried off and donned his best clothes, the couple would share the wine—under the watchful eyes of her family—during the midday feast.

Collan had learned from Carlon that this was a universal feature of St. Siralla's Fair—which honored virgin girls. "Personally, I find the symbolism a trifle vulgar, but it's been a courting ritual as long as anyone remembers. Only three weeks until Maiden Moon and St. Maidil's Day, after all."

Then, both the symbolism and the significance of the Saint's day had completely escaped Col. Now, at seventeen, he was certain that quite a few of these virgins wouldn't be by the Feast of New Lovers. There was much laughter and jostling when the handsomest youths climbed the ladder, and every so often competition among the girls to be first in line grew heated, but not even the dullest-looking boys lacked attention.

After observing the game for a little while, he became aware that people were observing *him.* Unused to being looked at, he tried to fade into the crowd.

And then he realized that most of looks came from eyes sparkling beneath crowns of roses and daisies, and *all* the looks approved.

Collan immediately relaxed into it with the sure instincts of a man born to please women—though he never looked at it that way himself. For a scant ten minutes he forgot his lowly status and lack of a name. He swaggered a bit, and eyed his admirers, and smiled—until, stepping back to avoid being splashed, he bumped into the First Daughter of the Slegin Blood Herself. Abruptly he was a seventeen-year-old former slave again. The stunning crash back to reality mortified him.

Lady Agatine was as nearly tall as he, and even lovelier close-to than seen at a distance in Sheve Dark. Her skin had a dark golden sheen and her strong features were dominated by gold-flecked brown eyes below a sweep of loosely piled black hair. Her dress was pale blue, her lacy shawl pale green, and two silver hoops in each earlobe were her only jewelry. Startled contact with him had unsettled her garland of lemon blossoms, the fragrance competing with some deeper, muskier scent. All he could do was stare.

She caught her balance quickly and met his gaze. He was about to stammer an apology when a voice from about the height of his ribs said acidly, "Have you always been so clumsy, or did you take lessons?"

"Sarra!" admonished Lady Agatine.

About to admit that the accident had been entirely his fault—which was only the truth—Collan suddenly felt a rush of anger. Bloods always thought they could say and do anything they pleased. Everybody knew that. Glaring up at him was a decidedly plain little face surmounted by a coronet of white rosebuds wilting in the midmorning warmth.

"Have you always been so rude, or did *you* take lessons?" he snapped.

The girl, no more than eight or nine years old, sucked in a breath through her teeth. That one of them was missing and another only half grown in did not improve her looks. Her eyes were so dark a brown as to be indistinguishable from black, and at present flashed fire like night lightning. Freckles dappled a sunburned, upturned nose and pudgy cheeks. Her sole redeeming feature was a wealth of pale blonde curls cascading down her back. Col had never seen hair that color before—like silk spun of equal parts sunlight and moonbeams.

Lady Agatine was frowning at both of them now. Collan dragged his gaze from the girl's and bowed as Carlon had taught him to do before a performance. Offending a powerful Blood was never wise, even if one of its members was a little shit.

"Your pardon, Lady. I *was* clumsy, and being unused to such noble company, I'm afraid I was also rude."

"Not without provocation," replied Lady Agatine, eyeing the child. "Sarra?"

Sullenly: "What?"

"Sarra."

The tone was of warning now, and Collan half-turned to

hide his grin from Lady Agatine. Young Sarra, however, saw every tooth in his head—just as he meant her to. Her jaw clenched, her eyes narrowed, and for a moment he thought she would kick him in the shins.

Then a complete transformation took place. A smooth social mask descended. Her lips curved—carefully, to hide the teeth—and her eyes became twin pools of melted molasses. He felt his own expression soften as he anticipated his gracious acceptance of a Blooded Lady's apology.

"I forgive you," she announced grandly.

Col's mouth dropped open. "You *what?*"

She lost her composure and began to giggle.

"Sarra!" cried Lady Agatine. The exasperation held the despairing note of frequent usage, indicating near-constant chiding of this miserable infant. Better she should apply the flat of her palm to that well-padded backside.

"Oh, all right," Sarra relented, grinning. "I shouldn't have said it—I guess anybody with feet that big can't help but trip over them."

An impressively tall man wearing an unfastened black coif stepped forward and picked the girl up by the belt of her dress. She squealed as he lifted her effortlessly to his eye level.

"Orlin! Put me down!"

"May I ask your name, young man?" the giant asked in a voice that rumbled like an earthquake.

Looking up a full eight inches, he stammered, "Uh—Collan."

"Honored. Mine is Orlin Renne. This is Lady Agatine of the Slegin Blood. The monster is called Sarra Liwellan." He fixed a stern gaze on the squirming child. "Say you're sorry for insulting *Domni* Collan."

"No!"

"Say it, or I'll tell Granna Felera—and you know how she feels about manners of the Slegin Blood."

"Sorry!" She grabbed for the coronet dislodged in her struggles. It fell into the dirt. "Damn!"

"Now you may apologize for your language."

"I'm *sorry!* Put me down, Orlin!"

Ignoring her, he turned to Col. "Damage repaired?"

"Yes, Lord Renne."

"Good." He lowered Sarra to the ground.

As she smoothed her rumpled dress, for all the world like a kitten inexpertly grooming, Collan bent and plucked up the

flower circlet. With another bow—mockery in every line of
his body—he proffered it.

"Yours, I believe?"

Snatching it from him, she jammed it askew onto her
head, gave him a look to wither grass, and ran off.

Orlin Renne sighed. "Not *my* begetting, thank St.
Geridon."

"Sarra's a distant cousin," Lady Agatine told Collan. "Orphaned daughter of a very old Blood, my husband's kin. My
mother took her in, and we've raised her since her parents
died—"

"—and done as bad a job of it as on our sons, too," Renne
finished for her, chuckling. "No, truly told, Sarra's a good
child. Just very ... um ... spirited." A grin finished the
characterization.

Col nodded noncommittally, wondering why they were
telling him so much. Lady Agatine's next comment put the
puzzle right out of his head.

"You'll be up there soon, I suppose," she said, eyeing him
with a smile. "Every lady in seeing distance will want to
share feast wine with you."

Abruptly the impossible gulf between him and everyone
else here opened wide at his feet. Plenty of girls would
clamor for him to climb the ladder—until he removed his
shirt and they saw Scraller's sigil on his shoulder. Slavery
was illegal in Sheve, but all would know him for what he
was, and point, and stare, and pity. And then throw him out.
For nothing about this place—from the Fair to the feast to
the honorable title of *domni*—was meant for slaves.

Something must have shown in his face. Orlin Renne
started to speak, but an upward glance from his Lady silenced him. She said, "But then, it may be that you're the
kind of man who doesn't enjoy making a spectacle of himself. Unlike my husband," she added with a wry grin.

"Careful, Aggie," he warned in that low, gravelly voice.
"Or I'll tell young Collan about the small fortune in rings
you tossed before you won me!"

The awkward moment was gone. Collan appreciated their
graciousness even while cursing its necessity. The day was
ruined for him. He stayed long enough to express his pleasure at meeting them, then excused himself by pretending to
spot a friend near a booth fluttering with ribbons. He es-

caped the Fair with all its reminders of what he could never be, and ran all the way home.

When he got back to the cottage, he was tired and hungry and nursing an emotional bruise that an entire evening of lute and songs couldn't ease. It was a week before he told Falundir about it, another week before he could think of it without wincing, and yet another before he didn't think about it every day.

By then it was Maiden Moon. At Sleginhold, Lady Agatine would preside with Orlin Renne over a moonlit feast in honor of St. Maidil, patron of New Lovers. There was a song cycle about it in Carlon's collection. Remembering the lyrics, Collan pictured the scene in the village meadow: more laughter and wine, more flowers and bright dresses, more pretty girls. But not one of them—not in small Sleginhold or all Sheve or anywhere else in the world—would ever share so much as a smile with him.

6

Gorynel Desse arrived during Last Moon, three days before the Wraithenday. He stayed in the snowbound cottage through St. Lirance's, first day of the new year of 956—which was made remarkable for being the very first time Col ever had a Birthingday celebration. He was eighteen—more or less—and between them Mage and Bard put together eighteen gifts as was proper to mark the manhood year. New boots, shirt, cloak, trousers, coif; two gleaming steel daggers; two bound books of blank pages, two pens, and a sturdy pot of black ink; a plain blue silk longvest of perfect fit; two sets of strings; and three final gifts that rendered him speechless: a map, an identity disk, and Falundir's lute.

In brief, everything he needed to make his way as a roving Minstrel.

"My friend who made the knives also does a brisk business in other forgeries," the Warrior Mage said, grinning blithely at his own pun. "The Rosvenirs really do exist, though there aren't many of them. They're Second Tier, rather obscure, and confine themselves to a smallhold twenty miles from the nearest village, so I doubt you'll ever encounter one." He warmed his hands at the hearthfire. "But avoid Dindenshir, and if you can't, try to avoid doing anything appallingly stupid—like getting arrested by the Council Guard."

It hit him then. They were sending him away.

Collan stared at the flat silver disk in his palm. About the size and shape of an almond, it was etched on the obverse with two crossed daggers, two names, date of birth, and Tier. The only word of it that was not a lie was his given name. The reverse was stamped with an eagle with crest feathers upstanding, an arrow clutched in the left talons. A long, thin silver chain was attached to the disk through holes at either end, the final links separated from the disk by a dark gray bead on one side and a turquoise on the other. Collan assumed these were the Rosvenir colors, and the copper daggers were their sigil.

"I would've been here sooner," Desse went on, settling back to sip mead, "but at Harvest a new design was authorized. The crafters went mad trying to fill the orders. Old disks must be exchanged for new by today."

Falundir grunted an interrogative. Desse refilled his mug before replying.

"You'll note that the Council's Eagle now holds the Anniyas Arrow. *Wields* it, more like—but I'm prejudiced." He gulped a huge swallow as if to rid his mouth of bitterness. "At any rate, with so many disks being struck, slipping in a few extra wasn't difficult—though they're keeping count of how many are turned in as opposed to how many are issued. Casting the blanks is the exclusive right of the Renne Blood."

The Bard snorted in amusement. Col glanced up.

"Renne?" he asked. "As in Lady Agatine's husband?"

"And also as in the mines and foundries of Brogdenguard, and Healer Mage Viko Renne of the cure for Kenroke fever." Desse shook his head, thick white mane swirling. "The First Councillor seems to think all the Generations since have purged the taint from the Renne Blood. In truth, they haven't turned out a Mage since the great Healer. Although the First Daughter," he added as an afterthought, "has a distinct magic of her own. She's an old friend of mine."

Again Falundir snorted, and this time the Mage grinned. Collan instantly concluded what sort of friend Desse meant.

"Hadn't seen the fair Jeymian in years," he mused. "I

must say she's aged as sweet and spicy as your mead,
Falundir."

The hint was taken. The Bard rose to get another clay pot
from the shelf—the third that night. If Collan was any judge,
it wouldn't be the last.

"The disk," Gorynel Desse resumed, "is genuine enough.
So is the map—which I expect you to make good use of, boy.
I've marked in blue the holds where Minstrels are welcomed
with mild extravagance. Reds have pretensions but shallow
pockets. Greens will give you a bed and a crust and no more."

They were giving him everything he would need to survive on his own. They were sending him away.

"As for the ones marked in purple—don't go anywhere
near them." He put his mug down and sat forward again, elbows on knees, hands clasped before him. "This brings me to
the brand on your shoulder. As often as you can from spring
to autumn, take off your shirt and bake your skin to its darkest
brown. Yellow ink will disappear under a deep tan. In winter,
don't sleep naked. Don't even bathe naked. I don't care if
you're in the middle of nowhere, if the door locks triple on
the inside, or if you're absolutely certain you're alone."

Collan nodded—mute, numb, not believing that the future
was upon him. He should have known. Falundir had brewed
no mead this summer. Last week he'd only shrugged when
Collan fretted that snow kept him from hunting. The peaceful years in the forest were over. He would be going out into
the world now. They'd thought of everything. . . .

"Something else," Desse said. "Swear off girls as your
sunburn fades and until you get it back. Sight of that mark
will mean it's back to Scraller's for you—and what you escaped years ago will happen with a vengeance."

The Mage sliced off another wedge of the tangy cheese-
cake he'd brought with him. They'd feasted tonight before
the gifting. Enough food remained for two or three days, no
more. Col assumed that what was left would go into
journeypacks.

What he didn't know was where Desse would take the
Bard. Obviously, Col would be leaving alone. *But Falundir
needs me!* he wanted to say. *And where can he go to be
safe? Anniyas marked him as surely as Scraller marked me!*

He knew he would not be told where the Mage would take
Falundir. What he did not know, he could not tell. So he
didn't ask. He merely sat with Falundir's lute at his knee

and his new disk in his palm, listening to Gorynel Desse explain his new life.

"Remember the coif—yes, I know you hate it, but society demands it. You're not a little boy anymore. Remember, too, that outlying districts are likely to be more conservative. So button that longvest to your neck and knees, and wear the coif at all times."

"They're blue," he heard himself say.

"Bardic Blue," the Mage affirmed. "There's no indication on your disk that you've earned it, but that matters less and less now. Bard Hall was lost with Ambrai. The Hall, but not the music," he murmured. "Nor the medicine, nor the magic. . . ." He paused for a swallow of mead. Suddenly it occurred to Col that Desse was trying very hard to get drunk. "And, by Delilah's Silver Sword, not the knowledge." He drained his mug and slammed it on the table. "Look at me, Collan Rosvenir, and speak your thoughts. Could it possibly be an old wreck like me can still teach swordskill to young Warrior Mages?"

The green eyes were fierce and sharp as shards of bottle glass. Col groped for a polite lie.

He never spoke it. Abruptly dizzy, and not due to mead, he felt as if he was falling off the chair, helpless to catch himself. A voice he knew he ought to recognize said, "Don't fight so hard, boy, you'll only make it worse. I'm not as young as I was the first time we did this."

"The first time?" What *"first time"*? Collan struggled, knowing the old man searched for something—

"Ah. *There.*"

And for just an instant Col saw a glorious blazing light just out of reach. Something precious, something he couldn't identify and had never known was there—but now he grabbed for it, crying out. His, this thing was *his*—and the old man was stealing it from him—

A voice he had never heard before and couldn't really hear now said, *You're hurting him, Gorsha.*

"He's fighting. After all the preliminary work I did, he still—all right, that's got it."

Thick black velvet muffled the light. As it wrapped sleep around it, a voice murmured, *Little singer, grown so tall . . . thank you for these years. But it's time you were on your own. My music is safe in your keeping. We will meet again . . . I promise we will meet again, son of my heart. . . .*

7

Collan Rosvenir woke shivering in the grip of a raging headache. The simple act of tugging up covers slammed through his skull. Opening his eyes was an even bigger mistake. Weak winter sunlight stabbed into him, and he sank back with a groan.

After a time the pain became manageable. He cracked one eyelid, then the other, and a cottage came into focus: clothes folded on a chair, lute in its case, journeypack hanging by the door. Between it and him was a table before a cold hearth. By St. Velenne the Bard, no wonder his head hurt: three empty jars lolled on the tabletop. The sticky taste in his mouth meant potent mead.

Groaning again as he slid from the covers, he stuck his legs into trousers and his frozen feet into boots. He'd slept with his shirt on; however much he drank, however alone he seemed, he never slept naked.

Fortified with the last few swallows of mead and the remains of a dry loaf, Collan touched the identity disk at his heart for luck, shrugged into wool longvest and cloak, and strapped on his swordbelt and the twin daggers that were not only weapons but reminders of his Name. Shouldering the lute and pack, he slammed the cottage door shut and set off through snowy Sheve Dark for Sleginhold with his hands fisted deep in his pockets. The Lady wasn't in residence this time of year, but her steward was said to be musically inclined. If nothing else, Col would get a hot meal and the chance to thaw out fingers and toes. It was snowing again.

About a mile from the cottage he saw a curious thing. A single stone the size of a galazhi fawn lay bare, as if some interior heat had melted the snow. Collan had the sudden thought that he'd left something behind at the cottage. He checked pockets and pack. All present and accounted for, everything he needed to survive. Shaking his head, he resumed walking.

Snow quietly buried the stone behind the young man who no longer remembered the wind.

Glenin

1

"What kind of name is 'Feiran'?"

Glenin had not yet heard that question often enough to prevent the stiffening in her shoulders that gave away her feelings. "My father's name," she replied, almost casually enough to offset the telltale posture.

The other eight-year-old girls in dancing class—newly met that morning, after the teacher's return from holiday—stared at her in shock. *Your father's?* was in their eyes; she gazed back as calmly as she could and ignored the writhing emptiness of loss inside her.

Barely four weeks ago her father brought her to Ryka Court from Ambrai, explaining that her mother and little sister were no longer her family and that she would now use his name. Despite the excitement of the journey, the wonders of Ryka Court, and the proud consciousness that Auvry Feiran was much more important here than he had ever been in Ambrai, she missed her mother. She even missed Sarra, who was outgrowing the annoying age and beginning to be an enjoyable companion.

Elsvet—plump, sallow First Daughter of the formidably wealthy Doyannis Blood—stalked closer and followed up her original question with, "What about your mother?"

"What about her?" Glenin shrugged.

This dismissal confused the other girls; Elsvet narrowed

her pallid blue eyes and said, "The only reason to have your
father's name is because your mother rejected you and took
her name away."

"My father and I rejected *her*," Glenin replied. "And I *discarded* her name."

This scandalous assertion was too much for the rest of the
class. They gasped and whispered among themselves, ten
proper young Daughters of various Bloods whose court-
formed notions of propriety had received a terrible jolt.

Elsvet, however, was made of sterner stuff. "Who was
she?"

For the first time, Glenin understood the uses of another's
curiosity. She played on it instinctively, giving another little
shrug. "It hardly matters. We don't speak of her anymore."

"Tell me who she was!"

Enjoying this newfound power, Glenin allowed the corners of her mouth to curve in a mysterious smile.

"She must've been Fourth Tier." This elicited gasps;
Elsvet smiled like a snake. *"Fourth Tier,"* she repeated.
"What are you doing in a class for Bloods?"

Her power and her temper snapped simultaneously. "She
was *not* Fourth Tier!" Glenin cried. "I'm just as much a
Blood as you!"

"Fourth, Fourth, Fourth!" Elsvet chanted.

"I'm not! I'm not!"

The teacher hurried over, distracted from giving instructions to three bored musicians who supplemented their
wages by playing for classes. He was just in time to keep
Glenin's fingers from Elsvet's throat.

"Ladies, ladies! What's all this, then?" he demanded.
"Who started it?"

The other girls melted away toward the mirrored walls.
Glenin shook off the teacher's restraining hand, haughtily refusing to answer. Elsvet struggled for a moment with her
Blood Honor and her grievance. The fact that the former
won was one basis for a truce that eventually developed into
a wary association between the girls. That evening at her
mother's table, Elsvet learned that Glenin was First Daughter of none other than Lady Maichen Ambrai; self-interest
dictated the establishment of diplomatic relations.

The pair never became real friends. Glenin never forgave
the initial insult, and Elsvet never forgot the momentary feel
of furious hands that might have crushed her neck. But with

the sharp insight of intelligent children, they knew they had two choices: become enemies, or unite and rule. This they did—not only over the girls in dancing class, but the rest of their age group.

At about the same time Elsvet was learning Glenin's maternal heritage, Glenin was learning why questions about her Name would be common for a while.

Hers was now the privilege of presiding over the evening meal. She was as proudly conscious of her status as she was painfully aware of how many people were missing from her table. It was just Glenin and her father now. Only the two of them. So small a table, and so lonely.

Auvry Feiran waited until the servant departed before indicating that Glenin should light the tall central candle. She did so with trembling hands.

"Someone upset you today."

His voice was deep and sonorous, tinged these days with sadness. She hadn't seen him smile since they'd left Ambrai, and his gray-green eyes never sparkled anymore. Though Glenin recalled painfully well the escalating battles with her mother that had preceded divorce and the remove to Ryka Court, she wondered suddenly if he didn't miss Ambrai as much as she did.

She sneaked a glance at him, then stared resolutely at the table. The candle cast a carefully planned glow over the artistry of plates, goblets, and flowers, touching each element of the design with exquisite regard to reflection and refraction. Silver flatware glistened; clear crystal flung delicate rainbows; the food, arranged just so on each square of white porcelain, looked delicious. But there was something too mannered about the table, too formal for a family meal. And there were so many people missing.

She remembered the great oval table at Ambrai: the formidable Allynis Ambrai at its head, servants hovering behind, waiting for her to light a great turquoise candle in the ugly black iron holder that had been in the family since the Waste War. On Grandmother's left, First Daughter Maichen and her husband and two daughters. Grandfather at the other end of the table. On his left, Tama Alvassy and her husband Gerrin Desse, who was Grandmother's nephew, and their little girl, Mai—Sarra's age and not quite civilized yet, according to Grandmother.

After Lady Allynis lit the candle, they would all listen as

she praised or (more often) criticized the evening's design of plates and flatware and flowers. Then would come talk of the day's events, politics, the girls' lessons, art, music. Allynis would scold her husband roundly for repeating gossip even while her black eyes danced with laughter at the antics of her court. If there were plans to be made for an upcoming Saint's day or a ball—Grandmother adored giving parties—Sarra and Mai would join Glenin in her pleas to be allowed to dress in their best and stay up late, and Grandfather would take their side: "Oh, just this once, Allie?"

But those last few dinners at the bronzewood table had been tense: nobody talking, nobody eating, the adults drinking too much, Tama Alvassy and her family refusing to join them, Glenin and Sarra hardly daring to breathe. . . .

To Glenin's horror, the candlelight suddenly shimmered and tears rolled wet and cold down her cheeks.

"Glenin!"

Her father rose from his chair and swept her up in his arms. She cried and cried, utterly humiliated. When at last she was spent, she found herself in his lap, snuggled into the big overstuffed chair in their suite's library. He stroked her hair with his large, strong hands, occasionally lifting the spill of dark gold to the last rays of sunlight through the windows.

"You're going to be so lovely," he murmured. "I saw it the minute you were born. Other babies are wrinkled and red and rather ugly, but you were perfect. I remember the very first time you looked at me. All big eyes and tiny hands—oh, you claimed me with a single look. You were always my daughter more than your mother's. I couldn't leave you behind. Do you understand, Glensha?"

She drew away slightly, knuckling her eyes, and nodded. "It's just—I miss home. A little."

"So do I." His smile was sad. "Can you tell me what happened today?"

She did, and his handsome face settled into stern lines. The furrows across his forehead deepened as heavy brows knotted, and the generous curves of his mouth thinned. She knew that some people in Ambrai were frightened of her father; watching his face now, she knew why. But he was never angry with her.

"Glenin," he said at length, "it's time I told you why we had to leave. I should have explained sooner, but I thought you were too young and wouldn't understand. I see now I was wrong."

"I can understand, Father. I promise."

"I know." He settled her more comfortably on his knee. "There are two things you must remember always. You are a Lady of Blood, a First Daughter. Anyone important enough to bother about will know. The others don't matter. Ignore them." When Glenin nodded agreement, he went on, "The second is a thing you must never speak of. You're Mageborn, Glensha. There's magic in you. And this you get from me."

"Magic—?" Her emotions swung wildly: surprise, pleasure, pride, puzzlement.

"Oh, yes. In a few years you'll begin to feel it for yourself."

"Wh–what's it like?"

"Nothing like the way it was for me. A restlessness, a pressure building inside that hurt like a Saint's curse, until. . . ." His eyes lost focus.

"Until what, Father?"

"Until a Mage Guardian found me. While I was a Prentice Mage, he taught me how to use magic, how to take what was burning inside me and do wonderful things with it. But it won't hurt you the way it did me. We know what you are, Glensha, and when it begins for you, we'll be ready."

"But why can't I tell anyone?"

Auvry Feiran's fine eyes clouded with sadness. "Because terrible times are coming. There are those who'll want to harm you for being Mageborn. All who use magic will be shunned and despised. It will be very difficult and dangerous, so you must never tell anyone what you inherited from me. Not from your mother," he added fiercely. "From *me.*"

She clung to his hand. "They'll hurt you, too! They'll—"

"Shh, don't worry. No one will harm me. Not here, not in Ryka Court where I'm Commandant of the Council Guard. Mageborns will have their uses in the times to come—and I had the luxury of choosing to what use I'd be put. But you'd be in danger if they knew about you, Glensha. I'll tell you why if you promise that this, too, will remain a secret."

Glenin nodded again, wide-eyed.

"Good. You know that we count the years from the establishment of the Council of Lenfell. Whatever existed before was wiped out by a war between the Mage Guardians and the Lords of Malerris."

"That's when The Waste happened," Glenin said. "Wraithenbeasts appeared then, too. I learned about it in school back home—" She corrected herself quickly. "—back in Ambrai."

He seemed not to notice the slip. "The Waste War unleashed horrible magic. Millions died. The Waste was the final battlefield, and after that battle something happened to the air and water. Sickness spread across Lenfell, as if lingering battle-magic took out its anger on everyone, even innocent children. Evil magic," he said quietly. "Babies were born without sight, without hearing, without limbs. Some seemed healthy, even grew to adulthood—before dying of terrible sickness." He paused. "And other children were born with Wild Magic."

"If Mageborns did that. . . ." She shivered. "I'm not sure I want to be one."

"It was a hideous accident, Glenin. Magic itself isn't evil, even though some of its uses are. The Guardians and Lords tried to destroy each other, and the magic they used was too powerful for them to control."

Glenin thought this over. "Papa? Why wasn't magic outlawed back then, and the Mageborns killed like the Fifths?"

"I've often wondered the same thing. But it turned out they were needed—"

"The Wraithenbeasts," she whispered.

"Yes. But before that, the Bloods and Tiers were established. What do they teach you in school about that?"

"After five Generations, some families were certified worthy," she recited. "But I always thought that meant they were powerful at court, or really rich, or had lots of friends or something."

"What it meant," he said grimly, "was that families that showed no defects for five Generations were judged clean of taint. The cleanest—the Bloods—gained land and riches by selling their sons in marriage to the Tiers, and sometimes allowed their younger daughters to be bought the same way. The price was ruinous, but worth it to have the next Generation bear a Blood Name."

The Tiers, he explained, had been established according to the number of defects per hundred births in that fifth, benchmark Generation. Any family with more than four was forbidden to reproduce itself.

"But of course they did, and fostered the babies with sympathetic friends of higher Tiers. No Fifth was killed outright, but within a few Generations all were extinct, their Names forgotten. Some of them were very powerful before the Waste War and the Lost Age. But everything changed, Glenin. Everything."

"It sounds very unfair," Glenin ventured.

"Unfair, brutal—and desperate." He shook his head. "It's said they regretted their cruelty."

"But if the evil magic had spread through the whole world. . . ."

"Yes. This must've seemed the kindest way. After all, they could have put the crippled children to death." Drawing in a long breath, he finished, "In any case, that was all a very long time ago. Babies aren't born deformed or diseased anymore. Actually, the worst I've ever heard of is short-sightedness in certain families."

That explained Lenna Ellevit's unattractive squint. Glenin nodded. "But if no one is born crippled anymore, why are there still Bloods and Tiers?"

"Consider it from a Blood's point of view. If there were no Tiers, what would happen to the marriage value of daughters and sons? That's why some Names try to convince the Council that they should be Blooded. And with every Name elevated, there's one more group wanting the system intact." He cleared his throat. "Truly told, Glensha, the First Councillor has offered this to me."

It burst out of her before she could think. "Then I'd really be a First Daughter of a Blood again!"

Her father frowned. "You will *always* be that."

"Yes, I know—I'm sorry, I didn't mean—"

"I understand, heartling. Ours is a proud Name, even though First Tier. I'm the only child of the last Feiran. And because you've taken my Name now instead of your mother's, like me you'll be scorned by the Bloods—just because all those Generations ago, one Feiran child of every hundred wasn't born perfect."

"It's *not* fair!" Glenin exclaimed. But she was wondering feverishly what this had to do with being Mageborn and hiding it, and the terrible days her father said were coming.

"Your grandmother was dead set against your mother's

taking me to husband," he went on bitterly. "Polluting the
purity of the sacred Ambrai Blood—even though that name
would be borne by our children and mine would vanish with
me, as forgotten as the Fifth Tiers. *She* would know, she
said—mighty Allynis Ambrai, whose Blood hadn't mixed
with a Tier's in thirty Generations!"

Glenin squirmed slightly as his arms tightened around her.
He gave a start as if he'd forgotten she was there. He smiled
again, but it was a cramped, forced thing.

"You have my name, Glensha, because in the world I'm
going to make for you, there'll be no more Bloods or Tiers.
No more unfairness, no more scorn. Only Mageborns taking
their rightful places at the Great Loom."

He laughed softly at her confusion. She hadn't heard him
laugh since long before leaving Ambrai. She wondered suddenly if the divorce had been due to his First Tier status,
then rejected the notion. Mother wasn't like that.

But Grandmother was.

"It's too long a story to tell on an empty stomach," he
said, hugging her. "For now, I'll tell you this: before you
and I and others who believe as we do can be what we were
meant to be, it will have to seem that all Mageborns are
gone. Magic is too powerful and dangerous to be left to
those who don't understand its true purpose. Think of the
world as a vast Loom, Glenin, and picture yourself as one of
the weavers."

"Because I have magic?"

"Because you have magic," he affirmed. "Whatever your
name, you'll always be the First Daughter of Auvry Feiran."

They went back to the table where the evening candle had
burned low, and ate in companionable silence a dinner long
since grown cold.

2

Magic woke in her just as he'd said it would. One blustery
winter night in 955, a week after her first Wise Blood, her
bedroom windows blew open. It was too cold to get up and
close them; she huddled into the quilts, wishing the shutters

would close and lock on their own. And they did—so securely that the next morning the servant couldn't open them.

But Glenin could.

The delight of knowing her magic had begun compensated for not having the same womanhood celebration as other girls. She had no mother or aunt or grandmother to send out invitations ready since her twelfth Birthingday, or to present her to the assembled guests as a woman grown. There were no presents, no congratulatory notes, no tributes of hothouse blooms—though Elsvet Doyannis gave her a nosegay of wildflowers, the First Councillor sent gold earrings, and there were verbal acknowledgments from other girls in class.

Elsvet's party during First Frost had been spectacular, as befitted her Name's wealth. Avira Anniyas, unable to attend, sent a fine gift of matching silver bracelets. Two hundred and thirty guests dined and danced in a huge chamber festooned, torchlit, and awash in Doyannis blue and green. As it was near the Feast of St. Tirreiz the Canny, remembrance tokens for the guests honored the patron of merchants and bankers: large leather purses stamped with the Doyannis Ship sigil in gold, jingling with double eagle coins. Glenin considered this display of largesse vulgar, and donated the money to the Compassionate Fund for Orphans of Ambrai. That Auvry Feiran had four years earlier helped to create these orphans troubled her not at all, nor was she concerned by the current sorry state of their lives. As a contributor, she was entitled to a copy of the yearly report on what had been done with the money, and for whom. It made interesting reading.

Elsvet's very public celebration was of her new womanhood (though she was none the wiser that Glenin could tell); Glenin's very private one with her father was of her new magic. It didn't even rankle that she could never share this more important event with anyone. She loved secrets, and cherished this one more than most.

Most people had two patron Saints. The one in whose week they were born watched over their lives, and the one for whom they were named influenced their characters. (No one was named for Kiy the Forgetful, though to be born in Harvest week omened well for a career in—or luck with—the law.) Some mothers sought extra favor by naming a child for the birth-week Saint. Unlucky persons were born during an Equinox or Solstice week, which had no Saints. Women

had another Saint, the one in whose week their Wise Blood
first flowed. A girl born during Velireon's week, named for
Delilah, who matured during the week of Alilen was protected by the Provider, the Dancer, and the Seeker all her
life.

Glenin had been named for St. Gelenis. That her Wise
Blood came during Weaver's Moon was a sign of Chevasto's
special regard; she had been born on the Saint's very day in
942. Not for her the riches omened in adulthood for Elsvet
by St. Tirreiz the Canny, or the health that the Grenirian
Blood hoped would come to their frail Velenna with St.
Feleris the Healer's patronage. With Gelenis First Daughter
looking out for her interests and a double mark of favor
from the Weaver, she would certainly take a prominent position at the Loom.

She understood much more now than when she first arrived at Ryka Court—five years ago this coming new year,
though it seemed much longer. Her father took her into his
confidence more and more, explaining Anniyas's moves in
Council as they advanced the weaving of the Loom. He gave
her the rare and secret books his unnamed Mage Guardian
teacher had given him long ago. Often she had to bite her lip
to keep silent in class when the official Council version of
events was discussed, for much of it was lies.

She knew, for instance, that although history ascribed
equal blame to Mage Guardians and Lords of Malerris, the
former were solely responsible for the Waste War. Glenin
had read an account reporting the words of the Mage Captal
himself, mourning what he and the Guardians had done.

> May the people of Lenfell forgive us. We will never
> forgive ourselves the folly of believing that use of such
> power could end in anything but misery. The fault was
> ours, the atonement never enough. Our oath of service
> must apply not to ourselves from now on, but to those
> we so grievously betrayed.

Glenin's reading did not tell her why magic had not been
outlawed and all Mageborns killed outright. She eventually
concluded that the Lost Age following The Waste War had
been so terrible that only Mageborns could have held the tattered remnants of society together. And after the First
Wraithenbeast Incursion ... well, proof enough that those

with power ought to be free to use the power that was their birthright.

It had been demonstrated to her early on that those with talent and wisdom were duty-bound to seek high position. It was Auvry Feiran's ineligibility for important office that had, in fact, caused the divorce.

From 931 until his death in 948 at age fifty, Lady Allynis's brother Telo had been Chancellor of Ambraishir. It was the only post in all Lenfell always held by a male: the father, uncle, brother, son, or husband of the ruling First Daughter. Thus it was expected that when Maichen Ambrai married, her husband would eventually take her uncle's position. But she had chosen a Prentice Mage, and therein lay the difficulty.

Mage Guardians did not hold public office. This dictate was nearly as ancient and exactly as absolute as the imperative that the Captal must survive. Governments had to be protected from Mageborn control—and Mageborns from the control of governments. This rule was especially necessary in Ambraishir, location of the Academy. Some First Daughters and Captals had loathed each other; some (as was the case with Allynis Ambrai and Leninor Garvedian) were personal friends. But whether their interests overlapped or they worked against each other, every Ambrai First Daughter and every Mage Captal scrupulously avoided even the semblance of interference in the other's jurisdiction.

Maichen Ambrai had chosen a husband her mother despised for his First Tier origins and for his failure to become a Listed Mage Guardian—but these things were incidental to his uselessness as a potential Chancellor. When Telo Ambrai died unexpectedly, all of Lady Allynis's rancor—softened somewhat by the birth of two fine granddaughters—was renewed. She needed a Chancellor, and Auvry Feiran was forbidden the office.

Her husband, Gerrin Ostin, had neither the training, the temperament, nor the inclination for public life. He was the perfect husband: adept at and content with making his Lady's home, hearth, and happiness. He shuddered at the very notion of helping Allynis govern the whole Shir. And because she hadn't married him with an eye to the Chancellorship, loved him exactly as he was, and treasured his talents that left her free to do her own work, she didn't cause him chagrin by asking.

There was one other candidate: Gerrin Ostin's namesake, Telo's son by Gorynna Desse. As Allynis's nephew, and husband to Tama Alvassy (Ambraishir's other great Name), Gerrin Desse had excellent Blood connections. He had already shown political savvy by helping his father restructure the tax code, earning the respect of all three fractious regions: fishing coast, farming heartland, and wild mountains. But in 948 Gerrin Desse was barely twenty-two. He had a pair of very young children to care for. And his beloved uncle was Gorynel Desse: Warrior Mage, First Sword, and most powerful Mageborn in a dozen Generations.

In desperation, Lady Allynis sent an appeal to Jeymian Renne, whose husband Toliner Alvassy was Tama's uncle. Toliner was Commissioner of Neele, so he had knowledge and experience. Ambrais and Alvassys had intermarried many times in Generations past, so he was more or less family. But in marrying the lovely and mysterious Jeymian Renne, whose Blood owned approximately half Brogdenguard, he had forsworn his allegiance to Ambraishir. Only divorce could return him legally to his home Shir. Lady Jeymian was willing to divorce him for appearances' sake and live with him in Ambrai as if they were still married. But Toliner, happy in his marriage and his duties, categorically refused.

A year went by, and then two, and Lady Allynis had no Chancellor. The irony of it was that Auvry Feiran would have been excellent in the position. His unofficial missions to other Shirs and even to Ryka Court had invariably met with splendid success. He was clever, intelligent, physically imposing, personally charming, socially adept, and both diligent and creative in pursuit of Lady Allynis's goals. He was also proud and ambitious, and nearing forty with little to show for his devotion to duty or his Mageborn gifts. He had been trained at the Academy and could never become Chancellor; he had left the Academy as a Prentice and would never become a Listed Mage.

And after seventeen years of having a trusted brother at her side, Lady Allynis could not have brought herself to make her daughter's husband Chancellor even if he had been eligible.

It was all so hideously unfair. Glenin had been not quite six years old when Telo Ambrai died, and over the next two years had watched the relationship between her father and her grandmother deteriorate until they were barely on speaking terms. Glenin knew who was right and who was wrong; what she would never understand was why her mother seemed stuck in the middle.

Her resentment had been that of a favorite child whose adored father has been slighted. Later she understood that her father was too valuable to be thwarted and pushed aside and stamped underfoot like a slave. He was strong, wise, clever, Mageborn, and husband to the First Daughter of the Ambrai Blood. That last would have been more than enough for most men. Auvry Feiran was not to be grouped with the common herd of males grateful to be told what to do by their mothers, sisters, the First Daughters of their Names, their own daughters, or the women they married. In government, in the vast trade Webs that spanned Lenfell, in village shops, in farm fields, in every facet of society, a man who held any position at all held it at women's convenience, and was answerable in all things to them.

Two women ruled Auvry Feiran's life and ambitions. Mage Captal Leninor Garvedian forbade him even to consider seeking the Chancellorship. Lady Allynis welcomed the Captal's word as adding weight to her own refusal to give any power to her daughter's upstart husband. Both paid dearly for this: in losing Auvry Feiran, they lost all his many gifts. On the day word came that Ambrai was destroyed as a city and a power and a Name, Glenin wondered if her tyrannical grandmother had cursed or cried as she died. Probably both.

It happened in 951, the summer after the remove to Ryka Court. One night her father came into her room very late. She half-woke as he murmured her name and stroked a finger lightly down her cheek, the way he'd done ever since she could remember. Then he was gone. Their servant gave her a letter at breakfast. Glenin was so surprised that she forgot to dismiss the man before she broke the green wax seal.

Forgive me for not saying a proper farewell. The Council orders me to Ambrai. I leave tonight. I'll come back just as soon as this matter of the Captal is settled. I don't think it will take long.

Stay well, First Daughter, and remember always that I love you and will strive to make you as proud of me as I am of you.

The "matter of the Capital" was serious, directly related to the divorce. In autumn of 950, the Council had proposed that Mage Guardians and Lords of Malerris hold office as their abilities qualified them and as it pleased their governments to honor them.

Everybody knew what it was all about. Anniyas wanted her recently acquired friend Auvry Feiran to be Chancellor of Ambrai. But he was a Mage Guardian—though officially still a Prentice—and Mage Guardians did not hold office. Warrior Mages did not direct the training of the Council Guard or the Watches; Healer Mages did not become resident physicians at Council or Shir infirmaries; Scholar Mages did not join the faculties of the various academies. No Mage—Novice, Prentice, or Guardian—served in any official capacity whatsoever. The same was true of the Lords of Malerris, though they kept to themselves in Seinshir by ancient choice and there were far fewer of them anyway.

Everybody also knew that Feiran was to be Avira Anniyas' wedge. She wanted Mageborns in government. Lady Allynis rejected the notion—and where Ambraishir led, seven other Shirs followed, with three more tagging behind. Allynis thundered her opinion at her family, at the Ambraishir Assembly, and indeed at anyone within earshot, oblivious to her daughter's white silences and her daughter's husband's set jaw.

By Candleweek the Council had withdrawn its proposal. Auvry Feiran would never become Chancellor. Allynis and the Capital congratulated each other. Glenin remembered hearing Grandmother laugh with satisfaction and then say a strange thing to Maichen: "I'm sorry if this incident has pained you, Daughter, but the Capital agrees we won't accomplish anything this way. We will stay on the original path. Tell him so."

At not quite eight years old, Glenin was unable to envision her parents, her grandmother, and the Capital in collusion. She did understand that the Council's move had been obvious and too easily thwarted. It reminded her of when she'd demanded Sarra's new puppy, been quite rightly refused, then asked for what she really wanted: a horse of her own. Grandfather Gerrin had obliged.

During early winter of 950, Glenin waited for Avira Anniyas to reveal what she really wanted, certain that the Council would oblige.

Next thing anyone knew, the Council had proposed registering all Mage Guardians and Lords of Malerris and testing their offspring for magic. New identity disks would then be issued them, lacking family colors and/or sigils, substituting a new classification: Mageborn. It was the Council's opinion that such persons were too important to Lenfell to be left unidentified. Each would decide for Mage Guardians or Malerrisi, and be educated by one or the other.

Lady Allynis was appalled. She knew very well that if this idea became law, her grandchildren might not be allowed to govern the Shir her family had ruled for thirty Generations. Should Glenin and Sarra turn up Mageborn, it would mean the end of the Ambrai Blood, unbroken in direct line since the Eighth Census. A fine vengeance for Anniyas—and Auvry Feiran. She said as much, but not to his face. She had that much concern left for her daughter's feelings.

One afternoon Glenin was on her way to a riding lesson when the Captal stormed past and nearly knocked her down, blind with rage, fist clenching her swordgrip. Glenin gaped in frank astonishment; never had the fiery Captal entered the Octagon Court armed, let alone in a black fury.

Leninor Garvedian was not just angry, she was frightened. Anniyas had all but announced that if Mageborns were forbidden government, then government would govern Mage Guardians. Unthinkable. Unprecedented. And—if she didn't talk fast—unstoppable.

Because it all made sense. Mageborns *were* an important resource. But no Mageborn had ever been compelled to become either Guardian or Lord. Some never even knew what they were, for powers varied and no one learned their use without extensive schooling. Some asked to be taught just the basics, balking when told it was all or nothing; others, terrified of their magic, asked to be Warded. The Captal regretted lost potential but would not accept unwilling students; indeed, it was expressly forbidden.

She also knew that Anniyas wanted Mageborns made distinct from their families, implying that their first loyalty was to other Mageborns. This would shake the very core of Lenfell's society. The Shirs were administrative conveniences; real allegiance went to the family. For a woman, the descending order of loyalty was her own family, then her father's, then her husband's. For a man, his birth-family was supplanted by the one he married into.

Almost every extant Name was Webbed across all fifteen Shirs. A Fenne of Shellinkroth might argue vividly in Assembly on behalf of Bleynbradden, even though Shellinkroth had no interest in or might even be injured by a vote in Bleynbradden's favor. It was the *Name* that counted, the Fenne Web of kinship and economics. Connect that Web with all the others of all the Bloods and Tiers, and the world held together.

Mages were as bright lights shining at intervals along the interlocking Webs. Their vow of service was not to the Guardians or to magic but to Lenfell. Identification and separation such as the Council proposed would cause that oath to be doubted and their families to suspect their allegiance.

Then there was the prospect of being set physically apart—and the Captal was sure that would be next. The Lords of Malerris wouldn't mind. They stuck to their island in Seinshir anyway. But the Captal knew that her Guardians would know it for what it was: a cage. And this was contrary to their credo, their heritage, and their very natures.

The Captal made her objections known to the Council at Ryka Court, and in such language that even those who were on her side blanched. The mildest of her statements was that she'd burn her own regimentals and melt down her Captal's sigil pins in public before she'd countenance governmental interference in the affairs of Mage Guardians—*or* the Lords of Malerris. She arrived ostentatiously by Ladder on the tenth of First Frost, spoke with a Mage Globe at her side to record her every word, and left by the same Ladder back to the Academy that evening. The next day she and Allynis Ambrai met to plan their next move.

They plotted for nothing. On St. Rilla's Day, the first of Snow Sparrow and only twenty-eight hours after she left Ryka Court, Captal Leninor Garvedian was arrested in Ambrai by the Council Guard and charged with treason: interference by a Mage Guardian in government was as illegal on the Statutes of Lenfell as it was in the Mage Code. The irony did not escape Glenin—especially when Lady Allynis expounded on it at length one night while the candle burned low at the bronzewood table. "Why didn't anybody ever have the sense to write a law forbidding the Council to interfere with the Mages?" she fumed, and Glenin hid a tiny smile. Anniyas, having asked for a puppy, had gotten her horse.

The Captal was spared the indignity of jail. She was confined to Academy grounds. On the Wraithenday that ended the year, Glenin's father returned to Ambrai from Ryka Court. Lady Allynis forbade him her table. Glenin considered openly defying Grandmother by refusing to be where her father was not welcome, but no one in the family had successfully defied Allynis since Maichen had married Auvry Feiran. For a time Glenin thought about pretending illness, then realized she could be more help to her father by hearing what Grandmother said.

Grandmother said nothing—as the Lords of Malerris had thus far, and as Captal Garvedian should have. The first four dinners of the new year were silent misery. Her parents' battles made up for it. Her elegant, serene mother; her composed, self-possessed father—raging at each other noon and night—Glenin's whole world was coming apart.

And then Glenin and her father left Ambrai.

In the summer of 951, he went back.

Eight days into Long Sun, the Mage Captal was found guilty of treason. Twenty-five thousand Ambraians marched on the Council House in protest. Leninor Garvedian had been born in their city; she was one of their own. She was said to be as astonished by the verdict as Lady Allynis, but only half as furious. Their joint appeals to the city prevented more than windows from being broken; only a few of the Council Guard were roughed up. The Justices locked themselves in chambers and didn't come out for three solid days.

By Allflower, things quieted down. The Captal's conviction was appealed to the Council, Ambrai settled to grumbling resentment, and Glenin—supplied with all the latest news at Ryka Court—guessed that Grandmother bitterly regretted not having made Auvry Feiran her Chancellor.

Sailors Moon was a favorite holiday, its full moon dedicated to St. Tamas the Mapmaker. After a long, raucous morning of boat races on the lake, Ryka Court met on the grassy parade ground for a banquet and the awarding of the Silver Anchor to the ship that had sailed farthest during the preceding year. A Doyannis vessel was in the running, and Elsvet was too excited to eat. Glenin, invited to sit with the family, endured her schoolmate's nerves with what she felt was remarkable patience. Well before the sweet was served around the trestle tables, however, she excused herself to go talk to her father. He sat with the Council—at the very end of the table, but with them just the same. Glenin quivered with pride at the sight of him. Dressed in green and black, he was ten times as handsome, twenty times as imposing, and a hundred times more worthy of sitting at that table than anyone else there.

He took her onto his lap so she could share the sweet with him. She was munching a spun-sugar anchor when all conversation died.

"Bard Falundir!" someone at the Council table whispered.

"But he never—"

"Has Anniyas seen him?"

"But Falundir *never*—"

"Not since that satire about her victory over the Grand Duke."

"I thought she'd have a seizure! He wouldn't dare offend her again."

"Must be a new song. Has he ever used Tamas as a theme before?"

"But he hasn't got his lute."

"Shh! He's about to start!"

The Bard wore plain blue. He wore no coif. Neither did he wear shoes. Glenin glanced quickly around to see if anyone else had noticed, her chest tightening with apprehension. Only those in mourning went barefoot.

All was silence. Falundir stood ten feet in front of the Council table, directly before Anniyas. The First Councillor smiled in pleased anticipation.

" 'Garden of the Long Sun,' " said the Bard, and began to sing.

His theme was not St. Tamas, or the sea, or sailors. The melody alone was enough to bring tears. The first stanza lovingly detailed the garden's gentle perfections of sweet green shade and glorious flowers, the delicate harmony of color and scent, the cool nurturing stream.

The second stanza told of danger that made grass blades tremble. Glenin felt her father tense.

The third revealed this danger to be poison seeping into the stream, polluting and then killing the garden, as surely as a long-ago war had destroyed The Waste.

By the middle of the fourth stanza, everyone knew that the garden was Ambrai and the poison was Anniyas.

She rose to her feet with her jeweled belt-knife in hand, a squat little woman made abruptly formidable by rage. Falundir sang a fifth stanza, tracing the pollution to its source.

The sixth would reveal Malerris. Glenin knew that as surely as she knew Falundir must be stopped. He must not link Anniyas to the Lords of Malerris. No one must know.

The First Councillor gestured curtly with the knife. Two Council Guards took Falundir by the elbows and dragged him to her.

"You have been warned before, Bard," Anniyas said, voice shaking with fury.

Auvry Feiran stood, Glenin caught close in his arms. Quickly he strode from the Council table.

"It is all Lenfell that needs warning," Falundir replied.

Glenin squirmed, looking back over her father's shoulder. "I want to—"

"*No*, Glenin."

"And that is your final word, Bard? Yes, I think it *will* be. Council? Your vote, at once."

Glenin heard the first few affirmatives before Feiran's long legs took her out of earshot. She heard very clearly the sudden gasp behind her, as if a thousand people caught their breath in a simultaneous, horrified hiss.

When she found out what Anniyas had done, she wept for the Bard's pain. But only a little, and only in secret. She understood why it had been done.

That evening an extraordinary person came to the Feiran suite. An old man she had never seen before—black-skinned, white-haired, and with eyes like green fire—entered without knocking and simply stared at Glenin's father.

"You've come for my help," Auvry said.

The old man nodded.

"This will settle all debts," Auvry warned. "I risk much—"

"So did I." The old man's eyes flickered to Glenin; she instinctively drew back. "And I lost. But not all."

"You think *that* fate reserved for me, don't you?"

Black-clad shoulders shrugged. "You do what you must."

"True of us all." He paused. "The Ladder, just after midnight. I'll make sure it's clear, and—"

"No. Now."

"Impossible."

The old man took but a single step. The effect was as if he'd leaped forward to grab Feiran by the throat. "Damn you, he's bleeding to death!"

"He'll do that anyway, inside his soul. We both know that." Another hesitation. "If it's any use to you, I don't approve of what Anniyas—"

"You're *no* use to me. Or to Maichen."

"How—how is she? And Sarra. . . ." A note of pleading entered his voice, and jealousy stabbed Glenin with a shard of ice. "Gorynel, please—tell me—"

"How the hell do you think they are?" the old man snapped.

Not even Lady Allynis spoke to Auvry Feiran with such contempt. Glenin thought that if she had, he would not have reacted. But he flinched from Gorynel Desse—for that was who this old man must be. And Glenin realized that this most renowned Warrior Mage was also her father's hitherto unnamed teacher.

"Glenin, stay here. Wait for me."

She half-rose from her chair. "Father—"

"No. I'll explain later."

But he never did.

All that summer at Ambrai, Lady Allynis dug in. Since the verdict and its subsequent disturbances, she had stationed her own well-armed Watch around Council House to prevent access to the Captal until the appeals process was complete. Depending on one's loyalties, this was seen two ways: as keeping the Guardians from rescuing their Captal before the Council ruled on her guilt or innocence, or as protecting her from possible assassination that would render any verdict moot. Allynis also closed every gate and every river dock, and restricted all Mages to Academy grounds.

This disruption of normal life—and especially of normal commerce—was endured with understanding by some and irritation by most. A few would not tolerate it. The interconnection of Lenfell's Webs worked in Anniyas' favor: trade must not unravel because of one recalcitrant city. All that was required to initiate proceedings against Ambrai was a complaint by a Blood Line—in this case the Doyannis, with their extensive shipping interests. Then, for the good of Lenfell, Anniyas could act.

She sent Auvry Feiran, and an army.

From Hunt week to Wildfire Glenin slept each night with

his note beneath her pillow. The battles of blood and magic she saw fought inside her dreams caused her to wake sweating.

When he finally returned three days after St. Caitiri's, it was not by ship but openly—daringly—by Ladder. He went immediately to the Council and begged leave to report that Ambrai would no longer annoy anyone with its intransigence. Ambrai was utterly destroyed.

Glenin expected to feel more than she did. She had long since stopped missing her mother and little sister. Being the center of Auvry Feiran's life more than made up for the loss. She did regret that circumstances had forced her father to do what he'd done. But had she been given a choice, she knew she would have chosen him instead of her mother—just as he had chosen her instead of Sarra.

No one knew the fate of Maichen Ambrai and her younger daughter; rumor was they still lived . . . somewhere. It didn't matter. Ambrai was gone. The Mage Academy, Bard Hall, and Healers Ward were charred husks; the bustling docks had collapsed into the river; wooden houses and stone public buildings and markets and even the Council House were rubble. Outlying farms were put to the torch, fields trampled. Surviving inhabitants—a tenth of the more than sixty thousand citizens of Ambrai—fled. Lady Allynis was dead, and her husband Gerrin Ostin. Tama Alvassy and her husband Gerrin Desse had been killed, and their three small children had vanished as surely as Maichen and Sarra. The Captal was dead, and at least a thousand Mage Guardians—even, it was said, the mighty Gorynel Desse.

Remembering how the old man had spoken to her father, Glenin nodded in grim satisfaction.

She fretted, though, about the Octagon Court. She loved the great palace, curious for its angularity in a world obsessed with circular architecture. At the age of six she'd earned a spanking at Lady Allynis's own hands for riding her pony across the gorgeous black and turquoise tiles of the audience chamber. When she learned that the Octagon Court had been spared on Feiran's order, she was glad. He'd done it for her, she knew. One day she would return and claim it and all Ambrai as hers, for one day she would hold all the powers of magic and the Great Loom.

And she would do it as Lady Glenin *Feiran*. And laugh as

the Wraith of Grandmother Allynis howled through the Dead White Forest with rage.

In later years, as she learned about the Great Loom and the tapestry of life woven upon it, she understood that Allynis Ambrai was a thread that had to be snipped and pulled. Snags, unravelings, random colors and textures—none of these flaws must spoil the magnificent design. Grandmother's fatal error had been to deny Auvry Feiran his rightful place as a Weaver. From this, all else had come.

She said as much, though not in so many words, to Elsvet when her not-quite-friend expressed tentative sympathy—a roundabout apology that her family's demands had led to the destruction of Glenin's home.

"My father should have been Chancellor, but they wouldn't let him, the Mage Captal and Lady Allynis. People of strength and intelligence should run things, no matter what they were born."

"Your father is certainly doing a lot in the First Councillor's service," said Elsvet. "My mother says he must've been born a Blood all unknowing."

Glenin rounded on her. "That's a stupid thing to say! Why is it you think that no one can possibly be smart or wise if they're not one of you?"

"*You're* one of us," Elsvet retorted.

"Only by accident of birth—just like *you*," Glenin snapped.

To reward his service at Ambrai, Auvry Feiran was elevated from First Tier to Blood. Others, most notably the notorious Scraller Pelleris, had bought Blood status like a trinket in the marketplace. But this time all Ryka Court agreed that it had truly been earned. As the celebration of Ambrai's fall and Auvry Feiran's rise continued long into a night ablaze with torches, Ryka Court further agreed that no one could have been so successful and done so much for Lenfell who had any taint in his ancestry.

3

Four and a half years after Ambrai's fall, Glenin came into her magic. Six weeks later, during the spring Equinox of 956, she acquired a new tutor.

The old one, a grim little man of vast scholarship and no patience, had augmented her classroom lessons with endless lectures and vicious tests. She was relieved to see the back of him. The new one was a tall, fine-boned, tawny young man, no more than twenty-five, handsome if one ignored the occasional squint that was a result not of weak eyesight but of a habitually piercing gaze. His name was Golonet Doriaz, and after Auvry Feiran greeted him and left on other business, he revealed himself as an emissary of the Lords of Malerris.

"I say this because I have every confidence in your secrecy," he went on in a voice that instantly fascinated her—like gravel stirred in a vat of cream, she thought, or a lion growling through velvet. "You and I will share many secrets. But only with each other."

"And my father," she said.

"To a point, yes." Doriaz laced long, thin fingers together. They were without rings, and his clothes and coif were plain unadorned gray. Current fashion at Ryka Court dictated the wearing of as many colors as one could work into a costume; Doriaz evidently believed with Glenin's father in the elegance of simplicity. "He is, after all, a Prentice Mage."

"Not now. Well, he is, but with the old Captal dead—"

"And the new one so foolish and ineffectual—yes, I know. But it remains that Auvry Feiran belongs to a Tradition vastly different from the one I will reveal to you." His eyes, a light brown that was nearly golden, regarded her narrowly. "Please tell me now if you feel compelled to share all with your father. I will add that he knows and agrees to the conditions of your learning."

"Oh." She paused, picking at a rose in the bowl beside her chair. "Are the two Traditions so different as to make his knowing what I know dangerous?"

"An interesting question. Dangerous for whom? You, him, or me?"

"*Domni* Doriaz—" she began, but he shook his head.

"Address me simply as 'Doriaz.' *Domni* is not a title we favor."

How very strange, she thought. First Daughters were always called "Lady"; their husbands, "Lord." Everyone else was a *domna* or *domni,* terms originally earned through accomplishment in the arts, sciences, law, and so on, but now promiscuously scattered among the ordinary populace like fallen leaves.

"Doriaz, then—if it would be dangerous to *anyone,* then I will keep what you tell me to myself."

"Very well. We begin in the morning, *Domna* Glenin."

Domni was forbidden to her, but he could call her *Domna?* She was a First Daughter, and "Lady Glenin" or nothing. But she decided to wait before correcting his manners, at least until she discerned whether he would teach her real magic.

So she smiled and asked, "Why not begin now?"

"You may have the day and the night to reflect on what it is you wish to learn."

Glenin almost retorted that it was generous of him to give her his permission to consider her own future—but something told her that sarcasm would be lost on him. Any other man with such abrupt manners would have been thrown out of her chambers and told not to come back until he'd learned proper courtesy toward women in general and a Blooded Lady in particular. But a Lord of Malerris was not just any other man. However . . . if they were all like Golonet Doriaz, what was needed most at Malerris Castle was a woman with a mind strict as an etiquette book and a hand ready with a switch cut from an apricot tree.

He unfolded his long frame from the chair. Most men found it necessary to adjust a longvest back into place with their hands—a gesture that could be awkward, furtive, perfunctory, mildly suggestive, or downright lewd. Doriaz merely gave a graceful shrug, and the thin gray material smoothed instantly from chest to thigh. A neat little trick, and one she appreciated.

"*A'verro, Domna* Glenin. That is the first thing I will teach you. It means 'truth.' You will, I hope, come to understand its significance."

That night she considered what she wanted from life. Or, more pertinently, from her magic. Problem was, she couldn't define her powers yet, and her father had warned against experimentation without supervision. *That,* he'd told her with a wry grimace, was how *he'd* gotten into trouble.

The first thing was to explore her abilities, with Doriaz's help. When she knew what was possible, she could make informed decisions about her future.

Her new teacher, however, obviously expected some sort of plan. One of the professions, perhaps? She was uninterested in the various arts and crafts, bored by the sciences, and saw no reason to waste her powers on medicine. The law, perhaps ... but the Judiciary was a notoriously slow path to influence. The one career closed to her was that of soldier. Women of Blood Names were too valuable to risk in warfare—not that there'd been much armed conflict lately, she reflected. Lenfell's only major military action this century had occurred seventeen years ago this summer. The Battle of Domburron had brought to heel His Exalted Grace the Grand Duke of Domburronshir, Heir to Grand Duchess Veller Ganfallin, Ruler of The Diamond Marches (which translated into about a half million square miles of snow in the Endless Mountains of South Lenfell). There had been fighting at Ambrai in 951, of course, but that had been a disciplinary action, not war. Female Mage Guardians could of course choose the Warrior side of magic. But Glenin would not become a Mage Guardian of any kind.

This led her to wonder why she'd never heard the phrase "Lady of Malerris." Surely there must be women among them. Nowhere on Lenfell was the natural order so overset as to place men in authority over women. She must ask Doriaz about it, for if accomplishments gained a woman no recognition, then the Lords of Malerris would have to do without her.

And yet ... *they* were the Weavers at the Great Loom, and nothing in life made so much sense to Glenin as the elegant, orderly, directed making of the tapestry.

Well, she'd simply reserve judgment and choice until she knew more.

This still left her with the problem of what she wanted her own thread to weave. A political career in the Assembly, and eventually a seat on the Council? Ah, but that would be to work with fools. By now she knew all the Councillors, not so much from personal acquaintance as from their dealings with her father. All but one or two were concerned only with the prestige and power of their own Names, and lacked true dedication to the greater good of Lenfell.

Glenin wondered suddenly why Anniyas didn't just get rid of them.

If she did . . . if the Council seats were held by those who understood as Glenin did . . . if one day *she* took the First Chair. . . .

Yes. That was what she wanted in life. Not to sit near Anniyas, as other Councillors did; not to stand at her right hand, as her father did; but to own that First Chair.

It was not something she could tell Doriaz. He would surely laugh at such an outrageous ambition. Auvry Feiran would not laugh—but she decided not to tell him, either. This was the first secret she kept from her father.

The next morning before her first class, Glenin met Doriaz in the lovely oval library of the Feiran chambers and said, "I've decided that I want to be in government." Not mentioning that she wanted to *be* the government.

"An interesting profession," he replied, crossing lanky legs at the knees. "Why do you wish to spend your life looking over your shoulder for knives poised to strike you in the back?"

"You speak metaphorically, I assume."

"I speak quite literally."

Glenin shrugged. "I won't have to look over my shoulder. I'll simply make my death unprofitable for anyone—and dangerous for all."

Doriaz rose with his little shrug—the longvest was dark green today—and gazed down at her from a great height. Glenin had to tilt her head back to hold his tawny gaze. She resented the necessity but learned something from it.

"*Domna* Glenin Feiran, born of the Ambrai Blood, it is my sincere wish that I will one day have the honor of addressing you as 'Lady.' "

4

"What about poor people, Doriaz? And sick people, and criminals, and those of the Fourth Tier whom everyone despises?"

"We will give everyone her own place, her appropriate place, and there will be no poor. The sick will be cared for. Criminals will be excised as the broken threads they are, for they endanger the strength of the whole. Tiers will be abolished, and everyone will be equal with her own place in the design."

"But that means that those who do the weaving will have to know everything about everybody, in order to decide which place is the correct one."

"This is being arranged. Slowly. It all takes time, *Domna* Glenin."

"Why can't it happen now?"

"Because there are Mageborns who do not see the design of the Loom, or who believe each thread should be woven as it desires, wild and unplanned, without regard to the larger pattern. Our weave will be fine and beautiful, strong and resilient—free of threads that knot and spoil the whole with improper texture or color, or those that are weak and may break."

"So until those Mageborns are gone, we can't begin the tapestry?"

"It was begun long ago."

"Doriaz—do you really think I'll be one of the Weavers?"

"Everything you and I do prepares you for the place even now being readied for you at the Loom. You must be patient, *Domna,* and learn all I teach you."

"I'm curious about something. Why have I never heard of any Ladies of Malerris? And you've never explained just what 'Malerris' is."

"It means 'Threadmaster.' Our women are honored with the title of Lady when they prove accomplished in craft, knowledge, dedication, and obedience."

"When they've whelped a Mageborn or two, you mean. That's disgusting."

"A child is a woman's greatest gift to the Loom."

"So all her magic and learning and everything else she does is worthless?"

"I did not say that, *Domna* Glenin."

"But you implied it, and I *still* say it's disgusting. I'm worth more than my ability to have daughters!"

"Of course. But to see your gifts continued . . . I think you shall have quite remarkable children."

"By the right man—a Malerrisi, naturally."

"Naturally."

"What if I don't *want* a Malerrisi to father my children?"

"Obedience is not your strongest virtue. But you will learn."

"Not in this, I won't! Have *you* done your duty to Malerris, Doriaz? Well? Or haven't they found the right girl for you yet?"

"As it happens, no. You are impertinent, Glenin Feiran. Consider, if your conceit will allow, the overall design instead of your own individual thread within it. The man—or men—who will father your children will be chosen for suitable bloodline, importance, position, and power. Are any of these things different from the qualities you yourself would seek?"

"He'd have to be handsome—I want pretty daughters."

"Willful, impertinent, *and* facetious. I can see we will have no useful discussion today."

"No, I'm sorry—please sit down. It's just—so *personal!* Surely you understand."

"Yes. But it is not a thing that can be left to chance. You will be no different from any other Blood in that you may love as you please. But your children must have the best possible chance of being Mageborn."

"Well . . . so long as I have a choice and I'm not just told it'll be this man or that."

"You *will* be told. And you *will* obey. Or you will be viewed as any other Mageborn not educated in Malerrisi ways, and dealt with accordingly."

"They wouldn't dare!"

"Glenin, think of who you are! The only surviving Ambrai, powerfully Mageborn, who can ultimately influence or even *become* the pattern of our victory! What is your private whim compared to that?"

"An ... interesting question, Doriaz. I begin to see what you mean."

5

Glenin learned much from Golonet Doriaz over the next four years, though he despaired of her ever learning proper obedience. He went with her and her father when they traveled, and taught her—among other things—how to recognize those secretly Mageborn and distinguish Mage Guardian from Malerrisi. The feel of the magic was different when she sent subtle probes into their minds. The Mages all felt like her father: flexible and even chaotic at times, utterly undisciplined compared to the Malerrisi.

In late spring of 960, Doriaz was summoned to the Castle in Seinshir. Deprived of his daily presence, Glenin moped. She daydreamed all through her other classes, traced his initials on her rain-fogged windowpanes, and in general behaved as exactly what she was: a seventeen-year-old girl deep in the throes of first love.

Her father made no remark on her listless distraction, except for one evening when she set up the shadow-glass lantern in their sitting room and projected painted views of Seinshir on the wall. She'd purchased the box of ten-inch square glass slides that morning: *Spectacular Seinshir: Fifty Views.* She stared for a full five minutes each at the three depictions of Malerris Castle—one with the waterfall below, one from the village road, and one from out to sea. Auvry Feiran murmured that he didn't know about there being fifty spectacular views of Seinshir, but there certainly seemed to be three of more than passing interest.

While Doriaz was gone, she practiced her magic. In just over four years she had learned (among other things) twenty different Wards, six calling/retrieval spells, firelighting, the basics of Mage Globes, and the theory behind Ladders—though not the actual location of any on Ryka, or the total number on Lenfell. He'd promised to take her through one on his return. She wondered why he hadn't used a Ladder to Malerris Castle to avoid the lengthy journey by sea, but on further reflection decided that avoiding suspicion was more important. No one but Glenin and her father knew what Doriaz was; while not conspicuous in and of himself, as tutor of the Guard Commandant's daughter he was mildly visible at Ryka Court. It was wiser to book passage—though not specifically to Seinshir—and endure the voyage rather than simply to vanish.

Auvry Feiran had been correct: it was becoming more and more risky to be known for a Mageborn. The Guardians kept to themselves, still not recovered from the loss of the Academy and the energetic if foolish Leninor Garvedian. The new Captal, an Adennos, was an ineffectual Scholar Mage, cowering amid his books in a ramshackle building the Council had provided in Shellinkroth. Formerly a law court, unused since a new Council House opened in a better section of Havenport, the marble hallways were said to be thunderously silent. The scant seven hundred Mage Guardians who remained—Novices, Prentices, Warriors, Healers, Scholars—were scattered across Lenfell: a body sliced to bits that didn't yet know it was dead.

As for the Lords of Malerris—this conclave at their great castle had been called to deal with their own rapidly deteriorating status. This had come about courtesy of the Councillor for Seinshir. He was the gray and glowering Risson of the Dalakard Blood, who always looked as if he'd swallowed something sour. And the Lords were a particularly bad taste on his tongue.

On Malerris Island—one of eight major and countless insignificant islands that made up Seinshir—Dalakard lands abutted those of the Castle. Two decades of petty arguments had degenerated two years ago into a fight over who owned a rich vein of iron ore discovered smack on the border. Risson battled for Dalakard possession with words and lawsuits, but never with arms—for who knew what the Lords would do magically if provoked? A Warrior Mage could be counted on to fight the non-Mageborn according to strict rules of war, without spells (at least that was the theory; recently revisionist histories speculated otherwise, another sign of magic under suspicion). But the Lords of Malerris had no special class of warriors, and indeed scorned Mages both for accepting those with martial skills and for subsequently forbidding them to use magic in pursuit of military aims. So Risson fought for his family's rights in the courts, and had been losing.

In the week of Maiden Moon 960, the Council declared itself fed up to the teeth with the whole tedious issue and decided in favor of the Dalakards. A few days later a summons went out from Malerris Castle. The Lords found it necessary to review their position—politically, economically, and societally. Glenin, more concerned with the absence of Golonet Doriaz than the reasons for it, for once did not make the proper connections.

Her father enlightened her on St. Fielto's Day. After riding all afternoon in raucous celebration of the Saint's famous hunt, Ryka Court would feast all night. Glenin was too depressed to join. She spent a desultory morning in the kennels, coercing a litter of puppies down a hallway and into her lap—until the hound bitch came looking for her offspring with hackles raised and teeth bared. In the afternoon, while Elsvet and her other schoolmates galloped wildly through the forest, Glenin took out her bad humor on the cooks from the safe distance of a stairwell. Rising bread collapsed, stews boiled over, milk soured as ice melted in coldboxes. Harmless little magics, and she knew she was being silly, but Doriaz was gone, and she was bored and lonely, and there was nothing to do.

That night as they finished dinner in their chambers, Feiran asked, "Well, Glenin, did you enjoy using your magic on helpless animals and inoffensive cookpots?"

She flushed, embarrassed to have been caught in her foolish little spells. Then she was angry. Who had told on her? No one—she'd been careful not to be observed. Besides, she thought, resentful now, she'd done no real harm.

Gray-green eyes accurately noted each emotion. She saw it, and this time blushed so hotly her cheeks felt blistered. Doriaz had warned her about controlling herself, especially her complexion.

"You're lucky," Feiran went on. "No one was around today who could sense your little games but me." When Glenin's jaw dropped, he continued grimly, "Did you think you and I were the only Mageborns at Ryka Court?"

"I—I didn't—" She gulped. *"Who?"*

"Find out for yourself. But don't try until you can work

with more subtlety than you showed today. I felt the back-wash all the way to the parade ground."

"Backwash?" she echoed, wits as thick as the milk she'd curdled that afternoon.

"So. Something Doriaz hasn't taught you yet." He half-closed his eyes and a few moments later their servant knocked on the door. "Yes," Feiran said, "you may clear the table now, thank you."

When the woman was gone, Glenin blurted, "You *called* her! I felt it!"

"Only because you were groping around for it. *I* felt *that*. You're as delicate with your power as a Healer whose cure for a hangnail is to saw off the hand." Leaning back, he sipped his wine before adding with a slight smile, "They said that about me, too—only I was accused of lopping off the whole arm. You've learned spells, Glenin. What Doriaz hasn't taught you is technique. He's been Warding you himself, I gather."

Thoroughly ashamed of herself, she managed, "I'm sorry, Father. I know what I did was silly—worse, it was danger-ous."

"Yes, it was. Especially now that things are happening ex-actly as planned."

"You mean about Mageborns." When he nodded, she said, "I won't do it again until Doriaz shows me—"

"I don't think he'll be coming back, Glensha," he said gently. "I'm sorry. I know you're fond of him."

"Not c—coming back—?" Her insides tied into ever-tightening knots.

"Malerris Castle was attacked this morning by the Coun-cil Guard and the Ryka Legion. The walls were breached at sunset. By now it will have been put to the torch."

"And—those inside?" she breathed.

"Many are dead." He looked anywhere but at her. "I gave orders to spare Doriaz if he was caught."

But the elite Ryka Legion did not answer to Auvry Feiran. He commanded the Guards. The Legion belonged to Anniyas. Would she give orders to spare Golonet Doriaz— the man Glenin wanted instead of Anniyas's own foolish, magic-less fop of a son? Ah, Chevasto help her, she should have been nicer to Garon, less obvious in her preference for Doriaz's company—

Then she realized what her father had truly said. *"You gave orders? You?"*

"I planned the action, yes." He set his cup down and met her anguished gaze. "At the request of the Council, which is to say Anniyas."

Glenin leaped to her feet. "No! You *couldn't* betray the Malerrisi the way you betrayed the Mage Guardians!"

"Sit down!" he snapped. "No one has been betrayed. What was done today was done with the assistance of the Lords of Malerris themselves."

She did not sit down. She reached for the silver carafe of wine and poured her waterglass full, she who was never allowed liquor. She drank it down, poured another, and finally pulled her chair back under her. Seating herself, she stared him straight in the eye.

"Explain this," she said flatly.

A heavy brow arched at this display of Blood arrogance—but she also saw a glint of pride in his eyes. In a neutral voice he said, "If you can tell me why it happened, then I will explain what it means."

She considered, then nodded. "The Council, which is to say Anniyas, gave the Dalakards the iron. The Lords gathered to decide how to deal with the insult to themselves and to the process of law. All in one place, they made an easy target. You, a former Mage Guardian, could warn the troops what to look for by way of Wards—except that most of the Wards were cancelled or weakened."

"Go on."

"The dead at Malerris Castle are either very old, not very powerful, or servants who don't matter. Expendable. Anyone important escaped by Ladder. No one but the Malerrisi know how many Ladders there are at the Castle or their destinations, so now no one knows where the Lords are. They can do as they please, safely anonymous."

"Very good. A few more items, though. By burning the Castle, the number of and identities of the corpses will be uncertain. As a former Mage, I could not participate personally, or it would seem as if the Guardians had approved it. But of course everyone knows who the Council Guard Commandant is."

"The Victor of Ambrai." She wondered if he knew that he was also called the Butcher of Ambrai. Of course he knew. He knew almost everything. She resumed, "Captal Adennos struck your name from the Lists, but that could have been a ruse to put you in exactly this position, using the Council's forces to destroy the Malerrisi. Several bodies will be identified as Warrior Mages, won't they?"

"Yes. Preventing the fires from burning them past recognition will be difficult, but there are always the identity disks. And you're right, the Mages will be said to be behind this. The ancient enemy, vanquished at last. And now Lenfell will wonder what the Mages will do next, lacking the Lords of Malerris to counter their power."

"A power greatly diminished since Captal Garvedian died," Glenin pointed out. "Weak as they are, it'll be hard to make anybody suspect them."

"People are accustomed to thinking of them as powerful. As individuals, they still are. As a unified force. . . ." He dismissed this with a shrug.

Glenin circled the rim of her goblet with a fingertip. "What excuse was used to attack the Castle?"

"Risson Dalakard asked what a meeting of hundreds of powerful Mageborns could mean. And answered his own question, of course."

"An attack on Dalakard lands."

"Precisely. He added that who knew but what the Malerrisi couldn't simply make the disputed iron vanish." He snorted. "Ignorance of what magic can and cannot do is a vital asset, Glenin."

She took a long swallow of wine. It was spicy and warm and felt wonderful sliding down her throat, settling her stomach and her nerves. "So this was as carefully planned as Ambrai."

"More so. And much easier. This time we had the full cooperation of those whose home we destroyed."

"What about the Ladders?"

"Fire is the one thing they cannot survive. They are as vulnerable to it as their wooden counterparts. That's why it was important to burn the Castle. Mage Guardians know about Ladders, too."

"Then . . . wherever the Lords went, they're stuck there."

"Each Ladder has only one destination, yes. Would you like me to show you?"

6

It was a wink at the corners of her closed eyes, a teasing tingle just beyond reach of her magic. The more she tried to see and the harder she tried to grasp, the less substantial it became.

"Oh, stop that," her father said, amusement in his voice.

Mindful of his chiding her for lack of subtlety, she stopped chasing the wink and opened her eyes to find his face in the darkness.

"Doriaz told you the basics, I assume?"

"How it works, but not how to work it."

"A conceit on his part. Nobody knows exactly how they work. Nobody knows how to build one, either. The knowledge was lost in the Waste War. As for finding those that still exist—you never know one's there until you're in the middle of it, as we are now. Even then it's a coy beast, quite often Warded."

"Keep Away? Danger?" she guessed.

"Too obvious. I'm told this one once had a rather insidiously clever Stain On My Shirt around it. Note the mirror on the far wall."

Glenin laughed nervously. "By the time you got through checking, you'd forget about the possibility of a Ladder."

"Vanity can be useful," he replied, smiling.

Taking her hand, he centered her with him in the circle. It was delineated by a pattern of pale green tiles set into the white floor of an insignificant anteroom near the Council Chamber. If he hadn't pointed it out to her with the aid of a Mage Globe, she would never have known it was there. No magical energy betrayed its existence. The circle pattern was repeated in several places to accent the circular room. Doriaz had told her that a Ladder was always situated within round walls. She'd asked why: he'd answered, "An interesting question."

Her father hadn't made her promise not to try the Ladder on her own; she might yet lack subtlety, but never intelligence. Council precincts were forbidden at all hours to any-

one not a Councillor—or the man who stood at Avira
Anniyas's right hand. Tonight was the exception to the rule
of constant and multiple sentries. Everyone was at the St.
Fielto's Day feast but for a few token Guards, none of whom
would dream of challenging the passage of their Commandant.

"First, center yourself as I taught you years ago," he said.
"Ignore what you almost sense. Calm yourself, close your
eyes, and forget where you are."

She clung suddenly to his hand, gasping. There was nothing around her—no tiled floor underfoot, no circle of walls,
no vast Ryka Court beyond this room.

"It's all right. Open your eyes."

She blinked. Her eyes stung and her nose prickled with
the smell of scorched wood. Clutching his arm with both
hands, she looked around wildly by the rose-red light of his
kindling Mage Globe.

"Wh–where—?"

"Ambrai," he whispered.

Glenin huddled close to him. They were still within a circle, but this time it was the central well of the famous Double Spiral Stair. Only a few days before she'd left Ambrai,
she and Sarra had played here. People climbing up one side
couldn't see anyone on the other, and the possibilities for
startling Grandmother's stuffy ministers had been endless.

Now the shining marble was stained by smoke and fire.
Oily black tongues of soot licked up the smooth walls.
Auvry Feiran guided her through the narrow access slit into
the grand hall. She wiped her eyes and rubbed her itchy
nose, and made herself look around.

The tapestries were gone. Of the gorgeous Cloister rugs,
chairs and tables, huge vases brimming with flowers, carved
wood window casings and panes of colored glass, nothing
was left but charred wreckage.

"But—but you said it had been spared," she blurted out.

"As much of it as I could manage, Glensha. I'm sorry."

Glenin knuckled her eyes again. "Why?" she demanded,
looking up at her father. "Why did they make you do this?"

"The Council?" he asked, frowning.

"No! Grandmother and the Captal and—and even Mother!
They made this happen, it's their fault—"

"Glensha—" He gathered her in his arms and rocked her

while she cried. "I'm sorry, I should never have brought you here, please don't cry, heartling—"

After a time she regained control. Drawing away, she tugged the hem of her shirt from her trousers and used it to dry her face. "I'm all right. It's just—I know you did your best to keep it safe."

"I'm sorry," he said again. "One day it will all be as it was."

"Better," she corrected, and he almost smiled.

He brushed at a step, trying to clean it off so they could sit. Hopeless, of course. Nine years of accumulated grit overlaid on the stains of soot and smoke could not be wiped clean. They sat anyway, his strong arm around her shoulders, her head against his chest.

"I suppose I could say I brought you here because there was no chance we'd be seen. I'm not much good at invisibility spells."

Glenin was. But that was one of those secrets she kept from her father.

"A Ladder's Blanking Ward cancels all other spells until one steps out of the circle anyway," he went on. "That's why I had to call up another Mage Globe. I judged this one the safest of all the Ladders at Ryka. . . ." He trailed off, and she waited. Then: "Truly told, I wanted to remind myself of the necessity of sacrifice."

Glenin considered. "Did someone you know die today at Malerris Castle?"

After a moment's silence, his answer was soft, sorrowful. "Many chose to be left behind, to sacrifice themselves for others. I knew some as teachers, some as friends."

Glenin said nothing, listening to the faint whisperings of a breeze through Ambrai's empty halls. At length, she stirred.

"How did we get here?"

"How—? Oh. The Ladder." He sounded as if awakening from a troubled sleep, and glad to do so. "You didn't get past the Blanking Ward, did you? It's unsettling the first time. But once you know where the Ladder goes, you can see that place past the Ward. It's set to keep the Ladder from use by unauthorized Mageborns, for you can only use a Ladder if you know where it goes. Ancient magic had a sublime elegance that we can't even hope to emulate."

"Will you teach me how it's done?"

"Not this time." He stood. "We should be getting back."

Glenin followed him to the narrow opening into the Double Spiral and looked up. The graceful, precisely matched curves would glow pristine white again one day. She vowed it. When *she* ruled Ambrai, and the Octagon Court was hers alone, and she became First Councillor and no one had to die or hide or pretend or—

—or sacrifice his life.

Five days later, word came of Golonet Doriaz.

"He was the last to reach the Ryka Ladder," said Auvry Feiran, holding Glenin's chill hands between his own, watching her shock-dulled eyes. "He helped everyone else first—clearing the corridor to the Tillinshir Ladder took over an hour. Just as he was about to leave by the Ryka Ladder, he was overcome by smoke. I'm sorry, heartling. I'm so sorry."

He could have gone to Tillinshir—but he wanted to come back to Ryka. To me. *I know he did. And he died because of it.*

"Glensha . . . I know how deeply this hurts you. I know you cared for him. But you must take pride and comfort in his courage. He helped everyone he could. He never thought once of himself, only of the others."

But at the last, he thought of me. *He was coming to Ryka.*

"I *am* proud of him," she replied stiffly. "His thread was strong enough to preserve the whole fabric of the Loom. He won't be forgotten."

7

Once again, it all happened just as Auvry Feiran had said it would.

Rumors lurched and spasmed worldwide. Assembly representatives and Council members went home to their Shirs, holding public forums and being interviewed for the local broadsheets, and anyone who bothered to read a sampling from each region was bound to notice certain similarities in what was said. Whether an individual was for Anniyas or deplored Anniyas, the subject of Mage Guardians was foremost on every agenda.

They had strongly protested the destruction of fellow Mageborns, even though the Lords of Malerris were their enemies. They avowed themselves innocent of complicity, but three circumstances argued otherwise.

First: Several burned corpses had been discovered with collar pins easily identified as swords: Warrior Mage insignia.

Second: Auvry Feiran, former Prentice Mage, commanded the Council Guard though he was not at the battle (he'd been conspicuous at Ryka Court, as everyone agreed). Was it so outrageous to think that the destruction of Ambrai and the Mage Academy had been a ruse to make people think Feiran's loyalties were now with the Council?

Third: Those few score Lords of Malerris who were not at the Castle, too old or ill to attend or unable to get passage in time, had been mysteriously murdered in their beds the very night of the attack. Who could get past Mageborn Wards but other Mageborns—namely, Mage Guardians?

Only see what they'd gained! said those for Anniyas. Whatever the Guardians lost at Ambrai, whatever their current state of disarray, the Lords of Malerris were utterly gone.

Only see how absurd the accusation was! said those who deplored Anniyas. How could the broken, disorganized, virtually leaderless remnants of the Guardians mount so overwhelming an attack? Moreover, as suspicion would invariably fall on them, how could they be so stupid?

The Captal dithered and protested to the Council and finally issued a formal denial of involvement. He reminded all and sundry that on accepting the post of Commandant of the Council Guard, Auvry Feiran had been stricken from the Mage Lists. Names had been so stricken only a few times before in the long history of the Mage Guardians. The dishonor was total, the erasure complete. It was as if that Guardian had never existed, not even in fireside grandfather tales. This was the fate Captal Garvedian ordered, and Captal Adennos reconfirmed, for Auvry Feiran. Proof of Feiran's loyalty to the Council—or a move to cover Guardian involvement.

Some said Feiran *was* loyal, but only to the First

Councillor—who played each side against the other in an attempt to obliterate all Mageborns.

Others said all fault lay with Risson Dalakard. Just as the Doyannis Blood's demand that the Council break the blockade of Ambrai's ports led to Ambrai's fall, the Dalakard Blood had been the instrument of Malerris Castle's destruction. (Both Bloods howled injury at this.)

No, official rumor agreed at last, there were no conspiracies, no deliberate malice, no wheels within wheels. The consensus among those who governed the Shirs, supervised the Guilds, and otherwise held positions of importance was that the whole sorry mess was due to a lamentable series of accidents. To view it as anything else led to discomfort of the acutest kind.

And so it was decided for the peace of Lenfell to cease speculations and get on with life. Truly told, what would be so different? In the nine years since Ambrai the Mage Guardians had not resumed their usual roles as teachers, healers, protectors. Their former influence was becoming a memory. Lenfell was doing fine without them. As for the Lords of Malerris—they had never been as involved in the world as the Guardians, anyway. For the most part they kept their magics to themselves inside their Castle. They had never had governmental ambitions; they were concerned with trade only insofar as the excess produce of their lands was offered for sale; they traveled rarely. Most of Lenfell didn't know anyone who had even met a Lord of Malerris. As with the Mage Guardians, the lack of them would not be felt.

The important folk of Lenfell asked themselves if magic of any kind was needed at all. Their confident answer was *No*.

The common folk of Lenfell would have answered differently. Magic had always been in their lives. Wards were set in high pastures to protect flocks; medicines were brewed by Healer Mages; Warrior Mages cleared out brigands; non-Mageborn teachers were taught by Scholar Mages at the Academy and returned to educate hometown children—for the common folk, magic was needful.

The common folk were not consulted. Those who ruled Lenfell foresaw benefits to the diminution of Mageborns; magic had always caused trouble in public affairs and there was always the risk of another war as long as both Traditions survived with their power intact.

The Mages were greatly reduced in numbers and influence. The Lords were gone. Whether or not there had been Guardian hands in the matter ended up mattering little—except that the Council and the Guard would keep a close watch on those Mages who were left.

Then, in the new year, Ryka Court had something else to talk about. Anniyas' only offspring, a son called Garon, was more and more often seen in the company of Glenin Feiran.

In the first weeks of 961, professional Advocates were engaged to negotiate the necessary contracts. That spring, on the Feast of St. Imili the Joyous, the pair were betrothed. Garon, not yet twenty-four, had just finished his formal education. At barely eighteen, Glenin had several years of schooling still ahead of her. They would be wed during Rosebloom three years hence, on Anniyas's sixty-fourth Birthingday.

The First Councillor let it be known that general rejoicing would not be frowned upon. News of the betrothal was disseminated across Lenfell by St. Sirrala's Day, and every Shir's celebration of the holiday included at least a mention of the happy event.

Anniyas described her son as the image of his long-dead father—whose Name she never divulged. It was a woman's privilege to reveal or not to reveal her children's paternity, but Garon's was a subject of constant speculation at Ryka Court. Anniyas had been thirty-eight when her only offspring, the darling of her life, was born. His looks were the opposite of her plump fairness: he was tall, slim, dark-eyed, raven-haired. But the set of the eyes, deep and shadowed beneath heavy brows, and the full curve of the lower lip that hinted petulance, were identical in mother and son—though Garon was handsome and Anniyas was decidedly plain. Glenin's schoolfellows fell all over themselves congratulating her on her betrothed's fine appearance. His position as son of the First Councillor was to them a secondary consideration.

To her own great pleasure, Glenin had grown up to resemble her father. Like him, she was tall, with gray-green eyes and strong bones. But the rest of her long-dead family showed in other aspects: thick, dark-blonde hair from her mother, a perfect oval face from Lady Allynis, a long, straight nose from her Ostin grandfather. Her figure was slender and supple, her gestures graceful, her rare smiles coveted, her taste in clothes slavishly copied by every girl her age. She and Garon made a handsome couple, and they both knew it.

They also knew—and never spoke about—the differences in their characters. The long betrothal was silently understood as time to accustom each to the other's quirks. Because each scorned as ill-bred the directness of a rousing argument, no complaint or grievance was ever aired. They were unfailingly, exquisitely, sometimes ostentatiously polite to each other. Garon deferred graciously to Glenin even when he seethed inside; Glenin smiled even when she wanted to spit in his face. She could smile because every time she felt like strangling him, she imagined Grandmother Allynis's rage at alliance between the sacred Ambrais and the family of Avira Anniyas. But at times even that trick came close to failing her when Garon was particularly annoying.

They had a single personality conflict. Garon wanted all the privileges of position and none of the work. Glenin wanted position *because* of the work, for through it came the accumulation and exercise of power.

Anniyas had been a power in Tillinshir and an Assembly member since before Garon was born. He'd grown up with his whims indulged, his conceit pampered, and his every desire granted, and saw no reason why manhood should differ from childhood. With the exception, naturally, of doing exactly as he pleased without anyone to say him nay, not even his mother. And certainly not the woman who took him to husband.

For, despite the fact that he was male, Garon took it as written in stone that he would succeed his mother as First Councillor. Had Glenin been less ambitious, he could have had the title while she wielded the power, and they would have been a perfect match. But that was not how her mind worked.

Still, she could be patient. There was much magic to be perfected in the next three years, and much to discover about how to govern Lenfell and her future husband. Sooner or later Garon would see things her way—and despite his position as Anniyas's son, he would indeed see things *Glenin's* way.

Eventually, she might let him stand at *her* right hand.

Auvry Feiran had no illusions about Garon or the reasons for Glenin's acceptance of him. He'd hoped for it, while saying and doing nothing toward its accomplishment. When it happened, he asked only one question.

"Could you learn to be content with him, Glensha?"

"I think so," she answered, and quite honestly. She considered it no part of her obligation of secrecy to keep from him her emotional truths. Only—thanks be to St. Chevasto he hadn't mentioned *love*. For love of Auvry Feiran, Maichen Ambrai had defied everyone and everything. Glenin could still recall how they had adored each other with a devotion that excluded everyone, even their daughters. With their example before her of how a passionate love could shatter hearts when it died, she had no wish to find such a thing of her own.

A similar but unconsummated devotion had shattered *her* heart when its object died.

"It'll turn out fine once we get to know each other better," she went on, "and, of course, after my First Daughter is born. Garon looks a bit like Golonet Doriaz, don't you think? Tall and thin, with black hair . . . I've even taught him that little trick Doriaz had of resetting his longvest." She smiled.

"I noticed," her father answered dryly. "Now, if you could only get him to wear something besides those garish reds and purples!"

"I'll work on it!"

They laughed, but a few moments later he took her shoulders in his large, strong hands and said very seriously, "If he ever makes you unhappy, Glensha . . . if he ever hurts you. . . ."

"He won't. We're learning to understand each other and that's the most important thing."

What she meant was that she already understood him, and over the next years she intended that *he* understand precisely what she required of him. Had he been any man other than Anniyas's son, she would simply have informed him. But Glenin must tread carefully, conscious always that her marriage would be different from those of other women: although legally the man would be hers and no longer his mother's, this man's mother was also the most powerful woman in the world.

For now.

After the betrothal ceremony, Garon returned to his amusements—he was an avid hunter, an excellent horseman, and a constant winner at cards—and Glenin returned to her schooling. While Garon enjoyed the social pleasures of his status, Glenin studied law, government, commerce, and magic. This last was done in secret, but it was done as thoroughly as if Doriaz were still with her.

In a way, he still was. In 960, shortly after the official report came that he had died in a shipwreck in the Sea of Snows, an elderly Advocate had delivered to Glenin a small wooden box.

"He didn't leave much, Lady," the woman said. "These scholarly types—well, that's to say, all he left were books. Except for this little box, which goes to you. He was your tutor, I understand."

When she was alone, Glenin turned the box over and over in her hands. Uncarved, undecorated, without a lock to guard the contents, yet it could not be opened until its Ward was negated. The Ward whispered quite clearly to her, as it undoubtedly had to the advocate: *Take me to Glenin Feiran.*

She dealt with the Ward—simple, because it had been set by the man who'd taught her such things—and opened the box. In it was a brass key. It also whispered, this time of a trunk in his private chamber. Within the trunk were piles of books and manuscripts. And below them, securing a hidden compartment, was another lock. Glenin almost missed it, and would have if she hadn't been looking with more than her eyes. This had no key but the word that canceled its Ward—*a'verro,* which Doriaz had used for all the Wards he'd taught her.

She murmured it, and the lock sprang open. Inside was the real treasure: *The Code of Malerris.*

This great tome—thirty inches tall, ten inches wide, and eight inches thick—became her teacher. She would have sworn it spoke to her in the voice of Golonet Doriaz, and every so often when she scowled bewilderment and muttered to herself by the light of her Mage Globe late at night, she heard him say, *An interesting question,* Domna *Glenin.*

One evening during her twenty-first year, she saw how few chapters remained to be mastered and wondered what would happen when she was finished. The remembered gravel-and-velvet voice whispered, *An interesting question, Lady Glenin.*

She put her face in her hands and wept—for joy, for grief, for honor, for pride, and for bitter knowledge that the one man who should have been her husband was lost to her forever.

"*A'verro,* Doriaz," she whispered at last, promising him that his truth would be woven forever into the Great Loom.

Sarra

1

It had been bothering Sarra ever since they'd come to Ostinhold at Maiden Moon, and at last curiosity got the better of manners.

"Will it ever rain again?"

What was to her a perfectly sensible question brought smiles and outright laughter all around the huge Ostin dinner table. The reaction startled her so much that she simply failed to comprehend it for a moment. No one had ever laughed at her in Ambrai.

But then, The Waste was as unlike Ambrai as a place could get.

"It's always raining *somewhere,* even during Wildfire," said Geria. As First Daughter she had special speaking privileges, but the smug superiority of her tone earned her a stern glance from Lady Lilen.

"Somewhere in the world," Taig added, "but not here." The sympathy in his gray eyes made Sarra's spine stiffen, but an instant later she realized what he really meant: *everything* happened anywhere but The Waste.

"Geria and Taig are both correct," said Sarra's mother, her soft voice like the brush of polished golden silk on Sarra's skin. "What you must remember is geography's effect on weather." And thus a lesson began, just as if they'd been at home seated around their own table, with Granna and Granfa and Tama and Gerrin and Mai and—and—

Sarra had been ordered never to speak of her father or sister again. But she couldn't help thinking. Or feeling. Neither could her mother. The sound of muffled weeping still came from her room at night. Ten weeks since they'd left Ambrai, and still she wept every night. So did Sarra. At Fifteenth, long after she was supposed to be asleep, she'd tiptoe into her mother's room and curl into her arms in the narrow bed and they'd cry each other to sleep. But Sarra always woke before dawn, in time to go back to her room and pretend she'd never left it. To be an Ambrai was to be proud; she'd learned it from Granna Allynis even if it hadn't already been in her Blood. Besides, Lady Lilen would be unhappy if she knew, and it was a guest's duty to show nothing but gratitude for hospitality. So Sarra and her mother saved their tears for late at night, and never let on to anyone that it happened. Not even to each other.

". . . so we must be very cautious about our use of water here," her mother was saying. Sarra nodded, listening with half her mind—alert as most people's full attention—while unruly memory spun pictures.

Her father. First and always, her father. Last summer, after a very public and very noisy fight followed by a very private and very tender farewell, he had gone away to Ryka Court. Maichen Ambrai explained it to her two daughters as a necessary deception. But on Wraithenday Auvry Feiran returned to Ambrai, and this time no gentleness followed the shouting. After five horrible days he claimed Glenin and took her away with him forever.

Sarra knew it was forever. She wasn't sure *how* she knew it, but she did.

"You can't! She's *my daughter, my Firstborn*—"

"I can and I will, Maichen."

"How can you do this? Have you begun to believe the pretense? What did Anniyas offer you?"

"That's none of your concern. The Council has agreed to our divorce—"

"You mean Anniyas has! What did she promise? Do you really think she'll let you share her power?"

"There's more to the world than Ambrai."

"And how much of it did you ask for, Auvry?"

"This is pointless. Stop it now, before we forget that we

*once loved each other. The divorce is a fact. You may keep
Sarra, but Glenin is* my *daughter now. Mine alone."*

"No! NO!"

Listening from her perch on the ledge outside her parents'
third-floor chambers, Sarra knew with absolute certainty that
she would never see her father and sister again. Frightened
by the strength of the knowing, certain of its truth even as
she rejected it, she climbed shakily down from her habitual
secret spot and said nothing to anyone about what she knew.

During Maiden Moon this year, on a night when thousands took to the streets of Ambrai in a blaze of torches and
a tumult of songs to celebrate Granna's Birthingday, Sarra
and her mother were hurried by First Sword Gorynel Desse
from the Octagon Court to the Academy. That night Sarra
traveled by Ladder for the first time. One moment she was
in Ambrai; the next, somewhere in The Waste. She didn't
know where, only that there had been long, hot days of riding and short, sleepless nights in the open before they were
welcomed to Ostinhold by Lady Lilen, she of the warm
voice and sorrowing eyes.

Everyone Sarra knew and loved—except her mother—was
gone. Grandparents, cousins, friends, schoolmates, everyone.
Sarra was forbidden to speak about the Octagon Court, but
she couldn't help thinking. Or feeling. Or missing the soft,
clean, cool rain—nearly as much as she missed her father
and her sister.

She wanted to hear her father's laughter. She wanted to
reach up and feel him gently enfold her fingers in his large,
warm hands. She wanted to sense him come into her room
late at night when she was wide-eyed and scared in the dark,
and hear him chant the words of a spell, and watch him
make the stars come down from the sky to guard her sleep.

She missed Glenin, too—playing with the Ostin girls
wasn't as much fun, and neither was squabbling with them.
Sarra wanted to ride her pony around and around the gardens of the Octagon Court with Glenin correcting her and
praising her when she got it right. She wanted Glenin to read
her bedtime stories at night, and share complaints about their
tutors, and have pillow fights, and—

"... barren of life," Lady Lilen was saying now, "but
you've seen for yourself that's not true. Plants and animals
here are very good at gathering and storing whatever water
they can find." She smiled. "Some even know how to purify

water. And with the help of these clever plants, we fill our cisterns."

"But it was beautiful here once, wasn't it?" asked Taig in a voice that held a strange note of yearning. "Before—"

"Yes, a long time ago it was very beautiful here. Almost as lush and green as Sheve. But Wasters—I trust you hear the irony in the name!—must deal with the present reality."

Though Lady Lilen's interruption was smooth as cream, Sarra promised herself to ask Taig what had been unsaid. Of all the Ostin brood—and there were plenty of them—Taig was the only one she felt comfortable with. At twelve, he was seven years her senior but never treated her like a baby. His sister Miram and brother Alin were near to Sarra in age; though she was content with them as playmates, only Taig seemed to understand her. He was like her. He questioned until he got answers that made sense to him. Restless and moody beneath his smile, he was frustrated by the plodding life of The Waste. Sarra, who had spent every day of her life at the center of Lenfell's liveliest and most sophisticated court, understood perfectly. But in escaping Ambrai, she and her mother had escaped death. Even at five years old, Sarra understood that most of all.

Talk at the Ostin table shifted to the coming journey to Renig, where the family usually spent several weeks in winter. First they would all go to Combel, where Lady Lilen had appointments with the stewards of Scraller Pelleris—an odious man whose herds of galazhi were run with the Ostins' own. The family's Web was an extensive one, and kept Lady Lilen moving like a migratory bird among her four major residences, trailed by some or all of her nine children, five siblings, and innumerable nieces, nephews, and cousins. The vast Ostin Blood was particularly ubiquitous in the Waste, sliding into gaps created by Scraller's wholesale obliteration of his Name. Herds were tended by Ostins; farms were run by Ostins; shops and inns were owned and staffed by Ostins; trade partnerships were overseen by Ostins; ships were captained by Ostins. The only thing they strictly avoided was government. Because politics was the Ambrai passion, inherited with the Name and the fortune and the Octagon Court, Sarra concluded that the Ostin Blood was lacking in real power.

Ostinhold, largest and most crowded of Lady Lilen's homes, was a sprawling, disorderly maze with additions tacked on as needed to accommodate an ever-growing population, currently numbering nearly a thousand. A wing protruded here, a second or third story rose there, a stairwell was crammed in any whichway, and old guard walls were constantly torn down and moved outward to expand the hired hands' living space. It was, quite simply, the ugliest dwelling Sarra could imagine. Accustomed to the cool white marble of the Octagon Court, the tall pillars and elegant domes and bright roof tiles of Ambrai, Ostinhold's chaotic exterior—walls of saffron, orange, or even pink as fancy had taken the builders—hurt her eyes. Sarra was generally bored by plants, and never appreciated Ambrai's lush parks until she walked through what Geria grandly called a garden—kitchen herbs and vegetables, a flower or two, but not a single tree. Still, as hideous as Sarra thought the place, all the Ostins—even Taig—loved it.

She supposed Ostinhold was all right if one's tastes ran to isolation. Descriptions of the town properties held more appeal. There was a seaside home in Renig, a small mansion in the outlying districts of Combel, and a house in Longriding that would be Geria's when she married. Sarra thought it a pity this hadn't yet happened. Geria mocked Sarra's long Ambraian vowels, her short Ambraian hairstyle, and her formal Ambraian manners—though not in Lady Lilen's hearing. One reason Sarra liked Taig so much was that he never hesitated to tell his sister, First Daughter or no, to shut up.

By all the Saints of Lenfell, Sarra wanted to go *home*. She'd asked her mother about it. Once. On St. Geridon's Day, the full moon of the Stallion who protected domestic animals in general and horses in particular, everyone helped light a bonfire with a burning twig (it was supposed to be gathered from the forest, but the Ostins had to import wood for the ceremony; The Waste had no forest, and precious few trees). Sarra made the traditional wish as she tossed her tiny flame onto the pile, then watched as Taig, eldest son, threw in braids made from the tail-hairs of the six Ostin studs. Later, as she was getting ready for bed, she told her mother what she wished. To go home.

"Can we?"

"No, Sarra. We can't go home for a long time." Maichen's eyes sparkled with sudden tears. Those magnificent black eyes had inspired the great Falundir to an admiring lyric when Maichen was but fifteen. Sarra had inherited her mother's eyes; Glenin had not. Sarra wondered suddenly if the new baby would.

"But why not? Guardian Desse could take us back on the Ladder—"

Fingers dug into Sarra's shoulder, silencing her more with shock than pain. "I told you once and I won't repeat myself again. *Never* speak of Ambrai, or Ladders, or Gorynel Desse, or our family, or who your father is."

Sarra struggled not to cry. Her mother had never spoken to her this way in her life. "You wished for the same thing, I know you did!" she accused.

"If I did, I'll keep it to myself—the way you must. What would Lady Lilen think of us if we were so ungrateful for all her kindness?"

"I don't care! I hate it here! I want to go home!"

It was the only time her mother struck her—a swift, sharp slap that stung her pride more than her bottom. The next instant she was seized in a fierce embrace, apologies tumbling into her hair. She accepted the slap, and the sorrys, and the holding, because she knew she deserved all three. But the hug was awkward, the growing bulge of the new baby ruining the comfortable cradle Sarra had always known.

Now, the day before St. Caitiri's, Sarra's mother was so big and ungainly that it took two people to help her out of a chair. Hugs happened sideways, if at all. She was constantly exhausted, her cheeks hollowing even as her body rounded. But nobody talked about the baby. It was as if it didn't exist, even with the evidence bulking large and larger each day.

"Lady . . . ?"

Everyone stopped talking and glanced around. Servants were not supposed to appear until Lady Lilen rang the little acorn-shaped brass bell beside her plate. The maid looked worried and nervous, but determined.

"Yes? What is it, Jonna?" asked Lady Lilen.

"A messenger, Lady. From Longriding, for Lady Maichen. He's ridden three horses nearly dead getting here."

Sarra watched in puzzlement as her mother and Lady Lilen exchanged quick worried glances. What could have happened at unimportant Longriding that would affect Maichen Ambrai?

"We'll hear him in my office," said Lady Lilen, rising.
"Has he been fed?"

"Yes, Lady. Though he's almost too tired to swallow."

Taig and Geria helped Sarra's mother to her feet. Lady
Lilen took her arm and they left the room. Geria, now the
ranking Ostin present, tapped a long fingernail against her
plate.

"Three horses," she mused. "It's a good four days from
Longriding at normal speed. The messenger must've done it
in two, maybe even less."

"What could be that urgent?" Taig asked.

"How should I know?" his sister shrugged.
"You're the Almighty First Ostin Daughter. I thought you
knew everything."

Sarra paid no heed to the bickering. Her mind took several
instinctive leaps—which as she grew older she would learn
to trust more and more, though it would be many years before she knew it for her magic. Maichen Ambrai could have
no interest in anything that happened in Longriding. Four
days was just the length of their overland trip to Ostinhold
from the Ladder.

With barely a logical thought to confirm it, Sarra knew
that the Ladder was in Longriding, the messenger was a
Mage Guardian, and the news was from Ambrai.

2

They didn't know she was listening, or they never would
have said so much.

Sarra had plumped pillows under the sheets to mimic her
sleeping form—Glenin had shown her how—and sneaked
out of her room, seeking the source of certain sounds. A tiptoe journey along the upper balcony outside the schoolroom
brought her to the corner of the wing. An easy slither by
storm gutter (for sand, not water, except for the acid rains),
a scramble across reddish roof tiles, a short climb to another
balcony, and she reached a sill. The window was half-open,
thin dark drapes drawn imperfectly shut. Wedging herself
against the brick frame, she peered within. And shivered.

She huddled outside the Ostinhold birthing chamber, source of the sounds she'd been following: the gasping cries of a difficult labor.

Someone was crooning soft words of encouragement. When low voices spoke from the other side of the draperies, mere inches from where she perched, Sarra nearly fell off the sill.

"From what you've told me of her first two birthings, this one won't be easy, either," said a voice Sarra didn't recognize, male and deep and concerned. "You'd best send for a Healer Mage, Lady."

"You've seen me through seven of my nine, Irien."

"You're built for it," the man said bluntly. "She's not. And this is a big baby even though she's not yet at term. Can't the Guardian send for someone?"

"Even if he could, we can't risk it." Lady Lilen's voice shook, as if her heart beat too fast. "No one must know about this birth, Irien. No one outside Ostinhold. Not even a Healer Mage."

"What they don't know can't be tortured out of them? I see." He paused. "Ambrai in ruins, her parents and most of the family dead—I can't believe it."

"She does. The shock brought on her labor. I hope never to see such horror again in anyone's eyes."

"And Auvry Feiran responsible for it all—" Irien paused. "Lady, I need to know something. Does she want this child? His child?"

Lilen Ostin said nothing for a long minute. Then: "Irien, I do not know."

Sarra hugged her knees to her chest, cold now to her marrow. Ambrai in ruins. Grandmother and Grandfather dead. Father responsible. Mother might believe it; Sarra did not. "No," she whimpered soundlessly. "No—"

When gasps became screams, the voices at the window went away. The sun rose a long, long time later, but could not warm Sarra's chilled, cramped body. A servant, opening windows in the next wing, saw her and called out in alarm. She was coaxed down, tucked into bed, given something hot to drink. It was poppy syrup to make her sleep, sticky-sweet, familiar from a brief illness last year. But in her sleep she heard her mother's screams.

When she woke it was late afternoon. Taig sat at the foot

of her bed, reading a book. She watched him through slitted lashes for a time as the fog gradually cleared from her brain.

"Where's my mother?"

Taig looked up, not at all startled. "Resting, I hope."

"Did the baby come?"

"Not yet. Don't worry, Sarra. It'll be all right."

Sarra gazed at him a while longer. Deep golden sunlight, hot and thick with dust through the open windows of her room, painted him in shadows. Dark-haired like almost all the Ostins; gray-eyed like his dead father, or so she'd been told. Would the new baby look like Auvry Feiran?

"I want to see my mother."

"Not just now. Maybe later."

"I have to tell her something."

"I'll take a message, if you like."

Sarra considered. Her muscles ached from a night huddled on the ledge, and the drug made her feel weak. "No, thank you. I have to tell her myself."

Taig nodded. "Maybe you ought to have something to eat."

"No. I'm—" Abruptly she changed her mind. "You know, I think I *am* hungry. Some bread and cheese?"

"I'll go see what they've got in the kitchen."

When he was gone, she pushed herself out of bed and pulled on her clothes. Her arms and legs moved so slowly; she fretted against the passage of time, knowing that if she was caught, Taig would not be fooled again into leaving her alone. At last, trousers fastened and shirt buttoned right, she peered either way down the hall outside her door. Empty. She couldn't risk last night's route, not with her muscles so stiff, but she had to *do* something. So she made her way as stealthily as she could to the wing that housed the birthing room.

There were no screams now. Sarra flattened herself against a corridor wall, edging around the corner. She heard a whimper, then another, and thought it must be the baby, born at last. She crept down the hall.

"Maichen, you must push, dearling, you must help us bring your baby."

Not born. More soft cries, and a thin wail: "I can't!"

"You must. Only a little while longer," Lady Lilen soothed. "Next time you must bear down, please, Maichen, you must try—"

"No—I *can't!* Leave me alone, I can't try anymore, I don't want to—"

Sarra ran to the door. A lean-shouldered man crouched beside the birthing chair. In the chair was a woman, white sheet draped over her swollen body. Her face was gray and exhausted, mottled with red marks like burns. Dull black eyes set in puffy bruises, mouth thin and colorless, she was completely unrecognizable as Sarra's beautiful, elegant mother.

"Sarra!"

Lady Lilen had seen her. Sarra fled.

A Healer Mage—the man said she needs a Healer Mage—I have to find one—please, blessed St. Fielto the Finder, you have to help me—and Feleris the Healer, and Gelenis First Daughter Who Helps in Childbirth and Imili and Caitiri Whose Day this is and—and—

She ran out of Saints halfway down the stairs. Out at the stables, three horses were tethered to a hitching post and waiting to be saddled. Three incredibly tall horses that scared her witless. She was infuriated by her fear. *Just imagine it's a pony. It's all the same, just bigger.*

She scrambled up onto a horse's back before she knew it. Yanking the reins free, she kicked with all her might and the horse obliged with a gallop through stableyard and gates, out onto the dry road.

As an adult, Sarra would believe with all her considerable intellect in the Mage Guardians' creed. That evening, however, formed in her a faith that went beyond logic and reason. She had ridden no more than a mile before another rider appeared, and became recognizable as Gorynel Desse.

Not a Healer Mage, true—but a Mage nonetheless. And she had found him. That he had already been on his way to Ostinhold had nothing to do with it in the mind of a five-year-old girl. She, Sarra, had decided what was needed and done it. Without thought to herself or the consequences, or indeed much thought at all, she had done what was necessary.

It would become the pattern of her whole life.

3

The baby was a girl. Born in the last hour of the night, she was given a version of St. Caitiri's name. Sarra, looking at her new sister for the first time the next afternoon, murmured, "Cailet, Cailet," and swore to Taig that the baby turned her head when she heard her name.

This time she didn't have to eavesdrop. Gorynel Desse sat with her after dinner that night and told her precisely what he proposed to do.

"Pardon an old man's lack of courtesy," he began, with a rueful gesture to his bare feet, soaking in a basin of cold water. "My bones have been rattling all over Lenfell these past weeks."

Sarra shook her head to indicate she didn't mind. Seating herself on a low stool, she folded her hands in her lap and waited.

"You know what happened in Ambrai," he said. "I grieve for your losses."

"Thank you," she whispered.

Desse paused for a sip of wine. "It's no longer safe for you here, Sarra."

She watched his green eyes, so startlingly bright in his dark face below uncovered, flowing white hair. "Everybody has to think we're dead," she told him. "Like Grandmother and Grandfather, and the Captal."

"Yes. Anniyas can't know—"

"You mean my father can't know. Or about Cailet, either."

He rubbed the bridge of his nose with a knobby finger. "Did you say you were five, or twenty-five?" he muttered. "Sarra, I know this has all been terrible for you. But you must trust me to know what's best. When your mother's well enough, I'll take you to live with some friends of mine in Sheve. You'll like it there. But you won't be able to talk of your old home in Ambrai, or that the Ostins are your kin, or that you visited here." He cleared his throat. "And ... you'll be given a new name."

She shrugged. Having lost almost everything else, what

was a Name—even the most powerful Blood Name in the world? "But Cailet can't come with us."

Desse blinked, and blinked again. "How did you—?"

"Mama doesn't want her."

"Whatever gave you that idea?"

"She said so. Because of what Papa did."

Leaning forward, he took her hands in his own. "Listen to me carefully, Sarra. I don't know what you think you heard, but what your father did has nothing to do with whether your mother wants Cailet. She *does*. You must believe that. Cailet is her daughter just as much as you are—"

"And Glenin?"

The Mage blew out a long sigh. "Make that *thirty*-five. My dear, Glenin had no choice. Your father took her with him and there was nothing your mother could do. And now . . . truly told, you're right. Cailet won't be coming with us. It will be safer for everyone if she stays at Ostinhold. Lady Lilen will say she's the daughter of a cousin, fostered here. There are so many Ostins that no one will remark on yet another."

Instinct had told her she was going to lose her second sister just as she'd lost her first. She gulped back the thickness in her throat and asked, "When can we see her again?"

"I don't know."

"Does that mean 'never'?"

"A difficult word, Sarra, and not one I like to use. There are a hundred million pathways, child. We can only hope that St. Rilla the Guide shows us one that will make everything all right again."

That was no answer. She nearly told him so, but what was the point? The adults would do what the adults decided. They always did, for reasons of their own. Sarra made a decision, too: she would *never* (she used the word in deliberate defiance) order people around or arrange their lives for them. It wasn't right.

The next morning she stood beside the cradle again, telling the baby her name. Lady Lilen said new babies couldn't see much. Sarra knew very well that Cailet was watching her. She could feel it. Like all babies' eyes, Cailet's were misty blue, but so dark that Sarra was sure they would turn black like her own eyes and their mother's. *But I won't be here to see it happen. I might never see her again. Like Glenin and Papa.*

No. She wouldn't lose Cailet, too. Not forever, the way
sure instinct told her she'd lost father and elder sister.

And mother, for Maichen Ambrai never left Ostinhold.
She died without ever waking from a coma compounded of
blood loss, exhaustion, and heartbreak. Her body was burned
in secret, and the next day Gorynel Desse took Sarra—no
longer Ambrai—to live in Sheve.

4

Sarra unpinned her bedraggled flower coronet and hooked it
on the bedpost. Swearing as she unhooked the multitude of
buttons down the back of her dress, she stripped the garment
from her shoulders and flopped across the mattress, scowling at the ceiling. The sheet beneath her was thick and
heavy, designed to keep straw from poking through the tick-
ing. Pinderon, despite being "Gateway to Cantrashir," was
undeniably rustic. It was said that Lady Velira Witte believed in old-fashioned virtues; Sarra considered her simply
cheap.

Still, she rather liked the smell of this bed, though it was
full of lumps compared to her feather mattress at Roseguard.
No need there for sheets sturdy enough for bean sacks; at
Roseguard, she slept on finest linen.

Sarra brushed strands of limp white-blonde hair from her
eyes and peered up at the wilting circlet of flowers. Tarise
would bring a fresh one to wear at tonight's banquet—more
pink roses. This time she'd make sure *all* the thorns were
sheared off. Her gaze shifted to the gown hanging on the
back of the door. Rose pink. Again. And if not that, then
peach or apricot or lavender. Every cloying, insipid pastel
from garden and orchard eventually found its way to her
wardrobe. When she protested that she was eighteen, not
eight, Agatine always replied, "But, Sarra, you're adorable
in those colors."

She didn't want to be adorable. She wanted to haul on her
riding clothes, track down Gorynel Desse, and tell him she
wanted to join the Rising.

Instead she was condemned to wear rose pink and pink roses to a banquet celebrating her sister's marriage.

Sarra glared at the flowers, wondering what Glenin would be wearing in Ryka. Whatever the style of her gown, it would be Feiran green and gray, not Ambrai black and turquoise. Few recalled now that Glenin had once had another Name, or that the Octagon Court had once existed. It was wiser not to mention such things. Sarra could have written a hundred-page treatise on all the things nobody talked about for fear someone might be listening. Not even Wards offered protection; if one employed a magical Ward, it was assumed one had something to hide. So nobody said anything at all about anything really important.

The Tiers, for instance. They would be abolished as of the first of next year—a wedding gift from the Council, with all honor and gratitude accruing to Glenin for asking this rather than for jewels or a private residence. No one remarked, and Sarra didn't point out, that she could have any jewels she wished now that she was marrying the richest young man in Ryka, or that a home away from Ryka Court would distance her from the flow of information and power. Sarra followed her sister's career assiduously if obliquely: a fact here, a rumor there, a mention of Glenin buried deep in some official news broadsheet. The portrait gradually painted by these random daubs was not encouraging.

Although the abolition was a good thing, and Sarra approved in principle, there were many who had vowed resistance to their last breath. Bloods, of course. Jealous of their privileges, but not seeing the real threat. The new law wasn't an end in itself, but only another step on a long, twisted road to a destination Sarra feared. The Bloods and Tiers had defined Lenfell's social structure ever since The Waste War. Something would have to take their place. Sarra was sure she knew what it would be.

When the old identity disks were turned in—as they had been once before to label those few remaining Mageborns for what they were—new ones would be issued. Name. Birthweek. Education. Occupation. Colored beads for one's Name. And a number. Everyone would be delineated more surely than even the Tiers had done. And more permanently.

How dare they tell me who I am? Sarra thought with the angry outrage of any girl coming up fast on adulthood—and

who had, as well, been forced to lie about who she truly was
since she was five years old.

She answered to the name Liwellan. She knew the names
and history of that Blood back ten generations, including the
"parents" who had so sadly died. She was adept in her ignorance of Ambrai and Mage Guardians, and showed only polite social interest in Lady Glenin Feiran—she who was so
beautiful, so clever, so accomplished, so much the model of
what every young woman ought to be. Sarra was very good
at lies.

But she never forgot the truth. Never. Ambrai was her real
home. Auvry Feiran, the Butcher of Ambrai, was her real father. Glenin Feiran, Sarra's only sister, was the real First
Daughter of the Ambrai Blood. Maichen Ambrai, her real
mother, had died of a fever on the journey to Sheve.

And Sarra herself was Mageborn.

This secret she kept most carefully of all.

"Sarra!"

The bedchamber door slammed open, slammed closed,
and Tarise leaned back against it to catch her breath. The
anticipated wreath of pink roses was tossed into Sarra's lap.
She examined it sourly, waiting for Tarise to impart whatever momentous news had brought her here in such haste.
Sarra shared Tarise's services as lady's maid with Agatine,
but it was always to Sarra that the girl ran first with any
news.

Tarise Nalle wore the Slegin household livery of ankle-
length blue skirt, matching full-sleeved blouse, and yellow
shortvest liberally embroidered with blue and gold rose
crowns. Her honey-blonde hair betrayed her haste, straggling down her back where it had escaped its pins. She
flapped a hand before her flushed cheeks to cool them,
sucked in a breath, and let it out in a whoosh.

"Well?" Sarra asked at last. "Death, birth, scandal, duel—
what?"

"Arrival!" Tarise hitched up her skirts and plumped down
on Sarra's bed. "The Ostin Blood—two of them, anyway—
Lady Lilia or Alila or something, and her son, who is *the*
most devastatingly handsome young man I've ever seen!"

"When we got here last week, our hostess' son was *the*
most devastatingly handsome young man you'd ever seen.
What makes the Ostin sprig so special?"

Tarise sniffed. "Dalion Witte is a mere child, a stripling,

a catastrophic bore—well suited to the deadly dullness of Pinderon. But this man—!" She ticked off attributes on her fingers. "Tall, lean, perfect shoulders, long legs, gray eyes like pools of silver in sunshine, cheekbones to sigh for, smile to die for, mouth luscious as a ripe plum—and as for what's beneath those *scandalously* undone lower buttons of his longvest—Holy St. Geridon!"

Halfway through the recital, Sarra began to laugh. At twenty-three, Tarise's tastes were still as completely indiscriminate as a schoolgirl's. She admired one man for his muscles, another for his ankles, this for his eyes and that for his nose. But never had so many charms been ascribed to a single male.

"I wonder you weren't blinded by the first sight of this marvel!" Sarra teased, and Tarise made a face at her.

"You just wait until you see him. His name is Taig, and he's twenty-five—and *un*married!"

"How many times have I told you—"

"Wait until you see him," the maid repeated, grinning.

"—I don't like older men," Sarra finished, and stuck out her tongue.

"Oh, be sensible! At the very least, he needs a partner at the banquet. Why not you?"

"I'm not Witte Blood. Depend on it, First Daughter Mirya will be stuck to him like sap on a tree if he's as handsome as all that."

"Mirya the Mare?" Tarise scoffed. "Don't make me laugh!"

Taig. Sarra repeated the name silently. The sense of knowing it was familiar, a frustration that had driven her half-mad at times over the years—things she ought to remember but couldn't. *Taig.* Not a common name, but not terribly unusual, either. Well, perhaps she'd read a variant of it in some history book or other.

Suddenly Tarise bounded off the bed. "What am I chattering on about? We have to get you dressed. I'll do your hair."

"You'd do better to fix your own. Whatever would Mirya say if she saw you?" Sarra primmed her mouth and arched her brows in lethal imitation of the Witte First Daughter.

"Oh, never mind that. Hurry! If you don't have any interest in him yourself, have pity on the poor man, forced to partner a horse at dinner!"

Sarra suffered herself to be helped into the pink gown.

"Tarise! You know it's useless to appeal to my better nature—I don't have one. What are the Ostins doing here, anyway?"

"Something tedious about trade. *Why* won't my hair curl the way yours does?" Tarise complained as she drew shoulder-length strands up into a loose tumble atop Sarra's head. "One night I'm going to sneak in and cut it all off, and have it made into a wig for myself. It's just about the same color as mine."

"Rillan *likes* your hair," Sarra purred.

Tarise blushed. "What he likes or doesn't like makes no difference to me."

For all her avid looking, Tarise was remarkably single-hearted. Rillan Veliaz, assistant Master of Horse at Roseguard, really *was* devastatingly handsome. He seemed unaware of it—indeed, was aware of nothing but his beloved horses. Certainly he never saw the charming, freckle-nosed maid who had lost her heart to him long ago.

That's something I'll never do to myself, Sarra vowed with a sigh. *I'm not going to "lose" my heart to any man. I'll give it where I please.*

It never occurred to her that someday a man might just steal it.

Taig Ostin was just as handsome as Tarise described. Tall, with broad shoulders and powerful legs, the rugged bones of his face were offset by a sensitive and humorous mouth. His eyes were indeed silvery, and he smiled with singular charm as he greeted Sarra. But there was something almost too intense about him, something burning behind his pale eyes.

She was seated directly opposite him at the banquet table. He partnered their hostess, Lady Velira Witte; his mother, Lady Lilen, was entertained by Agatine's husband, Orlin Renne. Sarra heard snatches of conversation between the leaden gallantries of Velira Witte's father, who was eighty if he was a day and tended to squeeze her arm or knee to emphasize his sallies. Evidently he thought his advanced age conferred certain immunities to civility. At length Sarra picked up her goblet of iced wine, smiled sweetly, and murmured, "Touch me again and you'll be wearing this." The old man subsided into silence and kept his hands to himself. Sarra had that effect on men, eighty or eighteen.

She gestured a servant to add more water to her wine. In the incredible heat of smoking torches and a thousand candles, it would be easy to drink too much. The banquet hall of Pinderon, the Witte estate which had given its name to the port city that had grown around it, was probably a pleasant place in cool weather. In summer, with a crowd of five hundred, it was an oven.

Sarra wished herself back at Roseguard, at one of the open-air banquets Agatine and Orlin loved to give. They were expert at expanding their own romance to enwrap their guests. Tables strewn across the vast lawns in the cool evening breeze; silver-soft moonglow and rose-gold torchlight making beauties of the plainest men; minstrels meandering among the guests; servants timing the courses to the needs of each table, rather than waiting for everyone to finish the soup before the fish was served. . . .

At Pinderon, Sarra's eyes stung with the merciless blaze of candles. Her ears hurt from the enthusiasm of the household orchestra, playing loudly enough from the gallery to be heard at the other end of the hall, deafening those closer to. Her stomach recoiled from the plate of venison, served ten minutes too cold with the sauce congealing into lumps.

No, Agatine and Orlin really knew how to give a party. Five parts careful planning, five parts solicitude for their guests, three parts imagination—and one very large part personal enjoyment: it was the perfect formula, adaptable to any activity. Even the Rising.

Five parts planning, five parts personality politics, three parts imagination—and one part personal ambition. Yes, that sounds just about right. Now, if only Gorynel Desse would show up, I could get started.

A dessert of lime ice in biscuit cups arrived melted and soggy. Sarra stirred it into soup, waiting for Lady Velira to signal the end of the banquet and the start of the dancing. Not that she intended to join the sets; she'd wander around for a time and then go raid Pinderon's library.

Of all the places she'd visited with Agatine and Orlin in the last few years, none lacked a volume or two overlooked by the Council's Education Commission. A Shir history, a Mage Captal's memoirs, a collection of songs, a bound volume of broadsheets, a biography—Sarra had searched miles of shelves and sneezed mountains of literary dust to find her treasures. These she tucked into her luggage and added to her growing collection at Roseguard. It wasn't stealing. Not really. She considered it rescue.

Just as she gleaned news of Glenin from a hundred divergent sources, she winnowed a fairly accurate history of Lenfell from nearly a hundred books. But there were always gaps, omissions, references that the writers of the time thought too obvious to explain. She had hopes that the Witte library would yield a few more precious facts, or at least some corroborations.

"Are you as bored by this as I am?"

The deep murmur just over her shoulder startled her. She turned in her chair and found herself staring up at Taig Ostin. Way up; he was very tall. Though he smiled, and his words were good-humored enough, a strange urgency lit his eyes, akin to the white-fire intensity she'd seen earlier.

"We'll have to join one dance, you know," he went on. "For appearances' sake. But then you'll be perfectly justified in showing me the gardens."

She glanced around to find everyone heading for the ballroom. Past the flirtatious chatter of the guests the orchestra could be heard tuning up. The last thing in the world she wanted was to dance. She opened her mouth to begin a refusal, couched in a sharp reminder that it was for the woman to ask the man to dance, not the other way around.

Then she saw it. Dangling from his left earlobe below the black coif was a small golden hoop, and from it hung a tiny silver flameflower. Without the book liberated from the Mettyn Residence library at Rokemarsh last year, she never would have recognized the pattern or its meaning.

He saw reaction in her face and nodded. She placed her fingers delicately on his wrist. "I'd love to dance," she said quietly. "Thank you."

As they whirled through the set, she barely noticed Mirya Witte's furious equine glare. It was impossible not to notice Tarise's sleek grin as the maid approached after the dance, carrying Sarra's shawl—pink, naturally—having accurately guessed that the gardens would be next. Taig Ostin draped cobwebby lace around Sarra's shoulders, and they made their way through the crowd.

Taig seemed to know everyone. Much time was wasted on greetings, introductions, enquiries about relatives (of which Taig had hundreds), and comments on the evening. The one thing constant to every encounter was expression of delight at the event being celebrated. By the time she and Taig reached the garden doors, Sarra had smiled agreement so often with wishes for Glenin and Garon's happiness that her face hurt.

"To be universally beloved must be a marvelous thing," Taig mused as they gained the terrace at last. "You notice they all used the same phrases."

"As if they'd memorized a page of appropriate sentiments," Sarra said. " 'Charming couple, fine future, lovely young woman, delightful young man—' " She snorted. "Why don't they just set it to music and have done with it?"

He nodded absently, trailing his fingers along the stone banister as they descended to the lawn. Noise and heat behind them now, Sarra gave a sigh of sheer relief. This was more like Roseguard—gentle light, soft shadows, cool air. A Minstrel sang to a small group of young people over by the lily pond, his voice deep and expressive, his lute as supple as any Sarra had ever heard.

But as captivating as his gifts were, Sarra had other things on her mind.

"So," she began. "When did you last see Gorynel Desse?"

Taig chuckled. "You don't waste time. Actually, he hasn't been to Ostinhold in quite a while." He paused. "You realize that if I worked for the Council, you'd be at the top of my list just for implying that Gorsha's still alive?"

"A man who wears that symbol—and calls a Warrior Mage by a personal diminutive—is more of a danger to the Council than I am. Besides, I know I can trust you. My instinct is never wrong."

"A useful talent—but don't rely on it too much." He slipped a hand under her elbow, warm pressure guiding her down a side path. The Minstrel's richly evocative voice faded behind them into the shadows.

"This meeting wasn't supposed to happen yet, you know," Taig said. "But I couldn't resist the chance to see how you'd grown up. I must say I approve."

Compliments had ceased to impress her at the age of twelve. "What do you mean, 'yet'?" She paused beneath a torch, wanting to see his expression. His fingers on her arm coaxed her away from the light.

"Let's walk on," he suggested.

"Let's not." She planted her slippers in the fine gravel of the walkway. "I mean to understand exactly what's going on before we go any further."

"Sarra." His grip tightened; she had a choice between

walking and stumbling. "What a pretty fountain," he commented, pointing with his free hand. "Is it a natural spring, or piped in?"

Sarra neither knew nor cared. Gardens bored her. "*Domni Ostin*," she began angrily, but he shook his head. A moment later she saw another couple stroll out from behind some trees, and bit her lip.

Fifteen long minutes and a quarter mile of winding gravel paths later, they were truly alone at the western corner of the huge Witte estate. Sarra could hear waves crash against the rocks far below. Taig sat down on a wooden bench, sprawling his legs, and squinted up at her in the dimness.

"You're too young. You must understand that, Sarra. You'll join us, never think you won't. In a few years things will be in place. But we must wait for the right time. Gorsha would run me through with my own sword for telling you even this much, but the minute I saw you I knew you had to be warned."

"Against what?"

"Doing whatever it's in your head to do in order to find the Rising." She sensed rather than saw his smile. "You want to be part of it. I already am. Why don't you tell me what you've learned, and I'll tell you—"

"—what it's safe for me to know?" She consciously relaxed her fingers from the tense fists that betrayed anger—a bad habit she was trying to break. "All right. I know there are Mages in hiding all over Lenfell. I've met a few, though they never admit to what they are. The only one I've ever talked to at any length is Gorynel Desse, and he hasn't been to Roseguard in years. He always comes disguised, and it's nearly impossible to track him down to talk to. But I've traveled, and I've heard things. And you can figure out a lot by the news broadsheets, even though they're the Council's voice."

"Go on."

"A specific?" Sarra gave a shrug. "These 'friendship' journeys Anniyas takes. The most recent to Bleynbradden fits the mold. She arrives, the locals welcome her, everyone is excruciatingly nice, she leaves—and inside of a week there's at least one unexplained, unsolved murder or disappearance. Every so often one of the victims is identified as a Mage. It's obvious that she ferrets them out for someone to kill later. What *I* want to know is how the Mages are caught. Are they that stupid?"

"No," Taig murmured. "They're the most courageous people I've ever known."

An easy leap of intuition, but one that left her gasping. "You mean they—they *sacrifice* themselves?" When he nodded, she burst out, "But *why?*"

"To keep Anniyas contented. Oh, she's not greedy," he added bitterly. "Not the way she used to be. She only needs a few every year to feel her power. News of the murders is allowed out as a warning. 'We've caught another of you—none can escape us.' The idea is that one or more will panic, make a wrong move, and be flushed out without Anniyas' having to leave Ryka."

"But how does she do it? How does she know where to look?"

"Haven't you noticed who she always takes along?"

She'd noticed. Of course she had. But it was only coincidence. It had to be. She felt her knees give and groped her way to the bench, sitting down hard.

Taig's voice was soft with sympathy. "At first it was just Feiran. But when she was old enough, and especially after Garon was betrothed to her—"

"No." She shook her head, trembling. "I don't believe—"

"Auvry Feiran is feared. Though nobody speaks of Ambrai, every body remembers. But a young girl—what threat is she, despite who her father is?"

"No! *No!*"

Taig was silent for long minutes. Then he touched her shoulder. She jerked back. "Sarra . . . I know you don't want to believe it. But it's true."

Huddling away from him, she nervously shredded the fringe of her shawl. Of all the things she'd ever deduced or suspected Glenin was, accomplice to murder had never—

"She's Mageborn, like her father," Taig went on. "Trained by a Lord of Malerris named Golonet Doriaz. He's dead now, caught in the destruction of the Castle four years ago. Glenin is—"

He broke off as running footsteps crunched gravel. An instant later a small, slight figure in black skidded to a stop before them. Fair hair shone like a beacon even in the dimness—like a dark candle lit with a golden flame, Sarra thought as the child gasped for breath, as if all available light sought itself in that short, girlish cap of straight blonde hair.

"Taig! Here you are! I had to come tell you—" She stopped, eyes narrowing suspiciously at Sarra.

"Slow down," Taig advised. "Get some air into you, little one. You can speak in front of my friend. It's all right."

A quick shrug: *If you say so.* Gulping the cool night breeze, she went on in the quick accents of The Waste, "There's Council Justices here from their own banquet, and Guards with 'em."

"How many justices and how many soldiers?"

"Two Justices. Twenty, maybe thirty Guards." Long fingers raked the sunny hair, then rubbed against the coarse weave of black trousers. "I saw from a balcony. At first I thought it was just courtesy with the Guards as escort but then I heard talk about the Minstrel—you know, the one who sailed with us from Renig and sang that song of Bard Falundir's nobody's s'posed to know—" She broke off and looked directly at Sarra again. "You *sure* she's all right?"

The world lurched as Sarra looked into the child's black eyes. All the forgotten things that had frustrated her for years welled up like ocean waves crashing over her head, drowning her in names, faces, scents, textures, a Ladder and a long ride, weeks at Ostinhold, Lady Lilen and her many children—*Taig!*—a sister's birth and a mother's death—and brilliant black eyes exactly like her own.

They stared at each other, the elder sister trembling, the younger sister wide-eyed with startlement—especially when a girl she'd never met before in her life whispered, "Cailet—?"

"Yes, this is Cailet." Taig's voice sliced between them like a swordblade. "The one I told you about."

He had done no such thing. But that didn't matter. She remembered now how Taig had always taken her part at Ostinhold against First Daughter Geria, how he had been her friend. Sarra shook her head sharply, but the world did not resume its previous shape. *This* was her reality. The other had been a lie. The small, fair-haired, dark-eyed girl standing in front of her was the sister she hadn't remembered—*why?* What had been done to her that she had forgotten?

She turned her head with an effort and met Taig's eyes. How could she not have recognized their fierce quicksilver glow? His father's eyes, they'd said back then. Thirteen

years ago. Weeks blocked out of her five-year-old mind,
Warded away, other memories substituted and some expanded to fill the void—how much did a child that age recall, anyway?

Plenty, now that the Ward was gone. It was as if scenes
and words and feelings had been locked alone in a tiny room
like a musician practicing a difficult piece in total privacy,
total dedication. She heard Lady Lilen and Healer Irien say
that Maichen needed a Healer Mage . . . she felt wind in her
hair and her fear of the powerful horse beneath her as she
galloped away to find—

Gorynel Desse! *He* had done this to her. He had taken
away a summer of her life. He had robbed her of her memories and her little sister.

"I saw our Minstrel by the lily pond," Taig was saying.

"Didn't see him there," Cailet replied, shaking her head.
"Didn't hear him anywheres, either."

"If the Justices are after him, Cai, we'll have to find and
warn him."

The child nodded. Her hair was a silken flame around her
thin face with its astonishing eyes. "We can split up and
look for him. Will she help?"

Taig smiled. "Count on it. Forgive my manners, ladies.
Lady Sarra Liwellan, *Domna* Cailet Rille—my charming if
pesky stowaway foster sister."

"They wouldn't take me, so I sneaked on board," Cailet
explained with a shrug. "I'll take the east, Taig, along the
meadow wall."

"You know what to look—and listen—for," he agreed.
"Tell him to hop the wall and go to the Feathered Fan, just
off Hawk Alley. I'll meet him there before dawnlight. Hurry,
now."

Cailet darted off, vanishing into the night. Taig rose and
drew Sarra to her feet. His grip on her shoulders was firm,
bracing. "Yes, I know who you are, and who she is, and who
you are together. We'll talk about it some other time. For
now, please keep in mind that you were made to forget—but
for Cai, there's nothing to remember."

Sarra nodded mutely. *Cai*—the nickname they used for
her, all the people who knew the little sister stolen from her
long ago. So much to learn about her, so much to talk about,
and no time for it now.

"All right. This Minstrel we're looking for—he's about

my age, a couple of fingers taller, reddish hair, no coif. His voice is incredible."

"I heard, earlier." She straightened the shawl. "Go. I know where to send him if I find him."

Taig smiled again. "You don't disappoint, you Ambrai girls," he murmured, bending to kiss her cheek lightly. Then he strode off down the gravel pathway.

Sarra tucked the new/old memories into a corner of her mind and picked up her skirts in both hands. Fashion had changed recently, and gowns were daringly short—rumored to be Glenin's doing, to show off exquisite ankles—but there was still enough volume to Sarra's dress to prevent a quick pace unless her knees were free. She'd drop the skirt back to modest length if she encountered anyone, but right now she needed speed. Hurrying through the night-shadowed garden, she shut out the sounds of conversation, laughter, and the occasional languid sigh (ridiculous noise) and listened hard for strings and singing.

Ah—*there*. A lute being tuned. Directly across a broad lawn was a little copse of birch trees sheltering a bench and an inferior statue of St. Imili. Sarra slid through a break in the intervening bushes, crossed the path, and wished for longer legs that would let her cover more ground with each carefully casual stride. Half the garden away she heard a few telltale clinks of metal. Soldiers were searching the grounds. What had Cailet said—something about a song no one was supposed to know? This Minstrel must be a fool, to sing it anywhere but atop a mountain or in the middle of The Waste or alone in a rowboat in St. Tamas Bay.

And she was an even bigger fool, to risk so much by warning him of danger. Her shoes slid on damp grass and she swore under her breath, catching her balance. Instinct assured her it was absolutely right to help Taig help this Minstrel, but that wouldn't preclude giving the idiot the sharp side of her tongue for his stupidity. He was probably one of those misty-eyed imbeciles who lived on dreams and music, wouldn't know a sword from a pine branch, and sat a saddle as if surprised it wasn't an upholstered chair.

Her feet connected with gravel again. She glanced around, saw no one, and raced for the copse. There he was: all alone, and the perfect portrait of a wool-brain who existed only for music. Delicate hands, sensitive profile half-visible by the moons' light, eyes closing as he sighed and brought a few notes from his lute—the shit-wit didn't even hear her approach.

Sarra, mindful that there might be someone listening from a romantic shadow beyond the birch trees, cleared her throat loudly. "Forgive the interruption, but I had to find the source of such glorious—"

The words dried up in her throat. The Minstrel's head lifted, and a stray shaft of moonlight fell on his head—modestly covered by a Bardic blue coif. He got to his feet, lute cradled like a child in protective arms; he was barely a head taller than she.

He bowed. "No more glorious than your beauty, which inspires me to a song." He positioned the lute and struck an opening chord.

Sarra called up her dimple, and a simper that would do credit to Mirya Witte. "I came to tell you that you mustn't hide such music away, good Minstrel, really you mustn't. I have friends who ought to hear you—people who appreciate music and look for fine talents to ornament their court. Go up to the east terrace and wait there while I fetch them, won't you? Please?"

"*Domna,*" he replied with another low bow, "I am yours to command."

She didn't watch him go. *Fool!* She should have heard the difference between his insipid playing and the remembered mastery of the man by the lily pond. A salutory lesson in more careful observation learned, she set out again, this time through the copse to the paths beyond, alert now for a truly Bard-worthy performance.

The only music she heard for the next fifteen minutes came from the ballroom orchestra, playing a succession of dances. After a complete circuit of the gardens, Sarra admitted defeat and trudged back toward the terrace.

Standing beside some potted orange trees were two Justices in formal robes, five Council Guards in red-and-gold regimentals, and Lady Lilen Ostin in a gorgeous green gown and cap studded with moonstones.

How could I not recognize her? Sarra thought. The answer came quickly: *Because Gorynel Desse does his work very well. If it hadn't been for Cailet and her unmistakable black eyes—Blood calling to Blood,* she told herself. *That must be the reason. But once I catch up with that damned Mage again. . . .*

"—sheltering a known subversive, Lady Lilen," a Justice was saying. Sarra melted into the shadows of the bushes to listen. "I understand, of course, that you had no way of knowing. But some are not generous in their interpretations."

"Then it will have to be explained to them, won't it? He cozened his way on board saying he'd earn his way by entertaining us. His songs were pretty enough, I suppose, but not worth the price of bed, board, and passage. You'll do me a favor by finding the wretched man. He still owes me money."

Sarra grinned admiration. Lilen spoke with just the right degree of Blood arrogance tinged with merchant's annoyance. But knowing what she now did, she could hear how precisely calculated the tone and words were. Lady Lilen Ostin was involved in the Rising right up to her jeweled headdress.

"I'm sure your grievance will be addressed in due course," said the Justice. "But there is also the matter of your son."

Sarra stiffened, clutching the stone lip of the terrace.

Lady Lilen heaved a martyred sigh. "That boy! Doubtless he's been chasing someone's First Daughter again. Not yours, I hope, Justice Ballardis? Or yours, Justice Rengirt?"

"Neither," Ballardis replied, sounding amused.

"Saints be praised for it. One tries so hard to turn out modest, mannerly sons, but—"

"This is serious, Lady Lilen," said Justice Rengirt in severe tones. "Your son has been seen with low and vicious characters since his arrival—"

"He works fast," Lilen observed dryly. "We've only been here five hours."

"—in a tavern known to attract the worst elements of Pinderon's populace."

"A *tavern*." Another sigh. "I should have known. His father had the same weakness for your famous wines. I did adore the man, and I'm afraid I see him in my son too much for proper discipline." She squared her shoulders and shook out her skirts. "Well! I'll tell you one thing, good Justices, and no mistake. Although they say youth must be served, this time it'll be on a pewter plate with peach compote!" She paused. "How much do I owe the innkeeper for damages?"

Sarra heard things in this conversation far beyond the Justices' threat of guilt by association. Lilen was, first and fore-most, brilliantly wasting their time. She was also painting Taig as a wastrel not worth the bother, and herself as a long-suffering mother afflicted with difficult offspring. But it was the subtlety of her disassociation from her son and any activities the Council might consider subversive that impressed Sarra, even as it angered and frightened her. Mages had sacrificed themselves, Taig had said. It was possible that Taig would have to be sacrificed to keep the Rising safe. And if this frightened Sarra, Lilen must be terrified. But there were more important things at stake than family or friendship. Sarra understood this immediately—and her instincts for once scared her thoroughly. Lilen would protect her son as best she could, but if it came to a choice. . . .

Well, Sarra knew how to make choices, too.

Her mind leaped with its accustomed suppleness, and before she was consciously aware of it she was tearing pink roses from her hair with one hand. The other ripped her shawl. She knelt to roll in the rich loam, stain ing the brocade of her dress. She almost threw the coronet away, then realized that her story would be seen for the lie it was if it was found here in the bushes. She closed a palm around the flowers, crushing them to get at the thorns. The sting prompted quite satisfactory tears. She left shelter, heading for the terrace steps in a ragged run, trailing little pink rose-buds behind her.

"Sarra!"

Lady Lilen was astonished into lack of caution. Sarra stopped in mid-step, turned to the little group by the orange trees, and said in a perfectly tremulous voice, "Lady—Lady Lilen? Forgive me, I'm not fit for company right now—" She turned so light spilling from the mansion glinted on her tears.

"My dear child!" Lilen rushed to her. The Justices followed, waving their escort to stay back. Sarra felt a warm arm encircle her shoulders and hid her face in a silk-covered bosom. She recognized the fragrance of lemon-grass perfume, which scent had always brought one of those odd glimmerings that so frustrated her through the years.

Damn Gorynel Desse.

"Oh, look at your lovely gown! What happened, child?"

"*Domni* Taig," she burbled, keeping her face lowered. "I couldn't believe any man would—but it happened so fast—"

Lady Lilen gasped. "*Taig* did this?"

"Oh, no. Not him! And the Minstrel, the tall one, who doesn't wear a coif—he was—"

"The Minstrel, you say?" This from Justice Rengirt, in tones so dark and dire that Sarra was certain she practiced them in private. Turning to Balardis, she continued, "What did I tell you, Tamasa, the man is lost to all decency! It doesn't surprise me that someone so immodest as to abandon the coif and sing such songs is responsible for this outrage!"

Horrified, Sarra realized they had used their imaginations and the "evidence" of her dishevelment to come to exactly the wrong conclusion.

"Where have they gone?" Ballardis put in. "Do you know, my dear?"

"Nothing happened," she said frantically, knowing it was too late.

"Don't you worry," soothed Rengirt. "Agatine Slegin's fosterling, aren't you? Well, we'll catch this Minstrel and lock him up good and tight, where he can never hurt you again."

"Which way did Taig go?" Lady Lilen said, and Sarra's ears, tuned for other meanings, heard the urgency.

"Toward the sea wall, I think. Oh please, Lady Lilen, take me away! Don't let anyone see me!"

"There now, child, calm yourself. I'm sure the kind Justices will excuse us. Come along, my dear."

A swift climb up the back stairs gained them the privacy of Sarra's room. She drew away from the supporting arms and locked the door herself. Lilen stood silently by, speculation wild in her eyes.

"I remember you," was all Sarra said.

Lilen embraced her. After a moment, voice thick with emotion, she said, "Oh Sarra, little Sarra! You're the image of your dear mother—much more so than Cailet. Did you see her? Oh, you must have. That child! Whatever happens, she's always in the thick of it."

"I got that impression," Sarra replied dryly. "Taig treats her as an officer of the Rising. The Minstrel, I take it, is not."

Lilen's mouth twitched in a smile. "If he continues on his present course, he will be—like it or not. Tell me what happened."

Sarra did. "I made a mess of it, though," she finished. "I didn't mean for them to think the *Minstrel* had assaulted me."

"I don't think it's too serious. If they do find him, you can correct their mistake. With luck, they won't be found at all."

"Pinderon proper is the other direction from the sea wall. How serious is the part about the song?"

"Well, it's not yet illegal to sing a song or visit a tavern. The Justices don't have any real evidence—but they don't need much, these days. Pity we can't warn the boys that they're supposed to be chasing down a vile and infamous seducer." She chuckled.

Sarra smiled a little. "It'll only matter if the Guard catches them, and Taig's smart enough to take whatever cues he hears."

"He does show signs of intelligence every so often," Lilen replied. "With luck, as you say, things will fall together. If not—we've done what we can."

The Minstrel dealt with, Sarra asked, "Tell me about Cailet. Please, Lady Lilen. There's so much I want to know about her."

Lilen sat on the bed and patted the coverlet. Sarra perched beside her. "She's lived with us nearly thirteen years now on the same footing as you live with the Slegins. And now here you are, all grown up. So beautifully, too!" She smiled, and Sarra was transported back to evenings at Ostinhold, when Lady Lilen's smile warmed all who sat at her table.

"Tell me about her—and Miram and Tevis and Lenna—" She pushed tumbled hair from her eyes. "I didn't recognize Taig at first, I didn't remember him. But Cailet—she has our eyes, mine and Mother's. I saw her, and I remembered everything." She caught at Lilen's hand, hard. "What did Gorynel Desse do to me? Why did he make me forget?"

"It was for your own safety—and ours. Saints, it's difficult to explain. You would have met Cai eventually, or perhaps Gorsha would have helped you remember. But of course that impossible child had to force events by stowing away!" She laughed, rueful and exasperated and loving. "No, she can't bear to be left out of things, our Cailet."

"I thought I'd only lost those weeks at Ostinhold—but what I've really lost is thirteen years."

Lilen hugged her once more, and began. First Daughter Geria had taken a husband. Margit, next eldest after Taig, had died two years ago in an accident that had been no accident. Her death prompted Taig's entry into the Rising.

"She'd been studying with a Guardian in Renig—on the sly, of course—"

"Margit was Mageborn?"

"My only Mageborn daughter," Lilen murmured. "One day her horse came back without her. The stableboy told Taig the saddle blanket burned his fingers. He went to wash his hands, and when he returned the blanket was gone. Gorsha thinks it was a slow-acting spell set into the wool. The horse bore no signs, but. . . ." She stared down at her hands. "They found her body three days later."

"Oh, Saints . . . I'm so sorry."

Lilen went on to speak of the other children. Lenna and Tevis were at St. Deiket's Academy in Combel; Miram, Alin, Terrill, and Lindren were still at Ostinhold. "And that's the list of them. Now tell me about yourself, Sarra."

She hitched a shoulder. "Nothing to tell. I go to school at Roseguard, I travel with Agatine and Orlin, I learn what I can where and when I can."

"How have you fared, with magic in you and no one to teach you its uses?"

"I don't seem to have much," she replied, uncomfortable with the subject. "Nothing to compare to my father—and Glenin. Is Cailet—?"

"Oh, yes. And strong, too, according to Gorsha. We won't know exactly until after her first Wise Blood. But she's been more than a handful this past year. Restless, discontented, not knowing why. She's wild to go with Taig every time he sets out on one of his little journeys."

"She—" Sarra broke off as someone pounded on her door. "Yes? Come in!" She huddled close to Lilen, ready to resume her portrayal of outraged Blooded Lady.

Tarise entered, breathless as usual. She ignored Sarra completely. "Lady, your son and the Minstrel are safely away, but the Guard is everywhere. Taig needs help getting the Minstrel out of Pinderon."

Sarra's jaw descended nearly to her lap.

"Typical," Lilen remarked, in the same tone she'd used to describe her son to the Justices; evidently her maternal exasperation was genuine. "Taig finds trouble as easily as a bee finds a summer garden, and invariably gets stuck in the thorns. Is there a way of returning a message to him?"

"Something simple and nonspecific," Tarise replied. "The boy we use doesn't attract much notice, but if caught he'd babble everything in his head. Which isn't much, but—"

"Let's not put him in danger. Well! I'll just have to fix the problem without warning Taig—who at least knows a signal when it bites him. Very well. Thank you." Rising, she looked down at Sarra and smiled. "Don't look so astonished, my dear. Did you think Gorsha would allow you to go unprotected? I hope we'll talk tomorrow. If not, then certainly one day soon." With a nod for Tarise, she left the bedchamber.

Sarra had taken about as many shocks as she could endure in one night without wanting to take it out on *somebody*. She glared at Tarise and burst out, "You never told me!"

"Well, of course not," she agreed. "Put yourself in my place."

"That's exactly where I ought to be—working for the Rising!"

With infuriating calm, Tarise replied, "As Lady Lilen said, one day soon."

"So you're my 'protection,' are you?" Sarra flung her bedraggled rose coronet to the floor. "The most unlikely rebel I ever saw!"

"Do you think only Mage Guardians have something to lose?" Tarise picked up the flowers and tore them to bits, speaking with a passion that surprised Sarra into silence. "If the Malerrisi have their way, everyone will be labeled like hothouse plants—rooted in place, pruned to specifications, torn up and thrown away if a single leaf doesn't conform!"

Sarra blinked at the vehemence. "But you could've *told* me—"

Tarise threw the roses into the bowl of potpourri on the dressing table. "Now that you've found out, I'll explain a few things. I know exactly four other agents of the Rising. Don't ask their names, I won't tell you. They in turn know four people each. We're organized as the Mages used to be when they traveled: Healer, Warrior, and Guardian. The terms are convenient but not really applicable, except for the Warriors. They really do have to do some fighting now and again. Healers—well, I guess in a way that's what they do with their political or financial influence. They smooth out suspicion, get people out of trouble, and so on. Guardians are mainly couriers."

A very simple jump this time. "You join Agatine in all her journeys, so you must be a Guardian. And because Agatine is wealthy and wealth is power, she's the Healer. But who's your Warrior? Not Orlin, surely."

"Please, Sarra. Don't ask. By the way, you're wrong about Agatine."

"But she *is* involved. Oh, don't bother to confirm or deny. I won't ask any more awkward questions. Just show me how you're organized."

Tarise hesitated, then sighed and scooped a handful of flowers from the potpourri bowl. She knelt on the carpet. Sarra joined her, forgetting her grudge in excitement at finally learning something real about the Rising.

Tarise picked out three different colors of flowers—white, pink, and red—and arranged them in a square.

"The connections go across and down, like this."

> *white—pink—red*
> /   /   /
> *pink—red—white*
> /   /   /
> *red—white—pink*

Sarra studied the arrangement. "But one person can be betrayed by four others—or betray four others herself. So in losing any one element, you potentially lose over half the square."

"Better that than all nine."

"You also cripple all the other units."

"Can you see a better way to do it? That's not an idle question—I know how your mind works."

"Do you?" Sarra studied the roses. "Where are the connections to other squares?"

"Along the corners, to form cubes."

"Thereby increasing the number of names those corners know." There had to be a better way—and Sarra was going to devise it. "It all depends on whether betrayal or communication is your biggest worry. What *I* want to know is how I can fit in."

"You?" Tarise laughed. "What else could you be but a Warrior?"

5

Sarra thought about that after Tarise left. A Warrior? She could probably learn swordskill without lopping off a finger or two, but she had no desire to gallop around looking for—or avoiding—a fight. Neither did she see herself as a Guard, running other people's errands (though gathering information had become a specialty). She was too young for political influence. As for the power that money gave—

By Maidil the Betrayer's Mask—what about Ambrai? With Allynis and Maichen dead, and Glenin now a Feiran, Sarra was First Daughter. In fact, if not in practice, she was Lady of Ambrai.

She couldn't use it. Not the power of her real name and identity. But she *could* use Ambrai. Single most potent symbol of the ever-growing dangers of Anniyas' rule, remembered as a center of learning and culture—remembered, too, as the home of the Mage Guardians.

Sarra was Ambraian, and Mageborn. And this told her what her role must be.

If she had to tell lies about who she was, she might as well make them useful lies.

I'm the orphaned daughter of Mages killed at Ambrai. The Lists were burned with everything else, so there's no record of their names—yes, that will do nicely. Of everyone at the Academy, I alone was taken to safety. That makes me the perfect symbol of all that was lost.

All she need do was use it—and live up to it.

Further, if Sarra stood for the past, then Glenin, newly married to Anniyas' son, embodied a possible future. Ah, yes—a very neat little pattern. Because there were three Mageborn sisters of Ambrai. Lady Lilen had said that Cailet's magic was strong. *She* was the other future.

Three living symbols. Which was, perhaps, what Gorynel Desse had planned all along.

Well, for her own part, she would give him his symbol, but for her own reasons. She would be the reminder of what Lenfell had been—like a statue in a shrine, robed and jeweled to be admired on feast day—but she was damned if she'd be that alone.

Five parts organization, five parts politics, three parts imagination—and one very large part personal ambition. She got out of bed, lit a lamp, and took out pen and paper. In the next hour she used her imagination to draw up a political organization that, not incidentally, defined her own ambition.

6

Sarra slept late, not waking until after Eighth—nearly noon. *Strange,* she told herself as she washed, *usually Tarise comes in at Sixth with my tea. . . .* Still, considering the events and revelations of the previous night, perhaps not so strange.

She dressed in riding clothes, aware that Lady Velira and Mirya the Mare would want her in attendance for the inevitable discussion, dissection, and discerning commentary that followed any grand occasion. Sarra had better things to do. Making quick work of herself from braids to boots, she went downstairs.

Clean-up was well advanced. Chairs were stacked, paper streamers and candle nubs gone. In the entry hall, Sarra wove a path through boxes used to store reusable decorations, barrels filled with trash, and buckets sprouting mop handles like shorn bouquets. Consultation with several servants finally yielded Lady Lilen's whereabouts, and Sarra descended the steps to the garden.

Beyond the rose-trellised portico, a dozen slaves were raking the gravel—churned last night by hooves and carriage wheels—into perfect interlocking chevrons. It was the whim of the Witte Blood to style everything from the decorations on their cornices to the layout of their gardens with the family chevron sigil. Sarra skirted the edge of the drive, winning sour glances from rake-wielders and gardeners alike as she crunched one boot into the gravel and the other into the border of flowers. *Neatly managing to offend everyone,* she told herself wryly, *while doing no real damage at all. I must work on that.*

The day was bright, warm, fragrant with roses. That last

was a surprise. Sarra had expected that the previous evening's decorations and coronets would strip the bushes of all but their leaves. She glimpsed Lilen's graying head beyond a four-foot wall of bright orange blooms and started toward her. Surely if she was so casually strolling the gardens, Taig was safely out of trouble. That fool of a Minstrel, too.

But she wasn't quite fast enough. Her foster-father's deeply resonant voice called out behind her.

"Here you are! I thought you'd sleep all day." Orlin Renne took Sarra's arm, steering her firmly down a walk leading away from Lilen. "Taking the long way around to the stables? I feel in just the right mood for a ride, myself. Out to the beach, perhaps."

Away from Lilen, now away from town. Conspiracy. "Pinderon has some cute little shops," she replied sweetly. "I thought I'd see what's in them."

" 'Cute'? *This* from the girl who flees in horror when Aggie even mentions the word 'shopping'?"

Sarra muttered, "I thought Tarise was the one who keeps an eye on me."

"Both eyes," he agreed, not even breaking stride. "You, daughter of my heart if not my loins, are like a cat who's sure there's a perfectly fascinating mousehole just around the next corner. And this afternoon my sole aim in life is to keep those pretty paws of yours out of mischief."

Making a face at him: "Mrroww!"

Orlin laughed and loosened the ties of his coif. "Come on, let's get some horses. I'll even take you into town."

"We both know I can lose you anytime I feel like it," she challenged. "I've been doing it since I was seven years old."

"So you have," he answered pleasantly.

"Why don't you spare me the trouble and yourself the embarrassment?"

"Because you haven't the vaguest idea of what you think I'm fool enough to let you get into."

"Tell me," she invited.

He shrugged. "You'd find out once you got in the middle of it. Personally, I'd put my money on you—any other day but this. Not against Council Guards interested in discovering if a Blood's blood is the same color as theirs."

Sarra thought about this as they went through the garden gates to the nearly empty stable yard. "Are we under suspicion, then?"

"*Everyone* is under suspicion these days."

"Damn it, Orlin!" she exclaimed. "I know about Taig and Lilen—"

"I gathered that when you mentioned Tarise," he said, still serene. He hooked a finger at the lone groom on duty, who sprinted the width of the yard at full speed. "Two horses, please—and none of this gorgeous saddlery the Wittes are known for, either," he added with a grin. "I don't want the local merchants to think I'm *that* rich!" When the boy ran to comply, Orlin went on, "Best forget what you know—or behave as if you've forgotten it."

"All I want is to help!"

"I understand, Sarra. But this is neither the time nor the place. When we go back to Roseguard, Agatine and I will tell you what you need to know—"

"According to whom? Gorynel Desse? Is he at the center of—"

"Yes," Orlin called to the groom as two horses were brought out to the yard. "Those will do us very well indeed. Thank you, lad."

Mounting the matched geldings—big, deep-chested Tillinshir grays—they rode out the main gates onto a cobbled road leading to the sprawl of Pinderon.

"Now you listen to me," Orlin said, and his voice had lost all its easy good humor. "You're eighteen years old. You don't even know how to use a knife to defend yourself, let alone a sword."

"Or magic," she said, and he twisted in his saddle to stare at her. "I know it's there. I've known since the week after my first Wise Blood. Coincidence, was it, that three weeks after, Gorynel Desse paid us a visit at Roseguard? Did he take my magic away as well as my memories of Ostinhold?"

"Damn," said Orlin Renne.

"I did a lot of thinking last night," Sarra went on. "Taig told me nothing, really—it was Lilen, and later on Tarise. Don't blame them. Once Lilen knew I remembered, she had to tell some of it. And neither she nor Tarise said much."

"Just enough to make you want to know more." He gave a long, heartfelt sigh. "Why weren't you born stupid?"

"If I had been, how could Desse use me as a symbol of all that was lost with Ambrai?"

This time he gaped at her.

"Not as who I really am, of course," she went on.

"Daughter of Mages killed at the Academy is the best way to present it. Any connection with the Feirans must be avoided."

"So you've got it all figured out, do you?"

"No!" she cried fiercely. "And unless somebody tells me what I'm supposed to do, what part I'm supposed to play, how can I do what I must?"

Orlin reined in atop a rise. From this vantage, they could have been admiring Pinderon's sleek prosperity, its intricately woven thatched roofs, its soaring domed temple to its patron, St. Tamas.

"You remind me of your mother—both your mothers, actually. Agatine and Maichen went to school together, did you know that? St. Delilah's, on Brogdenguard." He smiled into the distance. "Appropriate, though neither was ever any good with a sword. More like scalpels, the pair of them, slicing away what's rotten but leaving it to others to heal up the wounds. That's *my* job, where Agatine's interests are concerned."

Sarra could understand that. Orlin could charm the scales off a snake.

"But you're different," he went on. "You want to cure the whole world."

Slowly, almost without conscious volition, she said, "I remember once when I was very little, sitting on Mother's lap, watching the stars. She asked which one I wanted for my own—and I told her I wanted all of them."

"I'm not surprised. And I have the feeling that in pursuit of them, *you're* the one who'll turn into a sword." His smile turned sad. "Agatine and I wanted you to have a life of your own before the past caught up with you and claimed your future. We always knew it would happen one day. We're selfish enough to want you to be just ours a little while longer."

"I love you, too," Sarra said, her voice a little thick. "But the Rising won't be taking anything from me that I won't want to give."

"I'm very much afraid you're right. You First Daughters, you grow up with obligations and duties and responsibilities ... promise to remember one thing for me, Sasha," he said, and use of the childhood name made her bite her lip. "Remember always that your life belongs to *you*. Not to your Blood, or the Mage Guardians or Ambrai or the Rising.

However much you give of yourself, you have to take things back, too. Otherwise you'll use yourself up, like Taig Ostin."

"Taig?" she echoed, bewildered.

"He'll burn himself to ashes. It's in his eyes." He shook himself and heeled his horse gently. "Come, we're wasting a lovely day."

The city of Pinderon was surrounded by a low wall covered in flowering vines, a pretty boundary between it and the Witte lands. Broad avenues radiated in spokes from a central Circle, with narrower streets connecting at irregular intervals, angled so that a map of the place looked like the Witte chevrons. Pinderon boasted only one completely round building—the St. Tamas Temple in the middle of the Circle—but everywhere the angles of walls were gentled by curving turrets, arching walkways over wide streets, circular windows, and the intricate serpentine patterns of thatch for which the city was famous. Pinderon's maze of interlocking streets provided fascinating opportunities to hide—if one knew where one was going.

Possessed of a logical mind, Sarra had been scant minutes into Dalion Witte's tour the other day before she figured out and stamped in her memory the layout of Pinderon. Whatever else might happen, she would not get lost.

An itching at the base of her skull begged for something to happen. She shifted her shoulders against the impatience and placidly—for her—joined Orlin in touring the seaside walls, a shopping arcade, and a little gem of a Cloister textiles museum donated by the Wytte family. The Wittes cordially loathed and refused to acknowledge these distant cousins, who during the War of The Tiers defiantly split from the main family, changed a vowel, were classified as Fourths, and continued to use the Witte colors of yellow and red to irritate their Blood relations. During a tour given by the Wytte daughter in charge, Sarra praised the collection to the skies—both because she truly enjoyed it and because she knew it would get back to Mirya Witte. But lovely as the weavings, quilts, needlepoint, and wall hangings were, the itch to be *doing* something got worse.

It almost vanished inside the cool serenity of the St. Tamas Temple. A gentle silence washed over her as she walked the sea-green tiled floor beneath a gigantic blue dome. A wide font of sea water stood to one side of the altar, above which hung a fine old iron anchor on a massive chain. Be-

hind the gnarled wooden altar—said to be carved from the
very shipwreck the Saint had miraculously survived during
the Lost Age—was a modern fresco of sloops gliding to safe
harbor. Rarely had Sarra seen such beautiful work, and she
said as much to Orlin—right before she spotted a pair of tall,
robed-and-coifed sailors kneeling on the other side of the
font.

She would never be able to say what warned her. She'd
spent less than an hour in Taig Ostin's company as an adult,
and not a moment in the Minstrel's. She didn't even know
the man's name. But she knew who they were. She *knew* it.

Orlin pointed out a charming little statue of a dolphin near
the side door. Sarra admired it aloud, wondering feverishly
how she would contrive to tell Taig what he needed to know.
Although the Temple was empty but for the four of them,
anyone might come in at any minute.

She returned to the altar, telling Orlin she wished to pay
her respects to the Saint before departing. She managed to
trip over a seam in the tiles and stumble into one of the sailors. Sure enough, Taig Ostin's handsome gray-eyed face
looked up from the frame of a black coif.

"Taig—"

"Shh!"

Footsteps—one set light and soft, the other wooden
heels—sounded behind her. She cursed the untimely appearance of more suppliants and murmured, "Forgive me. I
didn't mean to interrupt your devotions."

He shook his head and placed a fist to his lips, signifying
a vow of silence. The other man, coifed head and broad
shoulders bent, didn't move.

"Come, Sarra," said Orlin, just as Taig mouthed *Horses*.
Sarra dipped her fingers into the font and touched the seawa-
ter to her brow, using her hand to hide the movement of her
lips as she replied, *Where should I meet you?*

Taig scowled. Sarra scowled right back. Turning, she
joined Orlin and together they passed by a barefoot child
and an old man, come with offerings of seashells to ask St.
Tamas' protection for a sailor.

Once they were mounted, Orlin said, "How's Taig?"

Sarra nearly dropped the reins.

"Give me some credit, girl," he growled. "Those two
were no more sailors than I am. Their hands gave them
away, for one thing. The calluses of a musician or a horse-

man aren't those of a sailor. And for another, it's on the day of a voyage that a sailor goes to St. Tamas. No ship will sail until Taig and the Minstrel are found."

"Umm—I see. He said they need horses."

"Good thing I asked for plain saddles, isn't it?"

"You *knew?* You *planned* to meet them?"

"Cailet's missing," he said unwillingly. "She shadows Taig like a galazhi fawn. He may know where she is. Now shush up, Sasha. Here they come."

Cailet? Oh, no—not when I've only just found her! Knowing she shouldn't, unable to help herself, she glanced over her shoulder. Two men, all right—but neither was in black, one limped on a short crutch, and the other had an empty left sleeve. She saw at once how they did it: voluminous robes reversible into green cloaks, coifs the same, the arm bound behind, the crutch easy to hide. They merged into the casual flow of people and vanished.

"We'll lose them," she said.

"No we won't." Orlin seemed to be struggling against laughter—over what, Sarra could not imagine. He led the way down a tree-lined avenue in the opposite direction from Taig and the Minstrel, made several turns down increasingly disreputable side streets, and eventually reined in.

"This is where you leave me," he said.

"Oh, no. Where you go, I go."

"Don't argue!" Orlin dismounted and lifted her out of the saddle with no effort at all. "Risk enough taking you this far. This is no neighborhood for a lady. Take this street back the way we came, turn left at—"

Beyond him, she saw two men. This time one leaned on the other as if too drunk to walk, both were in nondescript brown cloaks (how had they managed *that* switch?), and each was possessed of two good arms. "Look!"

"Keep your voice down—do you want all Pinderon to hear you?"

There was no more talk of sending her back. They walked their horses through several miserable alleys, finally tethering them in back of a tavern. Raucous music and a stink made equally of stale liquor and cheap incense wafted outside toward the trash bins where they belonged. Orlin collared a boy from the dozen playing in the alley and gave him two cutpieces.

"Another two if our horses are still here when we come out," he said.

"Three," the child demanded.

"Two, or a broken finger," Orlin replied, smiling gentle menace down from his great height. The boy shrugged, impressed but damned if he'd show it, and took up his post. Grasping Sarra's arm, Orlin muttered, "You stay close to me, and not a word out of you—or I'll break more than your finger. Understood?"

She nodded, gulping. This was a side of the equable, urbane Orlin Renne she hadn't dreamed existed.

And the Feathered Fan was the kind of place she had never thought to set foot in in her life.

A kitchen boy pointed them to the main hallway without surprise or comment. A door opened, and a stinking wave assaulted Sarra. She swayed against her foster-father's strong arm. Arrayed about a dim taproom were a dozen men in various stages of undress. A tall, thin woman wearing magnificent green brocade and a headpiece like tattered butterfly wings approached, lips split wide to reveal yellowing teeth.

"Ah, here's one too shy to come in the front door! Is it for yourself you need companionship, good *Domni,* or for the little lady here?" She fluttered a fan the size of a serving platter. It was molting.

Oh, Sweet Saints—Taig said the Feathered Fan—but it's a bower!

Orlin chuckled, his hand like steel around Sarra's arm. "With regret, mistress, I'm kept too busy at home to spare anything for your charming boys."

Sarra realized abruptly that a . . . companion . . . was being solicited for *her.*

"So it's the little ladybird," said the bower mistress. "Her first?"

"Of course." Orlin glanced around as if examining the masculine offerings, who preened and primped. "I need something tallish, darkish, and newish. A friend mentioned recent arrivals . . . ?"

"Country boys fresh as new-mown grass," she boasted, and when Orlin's brows quivered added hastily, "But well-educated, talented, and fully capable, I assure you, *Domni.* Youth just means they haven't had time to develop bad habits." She bent a stern gaze on a redheaded young man with a sulky mouth, who shrugged indifference. "They've just come back from a stroll. Let me call them downstairs so you can select which the young *domna* fancies."

Should I choose Taig or the Minstrel? Sarra thought, dizzy. Orlin smiled reassurance and she rallied, only to flinch back a trifle as the redhead sauntered over. His unbuttoned longvest revealed a shirt open to the buckle of a perilously low belt.

"Too bad you like 'em dark, little one. I'd be honored to be your first."

Sarra cringed in earnest, grateful that her role as nervous virgin gave her the luxury. Glancing wildly around, she noted for the first time that *all* the men were young, some no older than herself.

Like most women, Sarra would remain a virgin until she was ready to marry. But her husband would not be the first man in her bed. The services of a professional would be purchased some weeks before the wedding. With all the expertise of his trade, he would explore her needs and responses thoroughly, and she would receive her husband knowing he had been instructed in exactly how to please her.

The wealthy made their selections in elegant, Council-licensed bowers that kept at least twoscore young men of all shapes, sizes, and colors. It was a lucrative career for an attractive superfluous son; a few famous bower lads were even Bloods. Well-trained, well-kept, and well-paid, they were contracted at eighteen and spent the first year learning their craft from older women who made up a secondary clientele. If a man was accomplished, if his customers were generous, and if he managed to keep several married women and widows as continuing patrons, he could earn a lifetime's keep before the stipulated retirement age of thirty.

The Feathered Fan was not a bower where the wealthy arranged such services. It was, quite simply, a whorehouse.

"I'm Steenan," the man went on. "Sure you don't like redheads?" He was fingering the buckle of his belt suggestively. Sarra flinched once more—and then came close to gasping aloud. The buckle was cheap brass, crudely made, and decorated with a multitude of leaves surrounding a single tiny flameflower.

"Holy St. G—Geridon!" she stammered aloud, while inside the thought came wildly: *He's one of us!*

Orlin would have been appalled to know she had just

made herself a member of the Rising. But it marked an important change in her thinking. She was one of them now, she belonged to them—no matter what Orlin or Agatine or Tarise or Taig or anyone said. More importantly, *they* belonged to *her.* It had started with her impulse to help Taig any way she could. Now this instinct to aid and protect included the whole Rising.

Take something back for herself for everything she gave? She had enough and more than enough to give without ever feeling any lack. The cause for which she was determined to fight would never, could never, burn her to ashes; she was an Ambrai, Mageborn, inheritor of magic that flamed forever.

It would strike her as singularly amusing in later years that these noble sentiments had first swept over her in the middle of a whorehouse taproom.

Steenan grinned even wider at Sarra's exclamation— Geridon the Stallion was a compliment to what was below his buckle—and she blushed. Though Tarise's phrase for exceptional masculine pulchritude had come to her lips quite involuntarily, it was exactly the right thing to say; instinct again.

Having revealed that they were not without allies even in this incredible place, Steenan strolled back to a hearthside table laden with ale mugs. Nailed above the mantle was a sign:

THE FEATHERED FAN
Under New Management
(formerly The Bower of the One-armed Lover)

This was a reference to a ballad that gently-reared young females were not supposed to know, for it had nothing to do with a missing limb. She blushed again, even while realizing that Taig had impishly punned on his destination with his "amputation" outside the Temple. That was why Orlin knew where to find them—and why he'd laughed.

And Steenan is why Taig came here—Saints, the things he must learn from clients—but what a bizarre way to serve the Rising!

And there was a pun in *that* that she didn't want to think about.

Orlin was glancing around impatiently for the bower mistress. Sarra looked up at him, trying to tell him with her eyes that she wasn't as scared as she was pretending. In fact, this had suddenly become very exciting. *Taig or the Minstrel? Taig, so Orlin can help the idiot slip outside to the horses and get away. But then Taig will still be in danger—well, I'll think of something.*

Preparing herself to make her selection as natural as possible, she was totally unprepared when the streetside door burst open. Sunlight drizzled the floor through the thick haze of incense and seven women escorted by five men staggered through.

"Ale! Ale!" one woman chanted drunkenly. Another, disdaining to state the obvious, went directly to the barrels and claimed the nearest tap, kneeling so it decanted directly into her open mouth.

The bower youths quickly joined the merriment, providing mostly clean mugs. Three of the new arrivals started singing. Every occupant of the taproom not yet standing jumped up into what was soon a deafening din.

"Drinks all around!" someone cried. "Celebrate the grand occasion!"

"C'mere, cockie!" a blonde woman shouted. "I'll console you for not being in Lady Glenin's bed last night!"

Sarra winced, and not only at mention of her sister's name. Taig was among the raucous invaders. He clambered over a bench, reached for a mug, drained it, and roared for a refill. The Minstrel—at least, she assumed it was he, for he fit the general outlines of the man she'd seen in the temple—tottered over to where Sarra and Orlin stood. Grinning all over his florid face, he announced, "To hell with Glenin! I'll take this one!" and pinched her cheek.

Men who touched Sarra without her permission regretted it profoundly. A surreptitious hand on her knee was one thing. But—*He thinks I'm—that I'm a—!*

She slapped his face. It was not, in point of fact, the sort of masculine face she favored: every line of it proclaimed rogue, born liar, and devoted follower of Pierga Cleverhand, patron of thieves. The obnoxious face laughed down at her, and she drew back her hand, intending to slap him again.

Butterfly Wings came down the stairs with the promised farmboys—hulking, hunch-shouldered lads who might or might not have been de-loused. The Minstrel sidled around, dark gaze stroking Sarra's figure. The urge to slap someone

was transferred to Orlin. Why wasn't he being any help?
And where was Taig?

More importantly, where was Cailet?

Dark brown eyes laughed at her above the red mark of
her hand on his cheek. He chucked her under the chin. She
planted four dainty knuckles squarely on his jaw. His head
snapped back, teeth clacking; she hoped she'd broken a few.
It couldn't hurt his appearance any more than that smug
grin.

Success at last. He took a step backward, cradling his
abused jaw with long fingers. "Hellspawn!"

"Blood Daughter," she corrected icily, and proceeded to
ignore him.

"What's all this, then?" cried Butterfly Wings. "This is a
decent respectable bower, I'll not have you coming in
and—"

All at once the Minstrel was picked up by the shoulders,
swung around, and slammed facedown across a tabletop.

"Women are like peaches, friend. Never pluck them underripe," came a new voice—deeply melodious, fashioned
equally for speech and song. It belonged to a very tall, very
broad-shouldered man about Taig's age. Very blue eyes regarded her with a tolerant amusement Sarra immediately
loathed more than the other man's leer. "Besides," he went
on, "this one's not worth a tin cutpiece."

Orlin cleared his throat as if his coif—or laughter—were
half-strangling him. "Umm . . . she isn't—er—she's not—"

Not for sale? Sarra thought furiously. *Or not worth a tin
cutpiece?*

"On offer?" suggested Blue-eyes.

"Exactly," said Orlin. "Underripe, as you say. We're here
to remedy that, actually." He clasped the man's left hand for
a moment, leaving a quick glisten of gold in the palm.

Sarra stared. *This* was the Minstrel, his troubles to be partially cured by application of Agatine's gold? Recalling
Taig's description, she searched the edges of the black coif.
Ah—there, just at the right temple, a few curling coppery
hairs. Definitely the Minstrel. She considered her original
plan, then glimpsed Taig—reeling up the stairs with a boy
on each arm, bawling a drinking ballad. He'd probably give
them the slip and take one of the horses. That left the stupid
Minstrel to take care of.

"Papa?" she ventured, favoring Orlin with her best wide-eyed born-this-morning look. "I think I like *this* one. Buy him for me, please?"

Blue-eyes choked.

The taproom noise resolved into a popular ballad praising Lady Glenin Feiran's charms. Butterfly Wings was leading the chorus. More money to be made from many customers than one, after all; Sarra's transaction could wait.

Orlin's brows knotted over gleeful eyes. "But he's not a professional—are you?" he asked the Minstrel, who turned an interesting shade of purple.

"Oh, but he's clean—at least, he doesn't smell *too* bad," Sarra said sweetly. She took his hand as Orlin had done, making a show of inspecting his nails. He snatched his hand back, but not before she felt the fingertip calluses of the ardent lutenist. Absolutely the Minstrel. "If he's not a professional, he won't cost that much, will he?"

For someone who presumably made his living with his voice, the Minstrel was singularly silent. The very blue eyes expressed a very serious need to strangle Sarra.

She plied her dimples. "Unless, of course, you don't know *how*."

For another moment he struggled with some overpowering emotion. Then he found his voice in successively louder stages. "You—can't—*buy*—*ME!*"

"Now, don't try to run the price up just because I fancy you," Sarra scolded winsomely as she moved closer and kicked him in the ankle. The moron didn't even know when he was being rescued. Tucking her hand in the crook of his elbow, she finished, "I'll take this one, Papa. Let's go home."

Orlin nodded helplessly, tears of repressed mirth in his eyes.

"Our horses are out back," Sarra said, gesturing to the kitchen. "Papa, should you give the bower mistress something for her trouble?"

Recovering, he winked at her. "Don't leave without me, now that you're so eager." He threaded through the tables to Butterfly Wings.

Sarra prodded the Minstrel into the kitchen. "Hurry up!" she hissed. "We don't have all day!"

A peek out the kitchen door showed Sarra the urchin faithfully holding the Tillinshir grays—while he picked the meager brass decorations off the saddles. *Damn Taig—he can't actually be waiting for this dimwit to join him. Well, first things first—get the Minstrel out of here, and worry about Taig later. Do I have to do everything?*

And where's Cailet? If anything's happened to her, if anyone's hurt her—

Sarra started for the horses. Hard fingers around her wrist halted her in mid-stride.

"*Nobody* buys me!"

When she yanked at his arm, he flung her off so powerfully that she stumbled against the doorframe. "You idiot!" she hissed. "I wouldn't have you if *you* paid *me!*"

The insult was lost in the increasing space between them: he was halfway back through the kitchen. The commotion in the taproom had for some unknown reason subsided to a ragged hush. Sarra sprang for the Minstrel, getting both hands around his elbow. He merely dragged her along with him. The kitchen boy, watching avidly from the hearth, giggled; Sarra turned red to her toenails at the picture she presented of frantic virginal lust.

Clouds of incense swirled around six new arrivals wearing Council Guard uniforms and formidable frowns. Murderous lengths of silver glinted down their thighs from gold belts. Sarra yanked the Minstrel's arm. He freed himself vehemently. Straining on tiptoe, she glimpsed Steenan's red head and Orlin's towering dark coif—and Butterfly Wings, screeching as Steenan's fist connected with Orlin's jaw.

The taproom erupted into a free-for-all. Bower youths, drunken customers, roaring Guards—the Minstrel pushed up his sleeves, very blue eyes alight, and ripped off his coif. Sarra let all her weight hang limp from his shoulder.

"Get off me, you little shit!" he snarled.

This was without question the stupidest—not to mention the rudest and most hateful—man on Lenfell. Didn't know a rescue when it handed him money, didn't know a diversion when it broke out in a fight staged for his benefit—

Steenan battled himself within range, both fists flailing, one eye already blacking. The Minstrel, off balance and with only one arm free, slammed the heel of his hand into Steenan's opponent—the red-faced lout who'd accosted Sarra earlier.

Chivalry lives, she thought sourly, and scrabbled for footing; having decided he couldn't get rid of her, he'd wrapped an arm around her waist and lifted her off the floor, more or less out of his way.

"Thanks!" Steenan panted. "Now get out of here!"

The Minstrel laughed. "And miss the fun?" He landed a right to the jaw just as Steenan delivered a left to the stomach of a Council Guard. Sword, teeth, and coif were knocked awry. Sarra, swinging from the Minstrel's elbow like a rag doll, swore luridly and kicked as she sensed someone approach from behind.

"Get gone!" Steenan commanded. "Taig will follow later! Hurry!"

"After what Guards have done to me the last few years? Not fuckin' likely!"

"There'll be another time, and a better one! Don't be a fool!"

Sarra would have commented on the hopelessness of this admonition if she hadn't been half-suffocated.

"All right, all right, later," the Minstrel grumbled.

"Run for it!" Steenan craned his head around, grinning suddenly at Sarra. "So you *do* like 'em red-haired, eh, *Domna?*"

She glared. "Get me out of here!"

"Anything for a Lady," the Minstrel responded. And with a surge of muscles Sarra's world upended. He slung her across his shoulder, ran through the kitchen, and with completely consistent lack of ceremony tossed her across Orlin's horse.

"What are you *doing?*" Sarra gasped, trying to right herself.

"Kidnapping you." He was in the saddle instantly, one hand firmly on her backside to keep her where she was. "Scream, why don't you?" he invited, giving her a sudden thwack on the rump.

She obliged involuntarily.

"You call that a scream?" He reined around, giving her a sidewise view of the back door.

"You call this a kidnapping? What're you waiting for?" she yelled.

"Them!"

She had one good look at a pair of Guards with bloody noses colliding with each other on their way through the door. Then she hung on to whatever she could grab as at last he kicked the gray into a gallop.

They rode in a wild clatter through winding streets, curses in their wake as pedestrians scattered right and left. Shops, faces, laden washlines, patches of sun and sky all went by at dizzying speed. Sarra was sure she would throw up. The next thing she knew was the hay-and-horse half-dark of a stable, and a snarled command to stay put.

Naturally, she slid off the horse at once. The Minstrel was rummaging in a pile of straw, bent over. She took the opportunity the Saints provided and kicked him right in the ass.

"Don't you *ever* put a hand on me again!"

He rolled to his feet clutching a lute case in one hand. "Get b—" Menacing tone and threatening step were both marred by a slight slide in horse dung. "Get back on that horse."

"For a tin cutpiece I'd turn you in to the Council Guard myself!"

"I don't care what you do once you get me past the gate. Nobody'll stop me if I've got the First Daughter of—which exalted Blood are you, anyway?"

Sarra fiercely regretted there was nothing handy to throw at him—say, an anvil—to make an impression in his thick skull. Instead she marched up to him, careful even in rage to avoid dark plops on the cobbles, and stuck a finger in his face. That she must reach so far to do it improved her temper not a whit.

"I know Taig Ostin, I know who you are, and I've been *trying* to keep the Council Guard from nailing your worthless hide to the St. Tamas Gate! The man with me was Orlin Renne—husband of Agatine Slegin, which means you have powerful friends—which is obviously more than you deserve!"

He heard this speech without a flicker of expression. Sarra nearly spat with frustration. At last he said, "Lady Agatine Slegin?"

At last something had gotten through. Sarra tugged her clothes to rights and waited for the rest of it to connect.

"So who the hell are *you?*"

"Sarra Liwellan. Do you know of any other safe places to—"

"Sarra—? You silly cow, you're the one who accused me of rape last night!"

"That was a mistake. I—"

"You're damned right it was!"

It seemed she'd have to explain everything in words of one syllable or less. Well, what could one expect from someone who sang a proscribed song right out in the open? She drew a breath that left her in a whoosh as the Minstrel grabbed her. He tugged her vest down to pin her arms; silver buttons ripped free and tinkled to the cobbles. Then he kicked her feet out from under her. She sat abruptly on hard stone and soft stinky glop. Her struggles to rise gave him time to unfasten his longvest and whip the belt from his waist.

For a horrified instant she thought he was going to do what the Justices thought he'd attempted last night. He didn't. Seizing an ankle, he lashed worn leather around her boot and despite her frantic kicks quickly performed the same service for her other leg, fastening the buckle tight. Sarra let loose a string of invective. The Minstrel told her to shut up, and set about securing the lute case behind the saddle with reins cut from a pegged bridle.

"You Blood Daughters—always sticking your meddling little fingers where they don't belong—"

"How *dare* you do this to me!"

"Predictable down to the last platitude." He hauled her up. "Stop squirming!" he ordered, replacing her on the horse.

"Orlin will kill you for—ow!" Sarra yelped, the shift of the saddle as he mounted causing the horn to dig into her ribs. "If I don't kill you first!"

"I said shut up!" And he dealt her another whack on the rump.

She bit his knee.

"Do that again and I'll—"

"Don't you threaten me!"

Then they were galloping the streets again and with every stride her middle bounced against the saddle. By now the Council Guard would be doubly alert for him. Subversion, attempted rape, now kidnapping—Sarra hoped they caught him.

But they didn't. He seemed to know the streets of Pinderon as if a map were engraved on his eyeballs. Twists and turns, a mad gallop, a short rest in a dark alley—Sarra, who'd always thought her sense of direction superior and her instant comprehension of town plans unequaled, was thoroughly lost. Then again, she'd never seen a town at this angle, either.

She could hear nothing past the drumming of the horse's hooves. Faces blurred past—mostly shocked and startled. Infuriatingly amused, some of them. The men, naturally. Guard uniforms glimpsed in a flash of red and gold; the local Watch in the Witte Blood's yellow and red; garish inn signs, bright clothes, and the occasional burst of sunlight that half-blinded her.

Suddenly all was sunlight as they left the buildings behind and the Tillinshir gray broke into a flat gallop. Sarra saw the Minstrel's hand reach back to steady the lute. No such tender consideration was shown her. She slid and bounced, bruises compounding earlier bruises until her whole body felt raw.

I'll kill him.

No. That's too good for him. I'll keep him locked in a very small room for a very long time.

And make him listen to Tarise sing.

And I will learn the lute. Badly.

"Gatekeeper!" he bellowed all at once, reining in hard. "Open up! Unless you want to take the blame for the little Blood here getting hurt!"

Sarra craned her neck and saw that the gates were indeed closed. The Minstrel stuck a finger into her ribs and she yelped. The gates swung open.

"Much obliged!"

Sarra gasped as the gray leaped forward. At long painful last the horse slowed to a walk. They were miles and miles north of the city, up in the hills where in winter animals grazed. They and their herders were in high spring pasture now. The drowsy landscape of waving grass and murmuring trees was completely deserted.

Sarra tumbled to the ground. The belt was removed from her ankles. She sat up and tugged her vest tidy, rubbing her side and shoulder.

"Congratulations," she rasped. "Now the Watch and the Guard will want you for kidnap as well as attempted rape and sedition."

"There's worse on my charge sheet." He grinned as he rethreaded the belt through trouser loops. "Besides, who'd believe *I'd* have to use force to get a woman to do exactly what I want?"

Conceited pig! she fumed, rubbing her tingly-numb feet.

"It's a long walk back to Pinderon, *Domna*. Get moving."

She peered up at him. "You're not taking me with you?"

He paused in the process of finger-combing his hair, and his brows arched. "I'm flattered, Blood Daughter."

She stared blankly, sitting there in the dirt. Then she understood. *"You?"* she choked.

"Better me than some sleek, pampered bower cockie," he went on, raking a hand back through wildly curling coppery hair. "Admit it, sweetheart. You'd rather have a *real* man teach you what your husband—Saints pity the poor fool—will need to know."

Furious, she scrambled to her feet and took a wobbly step toward him, fists knotted at her sides.

"After all," he went on, very blue eyes wicked as he fingered into a vest pocket, "Orlin Renne already paid for the privilege of my knowledge and experience." He flipped the gold coin high in the air and caught it again. "Granted, I'm expensive, but well worth it. Besides, there's nobody like me in any cock-broker's bower. I'm one of a kind."

"Cock-bro—?"

"The vulgar vernacular, kitten. See, you've already learned something. There's plenty more I could teach you if you want to come along for the ride." He pocketed the coin, laughing down at her. "So to speak."

"You're disgusting!" she snapped. "Go on, get out of here! I hope you get caught! Even if they don't catch you, I hope you get lost in the Wraithenwood!"

"Been there, thanks," he drawled. Sweeping her a low bow, he ended with, "Now, Blood Daughter, with your permission—or without it—I'll be off. My thanks and apologies to Taig."

"And none for me!" She planted her fists on her hips.

"You? After the aggravation you gave me today?" He checked the lute case, mounted, and paused to rub his fingers through his hair once more. Sarra had rarely seen any man but Orlin uncovered—and she had never seen hair this color in her life.

He grinned. "That's right, darlin'—take a good long look, and regret what you'll miss! By the way, it's true what they say about a Minstrel's hands!"

And with that and a wink he galloped off, vanishing over a grassy rise.

Sarra stood there, so furious she shook with it. Eventually she brushed herself off, muttering all the while.

"*Men!* Stupid, selfish, foul-mannered—and the arrogance! Bad enough to know any man at all—but have one around all the time? No *thank* you! I'm never getting married. Why would any woman want a husband? Cailet can continue the Sacred Ambrai Blood, and welcome." She froze. "Cailet! Blessed St. Rilla, I forgot all about her!"

She started back toward Pinderon, and had gone about a mile when a lone horseman on a Tillinshir gray thundered toward her. Taig Ostin; another *man.* Wonderful. All she lacked.

He drew rein. "Sarra! Are you all right?"

"Just splendid," she snarled. "Give me a hand up."

"Sorry, I'm on the run myself."

"Why? And where's Cailet?"

"Safe. Which way did your Minstrel go?"

"He's not *my* bloody Minstrel! And why are you running? What happened?"

"Long story. Renne will explain when you get back to town." He looked over his shoulder. "Some think I'm after Rosvenir for kidnapping you. More think I'm *with* him. They'll've sorted themselves out by now. Delay them if you can."

"He rode east. I'll tell them south." *Rosvenir? That's an old name—and false. They died out years ago.*

"East to Cantratown? Smart man." Not explaining this reference, he leaned down to touch her cheek, smiling. "And you're a smart girl."

She jerked back from his fingers. "Stop patronizing me, damn you!"

Taig laughed and straightened up in the saddle. "Be patient, Sarra. Only a few more years and you'll be joining us."

"Lose the Minstrel and I may consider it," she retorted.

"Now, Sarra! He didn't hurt anything but your dignity!"

With that remark, Taig put himself firmly in second position on the list of men she would flatly refuse to marry—never mind that it included every eligible male of her own and any other Generation.

"Where did you find Cailet?"

"Upstairs in that whorehouse, if you can believe it. I don't know how, but she knows it for a hidey-hole of ours. Steenan—the redhead, he's with us—locked her in so she couldn't get into more trouble. I sent her back with Orlin, then came after you. Or so everyone thinks." With a sudden frown: "Tell my mother to keep Cai at Ostinhold if she has to tie her down. I'll send Gorsha as soon as I can."

Easy jump. "To free her magic? Damn it, Taig, why can't he do the same for me? I'm Ambrai Blood, I'm——"

"——meant for other things. My mother will explain. Tell her I love her, and kiss Cailet for me." Another glance behind. "I've got to go, Sarra."

And for the second time that day a man abandoned her in the middle of the road. According to folklore, one more such occurrence before sunset and she would remain unmarried all her life. Sarra found herself actively wishing for this sign of the Saints' favor.

Still, when the Guard and the Watch found her, she presented so piteous a portrait of helpless victim that, far from abandoning her, all eight of them escorted her back to the Witte residence. Well, she supposed, one couldn't have everything. Keeping her hands over her face, sobbing realistically every so often, she was given at last into Agatine's care.

Once they were private, and Sarra had rid herself of the torn, abused, stinking clothes, she made short work of her story—with a lack of aggrieved pejoratives that surprised even her—while Agatine poured wine. Orlin, sporting a black eye that made him wince with each grin, described the fight back at the bower with a relish that made Agatine snort.

But the promised explanations were not forthcoming. Fooled with a sleeping draught in the wine, as she drifted off her last thought was that she'd break every one of that fake Rosvenir's fingers in three places each if he ever put his damned "Minstrel's hands" on her again.

Cailet

1

To nearly all those living at Ostinhold in 951, Maichen and Sarra Ambrai were just people who came for a visit and then left, something that happened all the time. It was sad that the pretty blonde lady had died, and her baby with her, but sometimes that happened, too. Certainly no one connected the incident with the vanished Ambrai First Daughter.

Only five people of the nearly one thousand in residence knew the truth: Lady Lilen, her three eldest children, and her Healer. Margit Ostin's death in 961 reduced the number to four. The servants who waited on the family were later Warded by Gorynel Desse just in case. Lilen, her children, and the Healer were not. At some future date, Cailet's identity as an Ambrai would have to be established. Interrogation must reveal no trace of magic in their memories.

Cailet herself was heavily Warded—not against memories, for a newborn had none, but against the magic that curled within her, waiting. Shining. Growing, even as Desse Warded it with all the cunning he possessed. When he emerged from the work after almost nine hours, he muttered something to Lilen about Cailet's given name being appropriate, and then collapsed and slept for a whole day.

She grew up as Cailet Rille, and it was never quite clear how she was related to the Ostins. This was not unusual. There being only about three hundred extant Names, discerning close cousin from total stranger was naturally something of a problem. It had been thirty-three Generations since the defining Fifth Census; even if two people shared a Name, it was probable that they shared only a twenty-times-great grandmother. The tangle of kinship meant six years of apprenticing before one became even a junior clerk at Census.

Though Cailet's official status was somewhat vague, she was treated as if she had been born Lilen's own child. This, too, was common. Favorite nieces or cousins often grew up in a First Daughter's household instead of their mothers'. The Tigge Name for instance, made a point of exchanging offspring. But while in theory every Tigge was equal, children of First Daughters had primary inheritance rights. This kept holdings intact, but inevitably some Tigges were more equal than others.

Lady Lilen was, in the common parlance, a First Daughter Prime; that was, she was descended in direct First Daughter line—in her case, for seventeen Generations. The bulk of the Ostin fortune was hers to do with as she saw fit. And as she felt morally bound to provide for all the sprigs on her gigantic tree, she ran the largest, most complex, and least visible Web on Lenfell.

In the year Ambrai and the Ambrai Name were destroyed, more than twelve thousand Ostins were employed in nearly nine hundred ventures worldwide. The smallest was a bookshop in Firrense. The largest was Ostinhold. Between 951 and 961, all the Ostins laid as low as their phenomenal numbers allowed—for Lilen's mother's brother had been husband to Allynis Ambrai.

Scraller Pelleris, alternately shaking with rage and trembling in terror at his own business connections to the Ostins, enlisted Anniyas's help in attempts to ruin them financially. The First Councillor directed similar action against every known Ostin interest. Lilen allowed some of these efforts to succeed. To divert funds from the Rokemarsh fisheries into the failing Gierkenshir shipping line would be to invite inquiry as to why the latter was headed by an Eddavar (Lilen's cousin, who doubled the connection by marrying a Solingirt whose father was an Ostin). But Lilen could not and would not let Scraller wreck Ostinhold. After some lean years and some tricky financial juggling, at last Scraller—and Anniyas—gave up.

One result of losing businesses from the Web was an influx of unemployed relatives. Guilt-ridden, and conscientious as always about her kinfolk no matter how distant, Lilen gave welcome to them all. In ten years, the population of Ostinhold increased to over three thousand. They made themselves useful—no one idled in The Waste—but they also had to be fed. And, being Ostins, they kept breeding.

Thus it was that Cailet, born Ambrai but called Rille, grew up as just one among scores of children at Ostinhold. She was a rather plain child and for the most part went unnoticed. She did not distinguish herself in any way: she committed a normal amount of mischief, fell into the middle range of scholarship, and was chosen neither first nor last in games. She sang in the children's choir organized by Miram Ostin, but never soloed; she had no trouble with basic mathematics, but higher functions defeated her. Cailet was simply an average little girl.

Which was precisely what Gorynel Desse had labored to accomplish with his magic by Warding hers—the powerful magic of a child named for Caitiri the Fiery-eyed.

One morning a few weeks before her tenth Birthingday, Cailet was on her way to school when she heard a maid tell a groom to saddle First Daughter's horse. Geria was riding to Viranka's Tears, a nearby village that boasted the only sweetwater well (other than Scraller's) in a hundred miles. Cailet immediately abandoned class and raced up three flights of stairs to the chamber kept for Geria's infrequent visits. It was just up the hall from Cailet's own room, where she made a brief stop to scrounge in a drawer for her purse.

After a respectful knock elicited permission to enter, she found Geria finishing her makeup. During application of brown pencil to her brows—plucking had been popular for a time but now exaggerated arches were the rage—Cailet begged Geria to purchase a book she was wild to read. It was the third installment of an adventure set during the First Wraithenbeast Incursion, about a brave band of friends who fought the Wraithen horrors. Although it was only four weeks until Wildfire, she simply couldn't wait for Lady Lilen to give her the book as a Birthingday present.

"Here's money," Cailet said. "It won't take long, First Daughter, please?"

Geria—who reveled in her title and treated her siblings as if she had been born Lilen's only child—glanced down at

Cailet's palm. Five carefully hoarded copper cutpieces, tarnished and slightly sweaty, vanished into the First Daughter's purse.

"If I remember," Geria said, bending to check her hair in the mirror.

"The bookshop's in Eskanto Alley, where all the printers used to be before Scraller outlawed new books. Why'd he do that, First Daughter?"

"Because he's wise enough to know that anything worth writing has already been written and printed," Geria answered absently, applying a fingerful of rouge to her lips. "And most of that isn't worth reading, anyway," she added.

Cailet was long accustomed to Geria's total lack of interest in anything requiring even minimal mental effort. She thanked the First Daughter again, cast a last look at the embroidered purse where her precious cutpieces now resided, and bowed herself out.

Geria returned from Viranka's Tears that evening with her purchases: skin cream, fine-milled soap, candies, a lace shawl, and earrings made of Scraller's Silver (a vein discovered beneath the keep had yielded richly for a year before dying out; he parlayed the rarity into a demand—another "scrall"). But nowhere in the First Daughter's room could Cailet's small commission be found.

"Oh, that," Geria said when Cailet ventured a question. "I didn't get to the shop. It's a filthy street, I wonder that you're allowed to visit."

Cailet gulped back disappointment and asked politely for her cutpieces.

"I haven't got them," replied Geria, tossing her head to admire the swing of silver at her ears. "These cost more than I thought—Saints, the prices here, and practically nothing to buy! Anyway, I used your money. I knew you wouldn't mind. So you see even if I'd had time to look for your book, I wouldn't have had enough to buy it."

As it happened, Cailet did mind. Very much. It had taken five weeks to earn those cutpieces, doing errands for Ostinhold's harried steward. Now she had no money—and no book, either.

Cailet stared at her scuffed boots. "May I please have my money back, First Daughter?"

"It's not convenient for me to repay you right now. Ask my mother for it."

"Please, First Daughter, I don't like to do that."

"Whyever not? She can easily afford five cutpieces."

"I just—I don't like to ask her for money."

Times were tightening again, what with the galazhi suffering from some mysterious ailment. Now that Scraller and Anniyas had withdrawn from the financial battlefield in defeat, Lady Lilen's first rule had been reestablished: each Ostin property must be self-sufficient, never borrowing from the others unless destitution had one ragged foot already in the door.

"I don't like to ask," Cailet repeated.

"I do, all the time." Geria paused. "But then, I'm First Daughter. Very well, Cailet, the next time you come to visit me at Combel, I'll have your money for you."

"I'd like it now, please. I need it."

Swinging around from the mirror, Geria frowned. "For what? Some silly book? You'd do better to spend it on skin cream. Saints, how I *loathe* Ostinhold. I always come away looking ten years older. And I won't bring the children here, it's far too unhealthy for them."

Cailet, fair skin tanned brown and fair hair bleached white by the relentless sun of The Waste, said, "All the same, I need my money back."

"You'll have to wait." Geria resumed position before the mirror. "Just like me," she muttered.

Cailet understood the reference, and flushed with hot anger. Geria had married Mircian Karellos in 958 and moved to the Ostin house in Longriding. Barely a year later, after the birth of First Daughter Mircia, she persuaded her mother to give her the more elegant mansion in Combel. Having found its revenues inadequate for her growing family—Gerian had been born last year—First Daughter was at Ostinhold to ask for the large seaside residence in Renig. If she couldn't get the house, she'd settle for more money. Thus she lingered past her usual three-day visit, waiting on her mother's decision.

But Cailet knew what Geria really waited for. As First Daughter, she would inherit the management and the profits of the Ostin Web. Even after providing for her sisters and brothers from the Ostin Dower Fund, she would be the richest woman in North Lenfell. But first her mother would have to die.

"Y'know, Geria," Cailet said, deliberately using name and not title, "you're not a very nice person."

A blink of greenish-brown eyes. *"What?"*

"You're selfish and greedy, and if you didn't look so much like Lady Lilen nobody'd ever believe you're her daughter. I want my cutpieces back. Now."

Geria laughed. "Incredible! Get out of here before I have you thrown out."

Something inside Cailet began to burn and tremble. She did not like Geria; she never had, and she was sick of pretending respect for someone who didn't deserve it.

Geria happened to glance at her then, and whatever she saw in Cailet's face made her painted brows swoop down in fury. "Ungrateful brat—you've lived off our charity since the day you were born! Now that I think on it, I'll keep the cutpieces to start repayment of everything you owe—and I'll collect it all one day, see if I don't!"

Cailet locked gazes with her. Anger flared deep inside, but outwardly she was as cool and steady as frozen stone. And she knew of a stone-cold certainty that she did not want to listen to this woman anymore.

"Be quiet," Cailet breathed.

Geria's lips moved. No sound came out.

Still holding the First Daughter's gaze, Cailet calmly took the purse from the dressing table. Upending it, by feel she counted out five cutpieces from the dozen jingling on the glass tabletop and replaced the rest.

"So you're a liar as well as a thief," she observed. "We're even now, Geria. I won't tell anybody about this—and it *won't* happen again." Pocketing the money, she added, "You should've married Scraller. He's just your kind."

Only then did she relinquish Geria's eyes. A blink, a gasping breath—and Cailet's armbones nearly snapped as Geria grabbed her.

"What did you do to me?"

"Took back what was mine. Let me go."

"You *stole* from me! How dare you! Give it back, you thieving little whelp!"

Geria fumbled at the pocket of Cailet's shortvest, cursing all the while. Cailet struggled, more frightened by the surge of fire within her than by Geria's fists, then called out to the only defense and protection that had never failed her.

"Taig!"

He was there like magic, already drawn by the shouting. "What the hell—? Geria! Let her go!"

"Little thief!" She delved into Cailet's pocket and came up with two cutpieces. "She stole from me!"

"Did not!" Breaking free at last, she hurtled toward Taig. He caught her against him, one cool hand smoothing her hair. "It's my money, Taig, I asked her to buy a book—but she didn't, and said she spent all her money and mine, too—I won't go to Lady Lilen for it, Taig, it's not right!"

"Shh," he murmured. "Of course it wasn't right, Cai."

"She *did* something to me!" Geria accused. "Fixed those Wraithen-eyes of hers on me and—"

A chill washed over Cailet, shivering through her so swiftly that it was as if the hot fury had never existed.

Taig rapped out, "Shut up, Geria!"

"We all know she's a changeling!"

"I said shut *up!*"

He was tall enough and strong enough—and their childhood battles had been frequent enough—for even a First Daughter to back down.

Cailet stared up at him, shuddering with cold. "Taig? What's she mean?"

"Nothing, darling. She's just being herself—obnoxious as usual. Now tell me what happened."

She calmed a little, warmed by his solid warmth. "I gave her money to buy a book, and she didn't, and she wouldn't give my five cutpieces back."

"She's lying," Geria announced with a shrug.

Her brother eyed her. "Knowing you and money, I doubt that."

"You'd take her word over mine? You forget who I am!"

"I know exactly what you are," he snarled back. "You selfish cow!"

Geria sucked in a breath. "How *dare* you speak to me that way!"

"How dare *you* treat Cailet so! But I don't know why I'm surprised. You don't change, do you? Everything at your convenience, Saints forbid you should show any kindness—"

"I don't have to listen to this." She rose, preparing to storm out, then remembered she was in her own room. Cailet saw it all in her face. She could read Geria's every thought and emotion as if they were written in the air.

"You're damned well going to listen for once in your life! You're as cold as the money you love! You never even grieved when Father died. Never knew what Mother went through, never even tried to comfort her."

"I did so cry! I'm a very sensitive person, I—"

"Sensitive?" He let out a harsh laugh. "All you could see was yourself in the same position, barefoot beside a pyre with ashes on your head! If you wept, it was for the pleasure of all the attention you'd get!"

"That's not true! I loved Father!"

Cailet listened and watched, thinking that Taig was right about Geria: she was made of ice. And yet ice could burn: the sight of her face, the sound of her words and the feelings she flung into the room—Cailet shrank against Taig's warmth, trying to shelter in him. But suddenly his presence burned her also, with a fierce and angry fire like yet unlike the flames within her before.

"When he died, your first thought was how much of his dower you'd get! And even with the greater share of it yours, you complain that Mother won't give you more! 'While I'm young enough to enjoy it,' " he mimicked in Geria's whine. " 'To travel, and have nice clothes and jewels and carriages and furniture—' "

Goaded, she spat, "Why *shouldn't* I have more? It's mine! I'm First Daughter! I have expenses—a husband and children to provide for, a house—"

"A house Mother gave you! A husband whose dower pays for it—and who thinks you hung the moons, Saints help the poor fool! He's lucky, like Father—he doesn't really know you. The pretense must be quite a strain, Geria!"

Cailet inched away from Taig, unable to bear the proximity. He was ready to ignite right here beside her—surely in another moment she would see the flames rise up and engulf him and Geria and everything else in wild rage—

"As for the children—you only bring them to see Mother once a year. It's too far, the roads are too rough, you won't risk them—won't risk missing more than a few nights with your latest lover is more like it!"

"Oh, and you're a portrait of all the virtues! I don't see you giving Mother any grandchildren! Alin's bad enough, but to have *two* in the family—"

"Leave Alin out of this," he warned.

"I intend to! He'll never get a single cutpiece from me!"

"You think he'd take money from you, or even want it?"

Cailet's eyes filled with tears of pain. Taig was immolating her. She wanted it to stop—but the alternative was Geria's terrible ice.

"Oh, that's right. Alin's *sensitive!* He and you and Margit—"

Taig went white beneath his sun-browning. "Say her name again and I'll—"

"You'll what?" She laughed. "I'm First Daughter, Taig. I can't be displaced or disowned. But *you* can—and will be if you don't stay away from the Rising. Yes, I hear things, brother dear. While I work like a slave keeping the Combel Web intact, *you* consort with traitors and felons, spending Ostin money on schemes against the Council—"

"That's enough!"

"I'm the only one in this family with any sense! Lenna and Tevis won't even consider the husbands I've found for them—good husbands, willing to pay plenty for the Ostin Blood. And Mother's worst of all! Coddling that impossible Alin, giving shelter to renegade Mages, taking in stray cousins as if they're her own children, and an orphaned brat who'll be the ruin of—"

Taig slapped her, bringing a cry to her lips and blood gushing from her nose. Fire quenched and ice shattered with the crack of Taig's hand. Cailet's whole body spasmed in reaction, in relief. For an endless instant time seemed suspended, and Taig and Geria were only people again, not raging opposing elemental forces.

Taig's voice was curiously mild. "I said *that's enough.* Give Cailet her money. Now."

The First Daughter pinched her swelling nose and obeyed. Her eyes were sulky with hatred and the promise of vengeance. Cailet darted a hand out for the cutpieces and fled.

Taig caught up with her in the hall connecting the west and south sprawls of Ostinhold. "Slow down, Cai! It's all right, she won't eat you, I promise."

It was calm here, the air cool and quiet. No fire. No ice. She caught her breath and turned to face him, looking way up into his silvery eyes.

"I'm not frightened—not for me," she amended, having only now realized what she'd witnessed. She had never seen a grown man hit a grown woman in her life—had never even *heard* of such a thing. "Taig, you *hit* her!"

"Not the first time," he replied with a shrug. Then, smiling: "Saints, Cai, don't look so grim! She won't haul me up before the Watch at Longriding."

"But she'll take the Ostin Name away from you first chance she gets."

"Oh, I've expected that for years. And you're nothing to do with her reasons for it." Bending, he grasped her shoulders gently. "Don't be scared for me, lovey. If she complains to Mother, she'll have to explain how it started. She may have convinced Father she was the sweetest girl ever born, and Mircian may believe it as well—but Geria has never fooled Mother."

Then why does Lady Lilen give her everything she wants? But Cailet didn't say that. "If she takes your Name away, you can use mine," she offered. "You'd be my brother."

"Haven't I always been?" Taking her hand, he strolled with her along the hall. Hazy late sun—real warmth, soft and easy—seeped through windows pitted by a hundred years of acid storms. "Now, what's this famous book you're so eager to read?"

It seemed so silly now. "Just a story. Taig, why'd she say that about Alin? And the Mages? What'd she mean about me?"

"You're too little to hold so many questions. No wonder they overflow. What I want to know is, why am I always in the way of the flood?" He shook his head, still smiling. "If you were Alin, and only fourteen, would you like it if someone tried to marry you off? Lenna and Tevis are old enough to defend themselves, but Geria's trying to bully poor Alin into signing a contract now."

"That's dumb. He's not even interested in girls. He spends all his time with Valirion Maurgen."

"Just so. At fourteen, I didn't much like girls, either. Nasty, chattery things," he added, pulling a face to make her smile.

Still, she was not so easily distracted. "What about the Mages?"

"I can't answer that, Cai. And you know it's something you shouldn't ask."

Cailet sighed. Nobody talked about Mageborns except in whispers. "I know, I know. When I'm older. When *is* 'older,' anyway?"

"Well, I'm twenty-two, and they still don't tell me everything."

"But you know about the Rising, and what Geria meant about me. It's why you slapped her. To keep her from saying more."

Taig had a habit of gnawing his cheek when he was thinking fast; it screwed his mouth around. Cailet mimicked the expression. He noticed, smiled, and ruffled her short pale hair.

"Cai, she's wrong. You're no danger to any of us who love you."

She believed him, because she always believed everything Taig told her. But she couldn't forget the feel of the fire and the ice—and something else that had happened before them.

"Taig . . . I did do what Geria said. I just—I was tired of listening to her lie to me. So I told her to be quiet. And she *was*."

"A speechless Geria Ostin—I'm sorry I missed it!"

"I was glad I shut her up. She really makes me mad sometimes. But, Taig, it was scary. That I could do that."

"Did you? Or was she so astounded that you actually talked back to the high-and-mighty First Daughter that she just couldn't find anything to say?"

"I guess that was it. It'd have to be, wouldn't it?" She sought reassurance for her doubts in his eyes. If she mentioned the fire and the ice, he would have an explanation for them, too. Soothed, trusting his answer even though she had never even asked the question, she decided it had been what Lady Lilen called "overactive imagination" in Alin, and pushed it all aside. Taig was just Taig again, after all: tall and warm and solid and caring.

"I'm sure that was it," he said, then grinned. "And it's a pity that's all it was. Shutting her up is one of my life's ambitions! Come on, Cai, it's almost dinnertime and I'm starved. Besides, I want to hear how Geria explains her bloody nose!"

2

Just after Cailet's Birthingday (Taig gave her the book), a guest arrived at Ostinhold. Geria had long since gone back to Combel, so there were no protests when Lady Lilen welcomed another Mage Guardian to her home.

Few Mages admitted to their calling nowdays. Everyone knew that. There were very few Mages left. Since last year's horror at Malerris Castle, where the Lords were exterminated by Guardian treachery—or so it was said—suspicion of undisciplined magic ran rampant across Lenfell.

This Mage was a Scholar, clad in black and gray robes, even adhering defiantly to a hint of his regimentals: the severe cut of his longvest, a gray sash, the stitching at collarpoints reminiscent of rank insignia pins. He swept into Ostinhold with his graying hair uncovered by a coif and within the hour was alone in a private chamber with Lady Lilen and her second son, Alin.

The former emerged looking shaken. The latter remained with the Scholar Mage until well after dark. Over the next few days, Alin rode out with the Mage in all directions, returned at all hours, and ignored the rest of the family. Cailet's single encounter with the Mage taught her that he had no time or attention for anyone else; her glimpses of Alin's pallid face told her the boy was constantly exhausted.

"But what's he teaching Alin?" she asked Taig one day. Taig only shook his head. Mage things again, that she wasn't supposed to ask about. But Taig looked as worried as Lady Lilen.

So Cailet told neither of them that she didn't feel very well, either. She slept badly, dreaming strange dreams she didn't remember in the morning. As the days wore on, the prickly feeling behind her eyes gradually went away and the dreams stopped. Just as well she hadn't bothered Lady Lilen with what was obviously unimportant.

On the first day of Applefall week, all Lenfell observed the Feast of St. Agvir. Trestle tables the world over groaned under the weight of food to be devoured after the traditional competition among children to climb the tallest tree in the district. Ostinhold, however, had a problem: there were no real trees within a hundred miles. The Agvir Wood—twenty-five feet of solid oak imported at great expense by Lady Lilen's great-great-great-grandmother—was raised instead. Long silver ribbons were distributed to every child between the ages of ten and thirteen, the courtyard humming with anticipation. Alin, who had won three years in a row, was no longer eligible. For the first time, Cailet was—and determined to have the fastest time.

The ten-year-olds went first. "St. Agvir's Windfall Apple" was sung by the assembled crowd as one child after another scurried up the Wood like squirrels, knotted a silver ribbon around the apple finial, and shinnied back down to race for the finish line. One verse and the chorus was good time; one verse and part of the chorus excellent; last year Alin did it in four words past one verse. Waiting her turn, Cailet counted under her breath, fingers clenched around the stiff ribbon. This many beats to the midpoint, that many more to the top—where time was usually lost tying the ribbon to the base of the apple. Some tried to make it up on the way down by dropping the last few feet onto soft mats spread for safety's sake, but that was against the rules. You had to keep hold of the Wood until your feet touched ground.

"Cailet Rille!"

Her turn. Heart pounding, she stepped up to the line, rocking slightly back and forth in time to the tune. Lady Lilen always hired musicians from Longriding to keep the rhythm even throughout; people had a tendency to sing faster as the song wore on. Cailet heard the drumbeat that signaled the start of the verse, poised herself, and at Lady Lilen's signal ran for the Wood.

Leather gloves, trousers, and shortvests protected the children from splinters—as if after so many years the Agvir Wood hadn't been polished smooth as satin. Cailet had chosen to go barefoot so her feet could get a better grip. Teeth clamped around the ribbon, she leaped as far as she could and climbed for all she was worth.

Halfway up, they hadn't even finished the first line. Grinning, she climbed faster. Other ribbons were held out of the way down below by the children who had tied them; as she neared the top they formed a silvery trellis overhead. Only a little way—Saints, the Wood was slippery!—gilt apple within reach—

A long, thin wail cut like an arrow into her heart. *Alin!* She knew it, as surely as she knew she was about to fall. Twenty-five feet straight down—onto pads not springy enough to prevent a broken bone if she landed wrong.

Twenty silver ribbons—including, somehow, her own— were tight around the finial. She let go of the Wood and grabbed at them with both hands. Strips of silk woven with metal threads hissed through her gloves. She felt heat through leather and then cuts on her palms. She was flying, falling, frightened and exhilarated all at once. She heard screams, none of them Alin's. And then she lost her grip and slammed into the mats, breath knocked out of her, stars exploding into sudden darkness.

Cailet had been afraid of the dark ever since she could remember. Miram had told her once that even when she was a tiny baby, she cried frantically if no light was left burning in her room. Now there was darkness all around her, the stars were gone, and she had no breath in her lungs to cry out her terror.

Worse, she sensed someone else in the darkness with her—someone even more frightened than she, and in profound pain echoed by the stinging ache behind Cailet's own eyes. Alin—scared of the Scholar Mage, of darkness, of chaotic swirling images he couldn't even see. Cailet tried to find him, needing not to be alone, needing someone to help her against the Wraithenbeasts she was sure lurked in the dark. But Alin was beyond her reach.

Beyond anyone's?

The thought came unbidden, terrible in its implications. Gentle, comical, fiercely independent Alin—scared and alone and hurting—

I'm here, Alin! It's all right!

She couldn't find him. Her eyes opened to daylight and panicky faces: Lilen, Taig, Miram, Healer Irien. She tried to speak, to tell them Alin needed help more than she. Gasping air, she struggled to sit up and make sense of the world. Her head spun and her right arm buckled, refusing to support her, and her breath caught with the pain.

"Hold still," Irien commanded, fingers probing gently. "Somebody get some ice. St. Feleris, look at her hands!

Let's get the gloves off, Cailet. That's it, you lie down with your head in Miram's lap. Don't try to move."

"Are you all right, Cai?" Taig asked, voice shaking.

"Yes," Irien answered. "Sliced hands and a broken arm—a clean fracture, thankfully. The cuts are nothing a few stitches won't cure. You're lucky you didn't break your leg or your head."

"That thick skull?" Miram teased gently, stroking Cailet's hair. "Don't be silly. Don't you worry, sweeting. Lenna's gone for Irien's kit. You'll be just fine in no time. You scared us all, truly told! What made you slip?"

Cailet stared in mute bewilderment. Hadn't they heard? Didn't they know that Alin—?

"Stupid custom," Irien was muttering. "A real tree has branches to hold, rough spots to dig into. I've expected this for years." He reached without looking into the medical kit that had appeared at his side, and extracted a bottle. "This will sting a little. Will you heed me now, Lilen, and put footholds on that damned Wood?"

The salve smeared onto her hands stung more than a little. Cailet ground her teeth, fighting the threat of renewed darkness. "Alin—" she managed.

Lilen smiled down at Cailet, an obvious effort to mask worry. "Yes, you beat his time," she scolded fondly. "We didn't even get to the chorus!"

"Cheated, though," Taig put in, winking. "Cai, you know you have to keep hold of the Wood!"

"Swallow this," Irien said, and poured something sweet onto her tongue. She choked, coughed, swallowed. Almost at once the pain in her head went away. A minute later, just as she got her voice back, darkness swirled in again.

"It'll hurt, setting her arm," Irien's voice said from miles away. "This will knock her out while I do it. Let's get her to bed, shall we? Taig?"

Strong arms lifted her. She wanted to tell Taig not to bother, she was already floating. All he need do was nudge her where she was supposed to go and she'd drift like a cloud in a moon-dark sky. A nice dark, soft and sleepy like a fine wool blanket, all the more comfy for being wrapped in Taig's warm embrace. Cailet roamed the gentle dark for a time, wondering vaguely if Alin was in this one, too. She hoped so; it was a good dark, the first in her life that didn't frighten her.

Alin?
But she didn't find him.

3

Eleven very long days later, Ostinhold kept a quiet St. Kiy's.
Lenna and Tevis took the younger children and a horde of
cousins to Longriding to visit Senison relations; of the immediate family, only Lilen and Taig remained at the Hold.
And Alin.

Cailet, hands and arm healing nicely though still achy,
was at her window gazing moodily down at the courtyard.
Range hands and servants milled about, drinking from casks
of last year's vintage as usual, but the rollicking good humor
of Harvest was muted. Everyone was worried about Alin.

No one was allowed to see him but his mother and
brother. The Scholar Mage kept to his own chamber after a
single visit to Cailet the day after her accident. Glaring, he
said only, "It's her fault," to Lilen, and departed in an angry
whirl of black and gray and silver.

Cailet shrank back into the pillows. "M–my fault?"

"Nonsense," Lilen said, recovering from shock at the
Mage Guardian's words. "You had nothing to do with what
happened to Alin. He doesn't know what he's talking about.
He's only trying to shift blame to you. Pay him no mind."

"But what *did* happen? I heard Alin cry out, and that's
why I lost my balance. Why didn't anybody else hear?"

Lilen stroked her bandaged hands. "Dearest, that's a question only another Mage can answer—a better one than that
idiot. Be patient. Someone's coming who can tell us what
happened and put everything to rights."

Clinging to Lilen's hand, soothed as always by the scent
of lemon grass that surrounded the only mother she'd ever
known, Cailet asked, "Can this Mage help Alin?"

"I've never met the problem Gorynel Desse couldn't
solve."

Cailet's eyes went round as soup bowls. Gorynel Desse!
She'd read about him in one of the books Lady Lilen wasn't
supposed to own, and heard his name whispered ever since

she could remember. Listed Mage at eighteen, Warrior at twenty, First Sword—Commander of the Captal's Warders—at thirty. Staunchest opponent of First Councillor Anniyas, the most learned—and most dangerous—Warrior Mage Guardian in Lenfell's history, rumored dead these ten years . . . but he was alive, and coming to Ostinhold!

Her excitement died abruptly. Alin must be badly in need, to make the great Mage risk the journey. Cailet said nothing of this, however; it was in Lilen's eyes that she already knew it.

Now, watching the hold's desultory attempts to celebrate the Saint's day, Cailet fretted anew at how long it was taking Gorynel Desse to arrive. Surely there must be a Ladder or two still functioning—despite the Council's published certainties that all had been discovered and set ablaze. Even if compelled to travel by ordinary means, surely he ought to have come by now. Irien had told Cailet this morning that Alin was resting comfortably, but the circles of strain beneath the physician's blue eyes told another tale.

"Great Saints, child, close that window before you catch cold!"

Cailet turned quickly, bumping her splinted arm against the casement. She completely forgot to feel the pain—for something tingled in her mind, like the prickle of a blood-starved limb. It was in the same place as the pain had been, right behind her eyes, but this was nothing like pain at all.

Standing in the center of her small bedroom, dressed in an astonishing rag of a cloak, was a white-haired, green-eyed, black-skinned old man. He dragged the chair from her desk, settled himself, and waved her closer.

"Come, come, sit here by me," he invited. "And do shut the window. It's chill for autumn in The Waste. Well? What are you waiting for? Let me get a look at you, girl."

Eyes the color of wine-bottle glass sparkled cheerful curiosity from below great tufted brows. She'd seen those eyes before, she knew she had—the memory skittered like a clever mouse from a clumsy cat, escaping before she could catch it. Rising from the window seat, Cailet took a few wary steps toward him.

"Shy, eh?"

She took another step—just one, she would have sworn it—and the tickle in her head seemed to dance. When it faded, she was standing right smack in front of the old man.

"How'd you do that?" Cailet blurted.

"One of my many talents. I'm told you have one or two, yourself. Staring with your jaw wide open seems to be primary among them right now. My dear friend Lilen has neglected your manners."

"Sorry," she responded reflexively. "I'm Cailet Rille. Are you—?" Somehow she couldn't manage the rest.

"Gorynel Desse? Yes, I have that honor—or that affliction, depending on how you look at it." He smiled. "And your look now says that you don't think a Mage should let himself be seen so shabby. Well, that's the 'affliction' part."

"Sorry," she said again.

"No matter." He patted the bed nearby. "Sit down, *Domna*. To answer the question foremost in your mind, Alin will be quite all right."

"Then you helped him! Thank you!"

"It's an appropriate day for the work. St. Kiy the Forgetful. Learn to appreciate the ironies in life, *Domna*."

She understood none of this—indeed, barely heard it. Relief that Alin was safe had been immediately followed by suspicion. "How'd you know I was thinking about Alin? Did you—"

"—read your thoughts? Certainly not. No Mageborn can, so remember that if anyone ever tries to tell you differently."

She hesitated, then told him what she'd told no one else. "But I did—sort of, anyway, with Geria and then Taig."

"Did you hear the words they were thinking?"

"N–no," she said slowly. "But I knew what they felt."

"There, you see? You read their faces, *Domna* Cailet, the way I just read yours. People can be just like books. Reading them is a talent anyone can learn—and it's a good thing you've already started."

"But—it *hurt*. They were fire and ice, and—"

"Hmm. No need to ask who was what. Sit, Cailet. We're going to have a talk about reading people's faces."

She sat at the foot of her bed, tucking her feet under her. "Why?"

All at once he looked very sad. "You'll need your wits, child, because your magic won't be available to you for a long time yet."

She could not have heard him correctly. Her *magic?*

"Forgive me, Cailet," he murmured, and took her left hand, and caught her gaze with his shining eyes. She tried with all her might, but could not look away. "If I'd done my work properly when you were born, this wouldn't be necessary now. I should have guessed how powerful your magic would be."

Magic!

Cailet struggled in a frenzy of fear. She remembered this feeling, those green eyes looking deep into hers, the empty hollow that had opened in her worse than thirst or starvation or loneliness. It loomed now, the dark that had first frightened her mere days after her birth. Into it he would fling every glimmer of all the fire she knew was in her—the *magic*—

"We can't let them find you, little one," whispered Gorynel Desse. "You must be ordinary for a while longer. One day, I promise you, you'll not only touch that fire, you'll tame it. But I have to do this, Cailet. Forgive me."

No! She could only just sense the burning glow inside, he couldn't hide it away from her again—

But he did, and she did not find it again for many years. By then it was almost too late.

4

"How will Taig get home?"

Lady Lilen's sigh was lost in the rattle of the carriage. The one sent by the Witte Blood to take them from the ship to Pinderon had been a marvel of comfort (even if it did look like a yellow-striped tomato on wheels). This one was so badly sprung that every cobble jounced their bones. It was a sign of disapproval that Lilen had harbored, however unknowingly, a Minstrel who turned out to be so heinous a villain. Only one good thing about the whole mess: Lilen wouldn't have to think up a reason to refuse the Witte's offer of Dalion to husband Lenna. After last night's disaster, with Justices and Guards and the Pinderon Watch and half hell breaking loose, the offer would never be made. Geria would be furious.

"I don't know that Taig will be coming home for quite

some time, Cai. We may have to get used to missing him, the way we miss Alin."

Cailet rebelled at the unfairness. Alin had *chosen;* Taig had been chased. Thus far the younger brother's association with the Rising was secret—but the elder, no matter how much fast talking Lilen did, would be suspect from now on.

She wedged herself into a corner of the seat, bracing against bumps, and chewed a thumbnail. It *wasn't* fair, any of it. First she'd lost Alin—not that she blamed him for packing up and leaving last year, what with Geria nagging for a betrothal. Lira Vedde was *years* older than Alin, and so mad to have him that she'd argued her mother into offering the price of Alin's share of the Ostin Dower for the privilege. It was his duty, Geria kept saying, to use his charming golden looks to bring those charming golden double-eagles into the family coffers. She simply refused to acknowledge that Alin would never marry anyone—except in the unlikely event that Valirion Maurgen turned female. The two of them, seventeen and eighteen respectively, were off on their own now. Cailet knew that however they were living, they were happy with each other.

But how would Taig live? Alone, hunted, safe only when he found other agents of the Rising, never knowing where he would be from one day to the next. . . . Cailet's heart was with Taig Ostin, and the prospect of life without even hope of glimpsing him made her feel like an empty husk.

If not for that Minstrel and his stupid song—it was all his fault. And that blonde girl in the sickening pink dress, too. Cailet didn't trust her, no matter what Taig had said. At not quite thirteen, she was not yet old enough to realize that she would instinctively distrust anybody that beautiful who had been found alone with Taig Ostin.

Cailet voiced her complaints about the Minstrel—but not about the girl—to Lilen, who shook her head. "No, dearest. If there's blame, it falls on Anniyas. Everything traces back to her ambition. Even her hatred of Mageborns, which has caused so much grief, is a tool of her need for power."

"I don't understand. What d'you do with power once you get it?"

"If the power is vast enough, you can change the world as you wish."

Cailet thought about that for a time. The world was about to be changed, and it was said the Council was doing it as a wedding present. "Then it's the First Councillor and not Glenin Feiran who wants to do away with the Tiers?"

Lilen peered at her in the gloomy carriage. "Why do you say that?"

"Follows," she shrugged. "After all, Lady Glenin's just like the rest of Ryka and the Council and everybody—she does what Anniyas says. Everybody except the Mage Guardians and the Rising."

"You've been listening again where you shouldn't." The rutted cliff road jounced Lilen to one side. Righting herself, she continued, "I know you don't say these things to anyone but Taig and me. But I can't help feeling it would be better if you didn't say them at all."

"Not even to you anymore?"

Lilen toyed absently with the fringe of her beaded purse. "Cai . . . I believe the Council has ears even at Ostinhold."

She caught her breath. "Who?"

"I don't know. How can anyone know?" She parted the yellow curtain to see how close they might be to the docks. "Times are dangerous. We must be careful. And that means we must also be silent."

Silence would be no real hardship. With Taig gone, there'd be no one to talk to. Lenna, Tevis, and Miram would soon be back at school in Longriding; Alin was with Val Maurgen somewhere; Terrill and Lindren were nice enough, but. . . . Of the hundreds of other Ostins at Ostinhold, there wasn't anyone she could confide in. Loneliness hollowed her insides. She wrapped her arms around the hurt and closed her eyes.

The voyage back to The Waste did nothing to lighten anyone's mood. Day after day the ship wallowed in a windless calm, the cabins too stuffy for sleeping even in the depths of night. Finally back at Ostinhold, Lilen closeted herself with her stewards for days on end. Cailet sat in the schoolroom with the other children, did her chores, reread her favorite books, and rode out alone as often as she could sneak a horse past the grooms. But with Alin and Taig both gone for good, Ostinhold was a sorrowful place, as empty as the place Cailet's heart used to be.

Her restlessness of the past year grew worse. Her studies suffered, and so did anyone who got within range when she was in a particularly irritable mood. Generally a cheerful child, she definitely had a temper. Drygrass passed, and

Wildfire, and the terrific heat of The Waste set everyone on edge.

And then, the last day of Wolfkill, an acid storm blew in out of season. All Ostinhold was shuttered inside for three solid days while corrosive grit battered the walls and storm fittings. Cailet prowled from room to room, unable to settle, unable to sleep more than an hour or two at night. On the third morning of the tempest, she woke at Half-Fourth with a dull ache in her belly. Suspecting its cause, she curled around herself and listened to the growling storm outside, sullenly contemplating this pivotal event in her life.

As was done for all the girls at Ostinhold, Lilen would give a party to celebrate. A banquet, dancing, congratulations, gifts—and Geria complaining of the expense. *"It's not as if she's family. Besides, Rille is only a Third Tier Name. No one will be interested in even preliminary negotiations. In fact, I don't see how we'll ever husband her!"*

Cailet smiled grimly at the image of First Daughter's face if she knew that the only man Cailet wanted was Geria's own brother. But Taig was gone. There would be no flowers from him, no congratulations, no first dance in his arms as a young woman instead of a little girl. She'd dreamed of it all her life, it seemed, imagination painting her pretty and grown-up and worth dancing with . . . and now it would never come true.

She rose at Fifth, bathed, and steeled herself for the obligatory visit to inform Lady Lilen. Keeping her first Wise Blood secret was out of the question. The maids would know the instant they collected the washing; the householder would know when pads disappeared off-schedule from the bathroom. Besides, Cailet was supposed to be happy and proud. Other girls were. Staring at her reflection in her bedroom mirror—a face all broad cheekbones and wide mouth and black eyes, a face that couldn't remotely be called pretty—all she felt was depressed.

Resigned, she made her way to Lilen's private chambers. Just as Cailet was afraid of the dark, Lilen feared acid storms; she spent them locked in her rooms, not wishing anyone to see her tremble at the slightest change in the wind. She was convinced that the roof tiles would be eaten away, the stinging rain would flood down, and everyone at Ostinhold would be seared to bare skeletons. Miram told Cailet once that Lilen's childhood nurse had used such tales to terrify her into obedience; when her mother, Lady Taigrel, found out, she was so furious she'd actually sold the man to Scraller.

To Cailet's surprise, Lilen's antechamber door was open. She crept in, supposing a maid had brought breakfast in hopes the Lady would eat. The bedroom door also stood slightly ajar. Cailet was shocked into absolute stillness when she heard voices. Lilen had a visitor, and the topic of discussion was Cailet.

5

". . . child anymore. Her Wise Blood will come soon—and you know the effect that has. My poor Margit had a terrible time."

"The Wards I set for Cailet—"

"—you had to reset. Gorsha, you've always said she'll be the strongest of them all. We've *hoped* for it. I've watched her the last year, and what Margit suffered is ten times worse in Cailet."

"That bad? You were right to send for me, then."

"Will you Ward her again?"

"I must. She's too young yet."

"Every time you do makes for greater danger. If her magic suddenly breaks through, it might turn Wild. It's happened before."

"Not to Cailet. I'll be careful."

"You'd better."

"It isn't easy, is it? This changeling in your midst."

"Easy? No. But I love her as if she were my own. I've tried so hard—but she hates The Waste, Gorsha. I can't blame her. She was meant for Ambrai. This place starves her soul."

"She can hardly miss what she's never known."

"Saints, men can be stupid. My great-aunt Lindren never had children, but she ached for them all the same. Cailet aches, too—for green hills, forest, rivers, everything that's truest in her blood. I keep her safe, but I can't give her what she truly needs. And the rest of it, you've kept from her."

"If I'd let her have her magic, they would have found her—and that would have been the end of her. Or worse."

"Like Glenin?"

"A calculated risk, letting Auvry take her. An unexplained talent like his rarely breeds true. Who could know that all three of his girls would turn up Mageborn? I think he reinforced the Ostin gift, through their grandfather."

"Why do you think I married a Senison?"

"Because you adored him, of course."

"That goes without saying, and you know it. The point is that in marrying Tiva, I hoped to breed magic out of my children. I was right to worry. Look what happened—my poor Margit, and little Alin—"

"Calm yourself, my love. The boy is just fine. He and Val are having the time of their lives."

"They're too young for the Rising, no matter what you say. And now Taig—praise be to St. Miryenne *he's* not Mageborn!"

"I shudder to think what he'd do with real magic as well as the legendary Ostin charm—which doesn't fade, by the way. By Maidil's Mask, you should've taken *me* to husband, Lilen."

"And have *all* my children turn out Mageborn, and be even more frightened than I am now? You men, you never understand."

"Well, probably not. As for our Cailet—is she old enough to go riding out alone and just happen to happen upon the Mad Old Man of Crackwall Canyon?"

"The—? You mean he's *you?*"

"Second Rule of Magic. It would have been shockingly unsubtle simply to show up around here. I've been spreading rumors for—oh, going on five years now. And it's been a strain, what with all the other demands on my limited time and considerable talents. Luckily, I'm as fit and clever at seventy-one as I was at forty-one."

"*And* as arrogant and braggardly!"

"And *you* are as lovely at fifty as ever you were when first you stole my poor heart."

"Fifty-five, and your heart had nothing to do with it. I know you, Gorsha. So did Fler, which is why she married Niyan instead of you. And Jeymian, who had the sense to marry Toliner Alvassy. And that's not to mention—"

"Lilen! I beg you! This catalog of women who rejected me is too depressing for words!"

"Tell me what we're to do about Cailet."

"You already know. You've always known that one day Mage would call to Mage and Blood to Blood as it has with Sarra, and the safe days would be gone."

"I've always known it would break my heart. Must it be now, Gorsha? She's so young. . . ."

"But old enough to eavesdrop in perfect silence for the last ten minutes, and understand much of what's said. Come in, Cailet."

6

Some weeks later she rode out alone on her very own mare (a Birthingday present from Lilen) on an errand for Healer Irien. He gave her directions to a cottage snuggled into one of the many splits in the sides of Crackwall Canyon. Inside she found an old man she'd never met before, a hundred books, and the beginnings of her life's work. Not that she knew it as such for several years—because the first thing Rinnel Solingirt did was make her build a wall.

To be fair, the cottage—a generous term, considering its state of disrepair—really did need a retaining wall, if only to give the rose bush something to climb. The existence of this stubborn plant was astonishment enough to Cailet. That it was in constant bloom despite the multiple vicissitudes of The Waste led her to believe that Rinnel had talents more esoteric than brewing herbal remedies, carving jade, and telling stories.

Sale of the carvings to a shop in Longriding kept Rinnel fed. He was expert at using the natural striations of color in the jade to enhance a pattern. The most beautiful of all the pieces she ever saw him make was a jagged black pendant with a relief of volcanoes spewing red-orange lava; the week she turned seventeen, he gave it to her. Mostly he strung etched beads into necklaces and carved earrings and finger rings. Most lucrative were his large pendants of St.

Geridon's double horseshoes favored by bower lads; most popular were the other, more modest, Saintly sigils.

His herbal potions cured anything from snakebite to freckles. Healer Irien had, in fact, sent her for an ointment guaranteed to soothe acid-rain burns better than the remedy he'd been using. Although Cailet learned eventually the calming craft of carving jade, she had no interest in the Healing arts. Rinnel didn't press knowledge on her, though often he wielded mortar and pestle or mixed powders while exercising his third major talent: telling stories.

These utterly fascinated Cailet. He recited the Lives of the Saints with all the not-so-holy details other versions left out; the tale of Grand Duchess Veller Ganfallin; the deeds of various heroines and heroes; the histories of selected Mage Captals and First Lords of Malerris. He was a walking library, and when he ran out of stories for the day or Cailet was compelled to ride home for dinner, he shared with her his more conventional library of books.

By Deiket Snowhair and Eskanto Cut-Thumb, the books! Rinnel deplored her appetite for improbable adventure stories (she had a weakness for dragons), but his collection included several examples of popular literature. He corrected her total ignorance of Bardic literature, and sneaked in a few classic romances (his own weakness). She read about persons real and imaginary, events that truly happened and events that never could, high-minded poetry and sly ballads. Of philosophy, government, the sciences, and politics, she learned nothing except what incidentals were included in the other works.

Cailet's education at Rinnel's hands was eccentric, but he was not out to make a Scholar of her.

"People!" he declared again and again. "Learn about *people*—how they think, what they feel. The rhythms of their minds and hearts and bodies. What they'll give their lives for—and what they'll put up with. Learn people in all their wisdom and folly, their honor and cravenness, their courage and cowardice. Learn how to read them in an eyeblink—and how not to make snap judgments!"

Cailet accepted that the histories could teach her some of this, but was at a loss as to how novels, songs, poetry, and the like would be of use. Still, the histories became more interesting when she'd read the livelier tales and made connections between who people were and what they did and why.

Veller Ganfallin, for instance, figured as the villain in all the histories, but was never portrayed any more deeply than a layer of dust on a tabletop. Songs and stories made up for this, varying in their interpretations of her character but almost always giving Cailet some insight into avarice, amorality, and the grandest possible ambition.

So she read, and listened, and watched as Rinnel carved jade or concocted potions. But that was only after she'd built a wall.

The cracks in Crackwall Canyon were due to both erosion and earthquake and supported a surprising variety of life. In smaller crevices, animals—mainly rodents—made permanent dens. A mile from Rinnel's cottage was a family of silverback cats; once or twice Cailet saw the breeding pair herd four kits out for a hunting tutorial. In springtime residence were three couples of flightless cranes—ridiculous creatures with huge horny beaks, stunted wings, and long spindly legs capable of outrunning a horse at short distances. Plants that processed acid rain into fresh water sprouted in great clumps where rivulets collected in season.

People who thought The Waste was lifeless were wrong. There were vast flats, of course, where The Waste Water had been drained. It was murderously hot in summer and freshwater wells were few and far between. But galazhi thrived, and silverbacks, and a thousand other species of plants and animals.

Including humans, whom Rinnel termed the most dangerous by far. Not for him the protective walls of Ostinhold; he preferred the lonely wilds, and his cottage that seemed a part of the canyon itself. Two sides of the split formed the side walls. The back and front were made of stacked stones mortared to snugness, and the roof was layer after layer of sandstone shingles supported by five pillars inside the cottage. The southward slope of the roof fed runoff to the little garden of plants that purified just enough water for Rinnel's use (Cailet brought her own when she was to stay with him for more than a day).

Despite the bulk of the roof supports, the interior was quite spacious—if eccentrically shaped. Wide at the front, narrow at the back, the cottage followed the dimensions of the canyon crevice. There were shelves of various lengths and depths carved into the walls: some for books and storage, one for a bed, one with a deep firebowl in the center and a grill over it for cooking. (Cailet also brought her own food, for Rinnel was, by his own admission, the worst cook in North Lenfell.)

So what need for another wall? Cailet didn't pose the question in so many words, but Rinnel saw it in her face as he mixed a quantity of mortar while she stacked bricks.

"Your horse, my dear," he said. "That's why you're going to build a wall. It's my cottage, but the wall is to protect your property."

"But she's very well trained," Cailet objected, sneezed dust, and resumed, "and she'll stay put without even a hobble."

"Mmm. And what if one afternoon *Domna* Silverback decides she doesn't feel like prowling too far afield for her kits' dinner, eh? Horses are either very stupid or very smart, I've never figured out which. But moron or genius, no horse alive who wants to stay that way will linger where there's a big cat around and hungry. Mortar's ready," Rinnel announced, and seated himself on a flat stone with every indication he intended to stay there all afternoon. "Have at it, Cailet Rille."

She conceded the point about her mare. Even if Rinnel would be the primary beneficiary of the improvement to his home, she didn't begrudge him a wall in exchange for letting her roam through his books and listen to his stories. In the two weeks since her first visit, there'd been plenty of both. Besides, while she worked he would probably tell her another one.

So Cailet—who even at thirteen had helped repair more than a few of Ostinhold's walls—stirred the mortar experimentally, adjudged it of the correct consistency, lined up two dozen bricks in easy reach, and started in.

And, as she'd hoped and expected, as the wall took shape, so did a story.

Back before the Generations, (said Rinnel), the only walls on Lenfell were those to keep animals in or out, like the wall you're building now. None were needed for protection against other people, because there was no such thing as war. It wasn't that people then were any better or wiser than we, or less covetous of their neighbors' property. But war costs lives, money, and time much better spent in living. Our ancestors were

very practical people who liked things to be efficient,
and war isn't.

The way they prevented wars was to have Mage
Guardians work with the government. An individual or
family—this was when there were over five thousand
Names, remember—or a city or sometimes a whole Shir
would present a petition outlining the trouble. People
would testify—yes, this is the origin of our Court system. Where was I? Oh, yes. Mages would listen, evaluate for truth, and report to the government *without*
making recommendations. And the government would
make a decision. Sometimes they were just, and sometimes not so just, but that's the way of people and by
and large the truth won out.

There came a time, however, when the Captal began
to make her opinions known, and to say what ought to
be done. The government began to resent the Captal's
forceful presentation of her point of view. In one famous case where Mages were involved, she was
strongly suspected of tilting the facts to favor her
Guardians.

Now, what you must understand about them is that
since the Founding they have taken an Oath of Dedication. Not to the Captal, but to all Lenfell. The Captal
believed that by telling the government what it ought to
do, she was only doing her duty to our world. Many
Guardians agreed with her. After all, Mages had ways
of discerning truth so there could be no doubt. It is a
skill sadly lost, by the way—or so I'm told.

Anyway, after all the schooling and discipline and
testing undergone as Novice and Prentice, a Mage was
thought to be at least a little wiser than most people. So
I suppose it was natural that some Mages thought that
they ought to be doing the deciding.

As it happens, it was your own Name Saint, Caitiri,
who first told the Captal that there were Mages who
thought this way. The Captal shrugged, for it was the
direction her own thoughts were heading, and invited
the leading proponents to a conference. Caitiri was
present, representing the majority of Guardians who ad-
hered to the old ways of assistance without interference.

(I know you know the popular tale of Caitiri's life—
how she defended Brogdenguard single-handedly

against a flood by calling up the fires of her Hearth, but that's purely symbolic, as you'll discover.)

Where was I? Ah, yes. Caitiri listened, and so did the Captal, and when the Mages had argued their position, everyone retired until the next day. The Captal summoned Caitiri to her chambers, and though it's rumored she wept for shame, I don't believe it. What she *did* do was confess that she had been exerting her extremely subtle and terrifically potent magic on the other Mages as they spoke without their knowledge (for she was Captal, and Captals are always the most powerful of the Guardians). Anyway, she learned what they had *not* said: that they believed not only in their own superior wisdom in making decisions but that they should in fact be making every decision on Lenfell.

Education—how, how much, and who. Which Webs to allow, and which to unravel. How to honor each Saint, and which Saints were worth honoring. Which Bards to support, and which to suppress. What was published in the broadsheets and what could not be. Legend has it they even wished to decide who would marry whom, how many children they ought to have, and whether those children were girls or boys.

The Captal was horrified. So was Caitiri—for although she had suspected, she never thought the other Mages would be so bold as this. What they wished was, truly told, to decide the ordering of every life from cradle to grave.

Now, if you'll look at those bricks you're slapping on top of each other, you'll notice that no two are identical. Mostly the same size and shape, but by no means perfectly matched. There are even a few clinkers in the bunch—overbaked, chipped, flawed. So, too, with people, or so these Mages believed. Those who would not or could not fit into the greater pattern of life were useless. Not that the Mages advocated execution—they weren't evil, after all. They simply felt that such persons should be set apart where they could do no damage.

And this decision would, of course, belong to Mages. One word, and a girl destined to be—for instance—a bricklayer but who really wanted to be a bookbinder would be first cajoled, then ordered, then compelled to

follow the grand plan. If she did not, she would be sent
to a community of like-minded misfits, where she could
do as she pleased—as long as she didn't upset the overall pattern.

Now, it so happened that the Captal's own mother
had wanted her to follow the family trade of carpentry,
and the trouble when she turned up Mageborn was
something to behold. So she had personal knowledge of
how it felt to be ordered to do one thing when your
heart was leading you in another direction entirely. The
next day she announced her decision to withdraw from
public affairs, and flatly forbade Mages to serve in
government—which effectively squashed certain people's ambitions, for how could they enforce their notions of order without official position and the power
that goes with it?

Caitiri secretly wept for sure knowledge of what
would happen next. And she was right: the rebellious
Mages gathered together, fully four hundred of them—
there were many thousands of Mages then—and sailed
for Brogdenguard.

If you're wondering why Brogdenguard, and I see by
your face that you are, let me tell you a thing very few
people know. The beautiful mountains there, the ones
we call Caitiri's Hearth, are volcanic—and mighty they
can be when they're in a mood for it, too. But the vital
thing about them is that they form a natural shield
against magic. Some think this is due to sheer size, but
in my opinion, it's the masses of iron. Mageborns can
set Wards on almost anything, but they have a rotten
time trying to Ward iron—or so I'm told.

At any rate, off the rebel Mages went to Brogdenguard. Caitiri alone understood why: the barrier formed
by iron would prevent other Mageborns from sensing
whatever magic they cared to work there. And, considering their philosophy, ignorance of their activities
would be dangerous.

To be brief, because I see you're tired and running
out of mortar, Caitiri went by Ladder to Neele, rode the
fastest horse she could find up into the mountains, and
worked a little magic of her own. The "flood" she
burned away in the standard tale was the influx of ren-

egade Mages. You'll have to judge for yourself if it's true about the way she did it.

The defeated Mages took ship for Seinshir, where they built Malerris Castle—for this was what they decided to call themselves, the Lords of Malerris, although there were as many women as men among them. Caitiri died in the doing, but she accomplished what she set herself to do. For hundreds of years the Malerrisi could do nothing but plot and plan and try some very limited schemes, for someone was always watching.

But a century or so before The Waste War, one of them had a distinctly brilliant idea. They built a tower and ran iron rods into its walls, which smudged perceptions of what they were up to. Only the one tower, but it served to conceal what they wished to conceal. They could work no magic within, but neither could their words or maps or anything within that tower be perceived from without. And after The Waste War, the knack of Longsight was lost—along with how to make a Ladder, and how to read the truth, and much else that Mageborns once knew.

So the Lords of Malerris could speak and scheme and spell just as they pleased, and no one would be the wiser until the evidence of their magic appeared. Thus it remains to this day.

Cailet reached for another glob of mortar, heard the spatula scrape inside the bucket, and glanced around. She was astonished to discover the bucket was empty and the bright eastern sunshine of morning had become the dusky western light of afternoon.

All day? She'd been working all day? She blinked at the wall she had built almost without knowing it: fully five feet high and extending eight feet out from the canyon wall. Over half done, with only the weariness of her muscles and a few scrapes on her hands to show she'd done it all herself.

"I think that will do for today," said Rinnel, pushing himself to his feet. "Have something to drink and then ride on back to Ostinhold. I've a book inside you can return when you come back on the fifth to finish the wall."

She did, though it was much harder work this time. Rinnel told no stories, but instead sat near the cottage door grinding roots for some potion or other, and would not give in to her entreaties for another tale.

This time she felt every sore muscle, every drop of sweat wrung from her skin, every scratch and scrape on her ungloved hands. The work took forever, every moment of it drawn out in rough labor that numbed her mind even as her body clamored for surcease. The bricks were heavier, the mortar too runny or too gummy by turns, the rows damned near impossible to get even.

The six feet of wall forming the north side of the enclosure took her twice as long as the eight feet on the west. By sundown she was sodden with exhaustion. But the wall was done, and it surprised her that there seemed so little difference between this day's work and the previous construction. One had been nearly effortless, fashioned with automatic skill by her hands while her mind was engaged by Rinnel's tale; the other had cost her in energy, sweat, even blood. Still, had she not known which bricks marked the separation, she would not have been able to find it.

Rinnel let her stay the night after her mare was settled comfortably inside the new pen. Lady Lilen, he told Cailet, had sent him a letter saying that if it grew too late for the ride home, Cailet had permission to spend the night at the cottage. Giving her a simple dinner of bread smeared with a savory vegetable-and-meat paste, watered wine, and two fine plums for dessert, he stayed silent while she ate, watching the weariness drain from her.

"Ah, the young," he smiled, green eyes dancing in his dark face. "A full day's hard physical labor, but once you're fed and watered you're ready to add another two feet to that wall. Relax, child. Tonight we talk. How about another pillow? That bench is hard going on skinny bones like yours."

"I'm fine," she replied, licking plum juice from her fingers. "Are you going to tell me another story?"

"No, I'm going to tell you why you *really* built that wall."

"But—I thought it was for my horse—"

"First mistake." The old man leaned back in the one wooden chair he possessed, refilled his cup from the wine jug and did not add water, and regarded her with a smile. Lanternlight played white-gold over his dusky skin and his lank pale mane of hair. "You accepted everything I said without questioning. If you'd thought about it for just a minute or two, you'd've realized that no silverback worth her shiny golden whiskers would eat a horse unless she was starving half to death. There's game aplenty around here that she prefers—rats, cactus squirrels, galazhi, and so on."

Thinking of all that hard work, and glancing involuntarily at her bruised hands, Cailet burst out, "Then all of it was for—"

"—for nothing? Not at all. To begin with, my roses are already much happier. However—you remember the tale of St. Caitiri? She prevented the Lords of Malerris from using the natural wall of the Hearth. You didn't know it, but you were building *two* walls, my girl. One you can touch. One you can't."

It would give the old man no end of satisfaction if Cailet admitted that she hadn't the slightest idea what he was talking about. So she kept her mouth sullenly shut.

Grinning, he looked twenty years younger. "You don't know much about me, do you? Where I come from, my mother, what I've done with my life so far. You know I'm acquainted with Lady Lilen, I carve jade, make medicine, and talk more than any ten other people combined. But what do you really *know* about me, Cailet?"

Forgetting the politeness owed her elders—even male elders—she said tartly, "I know they call you the Crazy Old Man of Crackwall Cottage, and they're right!"

"On every count," he agreed cheerfully. "I do live in this misbegotten hovel, I am undeniably old, and opinions much more informed than yours long since judged me quite mad. But I'll let you in on a little secret, my dear. Look into my eyes."

She did—and all at once there was *something* inside her skull. A tickle, a tingle, a bright white light bouncing around behind her eyes—

"Stop that!" she cried, springing to her feet.

"Make me," Rinnel invited.

She closed her eyes; the sensations increased, as if a wild and gleeful lantern fly was zinging around in her brain. She tried to catch it; she could not. She looked at the old man again and, with hazy memory of an encounter with Geria Ostin, tried to make him stop. He didn't.

Frantic, she jumped from her perch on the shelf, intending to shake him or shout at him or *something,* anything to get that infuriating little light out of her head. With her first step, it was gone.

"Oh, *you* didn't do it," he remarked. "*I* did."

"How?!"

"I'm assuming you don't want me poking around inside your brain again? Just so. When I snap my fingers, I'll do it again. Try to keep me out, Cailet."

Her eyes squeezed shut and her fists clenched and the pain of broken raw skin reminded her of the wall—

"Oh, come now. You can do better than that."

—and she saw it again in her mind that wall *her* wall and his fingers snapped and she felt the tingling light batter at her—*but it couldn't get inside the wall.*

Cailet's eyelids popped open. So did her mouth. Rinnel was laughing softly at her—no, *with* her, enjoying her triumph.

"And that, my dear, is why you built that wall."

7

"It's been nagging you since you first rode out here, so to spare you further frustration I'll admit to what I am. Mageborn, of course. Largely self-taught, I might add. The Guardians got hold of me too late to impart any real discipline. They gave up. So I made my own way in the world, using my magic as it seemed necessary. And because these days Mageborns aren't what one would call welcome in all quarters, I decided to spend the rest of my years in peace and quiet."

Cailet, wrapped in an old blanket, sat on the bedshelf as Rinnel talked. It was past Fourteenth and she wasn't the least bit sleepy. Her body was tired, of course, and every so often her chin drooped to her drawn-up knees, but her mind was more alert than ever in her life.

"Now, I've encountered quite a few Lords of Malerris—and Ladies, too. There's a peculiar feel to them—a taste, I suppose, to their thoughts. No, I can't read minds, no Mageborn can. But what I showed you this evening, that's a thing I taught myself and then taught the Guardians, who'd lost it along with so much else after The Waste War. The

Malerrisi never did. And when one of them tries it on anyone—Mageborn or not—there's very little defense."

"Except a wall," Cailet said.

"Except a wall," Rinnel agreed.

"But what good is it? I mean, flashing a light inside somebody's head isn't very impressive. It's just a trick."

"It has been known to drive people mad, kept up long enough. You got a hint of that, I believe—unless my powers are as enfeebled as my poor wreck of a body these days. But back before The Waste War, this little trick could be used to agitate particular areas of the brain. Strong emotions start at the back of the brain, Cailet. Thinking and reasoning are at the front. Exactly where, I don't know. Nobody does. But observation of people whose brains have been injured in accidents or—well, I'm boring you, so let's just say that if you want to make someone incredibly angry, you'd direct that spark of light to the back of the brain."

"And if you want somebody to think really hard about something—or stop thinking altogether—!"

"That would be a little more complicated, not so crude as provoking emotion to wipe out rational thought, but I take your meaning."

"You ever tried it?"

"With indifferent success." A reminiscent grin tugged his lips beneath his beard. "While I was young, I quite earnestly pursued a quest for the ... um ... more primitive urges of the feminine mind."

Cailet frowned her puzzlement, then blushed and giggled.

"Never found it, though," Rinnel sighed. "The point is, the Mage Guardians didn't know how to do this until I showed them, but it can't be assumed that the Malerrisi forgot it as thoroughly. So I showed you how to protect yourself against them."

She lost all urge to laugh. "Because they're *not* all dead, are they?" she whispered. "What happened at their Castle—it was all a sham, wasn't it?"

"Indeed yes. They still live, Cailet, roaming Lenfell and working whatever magic they please. Their goal is still the same: precise, defined, absolute order, according to their own notions of what the world should be. That's the ultimate power, you know. It isn't being able to light a fire without a match, or cast a Ward, or heal the sick, or any of the other magical arts. True power is the ability to remake the world into what *you* have decided it ought to be. Not just to affect the lives around you, but to change *all* lives."

"Lady Lilen said the same thing, back in Pinderon," she mused. "I think she meant like Anniyas, or Glenin Feiran."

Rinnel looked puzzled. "Why do you say the name of the daughter and not the father? He is, after all, Commandant of the Council Guard."

"Yes, but ... I don't know," she replied slowly. "It's just—it's a feeling I have. I think she's ambitious, Rinnel, sort of in the way Veller Ganfallin was. But a lot smarter."

"And Auvry Feiran isn't ambitious?"

"Well ... he *did* want to be a big somebody in Ambrai, didn't he? Lady Lilen says when they wouldn't let him, he got angry and went to join Anniyas. . . ." She frowned. "But military power's just brute force. If he'd really wanted the kind of power *she* has, he would've done something else, right? Gotten on the Council somehow, or—I don't know. I just don't think he wants it for himself. Wants to change things himself, I mean."

"Rather, to help the people who do?"

She nodded. "Like Anniyas, or his daughter. Besides, he's Mageborn, and everybody with magic is under suspicion. I don't blame you for moving way out here. If I were Mageborn, I'd never *ever* admit it."

Suddenly she seemed to feel a flickering in the air, and instantly thought of her wall. Rinnel smiled at her.

"It's not necessary to visualize the wall consciously, you know. It's there now, even when you sleep. No one will ever be able to rummage around inside your skull again." He laughed at her expression of astonishment. "We both do excellent work, wouldn't you say? Now, get some sleep, little one. We'll talk more in the morning."

Cailet returned his grin with one of her own. "You mean *you'll* talk more!"

"Wretched child!"

8

Cailet learned more from Rinnel Solingirt than she ever learned at local schools. The old man had a genius for teasing her into a positive mania of curiosity. She simply had to discover the whys and hows and whats, and when he refused to provide ready answers she tore through book after book with a single-mindedness that sometimes made him laugh.

Over the next four years, she saw him as often as she could. She regularly left Ostinhold with the family for a few weeks in Renig or Longriding; he occasionally vanished for half a season at a time. There was always a present of some sort to be given after an absence—tangible apologies for being away so long, tokens of affection and how much they'd missed each other. The gifts told much about their characters. She'd bring a bottle of the Cantrashir red wine he loved, glass wind chimes, a spray of dried herbs tied with bright ribbons to hang over his door for luck. He'd give her a book, or cloth for a shirt, or something else eminently useful. Only once did he ever come back from a journey with anything impractical: a wispy length of turquoise silk to use as a belt or a neck-scarf. At not-quite-seventeen, after a depressing party at Maurgen Hundred (only Terrill Ostin and Biron Maurgen danced with her), Cailet needed something pretty to bolster her spirits. She kept remembering how that Sarra Liwellan girl had looked at Pinderon, all soft curves and golden curls and Taig hanging on her every word.

When beginning a story, Rinnel never said "Stop me if you've heard this one" because he knew she never had. Her education at Ostinhold and at the local schools was adequate to The Waste; she had not been allowed to join the Ostin girls at St. Deiket's Academy for advanced study. An indifferent scholar, she had no regrets and never questioned Lady Lilen's decision. Lenna, Miram, and Lindren had all loathed the place and Rinnel's stories weren't like school at all.

One afternoon during the summer of 965 a squall blew in from the east, one of the rare storms that climbed Deiket's Blessing from Ambraishir to gift The Waste with clean rain.

By the time it found the canyons around Ostinhold it was a mere sprinkle, but in the torrid week of Drygrass any coolness was welcome. Cailet sat on her wall with Rinnel beside her, damp and grateful, watching plants lift leaves and flowers as if inhaling water as it reached thirsty roots. Naturally, the old man used the sight as the beginning of a story.

Nothing ever really dies, you know. All life continues one way or another. Even if the rain hadn't come today, just in time to revive everything, there are always seeds waiting to grow.

But I'm at the wrong end of the tale. Let's begin again at the very beginning, with the First Truth: All Life is created and nurtured by First Mother. Women, who are Her image, are charged to guard the life they create. In other words, if you make it, you're responsible for it. You have only to look at Lady Lilen and Lady Sefana Maurgen for examples of the joys, frustrations, and sorrows of this awesome duty.

First Mother was not immune to sorrow, by the way. After She created the world and nurtured its new Life, a curious thing happened. She discovered She was lonely. Creation and Nurture were very fine things, and made her very happy, but it remained that She was lonely.

Then First Man came from the blue sky and bright stars, and saw all that First Mother had made, and was awestruck at Her power. She had made the whole of the world in all its beauty—from pine trees to dragonflies, from fish in the sea to birds on the wing, She made them all. This was a wondrous thing to First Man, and he sang Her praises as all males do if they've been brought up to be polite.

But First Man also felt as all males feel when faced with the power of women's works. "Teach me to do this," he begged. But She could not teach First Man to create. She *did* show him how to cherish Life by shining his sun's warmth and giving of his cool rain. And this is the Second Truth: men may cherish and even nurture the created works of women, but cannot create Life on their own.

Seeing that First Man was downcast, and filled with compassion for him, First Mother comforted him in the way of women with men—which I daresay you'll learn about one of these years—and in time First Daughter was born. This was a new type of Creation for First Mother. Her love and compassion for First Man formed a new entity that was partly of Her and partly of him.

First Daughter was very beautiful. Her hair and her skin were the rich brown of earth, and her Wise Blood flowed as the waters of the rivers, and in these ways she was of First Mother. Her eyes were the blue of the sky by day, shining with the twinkle of the stars by night, and her lips were the sweet crimson of the sunset, and in these ways she was of First Man.

Being a woman, First Daughter could do as First Mother did, and spent her time making wonderful new flowers and trees, animals and gemstones and rivers. Now, notice please that diamonds, for example, are rocks with fire inside. What First Daughter did in making diamonds and all the rest of her creations was use that of herself which was of First Mother and that which was of First Man. The new things were of both, as she was. And First Man was pleased as all fathers of daughters are when they see that something of themselves continues in new Life.

But it remained that he could only watch, with no one to understand and share his unique joy in what First Mother and First Daughter created. So one day First Man said, "There is none other like me." Once more he was comforted by First Mother, and in time another man was born.

Now, the man was also partly of First Mother and partly of First Man. His hair and his skin were the gold of the sun, and his seed flowed as the river of stars across the night sky, and in these ways he was of First Man. His eyes were the rich brown of earth, and his lips were the dark scarlet of leaves in autumn, and in these ways he was of First Mother. But when he looked upon First Daughter, he saw how different he was from her. In secret he considered the differences, and in time concluded that because her body was like that of First Mother, and his body was like that of First Man, that she was more first Mother's child than he, and thus she must be more beloved by First Mother. And envy was born in his heart.

To test his conclusion, he asked to be taught to create as First Daughter did. First Man explained, with the compassion learned from First Mother, that men could not do this. The man railed against it most bitterly, and he came upon First Daughter, and slew her for envy of what she was that he was not, and what she could do that he could not.

First Man came upon the slain body of First Daughter, and his grief caused the stars to darken and the sun to leave the sky. First Mother asked why he sorrowed, and when he told her, the ground shuddered with Her heartbreak. First Man wept so in his pain that the skies opened and rain fell and the murderer was drowned in the flood.

The world languished, for First Mother had no heart to nurture. Life struggled to survive, desperate and without hope. But First Man had also learned how to comfort, and in time new Life was born, and these were Second Children, whom we call Saints. Each was partly of First Mother and partly of First Man. Though they had their squabbles, they never forgot that they were sisters and brothers, and loved each other.

Second Children were born day after day for a whole year, one after the other, into the sunlight. As each opened eyes of blue or brown or gray or green or black, First Mother and First Man gave loving welcome and listened for the first word to be spoken. Caitiri said *Fire* and Geridon said *Horse* and Miramili said *Bells* and Velenne said *Music* and so on until all the elements and animals and crafts and arts were named. Sirrala, by the way, said *Diamonds,* and this is why she is especially beloved by First Daughter, whose creation diamonds are.

For as Second Children were born day after day, First Daughter stirred, and woke, and lived, and spoke the word *Rebirth.* First Mother cried out in happiness. First Man wept gentle, joyous rain. Second Children welcomed their Eldest Sister joyfully, and gave her the name Gelenis. And as new children were born of Second Children—except Sirrala the Virgin and Venkelos the Judge—and more children were born of them, Gelenis was kept very busy. First Mother and First Man watched their progeny multiply, and She thanked him for his kindness in comforting her sorrow. He replied that he had learned such from Her, and this is the Third Truth: Women teach men compassion, so that men may comfort women in their inevitable sorrow.

Now, the last born of Second Children was Venkelos, and alone of them all he was born into the darkness of night. And as he was born the rest looked at each other in worry, for his first word was *Death*.

Venkelos asked First Mother why at the moment of life he spoke of death. She replied that it meant that, with Gelenis First Daughter, he was the dearest of Her children, for it was he who would guide the return of all Life to Her. His was the judgment of what would live and what must die. Venkelos nodded thoughtfully. And he and Gelenis became close companions.

But one night he withdrew, saying he must contemplate anew his weighty responsibilities. And for a long time nothing died—not a blade of grass, not an insect on the wing, not a stalk of wheat, not a single animal or bird or any of the multitudes of people now in the world.

Consider what this means, Cailet. If grass cannot be bitten from its root, animals starve. If wheat cannot be harvested, people starve. If nothing dies, there is no food. In this way, life requires death.

First Mother summoned Venkelos. With all respect and humility, he told Her that his duties were meaningless as far as he could see. For had not First Daughter died, yet now lived? First Mother thought long and hard on this matter, and finally took First Daughter aside to discuss it with her.

"Truly told," said Gelenis, "I was dead, and now am alive. I would know why this is so, First Mother, if You will tell me."

From his favorite cloud, First Man let forth a polite peal of thunder to attract their attention. "If I may, Ladies," he said, "I think it is because you were reborn as She created Second Children. Nothing can withstand the power of Her creating, not even death."

"First Man is wise," said Gelenis. "But Venkelos has a valid point, and because I know him well I know he is sincerely troubled by this. He has attended many a birthing with me, and it grieves him when he is forced to reclaim a Life for You when that Life has barely begun."

First Mother nodded. "He is as gentle as Jeymian and as compassionate as Gorynel. That is why I gave judgment to him instead of, say, dear foolish Kiy—who would either bring a Life back to Me and forget why, or else forget to return any Life to Me at all!"

They laughed in fond exasperation. Then Gelenis said, "But, First Mother, why do I live again?"

Heavy of heart, First Mother and First Man traded glances, and he said what She could not bring Herself to say: "Firstborn, do you wish to die?"

"No, but it may be necessary. Venkelos's right to judge who must die was given after my death, but my renewed life makes for an unbalance."

First Mother considered. "Firstborn, you are wrong." And She summoned Venkelos once more to Her. "Gelenis First Daughter will live. Remember, Venkelos, her first word on waking: *Rebirth.* She who watches over birthings does in truth watch over each life being reborn from My original creation."

Venkelos knelt in gratitude. "I understand, and I am glad to hear You say it, because I have been sorely disturbed by Life's hatred of me."

She exclaimed in surprise. "Do you mean that you are feared, my son?"

"Truly told."

"I should have anticipated this and dealt with it sooner," said First Mother. "You must have suffered great pain, Venkelos. I am sorry for it."

"No matter. Henceforth I will not be so terrible a presence, or so dreaded. I am a man. I cannot create Life. I personify Death. But Gelenis's rebirth is proof that Life is ever and always returned to You to be renewed. If they will but understand this, I will find peace in their eyes when I come for them."

And that is the Fourth Truth: Venkelos the Judge is not to be feared, for he but returns us to First Mother, who creates and renews Life.

"But you said St. Caitiri was a real person, a Mage Guardian. How's that fit with being one of the Second Children?"

"Did I ever say that any tale I tell is the absolute, carved-in-stone truth?" Rinnel wiped silver rain from his dark face. "You are the most *literal* child! Still, I suppose that's to be expected in a matter-of-fact place like The Waste. No room for allegory or symbolism or—"

"I don't believe every word you say," she protested. "And I understand when a story's just a story! But why don't they all fit neatly together?"

"Does life?"

She had to admit it did not. Still, she grumbled, "They might at least *try* to keep their stories straight."

"Cailet, dear," he said in an oh-so-patient, oh-so-annoying tone, "getting the stories straight—otherwise known as figuring out what you believe—is *your* problem."

"What about Wraiths?" she challenged. "They're the spirits of the dead and they come back to haunt you—and that don't sound to me like they're reborn."

"*Doesn't* sound. Mind your grammar. And Geridon's Golden Balls, girl, who taught you theology? Didn't you hear a word I said? The idea here isn't that each of us gets literally reborn into another body. Our lives continue—what we think and feel and know, what we *are*. The most obvious way—obvious to everyone but you, it seems—is through our children. Have you got that much straight?"

"I understood that part of it, thanks," she muttered.

"Very well, then. We also live on in what we do. What we teach others. How we're remembered. Are you still with me?"

She made a face at him. "If all Life returns to First Mother to be reborn, then what *are* Wraiths?"

"Well, I suppose becoming a Wraith is a kind of rebirth into a different sort of existence. Personally, I'm not looking forward to it. But I could be wrong, and being a Wraith might be almost as much fun as being flesh and bone." He grinned suddenly. "I'll let you know!"

"I still say it don't—*doesn't*—make much sense."

"My very precious and relentlessly literal child, it's religion. It doesn't *have* to make sense."

9

Through the years her understanding improved (and her grammar), but she remained instinctively literal. Rinnel despaired of her other instincts; symbols meant nothing to her unless he explained them, and allegory was just as much of a struggle. Still, he always managed to get the point across. She wasn't unintelligent, he'd tell her, just woefully unimaginative at times.

They were out hiking one morning—Rinnel was remarkably spry for his years, and he had to be at least seventy—when they came across a galazhi doe huddled in tense misery five yards from a stagnant puddle. The old man left off his lecture on the erstwhile Grand Duchess of Domburronshir and knelt by the suffering animal. After a feeble toss of her horns in warning, the doe sank her head into his cupped palm and shivered. He stroked gnarled fingers down her flanks, probing carefully.

"She must've been desperate for water to take a drink from that." Cailet wrinkled her nose at the smell. "And now she'll die of it, instead of thirst."

"She won't die. Bring me a handful of that purple ruff up on the rocks—with roots, please."

Cailet did as requested. Rinnel fed the doe, who chewed rapidly as if fearing her strength wouldn't last. At last she gave a great sigh and laid her head on his knee.

"There now," said the old man, nodding. "We'll wait with her until she's up and about again."

"But isn't it too late? I mean, once they sicken on bad water, they always die."

"Only if they can't get to the cure. Look at the ground behind her, where she was dragging herself toward the rocks. She knew what she needed, she just couldn't get that far. They're stupid beasts, truly told, but instinct sometimes serves almost as well as wits." He petted the galazhi's long, supple neck. "Her belly isn't distended, which means she made her mistake less than half an hour ago. Another ten minutes and it would indeed have been too late."

Cailet sat on a flat rock and smiled at him. "And now you'll link this very convenient sick animal to the Grand Duchess."

Rinnel harrumphed irritably. "Learning all my tricks, are you? If you're *such* a clever child, you tell me what this poor little girl has to do with it."

"They both drank poison. Only there wasn't any cure for Veller Ganfallin."

"She wouldn't have taken it if there was. Ambition *is* poison of a sort. But I'd call it a disease. Like arrogance or ignorance. She was ambitious, and most of her advisers were morons."

"Now you sound like *Domna* Lodde."

"Who?"

"The healer First Daughter hired when Master Irien spent a year in Gierkenshir."

"Oh. Why do I sound like her?"

Cailet scooped up a handful of pebbles and began sorting them for likely bits of sand jade for carving. "She never referred to people by name. One person was 'fish allergy,' and somebody else was 'mild concussion' or whatever. I was 'simple fracture' even though she wasn't anywheres near Ostinhold when I broke my arm that time. We didn't have names, we had ailings."

"Physicians do tend to categorize people that way," he mused.

"But it's like it was the only thing she saw. As if everybody could be defined by a single trait."

"I see. If I were only 'arthritic knees,' she'd miss all my other aches and pains. One label obscures others, I think." Green eyes twinkled in his dark face. "I rather enjoy Crazy Old Man of Crackwall, though."

Cailet snorted and tossed away rejected stones. "First Daughter likes her label, too."

"So I've heard."

"It doesn't bother you? That people think so about you?"

He smiled, scratching the galazhi's ears. "Those who truly know me know the truth of me. And what about you? How do we label you?"

She thought it over. She was orphan and fosterling, and that was all. Neither said much about who she really was. Tentatively, she answered, "I don't know. Nothing seems to fit."

"Well, what do you do with yourself all day?"

"Study. Read. Go to school. Do my chores. Ride the herds, muck out stalls, and other suchlike."

"I'd hardly term you a scholar. You're no ranch hand, either."

"And I come visit you. Does that make me crazy, like they say you are?"

"Impertinent monster. And you've quite failed to define yourself, Cailet. What label do you *want?*"

With a little shrug, she said, "The ones I already have are 'orphan' and 'fosterling.' But I didn't have anything to do with either."

"Words other people have defined you with?" he suggested.

She nodded. "It's not exactly fair, is it? I think a label is just a convenience, so a person knows what place you hold."

"And sometimes it keeps others from seeing who you really are. From what you've said, Geria Ostin knows that on instinct. And uses it."

"Like you?" she asked shrewdly. "Nobody but me ever comes out here. They all think you really are crazy."

"How do you know they're not right?"

She laughed at him. "Did I say they weren't?"

"You're a disrespectful, ungrateful wretch who didn't get spanked half as much as she ought. Whatever Lilen Ostin's ideas on child-rearing, I've found little to approve thus far. I must say—"

Suddenly he gave a start as the galazhi doe leaped to her feet. She shook her head, pawed the ground—and simultaneously emitted a thunderous belch and a flood of purplish urine. Then she bounded away up the rocks to find the herd.

Cailet stared after her. "Who'd believe that skinny little thing could make such a great big noise!"

"Or such an appalling stench." Rinnel clambered to his feet, wincing. "Which I fear will be with us all the way back to my house. Her aim was not the best. Talk about lack of gratitude—!"

"Well, I've got a title for *her,*" Cailet laughed. " 'Rivermaker!' "

He chuckled. "May everything they call you in your life be as appropriate—and well-earned! Now, walk upwind of me, Cailet, and don't you even *think* of adding 'Stinky' to Crazy Old Man!"

A few nights later Cailet woke very abruptly in her pitch-black bedroom. Her heart pounded and sweat broke out on her skin: the tiny lamp always left on the corner table had gone out. Darkness—endless, suffocating, imprisoning—

Frantically she repeated Lady Lilen's advice: listen to the sounds of Ostinhold at night, regular soothing sounds of the breeze shifting the shingles and the house settling, the soft footsteps of her elders going late to bed, the yips of puppies in the kennels. She heard them, but none could block the rush and roar of blood in her ears. Sheets tangled around her limbs like jesses on a hunting hawk. She was paralyzed, she couldn't move or cry out, she could scarcely even breathe—there was nothing of calm or strength within her to combat her shaming, gibbering terror of the dark.

She didn't even know what she was afraid of. She only knew that she ached for light, that the darkness was a wall shutting her in—

A wall?

Rinnel had shown her how to build a wall. Perhaps she could put it between her and the darkness.

Brick by heavy brick, shaking with fear and sweating with the effort of concentration, she built it as wide as her shoulders and as high as her head. And it held. And it *glowed*. Darkness threatened on either side, but her wall protected her with softly radiant white light.

She collapsed against damp pillows, sucking in great breaths. Her heartbeats gradually slowed. She stopped trembling. Within a few minutes she was able to unwind the sheets and sit up, slightly sick and a little dizzy, but no longer terrified.

To relight the lamp, she had to see. She crossed to the door and opened it to let in what illumination filtered down the hall from the cresset lamp at the far end. Her eyes hungrily sought that distant light—but someone's shadow blocked it, lengthening with every stride, someone wearing a ragged black cloak she recognized.

Rinnel paused at the turning for Lady Lilen's rooms. Cailet watched in frank amazement as her foster-mother hurried into view, something clasped close in her arms. Rinnel accepted the bundle, shaking his head, then disappeared quickly down the stairs. Lady Lilen stood there for a long moment, her face both angry and sad. Cailet hesitated, then boldly stepped out of her doorway and ran barefoot down the hall.

Her sudden appearance made Lady Lilen catch her breath in a little gasp. "Cai! What are you doing up? Go back to bed."

"Why'd Rinnel come here? What'd you just give him?"

"Hush, you'll wake everyone." With a sigh, she went on, "Come to my rooms, dear. If you saw, then I suppose I'd better explain."

An hour later, sworn to secrecy, Cailet returned to her own chamber. She lit the lamp and lay back down in bed, but she knew she wouldn't sleep. What Lady Lilen had told her was too terrible.

Several days ago at Scraller's Fief, a slave had given birth. The infant boy had a maimed foot, the little bones twisted somehow in the womb. With care and a good healer's help, there was a fine chance that he would grow up with only a slight limp.

But at Scraller's, he would not be allowed to grow up. He had been born defective, malformed. Therefore, he would be killed.

"No, Caisha, I *can't* have it stopped," Lady Lilen had said in response to her horrified question. "It's not just Scraller. It's common practice all over Lenfell. Any child not perfect at birth is put to death. Some places are gentle about it—an overdose of sleeping drops is the favored method, I'm told. In other places, the babies are left on hillsides to die, or their throats are cut, or—I know, darling, it's hideous. But not all of them are killed. Some of us help as best we can. I sent word to Rinnel to come take the baby away to—to a place of safety he knows about. This little boy will live. Thousands die, and for imperfections less severe than a lame foot."

This wasn't the first time she'd saved a newborn's life. Just as it was never admitted that some children were born less than perfect, it was never acknowledged that a few people could be relied upon to spirit these babies away from certain death. But thousands more died—and no one ever talked about it.

"It happens rather more often in The Waste than elsewhere, or so Taig tells me. The pollution was worst here, of course. It lingers even now. Most people don't even know these babies are born. Those who do usually know only because it becomes their personal tragedy."

Collusion usually assured that no one discovered the truth. Birth of a flawed baby did more than shame and grieve the parents: it was an insult to Lenfell's collective sensitivities. It meant the system of Bloods and Tiers hadn't worked as perfectly as everyone wanted to believe. So everyone who knew kept quiet. Many healers who attended such births recommended choosing a different father for the next baby. Some comforted the stricken parents by telling them that the chance of repetition was very small, and even less for a woman who had borne a healthy child before the maimed one. Some took it upon themselves to sterilize the mother, lest she bear another defective child.

But all of them took the babies away, usually already dead, and left the parents to select a reason. Strangled by the mother-cord, too lengthy a labor—there were a dozen possible explanations for a stillborn child that would not reflect badly on the parents' heritage or the healer's skills.

Lilen would not tell Cailet where Rinnel was taking the boy. She didn't know and didn't want to. Ignorance was the best guarantee of secrecy. As for how many of these children survived in this mysterious haven, Lilen guessed their numbers to be around a thousand. Perhaps two thousand. Perhaps more.

"Who takes care of them?"

"I don't know. Caisha, I've told you all I can and all I'm going to. It's past First and you should be in bed asleep."

Cailet had one last question. "If they mend the baby's foot and he grows up all right, then could he maybe come back out into the world again?"

"Perhaps. It's done only when the disability can be explained away by injury." She paused. "There was one that I know of, a little girl with a winestain birthmark rather like a coif. She—"

"They would've killed her for a *birthmark?*"

"It was disfiguring," Lilen answered bitterly. "Her parents were Bloods. The Healer was a Mage Guardian, and he got the child to safety. She was about five, I think, when her hair was thick enough to hide the birthmark. Beautiful hair, black as a raven's wing. . . ."

"What happened to her?"

"Hmm? Oh. A woman of her own mother's Name adopted

her. No one ever knew." She smiled. "*I* know because my grandmother's brother husbanded her. We've been helping children like her ever since."

Now, as Cailet lay sleepless, it occurred to her that *she* might be one of the babies born maimed. There was nothing physically wrong with her—not now. But had she been flawed somehow, crippled, imperfect? Had her mother rejected her for some disfigurement that had been cured or had faded with time? Was that why Lilen had taken her in?

She knew better than to ride out to Rinnel's cottage for the next week or so. When she thought enough time had gone by for his return, she saddled her mare and went to visit him on a clear autumn morning.

There were no signs that he'd been gone. She hadn't expected to see any, though it would have been useful as an opening to the conversation she half-feared to have with him. He made her welcome as always, asking if she'd enjoyed the last dozen books she'd borrowed (a pointed reference to the fact that she hadn't yet returned them).

Knowing no other way to begin, she blurted it out: "You know about everybody and everything—did you know my mother?"

The green eyes were untroubled; he showed no surprise; he merely nodded as if he'd been expecting this question for a long time. "I know about most people and quite a few things, and I did meet your mother."

"What was she like? Why'd she give me away? Was I born crippled? Did somebody come when I was born and take me away like you did that baby? Is that why Lady Lilen took me in as a fosterling?"

He held up a hand. "Slow down! Whatever are you talking about?"

"I saw you that night. Lady Lilen told me all about it."

"Ah. I understand. And you think this is what happened to you? Saints and Wraiths, the ideas that find their way into your head! Cailet, my dear, you were born the most perfect and beautiful child who ever drew breath."

"Truly told?"

"More truly than anything I've ever said in my life. Your mother didn't 'give you away'—she died, poor lovely creature, and don't think you're to blame for it, either. She survived your birth but she couldn't survive a broken heart when she learned of your father's death."

"How did he die?"

Rinnel was silent for a long minute. "At Ambrai. He died at Ambrai. Your mother was a dear friend to Lilen Ostin, who wouldn't even consider letting you grow up anywhere else. Now, does that answer your questions?"

"Some," she sighed. "I know better than to ask where you took the baby, or how many there are like him. Lady Lilen says nobody can put a stop to it. But I bet Taig will, once the Rising wins."

"I wouldn't be surprised if he tried. You must remember, though, how much of our identity as a society is based on the success of the Bloods and Tiers in eliminating defects and diseases that run in families. For a for instance—I've never seen a single person under the age of fifty wear reading lenses. Bad eyesight often comes with age, it's the human condition. But to be *born* with it is a flaw no one will admit to. Which is why, even in an enlightened tribe like the Ostins, Terrill denies he can't read for more than an hour without getting a headache, squints when he thinks no one's looking, and does very badly in classes unless he's seated right up at the front closest to the writing board."

"But he's *smart!* And he's an artist, too, you should see some of the things he paints—he wants to go to school in Firrense when he's old enough. Why is he ashamed? It's just his eyes, not his mind!"

"Well, how did *you* feel for the last two weeks, thinking you were born with some similar flaw?"

She hung her head to hide her blush. "It's not right," she mumbled.

"No, it's not. And don't look for it to change all that quickly, either." He paused. "In the past, being Mageborn was considered a defect. It's getting to be that way again."

She looked up at him. "But—that's just what we were saying that day—that people put labels on other people for things they can't help being!"

Rinnel smiled and poured them both a mug of cider. "Here ends the lesson for today, little one."

"But—"

"It's too hot to do so much serious thinking. Drink, and catch me up on all the latest gossip. Is Riena Maurgen still juggling five boyfriends at once? And has the delectable Kania Halvos found a fourth husband? Ah, to be sixty again!"

Part Two

968–969

Ladders

1

Caitiri's Forge glowed hot with sparks
A million struck into the dark
A million more, the sky to fill
The night, so black and wild.
Sirrala laughed: the red-gold sparks
Turned to diamonds in the dark
White as ice, but fiery still
At night, so black and wild.
Lirance breathed wind into the dark
Blowing free the diamond-sparks
Warm wind she called against the chill
Of night, so black and wild.
Delilah caught sight of the sparks
And led them dancing through the dark
Across each sea and field and hill—
By night, so black and wild.
Velenne made Bardsong in the dark
To guide the darting shining sparks
In one vast dance, the sky to fill
At night, so black and wild.

Sarra hummed the old tune aloud, for there was no one to wince. It was a night for songs, even if she couldn't sing; every star close enough to touch, to pluck and scatter like dewdrops. It seemed a million or so had already been tossed by some generous hand onto the darkness of the sea. But millions more were there for the gathering. Tonight she felt she could reach them all.

She leaned on the carved windowsill of Roseguard's Have-a-Word Room—a whimsical name for a privilege held dear by everyone in Sheve. Lady Agatine spent several hours here every week; those wishing speech with her entered by any of six passages, none observable within or without the keep. Alone with their Lady in complete privacy, anyone could discuss anything for any length of time. Complaints, proposals, personal troubles, public disputes—and

succulent gossip—all were heard in the Have-a-Word Room.
And none of it was ever heard outside without specific permission in writing.

Sarra had been here just once. Shortly after she turned
eighteen, she came here to receive private congratulations
from citizens of Roseguard. But one day this room would
belong to her. Agatine, last of her Name, had petitioned the
Council to make Sarra her heir. In this, she secretly anticipated the time when "Liwellan" would be discarded and
"Ambrai" reclaimed—and all that went with it, for when
Glenin became Feiran, Sarra became Ambrai First Daughter.
The merging of Ambraishir with Sheve would protect Agatine's beloved land.

Though Sarra agreed to this, she was adamant about signing over Roseguard, Sleginhold, and other family properties
to Agatine's four sons. Just because they had the misfortune
to be born male was no reason to take their homes away.
Agatine and Orlin warned against trying to get this past the
Council anytime soon. Transferring primacy of a whole Shir
from one Name to another hadn't been done in at least ten
Generations; transferring sole ownership of such extensive
holdings to males would scandalize all Lenfell.

Which prospect bothered Sarra not in the least. It was her
first move as an important player in a game Anniyas had
thus far been winning, hands down. Sarra intended to shock
Lenfell quite a few more times on her way to victory.

She would, however, hold back on giving Riddon, Elom,
Maugir, and Jeymi the Slegin family lands. She would present herself meekly to the Council and be suitably grateful
for their favor—even if her stomach curdled.

Scrupulous search had already been made by the Census
Ministry for a female Slegin. Agatine was an only child
from a long line of only children—that she had borne four
offspring was an anomaly—and the closest the Ministry
came was an Alvassy cousin many times removed. As this
childless lady had just celebrated her ninety-fourth Birthingday, it had been decided that Sarra would be allowed to inherit.

Generous of them, Sarra thought acidly. *As if Agatine—or
any woman—should have to grovel for the right to dispose
of her property as she sees fit!* But irritation was quickly
subsumed into excitement and satisfaction. She had her excuse for going to Ryka Court. At last.

The excitement was ruthlessly quelled to a quiver. Between the ages of eighteen and twenty-two she had learned discipline—but no magic. It was unnecessary and dangerous for her to have use of her Mageborn powers. Accepting this was her greatest and hardest lesson in discipline.

The opening of the door behind her made her turn. She smiled at her foster parents. "No, I wasn't about to sneak away early! I can see the Sparrow best from these windows, that's all."

Agatine and Orlin joined her, gazing at a constellation low on the horizon. The two great wings, flickering tail, and uplifted head of St. Rilla the Guide's starry sigil flew eastward in the winter sky.

"I pray she watches over you and brings you safely home," Agatine murmured.

Sarra clasped her hand. "I'll be fine. Just so long as Telomir Renne doesn't put every eligible man in Ryka on parade!"

"Telo wants to see you happy. So do we," Agatine replied.

"You're a match for my brother and his schemes," Orlin said, a chuckle rumbling in his broad chest. "Besides, no man born is good enough for you."

Sarra laughed. "You raised me—you're *supposed* to think that!"

"Telo means well," Agatine said. "A 'parade' will be a useful distraction."

A small silence ensued. Then Orlin smiled. "Do you still want *all* the stars for your very own? After all, Aggie settled for just one."

"Conceited pig," Agatine accused, chuckling.

Sarra's Name-Saint had turned the stars into diamonds, according to the song. She hadn't kept even one. Sarra would, if only she could find one like Orlin. *Kind, strong, intelligent, considerate, thinks Agatine is the center of the universe—and without a braggardly bone in his body. But who do I meet? Morons like Dalion Witte, reckless independents like Taig Ostin, and that damned fake Rosvenir Minstrel. And now Telomir will march the whole roster of Ryka Court fops past me. Just as well I decided long ago never to marry!*

Besides, I don't have the time.

"If anything goes wrong, don't you go getting mixed up in a battle," Agatine warned suddenly.

"I won't get the chance," Sarra sighed. "Everybody else will do any necessary fighting. All I ever get to do is talk!"

Which, admittedly, she loved. She'd begun her career in meetings with Slegin stewards, then attended conferences with Council delegations, and just this past summer had spoken to a group of Council members—including Garon Anniyas. Unsettling, to hold forth to her sister's husband on the dangers of strangling trade (a thinly veiled reference to the crippling restrictions on Mageborns). But her petitioning carried with it the right to speak at Ryka Court. Sarra intended the First Councillor herself to listen this time.

Agatine drew her closer with a hand at her waist. "You have an honest and eloquent voice, dearest. Orlin and I taught you to shape the words, but the truths behind them are your own. Don't risk yourself if there's fighting. Promise me you'll obey Telo."

"I know my duty."

Relieved, Agatine nodded. "Be especially careful on the way home. It's the most vital part of your mission."

"I'll find him—if he's still alive." Doubt crept into her voice. "It's been years since anybody's heard from him or of him."

"Oh, he's alive," Orlin murmured. "He'll be around as long as he's needed."

"As long as *Cailet* needs him," Sarra corrected. "She still doesn't know, does she?"

Agatine shook her head. "I don't like to think of the shock when she learns the truth, Sarra. I hope you're there with her."

"I'd better be, or Gorynel Desse will answer for it." Then she brightened. "I can't wait to bring Cailet home. Once the Mage Guardians are safe on Warded Slegin land, she'll have dozens of teachers—and the Rising will have a central headquarters at last."

Orlin arched a brow. "Simple as a stroll through Roseguard Grounds, eh?" The edge to his voice was positively serrated. Instincts that had never failed her made an easy jump to guessing his thoughts.

"Don't worry. They're in Dindenshir." *They:* her father and eldest sister.

A discreet cough turned them all from the windows. "Your pardon, Lady Agatine, Lord Orlin. Time."

Sarra blinked as a young man appeared from behind a

tapestry—an entry to the Have-a-Word Room she hadn't known about. "Now? I thought—"

"This is Valirion Maurgen," Agatine introduced. "He and his partner will be your escort, Sarra."

"But I'm supposed to leave tomorrow morning!"

Maurgen shrugged. "Plans have a tendency to change, *Domna*."

She frankly looked him over. He was of medium height—though all men looked short near Orlin—muscular and swarthy, with a wrestler's square stance and solid build. Dark eyes sparkled above a curling mouth and a formidable chin with a rakishly offset cleft. Modestly coifed and longvested, he wore a heavy silver hoop in his right earlobe—and a heavy silver scabbard at his left hip.

"I, for one, am glad of it," Valirion Maurgen added. "It's time I got back to The Big Empty. All these trees make me nervous."

Sarra quickly sorted through her mental file. Maurgen: a Third Tier family connected by marriage to the Ostins—as indeed almost everyone seemed to be, including the Ambrais. So she and Valirion were cousins of a sort, she supposed, although as a "Liwellan" she could never claim the kinship.

"But—all my things, my clothes—"

"My partner has a cloak for you. That's all you need. Say your farewells, *Domna*. It's a long walk to the harbor."

And just that swiftly was it done: Agatine and Orlin were embraced, the tapestry was drawn shut, and the door was closed.

"Forgive the demotion in rank," Valirion Maurgen said, setting match to candlewick to light their way down an iron spiral of stairs. "As the Liwellan First Daughter I should call you 'Lady.' The insult to your status pains me. But we'll be going places where it's best if you're not *too* much of a Blood."

"Trivial," she replied, holding tight to his hand. The steps were slick and treacherous. "Call me Sarra if you like. Is it far? I could use that cloak."

"If my partner hasn't tucked it around some stray litter of kittens." He snorted. "Eyes like glacier ice, heart like mushy porridge, that's my Alin-O."

It couldn't be, but she had to ask; the name was not a common variant of Alilen. "Alin Ostin?"

"The one and only—and thanks be that there *is* just the one of him! You know him?"

She could hardly admit to having played hoop-a-roll with him at Ostinhold when she was five years old. "I've heard the name."

"He'll be crushed." Valirion shot a grin over his shoulder. "My clever cousin thinks he's the most cunning, secret, unknown, anonymous, stealthy and so forth agent in all the Rising. Ah, but you're Agatine's foster-daughter, so you'd know such things. That may console him a bit."

"I met Taig Ostin a few years ago." Sarra didn't tell him how ignorant she was of the essential names of the Rising. *Which appears to be largely an Ostin enterprise,* she thought with a smile. Lilen, Taig, and now Alin and this Maurgen cousin. *And me. At last!*

Eventually they reached a barred iron door. On the other side was an alley swathed in midnight. A slight, pale, intense young man was busy stuffing a mass of wheaten hair into a black coif. He glanced up as Valirion and Sarra emerged.

"About bloody time," he grumbled.

"No pun intended," added Valirion.

"Don't be flippant, Val. I'm freezing." He flourished a dark blue cloak around Sarra's shoulders. She returned the favor by tucking in stray wisps of hair almost the same gold as her own. Yes, this was definitely Alin: the only one of Lilen Ostin's brood with his father Tiva Senison's coloring. His dark-haired, suntanned siblings had teased him to fury about it back at Ostinhold, branding him a changeling for his blue eyes and fair, freckled skin. But also alone of them all, Alin had inherited their mother's ruler-straight nose (the others had anything from hawk's beaks to snubs) and Lilen's broad, lofty brow. Sarra reminded herself not to comment aloud on what she remembered. As far as Alin knew, they were meeting for the first time.

Still. . . . "You don't look much like your brother Taig," she said.

"Nobody's seen him recently enough to tell," Alin answered. "Consider us introduced." He didn't bow. Instead he turned to lead the way down the alley.

"He's not much for conversation," Valirion explained with a shrug.

"Val's eloquence intimidates me," Alin snapped.

"Or manners," Valirion added with a wink. "Pretty girls intimidate him, too." He escorted Sarra to the street, for all the world as if to the grand ballroom at Domburr Castle.

It had just gone Thirteenth—the hour after dinner and before bedtime. In summer, when daylight lasted until nearly Fourteenth, the streets were crowded with people strolling to and from shops, taverns, friends' homes, the docks, or nowhere in particular. But in winter, dark by Eleventh, everyone stayed by their own warm fires.

Some twists and turns later, just in case they were being followed—highly unlikely in the nearly empty streets, but Alin was evidently a worrier—they were dockside. Alin ignored three large sailboats Sarra considered possible for the journey. Almost at the end of the main wharf he swung abruptly over the railing and vanished.

"Ladder," Valirion whispered. Sarra's eyes blinked wide. He shook his head for silence, striking a casual pose with his arm around her. Two fishermen, a father trailing four small children, and a pair of lovers passed by.

"The nuzzlers," Valirion whispered, "are Council Guard."

She tilted her head back as if stargazing again. "Met them before?"

"In nasty circumstances. Alin really knows how to show a friend a good time in Roseguard. It's safe now. Down. Hurry."

Glad she had worn trousers instead of a skirt, Sarra did as Alin had done. She felt disappointed; it was just an ordinary old ladder, placed there to facilitate repairs to the wharf planking. Eight rungs down, with the sea lashing the pilings below, a hand closed around hers and urged her to sidestep.

"This way," Alin said.

She placed a cautious foot on a narrow board slung on chains between two massive support beams. Sea spray wet her boots and the hem of her cloak, splashed droplets onto her cheeks. When Valirion was balanced beside them, Alin lit a match without benefit of flintstrip. Sarra blinked. In Pinderon, Lady Lilen had said Margit was her only Mageborn daughter. Daughter—not son. By such delicate nuances, Sarra told herself wryly, were secrets successfully kept while telling the plain truth.

The tiny light revealed a huge support piling. Sunk beneath the waves to support the wharf like all the others, this one had a set of rusty hinges at one side. Alin's long fingers probed. He swore under his breath.

"Salt air," Valirion said, "is hell on the mechanism."

"Shut up, Val," Alin hissed, and sprung the catch. A door opened, two feet wide by three feet tall. He gestured Sarra inside.

She gathered the cloak tight and ducked inside. Val scrunched his way in behind her, begging her pardon for crushing her against the dank wood. Alin simply crammed himself in and locked the hatchway.

"Close your eyes."

Gorynel Desse had ordered the same on the flight from Ambrai. In the four years since Pinderon she'd set herself to remembering every scrap of what he'd caused her to forget—and she had vivid memory of the desperation in his voice. Desse had worked the spell in a moment. Alin seemed to be taking a long time.

As if her worry had been audible, Valirion assured Sarra, "He's really quite good at this—not half the lackwit he looks."

Alin muttered, "I love you too, Val."

Abruptly Sarra's senses blanked. The sound of waves lapping at pylons, the stinging salt-scent of the sea, the tickle of wind seeping through cracks, all vanished. She barely had time to be frightened before the strong, sharp smell of lemon sage filled her nostrils.

"You're Mageborn," Alin accused.

Sarra opened her eyes to an astonishing dazzle of sunlight through a window. Blessed St. Rilla the Guide, they were halfway around Lenfell!

"That's why I had trouble," he was explaining to Valirion. "She's Warded, and a fine job someone did of it, too. But she's Mageborn, truly told."

"Sorry," she managed, trying not to gape at her surroundings: the upper floor of a mill that hadn't ground grain in at least twenty years. Round, of course, like all Ladders. But what an odd place to put one. "I didn't think it would matter. Nobody's supposed to know, anyway."

"Nobody would, except a Mage who's looking for it—or trying to take you through a Ladder." Alin narrowed pale blue eyes at the sunlight that danced with dust and ancient chaff. "I *hate* this one," he said, and sneezed.

"It's a long walk to Roke Castle," said Val. "Do you want to rest, *Domna?*"

"I'm fine. What are we doing in Kenrokeshir?"

Alin, already starting down the rickety wooden stairs, jerked his chin at Valirion. "He'll tell you as we go."

The next morning—which was to say, the morning she would have seen in Roseguard but which was not the morning she was currently in; the morning happening around her was one that had already happened in Roseguard, but was still occurring in Kenrokeshir (with the feeling this could get very confusing, she decided not to think about it)—a ship would sail to Ryka, with a single stop at Shellinkroth. Sarra would in theory be on that ship, locked in her cabin, a martyr to seasickness. At Havenport she would recover enough to venture by night into the port for a walk. And when she was rowed back to the ship, seven new passengers would sneak on board with her.

"Alin, myself, and five Mage Guardians," Val said. "We'll collect two here, then go Laddering to Cantrashir, where another pair are waiting. The last is already in Shellinkroth. Then it's on to Ryka. Ladder to Ambrai, from there to Brogdenguard and Dindenshir, and join the ship again with ten more Mages."

"Why can't the Mages just use Ladders to get to Roseguard?"

"Because you have to know where you're going," Alin said.

Again, Valirion was the one to explain. Knowing the location of one Ladder was useless unless one also knew where it went. Not knowing, one would be lost forever inside a magical void called a Blanking Ward. Usually a Mage had to know just a few personally convenient Ladders. With the deaths of so many in the seventeen years since Ambrai, only a few Guardians now knew every Ladder.

"And one unofficial Prentice," Valirion finished, eyeing his cousin with combined fondness and worry. "In the vernacular, Alin's a Ladder Rat."

"I think I see," Sarra said. "The Mages we're collecting would have to do a lot of unnecessary traveling among Ladders they know, at tremendous risk."

Val stretched a shoulder. "I just hope they're not all as cramped as the one at Roseguard."

"So we're going a-gathering Mages. Do you know them?"

Meaning, did he know that one of the collectibles was Gorynel Desse?

He shook his head, fingers busy at the throat of his coif. "Oh—pardon, *Domna*," he said, starting to reknot the laces.

"Take it off if you like. I won't be offended. You too, Alin."

Blond hair was immediately revealed, shaken, finger-combed. Val, ever courtly, said their thanks to Sarra as he scrubbed his own scalp.

"Saints, that's a relief! A coif is torture in the best circumstances—and you don't know what it's like to wear one in The Waste in summer."

Sarra laughed. "I don't intend to find out, either."

"No chance of that." Val gave her a look perilously akin to an ogle, and grinned. "Of all the ways I could think of to disguise you, *Domna,* turning you into a boy definitely isn't an option!"

Sarra frowned. While it was true that her childhood pudge had redistributed itself most attractively—Tarise reported overhearing her described as being "built like a brick dollhouse"—Sarra disapproved of such remarks. Charming as Valirion Maurgen was, his manners needed some polishing here and there.

Alin gave them a glance over one shoulder, brows arching and lips twisting. "Hands off, Val. She's Blood."

"So are you, *Domni* mine."

To Sarra's surprise, Alin blushed bright red before setting his back to them and picking up the pace.

It was nearly dark, and Val had found them a sheltered little copse in which to spend the night, before it finally hit her. The cousins were lovers as well as partners; Alin was jealous. She clamped her teeth tight around a giggle. So Val still kept one eye open for the ladies, did he? She'd have to get it through to Alin that he could relax as far as she was concerned.

The blue cloak was quite warm enough to sleep in. Although it was winter in Sheve, here in Kenrokeshir it was soft summer. St. Lirance sang her to sleep, sighing through oaks and flowering trees and sage scrub. When Sarra woke next morning, her cloak and hair were drenched in dew and scattered blossoms.

After breakfasting from Val's journeypack, they started walking again. At length the cart track split in three like the tines of a fork; Alin led them to the west. Several more miles through low hills took them to an abandoned manor house by dusk. There they met up with the first two Mages.

Lengthy travel between Ladders was obviously impossible for the elderly Scholar in bedraggled black and gray cassock, silver Mage Globe sigils of his calling pinned to a frayed collar. His companion, a vigorous woman of about forty, was every strapping, healthy inch the Warrior Mage. Her black cloak lay folded on a chair back, red lining and Silver Sword badge clearly visible.

"Kanto Solingirt," the old man said, bowing gracefully over Sarra's wrist, his mustache tickling her skin as his lips barely grazed her pulse-point. She allowed him the liberty because she liked him on sight.

"Appropriately named, Scholar Mage," she replied, smiling.

He chuckled appreciation. "It was a sad day when Eskanto Cut-Thumb was removed from the Official Calendar. Alas, bookbinders now are lumped in with printers, judges, and other suchlike cripples patronized by St. Gorynel."

"I'll tell Gorsha Desse you said so, Fa!" The Warrior Mage smiled at Sarra. "I'm Imilial Gorrst. We didn't expect you until later today." She turned to Val, fair brows lifting. "Still advertising your sword, boy?"

"Both of them," he retorted, and smacked her a kiss on each cheek. "But no more fencing matches with you, Imi. I've still got scars from the last one."

Alin only grunted by way of greeting, which seemed to offend no one. Turning to Val, he asked, "Time?"

"Twelfth, less ten minutes."

Alin nodded. "We'll rest here until Half-Fifth. Scholar Kanto, I'm assuming you can wrap an Invisible around all five of us?"

The white mustache acquired a rakish tilt at each corner as he grinned. "My specialty, and my pleasure."

2

Valirion kept watch. He wedged himself into a window, profile and drawn-up knees vaguely outlined in starlight. At Second—or so he said when Sarra asked; she was never sure of the time without a clock—she joined him near the window, huddled on the single wobbly chair.

"Can't sleep?" he murmured, smiling in the gloom. "Have some of this." He held out a cup of tea thoughtfully spelled Warm by Imilial Gorrst.

Sarra drank, handed it back. "Why wasn't I told earlier about the Mages?" Then she made an annoyed gesture. "Silly question. Ignore it."

"Not silly at all. *Somebody's* got to know what everybody else is doing! And the system we use for it now is your design." He grinned, white teeth flashing in his dark face. "Alin and I are the first foundation blocks of your personal pyramid, Sarra. A few of the younger Mages we'll collect on this trip may be added as well. I don't know."

"You *can't* know. That's the whole point." Sarra was unsurprised that the Rising had adopted her pattern. It was practical, effective, and reasonably safe. "How did you and Alin get into this?"

"Taig."

"Why did I expect that answer?" she smiled.

"He's sort of a force of nature, isn't he? Lilen says his father was the same way. Rolls through your life like a storm, sweeping you along whether you want to be swept or not. . . ." He took another sip of tea. "Anyway, both Alin and I wanted to be swept. Night and day we are—in more than looks!—but we understand each other. No secrets. Sort of instinctive, you know?"

She didn't, but nodded anyway.

"It's been that way since school," Val went on musingly. "He's got this crazy memory—highest marks ever posted at Longriding Academy. Me, I'm hopeless at books. Naturally I made friends with him." He laughed low in his throat. "Then I discovered I actually *liked* the little wretch. And so

I got interested in what he liked, and that meant talking about our studies—so my marks went up without even having to cheat!"

"How mortifying for you," she remarked. "Go on."

"Well, one autumn a Scholar came to Ostinhold to teach him magic. I don't have any, unless you count always knowing the exact time. Not the most useful talent—unless you're partnered with a Ladder Rat."

"It *would* be inconvenient to appear unannounced at dinnertime."

"Such bad manners," he agreed.

"But you protect Alin, too."

Val patted his sword hilt to confirm it. "He's useless with weapons, is my Alin-O. Nicks himself on a butter knife. But don't ever get in range of his fists." He chuckled reminiscently. "There's a Council Guard in Dinn whose teeth will never meet each other again unless somebody uses 'em for shirt buttons."

Glad to know the sword wasn't just for show and the pair could be counted on in a scrap, she went on to the next topic on her list. "Tell me what other spells Alin can do."

"Fire—barely. You've seen that. It's the first one taught, preparatory to kindling a Mage Globe. But he can't. There's nothing else he can do with his magic. Oh, he knows the spells down to the last syllable. But he can't work them." Val shrugged. "Something about not being able to let a teacher in to tag power sources for him. Once they found out about his sense of direction—he's as good at that as I am with time. . . ." He stopped for a moment. "I'll never forget it. St. Agvir's Day it was, at Ostinhold. I'd come for the feast. Nobody heard him scream but me and Cai—the Ostin's adopted daughter, Cailet Rille."

"Mageborn?" she asked casually, knowing the answer.

"And then some, or so Alin says. Anyway, I'm not clear on Mage things, but the Scholar who taught him Laddering did it that day—quick, hard, and dirty. It hurt him in ways I'll never understand. Desse turned purple when he found out, and nearly crisped that fool Scholar's brains for him."

Sarra didn't know magic could be painful. Would it be so for Cailet?

"They needed him fast, y'see," Val went on softly. "The only Mage who knew all the Ladders was dying. The Scholar cleaned out the old lady's mind—with her permission, I'm told, but. . . . Anyway, they needed somebody to put all that Ladder Lore into. Alin ended up with no other magic but light."

Sarra shook her head. "That must hurt him most of all."

"Speaking from experience, *Domna?*"

She lifted one shoulder, dismissing the notion. "I've gotten used to the idea. Magic isn't my share—at least, not until it's safe to be Mageborn." Resettling herself on the chair, she went on, "And call me Sarra in private."

"I hope your name isn't as appropriate as Kanto Solingirt's?" His voice was light and teasing, and she wasn't sure if there was an offer in it or not. Doubt was removed a moment later. "If so. . . ."

Men, she decided, were becoming entirely too uppity these days. Still, she liked Val, so her reply lacked the sting it might have. "You'll never know, Valirion Maurgen. Besides, your Alin-O wouldn't approve."

She felt rather than saw his astonishment. "How did you—?"

"*My* talent," Sarra purred, "is coming to a correct conclusion based on fragmentary evidence. In the vernacular it's called 'gut jumping.' Pass the tea, please."

3

The next Ladder was forty-three miles from the abandoned manor house. Solingirt did his best, but at nearly eighty he could not be expected to hike along as swiftly as the rest of them. He was incapable of Folding the trail, and Imilial Gorrst could do so only for herself. Sarra filed this bit of knowledge away—Mage abilities varied among individuals, even within families.

They made almost half the distance, but they also made an early night of it when a shepherd's hut presented itself, empty this time of year with the sheep in high summer pasture. Alin roused them early the next morning. They started walking at Fourth, the sun not even a promise over the eastern hills. When the spires of Roke Castle came into view,

Sarra sent Imilial ahead to scout the Ladder's accessibility and secure it if need be.

"And can you get us something to eat?"

"Absolutely, *Domna*. Alin, love, show me the place we're staying tonight." She set a silver-green Mage Globe to burning between them.

He didn't flinch, but his pale skin turned sickly white—and not due to the glow of magic. "You won't need that," he said in icy tones, and proceeded to draw a map in the dirt.

The awkwardness lasted until Imilial was gone. Sarra walked with Kanto Solingirt while Val went ahead with Alin. She noted that no words were said, no touches given, no obvious comfort offered. But Alin's thin, tense shoulders soon relaxed, and eventually his hand sought Val's for a brief squeeze. When daybreak peered through the hills at them, he dropped back to talk with the elderly Scholar. Sarra joined Val to take the lead.

"You and Alin," she began a bit awkwardly. "You know, I've never seen—"

"—men like us?" he interrupted bitterly.

"Two people who care so much for each other," she finished quietly. "Except for Agatine and Orlin, you're unique in my experience."

Valirion shrugged. "Sorry. It's just—I get angry sometimes. Mighty First Daughter Geria Ostin doesn't approve of us." Dark eyes glinted dangerously. "She has a new lover every other week even though she's married. But according to her, *we're* immoral."

Sarra saw nothing unusual in Geria's sexual habits, although she personally deplored promiscuity. A woman took lovers as she pleased, causing scandal only if she had no children to carry on her Name, and if her husband disliked it . . . well, that was the husband's problem. But because she remembered Geria, she knew the real source of the First Daughter's disapproval, and thus knew what Val would say next.

"Alin could fetch a good price. He's Blood. They make expensive husbands. Geria had a girl all picked out for him and Alin told her to—well, let's just say he left Ostinhold."

"And . . . your own family?"

"Mother's glad she won't have to pay to make a husband of me."

So much for Glenin's wedding present, the abolishment of

Bloods and Tiers, Sarra told herself. The system survived because, of course, everybody knew what everybody else was. Sons with Val's preferences were still welcomed in lower Tiers; marriages need not be purchased for them. The marriage mart went on unchanged. It was obscene, almost as bad as slavery. It had long been on her List of What Must Be Changed for purely personal reasons; now she had another example before her.

Her mission to Ryka capsulized something else she intended to change. Attrition due to war, disease, or lack of female heirs had extinguished thousands of Names. Slegin would die with Agatine. Surely the Census Ministry—which had subsumed the Ministry of Bloods and Tiers—could trace descendants and encourage revival of lost Names. And for those in danger of extinction, sons could be allowed to pass their Name to a second or third daughter. . . .

Sarra became aware that her companion's mood had darkened still further. She smiled. "Cheer up, Val. I bet it just kills Geria to see her Blooded brother consorting with a son of a Third like you!"

He snorted, then laughed aloud. "Don't it just!"

Solingirt did his best to hurry, but even so it was nearly Tenth when they reached the Old Wall. During the rampages of the self-styled Grand Duchess Veller Ganfallin several centuries ago, Roke Castle's citizens had withstood a long siege by withdrawing to the innermost fastness of the keep. The Old Wall had been demolished by the Grand Duchess' army, but she hadn't taken Roke Castle. The stones of the Old Wall were later carted away to build new homes. In one of these, Imilial Gorrst waited.

Alin practically pounced on the dinner spread on a rickety table.

"Slow down, boy!" the Warrior Mage laughed. "There's plenty! I didn't dare buy enough of everything for five, but there's choice to make up for it."

"Oh, you know him," Val said. "If he sticks a fork in it and it stops wriggling, he'll eat it." Snagging a crab cake right out of Alin's fingers, he munched, swallowed, and went on. "It's Fifth less three minutes in Cantratown. We have plenty of time to eat before the place wakes up tomorrow morning."

Alin returned the favor by stealing Val's slice of onion

bread. "We've time for a rest as well. I plan to arrive in the middle of the night."

Temptation to ask *which* night was squelched by Sarra's original vow of ignorance for sanity's sake. If it was Alin's job to keep track of where they were, it was Val's to keep track of when. So she ate her share of food, and between mouthfuls asked why this house was deserted.

"Because we arranged it to be, of course," Val replied. "There are places like this all over Lenfell. Some more comfortable than others, truly told, but all Warded and safe. Imi took care of the Wards before we got here, and she'll set them again when we leave."

"Ah," Sarra said, as if she understood. *When I find Gorynel Desse, he's got a lot of explaining to do.* Turning to the Warrior Mage, she went on, "Is there a chance this place has some extra clothes? Especially cloaks. The ones you're wearing just beg the Council Guard to come after us."

Kanto Solingirt drew himself straight, mustache bristling and shaggy brows knotted over his nose. "I gave up my regimentals when the Captal ordered it for safety's sake, though it was a coward's decree. I similarly gave up my position at St. Mittru's Academy, even though I am a teacher born. But I will *not* give up my colors or the sigils of honored scholarship! I am not ashamed of being Mageborn, still less of the years I have served Lenfell as best I—"

"Fa," Imilial said softly. "We put the others in danger."

He harrumphed and looked sour, but eventually nodded. Privately Sarra both understood and deplored his attitude. She hated being unable to claim her own ancient name, colors, and sigil. Claiming them, however, was the quickest way she knew to get arrested. The choice of a coward, or the only choice for survival?

She changed the subject. "Have either of you ever been to Cantratown?"

"We left the Mage Academy when Mother died," Imilial said. "Hunt week, 941. We've been in Kenrokeshir ever since. A quiet life with few out-Shir visitors, so I doubt we'll be recognized—if that's what you're thinking."

"Exactly. I apologize for the indignity, but all four of you are now my personal slaves. Scholar Solingirt, my steward. Warrior Gorrst, you don't look anything like a maidservant, so I think we'll make you my guard, along with the cousins over there. Now, what was this about needing to be invisible?"

Valirion paused in emptying a wine bottle down his throat. He winked at Alin. "Told you."

His cousin shrugged. "What you told me was, 'She'll think of everything.' I haven't heard much yet about getting us into the Ryka Archives."

Sarra choked. "Where?"

"For evidence," Alin said. "We're to steal damaging documents."

"To win support for the Rising from those who need written proof," Val finished. "Any ideas, Sarra?"

"My dear children," Solingirt smiled, "that's what *I'm* for."

Alin traded a glance with Val, who cleared his throat. "Begging your pardon, but—"

"Oh, I won't skulk about by night. Nothing so energetic. There are easier ways of acquiring documentation. How do you think a Fourth Tier family like mine 'proved' they owned ten square miles of Rokemarsh?"

"Fa—?" his daughter asked faintly. "You *forged*—?"

He shrugged. "Simple enough. A good hand for classical calligraphy, a spell to age the paper and ink. The Vekke Blood never even missed the land, because we sold it back to them and used the proceeds as my dower. You see, Imi, your late unlamented grandmother wanted the Ladymoon wrapped in pink ribbon to compensate for wasting a Gorrst daughter on a miserable Solingirt."

Val grinned. "So you sold land you didn't own to the people who already owned it."

"No, we bought it first," the old man corrected. "Through the Vekkes, helped a bit by funds they provided."

"What about your share of the Solingirt Dower Fund?" Sarra asked, intrigued by the deception, irritated by its necessity—and more than a little confused.

"Ah, my dear, you don't know the Solingirts. Our Dower Fund has been a joke for three generations. All the First Daughters pay in as the law requires—but they pay in promises, not cash. And the year Imi's mother married me, sixteen or seventeen of my cousins also married. As the third son of a fifth daughter of a very junior branch, I was last on the list for my rightful share."

"But—that's illegal," Sarra protested.

"Easy to see you've never been part of betrothal negotiations," he said, smiling. "My predicament is nothing if not common. Besides that, the Gorrsts are odd about money. That which generates from land is vastly superior. If, for instance, I'd been a Talenir, with five barren mountaintops on Shellinkroth to our Name, it would've been a different thing entirely."

"But the Talenirs are Fourths—and one of the poorest families on Lenfell!" Sarra exclaimed.

"Their poverty is tied to land," Solingirt said. "My Name's money comes from trade. Tainted."

Val glowed with admiration. "Let me get this straight. You secretly bought land from the Vekkes with money secretly provided by the Vekkes which you then sold *back* to the Vekkes to gain a dower to marry a Gorrst. I love it!"

"Cousin Mittrian Solingirt's idea. He acted as my Advocate in the matter—he was Tevis Vekke's husband, you know. It amused them both no end to fool Mara Gorrst. By the way, you have a sister named for Tevis, Alin. And she was *your* great-grandmother," he added to the startled Valirion.

"Oh, Val! Does that make us too consanguineous to be married?" Imi teased.

He gave a languishing sigh. "Alas, darling *Domna,* let us simply enjoy each other, with illicity adding felicity—"

" 'Illicity?' " she echoed. "Is that a word?"

Alin pulled a face and rolled his eyes ceilingward.

Solingirt rapped his knuckles on a wall. "To return to the point! I expect to be busy with pen and paper until spring, once we get wherever it is we're going to end up."

Sarra thought it over. "Do you know Anniyas's handwriting? The paper she uses? The ink? The pen?"

"I've several examples of her signature—"

Oh, splendid. "Alin. Do you want official Council records or Anniyas' private papers?"

He went very still. Valirion started to say something; Sarra hushed him with a gesture. Alin's blue eyes began to sparkle wickedly.

"Very good, *Domna.* It's not the whole Council we want to discredit. They're mostly harmless. I was told to take whatever seemed suspicious. But if we—"

"Ha!" Valirion had tumbled to it. "Anniyas's quarters! Pick up a couple of her letters for our Scholarly forger, get out fast—and if we see anything interesting along the way, grab it."

Sarra nodded. "She may or may not have been foolish enough to have written down anything incriminating. If she has and you find it, good. If not—all we need is a sample of her handwriting to provide incriminations to order."

Alin grinned, a golden wolf. "*Domna,* you're a quick study."

"Gut jumping," Valirion muttered, dark eyes dancing.

"Thank you," Sarra replied. "We'll refine this when we get to Ryka. I'm still waiting to hear why we have to be invisible at Cantratown."

4

Alin sat the watch that night. Again Sarra woke in the early hours, and again she learned things about her unacknowledged cousins. Alin was slower to speak than Valirion, but when he chose to speak, it was with total honesty.

Still, it took Sarra half an hour to get him started.

She began at the logical place: Ostinhold. She asked about his mother, which led to Sarra's side of the story of Pinderon and the Minstrel, and thence to his siblings, and with Sarra's prompting to the topic of his sisters' marriages. Lenna and Tevis were now husbanded; Miram was resisting.

"She's just your age, *Domna,*" Alin said. "The whole idea bores her."

"I don't want to get married, either," Sarra admitted. "It seems an absurd amount of bother for very little reward."

"You're too young to be that cynical."

"Twenty-two—a year older than you!"

"You've traveled in state," he replied with a shrug. "Welcomed as a First Daughter, celebrated, honored. I sneak my way around the world's shadows, and the last thing I ever want is to be recognized as a son of the Ostin Blood. I prefer it so—but that sort of life makes five years to every one."

"Val seems to enjoy it."

"He's a Wastrel—in every sense of the word—whose one

saving grace is that he cheerfully admits it. The Maurgens are well rid of him." Alin laughed almost soundlessly.

"I hear you've known each other since you were children."

"I think we knew each other before we were born." He cast a quick glance at her, hunching a shoulder against the doorframe. "Does that sound . . . ?"

"No, Alin. It doesn't sound odd at all." *Agatine and Orlin are the same . . . and my own parents, before—before.* "It's a feeling I'd like to have one day. Except—I'd be so scared of losing it," she confessed. "Wearing it out. Watching it die."

"That's just it, Sarra. It *doesn't* wear out and it *can't* die. Nor can it be lost." He hesitated, picking splinters from around the lock for something to do with his hands. "Just after I learned about my magic, Val left The Waste for nearly a year—a conspiracy between his grandmother and my sister Geria. I didn't have an easy time with magic. When they sent him away, I expected I'd go mad. Actually *waited* for it to happen. But it didn't. Because Val was here." Alin placed two fingertips to his forehead, then his chest.

Did Auvry Feiran still remember Maichen Ambrai? Had he been a part of her until she died?

"You're lucky, you two," she murmured.

"I know. It isn't that neither of us is scared. But everybody is, one way or another. You just get on with things."

Sarra tucked her chilled hands into her pockets. "You're too young to be so wise, Alin-O," she said fondly.

For the first time she saw him smile—sweet, self-mocking, tender, his was a smile to mend hearts, not break them.

"If I were wise, would I be doing these crazy things?" He shifted to the window, peering through the grime to moonlit farmland outside. When he turned, the delightful smile was gone. "You were singing earlier. What was it?"

"Was I?"

He hummed a few notes. "D'you know the rest? The words?"

"It's just a song my little brother Jeymi was singing the morning I left Roseguard." *How many mornings ago?* Alin was right: this kind of life made weeks out of days. "It's a children's song."

"I know."

"Then why did you ask—"

"Do you know the verses?" he interrupted.

"Some of them." She searched for the beginning words, and when she had them nearly fell off her chair. "Alin! It's—"

"Yes. 'The Ladder Song.' Sing me what you know."

"Oh, you don't want me to do that. I couldn't carry a tune if it was strapped to my back. I'll just talk the verses."

The nonsense song accompanied a jumping game nobody played after the age of ten or so. She supposed the succession of repeating opposites made it a teaching song of sorts, but otherwise it made little sense.

> *Long or short, short or long*
> *This is called the Ladder Song*
> *Near or far, far or near*
> *Takes you there or brings you here*
> *Far or near, near or far*
> *Doesn't matter where you are*
> *Down or up, up or down*
> *Climb the ladder round and round*
> *Up or down, down or up*
> *Ladder in a rocky cup*

"So far, the same," Alin mused. When she looked blank, he continued, "Each couplet describes a Ladder. 'Round and round' is the Double Spiral Stair at the Octagon Court. 'Rocky cup' is a dry well in Bleynbradden."

"Of course! Alin, it's brilliant! Who'd suspect a list of Ladders hidden in a children's song?"

"Truly told, Sarra. But it has many versions, and changes in different parts of Lenfell. Children add or lose things, or mistake one word for another. Bards call it lyric shift. I want to hear the version they sing at Roseguard."

She began again, dredging up memories ten years gone. She'd gotten rather good at that sort of thing.

" 'Sick or well, well or sick/Ladder built with fingers quick'—" Sarra almost bounced in her chair with excitement. "St. Maurget Quickfingers!"

"That's how I read it, too, but I don't know the reference. Keep going."

> *Well or sick, sick or well*
> *Ladder in the shepherd's dell*
> *Big or little, little or big*

> *Ladder of the happy pig*
> *Little or big, big or little*
> *Ladder made of acorn brittle*

She broke off. "I always thought that an odd one. I mean, brittle-sweet is made with all kinds of nuts and seeds, but acorns are too tough. So if 'brittle' is an adjective, it's wildly inappropriate."

Alin wasn't interested in a culinary analysis. *"Acorn? Not almond?"*

"*Acorn.* As for the 'happy pig'—" She fell silent, and another jump landed her on both mental feet. "Where do acorns come from?" As pale eyes darkened under frowning brows, she laughed. "What's your Name sigil, Alin Ostin?"

He groaned faintly and covered his face with his hands. "St. Alilen, patron of crazies, have mercy on this poor madman! *Another* Ladder on Ostin lands?"

"Shake the family oak tree next time you're home, and see what falls out," Sarra advised. "Ever been to Domburron?"

Alin let his hands fall to his thighs. "Only when I can't avoid it. Why?"

"Just off the Circle there's a toy shop called the Pink Piglet. I never saw a happier grin on a shop sign in my life. Or on a genuine pig, come to that."

"The Pink—?" He rallied. "What were you doing in a toy shop?"

She fought a blush, wondering if Alin had gut-jumping abilities of his own. Almost fourteen when Agatine and Orlin took her to Domburron, she'd not been too old to scorn a new gown for her favorite doll. . . .

"Buying presents for my little brothers, of course. Let's go through the rest of the verses. We might end up solving them all tonight!"

5

They didn't, of course. Identification of the Ladders hidden in the big/little verse was the extent of their detections. But though Sarra was frustrated, Alin was as pleased as the piglet on the toy-shop sign.

Alin knew only those Ladders neither lost nor forgotten. Of the possibly hundreds once extant, a mere twenty-six Ladders—thirteen pairs—were still in use. Many were destroyed when Ambrai burned—that was why they'd burned it—and many more when Malerris Castle met the same fate. For, as the final line of any version of the song attested, *"Ladders set afire die."* Alin theorized that Ambrai and Malerris Castle were two of three major hubs—the former because centers for Mages, Bards, and Healers had been there, the latter because it was the home of the Lords of Malerris. He was sure the other hub was Ryka. Though he knew of only two Ladders there, to Ambrai and to Shellinkroth, for governmental convenience Ryka must have had Ladders to all the Shirs.

It made sense to Sarra. She was eager to get back to Roseguard and her purloined library and look for the oldest and most authoritative versions of the song. Then Alin wouldn't have to guess about lyric shift, added verses, or dropped lines. Her Ladder Rat would solve all the riddles, the Rising would have a network of swift transportation, and this journey would turn out even more profitable than she hoped.

Roke Castle Lighthouse *(North or south, south or north/ Ladder shines the lightning forth)* was easily approached and impossible to enter. Unless, of course, one happened to have along a Mage whose Invisibility spell had been the envy of three Captals. At Half-Eighth, while the keepers were in their common room eating lunch, two Mage Guardians, two power-blocked Mageborns, and a Wastrel climbed the winding stairs to the top floor.

Sarra went through the Blanking Ward much more easily this time, knowing what to expect. This made it easier on Alin. She opened her eyes thousands of miles, two seasons, and eight hours away in Cantratown.

As promised, it was the middle of the night. Kanto Solingirt immediately respelled for Invisibility, however, for the Ladder was located in a cellar of the Affe family compound. Fourth Tier, nearly as numerous as the Ostins, and staunch supporters of First Councillor Anniyas, an Affe discovery of fugitive Mages would be unmitigated disaster.

Once out the back door, however, the elderly Scholar let

the spell drop—and nearly dropped to the cobbles with weariness. His daughter and Val supported him to the main street of this rough part of town, where all five then mimed the results of a late drunken night. Sarra, leaning against Alin's shoulder, nearly leaped out of her skin when he began howling the unspeakably obscene chorus of "Bower Lad's Lament." Windows opened above to let down a rain of curses and a brick that narrowly missed Imilial. But no Constable of the Watch appeared to chastise, warn, arrest, or otherwise silence the group.

The boundary between Lesser and Greater Cantratown, though unmarked, was as clear as the winter moons in the cloudless night sky. The five staggered down a block lined with cheap stores and broken cobbles, crossed an intersection, turned left, and found themselves in a neighborhood in good repair. Trees lined the street in front of tidy shops, the paint was almost new, and a Watch post was visible two streets ahead. Alin shut up and everyone else straightened up. Six fast blocks later they were being warmly welcomed to Garvedian House.

"Sorry about the time, Luse," Imilial apologized to the young woman who let them inside. "It was noon where we came from." She settled her exhausted father on a soft chair in the parlor.

"Well, rest what's left of the night. Hungry? No, don't answer that, Alin Ostin!" Lusira Garvedian playfully poked him in the ribs. He pretended to collapse, mortally wounded, onto a couch—giving the lie to Val's remark that pretty girls made him nervous.

Although to describe Lusira as "pretty" was an injustice. She was, quite simply, staggeringly beautiful. No older than twenty-five, clad in a snowy nightrobe that did nothing to conceal a spectacular figure and everything to emphasize a dusky brown complexion, she had the kind of long-limbed, doe-eyed, full-lipped beauty that Sarra—round-cheeked, tilt-nosed, and uncompromisingly short—had always envied.

"Advar and Elomar arrived yesterday," Lusira went on. "They're asleep upstairs. As you ought to be!" she scolded Kanto Solingirt. "Val, make yourself useful and take him up to the corner bedroom."

After introductions all around, a servant came in with food. They'd eaten the remains of last night's dinner at dawn back in Kenrokeshir, so the array of duck-egg omelets, fried

venison strips, potato jumble, and tangy lemonade was more
than appreciated. Still, eating breakfast by lamplight when
her senses told Sarra it was afternoon warned her that she
was falling victim to what Alin termed Ladder Lag. Much
more of this leaping around the world and Sarra was convinced she'd want lunch at midnight.

After the meal, Lusira Garvedian escorted her to a small,
pleasant room at the back of the house. Sarra lay down for
a nap. And couldn't sleep.

All these people seemed to know each other so well. Why
had she never heard of them? Why had Agatine and Orlin
insulated her from the Rising? Or was it a more inclusive
conspiracy—with Gorynel Desse giving the orders? In any
case, what had they been protecting her from?

Or saving her for?

What, damn it?

It was no surprise to be in this house. Sarra remembered
Mage Captal Leninor Garvedian quite well. How many other
houses held relatives of Guardians killed at Ambrai? Did
they all shelter agents of the Rising? Or did the majority
shudder when their dead were mentioned, and shut their
doors?

Suddenly she jerked upright in bed, wide awake without
realizing she'd been asleep. Frail winter dawn outlined the
curtained windows, but the house was silent. No—some
sound had awakened her, alerted her. She rose quietly and
looked outside. Nothing but a little walled garden, bare but
for a few bushes and two beds of straggly winter herbs.
Along its dirt path hurried a tall, cloaked man. Valirion?
Yes—the long strides were familiar now, the jut of an elbow
as he kept one hand on the knife concealed in his right trouser pocket.

That he could betray them never crossed her mind; that he
could risk their safety on some private business was unthinkable; so it must be something to do with the Rising. Something else she hadn't a clue about.

Well, that was going to change. Now.

Hauling on her boots, Sarra slipped along a hallway to the
garden door. Lusira Garvedian stood there, exquisite beauty
framed in the open door against a winter as stark as her
black gown. She stared at nothing as she sipped tea from a
porcelain cup—Rine make, to Sarra's eye, and worth a small
fortune.

"Where did he go?" Sarra asked—rudely, she knew, but she'd had enough of not knowing what she had a right to know.

"He'll return in good time," Lusira replied, still watching something only she could see.

"Where from?" She paused, then added, "Please tell me, *Domna*."

Lusira closed the door and turned. The sadness in those huge dark eyes caught at Sarra's throat. With a graceful gesture she invited Sarra to follow her into the dining room, where the table was laid for another breakfast. The service was more of the same Rine porcelain: cups, saucers, plates, platters, and bowls in subtle tones of autumn green.

Sarra spared the service not a hundredth of the admiration it deserved, drawn instead to the sideboard where a silver clock, gears visible behind a glass door, ticked the last few minutes of Fourth. Such clocks that told the week as well as the hour were rare, but its uniqueness was not what caught Sarra's eye. To her, this clock was anything but unique. It was twin to one she'd seen a thousand times in Allynis Ambrai's bedchamber. On a round mother-of-pearl face each hour was marked by a tiny octagon of Ambraian blue onyx. The thirty-six weeks and the Wraithenday were shown on a cylinder that revolved around the bottom, each with the sigil of its saint or, for the weeks of solstices and equinoxes, many-flared golden suns. She knew it was not her grandmother's clock by the small lion's head week-marker; the one belonging to Lady Allynis had an acorn there instead, for her husband Gerrin Ostin.

"You recognize it, of course," Lusira Garvedian murmured. "A gift from your grandmother to her good friend the Captal. Friends spared it from what happened at Ambrai. Do you prefer your tea strong?"

Sarra turned to find Lusira at the serving cart. "Yes, please."

In total silence but for the soft tick of the clock she was privileged to witness Lusira turn a small ritual into a work of art. Delicate hands selected fresh leaves, ground them with a fine marble mortar-and-pestle set, tied them in an unbleached muslin bag, and settled the bag in a silver pot. Boiling water was poured, and as the tea steeped Lusira considered the array of porcelain cups on the cart. All were different, and the selection depended on a host's intentions toward a guest. The one chosen for Sarra had a pattern of wheatsheaves: sigil of St. Velireon the Provider.

Lusira offered the filled cup. Sarra inhaled the fragrance, sipped three times, and nodded approval. Grandmother had performed this ritual rather absently, usually too busy talking to pay proper attention to the nuances. But in some of Lusira's gestures, in the careful and elegant preparation of the leaves in total silence, Sarra was reminded painfully of her mother.

Manners now dictated that she sit at the oval table to indicate acceptance of Lusira's hospitality. She was barely seated when the lady spoke.

"He went to visit his son."

"His—?"

"His son," she repeated, "who is four years old and has no official father. Val must see him in more secrecy than any work he does for the Rising."

"Divorced?" *Like my parents. . . .*

"Never married. She's a Blood. He's Third Tier. Legally meaningless these days, but socially. . . ." Lusira ended with a small, eloquent shrug.

"A father has rights." *Even Auvry Feiran? Does he have a right to see me or Cailet?*

"Not unless his Name appears on the Census birth registry."

"But that's not fair! Unless a man is a criminal, or dangerous to his children, he ought to be allowed to see his child."

Until now she'd never thought about it. The issue hadn't even been one of those abstracts she loved to thrash out with Agatine and Orlin. But because Val had become a friend, the matter had become personal. And suddenly she wondered how many more social and political issues she'd find standing in front of her, made flesh and blood.

Worse, how many she'd never recognize *until* they stood in front of her.

Sheltered? Insulated? Protected? She'd been wrapped in a damned cocoon.

But—would I have been ready before now? Agatine and Orlin taught me the thinking part of it, how to reason through an issue without getting emotionally involved. Thinking is clean, logical. But people's lives are full of feeling, all convoluted and confusing, and—

"Valirion *is* a criminal as far as the Council is concerned. That's all the recommendation the Firennos Blood needs."

"But it's not *fair*," Sarra repeated.

"Much in life is not."

She felt her jaw muscles quiver—an outward sign of tension others could read, a habit she was trying to break—and consciously relaxed. "I promise, *Domna* Lusira, that things will become infinitely more fair very soon."

"How vehement you are!" She laughed, a sound Sarra would have found exquisite if she had not thought it directed at her. She flushed angrily. But Lusira's next words corrected her misunderstanding. "I thank the Saints for you, Sarra Liwellan! If anyone will make better this sorry world, it is you."

"You bet I will. I—" She started as five high, piercing notes rang from somewhere in the house. "What was *that?*"

Lusira winced. "Breakfast."

"Again?" Sarra asked, smiling. "It sounds like a shrine bell, summoning the starving!"

"If only it *was* limited to mealtimes!" She cupped her chin in her hand, elbow on the table, and sighed. "The silly thing rings every hour from Fifth to Thirteenth. It's an exact copy of the bell—*not* to scale, praise all Saints—at St. Miramili's near Wyte Lynn Castle. Our Name built the shrine ages ago, and with this house I inherited—to my hourly regret—that damned bell!"

Half an hour later they were all seated. No one remarked Val's absence. It was as if he'd never been there to be gone. Joining them were two men in Guardian black, both wearing the green sash and silver herb-sprig collar pins of the Healer Mage. Sarra bit back a warning to change clothes; Imilial would take care of it, and Sarra would not be compelled to tromp on them with her authority first thing.

For she *was* Authority on this journey. Not because she was a Blood or a First Daughter or Agatine's heir, but because she alone of them all was unhunted by the Council Guard.

And because she *had* been protected; because she *had* lived in a cocoon. Her thinking was clear and unimpassioned, not muddled by emotional conflicts and personal troubles.

Except for their regimentals, the two Healers were as opposite as pairs in the Ladder Song. Advar Senison, youngest

son of the First Daughter of the Prime branch of that Third
Tier family, was short, pleasantly plump, pink-faced, and a
true gallant. He bowed and flourished greetings to the
women, with many compliments on the obviously superb
state of their health as evidenced by Lusira's glowingly
flawless complexion, Imilial's delightfully sparkling eyes,
and Sarra's gloriously glossy hair.

Elomar Adennos, as grim and dry and uncompromising as
his Fourth Tier family's main holding in The Waste, was in
his mid-forties, perhaps six or eight years older than Advar
Senison. He said exactly nothing when introduced. He bent
his head over no woman's hand. Tall, thin-shanked, plain
and brown as an earthenware plate, he was an unlikely object for affection. When Lusira rose from her chair to kiss
him an extremely affectionate good morning, Sarra forgot
her manners and frankly stared.

After the meal they repaired to the bookroom. Lusira and
Imilial wrote letters; the three Mages talked with each
other—or, rather, Solingirt and Senison talked while Adennos sat silent; Sarra looked over the books and temporarily
considered trying to interest Alin in a collection of song-
sheets. But he ignored everything in favor of sitting at the
window, staring through lace curtains at the street.

When an informal lunch was served in the library at Half-
Eighth, Sarra was pleasantly surprised to find that this was
the meal her stomach was expecting. But Val, also expected,
did not show up. Sarra's head filled with all sorts of disasters and she ached with curiosity about this unsuspected son.
Four years old—what was his name? Which Firennos was
his mother? Did some sympathetic family member or nurse
sneak the child to a secret meeting with his father now and
then? She wasn't sure she ought to ask Val. She didn't dare
ask Alin.

It was getting on for a dusky Eleventh, and Sarra was getting frantic, when Val finally returned. He was loud with
false cheer and there were scars in his dark eyes. Alin took
him out into the back garden for a time while the others got
ready for the trip to Shellinkroth.

At length the pair returned. Lusira led them all upstairs to
a door guarded by a pair of carved lions crouching above the
lintel.

Sarra whispered to Alin, " 'Ladder in a lion's lair'?"

He nodded. "Garvedian family sigil, and a bad joke."

The circular "lion's lair"—featuring a fashionable Tillinshir Savannah decor that included a fresco of gamboling galazhi fawns, woven grass mats, and a brass lion head for a tub spigot—was a bathroom.

6

The Ladder on Shellinkroth was round, too, of course. Alin supplied the identification from a verse Sarra didn't know.

" 'Clear and fine, or rainy weather/Ladder of the silver feather.' "

Then he sneezed.

"Tell me, Kanto," Val asked, rubbing his own nose, "was the placement of a Ladder wholly dependant on its maker's sense of humor?"

"Not always." The old man brushed feathers off his cloak and mustache. "They worked with what they had—and because a dovecote is round. . . ."

The doves fluttered at their appearance, then fled in a flurry. Exiting by the keyhole-shaped door—through which pudgy Advar Senison barely fit—they stepped out into a sweet summery night. The sea was a star-sparked darkness far away. Once they descended a mile or two down the trail, it would vanish in folds of the Tarre Mountains.

"I imagine isolated Ladders are best," Imilial Gorrst said, picking feathers from her hair. "I'd hate to think what would happen, for instance, if someone arrived in Luse's bathroom while she was in it."

"You may hate the idea," Val retorted, "but it does wonders for me."

By the blue-white light of his softly kindled Mage Globe, Elomar Adennos favored him with a long, level look that quelled him instantly. Alin cleared his throat, mouth twitching in amusement.

"The cote-holder comes by a couple of times a week," he said to Sarra. "But this isn't one of his nights to sleep over. We'll wait in his shelter until daylight, then start for Havenport."

Sarra had forgotten all about the ship that supposedly was taking her to Ryka. What day *was* it, anyhow?

Val's happily malicious grin told her that asking was a mistake. "Count the night we left Roseguard as the first, or the ninth of Snow Sparrow. We spent the first, second, and third nights, which is to say the ninth, tenth, and eleventh, and the fourth night, which was first—of Candleweek—in Kenrokeshir. We lost the fifth and second between Kenroke and Cantrashir. We just came from Half-Eleventh on the sixth—or third—in Cantratown back to Half-First of the same day, which means that we've caught the night we lost."

"Everybody got that?" Alin inquired innocently.

"Very funny," Imilial growled.

When Advar Senison asked plaintively, "But what *day* is it?", Alin clapped a hand over his partner's mouth.

The nearby shelter, plain and spare, boasted a fire-ring and a hole in the roof in place of a chimneyed hearth, and a projecting shelf in place of a bed. Seven people cramped it almost unbearably. After six days—or four, or whatever the hell it was—Sarra began to feel the lack of a bath.

There was little to do other than talk. Imilial did not seem so inclined, preferring to polish her sword and various knives produced from unlikely locations about her person. The two Healer Mages busied themselves secreting their telltale sashes and collar pins in the lining of their cloaks. Kanto Solingirt stretched out on the bedshelf, arms folded on his breast like a corpse laid out for burning. Val took the watch outside, motionless on a rock. So Sarra fixed on Alin as the evening's source of information.

He saw her coming. A frown greeted her, but she was not one to let a little thing like masculine reluctance put her off. She sat down on the plank floor beside him, opening her mouth to ask her first question.

"Val probably wants some tea," Alin said, stood up, and took himself and his half-empty cup outside.

Sarra scowled, grabbed her cloak, and followed.

"You have to talk to me, you know," she informed the pair. "There's too much to be done, and too much I have to know before we can do it."

"It's cold out, *Domna*. Go back inside," said Alin.

She chose a rock and sat. "I know we're collecting Mages, but why these particular ones?"

Alin huddled on the ground, leaning back against Val's knees. "We can discuss it later."

"We will discuss it now."

Shrugging, he replied, "If you don't know, you can't tell."

Sarra gasped. "You can't possibly mean you don't trust me!"

"You already know more than is safe for Val and me—let alone Lusira Garvedian. If something happened—"

"Enough," Val said quietly. "She's right, Alin. She needs to know."

"It can wait."

"Oh? On board ship she'll be in her cabin playing seasick. At Ryka we'll hardly see her at all until it's time to leave, and then we'll be all over Lenfell again with hardly a breath to spare. Might as well get it over with."

Alin grunted, wreathing his arms around his shins. "You tell her, then."

"My thanks for your gracious permission, *Domni.* Sarra, the Mages we'll take to Roseguard are the best we can find. Scholars, Healers, Warriors, some of them just plain Guardians, but all of them dedicated to overthrowing Anniyas. Because all of them have personal knowledge of the Lords of Malerris."

Sarra nodded. "Then the rumors are true, and more than a few survived."

"Oh, they sacrificed a couple dozen when the Castle burned. The very old, the infirm, those who weren't soulbound to Anniyas—"

"Wait a minute. I've always known that she's working with them, but—" Sarra felt her bones freeze. Usually her gut instincts were like a sudden hot wind sweeping her mind clean of untruths and irrelevancies. This was different, this icy burning as vast and inexorable as a Wraithen Mountains glacier.

"Blessed St. Rilla," she whispered. "Anniyas *is* one of them! Mageborn!"

"Yes," Alin said in a voice that was almost a hiss. "And knowing that, you're in greater danger than you can imagine. If Feiran suspects you know anything, you'll be dead. Now do you see why ignorance was your best defense?"

Sarra hardly heard him as the words tumbled from her lips, as if the sounds must hurry to escape before the cold caught them. "When Anniyas led the Guard against that moronic Grand Duke of Domburronshir years ago, it was all arranged beforehand—to give her a great enough name and great enough power to do what she's done since—become First Councillor—and the same with the destruction of Malerris Castle, and Ambrai—" She choked on that, and her lips froze shut so that she could say no more.

Alin stared at her as if she'd gone mad. But Val was nodding. "Think it through, Alin," he said. "The Tiers were abolished for the same purpose. Likewise the persecution of Mage Guardians. It's all part of one gigantic scheme, with the purported goal of classifying and then eliminating Mageborns."

"Who told you all that?" Alin demanded. "And why didn't *I* know?"

"Ignorance is your best defense," Val quoted back at him. "There's a final piece to it, Sarra. When all magic seems gone, the Lords of Malerris will still be there. Unopposed, and unstoppable."

Sarra got her voice back somehow—and heard it fade to a horrified whisper halfway through her next words. "But before then, magic must be shown to be necessary. And history gives the example. Twice."

Valirion gave a blurt of surprise. Alin sprang to his feet as if needing physical distance between him and the implications.

"Val . . . Alin . . . there'll be a third Wraithenbeast Incursion."

And from the fear on Val's moonlit face, she knew this was something he had not been told. Perhaps Gorynel Desse didn't even know.

But it was true. She was certain of it. This was a harsh magic that had come to her, cold and dark and painful. But it had given her the truth.

"Who else could call them forth but those who long ago helped create them?" she asked, her voice hollow. "And when the whole world is terrorized and thousands are dead, and the Mage Guardians are nothing more than a memory, *then* the Lords of Malerris will be welcomed back and given anything they ask, if only they'll send the monsters back to the Wraithen Mountains and—oh, no, *no—*"

Alin scrambled to her side, supporting her while Val poured lukewarm tea down her throat. She coughed, waved them away, and rasped, "I'm all right. It just—once in a while it takes me by surprise—"

"It's your magic, trying to force its way out," Alin murmured. He warmed her hands between his own. "I know how that feels."

"Enough," Val ordered. "Go sleep this off. Alin, take her back inside."

Sarra made no protest. It had never been like this before. *Please don't let it be this way for Cailet,* she begged whatever Saint might be listening. *Don't let it hurt her.*

But as she curled on the wooden floor beneath her own cloak and atop Alin's, trying unsuccessfully to get warm again, her instincts—her magic—screamed at her to find Cailet and take her to safety. When the Wraithenbeasts came, it would be to The Waste. Where Cailet was. Where Cailet must not be.

7

The distance to the sea was much greater than it looked from the mountains. The first day, Sarra kept to herself, speaking rarely and joining the others only for meals. Exhaustion born of tired muscles and knees abused by steep descents should have let her sleep soundly that night. Instead she dreamed, and woke soaked in sweat with no memory of the nightmare.

They were due to meet their next collectible outside Havenport: Lusath Adennos, Elomar's cousin, the elderly Scholar Mage who had become Captal at Leninor Garvedian's death. Sarra was ambivalent about him: his reputation as a man, a Mage, and a Scholar was at best undistinguished, and she didn't see why they risked so much to take him back to Sheve. But he *was* the Captal, and as such knew things only Captals knew, and the Captal's survival was the duty of all Mage Guardians. Even if he was an idiot.

"Well, why do you think he was chosen?" Imilial replied when Sarra mentioned it. They were taking advantage of a sunny afternoon and a nearby stream to wash themselves and their travel-stained clothes. "The Captal's an embarrassment. Fa can't abide him. Elomar won't even speak to him, even though they're near kin." She paused. "But Elo doesn't speak to much of anyone."

"Except Lusira Garvedian?" Sarra asked innocently.

Imi actually giggled. "Saints, don't get me started on that!"

"Then tell me why Lusath Adennos was made Captal."

"Well, who better than a doddering, ineffectual old Scholar after a rampaging fury like Leninor?"

Sarra found the characterization a trifle extreme, but to comment on it would require explanation of how she knew the late Captal. *If secrets have been kept from me that I'm only now learning, I have one nobody will find out for a long while yet. I've got my nerve complaining!*

She hid a smile and knelt naked on a large, flat rock beside the stream to rinse out her shirt. "What I don't see is why what he knows can't be gathered from everyone else. Alin knows the Ladders, your father is an accomplished Scholar—Val said we're collecting the best of the Mage Guardians, in fact."

"Did he say that?" She splashed water all over her muscular body and shivered. "Oof, that's cold! I can't wait for Ryka and a hot bath!"

Sarra agreed, but any water to wash in was welcome after the searing sweat of her nightmare. "Why bring the Captal along?"

"Because there are things only a Captal knows. I'm not on the Mage Council, so I don't know the particulars. But some kind of ritual magic gives a Captal unique powers. Not that Adennos'd ever have the guts—or brains—to use them. Me, I'd like to see someone younger and more capable in the job, like Ilisa Neffe or her husband Tamosin Wolvar. Someone who isn't afraid of Anniyas."

"Like you."

"Me?" Imi laughed. "Sarra, there're two basic kinds of Warrior Mage. There's Gorynel Desse, who's fantastic with a sword but rarely uses it—because he considers using it a failure. Then there's me—all flash and fury, and when I get bored, like as not I'll pick a fight just to hear the swords ring. If he'd been Mageborn, Val would be in the middle—enjoys his skills, never gets beaten, but he'd really rather not exert himself!"

"What about Desse? Is he too old now to become Captal?"

"That may be partly it. I've heard rumors. . . ." She twitched a bare, muscled shoulder uncomfortably. "Some plan of his went awry. The Mage Council didn't favor it to begin with, and once it failed they were dead set against him."

Sarra mulled that over and was about to ask another question when Val shouted at them from a respectful distance.

"We've found a pool downstream! You ladies are welcome to first swim!"

"Not a hot bath," Imi remarked, "but it'll do. If I don't wash my hair, I'll scratch myself bald."

Leaving clean clothes draped on bushes to dry, they waded downstream. It never even occurred to Sarra that any of the men might peek; such things simply were not done. She washed her hair, then lay flat on her back like Imi to float and dream beneath the brilliant blue sky.

A commotion on the banks attracted their attention. Alin's voice was raised in outraged tones, joined by Scholar Solingirt. Both women stood in the pool—neck-deep for Imi; Sarra had to tiptoe to keep her chin clear—just in time to see Valirion race from the bushes and belly-flop into the water like a felled tree, naked as the day Sefana Maurgen birthed him and his twin brother Biron.

He surfaced laughing. "Didn't look like you were *ever* going to come out! Politeness to ladies can wait until I'm clean!"

Imilial pounced on him, forcing his head under. The battle that ensued soon engulfed Sarra—and Alin, who roared into the water to help Imi. Plump, pink Advar Senison picked his way across the pebbly bank, hands modestly covering his groin, stuck a toe into the water, then staggered with arms windmilling: Elomar Adennos—of all people—had given him a mighty push. As they joined the rowdy water fight, Sarra marveled that the grim-faced Healer could chortle like a schoolboy. She began to understand what Lusira saw in him.

In fact, she was seeing more—and more interesting—aspects of masculine anatomy than ever in her life. At first she was insulted that they should so blithely go naked before women, and moreover a woman of her rank; she was embarrassed for a few minutes more. But the atmosphere of play caught her and they were all as children together, wild and laughing and having wonderful fun.

Still, she and Imi at least showed manners and turned their backs while the men climbed out and went to dress. When they turned around again, there was a healthy glimpse of Val's bare backside as he hurried into the bushes.

"Nice ass, Val!" Imi called. "Alin has all the luck!"

Sarra choked on shock and laughter. The Warrior Mage winked at her.

"Men, my dear," she said, "are like flowers: they exist in this fair world to be admired. If we women didn't compliment them on their most admirable features, they'd pine away like roses in a heat wave, thirsting for water."

"Water, you say?" Sarra enquired sweetly. "Don't you mean fertilizer?"

"I heard that!" Val yelled from the trees.

Later, sloshing upstream to their sun-dried clothes, Sarra considered the four men's . . . features . . . and indeed found much to admire. Tarise would consider Elomar Adennos too skinny, but Sarra liked the way long muscles wrapped around long bones. Valirion was handsome and knew it, but where Imi had chosen to comment on his admittedly superior posterior, Sarra thought his shoulders more pleasing. She liked Advar Senison's solidity; not fat, but firm flesh beneath smooth skin that glistened in the water. Alin, though well-made, was bony and as narrow-waisted as a girl. Maturity might fill him out to a shorter version of his brother Taig. She fell to musing what Taig looked like naked—then tripped on a rock and landed with a splash when the image suddenly acquired coppery hair, very blue eyes, and the face of that smug, disgusting Minstrel.

"Careful," Imilial said, lending her a hand as she clambered to her feet. "These rocks are all over in Mittru's Hair moss. Makes for slippery footing."

They found their clothes and began to dress, lazy and warm in the afternoon sun. Sarra sat on a rock and drew her comb through her wet hair, eyes closed.

All at once Imilial said, "Saints, I wish I could get old Addy alone for an hour. Never knew he had such cute knees!"

"You mean you looked lower than—"

"Sarra!" The Warrior Mage pretended shock, then laughed. "You're too young to have such a mouth on you!"

"Well, it was kind of difficult to miss," Sarra responded

innocently. Then, after a moment's hesitation: "Imi, why is Alin's different?"

Now she pretended confusion. "Alin's what?"

Sarra cleared her throat. "Umm . . . his . . . *you* know."

The Warrior Mage grinned over her shoulder. "And where were *your* eyes, my girl?"

Sarra blushed hotly. "It's different," she insisted.

"Different how? Bigger? That's nothing to signify, you know. Matter of fact, the best time I ever had was with a man no longer than—"

"Imi!" She splashed water at the Mage. "You know what I mean!"

Taking pity on Sarra, she answered, "It's a custom with the Ostins and a few other families. They cut off that bit of skin at birth. No one knows why. But since it doesn't affect a woman's enjoyment, nobody thinks much about it." She laughed softly. "You can take my word for the enjoyment part."

Curiosity satisfied, Sarra nodded. A minute later she asked, "Imi . . . do you think men talk about women the way women do about men?"

Imi paused and developed a pensive expression. "You know, I've never considered it. I'm sure they notice, but. . . . Those with a proper upbringing don't discuss such things, of course. It's not decent. Some men probably *do* dissect us the way we do them, but only in private."

"When they give compliments, they always stick to eyes and lips and hair, that sort of thing," Sarra mused. "All the ballads are the same, with maybe ankles if the Bard is daring."

"Commenting on anything lower than the neck is vulgar," she agreed. "And a vulgar idea it is, that they'd say about our bottoms what I said about Val's!"

By the time they were clothed and combed and had rejoined the men, Kanto Solingirt was napping so peacefully that no one had the heart to disturb him. The men went foraging to resupply their stores of food. Advar Senison went fishing. Half an hour later, Imi wandered off. Sarra hid a grin.

They feasted that evening on fish stuffed with herbs and baked in leaves, a delicious vegetable stew, and berries soaked in liquor contributed by Healer Adennos (his flask of

Medicinal Purposes Only brandy). They slept under the open
sky, and Sarra had no dreams.

8

On the way down to the sea the next day, they passed a
pretty little All Saints Shrine of the triangular type popular
many centuries ago. Six slim, square wooden columns, one
at each apex and midpoint, were carved and painted with
Saints' sigils. Sarra had seen a similar shrine of marble in
the hills above Firrense, but that one had still had its roof.
This was open to the sky.

"How old, do you think?" Imilial asked her father.

Alin and Val kept walking. Sarra paused with the Mages,
interested in the answer, knowing the question was an excuse to let the Scholar rest.

"Count the Saints," he replied. "More than thirty-four,
and it dates back before the official Calendar."

"I thought age was indicated by the dedication of the entry pillar," Sarra remarked. "Fielto is on the one in Gierkenshir, they say it's very old. And very lovely as well, all
carved in marble."

"If it's that green-veined stone from Bleynbradden, date it
to 550 or so. The quarry wasn't opened until then." Solingirt
gave a self-deprecating shrug. "You pick up a lot of odd bits,
reading. I'm utterly stultifying at parties."

"Mother always said you could clear a room in a minute
flat," his daughter teased fondly.

Advar Senison—whose Healer Mage pins were symbolic
sprigs plucked from the wreath sigil of St. Feleris—was
gathering wildflowers, obviously intending an offering to the
patron of physicians. Sarra decided to honor her own Name-
Saint—and Caitiri the Fiery-Eyed, too, as long as she was at
it.

"Stay away from there!" Alin shouted.

So startled that by accident she tore a flower up by the
roots, Sarra straightened and stared at him. "What?"

"You heard me! Don't go near it!" he yelled back over his
shoulder, and kept walking.

Elomar Adennos spoke the first full sentence Sarra had ever heard from him. "There is a Ladder within."

"A Malerris Ladder," Imilial added uneasily, pointing at the carved entry column.

Squinting in bright sunshine, Sarra saw the wooden relief of Chevasto's Loom, complete with thread-heavy shuttles ready for weaving. Above it were the towers and spires of the great castle in Seinshir, rising over a craggy waterfall; impossible to mistake identification or meaning.

She took her scant handful of flowers forward anyway. After a moment Advar Senison followed. She found the right column—with Caitiri's Flameflower carved right below Sirrala's Flower Crown. Finding them together was a good omen, she swore to herself, and defiantly placed her offering.

Pausing, she squinted to see inside. Several circles were marked out on the floor, as expected. Most were tile, with grass and flowers springing up around. But in the center, free of encroaching greenery, a hollow circle of copper glinted in the sunlight, wide enough for four or five people to stand within.

"Sarra!" Val shouted. "Come on! Malerris Castle was torched years ago! The Ladder is dead!"

No, it's not, she thought, liquid ice trickling down her spine. The copper was cared-for, polished, untarnished. If the Ladder at the other end was dead, why was this circle so well-maintained?

She lengthened her strides to catch up with Val and Alin. "What happens if someone tries to use one Ladder in a pair when the other has been destroyed?"

Alin gave her an angry glance. Val asked mildly, "Are you volunteering? You sensed the magic around the Ladders we've used so far, right? That's the Blanking Ward. It's part of the connection between certain places. If there's no magic at one end, there's no connection. Nowhere to go."

Alin finished for him, "You'd end up with the Saints or the Wraiths, and as far as I'm concerned there's nothing to choose between them!"

They were being unconscionably rude—again—but she shelved the reprimand once more for a more appropriate moment. "We *do* know where the Ladder leads. Malerris Castle." Sarra clasped a wrist in each hand, halting them. And in an admittedly faulty voice, made the more so by excitement, she sang, " 'Spring or summer, summer or spring/ Ladder in the copper ring.' "

"So?" Alin almost snarled at her.

She described the copper circle within the temple. "Why should it be so carefully kept if the Ladder at the other end is useless?"

"Maybe the shepherds weed it."

"If so, Alin, then why not the tiles? Why just the copper ring? Have you ever heard of any other place with copper set into the floor like that?"

"Could be an inn sign, or a jeweler's, or any number of things."

"What are you so afraid of? If it's a Ladder, and it's usable, then—"

Alin tore his wrist from her grasp. "Because the damned Mage who shoveled Ladder Lore into me until I choked on it included some with no match that he knew of—and the last time I tried to pair two Ladders, Val and I nearly died!"

He stormed off, leaving Sarra speechless.

"I understand your curiosity," Val said softly. "But you have to understand his reluctance."

When they stopped for the night, Alin sat apart from them all. Not even Val spoke to him. He curled tight into his bedroll alone, far from the fire.

Sarra woke to someone shaking her shoulder. "Go 'way," she mumbled.

"Wake up, Sarra," Alin insisted. "I know which one it is."

Sleep-fuddled, she opened her eyes. A few delicate threads of sunlight wove through the trees, all of them seeming to seek Alin's bright hair. *Like Cailet,* Sarra thought, and was instantly awake.

"I know the matching verse. 'Fall or winter, winter or fall/ Ladder near the waterfall.' I've seen a waterfall in dreams, and Malerris Castle above. That kind of dream always scares me. That's how I know it's one of the unmatched Ladders. That has to be it, Sarra."

"But there are dozens of verses, and you said you weren't sure about some of them—how could you know that the waterfall one is—"

"I thought *you* were the one who wanted to try it!"

"Don't you snap at me again," she warned, completely out of patience with him. Nearby, Adennos stirred in his sleep.

Sarra lowered her voice. "Help me up, the chill's made me stiff."

When they had walked a little way from the others, she went on, "Convince me. Sing all the verses you know, and which Ladders match with which, and which ones you aren't sure of yet, and then *maybe* we'll go back to the shrine—" She caught her breath and swayed against him. "Merciful St. Sirrala! The carving!"

"What carving?"

"On the entry column! Chevasto's Loom, and shuttles— Malerris Castle was above it, above a waterfall!"

Alin nodded, fair hair gleaming in the predawn gloom. "All right, then. I'll leave Val a note, and we'll go back and—"

"The hell you will," Val said behind them.

Both swung around. Val's gaze scraped Sarra's nerves raw; he was angry with Alin for wanting to try the Ladder, but he was furious with Sarra for finding it in the first place. He retained enough decency not to direct his rage at her; she felt a little sorry for Alin, who would bear the brunt of it. Still, the set of Val's strong features and the fire in his eyes made her want to back up a pace just the same.

Alin gripped his cousin's arm. "I know where the Ladder goes!"

"Based on a bad rhyme in a children's song! You're out of your mind!"

"Based on my nightmares all these years—you remember my nightmares, Val."

"Better than you! Waking up in a cold sweat, shaking to rattle the bed down, barely remembering your own name—"

"The waterfall's always been one of the worst." Alin was nearly pleading with him. "If I can find it, identify it, maybe I'll never have that dream again. After all these years, Val, you of all people ought to trust me to—"

"All I trust in is that you'll get your guts strung on the Great Loom!"

They did not remind her of Agatine and Orlin now. They sounded like her parents during those frightening days before her father had taken Glenin away. Sarra repressed a shudder and tried to distract them by saying, "We're going back to the shrine to confirm our guess."

Incredibly, Val turned on her. "You'll try the Ladder, don't deny it! You're just as stupid as he is. Bloods! You're all alike!"

That did it. Of the very few people who had spoken to Sarra that way, none had been male and all had regretted it.

Then she saw that Alin was smiling slightly. Bewildered, Sarra took a few moments to recognize this as a signal that the fight was over and Val had capitulated in the only fashion he could. He was a proud man, as rigid in his way as Grandmother Allynis had been in hers.

It was beneath Sarra to match him for rudeness, no matter the provocation. Still, she had to show her disapproval, so her next words were a command: "You're coming with us."

Cleft chin thrust forward, he glowered. "Where he goes, I go."

"And you both go where I tell you to," Sarra reminded him. "Alin, tell Imi we'll catch up to them tomorrow. Arrange a time and place to meet in Havenport. Val, we need food and water. Not much, just something to gnaw on. Get moving."

9

They were back at the triangular All Saints Shrine well before noon. The carving was as Sarra recalled it. Alin spent a long minute staring at the central column before nodding confirmation.

"The way I've dreamed it is like a memory," he said. "Color and sound, even the feel of the spray. But it's the same angle, the same perspective."

"You experience all that in a dream?" Sarra asked.

"The Scholar took the images directly from another mind and put them into me." He moved slowly away from the column, bending now and then to pluck wildflowers from the thick grass. "Gorynel Desse told me later that Ladder Lore has been passed mind to mind for centuries, maybe since the Waste War. There were so many Ladders then, Sarra! Sometimes I think there must've been one in every village, no matter how small."

"Another reason you travel so much," she guessed. "On the chance you'll recognize a Ladder location."

"I never thought of it that way, but I suppose so. This is the first time it's actually happened." He straightened, a stalk of pale lupine clutched in one fist, the flowers nearly the same blue as his eyes. "If I can identify just one more Ladder pair . . . do you understand?"

Not to keep his name alive forever as the man who solved generations-old riddles, but for the Mage Guardians and the Rising. For those who might need those Ladders. She felt the same way each time she found just one more book, poem, song, or age-old broadsheet. But Alin also had a more personal need to match Ladder pairs, to stop at least one nightmare. Sarra resolved that when they got back to Sheve, they'd make a list of his dream images and compare them against the oldest version of the Ladder Song she could find.

Offerings made—Val's to Velireon the Provider, Alin's to Alilen the Seeker, Sarra's to Sirrala and Caitiri again—they sat in the tall grass, ate a hasty meal, and argued about the trip one last time. They took turns objecting and defending, but the conclusion was the same.

"So, we go," Val concluded. "But at mid-afternoon. Tenth here is First in Seinshir. I'd prefer a couple of sleepy guards to a whole castle wide awake."

"There won't be any guards," Alin told him. "It'll be Warded."

"Can you get past?" Sarra asked.

He shook his head. "I can't even set a Ward, let alone cancel one."

"I see. One of us will have to be on point. I volunteer. I must have enough magic to sense Wards—I felt the Blanking Wards in the Ladders, anyway. If I do, if there's a Keep Away or whatever, then I'll tell you immediately."

"What she's not saying," Alin remarked to his cousin, "is that the Wards at Malerris Castle are likely to be much nastier than Wrong Turn or Oops! I Dropped My Sword."

"What she's also not saying," Val agreed, "is that we're to prevent her from acting on whatever mad thing a Ward like that might urge."

Sarra made a face at them. "What I *am* saying quite clearly is that Val isn't Mageborn so he can't fight a Ward once it's got hold of him, and Alin's the only one who can get us back here, so I'm the logical choice. Pour out the last of that wine, Val, I'm still thirsty."

The warm, hazy shadows of the shrine columns were lengthening when at last they stepped into the copper ring. Even Val had to admit that its shiny-smooth surface argued for care not in keeping with the ruin. During their other trips by Ladder, he'd kept one hand on the knife in his pocket. This time he drew his sword.

"Waterfall," Alin murmured, eyes squeezed shut. "Waterfall . . . castle above . . . sea below. . . ."

Watching him, and resisting the Blanking Ward that hovered around her, Sarra loosened her grip on his hand. "Don't try so hard. Relax."

"Who's the Ladder Rat here, me or you?" But he smiled slightly as he said it, and the tension in his narrow shoulders eased.

She closed her eyes. After a minute or two, she heard Alin draw in a soft breath, and nothingness surrounded her. She let it come. Something inside her flickered like a distant star outshone by the light of the Ladymoon. *Magic*, she thought sadly—

—and then nothing became a deafening rush of water and a midnight wind needling her face with icy spray. She opened her eyes. Val was braced, sword at the ready. Alin wiped droplets from his cheeks and brow as if it was the sweat of fearful effort.

"We made it?" She couldn't even hear her own voice above the thundering water to her right and the crashing sea far below to her left. Moonlight made ragged by drifting clouds glowed off two hundred feet of white froth. They stood on a ledge within a small circle of white stones. Sarra peered over the cliff and gulped her heart back down from her throat: the toes of her boots were mere inches from a sheer drop to the ocean.

Val, naked sword in hand, led them back from the ledge into a cave. The roar receded and Sarra could almost hear herself think. Alin came up with a candle and lit it without a match. Wind and echoing water faded as they walked farther into the cave.

"I don't know who to thank—any or all of our Name Saints, Rilla the Guide, or Mittru Bluehair of the Rivers," Val said shakily.

"Just so long as it's not Chevasto," Alin said, shivering with cold and reaction. "Luring us into his very castle. . . ."

Not a cheering idea. Sarra pushed it aside.

Val slicked back his thick damp hair. "Almost makes me wish I'd worn my coif. Now what?"

"Up there," Alin said, waving one hand vaguely. "Do we go in, or go back?"

"All this way, and not look around?" Sarra smiled fiercely.

"So how do we get up there—let alone inside?"

"Alin-O," she replied cheerfully, "to use the Ladder they have to get to it. Where they can go, so can we. And this cave—so very handy to the Ladder, so very nicely carved out, and by human hands, if you'll notice—just begs to be explored."

Val cleared his throat. "I just hope none of them fancies a midnight trip to Shellinkroth. I'll keep my sword in hand, if it's all the same to you."

Alin produced two more candles and lit them from his own. They started walking, Sarra on point. The noise died away behind them, due partly to distance and partly to the sound-absorbing cushion of moss and lichen on smooth stone.

Not fifty paces into the damp tunnel, she nearly tripped over a Council Guard uniform that wrapped a rattling collection of bones picked clean.

Alin crouched to examine the remains. "It's been over eight years. I'm surprised the fabric hasn't rotted away, too."

"He didn't rot. He's not lying the way he fell," Valirion commented critically. "See where the trousers are torn, and the angle of thighbone? One arm's missing entirely."

Sarra looked, then looked away. "You mean . . . something gnawed—?"

"More than likely. Don't lose your lunch, Sarra, there'll be plenty more like this along the way."

"I'm fine," she lied, and kept walking.

My father did this. The Butcher of Ambrai. All that we'll see here, all that happened and everyone who died— attackers and defenders.

No. Not my father. Anniyas. And the Lords of Malerris who destroyed their own castle and their own people. But— merciful St. Miryenne, how could one of your own Mage Guardians do this? Auvry Feiran was a good man! I remem-

ber him from when I was little—what happened? What went so wrong?

Val was right about the bodies. Sarra had to step over or around piles of them, trying not to disturb the pale and empty bones in their ragged clothes. Council red, Malerris white, Guardian black—how cleverly it had been done, putting Mage regimentals on some of the corpses.

All included the red sash of the Warrior Mage. *Of course,* Sarra thought bitterly. The Warrior's Oath never to use magic in battle must be "proven" false. But of the Sword sigil pins there was no trace—nor of identity disks.

Even in war, custom decreed that if a body was not recoverable for funeral rites, the disk was retrieved and sent to the family. This was done for the Council Guard and the Malerrisi. But there was no such custom regarding the collar pins, and not one of the "Mage" dead had ever been identified.

The Council agreed to withhold the names to spare their families public humiliation. Orlin Renne, knowing how Anniyas' mind worked, asserted that she wanted the family of every Warrior Mage to live in dread—and not necessarily of that Mage's death at Malerris Castle. After the battle, no one admitted to having a Mage in the family; most made life easier on their Names by vanishing.

The identity disks were unnecessary. The sigil pins were proof enough of Guardian participation in this horror. But where had the pins come from? They were not susceptible to forgery; the Academy had had its own small foundry for casting such sigils. Sarra's instinct leaped and the landing sickened her. The Warrior Mages had been murdered in secret elsewhere, their regimentals and insignia taken, their identity disks destroyed.

It seemed Auvry Feiran—*No! Anniyas!* she reminded herself frantically—had thought of everything.

The tunnel sloped upward for about a quarter of a mile. Stairs appeared, cut into the living rock, with iron sconces at regular intervals and a torch nub in each. Why hadn't this place been cleared? If the waterfall Ladder was still used, why make people walk past all this horror?

Simple: if anyone came looking, Malerris Castle must seem untouched. Deserted. Lifeless. They had left the dead to rot in full view of those brave or foolish enough to venture here. Sarra guessed they would find the same in the castle itself. Or—perhaps not. How extensive was the deception? She *knew* they were here somewhere, but how could they have laid up supplies to last so many years?

She sighed at her own stupidity. She'd seen paintings of Malerris Castle and glimpsed the real thing tonight. The place was huge. With elaborate planning, they could exist in total secrecy for eight years or eighty.

And the Lords of Malerris loved nothing so much as an elaborate plan.

She knew they were here—somewhere. She could feel them.

Abruptly she stopped and turned to Alin. "I think I may have found a Ward. I feel people watching me."

Alin stepped to her side and frowned, concentrating. Then he shook his head. "Nothing. Val?"

He joined them, and after a moment shrugged. "Nothing."

"My nerves, then," Sarra said, annoyed with herself.

Stairs; more stairs. She had never wished so much for a Folding spell. At last they reached the top, where an oak door hung on one hinge. Uniforms and bones sprawled everywhere; she had no choice but to climb over them.

Sarra stopped cold an arm's length from the doorway, tottering with one foot on a tiny patch of floor and the other on a mound of uniforms. "Alin! Stay back! This *must* be a Ward—I feel that if I take one more step, I'll die!"

"All right, Sarra, take it easy."

There was nothing in the open doorway. All she saw was the space beyond: an expanse of plain gray flagstones, stairs rising about fifty feet from where she stood, a glimpse to the left of a wide foyer and a tall window empty of glass. Hissing in her head was the grim promise of death at a thousand eager hands. She trembled, unable to go through and yet refusing to turn back. *I'm Mageborn, even if I don't have my magic—I know this isn't real!*

"Alin!" She was ashamed of the thin whine that came from her throat.

"Nothing's going to hurt you, Sarra. Stay where you are. Val, talk to her."

"Sarra?" Val's tone was easy and calm. "Alin's coming around to your left. You can hear him, can't you? Don't worry. During the battle, the Wards were countered. They'd never have been able to get in otherwise. So what you feel—

careful, Alin!—it's leftovers of a dead Ward, Sarra. It can't hurt you."

"I *know* that, damn it!" she gasped. "But if this is a dead Ward, how did these people keep sane when it really w-worked?"

"Tell me what it's like. Come on, Sarra, you talk to me for a while."

She knew what he was doing: making her use the sound of her own voice against irrational fear. She took a deep, steadying breath that hurt her constricted lungs. "There's nothing here—no people, I mean, but—but the Ward's telling me they're waiting for me, to k–kill me—"

"How? Swords, knives, spells, what?"

"What do you mean, 'how?' " she shouted. "It's death, Val, people who want me to die!"

"Sloppy," Val announced scornfully. "If it'd been a really strong Ward you'd still feel the specifics, as detailed as the menu in the Compass Rose Inn. Ever been there? It's run by the Olvosian Web in Neele, and a finer venison steak and cheese pie I've never had in my—"

"Oh, shut up! I'm standing here like a damned statue and you're babbling about restaurants!" But anger was a good weapon against fear, and she knew Val knew it. "Alin, where the hell are you?"

"Right here, Sarra."

"He has to keep back from the Ward, Sarra, don't worry. Don't be afraid."

"Easy for you to say!" Alin's voice came from her right, and then he was holding her hand. He was still a pace behind her, balanced on piled bones. She heard him suck in a breath and knew the Ward had touched him. "Saints and Wraiths! Val, stay back. You're not Mageborn, you don't have any resistance."

Sarra clung to Alin's cold fingers. "What can we do?"

"I'm going to put my arm around you. On three, we jump through."

"No! I can't!"

"Yes, you can." Not leaving her any more time to think or fear, he said swiftly, "One—two—*three!*"

And he hauled her with him through the Ward. They stumbled and went down hard on the paving stones, bruising their knees. Sarra could breathe again, and her head and heart cleared of the terrible certainty that the door meant death. Still shivering, she wrapped both arms around Alin in wordless gratitude.

"Now, Sarra," he chided. "You'll make Val jealous."

"You wish!" called Val.

Sarra laughed at that, a bit hysterically. She bit her tongue and let Alin go, turning to look at Val. "Your turn to jump. Come get me, Val—pretend you *are* jealous and want to slit my throat."

"Nothing so messy, adorable *Domna*," he replied, taking a cautious step closer to the door, bones crunching underfoot. His bantering tone was belied by the apprehension in his dark eyes. Another step. "And nothing so quick. No, I'd make it something lingering, and—and—" His face went rigid and he dropped his sword. "Geridon's Golden Balls! *Alin!*"

"Jump!" Alin shouted. "Now, Val!"

He did, more on instinctive obedience to his cousin's command than from any real thought. He sprawled near them, panting and shaking. Alin propped him up and held him close. After a moment Val drew away.

"Your pardon, *Domna*," he managed. "I don't usually use such language around ladies."

After all the rude, ill-bred, mannerless impertinences he'd committed in her presence, *now* he was apologizing for swearing? It struck her as exceedingly funny. Hilarity proved contagious; the three of them rocked with loud and witless giggles. *Reaction,* Sarra told herself in a fleeting moment of sanity. *Laughter—better than tears for tension, or so Agatine always says. . . .*

Eventually they sobered. Val looked around and sighed. "Well, if all that noise didn't bring them down on us, I suppose they're not coming."

"Not here, or not interested," Alin agreed.

"Or waiting to see what we do next," Sarra added.

They helped each other up. Val slapped his thigh angrily. "Damn! My sword!"

"I didn't like to mention it," Alin said blandly, "but what use you thought it would be against a castleful of Mageborns is something I don't quite grasp."

Val gave him a look to boil a glacier.

Malerris Castle undulated over the southern cliffs of its island, a series of towers, turrets, outbuildings, and baileys surrounded by stone walls fifty feet high and fifteen feet thick. They could not hope to explore more than a small portion of it. Frankly, Sarra was ready to say she had been here and go back to Shellinkroth. The place made her thumbs prickle.

The window she had seen from the Warded door proved to be one of a score looking out on a cobbled courtyard. Deserted, of course, and scarred black by a conflagration that had blown the glass to shards. But within the castle signs of fire were few. The destruction was nowhere near as total as reported. Fire had come through, certainly. Still, as Alin said, it was odd to expect evidence of a blast furnace and find nothing wayward torches couldn't account for.

There were no more bodies. Perhaps the Council Guard had cleaned up. Perhaps this part of the castle was in use, and the Lords of Malerris had taken away the corpses. Or perhaps the door was the limit of the invasion. Recalling how it had felt to encounter the "dead" Ward, Sarra could easily believe it.

She indicated the stairs with a tiny shrug; Alin's shoulders lifted in the same fashion. Val made a multiple flourish of one hand toward the first step. Broad at the base, narrowing toward the landing, each riser was worn in the middle like a streambed. The stairs hugged the wall, no banister on the side open to the stones below; Sarra felt queasy at the idea of running sword fights.

"Investigate each floor as we go?" Val asked. "Or climb to the top and peek in as we come back down?"

"The top. I want to see the view," Sarra replied stoutly.

"Wonderful," Alin muttered.

"He's afraid of heights." Val nudged him with an elbow as they started to climb again.

"You bet I am! After that leap you made me take off the wall at Isodir—"

"That little hop?"

"Fifty feet if it was an inch! I might've broken both legs!"

"Thirty at the most, into a pile of straw."

Sarra nearly snapped at them to be quiet. Then she understood the good-natured acrimony: it kept fear at bay.

The tower was short compared to others spreading across the cliffs, a bit less than a hundred feet high. But the view was indeed spectacular, even at night. Sarra didn't intend lingering to see it by day. Light from the stars and the Ladymoon and her faithful companion illumined the sea far below and the rest of the castle mounting taller cliffs. An open balcony circled the tower. Sarra paced around it slowly, silently. The feeling of being watched was back.

"Let's go inside," she said. "It's freezing out here."

"Fine with me," Val said, eyeing the next spire over—a soaring stone needle sharpened to a wicked point snagging the starry sky.

The pair followed her back into the uppermost chamber, a single broad room charred to a crisp. Alin said they'd probably fired it to create the impression that the whole tower burned. All this deception—the bodies in the tunnel, the damage by fire—made Sarra even more certain that the Malerrisi still existed, and in great numbers, and almost certainly somewhere within this vast complex.

Damn it, she *knew* she was being watched.

On the way down they opened dozens of doors. Bedchambers, garderobes, tiled rooms with sinks and bathtubs, closets, storage space: nothing more sinister. Yet everywhere—carved into stone and wood, glazed on tiles, woven into tapestries and rugs—were the sigils of the Weaver and his servants. The Great Loom predominated. But spools and spindles and shuttles, spinning wheels and needles and scissors appeared over and over. Sarra shivered, wondering if Lords of Malerris would react with the same instinctive shudder to the repeated sigils of Mage Guardians and their patron Saints.

By the time they reached the ground floor again, Val remarked that the time was just after Half-Eighth, and considering the hour or so back to the Ladder, they'd return to Shellinkroth around Fourth—time enough for a nap before they set off to catch up with the others.

Sarra did not relish another jump through that doorway or another walk through that tunnel of bones. But she had another reason for wanting to stay a little longer: she had found exactly nothing.

What she had expected (hoped? dreaded?) to find, she could not have said. Perhaps the discovery of the Ladder pair and the confirmation of her suspicions were enough. Yet somehow she felt disappointed.

Ridiculous.

"Come on, then," she said. "I've had enough of this place."

"Y'know," Val replied, "I like you, Sarra. I mean, I *really* like you."

She shrugged this off as yet another masculine incomprehensibility—for it would never even occur to her that he wouldn't.

She approached the doorway with heart pounding—and sensed exactly nothing. *Idiot!* she chastised internally. *Of course it doesn't work from this side!*

Even so, she went through as quickly as she could, boots sliding on the piled uniforms and bones. The Ward clutched her for an instant, then let go. Alin and Val hurried, too. The latter stooped briefly to retrieve his sword, cursing under his breath. Down the long stairs they went, down into the damp and dark.

And emerged from a cave on the wrong side of the waterfall.

"What happened?" Val yelled over the liquid thunder, sword half drawn.

"So much for infallible memory," Sarra accused Alin—unfairly, she knew, because there had been no wrong turns to take in the tunnel. There had been no turns at all. "How'd we get over here? We're supposed to be over there!"

Alin's blue eyes narrowed against the waterfall's spray. He paced the rocky shelf, scowling ferociously, muttering and gesturing with both hands as if retracing their route below ground. Sarra was about to tell him to stop fidgeting and do something useful when he gave a sudden explosive "Ha!" and strode to the lip of the cliff.

Marching off a circle enclosed by black stones—shiny obsidian like that littering Caitiri's Hearth on Brogdenguard; Sarra had a souvenir from Neele—he pointed straight across to the cavern barely visible on the other side.

"See that?"

"See what?" Sarra demanded.

"It's identical!"

"It is?" Val joined him, squinting into the darkness. "To what?"

"Here! Except it's on the west side of the waterfall instead of the east!"

Sarra approached them, arms wrapped around herself, soaked by chill spray. "And you think this is significant."

"*Of course* it's significant!" Alin shouted. " 'West or east, east or west/Ladder at Viranka's Breast'! Here's the Ladder—" He nodded at the circle of stones, then at the cascade. "—and there's St. Viranka!"

Sarra, tired of trying to make herself heard, drew the men back into the relative shelter of the cave. "Alin, are you sure?"

He mopped his wet face and slicked hair from his brow with both hands. "I just *know,* that's all."

"Great," Valirion muttered.

"Shut up, Val," Sarra said. "Alin, do you have any idea where this one goes? Because if you don't, we'll have to go back to the tunnel and get over to the other side somehow. We'll have to do that anyway, to get back to Shellinkroth."

"Not necessarily." He gave a secret smile and began to explore the cavern, a tiny bluish Mage Globe kindling over his left shoulder. Sarra gave a start. Val only shrugged.

"He can, when he's not thinking about it," he murmured. "When there's need enough, and he's not—reminded."

"Oh," she said inadequately.

They watched his systematic search in silence. He was dogged by his Globe as faithfully as was the Ladymoon by her little companion across the sky. The odd light played over his features, reflected off each droplet clinging to cheeks and brow. Sarra glanced at Val, and nearly smiled to see bemused affection in his dark eyes—not unmixed with cheerful lust. It might be nice, she conceded, to have a man look at *her* like that, with tenderness and humor to govern passion. If she could find a man who could feel and laugh as well as desire, she might even think about thinking about marriage.

But why, she wondered with a forlorn inner sigh, were all the good ones either taken, like Orlin, or taken another way, like Alin and Val?

Alin swung around, gleaming eyes lit by more than the Mage Globe.

"He's got it," Val said.

The damp blond head nodded. "You'll never guess."

"But you'd like us to," his cousin replied, adding to Sarra, "He's always like this when he thinks he's been clever."

"I *am* clever," Alin retorted.

"Can we get out of here?" Sarra asked with exaggerated patience.

"As you command, *Domna.*" The Mage Globe vanished as Alin led the way back out to the cliff. Keeping them outside the black stone circle, he said, "I'll go first, just to be sure."

And before Val could lash out an arm to stop him, he was inside the circle and gone.

"Where does he think he's going?" Sarra cried. "If he doesn't come back, we'll be stranded!"

"If he doesn't know where he's going," Val told her grimly, "he'll never come back."

But he did come back, scarcely a minute later. And he was laughing quietly, his eyes all alight with glee.

"It's safe—the absolute dead of night. Come along, step inside. That's it. By St. Rilla, we're in luck! There's even a nearby Ladder to Shellinkroth!"

"From *where?*" Val roared.

"Ambrai."

And two blinks later, Sarra returned to the city of her birth for the first time in more than seventeen years.

10

She emerged from the round Ladder—this time a chimney—into a room she had never seen before but knew from her books. This was Caitirin Bekke's private hideaway, located in the highest tower of the Commandery. The fires that had destroyed the Mage Academy and its precincts had not climbed the thin round spire to this room, built two hundred years ago by the Third-Tier Mage Captal from Brogdenguard, a shrine to the home she had loved.

"The obsidian circle," Alin said as he stepped out of the chimney, Val close behind him. "I should've guessed just from that. But at first I thought it meant Brogdenguard." Carefully he touched the hearth hood, made of great sharp lumps of glassy black rocks mortared with black cement.

Sarra was drawn to a narrow window with a pointed arch. The shutters hung askew; years of storms had battered the frames and shattered the glass. Night wind swirled around her as she stared down at her city. In her memory, it had still risen proud and lovely across rolling hills on either side of the Ambrai River. Now that illusion was gone forever. She made herself see the ruin, barely hearing her cousins talking behind her.

"How did you know this one led to Ambrai?" Val asked.

"I read the sign."

"What sign?"

"The one carved into the cave wall." Alin sounded unbearably smug. Triumph evidently made him voluble. "Captal Bekke's initials entwined with Third Lord Escovor's. Their family colors even linger: red and crimson, black and orange."

Sarra knuckled her eyes and turned from the window. It would not do for them to see her crying over her moonlit glimpse of the Octagon Court. "A Mage Captal and a Lord of Malerris?"

"Lovers," Alin affirmed. "They were the scandal of all Lenfell at the time—except for Grand Duchess Veller Ganfallin, of course. In fact, they were hatching a plot against her when the First Lord, Warden of the Loom, found out about them and executed Shen Escovor. Rather messily, legend has it."

In all the books Sarra had stolen—*rescued*—she had never read about this. A Mage Captal and a Lord of Malerris? Lovers? Impossible! She sank into a dusty chair, one of an upholstered pair set near the hearth. Everything in this room came in pairs, in fact—tables topped with carved slabs of obsidian, brass lamps gone dull with lack of polishing, wrought iron braziers beside the chairs to warm chilled toes.

"Alin," she began, but he was still telling the tale.

"Caitirin Bekke built this tower the first year she was Captal, originally because she was homesick for Brogdenguard. Then she put in the Ladder so she and Escovor could meet in secret." He walked softly across the polished ceramic tiles, black filmed with a layer of dust and ash. "Everything is from villages near Caitiri's Hearth—the stone, the tiles, the furnishings—" He pointed to smoke-stained frescoes on the walls. "There are the mountains themselves."

"Alin," Sarra said again, "I have a question."

"So do I," Val interrupted. "If they were lovers, where's the bed?"

"Cousin, you have a prurient mind."

"Just practical. This is one hell of a cold hard floor."

"Alin!" Sarra snapped. "If Ladders die in fire, why does this one work? It's built inside a chimney!"

"See the braziers? No fire was ever lit in this hearth after Captal Bekke put in the Ladder."

"I still want to know where the bed is," Val insisted.

"And *I* want to know how you were so sure about this," Sarra said coldly. "I forbid you to do this again, Alin Ostin. You are *never* to risk your life on a guess, a legend, and a children's song again, do you understand me?"

Alin's spine stiffened. Sarra stared him down. Gradually resentment faded to minor grudge, then to acknowledgment that she was right.

"I'm sorry. But it wasn't really a guess. It's the only one that fits. 'Back and forth, forth and back/Stony Ladder shining black.' "

"A guess, a legend, and a children's song," Sarra repeated grimly. "If the whole Rising is run on logic like that, we'll need every Saint in the Calendar."

"We got here, didn't we?" Val's tone was not quite a challenge.

"Because the magic still functions on both sides," she retorted. "Why?"

That silenced them for a few moments. Surely both Mage Guardians and Lords of Malerris knew of this Ladder pair. Why would either allow the other access to their very stronghold?

"Maybe they Warded—no," Alin interrupted himself, "we would've felt it."

Val shrugged. "Ask Gorsha. He'll know."

Sarra's list was getting longer than she was tall. "What's the time?"

"Eight minutes after Second. In Shellinkroth, it's yesterday."

Definitely she was confused by Laddering. "Then let's get some sleep. Alin, where's this other Ladder? Have you used it before?"

"Yes. It goes from the Academy proper to St. Ilsevet's outside Havenport."

"Very well. *Domni* Maurgen, you have my permission to go find the bed." And with that she folded the cloak around her, closed her eyes, and slept.

II

It was not surprising that after her first view of home in so long she dreamed of Ambrai as it was before Father went away the first time and Mother became so tense and sad. To a child's eyes, Ambrai had been a wondrous place, all light and flowers and laughter. And with a child's eyes, she dreamed.

She saw Grandmother Allynis, pretending outrage when Grandfather Gerrin playfully tweaked her ear or sneaked a quick kiss.

She saw herself and Glenin, hiding inside the Double Spiral and making what they thought were authentic Wraithenbeast noises to scare courtiers until giggles gave them away.

She saw Mage Captal Garvedian, and Guardian Desse, and her Alvassy kin, and her friends, and the Bards and Scholars and Healers. And in her dream she did not weep, for she was a child again and all of them lived.

She saw a family picnic on the lawns, the Octagon Court rising majestically behind them, and beyond the trees the towers of Commandery and Academy, Bard Hall and Healers Ward. A string trio played Grandmother Allynis' favorite songs; Glenin and Sarra chased butterflies; Mother and Father sat on the grass near Grandmother and Grandfather, all of them laughing. Sarra knew this scene: the family was celebrating Grandmother's Birthingday.

She saw an elderly Scholar Mage in gray and black bow to Grandmother and present her with a large book, decorated in gold and turquoise and black. Lady Allynis exclaimed at its beauty; her daughter leaned over for a closer look.

What she saw next was no part of her memories. Auvry Feiran seized the book and behind him the Octagon Court burst into flame. Sarra then saw herself do a curious thing: she snatched the book from her father's hands and began to run.

She woke with a violent start. "Saints and Wraiths!" she exclaimed borrowing Alin's oath. "I'm a *fool!*"

"Sarra?" Alin hurried to her side.

"Huh? What?" Val struggled to his feet from the cold hard floor where he'd been drowsing while Alin took the watch. "What's wrong?"

"Quick, Val—what time is it?"

He scrubbed a hand over his face. "Uh—nearly Fourth."

"Are you all right?" Alin asked.

She ignored his concern. "When's dawn?"

"Less than an hour."

Sarra pushed aside the lingering emotions of the dream and got to her feet. "If we hurry, there'll be enough time."

"What did I miss?" Alin asked, bewildered.

"We *all* missed it," she said feverishly. "Oh, use your wits! The *books!*"

12

No deceptions here. No bones, no bodies, no uniforms, no Wards. Only blackened heights of stone, heaps of charred wood, rubble, and tragedy. Only the truth of what Auvry Feiran had done.

Alin led them to a row of columns that supported nothing. The roof had collapsed seventeen years ago.

"The library," he said.

"You knew," Sarra accused. "You could've just told me."

Alin shrugged. "You'd only have insisted on seeing it for yourself."

"You don't understand. I remember—"

Then she stopped. If she wasn't careful, they would understand all too much. What she remembered was coming here from the Octagon Court on very hot days; the lofty halls were relief from the heat, and the bottom of the cellar stairs was the coolest refuge of all. But to admit that would be to admit she was Ambraian. So she lied, and they believed her.

"When I was a little girl, a Mage came to Roseguard. She was studying to become a Scholar when all this happened. When we went through my library, she told me about a book vault in the cellar."

"Sarra." Val put a hand on her arm. "It's hopeless. Some-one would've come back for them long ago."

"I hope 'someone' wasn't a Lord of Malerris," Alin added. "No, *Domna,* there's nothing left down there."

"We have to look," she insisted. "We have to be sure. How else will Cailet learn what she must?"

Urgency had betrayed her. She knew the instant she spoke that she shouldn't have said her sister's name. Better to have given them a version of her dream, and explain the reminder it surely was (from her own mind? from a Saint? from Gorynel Desse—or Grandmother?). She brusquely excused herself the slip by deciding it was time Val and Alin knew, anyway. Some of it; not all.

"Cailet?" Alin stiffened reflexively.

In for an acorn, in for an oak, Sarra told herself. "She's Mageborn—I've heard it before, and you told me yourself, Val. The Guardians we're taking back to Roseguard will form the basis of a new Academy. They'll teach her and oth-ers. But we need the books. If they still exist, we have to rescue them."

Val chewed his lip. "What do you know about Cailet Rille?"

"More than you imagine," she said shortly. "Come on. We're wasting time."

The cousins went ahead to clear the way. Books burned with frightening efficiency, and wooden shelves with them: nothing left but ash and a few sticks that might once have been chairs or desks. Massive beams had fallen in, too, and a million roof tiles. Picking her way over the rattling mounds was very much like the journey through the tunnel of bones at Malerris Castle. There, people had died; here, knowledge. She didn't know which made her more furious.

Alin reached the cellar door first and stood there in si-lence. Sarra joined him. With her first glance downward, she felt her hands clench angrily. She'd forgotten that the steps of the spiral staircase had been made of wood.

"That's an end, then," Alin muttered.

It couldn't be—or why else had she dreamed, and woken with such urgent certainty of what she must do?

"How far to the bottom?" Val asked.

She frowned, trying to remember. At four years old, the steps had seemed endless. The equivalent of one floor? Two?

"With a spiral, it's hard to tell," Alin said.

Valirion braced a hand on the wall and leaned into the darkness. "The iron framework's still there, from what I can see. Support rails, banister ... it's just the wood steps that burned away."

"Don't get any ideas," Alin warned. "The frame's come away from the wall. It'll never hold you."

He rubbed his belly, grinning. "Well, I haven't been feeding as well as I'm used to. *Domna* Sarra, if you'll be so good as to hold my sword?"

Alin grumbled. Sarra hushed him. "I'm the lightest, I ought to go."

"I'm the strongest. Alin-O, keep your tongue between your teeth. You're lighter than I am, stronger than she is, and terrified of heights. By the way, Sarra, how do I open the vault? If the books are that rare, it'll have a lock."

"Or a Ward," Alin added.

She looked down into the blackness, cursing herself. She hadn't thought of that, either.

"Why don't I go down and see if it's open? That ought to tell us something, anyway. We can ask Scholar Solingirt if he knows anything about it."

Val got hand- and footholds on the framework. The iron creaked and groaned alarmingly, but held as he started the climb down. Sarra found a table leg charred only at one end, and Alin got it lit. The flames fluttered like frightened birds in the dark stairwell. Every so often iron squealed and Val swore, then called up that he was fine, just scraped a bit. At length they heard soft footsteps on ash-covered marble, and knew he was safely down.

"If the books are still there," Alin remarked almost casually, "we can bring a rope back from Shellinkroth."

"Mmm. Getting them all on board ship will be—" She broke off at the clatter below. "Val?" Her voice echoed back up at her.

"Maurgen, you moron, answer me!" Alin yelled.

"I thought I told you to shut up!" drifted back before Alin's echoes subsided. "I found it—and it's sealed. Can't feel a Ward, though."

"We'll come back later!" Sarra called down.

And, after Val clambered back up and Alin took them through the Academy's ladder to Shellinkroth, this was precisely what they did.

13

" 'First you see me, then I'm gone/Ladder on a clover lawn,' " sang Imilial as she stacked an armful of books on the floor. The tune she used was a variant of the one Sarra knew. " 'Wet or dry, dry or wet/Ladder caught inside a net!' " She looked around the candlelit shrine to St. Ilsevet, patron of fisherfolk, and grinned. "They had that part right enough," she added, gesturing to the thin woven latticework that overlaid the underwater scenes painted on the dome. "But I never would've guessed the greenhouse at the Academy was a Ladder!"

Sarra nodded from her nest of cloaks near the altar, and picked up another book from a nearby pile. "It must have been a beautiful floor once. Whoever painted those tiles to look like a lawn was a true artist. Oh, Imi! Look at this! I've read references to Steenan Oslir's memoirs, but I've never found a copy—and this one is signed!"

"*Not* one of my favorite Captals," Imilial said, crouching to take a look anyway as she dipped a cupful of water from the bucket at Sarra's elbow. "A real Slavemaster he was, according to legend."

They continued glancing through the books brought back from the vault. Sarra had been forced to stay behind by a sudden overwhelming nausea Alin said was classic Ladder Lag: common in someone unused to Ladders who'd traveled too many too quickly. She fretted until Alin and Elomar Adennos returned from the first trip staggering under the weight of dozens of books. Kanto Solingirt's advice about the vault's lock had been impossible for Alin to follow—being only a Ladder Rat, not a real Mage—but Elomar recognized the spell as a variant of one used to secure medicine cabinets. Val stayed behind to bind books for hauling up by rope; Advar Senison did the hauling and untying for transport, armful by armful, back to St. Ilsevet's Shrine.

They'd been at this for three nights now. At least, Sarra *thought* it was three nights; her time sense was skewed and she slept at the oddest hours. When she and Alin and Val first arrived at St. Ilsevet's, she was pretty sure it was the same night they'd left. More or less. She slept, resolving once more to let Val worry about what time and day it was. She slept while Val went to find Imilial and the other Mages at the rendezvous, and Alin went to find the shrine's votary, a secret member of the Rising. This ancient worthy, as weathered by sea and salt as his shrine, brought food and a sign for the front door: *CLOSED FOR REPAIRS*.

The Mages had arrived—and Imi was complaining that she felt like a trout in a fishbowl—by the time Sarra woke. After so much sleep, she should have been ready to return to Ambrai and help with the books. But when Advar Senison brought her bread and cheese, she disgraced herself all over St. Ilsevet's floor of sea-blue tiles painted with silver fishes.

Alin diagnosed her problem and told her to go back to sleep. The two Healer Mages made sure of it with a dose of poppy syrup. Faced with a choice between peaceful slumber and a vicious combination of dizziness, nausea, and chills, Sarra did the sensible thing.

The rest went on raiding the Academy library. Three nights, four—maybe even five—it was hard to tell in the dimness of the shrine with torrents of rain darkening the sky. The important thing was that books were stacked knee-deep all along the dome's perimeter. Solingirt had spent yesterday attempting to organize them all by subject, frustrated that they weren't brought here in tidy shelving order. He finally gave up and tucked himself against the wall, reading whatever struck his fancy. Time enough to catalog everything later.

Though Sarra was still a bit shaky, she, too, sampled every book in reach. She wasn't sure how to get them all home, but she knew one thing for a certainty: her dream had told her true. Cailet must and would have these books. Worth any risk—though it annoyed her that she was taking no risk at all.

Alin looked more ragged each time he popped into view in the center of the shrine. Imilial and Elomar made each trip with him, a little unsteady themselves by dawn. Alin, however, was the one whose magic worked the Ladders, and thus he suffered the most. In a very old book of Magesongs, Sarra learned why.

A Ladder leads from there to here
It brings you home from far to near
For trader's travel, or flight in fear—
You pay in magic, always dear.

"Hunh," Val grunted. "Bad poetry."

"Always the critic," Alin replied, but with little spirit. "You'd find fault with Bard Falundir. Is there more to the poem, Sarra? Is our Ladder Song in the book?"

They were snuggled nearby, Valirion providing a sort of living cradle of arms and legs for his exhausted cousin. Alin leaned back against Val's chest, drowsy-eyed, so slight that he looked like a child in Val's embrace. They made a sweet picture, Sarra thought, smiling.

"These poor old pages have seen hard usage." She held the book up from her knees. "They've been sewn back together five times that I can tell, judging by the different colors of thread. The cover and title page are long gone. But a Bard might be able to identify it for us. Which reminds me—I'll have someone search the Hall one of these days for other books."

"It's not that far from the Academy," Alin began.

"It's the other side of the river," Val said.

"Don't even think about going back to have a look," Sarra seconded. "If anything survived this long, another few weeks won't matter. Now, I'll read the rest of this only if you promise to go to sleep and not try to puzzle it out until tomorrow."

"You mean this evening," Val corrected.

"Whatever."

"Still can't keep track of what day it is?"

"Don't gloat, it warps your face," she retorted, grinning.

Alin shifted restlessly. "Are you going to read that or not?"

"Promise first."

He nodded, fatigue-bruised lids hooding blue eyes. The Mages were nested amid cloaks and books, tired faces lit by the blue-white Globe kindled above the small altar by Kanto Solingirt. It had hovered there all the hours except when he slept, light to read by and to cheer the cloudy gloom. The storm had eased up, but Imi was of the opinion that a new one would settle in tomorrow. They were due to go to another safe house soon. No one relished the idea of slogging through Havenport's muddy streets in the rain, but at least the rain kept potential visitors to St. Ilsevet's homebound.

Sarra made her voice a gentle sing-song, using the words as a lullaby.

> *Twice twenty-two the Ladders girt*
> *All Lenfell's Shirs, the Bards assert;*
> *But one is lost. Mage, stay alert.*
> *The broken circle's spell avert.*
> *Six Ladders each the Shirs possess—*
> *Though some have more, and others, less—*
> *When rungs are paired, the sum assess:*
> *Twice twenty-two. Mage, can you guess?*
> *Conundrum numbers; think them through*
> *To sum them in a total true:*
> *Six times fifteen, twice twenty-two—*
> *Halve the greatest. The last is due*
> *The new-struck coin of Captal's woe*
> *In payment to the timeless foe.*

"*Very* bad poetry," Val murmured. "But very nice work—you sent him right to sleep." Cheek resting atop Alin's blond head, Val followed his example.

So much for my womanly fascination, Sarra grinned to herself, then glanced up as Elomar Adennos unfolded himself from his cloak like a long-limbed cat and padded over. Crouching down, he squinted at the book on her knees.

"Twice twenty-two is forty-four. Six times fifteen is ninety, half of that being forty-five. Simple enough."

"Forty-four Ladder pairs," Sarra agreed. "With one pair lost."

" 'The broken circle.' And the line—ah, here. 'The last is due/The new-struck coin of Captal's woe.' Payment is implied."

"For what? Magic itself?" she asked, thinking of the first four lines.

"The Waste War." He rocked back on his heels, nodding to himself. "The Lords of Malerris would be 'the timeless foe.' A question, *Domna*. Is this circle lost because it's broken, or broken because it's lost?"

She felt her brows arch. "I see what you mean. Which leads into who broke it or lost it, and why."

"And if it can be mended—or should." With a polite nod, Adennos returned to his place near the altar steps.

Sarra covered a short stack of books with her bunched cloak hood and snuggled in for another nap. If Alin could match nightmare images with the children's rhyme, he'd be off to find the Lost Ladders unless someone tied him down. She'd have to warn Val, and issue another stern prohibition of her own.

That was what a leader did, wasn't it? Look out for the lives and safety of those she led? That, and use them as their talents indicated. Use them, the way she'd used Alin to rescue those books, until he was nearly used up.

Orlin had said that Taig Ostin would burn himself to ashes. Well, she'd take him in hand, too, once she got hold of him within the family business of the Rising. Soon enough now; by the new year. She fell asleep thinking of Cailet, vowing to permit no one, not even Gorynel Desse, to use *her.*

14

The night of the Winter Solstice, longest of the year, they cleaned out the rest of the rare book vault in Ambrai. His work done, Alin collapsed the whole of the next day, and therefore missed a lively discussion of how to get the volumes to Roseguard.

Kanto Solingirt wanted to box them as cargo on another vessel with himself as escort. There was always a ship or two doing the Havenport-Roseguard run.

"I'll buy other books to layer on top," he said, "to fool the inspectors. That way we can be honest about the contents. Always assuming the Council's functionaries can read," he ended with a disdainful sniff.

Val shook his head. "We won't have to disguise them at all if we make them part of Sarra's luggage. She has Shir privilege, no inspections allowed."

The Scholar Mage looked mulish. "Admit, boy, that I only slow you down."

"You won't be using any more Ladders," Val countered.

"You're staying on Lady Agatine's ship with Imi and the Healers."

"What does it matter which ship I'm on?"

Obviously, Solingirt trusted no one else with the precious books. Sarra could have ended discussion with an order, but she decided to let the men wrangle things out for her—unless they went totally off the trail in the usual maddening masculine way and needed a woman's guidance.

"Kanto," said Advar Senison, "with only book boxes for luggage, you'd be suspect. An itinerant Healer, on the other hand, travels light and could very well be overseeing the shipment of medical supplies."

Hearing this, Sarra knew she'd heard her solution. Senison would go in his itinerant Healer pose, with Imilial for protection. *Not to mention companionship,* she thought with an inward grin as Imi suggested straight-faced that they would attract less notice as a married couple.

The day after Solstice they left St. Ilsevet's. Imi and Advar went to the Havenport house belonging to the votary's daughter and her husband; Sarra recommended innocently that they ought to practice their parts by sharing a bedroom. When the rain finally let up on the sixth day of Midwinter Moon, a wagon took boxes to books and then the boxed books to a ship that embarked on the seventh for Bleynbradden, Pinderon, and Roseguard.

Meantime Sarra, Alin, Val, Kanto Solingirt, and Elomar Adennos crowded into the votary's own tidy little half-timbered home, which—not surprisingly—reeked of fish. The house stood creekside a mile below St. Ilsevet's on the hill, five miles from town. They would stay three days before boarding ship for Ryka—another period of total inactivity Sarra did not relish.

Healer and Scholar, on the other hand, spent the days in perfect contentment. Elomar sat hour after hour tying feathers to hooks, making lures for the votary to sell at the shrine and whistling under his breath all the while. Kanto Solingirt found in the votary someone his own age who remembered what he remembered, and the two old men entertained each other with long bouts of tale-telling. When the votary went to tend the shrine, the Scholar studied volumes he'd withheld from the boxes going to Roseguard.

Valirion was busy, too. The first day he slogged into Havenport to make certain arrangements. The second day he went duck-hunting—a soggy endeavor that netted him exactly one scrawny bird. The third day he climbed up into the attic to patch the votary's leaky roof. Sarra envied him the physical activity.

Deprived of another woman to talk to—for, like most votaries at shrines all over Lenfell, this one was a widower—Sarra applied herself to the Ladder Song. On blank pages torn from a broadsheet collection she and Alin wrote down every verse either could remember, glossed in a generous margin by variations.

"*How* many verses?" Val asked, serving himself with the last of the duck stew for lunch.

"Twenty-seven Ladders in twenty-four verses," Alin answered, unperturbed when his cousin groaned. "We can identify sixteen pairs."

"Or a little over a third of the total that other song says exist." Sarra rubbed the small of her back; the wooden chair was the wrong height for hunching over the bed where their books were spread out. The alternative was to share the small, rickety table with Elomar and his hooks and feathers.

"Exist*ed*," Alin amended. "Some were lost with Ambrai, remember. Ladders would be where someone needs them—Mages, Lords of Malerris, and Ryka Court for the convenience of the government."

Sarra nodded. "I think your three hubs theory makes good sense."

"As for the others—there has to be one from Domburron to Domburr Castle, to account for Anniyas's winning a battle against the Grand Duke and killing that Mage in the same day."

"So *that's* how she did it!" Sarra exclaimed. "I should've realized. The history books sort of slide around it, implying she set the order of battle and then rode like hell."

"Who took her through?" Val asked.

"Didn't you know?" Alin looked genuinely amazed. "It was Auvry Feiran."

Sarra felt her jaw drop and heavily picked it up again. "But he couldn't—I mean, he was barely thirty, and still a Mage Guardian—"

"I heard it from Gorynel Desse himself." Alin scratched his head with one hand—they were all in need of hot baths—and poured himself a mug of lukewarm tea with the other. "Feiran did it on his order. Gorsha was First Sword, remember. Discipline was his responsibility. Warrior Mage Lirsa Bekke was working for the Grand Duke, and—Sarra, what's wrong?"

"N–nothing. It's just—I didn't know the association between Feiran and Anniyas went back so far." She was babbling, and couldn't stop herself. "He didn't—I mean, I heard they didn't even meet until after Maichen Ambrai married him and Glenin was born, and that was years later."

"The length and strength of their teamwork is something to consider," Valirion muttered.

What she considered was screaming: *Damn it, how much hasn't anyone told me!* Then another thought landed on her like a lion on a limping fawn: she'd been traveling by Ladder for weeks, and it only now occurred to her that so could Glenin and Auvry Feiran.

They might be at Ryka Court after all.

How much did she resemble her mother? Lady Lilen had said there was a look of Maichen about Sarra. Would her father and sister see it, too?

She turned to Val. "You said I'd be hard to disguise as a boy. How would you disguise me as a girl?"

"Huh?"

"No, that won't work," she fretted, rising to pace. "Garon has seen me. He'd notice."

"What are you talking about?"

"Only this," said Elomar Adennos from across the room. "She is recognizable as someone she is not."

And that, Sarra thought, was as neat a way of putting it as ever could be.

"Don't concern yourself, *Domna*," he went on, not looking up from winding string around a feathered hook. "They won't see what you fear they might. You would never be risked in such a fashion, because of who you are."

"Who is she?" demanded Val.

"Who *isn't* she?" corrected Alin.

The Healer Mage raised his left hand, palm out, index and middle fingers upright and together, the other two fingers curled inward over the thumb. Sarra had never seen that gesture except in drawings in old books. But she knew what it meant: Mage-Right. The topic being discussed was to be discussed no more, except among Mages.

And that ended it as far as Alin was concerned. Val

opened his mouth to ask again; Alin silenced him with a single look.

Just before dawn of the next day, as they were readying to leave for Havenport proper, Sarra took advantage of a moment alone with Elomar.

"What did you mean by invoking Mage-Right?" she asked quietly.

"Only that Wards have been set." He finished arranging the feathered hooks in a segmented box, and closed the lid. "Trust in them to conceal who you are."

"And who do you think I am?"

He gave her a slow, whimsical smile. "Lady," he murmured, "yours was the first birthing I ever attended as a Healer Mage."

After a moment she managed, "How could you possibly remember one newborn?"

The smile grew wider, like dawn sunlight expanding on the horizon. "Because you were the loveliest, or cried the loudest? No, though you *were* a pretty child, with good lungs put to immediate use."

"Then how—?"

"I will answer with a warning. Of the formal gowns you wear at Ryka Court, let none go lower than—forgive me— *here*." And he tapped a fingertip lightly on her shirt between her breasts.

Dumbstruck, she watched him leave the cottage.

He had seen her stark naked in the stream—and seen the small, round, rose-colored birthmark. Her father had once told her that St. Sirrala had kissed her there to start her heartbeat.

Her father, whom she might see again at Ryka Court.

15

It rained again late that afternoon, a fat and lazy rain that fell until past midnight. By early morning Sarra was on board ship, and needed no excuse of seasickness to keep to her cabin. Ladder Lag had been replaced by a miserable head cold.

Although the ship from Roseguard was late—arriving not in the evening but before dawn the next day—the exchange was made with a smoothness that made Alin gnash his teeth with suspicions. At first light, two sailors rowed a skiff ashore, dropped off five passengers (wine merchants ignorant of how convenient they were), and waited at the jetty while "*Domna* Liwellan" stretched unsteady legs. Few people were about in the predawn gloom, yawning as they extinguished streetlamps, swept shop steps, or trod the last hour of the Watch.

The therapy for seasickness worked so well that "Sarra" felt able to have some breakfast. She entered a tavern the moment its doors opened for business. But after a single sip of mulled wine she clapped a hand to her mouth and raced for the toilet stall at the back of the inn. When she returned a few minutes later, the kindly innkeeper assisted her faltering steps to the skiff.

The sailors began rowing back to the ship minutes later. If the little craft rode lower in the water and the oars were stiffer than the weight of two men and a young woman could account for, there was nobody around to notice.

"Too easy," Alin kept muttering, and Val kept elbowing him under the stifling tarp that concealed the two of them and the two Mages. Already soaked from the rain, crouching in four inches of water meant little added discomfort beyond the cramped position—and the sea-and-sheep stink of the tarp.

They boarded on the far side of the ship, invisible from Havenport. It was difficult getting up the rope ladder, but they managed in good order. Sarra had no idea how the Mages, Alin, and Val would be explained to any curious crew—the swelling of her nasal passages made it torture to think about anything—but she trusted to Captain Nalle's discretion and imagination.

Agata Nalle, born a slave in Cantrashir, had been purchased and freed at the age of eighteen by Orlin Renne. The girl had gladly discarded her slave name and taken a form of Agatine's in gratitude. Tarise's family, the Fourth-Tier Nalles, had given her a home, a trade, and a Name. This last was in defiance of the Census Ministry, which still listed her as an unTiered former slave. Now thirty-one, Agata had been captain of the Slegin flagship, *Rose Crown*, for three years. She was as frequent a guest at her benefactors' table as sailings permitted; Sarra knew and liked her very well.

That evening Agata Nalle joined Sarra in her cabin for dinner—a habit established during the voyage from Roseguard with Sarra's double, when she came bearing potions to cure seasickness. This night she arrived with a gift from Elomar, a concoction supposed to make Sarra feel better. Though her fever was down, her head still felt stuffed and her nose dripped like a leaky faucet.

"Who was my double?" Sarra asked when she'd downed the foul-smelling brew.

"Mai Alvassy. Daughter of *Domni* Renne's cousin Tama. She's your age, blonde, small—there's even a good resemblance in feature. Blue eyes, though."

"I only got a glimpse of her in the tavern." Sarra paused to blow her nose. Similarities between herself and Mai Alvassy didn't surprise her in the least: their mothers were first cousins. *Let's see . . . Tama married Gerrin Desse, son of Gorynel's sister and Grandmother Allynis' brother Telo. Tama's mother was Orlin's father's sister—and their cousin was Gerrin's grandfather—sweet Saints, no wonder the patron of genealogists is Tamas the Mapmaker!*

"We traded cloaks so fast I barely saw the color of her hair, let alone her face," Sarra went on. "And then she disappeared. Do you know where?"

"Yes, but I can't tell you." Agata smiled. "Sorry."

"That's all right. I'm getting used to it. Can you at least tell me where she usually lives?"

"Domburronshir."

Of course—Enis Dombur was Tama's grandfather. His dower would've gone to her mother, and now to Mai. If I recall correctly, it's isolated out in the Endless Mountains. Might make a good base for the Rising. . . .

"Sarra dear, will you please stop thinking so loud?"

She blinked and then grinned. "You can't possibly hear the wheels spinning, they're wrapped in wool! Aga, my head is about to explode!"

"Have some more tea." She poured from a small pot into Sarra's cup. "Brewed just for you by that long, thin Waster who calls himself a Healer Mage." Agata's wide, sea-weathered face crinkled with laughter. "I don't know what Luse Garvedian sees in him. I like my men with something more on their shoulders besides a shirt."

"You and Tarise!" Sarra laughed, not adding that she was beginning to know just what Lusira saw in him.

"I thought we'd have two more guests," Captain Nalle went on, slicing cornbread. "But Val Maurgen says they took ship with a load of books."

Sarra explained. "It was incredible—all of it untouched and forgotten."

"I'm not surprised. What Mage would betray her Tradition by opening the lock for Anniyas?"

"Hmm. I hadn't thought of that." There was an appalling number of things she hadn't thought about. "Well, the books will be safe, anyway, and in Mage hands. Alin says the Captal came on board quite openly when you docked."

"Hard to hide him, silly to try. Officially, he's off to Ryka to beg better quarters. He whines rather eloquently, truly told."

"As bad as all that?" Sarra breathed tangy steam. "I didn't see him, you hustled me in here so fast. What's he like?"

"As for shoulders, his are stooped—from more than Scholarly pursuits. The weight of being Captal ... eh, he doesn't carry it well. I met him last time Lady Agatine was in Havenport. He doesn't improve on closer acquaintance."

Sarra listened, and learned. Though the Rising seemed comprised largely of Sarra's own kin, she had yet to discover its intricacies of personality and purpose. And this she must do in order to be an effective leader.

She'd spent the first twenty-two years of her life asking plain questions when she wanted to know something. Youth, and the innocence assumed to accompany it (plus a pair of very wide eyes), had worked well so far. But now she was a woman grown, and headed for Ryka Court, and it was time for subtlety. For saying what she meant without actually saying it; for telling the truth without telling all of it. (*"My only Mageborn daughter,"* said Lady Lilen's voice in her mind.) She had more secrets than her own to keep now.

Because Agata Nalle was an old friend, Sarra could use the direct method a little while longer. She forgot about her cold—or perhaps Elomar's potions were working—as she queried the captain on a hundred different matters and at least that many personal relationships.

By the time they reached Ryka Portside, Sarra felt reasonably confident. She had Elo's assurance that she would not be known for anyone other than Sarra Liwellan; she had her speech to the Council prepared and rehearsed; she had solved at least a bit of the Ladder riddle; she had shaken off the worst of her cold. Most of all, there was work to be done, *real* work for the Rising at last.

She went out on deck that evening and finally met the fidgety, ineffectual Captal. He treated her to a ten-minute recital of his woes: poverty, distrust of Mageborns, the pitiable facilities in Shellinkroth. Though Sarra agreed with everything he said, she agreed with Agata Nalle, too: he *did* whine very well.

The Captal himself rescued her from death by boredom when he excused himself to go watch their Portside approach from the bridge. After landing, they would rest for the night at an inn run by the Council, and then travel overland to Ryka Court.

Where Sarra might very well see her father and sister again.

She didn't look at Ryka. She looked northwest, where The Waste was. Where her other sister was.

Soon, Cailet. Very soon.

Betrayals

1

A petulant scowl marred Garon Anniyas's handsome face as he regarded the young woman he husbanded. "But you're *always* gone. How can I be expected to father a daughter when you're never here?"

Glenin gave him the briefest of glances, then returned to her packing. "Pregnancy would be inconvenient at this time, Garon."

"You've been saying that one way or another for four years! Mother isn't happy about this, Glenin. You should've had at least two children by now."

"Your mother contented herself with only one."

"My mother is not the issue."

She was, and they both knew it. This conversation, repeated at irregular intervals over the last two years, invariably annoyed Glenin. But because she still needed Garon, since through him she had his doting mother's ear, she made an effort to mask her feelings.

Turning, she smiled and said, "Come, husband, you know how much work needs doing. Pregnancy would keep me from the Ladders, and I hate being on board ship. The final six weeks before birth and until the baby's weaned, I wouldn't be able to travel at all."

"There are other people who can do what you do."

Even as he said it, she saw in his face that he knew this,

too, for a lie. And resented that she could do what he could not. For, despite a carefully chosen father in whose family Mageborns were quite common, Garon possessed neither a hint nor a glimmer of magic. He was in this respect a terrible disappointment to Avira Anniyas; in all others, however, she considered him the model of all the masculine virtues.

Glenin knew better. He showed his sweet, obedient side to his mother—and to Glenin herself, the first year of their married life. But Anniyas' hints about children had recently escalated into strong suggestions, and soon she would be making outright demands. Garon was, in short, caught between the two very powerful women in his life. And he didn't like it one bit.

"But there are few people who can do it so well," Glenin said in answer to his lie. "Smile, Garon," she coaxed playfully, loathing the necessity. "We're young and healthy. There's plenty of time for making babies."

And, because it *was* necessary to keep him contented, and because it was also necessary to remind him why she did what she did so well, she locked their bedchamber door with a single gesture. He gave a start of surprise. She didn't often use magic around him; it was all the more effective for being so rare.

"In fact," she suggested, "why don't we practice?"

Her hired bower professional had used much the same words during their time together a few weeks before the wedding. She'd avowed herself so in love with her future husband that she wanted to learn everything men liked in bed. *Everything.* The young man happily obliged, giving her plenty of practice.

Humiliating—but she'd known from the first that Garon could be held only through the senses. He was incapable of feeling an unselfish emotion, even for his own mother. Basically, he was a creature fashioned for pleasures. Some were innocuous amusements: riding, hunting, dancing. His gambling was mildly scandalous, his love of food and drink merely self-indulgent. His interest in other women was something else. Glenin had no objections as long as the women feared her too much to allow themselves to be caught. She would not share him sexually. She neither loved him nor found him physically compelling—though she had subtly taught him to be an agreeable lover. But she knew that her personal power could be enhanced by the absolute and obvious fidelity of her husband.

Besides, Anniyas would be unhappy if her darling boy was unhappy in Glenin's bed. And because Anniyas must be kept happy, so must Garon.

He came to her willingly, not from husbandly duty but because he truly wanted her. Why should he not? All who saw her agreed on her beauty. Thus far there had been no need for any esoteric and somewhat chancy Malerris spells of desire. One day she might have to use them, a prospect she accepted with a shrug. Indeed, she would have been mortified to be the kind of woman a man like her husband would fix on for the rest of his life. His eternal devotion was not among her ambitions. All she needed was his sexual faithfulness.

That their relationship was the antithesis of most marriages still angered her sometimes. It was for the *husband* to work at making the woman happy and keeping her desire for him fresh; it was for the *husband* to worry about the woman's straying. Glenin knew she was quite probably the most coveted woman in the world—wealthy, powerful, intelligent, beautiful. She could have any man she wished, merely by arching a suggestive brow. But the one man she would ever want had died years ago.

So she had taken Garon Anniyas to husband. That she should have to demean herself by catering to this man—to any man—was the ultimate humiliation.

But behind this man was the woman who ruled all Lenfell. So Glenin gritted her teeth and made herself as necessary to Garon as—for the time being—he was to her.

As he caressed her, she allowed her body to respond while her mind disengaged and calculated. Tomorrow she would leave by Ladder for Dindenshir. Two weeks later she would travel upriver to Isodir. Somewhere on the journey she could pretend symptoms of pregnancy. By the time she reached Firrense, she would "miscarry." Anniyas would be sad and sympathetic, and encourage them to try again. Garon would be relieved at evidence of his potency and eager to prove it anew. The only potential drawback was that Anniyas might forbid Glenin further travel. But timely discovery of another nest of Mage Guardians would outweigh dynastic ambitions; Glenin had several such enclaves in mind.

Secrets are such lovely things, she thought as Garon heaved and sweated beneath her. (She had allowed him on top only once; experimentation with unconventional positions was a thing to be used when and if his desire began to wane.) Power came from secrets: hoarding one's own and discerning those of others, both types to be used with exquisite timing to specific purpose. But for every secret used, another must take its place. If she exposed one Mage enclave, she must balance the loss by learning another secret of equal value. Because no journey failed to provide its cache of secrets, she wasn't worried.

But she was genuinely shocked when, on the barge upriver from the Calmwater to Isodir, she found she really was pregnant.

2

Glenin traveled extensively and was always welcomed with every honor. Her tour in the last weeks of 968 was no different from the others. But the secret journeys and the private welcomes were far more satisfying.

Officially, she was not Mageborn. Officially, she traveled by Council ship. Officially, she was Special Emissary from the Assembly of Lenfell—the hundred and twenty elected Shir representatives who convened in legislative session from Maiden Moon to Harvest of each year. Officially, as the Lady in whose gracious name the antiquated system of Bloods and Tiers had been abolished, she investigated and reported to the Assembly on that system's dismantling.

Unofficially, she was accomplished in the Malerris Tradition of magic, did a great deal of traveling by Ladder, worked for the First Councillor, and hunted down Mage Guardians.

She was very good at both her official and unofficial duties.

A ship would leave Ryka Portside with Glenin officially on it. At the first stop she would go elsewhere unofficially by Ladder. When the ship docked again, she would sneak back on board and pretend she'd been there all along. A marked facility at spells of Silence and Invisibility served her well.

She was said to prefer entering a port without fanfare, slipping in to talk to the common folk without being recognized. Thus her official arrivals almost invariably took place in the middle of the night, and any reception by local dignitaries was scheduled the next day—the later in the afternoon the better.

Her unofficial arrivals took place anytime. From the Ladder in Renig, for example, she would go to Malerris Castle and thence to Kenroke or Wyte Lynn Castle or Dinn or, indeed, almost anyplace on Lenfell. As long as she could get to a Ladder that led to Malerris Castle's central network, she could pick and choose her destination. The only stricture was getting to her ship's stated port in time to make her official arrival.

The Lords of Malerris—at the Castle and elsewhere—welcomed her visits with respect and affection. Many had become friends; several had named their children after her. She was known to be their future, for what Avira Anniyas gained, Glenin would use.

The First Councillor, not being stupid, knew who would succeed her, but at the age of sixty-eight she was nowhere near ready to relinquish her power. What Anniyas did not know, being too necessary at Ryka Court to visit Malerris Castle more than a few times a year, was that she would most probably not see her seventieth Birthingday.

Glenin knew it, and so did the Lords of Malerris.

Although it had long been planned that Glenin would bear a child before Anniyas' death, the pregnancy she discovered on the tenth day of Candleweek was no part of anyone's schedule. The Great Loom did not allow for it at this time. The interweaving of her thread with Garon's must not come until the Mage Guardians were annihilated once and for all, because of the danger of their subversion. There had always been tales of young scions of Malerris turned from the Weaver to the Mages. Auvry Feiran—whose pattern in the Loom was proudly termed the Great Seduction, even by him—was Malerrisi vengeance. It was unthinkable that the grandchild of their crowning success would be born into a world where any Mage Guardian survived. So this pregnancy must be terminated.

Besides, the child Glenin carried was a girl and it was imperative that she bear a boy.

Because she was dedicated to the Malerris Tradition, she accepted their dictates regarding the timing and sex of her offspring. Glenin's childbearing had been carefully planned by the Fourth Lord, Master Weaver; lavishly prepared for by the Third Lord, Threadkeeper; eagerly anticipated by the Second Lord, Master Spinner; and patiently awaited by the First Lord, Warden of the Loom. The Fifth Lord, the Seneschal with his golden Scissors poised at the first sign of a snag, was the person to whom she would report the difficulty. He would then arrange to solve it, as was his duty.

But because she was also the First Daughter of First Daughters going back more than a score of Generations, Glenin secretly rebelled at the sacrifice of her own First Daughter to the Loom. She knew she must not bear this child. But, despite the multiple discomforts of early pregnancy, she couldn't keep herself from wanting to keep it just a little longer.

So she did not use the Ladder in Isodir, nor the one in Firrense, to visit Malerris Castle.

In both cities, and at short stops in town along the rivers between, she did her usual work. She strolled quays and marketplaces; took afternoon tea in the houses of local notables; accepted petitions for delivery to the Council members for Dindenshir, Rinesteenshir, and Gierkenshir; visited infirmaries and schools and factories.

These carefully planned rounds established Glenin as not above mingling with the common folk; as mindful of the importance of each town's leading citizens; as a sympathetic intermediary between the people and their elected representatives; and as deeply concerned with health, education, and trade.

And they adored her for it.

Some of it she genuinely enjoyed. There was always something fascinating by way of regional handicrafts to pick up while shopping—and besides adding to her wardrobe, jewel coffers, and art collection, it pleased the provincials to see her buy and often wear some item of local crafting. She also liked her hours at the various academies. Small children worshiped her, older girls wanted to grow up to be her, and boys invariably fell in love with her.

Truly told, Glenin was a sociable creature, deft in the practicing of her wit and charm. There was no one she could not win over and she shone in both large gatherings and individual encounters. In this she was utterly unlike Anniyas, who, curiously enough, was extremely shy and needed a few stiff drinks before she could face even four guests at dinner. Though she had no such problems in political intercourse, her rural childhood in Tillinshir had left her with a dread of social gatherings—as if no gown, no matter how elegant or costly, could make her feel well-dressed and no amount of washing could remove the barnyard from her boots.

Glenin's advantages over Anniyas in this respect were nearly laughable. Not only was it in her nature to be gregarious, but she had lived the first years of her life in the most glittering, sophisticated court in Lenfell as the First Daughter of the First Daughter's First Daughter.

In Ambrai's glory days, Grandmother Allynis hosted one major party every Saint's Day and at least one minor one every week, mainly because she wanted to know what Ambraians were thinking. This information she used constantly in her governance of the Shir. Banquet, lawn picnic, garden tea, country dance, formal ball, morning poetry reading, afternoon musicale, evening concert, midnight supper— Allynis Ambrai had quite simply adored giving parties. Maichen attended all these events and still more at various city residences. She was her mother's link to the younger generation, but she also loved people and they loved her. Both women understood that social occasions had a variety of purposes: to gather news and gossip; to see and be seen; to flirt, court, and fall in love (which, in fact, Maichen and Auvry Feiran had done at a spectacular ball given by her cousin Gorynna Desse); to discuss and barter and politically maneuver in an atmosphere more relaxed than an audience chamber.

Barely eight years old when she left Ambrai, still Glenin had been a perceptive child, observing her grandmother and mother in action and instinctively comprehending what she observed. As the next heir, she had attended all social occasions (except those that started past her bedtime) from the time she was five. So she had begun with a vast advantage over Anniyas.

Besides, Glenin Feiran was acknowledged to be the most beautiful woman in the world (with the possible exception of

Lusira Garvedian), and Avira Anniyas would never be anything but short, dumpy, and plain.

"Plain" could never describe Isodir. Its nickname of the Iron City—said by its ruling eponymous family to be a tribute to their resistance to Grand Duchess Veller Ganfallin—was really a reference to the local mania for wrought iron. Doors, windows, gates, sewer grates; chairs and tables, benches and bookshelves and bedsteads; trellises, gazebos, catwalks fifteen feet above the streets—everywhere the eye was dizzied by twisted bars, curlicues, floral sprays, medallions, all of it painted either black or white. The Isidir Blood reserved exclusive right to use colors. Within and without their capacious residence, what ironwork was not painted Isidir purple was painted Isidir yellow, and motifs of violets, dark lupines, daisies, daffodils, and dandelions were rampant.

Glenin hated the Iron City. It felt like a cage for a reason other than the obvious. Iron and magic did not mix, except in ancient swords forged by the long-extinct Caitiri's Guild. The Sanctuary Tower at Malerris Castle, the one with iron rods in its walls, had the same effect on her and most other Mageborns. One could talk of magic and plan its use there, but working it was impossible.

As much as she loathed Isodir, the Iron City, that deeply did she love Firrense, the Painted City, where nearly every wall on every street was decorated with a mural. Scenes real or imaginary; portraits of persons living, dead, or legendary; geometric patterns that repeated a thousand times or never appeared twice—and there was always something new to see and admire. Despite eaves and awnings, weather eventually damaged the pigments. No wall lasted more than four years. The paintings were then either replaced with new ones or—in the case of those too wonderful to be lost—painted over exactly as they had been.

Everyone who visited Firrense toured the walls. Glenin did so her second day there, escorted by the Guildmaster of the Walls (twenty years in the post, a brilliant administrator and critic, but unable to draw a straight line with a ruler) in an open carriage. Glenin was constantly recognized and warmly welcomed as she made the rounds.

The first stop was the fantastical scene of the Saints—all 386 of them from the old calendar, one for each day of the year—that sprawled the length of High Street. For a full quarter mile it ran from All Saints Temple to the last shop before the great marketplace of Merchants Round. Lusine and Lusir guarded their flocks; Maurget fashioned a necklace for jewels held by Sirrala; Velireon scythed wheat; Tamas pointed to Firrense on a map; Tirreiz counted coins; Jenavirra smiled her sweet sad smile; Jeymian gathered forest animals around him; Lirance stood atop her tower, long black hair like a banner in the wind. Each scene flowed into the next with incredible skill, seeming to be all of a piece. Miramili rang wedding bells, Imili nearby with a basket of flowers; Steen raised his blade in salute to Delilah; Gorynel set type in a printing press while Eskanto sewed pages and Deiket shelved the finished books.

Even Saints whose names were long forgotten appeared on the wall, painted over five hundred years ago and repainted constantly since. Some part of it was forever being redone, for it took three years to get from one end to the other and by then it was usually time to start over. The artists never made mistakes, and the design never varied from the gigantic full-sized cartoon kept in All Saints. So many of the names and so much symbology had been forgotten that a small industry revolved around scholarly treatises arguing one way or another. Of these lost Saints, Glenin found most intriguing the golden-haired man setting a wooden ladder against a wall. No one knew his name, but she was certain he was either Mage Guardian or Malerrisi Lord. The ladder made it obvious.

Another of Glenin's favorite walls was being repainted. As her carriage passed by, she exclaimed in disappointment at the tarps and scaffolding covering a scene of Seinshir in spring. The Guildmaster began multiple apologies. Midway through the recital, Glenin ordered the driver to stop. She alighted, her escort close behind her.

"I'd like to see it, just the same," Glenin said. "Perhaps we could have something to drink as well." The Seinshir painting was on the wall of a tavern, and she was in need of something to settle her treacherous stomach. Damn Garon.

"Certainly, certainly," babbled the Guildmaster, and snapped her fingers at one of the outriders.

Glenin picked her way under the scaffolding past benches of covered paint cans. Lifting aside a portion of the tarp, she saw the familiar blue of the sea, the tall grass and flowers, the splashing stream. The Guildmaster, anxious to be helpful, yanked a little too hard on another tarp. Scaffolding rocked, bricks weighting the tarp shifted—and the drape fell away to reveal another scene encroaching on Seinshir's springtime charm. No, not encroaching; growing out of it, reaching from the green beauty in harsh splashes of hot color.

The Guildmaster wailed aloud. Glenin stood silent, transfixed.

Ambrai. Mage Academy, Octagon Court, Bard Hall, Healers Ward—yes, it was all here. All afire. Everything she had heard about the annihilation of her home was before her in livid color.

The person she'd heard it from was here, too. Auvry Feiran, tall and implacable, stood alone in the foreground. His was the only human figure in the composition. The fierce, triumphant smile on his face as Ambrai burned told Glenin everything she needed to know about the artist's intentions.

"Lady, I'm—I had no idea—" The Guildmaster was practically sobbing.

"Who did this?" Glenin asked softly.

"I'll find out—I swear I had no knowledge of—oh, immediately, Lady, I promise!"

Without another word, she climbed back into the carriage. The outrider, just emerging from the tavern, took one look at her face, and promptly dropped both crystal mugs of wine to the ground. As he hurried to mount, the innkeeper came out, ready to greet the distinguished guest. All he saw were his best serving pieces shattered on the street, the back of Glenin's carriage, and a half-finished painting on his wall that made his knees buckle.

"Cover that up!" he shrieked, staggering for the crumpled tarp. "What're you staring at? Give me a hand here! Oh, merciful Saints!"

Glenin stared at the driver's back, stone-faced and seething. *How had they dared? How? To paint an accusation that the Lords of Malerris were responsible for Ambrai and used my father as their tool—*

But the painting had only told the truth. The truth—for all Lenfell to see or hear about.

Ah, but who had seen? Only those who had gathered at Glenin's arrival in the district. None would dare speak of it.

"When I find whoever painted that—" the Guildmaster began.

"Will you?" Glenin inquired pleasantly.

The woman's jaw shut with an audible snap. Of course the artist would not be found. Someone would warn her or him. There were a million places in the world to become anonymous. And who would paint such an indictment without knowing the sensation it would cause—and planning in advance for a swift departure? It was akin to Bard Falundir's effrontery years ago, only the artist would probably have learned by example. No, she or he would not be found.

Glenin didn't much care, not even to learn the name. What shocked her was the gall of it, the slap in her father's face. She hadn't known he was so deeply hated.

So they blamed him for Ambrai, did they? And, beyond him, the Lords? What of Anniyas, whom Falundir had accused obliquely of the same guilt? Why had *she* not been in that painting?

"An interesting path of speculation," whispered a voice in her mind, and she closed her eyes briefly. *Yes, Doriaz— interesting, indeed. Does it indicate a campaign by the Rising to make my father the villain, with the Lords telling him what to do and Anniyas clear of blame? Or is Anniyas transferring responsibility to Auvry Feiran and the Lords? Or is it merely one rebellious, defiant artist at work here?*

"Do you wish to return now, Lady?" the Guildmaster ventured.

Glenin roused herself. "I've been invited to see several new compositions. There's no reason to let this incident spoil the day."

Pathetic in her relief and the implied absolution, the woman ordered the carriage to turn left at the next intersection. For the next hour Glenin praised and complimented and wished she could go back to the Council House and think this through in peace.

Finally back in her chambers, shock caught up with her. Instead of a quiet hour before dinner spent in thought, she hunched sweating and shaking over a sink, vomiting helplessly. *Damn* Garon.

By the time she could leave Firrense, she was well on the way to hating it, too. She cut her visit as short as decently possible without offending too many people—though most everyone had guessed the cause of her wan looks. The quiet sympathy she received irritated her even as she graciously accepted it and secretly cherished it as proof of how much she was loved. She didn't want to be pampered and catered to; she wanted to go to Malerris Castle, get this over with, and go home to Ryka Court.

Where she would have to battle a strong temptation to geld her husband—slowly, with his own nail scissors.

Curiously enough, while actually sailing up the Rine River and then down the Steen River, she felt fine. The sloop's gentle rocking on the wide waters soothed her. Besides, there was little to do but rest and read and watch the scenery go by. South Lenfell was a less diverse land than the North: there were ice fields and mountains, and rolling farmlands, and the soggy flats of Rokemarsh, and that was about it. Ambraishir all by itself was more varied than this whole continent.

Ambrai . . . she remembered its beauty from journeys with her parents and grandparents long ago. From Maidil's Mirror in the ragged Wraithen Mountains, the Brai River surged through magnificent gorges down to rugged hill country; farther south were broad wheatfields and grazing land before a twenty-mile stretch down to the sea where high winds were excellent for pushing ships upriver but terrible for any crop taller than a few inches. Glenin had traveled the whole of Lenfell and found much to admire, but in her secret heart Ambrai was still the loveliest.

Still, the South had its charm, mainly in the richness of its growing. For though it was winter in North Lenfell, here it was high summer. In the orchards, branches were bending with the increasing weight of fruit; fields of short grain like green velvet spread beside earlier crops glowing gold and rippling eight feet high in the breeze. Villages and small towns appeared at intervals, set far back from the river to escape the yearly spring flood that roared down from the Endless Mountains. One of Glenin's tasks this trip was to discuss the possibility of dikes and levies so the settlements could expand, but she was beginning to think a damming project might be a better idea. The thought pleased her, being quintessentially Malerrisi: to control, to bring into order, to tame the two great rivers, was better than allowing them to run wild each spring.

Rural visits were always easy for her—and one reason was that there were so few names to remember. No town of less than 500 inhabitants contained more than three family Names and a local Deputy of the Census who kept all the bloodlines straight. Although the purge of the Fifths after the

Waste War had culled out the majority of defectives, there lingered a strong prejudice against consanguinity. One of Glenin's other duties was to hear requests from villagers to find young men of other Names willing to relocate and husband the local girls for an infusion of fresh blood. These youths' Names would be forgotten, for their children would, of course, inherit the mother's Name. But the Deputy of the Census would keep track of it all, and fear of disease and disability would fade for another few generations. Glenin thought this silly, for there hadn't been a single birth of a defective reported in all Lenfell for centuries. But it was a simple enough matter, and created much goodwill, for her to send husbands to some remote village. All were eager to leave old homes behind; some brought dowries; and a select few, those who would husband First Daughters, were allied to the Lords of Malerris.

So Glenin had sailed up the Rine to Isodir, and then down the Steen to Firrense, doing her multiple duty while every day growing angrier at Garon.

On the fourth day of Midwinter Moon she boarded her seagoing ship once more. From Dinn it had sailed to Firrense's port on the Sea of Snows, arriving just in time to collect her for the scheduled journey to Domburr Castle.

Waiting for her on board was the Fifth Lord of Malerris.

Vassa Doriaz bore scant resemblance to his long-dead brother. Golonet had been a lean, elegant, tawny lion with a gravel-and velvet voice. Vassa was just as tall, but the similarities ended there. At forty-three, a husky body spectacularly muscled in his youth was softening. Dark hair and blue eyes icy as a mountain lake were fading to gray. But the evidences of aging were deceptive: in the five years since his elevation to Fifth Lord he had personally killed seventy-four Mage Guardians.

He rose and bowed when Glenin entered the cabin. She gestured permission to sit. She busied herself with setting a Ward on the door, counting her luggage, and removing hat, scarves, and gloves. Only then did she seat herself on the second chair in the stateroom and look her tutor's brother in the eye.

"You know, of course."

"Yes, *Domna*."

So they still would not accord her the title of Lady she coveted so much. Though she heard it regularly as a First

Daughter, it would mean nothing to her unless on the lips of a Lord of Malerris. Irritation made her voice sharp. "It will be necessary to arrange an excuse to sail for Seinshir instead of Domburr Castle. See to it."

"I shall."

At least he was polite enough to refrain from questions—unlike the Warden of the Loom. The First Lord did not consider himself superior to all other men; he considered himself superior, period. Anniyas remarked once that she doubted the First Lord's father had ever taught him any manners; Glenin earned roars of laughter when she replied that she doubted if the First Lord had *had* a father.

But Evva Doriaz, mother of Golonet and Vassa, had schooled her two sons rigorously. It showed now in the Fifth Lord's restraint despite what must be vast anger at this accidental pregnancy.

He did further credit to his upbringing by pouring her a cool drink from a pitcher set on the table between them, waiting for permission before serving himself. Likewise he waited again for her to speak first, as was proper.

"I didn't use the Ladders for a very good reason, Vassa," she said, giving him his first name because she could never bring herself to address him as she had his brother.

He nodded. "Miscarriage resulting from a Ladder is much more traumatic than the medical procedure. I understand. We all do."

"Good." The difficult part of the conversation over, she pointed out the advantages of the situation as worked out the very day Garon had caused the problem in the first place. When she was finished, Vassa Doriaz again nodded.

"Very wise, *Domna.* I hope you suffered no serious physical unpleasantness."

Eleven mornings of the last sixteen she'd lost the previous night's dinner into a sink; she was unable even to smell her favorite coffee blend without breaking into a cold sweat; a headache began every morning precisely at Half-Sixth and lasted until she managed to choke down some food. Her temper was dangerously short and she felt like eight kinds of hell.

"Nothing to signify," she said.

"I'm glad to hear it. When it is time, your carrying should be easy." He shifted in his chair, finished his drink, and changed the subject—not impolitely, but firmly. "If I may,

Domna, I should like to discuss something that has puzzled several of us. Have you any knowledge of Sarra Liwellan?"

"The girl proposed to inherit the Slegin lands? My husband met her in Roseguard last year, I believe. What's so puzzling about her?"

"The fact that she was seen at Malerris Castle when she was also on board a ship halfway to Havenport."

"Malerris Castle—!" Glenin sat forward. "By Ladder? Which one?"

"The Shellinkroth shrine. She and the two young men with her were diverted on their return journey to the Traitor's Ladder. But it was a near thing."

"They found nothing, of course."

"Bones and an empty tower. Still, the Mage Guardians now know two—that is to say, four—more Ladders. The question is, which of the three is Mageborn?"

"There's been no Mage or Lord named Liwellan in Generations."

"Fourteen, to be precise."

"Who were the men?"

"Not known. Both had the look of The Waste about them, I'm told—though observation was necessarily at a distance and nothing they said was overheard."

" 'The look of The Waste'?"

"Their boots were galazhi hide."

"A common enough material for the purpose."

"Acid-stained before tanning, not after."

"Ah." The scars of acid storms produced endless variations in the hide—Glenin's own gloves were of the rare Melting Snowflake pattern, perfectly matched—but the marks always showed up as white on the leather. Flaws acquired after tanning were invariably brown.

"Wasters, you say?" She mused a few moments, then smiled. "At least one of them was tall, dark, and very handsome."

"That was Lady Ria's opinion," he replied, lips twitching at one corner.

Lady Ria. Glenin had done a thousand times more work for Malerris than that simpering fool whose only talent was fecundity. Five daughters and three sons she'd borne to various Lords, all of them richly Mageborn, all of them nearly as stupid as their mother.

And yet Ria of the Third Tier Shakards was a *Lady,* while

Glenin Feiran, First Daughter of the Ambrai Blood, was merely a *Domna*—who must sacrifice her own First Daughter because she had been ordered to bear a son.

"How did you know?" he asked.

"Who else could it be but Taig Ostin?"

"That . . . had not occurred to us," Doriaz admitted slowly. "None of us have ever seen him."

"None of you travel as extensively as I," she retorted. "The last I heard, Taig Ostin was in Rokemarsh." With so brief a hesitation that not even the perceptive Fifth Lord noticed it, she added, "Six Mage Guardians live in one of those absurd stilt houses in Jenaton."

"Appropriate," he said, and for a moment his ironic smile resembled his brother's. "Jenavirra of the open book, patron of memories."

"All they have left," Glenin agreed, "perched at the end of the world like that. I've had them watched, of course, in hopes of catching bigger fish than Taig Ostin."

The excuse for not having revealed them earlier was given with a casual shrug of her shoulders. Technically, she need not even have mentioned it; she had advanced enough in the regard of the First Lord that he allowed her her own judgment in such matters. Humiliating to know she operated as an individual only with the permission of a man. Her father had explained it as being part of the discipline necessary to those who would become Weavers at the Great Loom.

Additionally, the fish all Malerris had been angling for these seventeen years was known to be the close friend and former lover of Taig Ostin's mother; if anyone could lead them to Gorynel Desse, Taig could.

Besides all that, it was not any Lord—or even the First Lord—who sat opposite her now. Vassa Doriaz was the Seneschal, with a power of life or death subject only to the consent of the Warden of the Loom. It was he who sought and excised flaws.

"If we deprive Ostin of one hiding place, he'll have to find another. You'd think he'd be running out of them by now."

"Eventually," Glenin said with another little shrug. "Kill the Mages in Jenaton. I've let them live long enough, and they've been small use to us. If it's done *correctly,* they may even be persuaded to speak before they die."

It was a deliberate reference, and Vassa Doriaz stiffened

slightly. He was skillful, ruthless, and lethal—characteristics imperative in a Fifth Lord, who must judge more sternly than St. Venkelos—but Anniyas had once told him to his face that he enjoyed his work too much.

"You welcome the necessity and never feel the loss. Regret the wasted lives, Doriaz. Regret the threads that are lost. Until you learn that, you will ever be too quick with those Gold Scissors of yours."

Seventy-four Mageborns in five years had discovered just how quick. Glenin wondered if he would add these six to his personal list or leave them to underlings eager for status. Well, it was none of her concern. She'd given up a secret according to prior plan—and damn Garon for making her lose a secret and a First Daughter and so much time—and she needed a secret to replace it.

"Where is Sarra Liwellan now?"

"She arrives at Ryka Court soon to petition the Council for inheritance rights to the Slegin lands."

"Well, she can't be Mageborn, and Taig Ostin certainly isn't—or he would never have come so close to death that time in Shainkroth. The other man must be the one taking them through the Ladders. What did he look like?"

"Slight, very blond. Nothing recognizable about him."

"Pity. You people really ought to leave the Castle more often." She indicated that he could pour her another drink. When he had done so, she said, "I'm rather tired. Perhaps we can continue this tomorrow."

"Of course, *Domna*."

Whatever delicate rudenesses she inflicted on him, he could always reply—in perfect courtesy—with that despised title. She forced a smile. When he shut the door she drained the cool fruit juice down her throat in five long gulps.

Several minutes later, while unpacking her nightrobe, she and the juice parted company. She barely made it to the basin in time.

Damn Garon! she raged weakly. *Damn him to Geridon's Hell!*

In that legendary location, men who were promiscuous, sexually importunate, or a bedsheet burden to the women who married them were condemned to the exquisite torment of a constant, total, eternally unrelieved erection.

3

The approach to Malerris Castle was from the north side of its island. There was no bay deep enough for an oceangoing vessel, but there was no treacherous current either, as occurred to the south with the outpouring from Viranka's Breast into the sea. Glenin regretted that she hadn't time to visit the waterfall. Now that the Mage Guardians knew of Ladders there and could appear at any time, it was too dangerous.

The fishing village that was the island's only settlement knew exactly nothing about the other inhabitants. Superstitious awe going back many Generations kept them from venturing to the Castle's precincts even before the destruction of 960. In days past, Malerris would send down servants to purchase produce: fish of all kinds, plus vegetables and fruits from the fields uphill from the village. Now they brought in supplies by Ladder, when they could.

"It would be nice," remarked Vassa Doriaz while he and Glenin were rowed ashore, "to have a steady supply of fresh food again."

Supply was the reason given for the change in course. The night of sailing, Doriaz loosened the bung of every barrel of water taken on at the Gierkenshir port. The captain was livid, vowing not only that he would never patronize that chandler's again, but that no other Council ship ever would either—and that Anniyas herself would hear about this.

The gilt on the coin was that the chandler's was an Ostin enterprise, and its ruination would suit the First Councillor up one side and down the other.

The reserves of fresh water would take them to Seinshir but not to Domburr Castle. Because Glenin was now known to be pregnant, the captain made all speed for the nearest populated island. Which, of course, was Malerris.

It had been renamed in 961 in Auvry Feiran's honor. Anniyas' suggestion, approved by the Council, a subtle reminder of the former Mage Guardian who had planned the destruction. Feiranin it became on all subsequently published maps. But few called it anything but Malerris.

Glenin suffered the amazed stares of the villagers as Doriaz lifted her from the rowboat to the sand. She smiled and gave greeting, wondering if she would have to plead fatigue in order to avoid a welcoming ceremony slap-dashed together at no notice. She need not have worried; the inhabitants had work to do before nightfall, and so after a brief speech by the mayor they dispersed.

Glenin and Doriaz went to the Council House for the evening. No town of any size on Lenfell lacked some sort of structure reserved for members of the government, itinerant judges, and the like. Feiranin's was surely among the most unimpressive: four brick walls, three windows, a thatch roof, and a rough wooden door with squeaky hinges. The whole building could have fit in Glenin's reception chamber at Ryka Court.

Inside was a little better. Someone had furnished the single room with two chairs, a cushioned settle, a standing lamp, and several small tables. A tall folding screen partitioned off a corner sleeping area that boasted a narrow bed with a trundle peeking out from beneath, a small brazier, a frayed Tillinshir rug, and a stand with basin and ewer for washing. There were no cooking facilities; the village supplied all food and drink.

Glenin arranged pillows on the settle and made herself comfortable with her feet propped on a chair. "I assume I'm going to become ill," she said.

Doriaz nodded. "We'll forbid this place to all after the sad news of your miscarriage. You, of course, will be up at the Castle. We leave tonight."

"I want to get back to Ryka Court immediately."

"Impossible without using a Ladder."

"Did you think I'd mention it without having a plan?"

"How do you intend to use a Ladder without revealing your Magebirth?"

It involved revealing yet another secret—and this grated her already raw nerves—but because the secret was not strictly hers she shrugged it off.

"What's more important," she challenged, "acknowledging that at least two Ladders still exist at Malerris Castle, or catching Taig Ostin at Ryka Court?"

Vassa Doriaz frowned.

Hating him, Glenin continued, "If Desse is the mind of the Rising, Ostin is the strong right arm. My father is waiting for me at Domburr Castle. Send my ship there—it'll take a good five days, but that can't be helped. He's a former Mage Guardian. He can use Ladders without much comment. This is a political emergency we'll say is a medical one. I'm going to be much sicker than you thought, Vassa."

Thus it was that Glenin was seen to leave the Council House five days later—pale, weak, leaning on her father's arm. He helped her into a small horse-drawn dray padded with blankets, and drove slowly up the hill to Malerris Castle. From there Auvry Feiran took his daughter back to Ryka Court by Ladder.

As for the large, dark-haired man who had accompanied Glenin into the Council House, he was never seen to leave it at all.

4

Auvry Feiran was sorrowful but accepting. Anniyas was heartbroken but determinedly optimistic for the future. Elsvet Doyannis, married now with two daughters of her own, was genuinely—if a touch smugly—sympathetic.

Garon was furious.

"How could you have been so foolish?" he cried, pacing her bedchamber. "It happened at last, and you ruined it!"

Glenin lay propped on pillows, reading documents. She must rest at least a day to give credence to reports of her fragile health, even though the Healer at Malerris Castle had done her work to painless perfection. There hadn't even been any cramping. Maddening as it was to pretend helplessness, Garon's tirade was worse. At least he had shown decency enough to confine his anger to privacy. It was proof of his real emotion that he yelled at her at all.

Glenin was not in the mood for it.

She set down her papers and glared at him. "How could I? How could *you!*"

He stopped pacing in mid-step. "What do you mean?"

"This journey was planned for weeks, and you deliberately got me pregnant! If I'm not pregnant now, it's no one's fault but yours! You know the risks to a Mageborn child on a Ladder!"

His lips tightened and he turned away.

"Guilty as charged," she fumed. "I could divorce you for this, Garon."

He spun around. The long, lavish ribbons decorating his shirt, designed to emphasize a slow and graceful movement, tangled about him like seaweed in a strong tide. He looked ridiculous, as most men did when they tried to follow a fashion they had not themselves set. If her absence produced such sartorial disasters as this, what else had he been up to?

"You'd *never* divorce me," said her husband. "Mother wouldn't allow it."

"She knows the Laws of Breeding as well as you do! And has more respect for them as well!"

The Laws stated clearly that a woman should bear a child only when—and if—she wished. It was a husband's responsibility to prevent untimely or unwanted pregnancy. There were various methods, ranging from simple abstinence to lamb-gut sheaths to sophisticated drugs used by the wealthy. Garon was not the abstentious type. He had tried a sheath once and said it spoiled his pleasure—as if that mattered.

"Husband, *dear*," Glenin finished, "would you care to let your mother inspect your medicine box?" Knowing full well that the bottle in question would give him away by being too full. "Rest assured that *I* will. Every full moon."

"I was justified!" Garon snarled. Sheer bluff; his eyes were scared. "You should have had a child years ago! Mother agrees with me!"

The old argument again—something else for which she was not in the mood. Needing an interruption, she reached for the thoughts of a servant down the hall—gently, softly, so fleetingly the girl would never know the idea was not her own. Aloud, she said, "Compose yourself, Garon."

"I suppose now you're going to punish me by denying me your bed?" he sneered. "That's no punishment, Glenin—and it isn't as if yours is the only one I've been in!"

She froze, and negated the summons so abruptly the servant's headache lasted into the next afternoon. "What did you say?" she whispered.

"Well, what's a healthy, normal man supposed to do? You're gone for weeks at a time. I don't fancy pretending

I'm a eunuch in your absence, with nothing upright about me but my spine!"

The emotion Garon mistook for shock was so profound that she simply could not move. Encouraged, he grinned at her.

"I'm young, handsome, rich, and coveted. What did you imagine, that I languished in my rooms, pining for you? No, by Geridon's Balls, not me!"

I have to get him to touch me, she thought within the icy facade that hid not astonishment but fury. *I have to get him to come over here.*

So she used a gambit more often employed by bower lads to melt the hearts of cooling customers. She buried her face in her hands and cried.

It was a minute or two before Garon made his approach. One step, then another, a long pause, a whisper of her name and "I'm sorry," another step. . . .

His hand touched her shoulder. Lingered in an awkward stroke meant to soothe. Descended once again.

"Glenin—please, don't cry. I'm sorry. I didn't mean—"

And she grabbed him.

He would never know what had happened to him any more than the maid knew the real origin of her headache. But Glenin knew. Glenin was one of the best spellbinders the Lords of Malerris had ever seen. The First Lord, Warden of the Loom, had admitted as much.

Garon left that room spellbound, and remained so for the rest of his life.

5

On the ninth day of Nettle-and-Thorn, the week presided over by St. Gorynel the Compassionate, Sarra Liwellan was due to speak before the Council at precisely Eighth in the morning. It was anticipated that once she had been heard and her petition for inheritance rights approved (few doubted it would not be), everyone would adjourn to the splendor of the Malachite Hall for a celebration of her new status.

She was on view everywhere around Ryka Court in the

days before the presentation. She rode out with courtiers her own age for an afternoon in the countryside, and was proclaimed by all the young blades to be a ripping fine horsewoman. She strolled the vast Council Gardens with ministers who afterward sighed that she was as charming as she was intelligent. She attended a small party given by Garon Anniyas in her honor, and the becoming modesty of her plain throat-to-heels blue gown sent other women shrieking to their dressmakers the next morning demanding similar garments. (The results were mixed; few ladies possessed Sarra's dainty waist and firm curves.) She took family dinner with the Trevarins, the Rengirts, and the Firennos Bloods, all of whom pronounced her the most delightful girl they'd ever met and began making plans for the likeliest of their unattached sons. In fact, every unmarried man of any standing at all within Ryka Court was frantic for an instant of Sarra Liwellan's time, a flicker of regard from her fascinating black eyes, even a glimpse of her shining golden head.

It was all precisely as Sarra had feared, and it was driving her crazy.

She favored her host, Telomir Renne, with twenty whole minutes of complaint early on the morning of her petitioning. He heard her out, watching as she paced the gorgeous Cloister carpets of his sitting room, and when she ran out of breath and invective laughed himself silly.

Telomir Renne held the post of Minister of Mining by virtue of his extensive experience on the Renne holdings in Brogdenguard. He was older than Orlin by six years, and their mother had never seen fit to enlighten anyone as to the identity of Telo's father. Her privilege, of course; the Census frowned on it, but Mother-Right was supreme. In childhood he had endured a certain amount of baiting at his unfathered status, but as his mother was a First Daughter of the Blood that owned most of Neele and half Brogdenguard, parents quickly mended their offspring's manners.

Jeymian Renne's beauty had caused enough windy sighs to turn a hurricane off course. Men from seventeen to seventy had vied for her favor; whichever of them had been Telo's father, his only visible bequest to his son was coloring several shades darker than Orlin's and a nose several sizes larger. But for those differences and the gap in age, they might have been twins.

Five years after Telo's birth, Jeymian Renne had met and married Orlin's father, Toliner Alvassy—great-uncle of Mai Alvassy, Sarra's cousin who had impersonated her from Roseguard to Havenport. The tangle of kinship meant, naturally, that Telo was in the thick of what Sarra now called "the Family Business": the Rising.

As he laughed over her complaints that winter morning, Sarra had to laugh, too. The young women she knew in Roseguard would kill for a chance at the young bucks of Ryka Court. Was it Sarra's fault she found the best of them foolish and the worst of them unspeakable?

"You're a spoiled brat," Telo remarked when he got his breath back. "Here I've arranged for you to meet the very flower of Lenfell's young manhood, and all you do is yawn!"

"I'm *not* a brat!" She threw a pillow at him, which he caught and threw back at her. "Oh, Telo, if you weren't here, I don't know what I'd do. I'm glad tomorrow is my last day at Court."

He folded his long frame into a chair. "Your two young Wasters have succeeded, then?"

They were free to speak in his chambers; Gorynel Desse himself had Warded the rooms against eavesdroppers. In fact, the suite had once belonged to the great Mage in the years he had been the Captal's representative at Ryka Court. No one, not even Auvry Feiran, had been powerful enough to cancel the Wards he had fashioned. And so they remained. Everyone knew it, just as they knew Minister Renne had not requested these rooms. They just happened to be the ones assigned the last person in Telo's post. Personally, Sarra had her doubts that it had "just happened" that way.

Anniyas's chambers weren't Warded at all. Sarra was astonished to hear Telomir say so when Val asked, though a minute later she knew she shouldn't have been. Wards directed at non-Mageborns could be kept secret only so long as visitors to the First Councillor's suite didn't compare impressions. Wards intended for Mageborns would be immediately obvious. Her well-known and growing dislike of things magical meant she could have no Wards at all.

But though a lack of Wards would make entry easier, it also indicated that Anniyas would leave nothing to the Rising's purpose in her rooms.

Luck had been with them, however. Sarra grinned at

Orlin's half-brother and replied, "They have succeeded indeed—and by visiting the library, if you can believe it! Val's crushed."

The pair had made extensive plans for a daring raid by night—complete with blackened faces, secret hand signs for silent communication, three different escape routes, and drugged needles ready to put any chance-met guards to sleep. The fourth day of Sarra's stay, after an idle remark of hers about books, a strapping young scion of the Doyannis Blood had organized a tour of the Council Library—of which his elderly cousin just happened to be Bookmaster. There, in a splendid display case in the main hall, was a letter to the Council in Avira Anniyas's own hand accepting the position of First Councillor.

"Thank all the Saints that she didn't just write, 'When do I start?' " Sarra finished. "She goes on for two solid pages about the honor and her unworthiness and how she'll try her damnedest to do a good job, and the duty she feels toward the people of Lenfell, and-humble-so-forth. Every letter in the alphabet, most of them in both capital *and* lower case, the way she slants her signature—everything Kanto Solingirt needs."

"But formal style, not personal." Telomir slid a wicker basket from under the chair, extracting balls of black and green wool and a gold crocheting hook. "She's not likely to use grand language in her private letters."

"You haven't heard the best part. In another case there was *another* letter—this one to her darling Garon back in Tillinshir. He's to pack up all his toys for a permanent move to Ryka Court and be Mama's good brave boy on the journey, and she can't wait to cover his dear sweet face in kisses—I almost threw up, until it occurred to me how it must gall him to have it on public display."

"What about the handwriting and so on?" Telo asked patiently.

"The same, just a little more scrawled, and shorter phrasing. She uses a thick paper made in Dindenshir. Easy enough to get, and Kanto says watermarks are no problem."

"Neither is her seal."

"Not for you, the man whose family commands the finest forges—and forgeries!—on Lenfell," Sarra agreed, grinning. "Elo Adennos is going to the Library this afternoon, and

he'll copy both letters into his Mage Globe. And that's all
there is to it."

"No wonder Val's disappointed." He paused to draw out
more yarn off the green ball. "Is your presentation to the
Council ready?"

"If I practice one more time, I'll sound rehearsed.
Everything's in order, Telo. Nothing to worry about at all."

"I'm glad you feel that way. In my experience, that's precisely when one ought to *start* worrying."

"You're as bad as Alin!"

He glanced at the mantle clock—a fine old piece made of
spruce and bronze, with a muffled tick and no hour chime—
and said, "Speaking of whom, I hope this time you won't
work the poor boy half to death. Laddering is all very well,
but too much of it, even for someone as experienced as Alin,
isn't healthy."

"We have stops at Neele and one or two other places.
That's all. I can't wait to get home and unpack those books."

"I thought you were more intent on giving Gorsha Desse
a lecture to burn his ears off."

"Oh, I'll do *that* first chance I get. In private, Telo!" she
assured him, laughing as his brows arched. "It wouldn't do
to cuss him up one side and down the other in public. After
all, he's the brains behind the Family Business."

"So he keeps telling me." Smoothing the complex web-
bing of yarn across one knee, Telomir frowned at it and
tugged a strand or two back into place. "I hate this damned
stuff. Never stays flat. Word is that the Council is favorably
disposed to your petition, by the way. You've done good
work here, Sarra. Those who were wavering came over to
your side after meeting you."

She gave an irritated shrug. "It's nothing to do with me
personally. Most of them have eligible sons and nephews."

"Granted, but you've been playing them off against each
other like a seasoned politician. You have the right instincts.
Agatine will be pleased to—"

Without warning, Elomar Adennos strode into the room.
He didn't even glance at Telomir Renne, instead fixing his
gaze on Sarra.

"If you are given to expressing shock, *Domna,* do it now.
You must reveal nothing when you enter the Great Chamber.
The Feirans, daughter and father, are here at Ryka Court and
will attend today's petitioning."

6

Glenin was not a member of the Council or the Assembly, and so sat with the other court notables in the balcony above the Great Chamber. Garon was in attendance—on his mother, not her, though he had escorted her most tenderly to her seat, sent a page to fetch an extra pillow for her back, inquired if she felt up to a long session, and detailed Elsvet Doyannis to keep watch over her.

"You're so lucky," Elsvet whispered after he had left them. "He absolutely adores you, Glenin."

She gave a little smile and a shrug, hiding mingled satisfaction and annoyance. Yes, he absolutely adored her now—body, heart, and soul—and would for as long as he drew breath or until she canceled the spell. His smothering concern was tiresome, but it was preferable to the alternative. Anyway, she told herself, better now than later, after someone had noticed he was cooling. It was easier to believe devotion renewed now, after the sorrow of losing a child, than after a period of near-indifference.

She and Elsvet were seated front row center in the gallery. The Council had not yet entered; all fifteen plain pine chairs with red velvet seat cushions were empty. The Council would come in through a door on the left, where Auvry Feiran stood ceremonial duty wearing the bemedaled dress whites of Commandant of the Council Guard. Garon was beside him, dressed as a lieutenant. Strictly honorary: soldiering bored him. Along two sides of the triangular white marble table, Guards of lesser rank were carefully placing paper, pens, small crystal pitchers of water, goblets, and, for Flera Firennos of Cantrashir, a bowl of fruit lozenges to soothe her chronically scratchy throat.

The Council met in the Great Chamber only on occasions such as this. Their regular sessions were conducted in a room half the Court away, where they could all look at each other across a wooden table made of planks from Grand Duchess Veller Ganfallin's flagship. The marble slab they would sit at this morning had been a present from the now-defunct Channe Blood ten Generations ago. Likewise the white marble plinth of the Speaker's Circle had come from the Channes, but unlike the stark table it was carved with the sigils of all the Saints.

Hanging from the balcony rails and around the walls were the colors of every extant Name on Lenfell. The banners were each a foot wide and three feet long, and appeared in strict alphabetical order with no precedence given the (former) Bloods—one of the changes made when, for Glenin's wedding present, the Council had abolished the Tiers. The sigils stitched on the banners of former Bloods, Firsts, and Seconds were the sole indication of rank. The flags of each Shir were draped in luxuriant folds behind the chairs where their Council members sat. With all that color screaming at the eyes, the plain white marble of table and plinth and floor was a relief.

"Have you met this girl yet?" Elsvet murmured.

Glenin shook her head.

"My husband says he can't understand the fuss. She's a shocking flirt with outrageously bad manners. Oh, I suppose she's marginally pretty in a washed-out sort of way, but nothing at all fashionable."

By all of which Glenin instantly understood that men were panting and Elsvet's husband was one of them, the girl's manners were charming, and she was a mere breath short of gorgeous.

"There's a reception after," Elsvet went on. "Are you up to attending?"

"I think so. You're sweet to worry about me, Elsha, but it's not necessary. I'm quite recovered—in all but my heart."

"Poor darling," her old schoolmate sympathized, patting her hand. "I was so looking forward to watching your little one play with mine. Did I tell you I'm pregnant again?" She placed a protective hand over her belly.

"Congratulations," Glenin said, smiling, wanting to slap the smirk right off Elsvet's mouth.

"Well, one day soon, I'm sure. You're young and healthy, and so is Garon."

"Yes," Glenin said, and then: "Shh, here they come."

The Council entered the Chamber in strict order of seniority and took their seats. The chair at the apex stayed empty, reserved for Anniyas. The ten women and four men

were dressed in plain white robes that billowed to the floor,
with stiff standing collars to the ears. The robes were open
at the front to reveal clothes in the colors of each Council
member's Shir. Someone had proposed once that they should
remain standing—and so should the spectators—until the
First Councillor's entrance. She had flatly refused to countenance this, although Glenin knew the suggestion had originated with Anniyas. From this Glenin learned that honors
were on occasion most effective when turned down.

Glenin's father and husband flanked the open door, and in
a hush more potent than the blaring of trumpets the entire
Chamber waited for Avira Anniyas, First Councillor of
Lenfell.

Down below the gallery were all the members of the Assembly, ten from each Shir; the Ministers of Mining, Agriculture, Commerce, Roads and Public Works, Census, Ports
and Shipping, and so on; and the Prime Justice and as many
of the Itinerants as were in residence at Ryka Court. Glenin
could see the first four rows and the two seats that were still
empty, reserved for her father and her husband. Garon had
no title but the "Lord" that had come to him on his marriage
to a First Daughter, but he had been allowed to sit with the
officials since his twenty-first year.

Auvry Feiran nodded once to the Council. Garon extended
his fist to his mother. She placed her beringed hand atop it
and entered the Great Chamber: short, plain, unimpressive—a curious guise for the most powerful woman in the
world to wear, but Glenin knew full well that her very in-
nocuousness was a strength. Who would believe that the
source of so many lethal schemes and secret murders was
this smiling little woman who waved one plump glittering
hand to acknowledge the crowd's cheers?

Being nondescript and unremarkable was not an option
available to Glenin, though she understood the advantages.
Her own guise was more effective the more she used it. Her
advantage was that one day, when *she* became the most
powerful woman in the world, she would look it.

She didn't listen as Anniyas spoke an ancient formula
summoning petitioners to the Speaker's Circle. Instead, she
watched the Council. They were seated according to years of
service, an invisible line of descending rank crisscrossing
the table as if it were a loom:

ANNIYAS

Tillinshir

Kenrokeshir METTYN -   - ELLEVIT Bleynbradden

Ryka	DOYANNIS -	- FIRENNOS	Cantrashir
Gierkenshir	FELESON -	- DALAKARD	Seinshir
Ambraishir	RIGGE -	- NUNNE	Dindenshir
The Waste	LUNNE -	- SENISON	Sheve
Rinesteenshir	ISIDIR -	- FENNE	Shellinkroth
Brogdenguard	BEKKE -	- DOMBUR	Domburronshir

Glenin had an excellent view of all their faces. *A portrait of Lenfell,* she thought sardonically. *Edifying, if occasionally nauseating.*

Sharp-eyed, silver-haired Tirri Mettyn, First Daughter Prime and great-great-grandmother, had worn out five husbands and eleven official lovers in her eighty years, over half of which she had spent on the Council. Elected in 926, she was senior to everyone, including Anniyas. They loathed each other and whichever way Anniyas voted, Tirri Mettyn voted the other from sheer habit.

Seventy-four-year-old Kanen Ellevit was another fossil and had been on the Council since 935. He had three interests in life: Bleynbradden, money, and pretty girls. In defense of the first, he was at times so tigerish that the Council often capitulated to spare the old man an apoplexy. His concern for the second had helped his Blood double its fortunes in the last fifty years. Regarding the third, at his age he was relegated to looking. It was asserted that Sarra Liwellan had his vote purely because of her looks. But Kanen Ellevit undoubtedly saw her as helpful to his other two interests: Bleynbradden had extensive ties to the Slegin Web, and these ventures were highly profitable.

Veliria Doyannis, Elsvet's mother, had held the Ryka seat since long before Elsvet's birth. She was limned in shades of gray: eyes the color and chill of steel, a formidable pile of iron-gray braids, a will of granite, and all the personal warmth of week-old funeral ashes. Her vast Name—almost as numerous as the Ostins—swarmed all over the island and most of North Lenfell. Her sources of information were envied even by Anniyas, whose wary ally she was. Proudest and most reactionary of Bloods, she hated the lower Tiers and had it not been impolitic would have hated Glenin for being the reason the system was abolished and the lower orders enfranchised. Sarra Liwellan's Blood was the only thing Veliria Doyannis found in her favor. Allowing Agatine Slegin to designate her as heir was too shocking to contemplate—yet here Lady Veliria was, forced to contemplate and even vote on just that. In simple terms, she was not pleased.

Flera Firennos ought to have retired years ago. She was seventy-two and almost completely deaf—though she would never admit it, for Bloods were emphatically immune to physical infirmities. When her thoughts wandered, the twin granddaughters who were her assistants explained her abstractions as "concentration on higher matters." When she addressed remarks to Council members dead twenty years, it was, "Incisive irony to remind colleagues of similar circumstances in her long career." When she nodded off during sessions: "Subtle commentary on the discussion." Whether or not she heard, let alone understood, today's proceedings—or anything else that happened in Council—was immaterial; the granddaughters would decide her vote as usual. Not being in their confidence, Glenin was unsure which way the vote would go.

Jareth Feleson was ungrayed and unwrinkled at sixty-five: a direct result of never having made a single decision about anything at all. He was husband to Marra Feleson, his distant cousin and publisher of Feleson Press, the only broadsheet still distributed worldwide. Though the Press claimed strict impartiality, it was taken for granted that it printed Anniyas's line. In Council, Jareth cast his vote as Marra told him; she found the Council less congenial than the luxurious Ryka Court offices of Feleson Press. Her feelings about the Liwellan girl were as yet unknown, but Glenin guessed the vote would be with Anniyas.

Solla Dalakard's elder brother Risson had engineered their Blood's victory over the Lords of Malerris—for which Glenin detested the whole family despite knowing it had been necessary. Fifty-nine, Solla admitted to forty-six and believed lavish use of cosmetics and lurid red hair dye made the lie plausible. She detested men in general and in particular any who dared call himself a "Lord" even if he was married to a First Daughter, and was eternally grateful that being a fifth daughter excused her from a duty to bear more Dalakards. She swore exclusively by St. Sirrala the Virgin—

Court wags had it that she'd vote in the Liwellan girl's favor because of her name alone—and each year proposed that all male Saints be removed from the official calendar.

Glenin's lips thinned once more as she contemplated the woman beside Feleson. Ambraishir had been represented by Glenin's family for fifteen Generations. The seat was now occupied by the skinny posterior of Lirsa Rigge. The first non-Blood on the Council, she had been seated the year Ambrai was destroyed. Her election had come by default. The Shir's three Bloods—Ambrai, Alvassy, and Desse—had been tainted by rebellion; of the Firsts, Feiran was extinct except for Auvry—who had other duties—and Garvedian was the Name of the late Mage Captal. Among Second Tiers, Rigge was the only one certifiably lacking traitorous ties. Their lands were in the far north of the Shir and they attended the Octagon Court only when ordered. After sixteen years on the Council, Lirsa Rigge still voted with prevailing opinion and still looked startled at being allowed to vote at all. Now that Glenin thought on it, though, perhaps astonishment was the only expression one could manage with eyes that big in a face that thin.

Semal Nunne, forty and never husbanded, sulked across the table from Lirsa Rigge. Nunne fancied himself a military expert. His knowledge of matters martial began and ended with a fascinated interest in men wearing uniforms. He was known as the Bloody Blood, for his initial response to any crisis, large or small, was a demand to send in the Council Guard. The resentment now on his handsome, moody face was directly attributable to the fact that the Ryka Legion in all its splendor was at formal drill on the parade ground, and he was stuck inside. He might vote against Sarra Liwellan from sheer spite.

Representation of The Waste had been problematical for a century and more. Of the Shir's two Bloods, the Ostins shunned politics and there was only one Pelleris left: the infamous Scraller. Branches of the Renne, Halvos, Somme, and Grenirian Bloods living in The Waste had all provided Council members during the preceding century. But in 964, after Glenin's wedding present opened the Council to all, Fiella Lunne had been elected—to the scandal of half Lenfell. She was not merely a member of a former Tier, but of the *Fourth* Tier. That her father was an Ostin and her grandfather a Grenirian counted for exactly nothing. In four years she had been snubbed often, and most often by Veliria Doyannis, who never addressed a single word to her in public or private. Fiella Lunne was a sturdy and stubborn fifty-three, well past the age when humiliation could cut personally. But on behalf of her Shir she demanded respect—and one piercing look from those hawk-green eyes set in a deceptively mild face ensured it in most cases. Childless, since the death of her adored husband in 946 she had mothered and mentored a dozen young nieces, several of whom had followed her into government service. One of them was now Minister of the Census. The Slegin and Renne ties to the Ostins, to whom the Lunnes were closely related, guaranteed Fiella's vote in favor.

Piera Senison, not yet forty and three times divorced (her short attention span was often exhibited in Council as well) was about as closely related to the Tiva Senison who had married Lilen Ostin as Glenin was—which was to say scarcely at all. Senisons usually supported Slegins, but Piera had a grudge against Agatine: she'd wanted Orlin Renne for herself. Her golden-brown eyes flickered constantly to the door where the Liwellan girl would enter as if she could hardly wait to humiliate Agatine's proposed heir.

Lean and predatory Granon Isidir was, at only forty-one, the darling of the proudest family in South Lenfell. The Isidirs had for ten years resisted the best that Veller Ganfallin could throw against the walls of their city, and they had never let anyone forget it. Granon was Anniyas's most vocal opponent for the sheer delight of the opposition. His name had been linked with many women, but he had never married; his devotion to his Name, his city, and his Shir was such that no woman could compete. His formidable grandmother allowed him to remain unhusbanded; a truly valuable male was never wasted in marriage to another family who would then have the benefit of his talents. In the Assembly since his twenty-fifth year, Granon's election to the Council had come with an unprecedented ninety-six percent of the popular vote.

Deiketa Fenne was nearly Anniyas's age, looked twenty years older, and had known her for the forty-odd years of their mutual public service: Fenne in the Assembly, Anniyas on the Council. They were the closest of personal friends and the staunchest of political allies. Deiketa was one reason Anniyas had wanted the Tiers abolished, so her old friend's status as a First would no longer prevent her from taking a

Council chair. It had been briefly rumored years ago that one
of the Fenne granddaughters was being considered to husband Garon, but shortly after Glenin Feiran entered the
scene the girl had died. Garon never knew what exactly had
happened to the charming twenty-year-old he'd been half in
love with. But Glenin did. So did Anniyas.

Last on the left was Gorynna Bekke. She held the seat
through special appointment after her aunt (also a Bekke,
and also a Gorynna) changed her mind about government
service and resigned shortly after election in 963. The
Bekkes owned what parts of Brogdenguard the Rennes did
not, and their partnership was the envy of all Lenfell. What
one produced, the other marketed. Yield from Renne mines
and Renne vines was shipped on the Bekke merchant fleet;
glass from Bekke factories and grain from Bekke farms were
distributed through a Renne consortium, and so on. Gorynna
had spent her twenties learning and her thirties chairing the
Bekke's hugely lucrative ceramics division (tableware in one
hundred and thirty patterns; bathtubs in five styles, eight
sizes, and sixteen colors; twenty-seven models of commode;
and countless varieties of industrial ceramics). Now in her
forties, she viewed government as a business, its profits
measured by a surplus in the treasury. Because Sarra
Liwellan was the fosterling of Orlin Renne, and Orlin was
Agatine Slegin's husband, the transfer of the inheritance was
more or less Bekke family business; so Gorynna was firmly
on the girl's side.

Youngest of them all, and least in seniority, was the darkly
gorgeous and utterly ruthless Irien Dombur, a playmate of
Garon's. He had been elected two years ago to replace a
cousin killed in a carriage accident. Rumor had it that this
had been no accident; that his branch of the Domburs had
designs on emulating Veller Ganfallin's conquests, only they
would do it with money, not soldiers; and that Irien found
the Liwellan girl so delightful that he had hopes of becoming her husband. Glenin, knowing Irien well, knew he
was attracted not by the girl's person but by her Slegin-
augmented purse.

And yet as Anniyas finished her invocation and the center
of attention walked alone and calm into the Chamber, Glenin
considered revising her opinion. Sarra Liwellan was radi-
antly blonde, delicately made, elegantly clothed, and undeniably lovely. Creamy skin, dark brown eyes, a wide mouth

that tilted slightly up at the corners—Glenin's discerning eye
noted that her nose tilted a bit as well, and a too-wide brow
spoiled the otherwise perfect oval of her face. Her gown,
high-necked and sliding down her slim figure to the floor,
accomplished several things Glenin saw at once and most of
the Court did not: that the cut and the thin vertical stripes of
Liwellan blue-and-turquoise and Slegin blue-and-yellow art-
fully disguised a short-waisted figure, and that the unfash-
ionable length hid high heels that added two inches to her
scant five feet of height. But who would notice imperfections when captivated by that glory of curling golden hair
cascading down her back?

For herself alone, Sarra Liwellan was a prize. With the
Slegin properties in hand, she would be the most sought-
after woman on Lenfell. Glenin did a quick total of the vote
in her head. Five in the girl's favor; three definitely against;
three who would vote with Anniyas and two who would vote
against Anniyas; one genuine unknown.

But how would Anniyas vote?

The girl paused to bend her head the precise degree necessary for a Blood to show respect for the Council. Onto the
table she placed the leather-bound folio of her petition. Then
she proceeded to the Speakers Circle at the far right. Her
hands were empty now; she would address the gathering
without notes. Such poise was surprising in one only twenty-
two, but Sarra Liwellan had been constantly at Agatine
Slegin's side these last few years. She placed both dainty
hands on the golden rail, standing so that she could with a
slight turn of her head address either Council or assembled
notables, and began.

"I come here today as a humble petitioner before the
Council. For myself, I am truly humbled by the honor of addressing you, and by the trust and faith placed in me by my
foster-mother. But on Lady Agatine Slegin's behalf, for all
those of her Name, I am proud that she finds me worthy to
represent her here today."

Glenin arched a brow at this intriguing start. The girl had
acknowledged the privilege, professed humility, and reminded everyone who she was. Her voice was clear, carrying, lacking both nervous stridency and any trace of the
slightly nasal Sheve accent. She did not tell the Council
what it already knew. She did not remind them that Agatine
Slegin was the last of her Name, or say what a sad occasion

it always was when an ancient family died out. She made no mention of the fact that she had studied and traveled and learned governance. Instead, she paid Glenin a compliment.

"Several years ago the Council abolished the system of Bloods and Tiers that long prevented many talented persons from holding office. This was wisely done, and Lady Glenin Feiran's doing."

For a fleeting moment during applause that belonged to both young women, the dark brown eyes of Sarra Liwellan sought and found the gray-green eyes of Glenin Feiran high above her. For that instant, Glenin could not look away. Her magic quivered oddly inside her. But when the girl relinquished her gaze, the tremor faded, leaving her puzzled and pensive.

"I say wisely done, for the wisdom of opening the Council to all has become obvious. It is now a Council more honestly representative of Lenfell in all its diversity. My petition is a result of that opening, and of that diversity. Assigning inheritance to another Name is a thing rarely if ever contemplated, yet here I stand before you, asking just that. In many ways this request goes to the heart of Lenfell's traditions. It speaks not only to property right, but to Mother-Right."

"What does she mean?" Elsvet hissed.

Glenin shook her head.

"A mother's gifts to her children are her Name and her property—unless circumstances force withdrawal or renunciation."

Her face and thoughts froze. *"Withdrawal or renunciation"—right after mention of* my *name!* She heard Elsvet whisper, "Cunning little bitch!", and wanted to kick her old "friend."

Sarra Liwellan now divided her gaze slowly and equally among the Council members as she spoke. "Long ago, Lady Agatine Slegin took me in as a fosterling. My own birthmother could not have been more tender in her care of me. So in every sense but that of Name, I am Agatine Slegin's daughter."

Glenin's eyes narrowed. She now had a fair idea of where this was going. It might be clever, and it might be exceedingly stupid; she'd know when the vote was taken.

"If the Council agrees," the girl went on, "I will one day inherit as if I was born her daughter. But what of her sons? They were born of her body. I was not. They bear her Name.

I cannot. Yet they cannot in law inherit anything but their shares of the Slegin Dower Fund. Where is Lady Agatine Slegin's Mother-Right when it comes to her four beloved sons?"

"Men *never* inherit!" exclaimed Veliria Doyannis. "Never! Outrageous even to speak of it! First Councillor, I demand—"

"Veliria, dear!" Anniyas sounded gently shocked, as if at a lapse in good grammar. "*Domna* Liwellan is in the Speakers Circle. I should like to hear her."

"Thank you, First Councillor," the girl replied with a graceful little nod. "As it happens, I agree with the distinguished Lady. Men have no right to inherit as if they had been born women. But I've been thinking about this, especially as it applies to my own situation. And doesn't it seem to you that this denies Mother-Right? Shouldn't every woman have the privilege of dispersing her property to the children of her body and her Name? *That* would be true Mother-Right, which is at the heart of every law of Lenfell."

"First Councillor," drawled Irien Dombur, "may I ask a question?"

Anniyas nodded permission.

"*Domna* Sarra, it was my understanding that you are here to argue your own case for inheritance, not those of your foster-brothers."

"Indeed I am here for myself," she agreed readily. "But it is by no means certain that the Council will decide in my favor. I decided on the journey here that if Lady Agatine were not to be allowed what I may call Foster Mother-Right, then I would place an option before the Council that clearly favors her Blood Mother-Right."

"You love her sons as if they were your brothers," said Flera Firennos, startling everyone. The ancient had not spoken coherently in Council in years, except to mumble her vote as dictated by her granddaughters. She further disconcerted the throng by adding, "Very commendable, child. You have my vote."

Glenin adjusted her mental for and against columns. Six squarely in favor now—and did Granon Isidir look thoughtful, deciding his vote before Anniyas cast hers and he automatically countered her? As the darling of his Name, if Mother-Right were extended to granting outright inheritances to sons, he stood to gain quite a bit.

Dombur was speaking again. "It is legal for a First Daughter to make an additional dower gift to a son if she pleases. So in essence a man may possess property, though he may not actually own it. But this is all connected with marriage, when the dower—whatever it may be—becomes the property of the woman. In the unhappy event of a divorce, the dower remains hers."

The Liwellan girl looked him straight in the eye. "Not if a husband retains sole ownership of what his mother gave him."

Pandemonium.

Veliria Doyannis was on her feet, shrieking; Piera Senison pounded a fist on the table in fury; the Ministers and Assembly babbled wildly; the gallery rang with yells. And more than a few cheers. Glenin listened, watched what she could see, and ignored Elsvet's splutterings. One day Glenin would bear the son required of her. By then she intended to be firmly in possession of Ambrai. Would it not be a very good thing to leave the whole of it to him, with no woman—no *Lady* of Malerris—able to claim it as dowry?

Glenin was impressed by this brilliant move. However noble the avowed motive, by suggesting this incredible alternative Sarra Liwellan had secured her own unorthodox means of inheritance. Better to give the Slegin lands into a Liwellan's hands than those of men. A very clever young woman. Pity she wouldn't live to see Roseguard again.

At last Anniyas signaled to Auvry Feiran, who took precisely one step away from the doorway. Glenin sensed the subtle touch of his magic. He didn't calm everyone instantly, for that would make them suspect magic. He merely damped tension in those who had been running out of steam anyway, and the step was reminder enough of his presence to silence everyone else. Glenin hid a smile. What Gorynel Desse had taught him in his youth, a Malerrisi education had honed to perfection.

"Dear me," Anniyas fretted. "All this noise! My dear," she said to Sarra Liwellan, "I understand perfectly that your affection for your brothers prompts this proposal, but—"

"I refuse to consider it!" Veliria Doyannis snapped.

"—*but,*" Anniyas went on with a mildly chastening glance sideways, "this isn't something we can decide in Council. It's a matter for the Assembly."

"Yes, First Councillor," the girl replied. "I'm sorry if I caused a commotion."

"Hardly your fault." Anniyas smiled warmly. "Is there anything else you desire to say?"

"Only that whatever the Council may decide, Lady Agatine and I will follow your wishes."

Glenin, wondering if anyone else heard the delicate distinctions in that little speech, smothered another smile.

"Very well, then. My friends, are we prepared to vote?"

They were. Garon rose from his seat and took the leather-bound petition from the table. He handed it to Irien Dombur, who opened it, took up a pen, and scrawled his signature. Someone in the gallery applauded, a sound swiftly muted as someone else hissed for quiet.

Garon presented the petition to Deiketa Fenne, who bit her upper lip before shaking her head. She would not sign; she was voting no. Up one side of the table the folio went, with each member of the Council indicating her or his choice. The order of signing—or not signing—was most unusual. Customarily Anniyas voted first. Glenin wondered what she had in mind by doing it this way.

Piera Senison actually slapped the leather halves shut. Glenin saw on Sarra Liwellan's face that she expected this. Anniyas, too—but was there the faintest frown of disapproval on her brow? Was she going to vote in the girl's favor?

Anniyas waved her son past her, saying, "I abstain for the moment, if my friends will allow me."

Lirsa Rigge looked slightly panicked at this lack of guidance. Tirri Mettyn looked annoyed. She signed, however, even though she had no indication of whether her vote in favor would agree or disagree with Anniyas's. Perhaps, Glenin mused, that was what the First Councillor had intended: a more-or-less honest choice of individual conscience, rather than voting to please or displease her. Glenin wondered what was so special about Sarra Liwellan to merit the oddity.

Dombur, Dalakard, Firennos, Ellevit, and Mettyn signed. Fenne, Senison, and Nunne did not. Elsvet's mother not only slammed the folio shut, she leaned back and folded her arms and glowered at Sarra Liwellan—who responded with a look of utter serenity.

Garon reopened the petition, his face showing as much irritation as he dared. He was being made to look the fool by having to open the thing again and again. The slow smolder in his eyes was the funniest thing Glenin had seen in weeks. Jareth Feleson was polite enough merely to shake his head, and in fact sent a glance of tentative apology toward the girl standing at the marble plinth. Lirsa Rigge also declined to put her signature to the document. Fiella Lunne signed. Granon Isidir—still looking thoughtful—did not. Gorynna Bekke scratched her name across the page with a flourish. And the vote stood at seven for, seven against, with Anniyas abstaining.

Precisely as Anniyas intended.

Glenin was lost in awed admiration, leavened with genuine humility. There was still much to be learned from Avira Anniyas. When Garon once more presented the folio to his mother, she picked up her pen and signed.

Sarra Liwellan now owed her inheritance to the First Councillor.

Which made Glenin think that perhaps she would be allowed to live, after all. One did not incur debts from a person one planned to dispose of.

Eight to seven, a simple majority. Garon announced the obvious, then ostentatiously presented the signed petition to *Domna*—now Lady—Liwellan. She thanked him, wrapped her arms around the leather, bowed her head, and left the Great Chamber.

The Council also departed, Anniyas first, the rest trailing after. Only then did the hall erupt in chatter. Elsvet said something about her mother's being unfit to live with for the next three weeks, and would Glenin mind *terribly* if Elsvet came to dinner a few times? Glenin nodded, not having to feign sympathy; Veliria Doyannis could have given lessons in snobbery to Grandmother Allynis—and a swearing tutorial to a Guards trooper.

The gallery emptied. Glenin waited for Garon to come collect her, appreciating the time in which to analyze the voting. The order had been such that by the time it got around to Jareth Feleson and Lirsa Rigge, it would be known that two more in favor waited at the end of the table—Fiella Lunne and Gorynna Bekke. The only questionable vote was Granon Isidir's; had he voted for, Anniyas's ploy would have been ruined and she would have been merely the ninth, unnecessary vote. A risk, Glenin thought with a scowl. Risks did not ensure the orderly weaving of the tapestry. But

Anniyas's whole career had been an exercise in winning against odds. This was why the Lords of Malerris had long ago chosen her—for this unpredictable, dangerous, rare quality that they simultaneously feared, despised, and used: luck.

Later, at the reception in the Malachite Hall—four thousand square feet of green-and-black stone floor gleaming beneath a dazzle of crystal chandeliers—Anniyas laughed when Glenin obliquely referenced the risk.

"My dearest, there was no risk at all. I knew how Granon would vote before the girl arrived! You see, the Isidirs want her to marry him, so he had to vote against inheritance."

Glenin blinked over her wineglass. "I beg your pardon?"

"The Isidir thinking goes this way. With the Slegin property, she can pick and choose a husband. Without it, considering her abilities and interests, she'd be compelled to find a man with a rich, politically prominent family. The Isidirs are all that, with an important city and most of a Shir in their pockets besides. Lacking other family to worry about, she'd concern herself with the one she and her husband would build between them. And though their Name would be Liwellan, the property would be Isidir."

"I thought his grandmother wants Granon to remain unhusbanded."

"Not if the woman is Sarra Liwellan."

Glenin frowned, and the courtier who had been about to approach backed off. No one disturbed the First Councillor and her daughter-at-law. "But with the Slegin property she's a much greater prize, if Granon can win her affections."

"Oh, he's charming enough when it suits him. He could probably attach her if he tried." Anniyas winked. "Which he won't. He voted no because his grandmother told him to. He also voted no because he has no intention of husbanding any woman, rich or not. And especially not Sarra Liwellan—"

"—who would naturally want the Rinesteenshir seat on the Council," Glenin finished, nodding enlightenment.

"Which Granon intends to hold until he keels over in it." Anniyas laughed again. "Nice that he could vote his own wishes as well as his grandmother's, isn't it? One sees so few examples of filial devotion these days."

Linking elbows, the two women walked the length of the room, smiling and giving greeting, but not lingering for conversation. A slave in Council livery approached with a tray of glasses; Glenin served Anniyas before taking another for herself, and they toasted each other silently with frothy pink wine.

"I'll say this now," Anniyas murmured, looking away, "where neither of us can afford to reveal our feelings and so may not cry. I want you to know, my dear, that I understand your pain. I, too, was forbidden my First Daughter."

Every muscle in Glenin's body stiffened. Her smile felt locked onto her face. Anniyas glanced at her, nodded approval, and went on.

"I was very young—younger than you are now—and deeply loved the child's father. But it was not permitted. I was to bear a son, and by another man." She sipped her wine. "It hurt for a very long time—until you came to us here at Ryka Court, and I understood the wisdom of my sacrifice. Will you permit me, Glensha, to see you as that First Daughter I could not have?"

Unable to speak, she looked down at this plain, plump, unremarkable little woman who held all Lenfell in her grip.

"One day you will understand also, and forgive, when you meet the girl who will take to husband your son." Anniyas paused. "Now, Glenin! I said no weeping, and I meant it. Whatever will people think?"

She forced back the tears and tried another smile.

"There, that's better. Let's go find the Liwellan girl, shall we? I'd like you to meet her. I find her quite charming."

7

Sarra had drained one glass of pink bubbles quickly, for the sake of her parched throat—and her nerves—before the reception. Telomir Renne had provided it. He caught up with her in the corridor leading to the Malachite Hall, gave the leather folio to his attending servant for storage in his suite, and led Sarra to an alcove where a sheet-fountain slid down a wall below a window overlooking the lake.

"Sit," he ordered, giving her the glass. "I snagged this from the pantry. Drink fast, the mob will be along in a few minutes."

"I need to go comb my hair—"

"It looks fine," he said impatiently. "Drink. You look like you need it. Saints witness *I* did, when you began that business about sons and Mother-Right! Sarra, whatever possessed you?"

She drank, glanced around to see who might be listening—a few servants and an honor Guard down the corridor—and took another swallow. Despite the oh-so-cutesy color, the wine was bracingly chill and dry.

"They'll have to do it eventually. I'm just getting them used to the idea in advance. Telo, why did Anniyas break the tie in my favor?"

"Why don't you ask her? She'll be here in a few minutes."

"Telo! *Why?*"

He flicked a glance down the corridor; footsteps and voices echoed, growing closer. "Because now you and Agatine and Orlin and I—and everybody else with a stake in your inheriting the Slegin fortune—owe Anniyas a very large favor."

"She thinks she *bought* us?" Sarra spluttered and brushed droplets off her gown. "How *dare* she—?"

"Actually, I'm comforted by how it happened. It means she intends a future for you."

Sarra mulled this over. Then she gulped down the rest of the wine.

Telomir spoke swiftly and softly. "It's certain she plans to use the Slegin holdings to manipulate you. Think what a position you'd be in if it came to a choice between all the people of Sheve, for whom you'll be responsible, and—other people with claims on you."

"I'm not worried about it," she said, more or less truthfully. "Soon everyone in Sheve will be . . . protected."

"I hope so." He glanced up as the first guests passed the alcove. "Listen, Sarra. The Council will arrive late—they have to get rid of their robes. By the time they get here, you can be hip-deep in men. Use them. I'll help, but I can't glue myself to your side. Don't drink too much and don't say anything serious."

"And don't make any rash, drunken promises of marriage," she finished, making a face at him. "I'm not stupid, Telo."

"Just forgetful. You know who you'll have to talk to,

don't you? For a few minutes anyway. I'll keep watch and if you're in trouble, I'll be there as fast as I can. But this meeting is up to you, Sarra."

She nodded grimly. "I'll be all right. But I'm glad you're here."

"Never doubt it. Can you feel the wine yet? Good. Smile for me. Yes, that's it. You've just won a huge victory and you're going to be one of the richest women in the world, and you can't *wait* to see a hundred men crawl on their lips across broken glass just to have you kick them with your dainty little foot!"

She giggled at the image he evoked; there *were* a few of the Court fops she'd love to see in exactly that position. By the time he escorted her through the double doors of the Malachite Hall, the wine bubbles were in her blood and she tilted her chin arrogantly and smiled her sweetest smile—hiding scorn, panic, and a ravening need to go home.

True to Telomir's prediction, she was instantly surrounded by eligible young men. She flirted, laughed, teased, took tiny sips of wine, and wondered how long she would be compelled to stay at this celebration of her triumph.

Garon Anniyas parted the crowd to offer congratulations; she smiled at her sister's husband as if she truly liked him. A young Doyannis blade, defying Aunt Veliria's condemnation, begged the privilege of escorting her all the way to her ship when she left on the morrow for home. This elicited howls of protest. Why should *he* have the luck, she mustn't leave Court so soon, whatever would they do without her beauty to gaze upon, she simply could not abandon them and break their hearts—and-pitiful-so-forth. Irien Dombur, no longer wearing his Council robe, took a liberty by taking her hand to his lips and kissing the center of her palm—not the pulse over her wrist, as was mannerly, but a lingering caress that included the tip of his tongue. She felt her eyes go wide at the boldness, but the urge to giggle was stronger. Repressing both outrage and mirth, she simpered and dimpled.

For a solid hour, all the greatest Names of Lenfell, incarnate in young, comely, virile masculine form, were intent on her. She had never suffered a worse headache in her life.

Then, in the momentary space between two embroidered longvests, she saw Avira Anniyas and Glenin Feiran heading toward her. As the knot of young men untied to admit the

First Councillor, Sarra saw Auvry Feiran approach, with antiquated Flera Firennos supporting herself on his arm.

Sarra felt sick. Whatever spell or Ward protected her, let it be strong—yet not so strong as to be sensed by three powerful Mageborns. For she was sure about Anniyas now, absolutely sure. Nothing else made any sense.

The First Councillor was two inches taller than Sarra, weighed about twice as much, and looked every minute of her sixty-eight years. Her light brown hair was heavily grayed, and her eyes were as flat as a shallow pan of water. From six feet away, Sarra could smell the cloying floral scent of her perfume.

Glenin Feiran was magnificently beautiful, though a little pale. Elomar had told Sarra that a recent miscarriage was the reason for her early return to Ryka Court. By Ladder, from the ruins of Malerris Castle—which shocked one and all. But it was understood that Auvry Feiran's concern for his daughter's health necessitated the use of the only Ladder still functional at the Castle. And if he had been able to use it, surely no Lords of Malerris lurked there still. They would have killed on sight the architect of their destruction.

And him, this man who was her father—Sarra fought memories of the tall, laughing man who swung her up into his arms and read her stories and helped her pick wildflowers in fields far beyond the Octagon Court—

Memories, too, of playing with Glenin in the well of the Double Spiral, squabbling with her, their riding lessons, the family picnics, going to sleep with her head on her sister's shoulder—

She fled the images, then abruptly changed her mind and chased them all down, tucking them in a corner of her heart so they could not escape and betray her. At least she *had* memories, good memories, of father and sister and mother; it was so much more than Cailet had.

So much more than she had of Cailet. . . .

"Here she is!" Anniyas cried brightly. "Glenin dear, I must make known to you Lady Sarra Liwellan. Lady Sarra, my daughter-at-law, Lady Glenin Feiran."

She barely had time to meet her eldest sister's gaze when Anniyas reached out a hand to Auvry Feiran, saying, "Commandant! Come at last to attend your daughter, I see. We need only Garon to make our family complete. Where is the boy, anyhow? Flera dear, you really shouldn't be standing so long. Where are your charming granddaughters?"

"Charming," the Council member agreed, nodding and smiling at Sarra.

Taking the old woman's hand, Sarra said, "Let me find a place for you to sit down, Lady. If you'll excuse me for a moment only, First Councillor?"

Telomir Renne caught up with them halfway to a chair by the wall of windows. "Nice catch," he muttered. "I'll go back with you and help."

"Charming," reiterated Flera Firennos. "You remind me of someone, child. Can't think who. I'm sure she was charming as well. I wonder who it was." Sinking into a padded seat, she looked up with mischievous old eyes. "Wouldn't do for Avira to know, though, would it?"

Sarra smiled and winked. "We'll let it be our secret."

"May I offer you some wine, Lady?" Telo asked.

With flirtatious severity: "Young man, are you trying to get me drunk so I'll agree to marry you?"

Giggling—a bit hysterically, to be sure—Sarra said, "Isn't he dreadful? His mother ought to've given him a good paddling!"

The bright eyes turned positively wicked with glee. "His *mother* was never the question, child. As for that so-called Nameless father of his—"

"Who shall remain Nameless, if it please my Lady," Telo interrupted, his smile a trifle strained. Sarra shot him a sharp glance as he went on, "Allow me to find your granddaughters to attend you."

"I'm quite happy here by myself, without their natterings," she snapped, then cackled softly, rocking back and forth. "Oh, if Avira only knew what I know about the two of you!"

"Our secret," Sarra repeated conspiratorially, giving the old lady a wink and a curtsy before Telo led her away. In an undertone, she asked, "Do you think she really knows—?"

"Who can say? Smile. You won't have to talk with them long. Just be ready to follow my lead."

She wanted very badly to ask who his father was. Later—when she wasn't looking her own father right in the face.

"Please excuse the interruption," she apologized to Anniyas. "But she really was looking rather unsteady."

"Oh, she's been that way for years," said the First Councillor. "It was kind of you to see to her comfort, my dear Sarra—may I call you Sarra?—and only confirms the wisdom of the Council vote. You'll make a fine ruler for Roseguard and all the Slegin holdings."

"You honor me, First Councillor." How bizarre it was, to be exchanging polite chat with this woman. It was difficult to believe her the cause of so many deaths.

"She knows worth when she sees it," said Auvry Feiran, with a smiling glance for Glenin. "We haven't met, Lady Liwellan. I'm Auvry Feiran, father of this Lady here, whom you so generously complimented today."

"A pleasure." She did not extend her wrist for him to kiss. "Both to meet you, and to speak nothing but the simple truth about your daughter." Sarra directed her most guileless smile at her sister. It was a heady game, this; she was beginning to enjoy it. *I am not who you believe I am—and who I am, I know you would not believe.*

Glenin said, "I regret I was unable to meet you before today."

With perfect honesty—for it was Sarra's own niece or nephew Glenin had carried—she replied, "I heard of your loss. I'm very sorry."

"Thank you. In fact, I'm a little tired. If you'll forgive me. . . ."

Auvry Feiran looked worried. "Would you like me to find your husband? Or will a mere father's escort do?"

She placed a hand on his arm and looked one last time at Sarra. "I'm certain we'll meet again, Lady Sarra."

"So am I, Lady Glenin."

And, that simply, it was over. They left, and Sarra was left with Anniyas on one side, Telo on the other, and a score of eager young men hovering nearby.

Not quite over. Not yet. Anniyas tilted her head like an inquisitive sparrow and said, "See any you fancy?"

She must have caught Sarra's quick glance at her admirers. "Not a one," Sarra answered forthrightly.

The First Councillor laughed. "Beauty, brains, and taste! Forgive my frankness, my dear, and rest assured I appreciate yours. And now that we have established that we may be blunt with each other, may I give you some advice?"

"Please."

"Have children as you please, but marry no one. My

mother used to sing an old song about it—I've forgotten most of it, but—" She paused, then recited:

> *Though he seem as solid as oak*
> *Yet recall that oaks draw lightning*
> *Though he seem as beautiful as roses*
> *Yet recall that roses wither*
> *Though he seem as strong as daggers,*
> *Yet recall that steel may shatter*
> *Though he seem as true as—*

"Oh, bother, I forget the rest. And now that I've begun, it will drive me mad until I remember it all! Minister Renne, have you heard this song?"

"With regret, First Councillor, no." He smiled. "Truly told, I've about as much ear for music and poetry as the average cart horse."

Sarra smiled pleasantly. She'd known from the instant Anniyas said "advice" that a warning was coming. She also knew there had been no song sung by her mother; Anniyas had made it up, perhaps on the spot but probably prepared in advance. She was, in fact, telling Sarra precisely whom not to marry: any young sapling of the Ostin Oak Tree; any young bud from the Slegin Rose Crown; any young blade of a Rosvenir—

Rosvenir? Had that idiot Minstrel become an agent of the Rising? If so, Roseguard had better not be on his itinerary.

"How maddening not to remember all of it," Anniyas said.

Meaning other tainted Names? Alvassy, Garvedian, Desse, Gorrst, Maurgen, Adennos, Solingirt—Sarra knew a dozen by now, many of them with sigils to play on in this little song.

Sarra plied her dimples. "Oh, but you *will* remember, you know. You'll wake in the middle of the night knowing every word—and then be unable to get it out of your head for days! That's how it always happens to me."

"You're far too young to suffer lapses of memory, my dear!"

And *that* was a reminder not to forget exactly who was responsible for the inheritance. "I never forget the important things, First Councillor."

"Ah. And what, in your experience, is truly important?"

So innocuous a question, so dangerous. Sarra began to see why Avira Anniyas was so formidable.

"Family, of course," Sarra said, "and—"

"Mother!" exclaimed Garon Anniyas. "Here you are!"

Sarra would have wagered the Octagon Court that she would never be happy to see her sister's husband.

He kissed his mother's cheek, nodded at Sarra and Telo, and said, "I've been looking for Glenin."

"She wasn't feeling well, and left." Anniyas looked irked at the interruption, but only for a moment; as she gazed up at her son, it was obvious that she adored him.

It was not the emotion Sarra had seen in Lilen Ostin's eyes for Taig; she loved her son deeply, all the more so for knowing him down to his marrow. But Lilen would have sacrificed Taig, back in Pinderon—though her heart shattered, she would have done it. Not because her loyalty to the Rising was stronger than her love for her son, but because she knew that to betray others to save him would mean to betray what Taig was.

No such complications of knowledge shadowed Anniyas's feelings for Garon. He was her only child, her "good brave boy," her precious darling; her love was encompassing, absolute, and blind.

"Why didn't someone send for me?" Garon asked anxiously. "How long ago did she leave? Never mind—I'll go to her at once."

Anniyas grasped his hand firmly in both her own. "Auvry is with her, my dearest. I'm sure she's just fine."

Ah! Sarra thought. Not so blind after all, that she could not see his love for Glenin taking precedence. Anniyas was not yet jealous—from which Sarra instinctively knew that this husbandly devotion was recent, probably dating to the miscarriage. But Anniyas was most definitely determined to keep her son at her side. Not Glenin's; hers. *Power play,* Sarra told herself, and decided to tweak the First Councillor a bit.

"Of course she is," she told Garon. "A bit pale, and she said she was tired. The gallery must have been quite warm and stuffy—and Saints, the crush in here now! She probably just needed some fresh air."

"You see, Garon?" his mother soothed. "Listen to Lady Sarra."

"You mustn't worry," Sarra went on, ignoring a sharp

glance of warning from Telomir Renne. "She had her father's arm to lean on." As the conjured image of his beloved's faltering steps sank in, Sarra finished, "It's sweet of you to be so concerned. If I ever *do* decide to take a husband, I hope he takes as good care of me as you do of Lady Glenin."

That did it; duty to his darling came first. He apologized to all and escaped his mother's grip. "I'll be back once I've seen to Glenin's comfort," he said, and left the Malachite Hall.

Telo made some jesting remark about besotted young lovers. Sarra smiled. Anniyas did not. After another few minutes of polite inquiries about Agatine, Orlin, the four boys, the charms of Roseguard and wishes for a safe return journey, Anniyas excused herself to talk with Kanen Ellevit.

One more hour and it really was over. Sarra's feet ached in the high-heeled shoes and it was a real strain not to limp out of the Malachite Hall. As soon as she and Telo were in more private corridors on the way to his chambers, she kicked off the shoes and carried them. Her skirts, two inches lower now, threatened to trip her.

At length, safely within Gorynel Desse's Wards, Telo doffed longvest and coif before sprawling in a chair. "That's the first time I've ever heard anyone call Garon 'sweet.' "

"When did he decide he's passionately in love with Glenin?"

"He isn't. Everybody knows—" Then he paused. "Ah. But he looks like it now, doesn't he?"

After throwing her shoes in the general direction of her bedroom, Sarra stretched full-length on a couch. "I *thought* it might be fairly recent. Did you see his mother's face? Right on the edge of jealousy."

"So you gave her a nudge."

She grinned over at him. "Just a little one. How did you like her song?"

"I've another line for it. 'Though he seems as true as an arrow/Yet recall that wood may warp.' Now, *that's* Garon, down to the ground."

"Yet he flies straight and true enough to Glenin." She glanced around as the door opened to admit Alin Ostin and Valirion Maurgen. "Well? What did you think of my speech?"

"Marvelous—as if you needed us to tell you!" Alin smiled and gave her an elegant bow.

"You *looked* superb, at any rate," Val teased. "I'm to be congratulated for designing the gown."

"You ought to be flogged," Sarra retorted. "Do you know how long it took to get into it?" She raised both arms, each sleeve boasting twenty-five tiny pearl buttons from wrist to elbow. There were fifty matching buttons down her back.

"Dare I hope my Lady is requesting assistance in getting out of it?"

With a show of supreme indifference to his cousin's flirting, Alin sank into a chair, folded his arms, and closed his eyes. "Wake me when it's time to hike back to the boat."

Sarra laughed, relaxing for the first time that day. She'd never had any really close male friends, and was discovering how much fun they could be. The warmth was different than that shared with Orlin and her foster-brothers, and despite Val's occasional outrageousness there was none of the woman/man undercurrent there'd been with Taig. And that idiot Minstrel. Certainly none of *them* would spend so much time and energy creating just the right dress for her.

Val had carefully observed Court fashions for three days before deciding that Sarra must flout every current trend. No expanses of skin; she must be covered from chin to wrists to ankles. No embroidery or decoration; no jewels; no separate laced bodice or slashed overskirt or ribbon-festooned flounces gathered up to show filmy lace-trimmed petticoats beneath.

"Give 'em only what you want 'em to see," he'd said when she modeled the gown for him two days ago. "In this case, the Liwellan and Slegin colors in harmony, all that hair, and your face. You're on display. You, not your clothes. Don't distract them with jewels or needlework or some complicated cut to the gown—or by exposing your charming bosom. Give them something to look at, and then when they've finished looking, they'll *listen*."

Sarra thought the gown's severity made her look a hundred years old. Its plainness made her feel a frump next to the elaborately gowned Court ladies. But she had to admit it had done exactly what Val had said it would. She'd seen and sensed people looking, noticing what they were supposed to notice—and then begin to listen.

But it was still going to take her half an hour to get out of the damned thing.

"So," Telomir said, "how went your little exercise in thievery?"

"Perfect," Alin replied. "Everyone who couldn't fit into the Great Chamber was at the reception after, so Ryka Court was about as deserted as it can get."

"I don't think anybody visits the Library much anyhow," Val added. "It's not as if most of the people around here can read."

"What a shocking thing to say about the flower of Lenfell's society!" Telo chuckled.

"Present company excepted, of course," said Alin.

"Don't state the obvious." Val lazed across a chair, long legs dangling over its arm. "Elomar's cuddling the memory Globe he made for Kanto Solingirt like a newborn First Daughter at her mother's breast. Speaking of First Daughters, Sarra, what about Glenin Feiran?"

"She and her father were at the reception. It was all very polite and no trouble at all. But Anniyas said a few things you may want to keep in mind." She told them about the "song" and its implications.

Val was unimpressed. "Those are just the Names everybody knows to be connected to the Rising."

Alin reacted differently; his brother was the "oak" Anniyas had warned against. "She was that open about it? I don't like the sound of that, Sarra."

"Not open, exactly, but I knew what she meant, and she knew I knew it. I wouldn't worry. Soon we'll all of us be safe in Sheve."

Valirion turned to their host. "Which reminds me. You ought to come with us. Things are going to get uncomfortable around here, and I'd rather you left now, with us, than have to come back for you later. You can say that your brother wants to confer with you in person—"

"Oh, and wouldn't Anniyas just love that?" Telo interrupted. "She's none too certain of me as it is. If I tried to leave—"

"What do you mean, 'tried'?" Sarra demanded, sitting up straight. "You're a Minister of Lenfell. You can go where you like."

"Yes—and with minions of the Council tagging right along behind me. I assume you *don't* require Anniyas's friends poking around this ship you're supposedly going to be on all the way back to Roseguard?"

"That," Alin murmured, "can be easily taken care of."

Telo gave Alin an odd look. Sarra hid a smile. Slight-shouldered, soft-spoken, innocent-looking Alin, with his little-boy shock of pale hair and his big blue eyes, seemed incapable of doing violence to a fly.

"Be that as it may," Telo finally said, "I'm still useful here. I'll join you in Sheve if life in Ryka Court gets too . . . uncomfortable."

He changed the subject to discussion of Court personalities. Dinner arrived. Sarra did the honors of the evening candle. It was barely Fourteenth when Telomir shooed the three young people off to get some sleep before their early start the next morning.

Val and Alin were next door to Sarra. She tapped on the connecting door and when Alin appeared she asked a single question.

"Who was Telo's father?"

He blinked. "You don't know?"

"If I did, would I ask?"

"Sarra, if he hasn't told you. . . ."

"He hasn't. But *you* will." She scowled up at him. "Alin. Now."

"Well . . . but you didn't hear it from me."

"I didn't hear it at all. Who was he?"

"Gorynel Desse." The corners of his mouth quivered in a little smile. "Good night, Sarra," he said, and shut the door.

8

They were ready to go at Fifth of a cold gray morning that threatened rain before midday. There was a small leave-taking ceremony in the Cobbleyard, an enclosed circle near the stables that served as a reception area for Ministers. Sarra's admirers and the Council members who had voted for her—and several who had not—sent servants or slaves with the traditional saddle-charms. These were tiny bouquets, tied with ribbons in the colors of the well-wisher's Name, that symbolized wishes for a safe journey.

Telomir identified them for her. All she knew—or cared to know—about Lenfell's flora was how to tot up the bushel yield at harvest.

"The usual," Telo said as they were tied on her saddle. "Marigolds for sadness-at-parting, rosemary for remembrance, fresh geranium leaves for protection, and so forth. Ah, now *here's* an interesting suggestion."

Some well-wishers had added a few herbal and floral hints, indicating that they actually knew the language of flowers rather than simply followed custom without understanding the meaning. Several bouquets from those who professed themselves heart-stricken featured blue violets for lover's faithfulness. One included chervil for sincerity and a tiny hazel switch for reconciliation. Another featured a dried ear of corn, symbolizing riches. None, she was relieved to learn, contained any herbs or flowers associated with marriage. All the saddle-charms included rue; the odor was said to be a Wraith Ward.

After Sarra conveyed her thanks to the gifter's representative, Alin and Val tied each nosegay to the back of her saddle. By the time the last had been placed the poor mare was bedecked like a Saint's shrine on festival day and positively dripping ribbons. Sarra hoped the silks were colorfast; it looked like rain before noon, and her pale Tillinshir gray would be a horse of many another color.

At last they were ready to mount and be off. Telomir would accompany them to the first inn, then return tomorrow to his duties. With all the servants and slaves gone, the quiet grated on Sarra's nerves—especially after weeks of the Court's constant noise. Aside from two grooms, it was just the five of them in the Cobbleyard now: Sarra, Telo, Alin, Val, and Elomar Adennos—disguised as he had been since Portside with a cousin's Saint-name and humble secretary's identity, which rendered him nearly invisible.

"Oh, you're still here!" a sweet voice called from the main porch. "I was afraid I'd be too late!"

Contrary to all custom that dictated saddle-charms never be given by any hand but a servant's or slave's, Glenin Feiran trod lightly down the steps. She held a tiny bouquet in one hand and a small black velvet pouch in the other.

"My Lady!" Sarra exclaimed. "Surely you should be abed still—"

"I'm feeling just fine this morning. It's kind of you to worry about me." Glenin presented the flowers: delicate blue rosemary blossoms and nothing else. "I'm sorry it's so monotonous," she said with a smile. "You've smitten every man at Court and they stripped the greenhouse bare!"

"These are lovely," Sarra responded. "Thank you."

"I have something else for you as well." The drawstrings were undone, and into Sarra's open palm spilled a glass globe. Inside, swirled about with bright blue crystal chips in clear water, was suspended an exquisite little gold hawk with yellow topaz eyes. In the silver talons was a wreath of gold roses.

"The First Councillor's gift, actually," Glenin said. "But I insisted that I be the one to give it to you."

The Liwellan Hawk, the Slegin Rose Crown. Anniyas had known several weeks ago how the vote would be cast; this globe was not the work of a day.

Unwanted and unbidden, a corner of her mind was illuminated by a memory: her own fourth Birthingday, the last she had celebrated in Ambrai, and the new doll clothes Glenin had sewn with her own awkward seven-year-old hands.

"I—I don't know what to say," Sarra admitted honestly. "It's beautiful. I'll treasure it. Thank you, and please thank the First Councillor for me."

"I shall, my dear."

Alin came forward to take the last charm and tie it to Sarra's saddle. Two curious things happened then. Glenin's eyes narrowed as she stared hard at Alin. Her lips parted and she gasped an almost inaudible breath. And Alin, perhaps due to the intensity of her regard, tripped on a cobblestone and bumped Sarra. The glass globe slipped from her fingers and smashed on the stones.

Paralyzed, instincts screaming, Sarra saw the golden hawk lose its grip on the roses and fly into a rain puddle. Alin backed away, babbling apologies like a terrified child. Telo picked up the hawk; Val knelt to gather glass shards.

"What rotten luck!" said Telo. "Slippery cobbles—"

"Cobbles, hell! He's clumsy!" said Val. "Begging your pardon, Ladies."

"I'm sorry," said Sarra, nearly mindless with shock—

surely unwarranted by something so unimportant. "I'm so sorry."

If Glenin was angry, she gave no sign. "What a shame! But don't bother yourself, Lady Sarra. I'll have the hawk and wreath repaired, and send a replacement to you at Roseguard."

Val gave the shards to a groom for disposal. Alin hid behind one of the horses. Glenin pocketed the hawk and wreath.

Five minutes or five hours later, Sarra would never be able to tell, they rode out of the Cobbleyard. Ten miles out of Ryka proper, on the cold gray road to the northern port, Sarra could at last breathe freely again. But when she glanced around, the first person she saw was Alin. Her whole body spasmed in a flinch she could barely control.

Magic. Fighting to get out—Alin's right, it can *hurt—*

He kneed his horse closer to hers. "What is it?"

"She—she recognized you." To her shame, she heard her voice tremble.

"That's impossible." Blue eyes darkened beneath frowning brows. "How could she? She's never seen me before. And even if she knows what Taig looks like, I don't resemble him at all."

"She recognized you," Sarra repeated. "I saw it in her face. I—felt it."

He said nothing for a few moments. Then: "I trust your gut-jumping, Sarra, but this time I think you must be wrong. Though *I* wasn't," he added grimly. "I broke that glass globe on purpose."

Once more unable to speak, she shook her head helplessly.

"Inside it was a Mage Globe. *I* felt *that,* stunted as my magic is."

So he had shattered it—at Saints knew what risk as the magic was released. Neither he nor Elomar, Mageborns both, had touched it. Val had taken care of the shards; Telomir, the hawk and wreath. Sarra tried to recall if she'd felt anything. No; she'd been too stunned—*because* of the freed magic.

"She would've used it to watch us," Alin added.

So that was why she'd felt the hawk's yellow eyes staring at her—just the same feeling she'd had at Malerris Castle.

9

The flagship of the Slegin fleet was the fastest vessel Lady Agatine owned. While Sarra was at Ryka Court, Captain Nalle had taken the *Rose Crown* back to Havenport with cargo from Ryka Portside, loaded a holdful of odds and ends and a few paying passengers, and sailed up to Ryka Northport to await Sarra. The new cargo of cloth, wine, and foodstuffs was bound for Renig. There the ship would offload, take on timber from the forests below Maidil's Mirror and a herd of galazhi for an experimental project in Cantrashir (fronted by Gorrsts, funded by Ostins), and make for Roseguard. No matter what its other purposes, no voyage of the *Rose Crown* ever failed to turn a profit.

After boarding—without subterfuge this time—Sarra's reunion with Kanto Solingirt consisted of a nod and a smile. He vanished out of the rain and into his cabin with Elomar Adennos, and the pair went unseen for days as they planned the Scholar's forgeries.

Mage Captal Lusath Adennos had left Ryka Court a week earlier, his requests for more money and better quarters denied. He'd stayed with an elderly aunt at Northport, waiting for the *Rose Crown*. Now he, too, kept to his cabin—Agatine's own—crushed by the Council's rejection. He might have perked up had he known Sarra's true mission. But for the first time in their history, the Mage Guardians had kept the Captal in total ignorance.

The rainy deck held only one fascination: the retreating view of Ryka. Val and Alin went below at once to their shared cabin. Sarra had private quarters as well—although two of her were in it.

Mai Alvassy wasn't quite Sarra's double. Her hair was only a few inches longer than the chin-length Ambraian style Sarra had long ago abandoned; impersonation required her to pile it atop her head and add false braids. Mai was two inches taller than Sarra, her eyes were dark blue, and her complexion had a dusty-rose cast—legacy of her grandmother, dark-skinned Gorynna Desse. Her voice was a little higher, her face a little thinner. But observed separately, they were enough alike to make the trick possible.

They took turns appearing on deck for short strolls, huddled and hooded in Sarra's blue wool cloak. Although all on board were with the Rising, it was safer to keep most of them as ignorant as the Captal. Agata Nalle joined the pair each night for dinner; Val played servant by waking them each morning for breakfast. He kept pretending not to know which was which—absurd, with their different hair and skin tones, but it made for a laughing start to the day.

Except for these visits, they had only each other for company. Having no idea who Sarra really was, Mai had no idea why the resemblance was so marked. She was, in fact, rather shy at first. But Sarra was grateful for Mai's presence, even when she was silent. Considering the implications of the Mage Globe, left to herself Sarra would have gone mad. She and Mai were the same age—Sarra was nine weeks the elder—born in the same city of mothers who were first cousins, and until the age of five, their lives had been nearly identical. Since Ambrai, the divergence had been total except for one thing: fierce opposition to Anniyas and the Lords of Malerris that had led them to the Rising.

Neither Tama Alvassy nor her husband Gerrin Desse had survived Ambrai. Shortly after Gorynel Desse took Maichen and Sarra to safety in The Waste, Mai, her sister Elin, and her brother Pier sailed in secret for the Alvassy villa in Bleynbradden. This seaside retreat had been the dowry of their grandfather, Piergan Rille—whose family had agreed to provide Cailet's Name.

Then in the middle of the night that Mai later knew was the same on which Ambrai burned, a beautiful woman had come and bundled her and her siblings into a carriage along with their grandparents. The children slept, and when they woke again they were heading for the small estate brought into the family by Enis Dombur. A Ladder had taken them from Bleynbradden to Domburron, but Mai had no memory of the location.

"I remember the Mage, though," she confided to Sarra one evening. "Elseveth Garvedian. She was even more beautiful than Lusira, if you can believe it. She left us at Domburron. I never saw her again."

"Lusira's mother?" Sarra guessed.

"No, but all Lusira will say is she was a cousin of some

sort." Mai shrugged her left shoulder—a gesture Sarra was trying to acquire, just as she was teaching Mai her own habit of clenching her nails into her palms. They had decided to exchange idiosyncrasies just in case. "We weren't supposed to ask, anyhow. My grandparents told us never to talk about anything we remembered from before. Especially after we lost Uncle Toliner to the Lords of Malerris."

"Jeymian Renne's husband, Orlin's father," Sarra said.

"Agatine's sons are my cousins." She smiled shyly. "That kind of makes *us* cousins, too."

Glad to acknowledge kinship—though Mai didn't know it was fact, not courtesy—Sarra smiled back. "We look enough alike to call ourselves sisters!"

Mai nodded, shining hair moving like liquid silk by lamplight. Cailet's hair would move that way, Sarra thought, aching suddenly for long nights of sharing secrets with her real sister. Someone who looked like her, thought like her, believed what she believed, as Mai did—and Glenin did not.

In Domburronshir, Mai's life had been as narrow and ordinary as Cailet's must be in The Waste. Elinar Alvassy and Piergan Rille raised their three grandchildren on the little Dombur farm that had been her father's dowry. They didn't exactly vanish, but they were far from Ryka Court and as long as no crimes could be proved against them, they were largely ignored.

"Anniyas planned for the Ambrais, the Mages, and anyone connected to them to die 'by mistake' that night," Mai said. "We're lucky to have escaped."

So was I, Sarra told herself, realizing it full-force for the first time. Looking at Mai, listening to her tale, Sarra understood at last what would have happened had she and Maichen been caught.

Another abstract idea now wore a human face: a face nearly her own. *Mother and I would've died, Cailet never been born. Father would've—no, Anniyas, damn it! He loved us, he could never have ordered us killed—*

How much worse if he'd killed all the others . . . and spared Mother and me.

There wasn't much more to Mai's story. The three children had grown up with their Name, if not their fortune. It was just Mai and her grandfather Piergan in the echoing old farmhouse now. Elinar had died in 966. Elin, twenty years old and a talented Mageborn, had been spirited away by

Gorynel Desse when she turned fourteen. Mai hadn't seen her since and didn't even know where she was. Pier, just seventeen and also Mageborn, was with the Rising somewhere in Cantrashir.

"You'll see them both again soon," Sarra promised. "And you'll like Sheve. It's not Ambrai, but. . . ." She stopped, in danger once again of saying too much.

"I don't remember much about home," her cousin mused. "But don't believe everything you hear about it, Sarra. The Octagon Court was a wonderful place, and I was very happy there. But people remember it as more than it was. They always talk as if it was . . . perfect. It wasn't."

Thumbing through her own memories, thinking about the refugees she'd met through the years, she knew Mai was right. Which, considering her own plans, was no very bad thing. "Don't you think people *need* to remember it that way? Perhaps everybody needs to remember it. As a symbol."

"Oh, for the sake of the Rising, yes. As a reminder of what was lost. But Ambrai was my home, Sarra, and it should be remembered as it was. This fantasy of perfection some people talk about never existed. Even if it had, it's gone forever. It'd be hopeless to try and remake something that never was. A waste of time and effort on a lie."

Though Sarra nodded, within her something insisted on substituting *dream* for *lie*—and this made the rebuilding of Ambrai neither hopeless nor futile.

The fifth night of the journey, Elomar Adennos came in while Mai was up on deck. He explained that she would stay there until he bade her return, for there was much to discuss with Sarra in private. Judging by the large pitcher of mulled wine he brought with him, it would be a long evening.

They got comfortable, drinks in reach. Sarra sat cross-legged on the lower bunk, the Healer Mage facing her in one of the two wooden chairs. He began without preamble: "The Mage Globe was not a common spell nor an easy one."

"It was ready before I arrived on Ryka," Sarra mused. "You don't make something like that in a day. Was the glass blown around the Globe or the Globe inserted into the glass?"

"Either would be formidable work."

"Meaning you don't know. Well, it doesn't matter, I suppose. Alin said she wanted to watch me with it."

"Of itself, the Globe was benign. Had it not been, the escaping magic would have wrecked the Cobbleyard. What little magic I dared touch told me that observation was indeed its purpose. Alin is more perceptive than he knows."

"And Glenin is even smarter than I gave her credit for. It's the kind of gift one puts out for visitors to see—token of Anniyas's favor and all. Even on board ship, every time I took it out to admire it...."

Adennos nodded. "Just so. You will be very wealthy and therefore very powerful one day. Perhaps this Globe is a usual gift to important persons."

"Mmm. I don't think so. I've visited quite a few Names, and nobody's ever pointed one out—and they *would*, for pride. Why did Glenin give it to me? What does she suspect?"

"Or Anniyas," he reminded her. "It was given in her name, though it was Glenin's work."

"How do you know?"

He hesitated. "The *taste* of the magic, if you will. Alin is unable to discern subtle differences in Mageborn work, but I can. It's like a signature."

"Can it be forged, the way Scholar Kanto will with Anniyas's writing?"

"An extremely skilled Mage might."

One more for Gorynel Desse! Sarra smiled at Elo. "I'm interrogating you like a Justice with a criminal, I know, but you're uniquely talkative tonight and I'm taking advantage of it!"

"Ask," he said, and actually grinned.

She laughed, appreciating the one-word reply. "All right, then—do *you* know why Glenin recognized Alin?"

"Did she?"

"Right before he broke the Globe. She wasn't noticing him for the first time, Elo, or seeing a family resemblance. There isn't much of one to see. She looked as if she'd seen him before. He says she hasn't."

"I can't be any help there, *Domna*. I saw nothing of this."

"Hmm. Too bad. Next question...." She paused, staring into her wine. "Elo ... what do you think they know about me?"

"Nothing. Recognition would have been instantaneous."

As it had been with her first sight of Cailet.

"As for the Rising...." Adennos leaned back in his chair,

crossing long legs at the knees. "They have nothing on which to base suspicions because you've done nothing suspect. But their eyes have been on Lady Agatine these several years. Perhaps the Globe was meant to watch her, not you."

"Something else we may never be sure about."

"One becomes accustomed to such things, in the Rising," Adennos said dryly.

She made a face at him. "Has Kanto decided what Anniyas will have written to condemn herself? No, wait— Gorynel Desse will think up something, right? Is he really Telo Renne's father?"

He choked on his wine. "Who told you that?"

"Never you mind. It's true, though, isn't it? Has he any magic?" She shook her head, impatient with her own foolishness. "He's Desse's son, of course he does. But he's Warded, just like me."

"How did you—?"

"Oh, it's obvious! How could he have gone so far in government if Anniyas knew who his father was? Besides, he touched the remains of the Globe, and neither you nor Alin went anywhere near it. So he's Warded, right?"

Recovering, the Healer Mage bowed slightly in his chair. "Are there any other questions you don't need me to answer?"

Sarra laughed. "Only one thing more, and then I'll have mercy on you. I'll bet you've said as much in the last hour as you said the whole of last year!"

A wry smile lit his long, thin face. "More."

"Very funny. Just tell me this—is there anything else I *ought* to ask?"

His smile changed slightly, and he did not answer. Instead he bowed slightly and made for the door.

Sarra slammed one fist into a pillow. "Elomar! Don't you *dare* tell me to talk to Gorynel Desse!"

10

Ten miles to Roseguard and yet another favor for the old man—*Well, hell,* Collan thought sourly, *I was heading there anyhow.*

This had become a familiar refrain the last few years. Ever since the debacle at Pinderon he'd crisscrossed the whole northern hemisphere. Always to places where "Minstrels are welcome and can earn good coin," always "only an hour or two of your time," always "just a small favor."

Always to someplace he was heading anyhow.

They knew him well in Roseguard. He was, in fact, modestly famous from Cantratown to Renig to Shainkroth. His reputation had even spread as far as Wyte Lynn Castle—though he wouldn't be going back there anytime soon, due to a tiny misunderstanding about how a fifteen-year-old Ellevit daughter got locked stark naked in a closet. (Not his fault; he'd honestly thought her request for a private performance meant to bring his lute. She was a schoolgirl and half his age, for Geridon's sake!)

When first Col began his career, earning his bed and board took a whole evening of songs, with all profits from increased business going to the innkeeper. Now when he rode in, word flashed through town, manor, or keep, and whatever tavern he graced filled rapidly. He brought in so many patrons that he could claim equal share of the profits. For a man who traveled with only a lute and a Tillinshir gray (the Witte gelding from Pinderon, which—with appalling lack of imagination for a Minstrel—he named Dapple), he was a wealthy man. And all of it, aside from the coin he needed on the road, was safely deposited with the Healers Guild in every major city in North Lenfell. He didn't trust banks; they were notoriously easy for the Ministry of Commerce to investigate, confiscate, and eliminate. What should have been his own Guild—the Bards—was a disorganized collection of lackwit rhymesters these days. Col judged the Healers a certain bet for survival whatever laws the Council passed. People always needed doctoring.

Had he known that management of the Guild coffers was the charge of a branch of the Ostin Web, he would have fainted.

After Pinderon, Col had laid low for quite a while. Taig Ostin, finally catching up with him halfway to Cantratown, had done his best to recruit Col to the Rising. Col would have none of it. He owed Taig, though, and he'd learned long since that a debt not swiftly repaid tied a man down. So he agreed to take a message to a house in Cantratown—since he was heading there anyhow—confident that this would be the end of it.

But gorgeous *Domna* Garvedian in Cantratown had asked so sweetly that it would have been churlish to refuse her. So he and Dapple sailed down to Neele—a good idea in any case. The Council Guard still had his name at the top of its list weeks after the incident in Pinderon. Delivering the *Domna's* message was the work of an hour; getting off Brogdenguard was the frustration of two solid weeks, until another woman connected with the Rising smuggled him on board a ship of her Name's line. On arrival in Ambraishir, he'd paid for his passage by slogging poor Dapple through a thunderstorm to hand over a leather sack of he knew not what to a little old man living at the mouth of the Brai River. As it happened, the ancient ended up nursing him through a miserable cold. He also restrung Col's lute and gave him a sheaf of rare songs dating back before the First Incursion. So when he was asked to take the same leather sack, contents again a mystery, to a farm on Blighted Bay, honor demanded that he do it.

Before he knew it—and certainly without his agreeing to it—he was a courier for the Rising. His roving life made him a natural; his attitude of "Don't tell me, I don't want to know" made him invaluable. If caught, he could reveal next to nothing.

He hadn't planned it. But no sooner did he rid himself of one obligation than another took its place. It was infuriating. Still . . . as long as no one asked him to visit Pinderon, and no connection with the Rising was suspected, he did favors to repay the favors done him. That this chain turned out to be endless caused a sardonic snort every now and then. The process also caused him to become a famous Minstrel and accumulate a hefty balance in numbered accounts in Healers Guild vaults.

Now he owed a favor to Warrior Mage Guardian Gorynel Desse Himself. Col knew a setup when he saw one. How else to explain the convenient appearance of Dalion Witte? The old man assured him it was mere coincidence; in Cantratown to court a Firennos girl, Witte was drowning his failure in a classic tavern crawl. But why had he just happened to show up in the tavern Col was performing in—and why had Gorynel Desse just happened to be there to save his skin? And singe it as well—the very instant Collan and Dalion Witte recognized each other, the hearthfire at Col's back flared, dazzling all eyes except his. A quick exit to the alley, a moment to pack the lute in its case, and Desse had been beside him demanding to be thanked for his timely magic trick.

Collan rode to the stable near his usual Roseguard haunt still grumbling over the errand the Mage had given him. "Just a message," he'd said. "One day, that's all it will take. You're heading that way anyhow. And they're generous in Roseguard, they appreciate music. You won't be the poorer for the trip."

But this time was different.

Always before there had been wrapped items to deliver— which he never asked about because he honestly didn't care—or a verbal message in code that made no sense to him, which was how he preferred it. This time, however, the items to be delivered were right out in the open, with no spoken message: the code was not made of words, but of flowers.

"A recent innovation," Desse explained carefully, "making use of a tradition long out of fashion. You'll recognize the meanings, I'm sure."

He did, and didn't much care for it. A few old songs used the intricate language of flowers and herbs, but most people only knew the basics: common saddle-charms, nosegays for first Wise Blood and courting. Floral metaphor was a brilliant code that nearly guaranteed secrecy.

Or it means the message is so dangerous it has to look as innocent as possible—and what's more innocent than a bunch of flowers?

Collan snorted. *Innocent, my ass.* This was the first time he'd ever understood what one member of the Rising was telling another. And that made him vulnerable if the Guard caught him.

The way he saw it, he hadn't much choice but to deliver the message. But it would be the last time. Absolutely the last favor he did anybody.

Naturally, the old man hadn't considered how difficult gathering so many different flowers would be. First of all, it was winter. Second, though there were plenty of places to buy flowers, purchasing all of them at once would mark him as eccentric—at best. But neither could he alight at every flower stall and shop in Roseguard like a demented bee.

After stabling Dapple, he entered the Thistlesilk Hostelry (saying it three times—fast *or* slow—was the proprietor's test of drunkenness). Col was tired from the long day's ride and begged off singing. The *domna* agreed, knowing she'd reap the profits of his rest tomorrow night. After supper Col bedded down with his host's charming niece and just before he slept decided that the easiest—and cheapest—way to acquire his needs would be to steal them from Roseguard Grounds. The message was for Lady Agatine; might as well use her flowers to send it.

Accordingly, the next morning he was first in line at the entrance. This was a pair of ancient barbicans, roofless and half-ruined, the stones held together by climbing roses. *Guarding the Roses,* he thought, and winced. In song he was used to wordplay; encountering it visually was just a smidge too clever for his tastes.

It was warm for winter, with a clear sky and a cheerful sun promising a splendid day. Collan paid the admission fee of a cutpiece, received a paper garden map, and prepared to search. Five steps later he forgot what he'd come for. Even in winter, Roseguard Grounds was a wonder beyond imagining.

Millions of flowers in a thousand colors and shapes and sizes, breathing fragrances to make a man drunk. Herbs, snuggling into tracery beds and growing in serried ranks on tall, broad-stepped, freestanding walls, giving forth yet more scent and a subtle shift of greens from near-black to silver. Down the center, a half-mile alley of velvety grass was bordered by matching pairs of trees, one on each side like candles, receding to a faraway blaze of coppery shrubs. To either side of him, arches cascaded purple, white, and crimson roses. Airy plumes of white and bronze ornamental grasses fountained behind massed flowers, and behind the grasses were more trees bearing all manner of fruit. Vegetables both practical and ornamental were laid out with the precision and color-care of a Cloister carpet, surrounded by thick, stunted hedges barely ankle-high. Throughout, bees hummed happy satiation and even the birds warbled on key.

And this was only what he could see after five steps into the garden. The map told him the entirety of it covered five square miles.

"First time, eh?"

The voice startled him from his waking dream of color and scent and sound. Slug-witted at the glory before him, he turned his head. A tall, muscular, pleasant-faced man of about his own age stood nearby, holding a pair of pruning shears in one gloved hand.

Collan nodded. "It's—" And then he stopped, at a loss. Fine Minstrel he was, lacking a single word of appropriate praise.

But the gardener understood. "Yes, it is, isn't it? I'm off on my morning rounds. If you've time, you're welcome to come along. New visitors make me see with new eyes." The shears were transferred to his left hand, and the upraised right palm was offered. "Verald Jescarin, Master of Rose-guard Grounds." He grimaced suddenly and pulled his glove off with his teeth. "Sorry," he mumbled around the thick leather.

Collan belatedly recalled the reason for his visit. Who better to guide him to the required plants than the man who grew them? Accepting the salute with his left hand matched to Jescarin's, he smiled. "If you don't mind a lot of stupid questions, I'd be glad to join you."

They strolled meandering paths, Jescarin describing what was placed where and why. This herb to repel insects, that to attract them; one section designed for summer in graduating shades of red from ground to archway, another in the same artful triumph of winter blues. Rounding a tall hedge, Collan caught his breath at the shimmering beauty of a small enclosure. Every leaf, grass to bush to tree, was silvery; every flower, ground cover to tall lilies to wall vines, was white.

"The Garden of Ever-Snow," Jescarin said. "Lady Agatine's favorite. Took my Fa *years* to get it blooming all year long. You should see it when the white cherries are ripe."

" 'And branches conjure Mage Globes/Of sweet white snow,' " Col murmured.

"So you've heard that song! But it wasn't written about Roseguard, you know. It's Ambrai that Bard Falundir sang of in that lyric." Jescarin knelt to finger through a heavy fall of trumpet-shaped blossoms. "Aha! Got you!" He held up a stalk dripping a few pink flowers. "I dig him up every year, but every year he pops up again, blushing with shame for spoiling all this white."

"Ambrai?" Collan felt a telltale throb begin in his temples. The name of the dead city he'd heard a million times; that couldn't be it. But *Falundir* was rarely heard, owing to the Bard's long disgrace. The sound of his name had triggered a familiar headache.

Verald Jescarin stood, tucking the offending plant carefully into his satchel for replanting in another bed. "That song cost him his music forever."

Collan turned away to hide a flinch as the pounding grew worse. "I know Roseguard is a liberal place, but is it wise to say things like that?"

"Nobody within hearing distance but you. And I recognize your name, Minstrel. Tell me, how was old Gorsha when last you saw him?"

"Annoying, dictatorial, and ornery," Col replied without thinking.

Jescarin laughed—a rich, deep sound that seemed to come all the way from his toes. "Which is to say he's healthy as a horse. I'm glad to hear it. Now, how may I help you, *Domni* Rosvenir? Which is to say, why are you stealing bits of my oleander, lavender, and white poplar?"

He had just enumerated the items Col had already slipped into his pockets—secretly, or so he'd thought. Surprise helped chase away the headache; if the triggering word was not repeated, it would not return. But he had never known why some words brought pain and others didn't—there was no pattern to it he had ever been able to discover. Just thinking about a possible pattern brought a threatening twinge.

Jescarin was smiling. "Why don't you just give me the list and we'll go hunt up the rest, and save ourselves the bother of a grand tour?"

Collan shook his head. "Touring is natural. Racing around to specific plants isn't. Besides—" He grinned. "I want to see this place."

"Can't blame you. Fa did good work, and I'm not bad at it either, even if I do say it myself!"

They left the Garden of Ever-Snow for an alley of trees spreading down to the river. After a moment, Collan asked, "How'd you know, anyway?"

"Plants talk. What do you need next? This is the Hall of Green Shade, by the way. You'll notice that leaf-color darkens toward the water, to contrast with the stand of aspens on the opposite bank. In autumn it's solid gold over there, and quite spectacular."

Col took a moment to imagine it. "Must be. What I'm looking for is goldenrod, broom, rhododendron—"

"Who needs protection against danger?" Jescarin gestured the question away with the shears. "Never mind. Forget I asked."

They strolled on. The turf underfoot was springy and uniformly dense, but Col counted at least six kinds of grass, differenced by leaf shape and greenness, making a subtle quilted pattern down to the river. "How do you get all this the same height and thickness?"

Jescarin snipped the shears in the air. "By hand, Minstrel! By hand!"

At that precise moment, as if cued onstage, two gardeners came along with scythes and started in on the area surrounding a chestnut tree. Collan eyed his host, who laughed uproariously.

"And now I owe you a cutting of bramble, as apology for the lie!"

"I'd rather have some more leaves—ash, oak, and thorn, to be precise."

All humor died in the expressive eyes. "Those three? All together?"

Collan nodded.

"Things are that bad?"

"Getting that way, seems like."

Jescarin closed his eyes for a moment. " 'Summon the Guide.' May St. Rilla protect us all, especially my good Lady and her husband."

The morning passed quickly. They followed Verald's usual route with a detour to the greenhouses to find the plants Collan required. Lavender stalks were taken from a drying shed, and a twig with hazelnuts was finally discovered in the pantry of the gardeners' day-kitchen. The Master of Roseguard Grounds provided commentary, naming the flowers and trees and bushes, pointing out their color effects, detailing his future plans for this area or that. Collan listened, and deposited each needed plant in his pockets, and nothing more was said about the Rising.

"Nearly Eighth," Jescarin observed at last. "Sela will be wondering where I am. Come back to the house and eat with us, *Domni*. We have an excellent cook."

A quarter-mile from the river was a trim thatched cottage of two stories and many windows, each with a bright flowerbox overflowing below. The gravel path was bordered with a dozen tree-roses, and on either side of the door were wooden tubs gaily painted, bound in polished brass, frothing with white Miramili's Bells like soapsuds on washday. Collan leaned down to sniff their fragrance, and immediately sneezed.

As he straightened, rubbing his nose, he caught Jescarin frowning at him. The next moment the door opened. A long-limbed, dark-haired, very pretty, *very* pregnant young woman blinked at Col with wide green eyes. He sneezed again.

"I *knew* I'd seen you before!" Jescarin exclaimed. "Sela! Do you know who this man is?"

Sela inspected Col's face narrowly and gave a sweet peal of laughter. "My First Flowers!"

Mystified, Collan took a step back. But Sela had seized his arm and was pulling him into the cottage, chattering all the while. Jescarin talked over and around her.

"—familiar, but I couldn't place the name except as a Minstrel—"

"—just a child, and my mother told me not to expect—"

"—inside the archway, sneezing your head off—"

"—always remembered how sweet you were to a little girl—"

"—turns out to be *you*—"

"—I bragged about those flowers for years!"

"—and an agent of the Rising into the bargain!"

Tempted to clap a hand over each mouth, Col settled for a piercing whistle instead. "I'm *not* an agent of anything!"

Instant silence. Sela stared with those big green eyes of hers.

The awkward moment was punctuated by a sudden pounding inside his skull. Col said, "I'm sorry, but you've mistaken me for someone else. I've never met either of you before, and I don't know what you're talking about."

"Of course you remember!" the young woman exclaimed. "St. Sirrala's Fair at Sleginhold, when—"

"If he says he doesn't," said Jescarin, "then he doesn't."

Sela frowned. "But—" She gulped back the rest, and put a bright smile on her face. "Well, certainly. That's the way of it, truly told. Be welcome to my house, Minstrel Rosvenir. Please, sit down."

III

Col stayed for two pleasant hours. At Half-Ninth Sela's First Daughter Tamsa, not quite four, arrived with a tribe of other children who'd been on an outing. The cottage became an immediate chaos of grubby hands, red-cheeked faces, discarded gloves and hats and coats, squeals, giggles, yells, and demands for water, juice, and the direction of the toilet. Collan was inundated in stomping little feet (ruining the polish of his boots), jabbing little elbows (too low to damage precious parts of his anatomy), and grabbing little hands (attached to aspiring lumberjacks who tried to climb him like a tree).

Sela and Verald worked frantically, assisted by three young and two older men who scooped up children and deposited them on the rug as fast as they could snag them, with orders to "Stay there!" The only inhabitants of the cottage viewing the invasion with supreme unconcern were three lion-maned cats, each occupying a windowsill well out of reach of eager little fingers.

"The husbands take turns giving the mothers a day of peace every week!" Verald shouted at Collan over the din. "We try to run the legs off 'em so they're tired enough for a nap! Sometimes it works!"

Col peeled a climber off his leg and held it out from him by the shoulders. Big brown eyes in a small brown face met him stare for stare. Looking around helplessly, he spied one of the older men and extended the now squirming child. "Can you—*unh!*" For something this age, it had long legs; Col had just gotten a little foot in the stomach. "Do something with this, will you please?"

"Maidalin!" the man exclaimed, relieving Col of the girl. "Go on and sit by Tirez, there's a sweetheart."

Verald was grinning. "*You've* never been a father, truly told!"

"Never more truly," Col replied with feeling. No matter what a bedmate's plans might be, he was always scrupulously careful.

"Viko!" Sela called out, and a twinge stabbed at Collan's left temple as his rescuer of before glanced around. "Help!"

"Do you want a story?" Viko asked the children, and winced at the raucous chorus of "NO!"

Not the face, the name, Col thought, and applied his usual remedy: calculating the area of the room in square inches.

"How about a song?" Verald said desperately. "We've even got a real Minstrel here today! If you're all very quiet, maybe he'll sing for you!"

"Song! Song! Song!" one of them chanted, and the others joined in, and it was worse than before.

When necessary, Collan could make himself heard above tavern brawls. This was the greater challenge.

"QUIET!" he bellowed.

Little mouths rounded with astonishment. Big eyes widened with shock. And adult lungs heaved with sighs of sheer relief.

"All right, then," Col said in his normal tones. "And stay that way. *Domna* Trayos, you wouldn't happen to have a stringed instrument handy, would you?"

Verald raced from the room and came back an instant later with a child-sized mandolin. "It belongs to—"

"*Mine!*" a little girl shrieked.

Green eyes, dark skin, high cheekbones—Sela's daughter, all right. Col bowed to her. "Will you do me the honor of allowing me to borrow your very fine mandolin, *Domna?*"

Thrilled by this dignified grown-up title, her head bobbed up and down.

"My thanks." He caught her parents' grins from a corner of his eye. The six fathers had escaped to the dining room for sustenance—of the liquid variety, Col surmised, and if they were smart, it'd have a considerable kick.

He adjusted the instrument to an open tuning, so all he'd have to do was move the flat of a finger up and down the strings to change major chords. The mandolin was half the size of any he'd played before, and his hands were much too big to attempt any fingering.

He gave them "Little Blue Pig" before asking them to help sing "How Many Mice?" because he'd forgotten some of the words. Then he slowed things down with "St. Jeymian and the Bear" and the "Lisvet Lost Her Shadow" before finishing with the old Ambraian lullaby "Moons in My Window."

It worked. Heads nodded, eyelids drooped, and several children simply curled up on the rug for a nap. Col bowed once more to Sela's drowsy daughter, set the lute on the mantle, and tiptoed his way to the door.

Verald followed him. "*Thank* you," he murmured feelingly. "And while you may not be a father yet, you'll make a damned good one."

"Not if I can help it." Col chuckled. "Fathering's one thing. *Being* a father—that means one woman, one place, and no more taverns!"

"Talk to me again when you've met the *one* woman," advised his host with a wry grin. "You've got all the plants you needed?"

"Yes, thanks." He patted the muslin bag Jescarin had lent him and paused in the doorway to wave farewell to Sela. She gave him a smile and a nod on the way to carrying Tamsa off for a nap. "How long will you be hosting this lot?"

"Mercifully, no more than an hour. They all belong to people who work for the Slegins. It's a good life, though it may seem dull to you," he added as the door snicked shut behind him and they started down the path between rose trees. "Lady Agatine provides schooling and a start in a profession, and helps with dowries and marriage negotiations. If we're sick, her Healer tends us. When we retire, there's a cottage waiting at Sleginhold or another of her properties."

"She's a good, kind Lady," Collan said, thinking of the frightening message he must deliver to her tomorrow.

"That she is. And *Domna* Liwellan will follow her example, though please St. Venkelos the Judge that won't be for a long, long time yet."

"*Domna* who?"

"Sarra Liwellan. She's our Lady's chosen heir, if the Council agrees." He paused to nudge a border stone back

into place with his boot. "She's at Ryka Court now, presenting the petition."

Sarra Liwellan. While this name brought no headache, it
had distinctly unpleasant connotations—except for the satisfaction of smacking her rear after she kicked his.

"If you've time before you leave," Verald was saying, "do
us the honor of coming to dinner."

"If I can, I will."

"And bring your lute. I'd like to hear you sing something
a little less cute than 'Little Blue Pig'!"

Laughing, Collan agreed and made his way back to the
entrance to Roseguard Grounds. *Nice people,* he thought as
he walked back to his lodgings. *Nice house, nice little girl,
nice life.*

And dull as a day in Domburron.

12

Collan's understanding with the Thistlesilk's owner was that
he'd perform for an hour and a half in early evening when
the dinner room filled with high-class customers. His understanding with the Thistlesilk's owner's niece was rather less
formal. Both ladies were seriously disappointed by his stuffy
nose ("All those damned flowers—I should've known better!"). Singing was impossible, and the music tonight would
be instrumental only. Dalliance was impossible, too—
although his nose was just an excuse. He needed the night
free to assemble the message. With regret, for the niece was
inventive as well as pretty, he promised to make it up to her
soon.

So he meandered among tables with his lute slung on a
shoulder-strap, strumming or plucking as the mood took
him, winking at married women to make them blush and
keeping his eyes strictly off their unmarried daughters.
Roseguard was no conservative country town where even a
glance could earn a man a fist in the jaw; neither was it so
"sophisticated" that a man could openly admire any woman
he fancied. The patrons of the Thistlesilk were solid, forthright, upstanding citizens, successful merchants and crafters

for the most part, whose daughters chose a bower lad, took a husband, had a few children, and only *then* did (discreetly) as they pleased.

Minstrels, no matter how famous or attractive, were not what the worthy *domnas* of Roseguard approved of for their daughters. For themselves, however, they enjoyed a sly look or two, and some giggled like schoolgirls under Col's grin.

He played for two hours that night, figuring he owed it to his host. When he indicated he was finished for the night, he accepted the Bard's Cup of wine and drained it in four long swallows, as was customary. The Thistlesilk possessed a very fine Bard's Cup made of beaten silver with inlaid circles of lapis around the stem. He paused to admire it, then drank while the owner chanted the Minstrel's Rhyme, lutenist's version:

> *First to thank good St. Velenne*
> *Whose gift has kept me fed;*
> *Next to thank the worthy Bards*
> *Whose songs have bought my bed;*
> *Third to thank my Lady Lute*
> *Whose strings control my purse;*
> *The last does not thank you, kind friends—*
> *Instead, I thank my horse!*

There were other versions, depending on what instrument had been played. But one thing remained constant: a Minstrel who did not finish the Bard's Cup in the prescribed four swallows before the verse ended was compelled to play another song before trying again. And again. Until he got it right. Collan had on occasion become splendidly and inexpensively drunk by purposely failing—but only where he knew the innkeeper would indulge him, and only where they served good wine in the Bard's Cup. Early in his career he'd learned that most did not; indeed, the absolute dregs, sometimes one step removed from vinegar, was often poured for Minstrels—who must drink as custom demanded or risk more songs. And more wine.

Belly full of excellent Cantra red, he stopped in the kitchen to pick up a tray: roast lamb with lemon sauce, potatoes seasoned with thyme, and a salad of greens and apples. A bottle of wine awaited him in his room, and in a little while the kitchen boy would bring up hot tea and the Thistlesilk's specialty: orange and almond torte.

By Fourteenth, with the meal only a delightful memory and the wine long gone, he wished he could have indulged in several more Bard's Cups. Confronted by the full implications of the message he would deliver tomorrow to Lady Agatine Slegin, getting blind drunk tonight was a real temptation.

Gorynel Desse had made him twice repeat the plants, their groupings, and the ribbons that went with each—an insult to a man who had only to hear a song once before being able to play and sing it perfectly. The insistence on repetition had served to impress him with the importance of the message. On his way to Roseguard, he'd tried to forget what the bouquet would say to Lady Agatine, and mostly succeeded. But now, as he assembled its parts, it was as if the meaning of each flower, leaf, seed, and root was inscribed in fire.

Pennyroyal—*Flee*—hid beneath the giant pink rhododendron that meant *Danger*. To its stem Col wired white poplar leaves, three at the top and eight below. *Time;* an indicator of when Lady Agatine should leave Roseguard. Third day of the eighth week? Eighth day of the third? It was the last night of the first week of the year. . . . He would have bet his numbered accounts in Neele *and* Shainkroth that departure would be sooner rather than later. The message was urgent; why tell someone to flee seven weeks before the fact?

Which meant Lady Agatine had nineteen days to plan an escape—assuming the leaves weren't meant to indicate days and hours instead of weeks and days. Col thought not; nothing else in the bouquet had anything to do with time.

He gave a start, realizing St. Lirance's had come and gone, and he'd forgotten his own Birthingday, or at least the one he'd chosen for himself. His thirty-first, give or take. Glancing over the plants again, selecting the next part of the bouquet, he had the feeling that if he didn't deliver this message and get out of town fast, he wouldn't be around to forget his thirty-second.

He braided the stems of ash, oak, and thorn leaves with more wire to hold them firm, combined with a juniper sprig symbolizing *Succor*. Two finished, two to go. He bound the dozen or so marigolds—white, not the orangy-yellow used to express sadness at a separation—at various places on the sprig of red oleander, and bunched tall lavender stalks around the whole. Together, they counseled distrust and predicted deceit. *With no indication of the traitor's identity,* Collan thought, shaking his head as he worked. Maybe the next bunch was meant to be comforting: yellow carnations, purple broom, and the twig of hazelnuts emphasized the knowledge and protection given by magic.

With all four segments of the bouquet assembled and laid out on the table, Collan flexed his fingers before digging into his journeypack for the ribbons. These had been supplied by Desse with specific instructions as to which bundle must be tied by each.

Col smoothed the bright lengths of silk onto the table. Some were wide, others very thin. He arranged them according to directions for their placement around the smaller bouquets, knotted them together at each end, and tied the first set in a multicolored bow.

And stopped. And stared. And then laughed, though there was no humor in the sound. The rest of the message was right in front of him.

Each wide ribbon was a Name's first color; each narrow ribbon was that Name's secondary.

Around the order to escape he had knotted ribbons of black and purple, blue and yellow, crimson and gray, and brown and green. He knew the first two: they were on pennants flying above Roseguard. And although the others had been unknown to him this morning, now that he had seen the cottage in the Grounds—with its pillows and curtains and the napkins at the lunch table—he knew to whom they referred.

Gray and orange bound the oak, ash, and thorn leaves with juniper. A green ribbon with a thin gray tied marigolds, oleander, and lavender.

And then there were the colors for the magical portion of the message: blue and turquoise, wide gray and narrow green, gray and turquoise.

The whole thing was to be bound with gray and crimson: the colors of the Desse Blood.

Assembled, the message was a masterwork of nonverbal communication. It was also terrifying. And it made him madder than a spider-spun hornet.

Renne, Slegin, Jescarin, and Trayos must leave Roseguard on or by the eighth day of the third week. A Guide named Ostin would be summoned to succor them in their flight.

Feiran was associated with imminent deceit. Knowledge, protection, and magic were available—and Col knew damned well who was expected to provide the protection. That Liwellan girl must be the knowledgeable one; Taig had told him she wasn't Mageborn. Which left some total unknown named Rille to furnish the magic.

He caught himself shredding the ends of the Rosevenir gray and turquoise, and swore. How *dared* that motherless old son of a Fifth involve him in this? He was about to untie the offending colors when the personal import hit him. He was in Roseguard; he was the messenger; he was in danger; he was to be included in whatever plan Lady Agatine formed to get everyone to safety.

He put the bouquet in his journeysack, locked his door behind him, and went downstairs to get good and drunk.

And thus it was with bleary eyes and a mouth tasting worse than Blighted Bay that he presented himself at the Slegin residence the next morning at Seventh.

It was Lady Agatine's regular day for receiving visitors from outside Sheve. In a brazier-warmed antechamber, Collan cooled his heels in company with a goldsmith from Neele, four cloth merchants from Firrense, a netweaver from Seinshir, a furrier from Tillin Lake, two inkmakers from Wyte Lynn Castle, and a mother-and-sons delegation from the Roke Castle Instrument Makers Guild. All wanted contracts, and all carried samples of their work. The goldsmith and inkmakers were the luckiest in this regard. The furrier was sweating, the netweaver was entangled, and the cloth merchants were burdened like pack horses. The collection of lutes, mandolins, flutes, drums, trumpets, and other assorted noisemakers clattered and rattled and rang until Collan wanted to break every string, slash every skin, and muffle all the metal in all that very handy wool.

He carried only the bouquet. Which was bad enough, for the broom and lavender were doing dreadful things to his nose. It was all he could do not to sneeze. Adding to his discomfort was the blue coif fastened tight at his throat. Whenever he was compelled to wear it, he was tempted to join the Rising if only they promised to outlaw the damned things

Orlin Renne—massively tall, casually dressed, and armed with a list of names—appeared at the door to welcome the visitors. Collan had not applied for an audience in advance. A Minstrel could show up anywhere and expect admittance anytime. Besides, Collan was no stranger in Roseguard and the gatekeeper recognized him.

So did Orlin Renne. Had Col not been looking for it, he wouldn't have seen the slight fading of the man's smile, the downward flicker of his brows. *Good,* Collan thought, *they know something's up.* So much the better. This was not the kind of message he cared to deliver to people completely unprepared for it.

Still, because he was not on the official list, he would be last of all to see Lady Agatine. To his relief, the instrument makers went in first. Renne took pity on the furrier and cloth merchants, admitting them second and third. It was nearly Half-Eleventh by the antique longcase clock before Collan, all alone for some time after the inkmakers were shown in, was at last escorted to the Lady's presence.

Her pretty oval reception room was furnished with a fabulous Cloister rug in Slegin blue and yellow patterned with roses, a brace of unlit bronze candle strands, and a desk of aged golden oak with a carved medallion of flameflowers, graceful tribute to her husband's family. At this desk sat the Lady herself: elegant, lovely, and worried.

Orlin Renne dismissed the hovering secretary with a nod. When the door had closed and the three of them were alone, Collan bowed a second time, crossed the rug, and laid the bouquet on the desktop. He said exactly nothing.

Agatine's slim fingers stroked each set of ribbons in turn, sunlight dancing from the gold sigil ring on her thumb. She spent a long time looking, touching each element of the arrangement. Her husband stood at her side, one hand, wearing a matching ring, resting lightly on her shoulder. At length she lifted her head and met Collan's gaze.

"So," she murmured. "It begins at last."

He didn't much like the sound of that.

"I'm sure you understand most of what's here," she went on more briskly. "Is there anything you'd like clarified?"

"No, Lady. I'd rather not know."

She frowned and glanced up at her husband, who said, "You're part of it, friend Minstrel, like it or not. The Rosevenir colors—"

"—aren't my problem," Col interrupted. "It's not even my Name."

"No?" Agatine asked, with an odd note in her voice.

"I took it and the identity disk from somebody who's

dead." He hesitated, then shrugged. He'd liked these people on first meeting—five years ago now—and they'd been both kind and generous the several times he'd played for them here. He decided to share the truth. "I was born a slave."

"Whose? Scraller Pelleris'?"

"Yes." Collan shrugged. "It was a long time ago. I try not to remember it."

The strange thing was that he didn't remember much about his childhood as a slave. His survival depended on forgetting so thoroughly that no one could tell from manner or speech what he had once been. But although he dreamed sometimes about those years, dreams that woke him in a shaking sweat, he avoided all attempts at remembering. At this moment he couldn't seem to remember his slave days at all. This might have been a blessing, except for the sudden telltale headache. Well, he'd paid his duty and more to St. Kiy the Forgetful last night, and this was only the usual morning wine-head.

First hangover he'd ever had that hadn't begun the minute he opened his eyes in the morning.

Orlin Renne said, "No one would want to remember such things, Agatine." He tightened his grip on her shoulder, as if in warning.

"We've purchased and freed several of Scraller's slaves. One of them tutors my sons. Perhaps you knew him—his name is Taguare."

Another squeeze to her shoulder; Collan was mystified. He also felt a worse throb in his head.

"The Minstrel would doubtless prefer not to be reminded of his past," Orlin Renne said, his deep voice grating.

"I think it may be necessary," she replied, softly but firmly, and after a moment's silent resistance he nodded once and removed his hand.

"Taguare?" Collan repeated—daring the pain, in a way. Mistake. "*Damn* it!" he muttered, rubbing at his temple where a vein pounded.

"Your head hurts, doesn't it?" asked Lady Agatine.

"It's the flowers," he said stubbornly. "Strong scents bother my—"

"No, it's not the flowers."

"Agatine!" Renne growled. "Don't!"

She ignored him. "If I say that name again, or if you try

to figure out why a mere sound brings pain, the pain doubles—doesn't it, *Domni* Rosvenir?"

"How did you know that?" he demanded.

"But if you avoid the sound that caused it, the headache goes away."

Though she had not moved, though no one could seem less threatening than this serenely lovely woman, Collan backed away across the Cloister rug.

"It's a terrible irony," she went on. "That a Minstrel, a man who can make such beautiful sounds with his voice and his fingers, can find some sounds so painful. But it's symptomatic of Wards."

He nearly choked. "M–magic?"

"When one has seen things, done things, or knows things it's not safe to remember, a Mage will set Wards. In your case, it was Gorynel Desse who—"

Had he been wearing his sword, its point would be at her throat—Orlin Renne or no Orlin Renne. "You mean that old—he *did* things to my head?"

"For your own safety, Collan."

"You're crazy," he snarled. "I'm not listening to any more of this. You got your damned message, I'm—"

"The name Taguare hurts," she said softly. "And Viko. And Elseveth."

Sounds, they were just sounds—and they meant blinding pain. The coif strangled him, he couldn't breathe. He heard the sounds again and he heard himself cry out with the agony; he heard Renne's heavy tread, and the sound of his own body thudding to the carpet.

A day or a week or a year later, he became aware of small sensations: silk beneath his cheek, a sticky taste in his mouth, an aching lassitude throughout his body. The excruciating throb in his head was gone. But when he cracked his eyelids open, the sunlight made him wince.

"Hush," a gentle voice told him. "You'll be all right."

"Will he?" This was another voice, deep and angry.

"Gorsha gave me the mixture a long time ago, Orlin. It's prescribed in such cases. We never had to use it with Sarra."

"You mean you *planned* this?"

"The gatekeeper sent word Collan was here."

"But you didn't see fit to tell me. Thank you for your trust, Lady."

"Stop it," the woman said wearily. "I had to know."

Col wanted to ask what, but couldn't hunt down the right words. Fingertips stroked his forehead, ran motherlike through his hair. No coif; small mercy.

"I remember what Gorsha said about this stuff, too, Agatine," said Orlin Renne. "It plays hell with the Wards until it wears off. Sarra's guard her magic. You know damned well Collan's are totally different."

Wards? Him? Oh—something about magic, and Desse, and the headaches—

"I had to know exactly when the Wards take over," she insisted. "They've never been tested. If I'd known it would be this bad, I never would've told Gorsha I'd do this."

"He told you to do this to *Collan?*"

"He'll be with the Rising from now on. We had to know."

With the Rising—? he thought in puzzlement, then realized what she was saying. *Oh, no—not me, Lady!* His struggles to move produced a single twitch in one shoulder. It should have frightened him, but fear seemed as distant and alien as the sound-triggered headache.

"Evidently," Orlin Renne said with heavy sarcasm, "these Wards were one of Gorsha's subtler efforts. And until Collan sleeps this through, any of a dozen names will hurt like nails driven into his skull."

"He'll be all right tomorrow."

"You think so? Consider how much of that you poured down his throat. All right, Aggie, I'll shut up about it. I'll even find out where he's staying and send for his things. Staying here while he's in town is perfectly natural."

Tongue swollen, lips pulpy, somehow he managed to say, "Not st-staying...."

"You must," said Lady Agatine; "You have to now, Collan," said Orlin Renne. There was sympathy in both implacable voices.

"No...!"

A sigh, and a soft murmur: "If not for us, then for ... Falundir."

Not nails.

"Agatine—!"

Knives.

"For *Falundir.*"

One into his head, its twin in his heart. He screamed. Between his parted lips trickled more of the "something prescribed in such cases." He passed out.

13

Sarra Liwellan and Mai Alvassy said quick farewells as the ship docked in Renig. Both would go ashore—Mai as Sarra, Sarra as a rather short sailor. One would return to the ship. Agata Nalle had timed the arrival perfectly: before dawn after the Feast of Lusine and Lusir. The night Watch was just going home, the day Watch was not quite awake, and the whole town was well-nigh deserted. What few faces they saw belonged to servants and slaves on daybreak errands, and the lower echelons of the port authority who were grumpy with too much wine, not enough sleep, and too little rank for cushy afternoon duty.

Only three horses were ready for them. Elomar Adennos had not been expected to come along, but he insisted. Sarra couldn't blame him; anything rather than attend the querulous Mage Captal, cousin or not. Searching for another horse to hire would attract attention, so Sarra mounted up behind Alin. They were well out of Renig before its citizens were yawning over their breakfasts.

"It's not customary to get drunk on the Twins' day," Alin observed, "not like St. Kiy's. But Renig will take any excuse it can get."

"If I lived in The Waste, so would I," Sarra said.

"Why do you think I left?"

Val laughed. "Stay long enough, Sarra, and you'll end up either drunk or crazy. Alin-O and I are living proof!"

She could believe it. For the next ten days they rode through progressively more barren country. The south was fairly civilized: small farms, weaving towns, water mills. Rivers were drinkable only after treatment, so mainly they powered grindstones, furnaces, and looms. The Ostins had made one of their many small fortunes investing in replacement gears.

As they left the coast and rode upcountry, the land began to deserve its name. Cattle became scarce, then vanished. Alin explained that any cow with half a brain between its horns refused to eat what grew here, and no cow was equipped to rip up the nutritious water-storing roots. Sheep didn't bite, they tore—and were even more stupid than cows—so sheep country this was.

"Where Alin and I come from," Val said one evening by the campfire, "it's just galazhi. Their hooves and horns dig trenches, and they can chew anything."

Alin grimaced agreement. "Teeth to dent a copper pipe. I've seen it. And they're almost impossible to catch. You saw the range riders with the cattle? Useless with galazhi. They can outrun a horse for over a mile, and laugh at you the whole way."

"Then how do you people herd them?"

"People don't," said Elomar.

Alin elaborated, smiling. "We use the descendants of Fa's dowry. We used to tease Mother that she only married Tiva Senison because she wanted a stud—not him, his dog!"

"Of course!" Sarra exclaimed. "Senison hounds!"

"There's nothing a galazhi can't outrun, even the big cats. But they're terrified of dogs. They even catch the scent, and they freeze."

"Which is really funny," Val added, "because all you have to do is smile at anything descended from a Senny and he's yours for life—all wriggles and slobbers and wagging tail."

Alin leveled a blue-eyed glare at him. "You say it, you die."

Val grinned innocently. A bit belatedly, Sarra got the joke, and giggled.

The occasional clouds of dust on the horizon were galazhi herds. Sarra had many times dined off steaks, chops, or sausage made of the delectable meat, but had never seen one of the animals on the hoof. Galazhi were approachable only when they gave birth and were helpless, but butchering new mothers and fawns was not only a nauseating idea, it was bad husbandry. Before the Senison hounds were perfected— yet another Ostin enterprise, made possible by Alin's father's dowry—the only way to catch them was to stampede them off a cliff to butcher on the spot. But for twenty years now the big dogs had herded them very tidily. From postures of petrified terror the galazhi would bounce a few nervous times before freezing once more, one eye always on laughing-eyed, brown-striped dogs who only wanted to make friends.

They reached Combel at sunset on the tenth of Shepherd's

Moon. All Sarra desired in the world was a bath, the hotter the better. After skirting the outlying districts, where wide streets were lined with comfortable homes, they finally reached a hostelry in a dismal section of town.

"The Watch still patrols here," Valirion murmured. "I'm surprised."

Alin shook his head as he tied up the weary horses. "Look down the street."

Sarra peered through the dusk. What Alin saw, she didn't, and said so.

"The boundary between this district and the next—the really rough part of town—used to be five blocks farther on." Val exchanged glances with Alin. "A year from now, it'll be *here*."

The hostelry boasted what the owner called a "suite." This consisted of two tiny rooms with a connecting door that didn't lock. No tub was available. Sarra made vigorous use of ewer and basin. She slept in a real bed for the first night in the last ten, and so soundly that only during her morning wash did she discover the bug bites. Val, Alin, and Elomar joined her for breakfast in her room, the only one with a table. The Healer Mage and Alin had slept in the second bedroom the previous night. Val had gone out prowling.

Expecting a scarcely edible breakfast, Sarra was surprised by its freshness and flavor: porridge and fruit, fried galazhi sausage, egg-batter toast, minted tea. Between mouthfuls, Alin said, "Val takes his Name Saint very seriously."

"So he 'provided,' " Sarra said with a smile.

"Easy enough, with money," Val muttered, attacking a sausage with his fork. "Times are bad. Between taxes and trade quotas. . . ."

"Quotas?" Sarra blinked over her tea mug. "What do you mean?"

Alin heaved a sigh and shook his blond head. "Now you've done it. Never ask a Maurgen about trade."

Valirion spared him a glance before launching into his explanation. "The Waste doesn't have a local government, Sarra, not like the other Shirs. We have a Council seat and the proper number of Assembly members, but that's pretty meaningless. It's the Web that runs everything."

"That's true all over Lenfell," she pointed out.

"Not like here. Our Trade Web isn't run by a family or group of families with holdings in The Waste. It's all outsiders. Take the Maurgen Tannery. We sell leather to cobblers, glovemakers, saddlers, and so on. The rest goes to the Trade Web. A deal is made with another Shir in exchange for something we can't produce here. The Web returns profit from the leather in cash, so we can buy tools, hire more workers, pay into the Dower Fund."

Sarra didn't see the difficulty. "So you get rid of the surplus that the local crafters can't use. That's how trade works, Val."

Alin gave a complex snort as Val continued, "You think Web quotas are optional? Say the Obreic Cobblery gets an order for special boots to outfit Brogdenguard miners, and wants to buy every scrap of leather the Maurgens can make. Too bad! We *must* fill our quota, even though the price the Web gets might be less than that offered by the Obreics."

"And we never see the profits," Alin added. "There're salaries for Web officers, payments to port authorities, tariffs—"

"—and the inevitable bribes," Elomar finished for him.

Val nodded. "Besides, the Web has first call. Nothing left over? Too bad! Rotten year and you can't make quota? The difference is added to next year, or you make it up in cash. Some families owe two or three years on their quotas."

"Or more," Alin said. "Remember when the Oslir Glassworks blew up in '64? I heard in Ryka that Jaym tried to sell himself to Scraller for money enough to rebuild." Hastily, he added, "He didn't. His grandmother found out."

"We were at school together," Val said, looking sick.

Sarra felt the same after this tutorial in the school of specific example. Of the associated evils, strangled trade, theft, embezzlement, and bribery were the least. Daughters sold to unwanted husbands for the dowry; sons unhusbanded for lack of funds; women and men working like slaves for little or no return; women and men who sold themselves as slaves because they had no other choice.

And all while others grew rich off the corruption.

Lusira Garvedian had charged her to *do* something. As she finished her tea, she added the economics of The Waste to her ever-lengthening list of Things To Do Something About.

Elomar Adennos correctly read her expression. "Right Lenfell's wrongs once you're in a position to do so, Sarra.

At the moment, we have an appointment that I hope will help get you there."

Val had sold the horses to a Vekke cousin, so the four walked from the inn to the prosperous district of Combel, near the main circle with its temple to Gorynel the Compassionate. Sarra glimpsed the small stand of the Saint's thorn trees in the middle of the circle and the domed sanctuary rising beyond. Anywhere else, there would have been gilding and glass and carvings. Here, where acid storms blew in at least twice a year, decoration was folly. And in that necessarily plain, unornamented facade, Sarra saw a problem that no one could solve: the ancient and continuing devastation of The Waste.

Or—perhaps she was wrong. Magic had done this. Perhaps magic might *undo* it. She added *that* to her ever-lengthening discussion with Gorynel Desse.

The Bower of the Mask ("Truth or lie, lie or truth/Ladder made in Maidil's youth"), though a licensed and elegant establishment, reminded her of her experience in Pinderon. She was older now; she did not blush. But surely such display of masculine charm this early in the morning bordered on the indecent.

The bower mistress evidently had a mania for black and white. Across a broad floor of chessboard tiles were scattered a dozen languid lounge chairs, in whose black or white depths a dozen young men were draped in various states of black or white undress. Dark-skinned boys in white robes; blonds in black longvests open to the waist; muscular youths in mists of white trimmed in black beads. All faces were hiden behind long-handled masks, features painted black and white, with dangling ribbons tied loosely about their wrists.

Sarra told herself to think like Imilial Gorrst: this was a restaurant and the men were on the menu. She assumed her role was potential customer, with Elomar in Orlin's part. All Val had said was, "Follow my lead." Sarra called up her best dimples, tried to look charmed, and waited for a lead to follow.

The bower mistress, wearing a gown that matched her floor, took one look at her guests and shrieked. "Valirion! Where have you been, you naughty boy?"

Val kissed both lacquered cheeks. "Lovelier than ever, *Domna!*" He tore off his coif, unbuttoned his longvest, and shooed a sulky bower lad off a black velvet chair. Sinking into it, he went on, "Lost some weight, changed your hair—"

The walking chessboard was still scolding. "If only I'd made you sign a contract! One week you were here—*one week*—and my customers have been heartbroken ever since!"

"I got a better offer," said Val.

Sarra sneaked a quick glance at Alin. He stood beside Adennos, stone-faced.

"I'll match it—I'll double it!"

"Not even you could do that, *Domna.*"

And that, Sarra thought with a smile, *was for his Alin-O.*

"Tell you what, though," Val added, "I'm in the mood for a little party." He waved an idle hand at his companions. "Is the Plum Room available?"

"For you, certainly—and at a discount, if you'll take on just one client."

Val winked. "Not even tempted, *Domna* darling. The Plum Room, regular rates, until tomorrow morning."

She chewed her lip, then nodded. "Oh, very well. But out by Sixth, I've a special client tomorrow night and the room will need a thorough cleaning once *you've* finished with it." She pinched him affectionately on the ear. "Will you need any of the boys?"

Several looked hopeful. Several looked at Sarra. One looked at Alin—who gave him a look to freeze a volcano.

"No, but thanks all the same. I've got a few more friends coming later. Be sweet to them, sweetcheeks. They're shy."

"Ah. Of course. Well, then come upstairs, my fine Wastrel cockie, and let's get you men and your lovely little *Domna* settled in."

Five minutes later they were inside a room remarkable for being exactly as advertised. Walls, rugs, curtains, bed-clothes, bedstead, goblets and wine pitcher on a marble table—it was all decorated with motifs of plump, succulent plums. And it was all purple. The sensation of being inside a fruit pie was multiplied a hundredfold by two walls of mirrors and another on the ceiling over the biggest bed Sarra had ever seen in her life.

"Geridon's Holy Stones," Val muttered. "She hasn't changed a thing."

Alin, turning from contemplating a purple ceramic figurine of naked lovers, asked mildly, "Since when? Oh—since you made the *sacrifice* of spending a week here to establish your credentials?"

"Don't start," Sarra ordered. "Alin, where's the Ladder?"

"Through there." He pointed to a half-open door. "It's just a closet."

" 'Just'?" Val snorted. "In the Bower of the Mask, Alin-O, nothing is ever 'just' anything."

"You should know," his cousin shot back.

"I said don't," Sarra repeated. "Be jealous on your own time, Alin."

"He's not jealous," Val said. "He's envious."

"I suggest you take the Lady's advice," said Elomar. He stood before a bay window paned in lilac-tinted glass. "We have visitors."

Sarra parted two panels of lavender lace drapery. In the street below she saw four cloaked, hooded figures slinking through the bright sunshine.

"In this case," the Healer remarked, " 'shy' translates as 'nervous.' "

"They're practically begging people to notice them," she agreed.

"You be sweet, too, Sarra." Val stood at her shoulder. "They weren't supposed to arrive before noon. Something must've happened."

She looked up at him. "And what, precisely, did you have in mind to do until noon?"

"Well ... this room has some interesting possibilities." Then he shrugged an apology. "My mother'd ship my hide to the tannery with me still in it, the manners I've used around you. But, truly told, you said you'd love a bath. It's down the hall."

She could just imagine.

Up the side alley privy stair came the four Mages. Elomar welcomed them, then performed quick introductions. "Scholar Mage Sirralin Mossen, her son Prentice Tiron Mossen. Healer Mage Truan Halvos. Prentice Keler Neffe."

They, too, were a trifle off their manners—Truan Halvos because he was utterly mortified at being inside a bower for the first time in his sixty-plus years. He twitched every time his dark glower alighted on some new purple perversion. Sarra kept her face sternly composed—a task made more difficult by the look on Tiron Mossen's fifteen-year-old face. A slack-jawed stare around the Plum Room left the boy

quite simply stunned. Brown eyes blinking, dark skin blushing, throat gulping, he was simultaneously embarrassed and
fascinated.

Prentice? Sarra thought as he finally remembered to bow
in her direction. Ambrai had been destroyed before he was
born, so it was impossible for him even to have seen the
Academy, let alone studied there.

His mother's reaction to the room was one of amused delight. Sirralin Mossen looked like nobody's idea of a Scholar
Mage. Tall as Imi Gorrst and more generously curved, she
had skin the color of coffee and cheekbones so prominent
they tilted the corners of her eyes. Though she must be nearing forty, she looked thirty—and the glance she threw at
Keler Neffe said she'd purely love to get him alone in here
and pretend she was still twenty.

He replied with a wink. Neffe was about thirty, so must
have begun his studies at the Academy, but his subsequent
education in magic had probably been sketchy at best. As he
bowed over but did not kiss Sarra's wrist, a thick lock of
honey-blond hair escaped his coif to droop into gray eyes.
He stuffed it back into the coif and apologized.

"No need," Sarra replied. "We're scarcely formal, this little group."

"You're very gracious, Lady," he said. "Aunt Mairin
would have my head shaved for the infraction."

"Having met your Aunt Mairin, I can believe it," she said,
smiling. She knew the Lady, and the Neffe Name—the family owned every leaf, twig, pebble, drop of fresh water, and
vein of gold on Neffen, the smallest inhabited island of
Seinshir. "Please sit down," she continued. "Val, pour some
wine. How is it you're here so early?"

"We were warned," Sirralin Mossen replied. "Rather
charmingly, too—a bouquet of flowers and herbs tied with
the Desse colors. It's the latest fashion in secret messages."
Nodding thanks to Val for the winecup, she drank and went
on, "Truly told, Lady Sarra, I was losing my mind in that
hut outside town. We were there five days, after a week on
the road from a similar hovel on the Ambrai border. I've
been languishing in that miserable frontier town since last
Candleweek. No books, nobody worth meeting, no conversation beyond crops and rain. How do ordinary folk stand it?"

She had summed herself into a total that Sarra did not find
impressive. Scholar Mossen thought Mages in general and

herself in particular superior to "ordinary folk." Well, at least she wasn't whining like the Mage Captal. And somebody thought her worth saving, or she would not have been summoned to Combel. Sarra sternly reminded herself not to judge in advance of real knowledge, and seized on the important point of the Scholar's tale.

"A message in flowers and herbs?"

"Why, yes. I sneezed for two solid hours. The pennyroyal and water willow weren't bad, but the roses—! I may be named for the patron of flowers, my dear Lady Sarra, as you are, but I hope she blessed you with a more tolerant nose!"

Sarra glanced up at Elomar. "Flee, and Freedom," he supplied in answer to her silent question. Then he asked the Scholar, "What kind of roses?"

"What kind?"

"Red, yellow, white—"

Her son answered. "The white ones were Maidil's Favor. And almost black ones, too, called Masked Moonlight. That's how we knew to come here. I *like* flowers," he finished shyly, and blushed again.

Sarra looked once more to Elomar. He shrugged. "As Scholar Mossen says, flower language is a recent trick of Gorsha's. But I must tell you, Lady, I do not like the implication."

"Or the haste. Val, what time is it in Neele?"

"Neele?" exclaimed Sirralin Mossen.

"Seven after Half-Fifteenth. It'll do."

"Someday," she said, "I'm going to check these so-called exact times of yours against a clock. How can you possibly know how many minutes—"

"Why are we going to Neele?"

"Have faith," Val intoned. Then his dark eyes developed a wicked glint. "You'll love this Ladder, Sarra. It's . . . unique."

"Neele! Why didn't you tell me before? A very dear schoolfriend of mine lives just two streets away from—"

"Oh, *do* hush, please!" burst out Truan Halvos. "The sooner we're out of this despicable place, the better!"

As they crammed into the round closet, Sarra eyed Alin. "*How* unique?"

Val replied, "Completely."

"Shut up, Val," his partner snapped.

And after a moment of now-familiar blankness, Sarra

found out what he meant. The Neele Ladder was a platform of iron grating inside a gigantic vertical drainpipe emptying into the city sewer.

14

Collan wasn't being held prisoner. He simply wasn't being allowed to leave.

Which was pretty much the same song, to his ears.

Not that he'd never been in a jail. Wyte Lynn Castle's was a real old-fashioned dungeon. Kenroke's was at the top of a spindly tower. Dinn used an offshore island. He'd gotten himself out of all these and one or two others—most readily when the jailkeep was female. His experience was of honest jails with steel locks and iron bars. Deep stone holes. Five-foot-square windowless rooms. Being forced to accept Slegin hospitality was a lot more pleasant, admittedly—and a lot harder to escape from.

He was given a fine, airy room down the hall from the Slegin sons. Those who stood watch over Lady Agatine's four offspring also kept watch over *him*. Locks and bars lulled captors into complaisance; human eyes had human brains behind them. Outside his room, he never went anywhere—not even to the toilet—without being watched.

It was maddening. They were all so *nice* to him, as if he was exactly what Orlin Renne said he was: an honored and valued guest. He was allowed free run of the residence and private garden, though not Roseguard Grounds. He ate dinner every night with the family, performed afterward, and was beginning to teach Riddon Slegin how to play the lute. He spent whole days in the library, learning new songs and variants of old ones from the vast shelves of folios, and was even allowed to raid Sarra Liwellan's private collection for songbooks. He did all these placid, genteel things instead of trying to escape because Orlin Renne had not been at all nice that first evening.

"You have two choices," Lady Agatine's husband told him when he woke from whatever potion she'd given him for reasons he couldn't quite recall. "You can make life mis-

erable for yourself and everyone else at Roseguard by repeated acts of foolishness, or you can enjoy your stay. Because you *will* stay, Collan Rosvenir. If I have to truss you
up head to foot in our best Cloister carpet and cut holes for
you to eat, breathe, piss, and shit from, you *will* stay."

Thus presented, he saw Renne's point.

Besides, they'd be leaving soon, and out on the open road
with a horse under him, escape would be simple.

He hoped. That business about the Mageborn Somebody-
or-other Rille worried him some. He'd heard what effect
magic could have on a blind-mind like him.

Seventeen days into this velvet captivity he really started
to worry. Two more days before they were supposed to
leave, yet no preparations had been made that Col could discern. Life went on as usual at the Slegin residence. What
were they waiting for?

He didn't ask. Lady Agatine and Orlin Renne might risk
their own safety but never their children. Col figured they'd
get out in time and take him along.

He liked the four Slegin boys—three young men, really,
and eleven-year-old Jeymi. Riddon, twenty-two come spring,
had a natural affinity for the flute and owned eight different
kinds. Had Bard Hall been standing, he'd be there; as it was,
he learned from whomever he could. Jeymi was all thumbs
and had a voice like a tail-trod cat, but was an enthusiastic
listener and amused Collan with an ardent case of hero wor-
ship. Elom was nineteen and girl-crazy; Maugir, nearly seventeen and horse-crazy. Musically, the two had tin ears, but
Col's fund of lore about both girls and horses won their un-
dying admiration.

"My eldest has recovered from the rebellious stage," Lady
Agatine sighed one evening while Col tuned up, "and my
youngest hasn't yet reached it, but my middle pair make
enough mischief for six."

Riddon gave his mother an overdone bow; Jeymi grinned
as if to say he was taking notes while waiting for his turn;
Elom clapped a hand to his heart in injured innocence;
Maugir simply looked smug.

"Saints, the faces on those four!" said Renne. "Can you
imagine what our lives would've been like with *girls?*"

"I forbid you even to think it!"

Col had never encountered a daughterless couple who didn't
bitterly regret it. He supposed they thought of the Liwellan

brat as theirs. Certainly the four brothers spoke of her as they would a real sister: they loved her, made fun of her, tolerated her foibles only so far, and assured Collan that after an unpromising adolescence she'd turned out pretty enough to do them credit. They didn't resent that she and not they would inherit the Slegin properties and wealth. Riddon seemed relieved for the weight it took from his mother's mind.

The newly confirmed Lady Liwellan was due back in Roseguard soon—before the eighth, Collan hoped. All they lacked in this little enterprise was a week spent chasing around Lenfell trying to find her. And quite the parade they'd be: Lady Agatine, Orlin Renne, their sons; *Domna* Sela Trayos, Verald Jescarin, their daughter; Sarra Liwellan, the mysterious Mage Rille, Collan himself—plus an Ostin as guide. Thirteen people traipsing about Sheve, one of them extremely pregnant. Madness.

Col shrugged mentally and sang a ballad learned in the Slegin library. A nod to Riddon signaled their surprise for his parents: a duet for mandolin, flute, and two voices, perfected just that afternoon. And thus went another family evening. Col was yawning before the mantle clock struck Fourteenth, Jeymi's bedtime.

It took all three big brothers to get one little brother to bed. Collan nearly dropped his borrowed mandolin when affectionate Jeymi included him in his good night hugs. Lady Agatine laughed aloud after the boys were gone.

"You really can't run once we're on the road, you know," she said, startling him so much that his flatpick slid from his fingers. "Jeymi would be off after you. Whatever would you do with an eleven-year-old tagging along?"

He thought it politic not to mention that she'd guessed his intention—though he knew his face had been admission enough—and instead took the attack. "It's the sixth, and I'm packed. Are you?"

"Almost," she replied serenely.

"I must say," Renne commented, "you've been remarkably patient. Or remarkably stubborn. You haven't said one word about our departure."

"Would it do me any good?"

"I like practicality in a man," said Lady Agatine. "One more song, please, before we retire for the night? I've an early day tomorrow."

So he sang, and said good night, and paced his bedroom

for half an hour before unpacking everything and then packing it again for something to do. Just for the snideness of it he parted the curtains and waved to his guards outside the windows.

This was the most charming jail he'd ever been in. He just wasn't quite sure how he'd been caught. He remembered taking the bouquet into Lady Agatine's office, and drinking something. That had been his mistake. They wanted him to stay until it was time to leave, and had done it very efficiently.

Well, they couldn't watch him constantly on the road. He'd tie Jeymi up if he had to.

And St. Alilen damn him for a total fool if he ever accepted a favor from a member of the Rising again.

15

Sarra was feeling twinges of Ladder Lag again. She'd been from Combel to Neele, Neele to Dinn, and Dinn back to Neele in the space of four days. Because the latter two cities kept the same time, there was no one-minute-morning, next-minute-midnight confusion. Perhaps her discomfort—a slight but nagging headache and a general weariness—was due to the constant exposure of her Warded magic to the Ladders. Or maybe it was just a relapse of her cold.

Once they climbed out of the Naplian Street sewer, they collected three more Mages: Deikan Penteon, Dalia Shelan, and Geris Mirre. There had been not the slightest difficulty which, of course, had Alin in a state of nerves. None of the three knew each other and each had been contacted at a different location. By the time everyone was assembled for the long walk down Bekke Farm Road, it was dusk. Valirion was in favor of stopping for the night at a local inn. Sarra told him she would favor it, too, if their party of eleven looked like anything other than a Mage Guardian convention. So they walked on as the moons rose. And as concrete gave way to gravel, and gravel to dirt, Deikan Penteon endeared himself forever to Sarra by Folding the road.

"I'm not half as good at it as Gorsha Desse," he apologized. "Plain ground is simple, and I can manage cobbles because the stones haven't been combined with anything. But *he* can work the spell on pavement."

So instead of three hours, the trip lasted a little over one. Their goal was a well halfway to the Bekke Farm for which the road was named, where travelers could rest and refresh themselves. Alin took them in three groups down a metal ladder ("In or out, out or in/Ladder steps of shiny tin") into the magical Ladder. It lacked a few minutes before Thirteenth when Sarra, last to go through with Adennos and Shelan, found herself in a place blessedly different from her arrival in Neele. This Ladder was the circular pantry of the Knife and Fork Inn, where the air was fragrant with spices rather than pungent with smells better left unidentified.

Val had already alerted the proprietor, a former slave who ran the tavern for Lady Agatine, and rooms were ready for them upstairs. The taproom patrons never even knew they'd arrived.

Waiting were the last three Mages: Ilisa Neffe, her husband Tamosin Wolvar, and Tamosin's uncle Tamos. There ensued a family reunion of sorts, for Ilisa was Keler Neffe's sister and these Wolvars were close kin to the Shelans and Mossens. Sarra left them to it in one room, repairing to another with her own unacknowledged kinfolk.

Val poured wine. Alin paced and fretted in silence. Sarra sat on the bed, back propped with pillows, and drank half the wine in two swallows.

"This isn't the itinerary you originally told me about," she said.

"Well, no," he admitted. "We had to make a few adjustments, based on information received at Ryka. Alin, sit *down.*"

Alin ignored him, and kept right on wearing the polish off the planks.

"Information you didn't see fit to share," Sarra observed. "Where do we go from here?"

"Back to Neele, where a boat's waiting to take us up to Roseguard. We may get there the same time as Captain Nalle and the *Rose Crown,* and we may not. Doesn't much matter."

"We won't be arriving as ourselves," she interpreted, "and in any case, I will already have arrived in the form of Mai Alvassy."

He snagged Alin's arm, turned him around, and pushed him into a chair. "I said, *sit*. And tell me what's bothering you."

"You wouldn't believe me if I told you."

"Try us," Sarra suggested.

Alin drained his wine and stared into the dregs. "It's too damned easy," he muttered. "I don't like it. Did you know that these two groups got flower messages as well? Same as the ones we picked up in Combel."

"So?" Val shrugged. "We learned at Ryka Court that we might have to move faster than planned."

"I don't *like* it," Alin repeated.

"Would you rather be a half-step ahead of the Council Guard, or have the local Watch breathing down our necks, or—"

"You see?" Alin burst out. "You don't believe me. I told you you wouldn't."

"Alin," said Sarra, trying to soothe without patronizing, "we're here, we're safe, there've been no mistakes and no problems. It seems to me we ought to thank St. Miryenne for her favor and hope she continues to smile on us."

He looked up, eyes dark. "And if she doesn't."

Val answered lightly, "Then we'll change allegiance to Garony the Righteous and Pierga Cleverhand, the patron of prisoners and the breaker of locks."

Casual as his voice was, yet there was worry in his eyes—not for what Alin feared might happen, but for Alin himself. Sarra felt a small, poignant ache center somewhere around her heart. To love someone that much, so much that every hurt was instinctively shared . . . to be loved that much, so much that no hurt went uncomforted. . . .

It might almost be worth it.

Maybe that sort of loving happened only with a member of one's own sex. Sarra thought about it for a minute, picturing women she knew and liked. She felt friendship, affection, pleasure in their company—but no desire for physical contact more intimate than a hug. Certainly not what she'd seen in Val's and Alin's eyes sometimes. Or Agatine's and Orlin's—or her own parents'.

Well, hell, she thought with an inner sigh. *Women don't interest me. It'll have to be a man. One of these years I really must do something about it.*

After all, she'd be twenty-three soon and that was posi-

tively ancient to be still virgin, even for someone whose
Name Saint was Sirrala.

The next morning she was again trudging the Bekke Farm
Road, this time back to Neele. The fourteen of them split
into three smaller groups an hour apart. They were to meet
at the St. Mittru dock by sunset, there to board the *Summer
Star*—captained by an Ellevit, owned on paper by a Senison,
and owned in fact by Lilen Ostin.

But when they converged on the rickety wharf, no mast
flew the white and brown Senison flag with its coiled
hooded Snake sigil; no pennant trailed from any stern bearing the Ellevit Dagger on green and crimson; and there was
no ship named *Summer Star* in the whole of Neele Harbor.

16

Collan woke with a vicious headache—as if his dreams had
been filled with all the names that had ever pierced his skull.
The pain was so bad that he didn't bother with shoes or shirt
before seeking out Lady Agatine's Healer. A potion tasting
like what she'd given him that first night sent him back to
bed until nearly noon.

Bathed, shaved, and decently dressed, Col took a purposely meandering path to the kitchen to scrounge something to eat. Even though the day of departure was—*must*
be—tomorrow, he saw no indication that anything was other
than perfectly normal. Just another day at Roseguard.

But as a cook sliced bread and tomatoes, a trio of grooms
came into the kitchen, snatched up journeypacks, and left in
haste. Collan sauntered to a window. In the back courtyard,
the three mounted up on the finest horseflesh Col had ever
seen. Orlin Renne and Rillan Veliaz, Master of Horse, were
there to see them off. Both men looked grave as the grooms
clattered out the gates.

The cook produced a plate of bread, cheese, tomatoes,
liver paste, and watered wine. Col sat down to eat, and after
a minute or two said casually, "Long road to Sleginhold."

"Truly told, Minstrel. They'll sleep as well as eat in the
saddle the whole way." The cook didn't even look alarmed

at having revealed the information. Maybe he thought
Collan privy to Lady Agatine's plans.

Jeymi Slegin ran in, skidded to a stop, and exclaimed,
"*There* you are! Mama says to attend her at once, but you
can probably finish your lunch first."

"I'm done," Col told the boy, slathering liver paste on
bread and folding it around cheese and tomatoes. "Not polite
to keep a Lady waiting."

Agatine was in her oval reception chamber, clearing out
her desk. She was unhurried and unworried as she stacked
papers into a box held by her personal maid—a pretty
blonde Col might have been interested in had she not been
so definitely married to the Master of Horse.

"And these to the Temple," Agatine was saying as Col
and Jeymi entered. "That's the last of it, Tarise."

"Yes, Lady." Tarise looked up and saw the new arrivals.
"He's here."

"Good. That will be all for now." Tarise went out, carrying the box, and Agatine turned to Col. "*Domni* Rosvenir,
you said you were packed."

"Yes, Lady."

"Good. Jeymi, go find your brothers. Tarise will join you
in your rooms and tell you what to do."

"Yes, Lady," her youngest son said, serious as a courtier,
and shut the door behind him.

"Is Taig Ostin here yet?" Col asked.

"Taig? Saints, no. Why would you think—oh. The message with the Ostin colors. No, it's Ostinhold we're bound
for. Taig has no part in it."

"Then who's the Guide?"

She smiled slightly and nodded to a tapestry to Col's left.
Its folds parted, and Gorynel Desse stepped into view.

Naturally. Who else? Collan thought, then stopped thinking as anger claimed him. "You son of a Fifth!" he snarled,
advancing on the elderly Warrior Mage. "You got me into
this—"

"Yes, I did," Desse replied. To Lady Agatine, he added,
"Any more headaches?"

"What do you know about—" Col began.

"Calm yourself, boy. You'll understand in good time. Yell
if you like, get it out of your system. You have one minute."

"Why don't you just spell me to silence?" Collan spat.

"Go ahead, work more magic on me—I won't know the difference!"

"Well, as a matter of fact, you would. But that's another conversation. Are you finished? Ready now to listen to what must be done to save your life?"

17

Sarra ordered her charges to scatter all over Neele in their original groups. Sirralin Mossen, Deikan Penteon, Tamos Wolvar, and Elomar Adennos kept tiny Globes tucked in a cupped palm as links. These small wonders, set by Wolvar, would flare at Adennos' command when it was decided where they would meet again. A picture of the rendezvous would appear for less than a minute before the Globes winked out of existence. No one, not even Gorynel Desse, could match Tamos Wolvar's artistry with Mage Globes.

Returning to Dinn was out of the question. Although the owner of the Knife and Fork Inn was Rising loyal, Dinn was even farther from Roseguard than Neele. What they needed was a Ladder to Roseguard. But the only one Alin knew was the Old Kenroke Mill. Nobody wasted any time trying to plot a way to get there.

Sarra led her own little group on a shopping tour. All of them pretended to scrutinize window displays; none of them saw a single thing. They were too busy not looking over their shoulders.

"It'll have to be Combel," Sarra said, staring at a display of cutlery on black felt.

"I agree." Valirion angled himself so the window reflected the street behind him. "I don't see anybody watching—which means bloody damn-all." He had succumbed to Alin's jitters. "You heard what Keler Neffe said about the flower messages everyone received."

This was what had finally convinced him—and Sarra—that Alin was right to worry. Huddled at the docks and trying to digest the fact that there was no *Summer Star* to board, Keler Neffe had suddenly torn off his coif and ripped it to shreds in fury. Sarra snapped at him to calm down and explain himself. So he did, and his tale made grim hearing.

Jenira Neffe, Keler's great-grandmother, had been a sometime poet whose most famous work was *Rose Rhymes*. Its hundred verses gave personalities to nearly every variety of rose on Lenfell, based on ancient ballads collected over twenty years. Every Neffe of her direct line was required to memorize it by the age of ten; Bard Falundir had even borrowed some of her images for the song that had been his downfall.

The point was that where to young Tiron Mossen, the black and white roses had indicated the Bower of the Mask, *Rose Rhymes* taught that this pairing of colors meant "The Sender Betrays."

Tiron's panicked remorse was quelled by Sarra. "It's not your fault, and I forbid you to think that it is. Guardian Neffe, that goes double for you."

"Whoever sent those flowers is *laughing* at us!" the Mage fumed.

"And who says we can't laugh right back?"

"You remembered," Val put in. "At least we're warned."

"Too late," Neffe muttered.

"Are we dead yet, or in chains?" Sarra scoffed. "Very well, then. Hush up about it."

The flowers had been tied with Desse colors; that Gorynel could be the betrayer was a stark impossibility. Also in all cases, the bouquets had simply shown up on doorsteps. There was no name or face to connect with the sender.

Two things only were certain: the floral code was hopelessly compromised, and there was a traitor in the Rising.

They did not linger at the docks to ask if a ship named *Summer Star* was due in port. The fourteen split up and vanished into Neele, connected only by Tamos Wolvar's little Mage Globes, still safely anonymous.

It was Sarra's responsibility to get them all to real safety. As she paused to look unseeing into shop windows, she decided they would use the drainpipe Ladder to Combel and then travel overland back to Renig.

"Longriding would be better," Alin murmured. "There's a Ladder there that goes to Ambrai."

"Is there?" she asked, knowing there was. Gorynel Desse had used it to get Sarra and her mother to safety long ago. "Then that's where we'll go."

"What?!" cried Val, then bit his tongue between his teeth.

Taking Sarra's arm, he steered her across the street to the greenswath median and practically shoved her onto a bench under a linden tree.

"That's insane! Ambrai? The Captal's own quarters? What makes you think the traitor won't be watching? And following! We have to assume *all* the known Ladders are compromised."

"Where's the first place a Mage in trouble would go? The Mage Academy! Which is precisely why Glenin Feiran won't look for us there!"

"Glenin?"

"Do *you* seriously mean you don't think she's the one behind this?" Sarra knew it without thinking about it—which meant she was certain it was true.

Val sank back against the wrought iron bench. "All right," he said. "I understand. But it's going to take a long time to get there."

"So? We'll be in The Waste—the land you and Alin and Elo know best." She grasped the fingers that still held her arm, taking them between both her hands. "Val, every minute we spend here gives her another minute to get here—for all I know, she already is. We have to get to Roseguard with these Mages."

"And you want to go by way of The Waste—to pick up Cailet."

"Yes!" She felt her eyes sting suddenly, infuriatingly.

"But she's in no danger at Ostinhold."

"We have to take her under the protection of the Mage Guardians."

"Gut-jumping."

"If you like. And even if you *don't* like. Just don't get in my way."

They returned to Alin and Elomar, who had been making plans.

"It's daylight, so we can't climb out of the Ladder right in the middle of Naplian Street," Alin said. "But I know of a maintenance tunnel in an alley."

Elomar added, "I'll send the image to the Mage Globes. The rest should join us within an hour."

"Excellent. We'll go to Combel at once to secure it, then send Alin back to bring the others through."

Val nodded unhappily, not liking this at all. But he didn't get in her way.

She nudged him with a shoulder. "You really do have the worst manners of any man I've ever met—except one. But the rotten truth is that when you yell at me, it helps me think!"

18

That evening, Collan traveled by Ladder for the first time in his life.

It was a real shame that he was unconscious when it happened.

Lady Agatine's eyes were suspiciously bright as she lit the evening candle at her dinner table—perhaps for the last time. Orlin Renne's timely fit of coughing distracted their sons from their mother's distress. By the time slaps on the back and a glass of water had been applied, Agatine was calm again.

Gorynel Desse did not share the meal. Officially, he didn't even exist. But later, while Col tuned his lute as usual, the old Mage slipped into the room and sat down to listen. No one did more than glance at him.

Shortly after Thirteenth, more guests arrived. Sela Trayos, Verald Jescarin, and their little girl came in and took seats on a blue velvet couch. Tamsa waved at Col; he winked at her, and she giggled.

Domna Sela was no longer just very pregnant. She was hugely pregnant, ready to deliver at any moment. Col despaired of making any kind of speed from Roseguard with a woman so close to term, but no one seemed worried. And why should *he* be, anyhow? It wasn't his problem.

Two songs later two more people came in: Tarise Nalle and her husband, Rillan Veliaz. Col's glum thoughts infected the folk tune he played; here were gathered the foremost members of the Rising in all Sheve—plus its worldwide Mageborn mastermind. Though Collan wasn't exactly an innocent bystander after all the favors of the last few years, this company could get him not just arrested but executed.

He sang on, wondering if he was easing adult nerves or distracting the children. At just past Fourteenth, Gorynel Desse got to his feet.

"I thank you for a lovely evening, Agatine, my dear. It will not be the last we spend like this in Roseguard, I promise you."

"I'm relieved to hear you say it, Gorsha," she replied softly.

So it was time to go. From various cabinets the four Slegin sons produced stuffed journeypacks, including Collan's own. There was one for each person present, even a little one for Sela's daughter—excepting Sela herself, who already had enough to carry. Col cased his lute, pocketed his picks, shouldered his pack, and put on the cloak and coif Jeymi produced from a cupboard. Desse led them all into a between-walls passage barely one person wide.

They emerged through a stone door into a small room overlooking the harbor. Jeymi whispered in awe that he never knew the Have-A-Word Room had a Ladder.

"A Ladder—?"

It was all Collan had time for. Verald Jescarin, standing just behind him, said, "Sorry, friend," and hit him gently but efficiently on the head.

19

Luck favored them—or perhaps St. Maidil: the Plum Room was unoccupied. Its closet Ladder being as cramped as the sewer Ladder in Neele, Alin brought the eleven Mages through in two groups. Val made both journeys with him, flatly refusing to leave his side.

Nobody could decide which Saint to blame for making each trip singularly memorable—perhaps Viranka, patron of wells, though she had never been said to have so perverse a sense of humor. Maybe it was just bad timing. For it was morning in Neele, and residents of Naplian Street did what everybody did first thing out of bed. Mercifully, some early risers were also just finishing their baths, so it wasn't as bad as it could have been—or so Sarra told herself. But she and everyone else arrived in Combel splattered, sopped, and stinking six ways to the Wraithenwood.

"*Damn,*" said Keler Neffe. "This was my last clean shirt!"

"At least you're wearing a coif," Sarra reminded him, and once again resisted the urge to run fingers through her soggy hair.

Elomar had uprooted a huge plant—with purple flowers, of course—from its tub for use as a washbasin, filling it with water from the nearby bathroom. He thought it unwise, and Sarra agreed with him, to send the Mages trooping down the corridor. So in the silent expanse of purple and mirrors, they took turns cleaning up as best they could while waiting for Alin and Val to return with the other Mages.

"We *had* to come back here, I suppose," sighed Truan Halvos.

No one answered him. A few minutes later they heard more voices—Geris Mirre's, mainly, telling Deikan Penteon to get off his foot. As they emerged into the Plum Room, both choked in astonishment. Dalia Shelan, right behind them, clapped a hand over her mouth to muffle a fit of giggles. Ilisa Neffe, Tamosin Wolvar, and Tamos Wolvar had equally abrupt reactions.

"Holy St. Geridon," whispered Ilisa in genuine awe.

Her husband gestured to the gargantuan bed and asked, "Want one for our next house?"

His uncle snorted. "It's big enough to *be* your next house!"

In Combel, halfway around the world from Neele, it was Fourth. The Bower was asleep all around them. Sarra had listened carefully for sounds from other rooms and heard nothing. She dared to relax a little. All the Mages were assembled, they were safe and undiscovered, and they had three native Wasters to take them to Longriding.

A sudden chill draft, which she might not even have felt but for the dampness of her hair and clothes, warned her an instant before a voice spoke.

"Crawled out of a sewer, I see. How appropriate."

From a mauve shadow stepped a tall young woman. Glenin Feiran. Beside her was a smaller figure, arm grasped in Glenin's strong fingers. Sarra's heart lurched. Cloaked and hooded as the girl was, still Sarra recognized the cloak: Liwellan blue.

Glenin took another step into the room, tugging Mai Alvassy with her. Her gray-green eyes caught and held Sarra's. For all the attention she paid the others, they might not have existed.

"My little toy may have broken, but magic has other uses. When applied to an unWarded mind—say, Captain Nalle's?—much can be learned. Unfortunately for the captain, few survive such questioning."

Geris Mirre caught his breath. "You wouldn't *dare*—"

"And *you* are going to tell me no?" Glenin raised her free hand and pointed at him. His long body crumpled soundlessly to the violet carpet.

Ilisa Neffe knelt beside him. The stricken face she raised to Sarra was indication enough that the man was dead.

"Where was I?" Glenin asked. "Ah, yes. Did you know this girl is my cousin? But her resemblance to *you* is truly remarkable, Lady Sarra. You've been very clever." Her gaze flickered to Deikan Penteon. "Must I make an example of you as well? I dislike interruptions."

"Do nothing," Sarra commanded, finding her voice at last. "She's Warded. No one would confront so many Mage Guardians without powerful protective magic."

Glenin nodded approvingly: a teacher pleased at a rather slow student who had finally worked out the answer.

Keler Neffe spoke coldly. "Only a Lady of Malerris would know such spells."

A corner of Glenin's mouth twitched downward. Sarra noted it, and put aside curiosity about its meaning and potential use. She had more urgent concerns.

Specifically, the remaining Mages—and Valirion and Alin, who were still within the Ladder closet. She begged all the Saints to make them stay there.

Quietly, Sarra went on, "There's no one to respond if we call for help. She's cleared every room in the building."

"An excellent guess. You impress me, Lady Sarra."

"It was no guess. It's what I would have done."

"*If* you had any magic."

Never in her whole life had Sarra so bitterly regretted it. "If I had your ethics—or lack of them."

"Now, let's not make this any more unpleasant than it needs to be."

"I assume there's a Ward from roof to cellar, too."

"Of course."

"But no Council Guards."

"Not one. Right every time! Do you pretend to understand me, then?"

"Your reasons—no. Your methods. . . ." She let herself

smile slightly. "Let us say that I know you better than you might think."

Elomar Adennos glided quietly to Sarra's side, his presence a silent warning to drop this line of conversation at once. He asked Glenin, "Have you a purpose beyond an attempt at entertainment? I find myself singularly bored."

Glenin deigned to notice him. "Lusira Garvedian's lanky charmer, aren't you? Her family has appalling taste in men. Yes, I have a purpose, one to capture your full attention. As that young man surmised—" She nodded to Keler Neffe. "—I represent the Lords of Malerris. Every one of you is an enemy of my Tradition—and within a day or two, of all Lenfell, by Council Decree. You will be taken to Seinshir, where those still capable of bearing or fathering Mageborns will live. The rest of you will die." She smiled at Sarra. "Is *that* what you would have said?"

She didn't answer.

"Oh, of course. Ethics. Well, you and I can discuss it at Malerris Castle—which I understand you've already visited."

Someone behind her gasped. Sarra did not. So she'd been right. They'd been watching.

"I'm afraid you won't be going there just yet, however. You and I and my cousin here are going to Longriding."

"To trap Taig Ostin," Sarra said.

She had the satisfaction of seeing her sister blink in startlement. "You know, you're really very good," Glenin admitted.

"Thank you. But I'm not quite clever enough to know just how you got here."

"Captain Nalle's ship never left Renig."

Sarra saw Mai bend her bright head, and knew that Agata Nalle and every woman and man on board the *Rose Crown* was dead.

"The ship will dock today at Roseguard. Its new captain is a Lord of Malerris with a feel for the sea, and its crew is loyal to the First Councillor. They'll be part of the forces that deal with Lady Agatine and her hive of traitors—captured or killed, I've no real preference."

"Because none of them are Mageborn," Sarra said, sick with loathing and already knowing what Glenin would say. Instinct. Gut-jumping that twisted her guts into knots.

"And therefore of no value," Glenin replied.

"The Mage Captal," Elomar Adennos asked. "Lady, does he live?"

"A cousin of yours, as I recall? Yes, the doddering old fool is still breathing. He's waiting in my carriage downstairs, in fact."

"To lure Taig Ostin," Sarra added. Glenin had just made a severe tactical error. In danger, the overriding duty of any Mage Guardian was to ensure the Captal's survival. Whatever happened to any or all other Mages, the Captal *must* survive. Those in this room now knew of his captivity, and would do everything in their power to free him.

Glenin Feiran was equally determined to keep him. Sarra did not intend these Mageborns—including a fifteen-year-old boy—to die for Lusath Adennos.

She could win this. Instinct sang in her, this verbal sparring with Glenin as intoxicating as the game she'd played with Anniyas. At Ryka Court, it had been for amusement, for the stimulation of flexing her wits; here, it was for lives. Yet it remained a game—one Sarra could win.

Glenin did not yet know about Val and Alin.

She didn't know about Sarra herself.

Or Cailet—

Something was glinting at the edges of Sarra's mind, something of power she could sense but not share. Warded as she was, still she knew it for Mage Guardian magic—just as she knew what emanated from Glenin was not. Elomar had spoken of a "taste" to magic. Now she knew what he meant.

What Sarra sensed from Glenin was *Malerris*—but it was also *Ambrai,* and it was *Feiran.*

"Once you capture Taig in Longriding," she said to Glenin, "You'll Ward him and send him back to the Rising, to betray it from within."

"You really *do* have a flair for this! Yours is a thread I'll regret seeing cut and pulled from the Great Loom."

"But you'll never allow that," Sarra murmured.

"Not until you've had several children, no."

"You will *never* allow it, Glenin." She felt Elomar's fingers touch her spine, another silent caution. But she knew what she was doing, she knew that she need only gain time and Glenin's absolute shocked attention, and the *something* that shone just out of reach would happen.

"It's not my decision to make. I'm not the Warden of the Loom, or—"

"Never," Sarra said one last time, and drew breath to tell her why.

She never spoke the words. Tamos Wolvar, master of Mage Globes, had finished his work: a great shimmering sphere of magic that encased Glenin and Mai in swirls of white and rainbows. The Mage Globe shone opaline and spat sparks of fire, and within it Glenin staggered.

Sirralin Mossen acted first. She grabbed her son with one hand and Keler Neffe with the other, and ran for the Ladder. Truan Halvos had to be shoved along by Dalia Shelan and Deikan Penteon together. Ilisa Neffe stumbled after them, pushed by her husband—who was supporting his uncle the Scholar Mage physically as he swayed with effort. Within the sphere, Glenin had begun to fight back.

"Sarra! Hurry!" Elomar Adennos dragged her back as the huge Globe sparked and crackled with flashes of barely controlled magic. Mai Alvassy collapsed, arms wrapped around her head and face buried against her knees. She rocked back and forth; somehow, Sarra knew she was screaming.

"Tell Alin to get them out of here! Back to Neele, it doesn't matter—"

"He already is," Elo said. "I'll get the Captal."

Tamos Wolvar's magic-filled sphere was shot with lightning tinted blue and green and red. His eyes were squeezed shut and he sagged against his nephew, but despite Glenin's attacks the Globe held firm. She had conjured a hand-sized Globe of her own, and from this the lightning spurted.

Sarra stood helpless, waiting for a chance she didn't know whether or not she'd have. Mai raised her tormented face and her mouth formed the words *Leave me!* But Sarra shook her head vehemently.

Wolvar suddenly groaned, and within the Globe harsh lightning flashed. Glenin's face was rigid with strain, her eyes fierce with triumph. The Scholar Mage was weakening. Soon her prison would shatter.

Glenin's small Globe shattered first. Mai Alvassy, surging up from her knees, reached for the sphere of concentrated magic. She wrapped her fingers around it, and her lips parted in a shriek Sarra felt rather than heard. Glenin fought her, kicking with polished riding boots. Mai held on, wrenching the Globe from Glenin—and as it left its maker's hands, it exploded.

Glenin fell. Tamos Wolvar's Globe splintered—and with it,

every mirror in the place. Glass spewed off the walls, spattered onto the absurd purple bed. Windows blasted outward, dragging lace curtains with them. Sarra threw her arms up to cover her face too late; tiny shards pricked her cheeks.

She only realized she'd closed her eyes when she heard Tamosin Wolvar's shaky voice. "It didn't kill her, Lady Sarra. The magic in her Globe was hers, and Uncle Tamos would never use lethal magic even against a Malerrisi."

Sarra looked at him, not quite comprehending. He cradled the old man in his arms, and as he walked toward her she heard glass fragments ring down to the littered carpet and crunch beneath his boots.

"I can still feel her Wards," the young man added, "even though she's got to be unconscious." So was Scholar Wolvar, limp in his nephew's strong arms.

"Is—is he all right? Will he be?"

"Yes. He's no longer young, but he's the best." He cast a glance of loathing at Glenin's sprawled body. "Even against such as she. Miryenne be merciful, our old enemy has returned."

"Her Wards still function?" Sarra had never heard of such a thing. A Mageborn must be awake and aware to maintain Wards, mustn't she?

Tamosin nodded confirmation.

"Then—she can't be killed," Sarra heard herself say.

"No. We must hurry, before the Malerrisi recovers."

The Malerrisi. That was what her sister was now. And in that moment Sarra no longer had two sisters. She had only one.

At Ostinhold. Please, let her be at Ostinhold, and not in Longriding where Glenin knows Taig will be!

"Get to the Ladder," she said. "I'll bring Mai."

"Lady," Tamosin murmured, "she is dead."

"No—!" But when Sarra turned for her, she saw the blood seeping from Mai's delicate nose and parted lips. She was dead, sacrificing herself to free them—killed by Glenin's magic.

"Sarra!"

Familiar hands on her shoulders turned her from the sight of her cousin's death. She looked up into another cousin's living face.

"Sarra, listen to me." Val shook her slightly. "Listen! Alin took the others back to Neele. They'll find safety as they

can. Elo's taking care of the Captal. We have to get out of
here. *Now,* Sarra!"

"Mai's dead," she whispered.

"I know. I'm sorry."

"Glenin—" Sarra choked on the name.

"We can't kill her, and we can't take her captive. None of
our Mages is powerful enough against her—maybe not even
Gorsha. We've got to hurry, Sarra. Help us."

That was what a leader did. Helped people do what they
had to—and kept them safe while they did it. Tarise had
been wrong: Sarra would not be a Warrior in the Rising,
making battle with words or swords. Nor a Healer to make
things right, or a Scholar to make wise counsel. She would
be what she had designed for herself to be in that chart
drawn up years ago in Pinderon. She would be the one who
made things *happen.*

Just like Glenin.

The Malerrisi.

Sarra had Mage Guardians behind her, and the Rising;
Glenin had Lords of Malerris and the Council. *An even
match—but for two things. I know who I am—and I know
about Cailet.*

"Sarra—"

"All right. I'm all right." She pulled away from Val and
glanced around—everywhere but at her sister. Tamosin
Wolvar had taken his uncle downstairs. Sarra went to the
landing and called down, "Elo! We need horses! Six, and
right now!" She remembered something. "No, wait—Glenin
said she came in a carriage, didn't she? We'll use it instead.
Scholar Wolvar can't sit a saddle anyway."

"Alin's already up in the coachman's seat!" Elomar
shouted back.

Alin had come back from Neele? Of course he'd come
back from Neele. Neele was not where Valirion was.

Val was ripping bedsheets to tie Glenin's wrists, ankles,
and mouth. What good he thought it would do, she had no
idea. Perhaps he merely needed to do it. "Sarra, get downstairs before she wakes up!"

*She. The Malerrisi. Would I kill her if I could? Would
Auvry Feiran have killed Mother and me? "If I had your
ethics—"*

She went to Mai's body.

Behind her, Valirion exclaimed, "What are you doing?"

"Help me. We have to leave her and Geris Mirre where they'll be found."

"For a decent burning?" He yanked the last knot tight and stood up from the bed. "Sarra, we don't have time!"

"For that, we do—and to make her look more like me in death than she did in life!" She unfastened Mai's small gold hoop earrings and substituted her own pearls, took the long gold chain with its identity disk from Mai's throat and replaced it with her own.

"But—Glenin will know!" Still, he took Geris' disk and pocketed it for his family, and undid the single Herb Sprig sigil pin of a Prentice Healer from the dead Mage's shirt.

"Yes. Glenin will know." *What else of mine should Mai be wearing?* Her ring, with the Liwellan Hawk—loose on Mai's finger. The gold ring carved with the Castle Spire sigil of the Alvassys didn't fit Sarra. She put it in her pocket with the disk. She'd send both to Piergan Rille in Domburronshir—no, she would give them to Elin and Pier Alvassy, who were part of the Rising.

"Glenin will know," Sarra repeated absently. "But that's why we have to leave Mai where she'll be found by others. The bower mistress, the Watch, neighbors—" But not the Council Guard, who would never return the body to Roseguard for proper rites. Roseguard—Glenin had said that Lady Agatine's own flagship was there even now, stuffed with the enemy—

"Sarra . . . anyone who knows you will know the difference."

"What?"

"You're very alike, but not identical."

"I don't underst—" But then she saw in his eyes what he meant to do, and cried out.

"Go downstairs, Sarra."

"No! You can't, I won't let you—"

"Sarra, *now!*"

And because she knew he was right, and hated him for it, she took one last look at the bodies on the floor: the Prentice Mage, dead too young; the Malerrisi who had been Sarra's sister; the blonde girl with Sarra's face.

Who soon would have no face.

From now on Glenin is dead to me. There's only Cailet left. Only Cailet. . . .

Flight

1

The only evidence of Glenin's fury of frustration was a frown. The escape of Sarra Liwellan and the Captal, and by extension Taig Ostin—and by further extension Gorynel Desse and the whole Rising—was enough to make better women than she scream and curse and rave. Glenin did not, even in the privacy of her own mind, as she picked at knotted purple silk. In the first place, there *was* no better woman than she. In the second, she considered screaming a waste of breath, vulgar language indicative of a poor vocabulary, and raging a shameful demonstration of faulty self-control.

And in the third place, even if she had been so inclined, there was no one to hear her.

This changed abruptly. Shouts were followed up the stairs by running footsteps. Still negotiating the last knot, Glenin wrapped herself in a spell of Invisibility just as a red-haired young man burst into the room. He stopped short and blanched, freckles standing out on his nose. A moment later he staggered forward nearly onto the Mage Guardian's corpse as a woman wearing an amazement of black and white pushed in behind him and began to scream.

Discovery of the bodies was closely followed by discovery of one identity disk. Huddled on the bed, hoping that in the welter of sheets and blankets no one would notice the telltale depression her body made in the mattress, Glenin

gritted her teeth with the strain of repressing her rage. To
reveal the truth—that Mai Alvassy lay there, not Sarra
Liwellan—would mean revealing herself. This she could not
do. But neither could she leave. Not until the bodies had
been removed and she was alone in this putrid chamber, and
could escape.

And not until she worked loose the purple silk still binding her wrists.

The redheaded bower lad urged the woman out onto the
landing while others crowded in to begin cleaning up the
mess. One young man took a long look at the bloody ruin on
the floor, lurched to the marble table, and was thoroughly
sick into the violet pottery basin.

Glenin could scarcely blame him. She had seen people
die, and die horribly—a few by her own magic. But this was
beyond horror. She understood why it had been done. But
though she believed in no Saint but Chevasto, she directed
a prayer to St. Venkelos now: that the Judge would mete out
the punishment the defiler of an Ambrai's corpse deserved.
Never mind that Mai had not been so Named; in her had
flowed the Ambrai Blood.

And Desse Blood, she reminded herself. Mai's loyalties
had condemned her. It was neither Glenin's responsibility
nor Glenin's fault that she had died.

Amid much wailing and terrified babbling, they carried
out first the Mage's corpse and then the girl's small body,
both wrapped in purple curtains. Glenin finally got the last
bit of torn silk unwrapped from her wrists, rubbing her
chafed skin, and shrugged away all thoughts of her cousin.
It was Sarra Liwellan who demanded attention now. Glenin
had underestimated her, believing the dimples and the innocent simper. It was a mistake not to be repeated.

But if Glenin had lost, Sarra Liwellan had not entirely
won, either. She would be hunted and she knew it. Where
would she go?

Most of the Mages had undoubtedly been taken back to
that sewer in Neele. The Council Guard—and in some cases
Lords of Malerris—stood ready at every access to every
Ladder on Lenfell. From dawn this morning until every
Mage Guardian was accounted for, the enemy would be
sought out where they lived and worked and especially
where they might attempt to escape justice. If Sarra Liwellan
had guessed so much about Glenin, then Glenin believed she

could intuit much about Sarra—certainly enough to know
that she would shun all Ladders as more dangerous than the
Wraithen Mountains.

For herself, Glenin instantly rejected the idea of returning
to Renig—or going to Malerris Castle or Ryka Court. She
had no intention of facing her father, any Lord of Malerris,
or Anniyas without some sort of victory in her palms. What
could she salvage from this debacle? Where could she go to
lay hands on Sarra Liwellan or Taig Ostin or Gorynel Desse?

Anniyas would never have said *or;* Anniyas would have
said *and.* Anniyas and her wild, unpredictable, damnable
luck.

Glenin was not less than Anniyas. She was more. Here
was her chance to prove it. The Liwellan girl had shown a
remarkable facility for guessing Glenin's plans. Now Glenin
would guess hers.

Striding to the window, careful to avoid the blood, Glenin
drew the lace curtains shut. Bending to reach beneath the table where she'd kicked it, after a moment's fumbling she retrieved a circle of white velvet three feet across. She spread
this carefully on the purple carpet, fingers light and soft on
its embroidery of gold bullion, freshly stitched over a pattern
ancient before The Waste War.

Swift she was, but not swift enough. The door squeaked
open. The redhead entered, his gaze on the stained carpet as
if his was the nauseating task of cleaning it up. Glenin could
almost follow the path of his thoughts as well as the path of
his eyes: from the discarded strips of sheeting to the velvet
circle to the lace curtains.

The man opened his mouth to shout a warning. She stood,
let the spell drop, conjured a Globe, and exploded it in his
face.

This time she did curse as his brains were added to the
bloody mess on the rug. The sphere had been half the size
this spell usually yielded. Efficient enough, but hardly instantaneous; worrisome in its feeble red-orange glow. Suddenly afraid, she stared down at the white circle. Would
enough power remain to work the Ladder?

More people were coming up the stairs. There was no
time. She stepped onto the velvet. The Blanking Ward coalesced into a perfect cylinder seven feet high; a murmured
word, and she and the velvet Ladder vanished.

2

Seven people—one of them unconscious—stuffed into a carriage meant to hold four would not make for one of Sarra's pleasanter memories. The pace at which the horses hauled the overburdened carriage made for torture.

After one particularly perilous corner tossed them all like marbles in a bottle, Ilisa Neffe picked herself off Captal Adennos and observed, "Val's driving has improved. Last year that turn would've tilted us clean over."

Alin righted himself and Sarra. "Drives within an inch, compared to then," he agreed. "And it's only his second time with a four-horse team."

"Second—?" Sarra echoed. "Why didn't you *say* something?"

"Because the rest of us never had a *first* time with a four-horse team."

Elomar had Tamos Wolvar braced in a corner of the carriage. When no more wild turns occurred for some minutes, he said, "Help me get him comfortable on the floor. There should be blankets under the seat."

Alin, Sarra, and Ilisa wedged themselves as small as possible while the others worked. Tamosin sat with his back to the door, long legs folded to one side, his uncle's head cradled on his knees. The Captal dragged out blankets. Elomar nodded thanks to his cousin, tucked warm wool around the Scholar, and then checked pulse, respiration, and his eyes' reaction to the light of an inch-round Mage Globe.

"What happened?" Ilisa asked.

Elomar hunched on the floor at Sarra's feet. "When the Malerrisi's Globe shattered, so did Wolvar's. Uncontained, her magic sought his."

"He knows how to defend himself," she retorted. "No one is more accomplished with Globes."

"Against a Malerrisi?"

Ilisa had to shake her head.

"I've done what I can. He needs sleep, quiet, and half the pharmacopoeia."

For the first time the Captal spoke. "He needs another Scholar with knowledge of Mage Globes. Tamosin, if I may trade places with you—?"

Sarra learned then a little of why it was imperative to preserve a Captal's life and freedom. Within five minutes Tamos Wolvar's breathing was even, his features had relaxed, and his heartbeat was steady. Elomar bowed silent homage to the Captal.

A short time later the carriage slowed, then stopped. Alin unlatched the window covering and slithered halfway out, sitting on the frame to consult with Val. Sarra heard something about "rest the horses" and "figure out where the hell we're going."

I'm working on it, she muttered silently. None of the Mages, including the Captal, had offered any suggestions. Getting them to safety was her responsibility. *"Safety?" That's a good one.*

Alin squirmed back into the seat. "Sarra—"

She was ready for him. "Where's the nearest Ostin property?"

"Here in Combel."

"Anybody home?"

"Probably my sister Geria." He made a face.

"We have to get rid of this carriage," Ilisa said.

"And find a place for Scholar Wolvar to recover," the Captal added.

"And warn Taig," Alin finished. "But he's in Longriding."

Sarra addressed herself first to Guardian Neffe. "The carriage is marked as Council property from Renig. That alone will get you through Geria Ostin's gates. Once you're in, how you identify yourselves is up to you. As is how you convince her of who you aren't. Send the carriage back to Renig. You, the Wolvars, and the Captal stay here as long as you judge it safe."

Ilisa nodded. "*Domni* Ostin, your sister's not Mageborn, is she?"

"St. Miryenne forfend!"

"Good." And she smiled a predatory little smile.

Sarra turned to Elomar. "Stay with them, or come with us? Your choice."

"The Captal knows more than I. Use me as you will, Sarra."

Use him—the way she was about to use Alin and Val to keep Taig safe. And find Cailet.

But first take care of this lot. She asked the younger Wolvar, "Can you drive this thing?"

"If Val Maurgen can do it, how hard can it be?"

Alin gave a snort of derision. "Don't let him hear you say that."

"Climb up on the box," Sarra said, "and have him teach you." As Tamosin wriggled out through the window, she finally looked again at Alin. "It's the four of us, then. We need horses to get to Longriding—fast ones, if we're to arrive before . . . the Malerrisi." She couldn't bring herself to pronounce her sister's name. "Along the way we'll have to find out what happened to make the Council outlaw all Mage Guardians."

"Mageborns," Elomar corrected. "She said 'Mageborns.' "

"Lords of Malerris, too? So it begins," Alin murmured.

" 'Begins'?" the Captal echoed, then shook his head. "No. Don't tell me. I don't want to know."

"A wise decision, Cousin," Elomar told him.

Sarra was so made that she could never wish not to know. But she might have made an exception in this case. With all remaining Mage Guardians imprisoned or dead and a few Malerrisi thrown in for appearances' sake, magic would "vanish" from Lenfell. Then the Wraithenbeasts would come. And the Malerrisi would demand—and receive—the whole world and the chains to bind it in return for penning the monsters up again.

She felt her ragged nails dig into her palms and reopen the cuts made by flying glass. "They've begun it," she said curtly. "But *we're* going to finish it. *Our* way."

3

The Golden Bean ("Combel's Finest Coffee Bar! The Last Word in Elegance!") offered a choice of twenty-six different brews ("Imported from the Best Brogdenguard Plantations!") accompanied by pitchers of cream ("Sweet! Fresh! Wholesome!") and little bowls of condiments ("Rock Sugar!

Cinnamon Sticks! Chocolate Drops! Raspberry Sugar! Crystallized Violets! Try All Eight!").

Sarra's notions of elegance did not include the dim and dismal low-ceilinged room she and Elomar now sat in. The black liquid presented to them could have doubled as paint remover. The mugs were dented, the cream curdled, the condiments ossified. Elomar chipped away at a pile of purple lumps that would not have been out of place in the Plum Room and eventually spooned a few into his mug. Sarra gulped her scalding coffee ("Almond Surprise!") black, and mercifully tasted not a drop of it.

Ilisa Neffe had easily gained entrance to the Ostin residence for herself, her husband, Tamos Wolvar, and the Captal—by what spells cast on whom, Sarra neither knew nor cared. She had watched it happen from the shelter of a nearby corner, and felt only relief that here were four fewer people to worry about.

Alin and Val were off somewhere acquiring horses—how and from whom she similarly neither knew nor cared. She had more important worries, and they were written out before her on the broadsheet that covered what little of the table the mugs and bowls did not. Combel might be in the middle of nowhere as far as the rest of Lenfell knew or cared, but news came to Combel just the same.

The headlines of the Feleson Press broadsheet might have been written by the same superior mind that had composed the coffee bar's menu.

KILLINGS IN KENROKESHIR!
MURDEROUS MAGIC RUNS WILD!
COUNCIL DECREE: MAGEBORNS OUTLAWED!
ANNIYAS OUTRAGED!
EYEWITNESS ACCOUNT OF FATAL DAY!

Sarra read it over and over again, huddled around two separate agonies: one of knowledge, the other of ignorance.

Knowledge was bad enough. Expert at gleaning kernels of truth amid sensationalist broadsheet chaff, Sarra knew what had occurred in Kenrokeshir.

During First Moon, in a minor town called Jenaton, a Warrior Mage Guardian—unsuspected as such by her neighbors—issued public challenge to a Lord of Malerris hitherto just as anonymous. Right there in the middle of Market Circle, before a hundred horror-stricken bystanders, they fought it out with Battle Globes. A spire toppled from St. Telomir's Shrine, killing the votary; several horses dropped dead in their tracks and several more ran wild, trampling to death five persons; fires broke out in shops and stalls, killing many more. These scenes were illustrated with woodcuts on the inside page. Sarra had no reason to doubt any of it.

What she did question was the manner in which the Malerrisi was reported to have died. Feleson Press said that the Warrior Mage's final blast incinerated him from the inside out—and a score of petrified onlookers as well.

When the magic faded, the crowd bludgeoned the Mage to death.

Sarra accepted that as truth, too.

In the twenty-six days since, rumor had spread throughout Lenfell. The broadsheet was the first official version of the facts and also printed the authorized announcement of a Council Decree: Mageborns must be taken into custody. All Lenfell was exhorted to vigilance. The Council was doing everything in its power to assure the security of honest citizens. In all Shirs Council Guards were arresting Mageborns for swift arraignment by the Justiciary. Additionally, a large force had been dispatched to Roseguard, a city sympathetic to Mage Guardians.

Sarra—and the rest of Lenfell—also knew that Marra Feleson's editorial was direct from Anniyas herself. Mageborns were dangerous. Destroying the Academy and all Ambrai had not been enough. Putting Malerris Castle to the torch and killing its inhabitants had not been enough. All remaining Mageborns must be found and imprisoned. Only then would Lenfell be safe from magic.

Knowledge was bad enough. Ignorance was worse.

Who was the Warrior Mage? The Lord of Malerris? Why had they broken cover? What had prompted the Mage to attack? Insanity was too obvious an answer. What threat or perceived threat had made her do such a thing? Well, no; that was the wrong question. Sarra knew in her guts that this oh-so-opportune event had been planned by the Lords of Malerris, but how they had managed it was beyond her comprehension.

Not that her personal understanding mattered. The Malerrisi had died—almost certainly sacrificing himself and making sure he took as many people as possible with him.

Sarra understood that much. It provided final proof of magic's evils. It was Anniyas' excuse for open persecution of Mageborns.

And the Rising. All those sly hints in her little song, all those Names connected to the Rising . . .

. . . and Roseguard.

This was the crux of Sarra's ignorance, where knowledge of Anniyas' assault on Roseguard intersected with knowledge of Agatine's involvement in the Rising. At the point where these met inside her was a vast emptiness that she must struggle not to fill with images of Ambrai. She had lost one family, one home. She begged every Saint in the Calendar—excepting Chevasto the Weaver—to protect her second family and her second home, perhaps more beloved than the first for being hers so much longer.

St. Chevasto, she cursed.

"They will flee to Ladders," Elomar Adennos murmured suddenly, and Sarra flinched. "And be slaughtered. The Malerrisi know Ladders, too."

More knowledge, bringing with it its burden of ignorance: which Ladders, if any, were still safe to use? How many Mages would die? The print blurred. She told herself it was steam from her coffee.

A strong brown hand descended to the broadsheet, splayed fingers abruptly clawing the paper into a ragged crumple.

"We can still help Taig and Cailet," Valirion said quietly. "Don't torment yourself, Sarra."

"The horses?" Elomar asked.

"Outside."

The Healer Mage clinked a few coins onto the table. "Come, Sarra."

She went with them. Numb. Helpless. Taig, Cailet—how remote they seemed, how unclear their faces compared to the immediate images of Agatine and Orlin and her brothers. . . .

Cailet is my sister in Blood, but we've spent our lives apart. She's not quite real to me yet. She's an idea, not a person.

And I'm not even that much to her. . . .

Outside in the street, Alin usurped Val's usual role of determined cheerfulness. "Didn't even have to steal 'em," he said as he boosted Sarra into a saddle. "I just walked in to a livery owned by a Senison cousin of mine and asked for four of the Ostin horses."

"Scraller and the Council be damned," Val said as they turned up Shainkroth Road that led west to Longriding. "Lilen Ostin is the *real* power in Combel."

"And everywhere else in The Big Empty," Alin added proudly.

Thus it was in Sheve with Lady Agatine Slegin. Or—had been. Where were they? And all the Mages—and Imi Gorrst and Advar Senison and the books, and Lusira Garvedian and Telomir Renne and—

"Sarra, stop it," Val ordered.

She turned her head dully. "I can't."

"Are we dead yet, or in chains?"

As he quoted her own words back at her, she felt a small flaring of temper. But not enough. She needed more to make her angry enough to stop thinking about what she couldn't do and start thinking about what she must do.

Knowing her by now, he obliged. "Did I mention that I think going to Longriding is a real shit of an idea? What were you planning to do—give a welcoming party for Glenin Feiran?"

"She knows that you know Taig's there," Alin put in.

Elomar's turn: "You inferred her moves—why should she not infer yours?"

"Shut up, all of you," she snapped. "I know damned well what she'll do."

Her magic, victimized by fear and helplessness, sparked along with anger. *Splendid,* she thought sourly. *The only time I'm usefully Mageborn is when I'm furious. What a comfort.*

"Really?" Val pretended polite astonishment. "Might one inquire . . . ?"

Taking advantage of the opportunity to repay him for all those convoluted answers to *What time is it?,* she said with vicious sweetness, "I know what she knows and she knows that I know it. Either of us, or both of us, or neither of us will go to Longriding. If neither go, Taig is unwarned and uncaptured. If I go, he's warned; if she goes, he's captured. She can't afford to let me warn him. I can't afford to let her capture him. Therefore, both of us will go to Longriding."

Alin was the first to react. "I'd applaud, but you'd probably hit me."

"I'd applaud, too," Val retorted, "If I knew what the hell she just said."

"Perfectly simple," Elomar told him.

"Then explain it to him," Sarra said, and kicked her horse into a gallop.

4

"No," said the Fifth Lord of Malerris, flatly and absolutely. "Not into the middle of an acid storm."

Glenin, furious enough at being forced to consult Vassa Doriaz, finally lost her temper. "How dare you dictate to me what I can and cannot do? Show me the safe house in Longriding and get out of my way!"

"You misunderstand, Lady Glenin," said a musical voice behind them, and Glenin whirled. No one at Malerris Castle ever called her *Lady*. She wondered if Saris Allard used the title now to mock her or cozen her.

Moving gracefully into the room, Saris placed a wine tray on a low table and spared a single glance for her husband. "Acid storms are still fraught with Wild Magic, even after all these centuries. It would be dangerous for you to use any Ladder, and especially the velvet one."

The *Code of Malerris* had made no mention of this; neither had any of her various teachers. Glenin frowned.

"Malerrisi avoid The Waste as a matter of course," Saris went on. "We so rarely go there that few ever bother to mention the problem. And it is a potentially deadly omission. I wish, Vassa, that you would occasionally recall who Lady Glenin is, and how valuable."

"After Anniyas," he appended, smooth as fresh butter.

"*Before* Anniyas," she corrected sharply, hazel eyes narrowing in her darkly lovely face. "She has freedom of movement, stronger magic—"

"—and rotten luck," Doriaz interrupted, getting to his feet. "Please excuse me, *Domna*. My son and I usually spend this hour together. Good evening."

When he had gone, Saris calmly picked up an embroidered pillow and flung it at the closed door with a force that made her multitude of black braids quiver.

"Sometimes," she said with perfect aplomb as Glenin stared, "one wishes for a knife. I apologize for my husband's manners. In recent days he has killed many Mage Guardians, an activity he has always enjoyed—as you may know. It makes him arrogant."

"*His* son," Glenin said by way of agreement.

Saris nodded and began pouring wine. "Chava turns fourteen this spring. Soon his magic will make itself known. Between you and me, Vassa is both proud and frightened of the boy."

"Chava's magic is stronger than his?"

"I believe it will prove so." Her smile told Glenin that Vassa was right to worry. Glenin smiled back. "As you are stronger than Anniyas. You didn't know that, did you?"

"She so rarely uses it." Glenin shrugged and accepted a winecup. "I suppose 'luck' suffices."

"In some things. Not all." Seating herself in the chair her husband had vacated, Saris continued, "What she calls luck is but an ability to take advantage of opportunities gained her by the hard work of others."

"I think you're right." And she wouldn't have said so if they hadn't been in the Iron Tower, safe from prying spells. "For me, however, hard work alone must provide. Lady Saris, I must get to Longriding. The acid storm will slow down the Liwellan girl, too, but I must be there before her."

"I had thought it was Taig Ostin you were after."

"I want *all* of them," Glenin stated.

The Lady of Malerris sipped delicately at her wine. "Will Sarra Liwellan not expect you in Longriding, and plan accordingly?"

"Certainly. She has no choice but to go there. If I were in her place—" Glenin stopped. Would—*could*—either of them outsmart the other? Or would each merely chase her own tail trying to be the more clever?

"In her place," Saris Allard remarked gently, "I would expect you at any instant and go half-mad with looking over my shoulder. Lady Glenin, do you really need to go to Longriding?"

"What do you mean? Of course I—"

"You've met her, so you would know better than I, but . . . it seems to me that nervousness alone may cause her to make a mistake. Overcaution is as foolish as recklessness. But even if she makes no mistakes, she can't stay where she knows *you* know her to be."

Glenin nodded slowly. "Longriding is obvious. *Too* obvious, truly told. The real trick is to figure out where she'll go next."

"Is that not the place you ought to be waiting for her?"

"But where will she go?" Glenin tapped the rim of her winecup. "No, I think the question is whether it will be a place of her choosing. There will be Mages with her, after all."

"Of course. I'd forgotten that. Probably even Gorynel Desse—" She broke off with a comical shudder. "I don't envy you this one, Lady Glenin! Thinking like another woman is one thing—but like a *man?* Who knows how their minds work?"

"At times," Glenin confided wryly, "I doubt that they *have* minds. Usually after an evening with my husband."

"In a contest, mine would win. One day you and I must sit down and decide what we did to deserve them. But before then, you have the appalling task of thinking as Gorynel Desse would."

Glenin rolled a tongueful of wine against her palate, savoring the taste as her father had taught her, then swallowed. The Mages needed a hiding place remote enough to be secure—but such a place would be too remote for easy supply and communication. Unless there was a Ladder. But she'd never heard any rumors that they'd planned for this eventuality. The Mage Guardians didn't have a Malerris Castle—remote, secure, and replete with Ladders.

"Mage Guardians don't plan," Glenin mused. "They react. It's a most untidy way to live."

"I must say that imagination fails me," Saris admitted. "Where could any Mage Guardian go now to find real safety?"

A Malerris Castle. . . .

"As for Desse," she went on, "no one knows him better than your father."

Malerris Castle. To all outward appearances, a place dead and abandoned long ago. . . .

"Lady Glenin, I believe you ought to return to Ryka Court and consult your father about Gorynel Desse."

"Lady Saris, I believe you're absolutely right."

5

It wasn't until Verald Jescarin was dead that Collan realized he'd lost a friend.

He knew hundreds of people. He called none "friend." When Verald fell to a knife out of nowhere in the dark, Collan felt a hole open up inside him.

He filled it with other deaths.

It happened so fast. One minute the pair stood guard outside a farmhouse. Collan was rubbing his nape, saying, "You *had* to hit me that hard, I suppose?"

Verald chuckled. "Your skull's rumored to be thick."

The next minute a knife thudded into his chest. He gave a soft, startled grunt, toppling sideways into the woodpile, dead before he hit the ground.

Black-cloaked shapes surged forward from the snowy forest. Collan began to kill.

Orlin Renne and his two elder sons and Rillan Veliaz burst from the farmhouse. They killed, too, swords ringing like chimes.

Col resented every death he didn't claim himself on Verald's behalf. He could not have said how many Council Guards it would take to assuage his need. More than were available to him, certainly. The sudden lack of swords lifting to meet his own was a bitter disappointment.

Into the abrupt silence spilled an impossibly roseate light. Col turned and saw Gorynel Desse appear from the trees, seemingly carrying a large ruddy-gold sphere that cast a sunrise glint across glistening snow.

"Orlin?" he called out.

"Here. And Riddon and Maugir—both wounded." Renne joined Collan, his sons in tow. "Rillan's checking the perimeter."

"Verald?"

"Dead," Col replied, wiping his sword on a Guard's cloak and kicking the corpse for the pleasure of it. Wishing it was Gorynel Desse lying there. "Where the hell were you?"

"Not where I should have been, obviously." He didn't look just old, he looked ancient.

The answer absolutely infuriated Collan. "What about your famous Wards? All that Warrior Mage magic you're supposed to have? Why didn't you protect—"

"Enough," Orlin Renne commanded. "Riddon, Maugir, come inside. You need bandaging."

"I'm all right," Maugir protested, but his wince as he limped through the door said otherwise.

Desse and his Mage Globe drifted into the winter night, touring the battle scene like any general who'd sat high on a hill out of the fray.

It had happened so fast. It hadn't lasted long enough. Collan started piling corpses to either side of the front walk. Rillan Veliaz showed up, dragging another. It was grim work by the silver of the Ladymoon and the feeble wash of starlight. Eventually Desse returned and surveyed the stacked bodies—and the single figure off to the side, wrapped in a dark blue cloak.

"I set Wards," Desse said to Collan. "That's why we were found. They had a Mageborn with them, a Lord of Malerris."

Col backed up an involuntary step.

"He's dead. The only magic now in the air is mine."

"And a big help it was too," Collan replied bitterly.

Veliaz cleared his throat. "We'll have to burn them, Guardian Desse. Inside, with the Ladder."

"Yes," said the Mage.

"No," said Col. "The others if you want—but not Verald. Not with them. He stays outside."

Fierce green eyes, oddly reddened by the Mage Globe, searched Col's face for a moment. Then he nodded. "Yes. I understand." He glanced around. "I assume you're responsible for much of this litter?"

Col shrugged, wishing he could claim all the dead as his own work. "Only nine or ten."

"Respectable," Desse murmured absently. "Not unworthy. . . ."

"Of *what?*"

He was ignored. "Twenty-five Guard dead?"

"Yes," Veliaz said. "I counted."

"Then the whole squadron is accounted for. When they

don't return, someone will investigate. We must leave soon. It's half a day to Ryka Court if I Fold the land."

"*Ryka—!*" Collan exploded. "I'm not going anywhere *near* Ryka Court!"

"You'll go where I tell you, boy," Desse snapped. "Or do you forget that my magic will *always* be swifter than your feet—or your sword? Geridon's Stones, you're even more stubborn than your—"

"Gorsha!"

Agatine's urgent cry sent all three men running into the farmhouse. Sela Trayos lay on a cot near the hearth, gasping, both hands pressed to her belly. Agatine and Tarise hovered beside her.

"Her water hasn't broken," Tarise said, "but if the pains continue and she goes into labor—"

"I'm surprised it didn't happen before now," Agatine said angrily. "Taking a pregnant woman through a Ladder!"

"Couldn't be helped," Orlin reminded her, busily tying torn cloth around Maugir's leg.

She flung a scowl up at him. "With two more Ladders to go, her baby may be in real danger."

"Only if she's Mageborn," Riddon said. He was pale, his arm tightly bound, but he didn't seem to be in pain. "There's no magic in the Trayos or Jescarin lines that I've ever heard of."

"Yes, you're right," said his mother; "Of course," said his father. They did not look at each other or at Gorynel Desse. Collan got the shivers from that determined absence of eye contact. Sela's baby *would* have magic—although how any of them knew it was beyond him. He wondered if Sela knew it. And what the danger was in taking an unborn Mageborn through a Ladder.

The old man stood beside the young woman, taking her face between his hands. Orlin drew Col away with a touch on his arm.

"Let him do what he can for her. We ought to do what we can for Verald."

The loss opened in him again. Nine or ten deaths, nine or ten thousand—nothing would ever make up for the loss of this one life. This *friend*.

It wasn't as if they'd known each other long or had much in common, a part of him argued.

Instinct said otherwise. There were people one simply *knew* on sight. Strangers one instantly recognized as friends.

He followed Orlin back outside. While Renne and Veliaz built a pyre of rocks taken from the path border, Col took the identity disk from Verald's neck and the small gold-and-amethyst pendant from his right earlobe. There was a wristlet as well, made of gold links set at intervals with chips of dark green jade carved into flowers. When he tried to give the items to Renne, the man shook his head.

"You take them," he said. "You were friends."

"I hardly knew him," Col replied gruffly. But he didn't refuse the jewelry. He'd give it to Sela—but not now. In a week perhaps, once the new baby was born and the shock of her husband's death had worn off. If it ever did.

Elom and Jeymi came out to help gather more rocks. Veliaz placed them as they were brought to him, constructing a flat stone mound as long and wide as a man. Jeymi then asked if he ought to bring wood from the pile.

His father replied, "No, Gorsha will see to the fire."

And so it was, once Sela's pains eased, slowed, then finally stopped. She and Tamsa slept while Verald's body was set alight by Magefire. No words were spoken, no dirge was sung; no one had the voice for it, especially not the Minstrel who'd been his friend. The only tribute paid the Master of Roseguard Grounds was the handful of flowers Collan threw into the fire. Another bouquet. It made him sick.

The body was scarcely burning when Desse faced them all across the fire. "We must go to the one place they will not seek us. Ryka Court."

Col waited for someone to protest. No one did. He couldn't believe it; they all trusted this crazy old man who'd abandoned them at dusk and returned too late to use magic in their defense.

Riddon collected his brothers with a glance. "We'd better see if they've got a wagon."

"And blankets for *Domna* Trayos," Elom added.

A minute later only Collan and Gorynel Desse remained, on either side of the fire. The young man watched the old man; the old man watched the flames.

"It isn't so great a risk as you think," the Warrior Mage said at last. "The Ladder is accessible. I found that out tonight."

"Forgive me if I don't sing your praises," Col snapped.

"It was necessary. I did what I could to keep you safe. I went as quickly as I could—and when I heard the swords and shouting I—"

"You didn't get here in time. Verald's dead. What're you going to do with me, now that he's not here to knock me over the head?"

"I understand your loss—"

"*My* loss? What about that girl in there? She's lost her husband—and she might lose her Mageborn baby as well! I don't know what you're talking about with Ladders, but—"

"No, you *don't* know what you're talking about. The child will be Mageborn," Desse replied, not appearing at all surprised that Col knew. "And safe-born."

That was something, anyhow—if he could trust the white-haired old madman. Col held his tongue for all of two minutes, seething. At last he said, "If what you said when we got here is true, and every Mage is in danger of death, why are you here? Why Lady Agatine and Orlin Renne? Why *me?*"

"For reasons I hope you will never know."

"Damn it, that's no answer!"

"It's all you'll have from me, boy." The Mage Globe changed color, from rosy-gold to white and then to a brilliant green sharp as bottle-glass shards in sunlight. Just the color of the eyes that suddenly stared into Col's, and although green was not a color of fire he felt singed to his soul.

"Do you understand, Collan?"

As he felt himself nod, he wondered what he was agreeing to.

A short while later, a wagon was brought around to the back door. The mare between the traces shied at the smell of smoke, but Veliaz held her head and talked to her, and she soon settled. After Lady Agatine and Tarise arranged a bedding of blankets, Veliaz lifted Sela in, then went back for Tamsa. Both were still asleep.

Col and Orlin Renne hauled the Council Guard dead into the farmhouse. Elom came to help once he shooed the last of the animals from the barn into the fenced field beyond. This time the fire came from a match; the bodies, the farmhouse, the barn, and especially the tool shed must burn more quickly than Magefire, and burn to the ground. No one would ever use this Ladder from or to Roseguard again.

6

"Which way did they go?"

Auvry Feiran shrugged. "There are four sets of wagon tracks beneath this morning's snow, all of them reeking of magic, all leading in different directions."

Glenin kicked at a large stone that had been part of someone's funeral pyre. Magefire could not be smothered by snow, and nothing was left of the corpse. Not even the large bones. But the farmhouse had not burned completely, nor the barn, and even from fifty feet away Glenin could practically smell magic coming from the tool shed.

"Gorynel Desse is no fool," Feiran went on, idly stroking his horse's neck.

"No—*we* were, for not coming here ourselves."

"The risk was too great. I won't put you in danger, Glenin. Not again."

"I'm Malerris trained, Father," she reminded him. "I know things he doesn't, I can do things he can't, and—"

"You've never faced a true Warrior Mage," he snapped. "Tamos Wolvar was a *Scholar*. He'd never applied his knowledge to a real Battle Globe in his life—and he would never, ever use lethal magic. Gorsha Desse has no such compunctions, I assure you. Your knowledge may or may not exceed his—but don't ever underestimate him."

She changed the subject. "What about the Ladder? Where does it go?"

"I had no idea it even existed. It's useless now in any case. But it proves you right, Glenin. Their destination is Ryka Court—the last place we'd expect them to go." Pride deepened his voice as he added, "Thanks to you, it's the first place we'll look for them."

"Now all we need do is find them." She grimaced, tucking her gloved hands inside her trouser pockets and kicking once more at the rock. "How many thousand people are at Ryka Court these days?"

"It won't be that difficult. They'll hide for a few days, trying to make us believe they've gone elsewhere. It may take some time, but they'll show up. This is the only set of Ladders available to them."

"We can't use the Council Guard to watch every one," she mused. "We need Malerrisi. I'll send to the Castle this afternoon."

"That's where you're wrong. We can't use any of the Lords—Gorsha would sense them half a mile off."

Glenin frowned slightly, wondering if he'd even heard the second use of the diminutive. If he still thought of the great enemy by an intimate nickname. . . .

"He expects only three Mageborns: you, me, and Anniyas," Feiran went on. "If he discerns any more—"

"Where can he go?" she challenged, spinning on her heel. "He *has* to use a Ryka Court Ladder. You and I and Anniyas can't watch them all. We can't Ward them—he'll feel that, too." She stopped, catching a breath that froze her lips and tongue for an instant. "By the Weaver, we don't *have* to watch every Ladder—or any Ladder at all!"

"What do you mean?"

She laughed softly, and made a sweeping gesture toward the farmhouse. A score of tiny fireballs, none of them larger than a cherry, flew from her fingertips to the smoldering half-ruin. It took fire, and this time would burn even in a blizzard.

"Let's go back home. I'll tell you along the way."

7

Collan had never been to Ryka Court. He didn't want to go there now. But he went, because honor said he must.

Not that he owed the Rising anything. He'd rendered up dead Council Guards in payment for getting him out of Roseguard. All accounts were settled. But he owed it to Verald to see Sela and Tamsa safe.

Survival had a lot to do with it, too. He followed Gorynel Desse to Ryka Court because he had no other way off the island. If that message in flowers and herbs was correct, Rosvenir was a Name on Anniyas's list. Heading straight into her lair was the very last thing he wanted to do, but he had to admit it was also the very last place she'd look for him.

Because of the horse, the Warrior Mage could not Fold the road. Horses, he explained, refused to believe that ten miles wasn't really ten miles. Desse walked ahead of the wagon—casting no spells or Wards lest they attract Malerrisi, but ready nonetheless to do so if necessary for safety's sake. Col hoped he would, anyway. He kept a hand on his sword under his cloak all the same. Orlin Renne did likewise.

Just before dawn it began to snow softly. Sela woke with a stifled groan. The jostling of the wagon was doing her and her unborn baby no good at all. There was no shelter, no hope of any within miles. So they pulled to the side of the road, tented a blanket over the wagon, and waited out the snow.

By midmorning they were moving again. By late afternoon they had reached a modest little manor, empty as the farmhouse had been empty. A crimson ribbon was stretched diagonally across the door, secured at either side by the large seal in wax of the Council Guard.

When Collan asked, Orlin replied grimly that this had been the home of a prominent family secretly connected to the Rising.

"Obviously not so secret," Col remarked.

This earned him a furious glance from Tarise Nalle, and he shut up.

All doors were similarly sealed. Collan showed off a talent for burglary by opening a back window without leaving so much as a scratch on the casement—thanking Pierga Cleverhand for the childish simplicity of the lock. His previous experiences with windows had more often been to get out rather than in, but the principle was more or less the same on either side of the glass.

The place was pitiably abandoned. Dinner rotted on the kitchen table, the evening candle unlit. A child's cloak puddled at the bottom of the stairs. A book lay open on the floor near the main room's cold hearth, and an overturned basket spilled bright yarn onto the rug.

The basket suddenly gave forth a sound that nearly stopped Col's heart: a plaintive *mew?* followed by a low and unmistakably canine growl. He clenched his fists to stop their shaking and knelt, whistling softly. The basket moved, and from its warm woolen depths slunk a spotted hound puppy and a round of tawny fur that looked like a baby lion.

Collan smiled as the kitten arched against his outstretched hand, purring. The pup was warier, nipping at the finger he extended. Neither had gone hungry very long, but there was that in their eyes which pleaded for more than food. He thought at once of Jeymi and Tamsa. Delighted by his inspiration, he scooped up a wriggling fur-ball in each hand—trying not to think of the child whose cloak lay on the stairs.

They stayed four cold days in the house. They lit no fires, lest the smoke be seen; Desse cast no spells, lest the magic be sensed. The bedrooms yielded blankets, quilts, and clothing the owners would never need again. There was food in the larder, cold fare but adequate to their wants, and the cellar was stocked with wine enough to warm the adults. As Collan had hoped, the two small animals warmed the children.

Jeymi gave the puppy a grandiose name from an adventure story his sister Sarra had read him, but this noble moniker was soon replaced by plain, simple, eminently appropriate Spot. Tamsa was slower to accept the kitten, though the kitten immediately established ownership of Tamsa. A nudge here, a purr there, and a night curled beneath the little girl's chin were all it took for Velvet to acquire a name and a fiercely reciprocated devotion.

Sela, watching the miniature lion pretend to stalk Tamsa across the rug, smiled quietly at Col. "Thank you."

"I had nothing to do with it," he said at once.

"All the same—" She bit her lip. The pains were controllable, not so much through any art of Magelore—Desse was not a Healer, after all—but because Sela feared birthing her child in a place where they couldn't even boil water. Simple determination was, Collan discovered, a powerful thing.

The morning of the fifth day, they left. Nobody bothered to ask the Mage if it was safe to do so; they'd run out of food, another storm threatened, and time was against Sela. Her baby would come soon no matter what happened. They had to get her to safety.

Ryka Court was a classic spoked-wheel city, centered on the All Saints Temple at its hub. Around this were the wedge-shaped blocks of Guildhalls, law courts, great merchant houses, and banks. The real center of Ryka Court, however, was on the edge of the city overlooking Council Lake. Here were the domed edifices of Assembly and Council, military barracks and parade ground, and residence towers for senior officials.

Rillan Veliaz drove the wagon the long way around, taking the Ring Road so it would seem they had come from the northeast and not the west. Collan could hardly control the nervous shift of his shoulders as he walked past pile after vast round marble pile, most of them inhabited by persons he'd rather not meet. Morning traffic on the Ring Road was sparse, a manifestation of uncertain times. With Mages and adherents of the Rising rumored to be anywhere and everywhere, most people stayed in their houses. Only the produce wagons rolled in from outlying farms, brightly painted with pictures of their contents: fruit, vegetables, flowers, fodder.

Their own wagon—decorated with a cornucopia of root vegetables—merged anonymously with the others. Collan wondered at that: surely the other drivers saw that their cargo was women and children, not sacks of potatoes. Then he noticed that each driver stared only at the road between his horse's ears. No greetings were called back and forth, no eye contact was made, despite the fact that these men must know each other, having come this way every day for years. The silence was numbing, oppressive. Col wondered if it had spread throughout the world—a horrifying thought for one whose life and livelihood were music.

Desse took a sudden turn off the Ring Road down a narrow street like a gully in a white marble canyon. Another turn took them into an even narrower alley. This led into a small kitchen courtyard where another wagon was being lightened of its burden of winter melons. A man in faultless white who looked more like a wrestler than a cook supervised, thundering condemnations as he inspected every crate.

"Help them unload," the old man murmured to Orlin Renne, who slapped Col's shoulder and gathered two of his sons with a look.

Two large wagons and two big dray horses and ten busy men made for admirably cramped quarters. Col saw Rillan Veliaz disappear, supporting Sela. After handing off another crate, he followed.

Orlin, Riddon, and Maugir were close behind. Renne led the way up a curving service stair, which led to a curving hallway, which led to a door with a sign above it: MINISTER OF MINES. Through the door, along another small passage, and Collan entered an office cluttered with maps, books, and piles of documents.

The big, handsome man who emerged from a tangle of Slegin sons strongly resembled Lady Agatine's husband. Brothers? Col wondered. The relationship was confirmed when the two giants embraced hard enough to crack spines.

"You look like hell, Orlin."

"So do you, Telo."

Lady Agatine was enfolded much more gently in the elder Renne's arms. "You, on the other hand, are more exquisite than even my most evocative dreams."

She managed a smile. "Still trying to convince me that I married the wrong brother?"

"After twenty years with him, it's my turn." He kissed her cheek, then said, "Before you ask, Sarra's safe as far as I know."

Gorynel Desse broke into the reunion. "We must move quickly, Telomir. I had to spell a few people getting here."

The Minister nodded. "The Ladder's still a secret. But they'll know when you go through." He stopped, a tiny smile touching his lips. "Is that Collan? Yes, I see it must be. Well, well, well."

Well-well-well what? Col thought.

Before he could open his mouth to ask, Telomir Renne continued, "Be gentle when you knock me out, little brother. I'm not as young as I used to be."

Orlin shook his head. "You're coming with us. Telo, you have to! I won't leave you here—"

"You need somebody at Ryka Court. That somebody is me."

"Damn it, Telo—" growled Orlin.

Desse interrupted. "Listen to me, son. He's right. It's no longer safe for you to be here."

"Is it safe anywhere, Father—for any of us?"

"No," intoned another voice.

Until the day he died Collan would never be certain what happened next. He had the impression of another massively tall man, and angry lightning that flashed from a pair of glowing spheres, and the flash of swords almost as deadly bright—including his own. But his vision was clouded, his perceptions muddied, the pain in his head crippling.

Somebody was dragging him somewhere. Every moment

set a new agony stabbing through his skull. There was darkness, and dizziness, and he felt his stomach heave.

Strong hands persuaded the sword out of his fist. He let it
go. The same hands guided him to something blissfully soft
and warm. He fell onto it, into it, wanting nothing but oblivion.

A voice snared him back to consciousness. Raw with
grief, thick with weeping, stammering out names: "... Agatine ... Orlin ... Verald ... Elom...."

And one other name: "Auvry Feiran—"

Col struggled to sit up. Someone else lay beside him on
the bed. Sela and Tamsa—thank the Saints, once again in the
merciful sleep Desse could spell for them. He wished he
could join them. He smoothed the little girl's hair, winning
a defensive hiss from the kitten tucked into her coat pocket.

Col swung his legs off the bed and swayed to his feet.
Over in a corner was a little knot of people. He peered into
the dimness, trying to identify each.

Jeymi Slegin, huddled in a chair with his face buried in
the puppy's neck. Tarise Nalle. Rillan Veliaz.

His temples throbbed suddenly, and in the center of the
room three more people appeared. Riddon and Maugir
Slegin stumbled immediately toward their brother. Telomir
Renne supported Gorynel Desse. A Mage Globe flickered,
died. The old man collapsed against his son's shoulder.

Pretending his legs didn't wobble, he went to help the pair
over to the bed. "What happened? Where the hell are we?"

"Ambrai. The Mage Academy. Feiran knows about the
Ladder now, but he can't possibly know where it goes.
We're safe enough here for the present."

Col considered reminding him that it had been only minutes since he himself had asked if it was safe *anywhere*.
"What happened?" he repeated instead.

"Auvry Feiran!" Tarise spat, knuckling her eyes—
uselessly, as new tears welled. "He killed my Lady and my
Lord and—and Elom—"

"Why didn't Desse kill *him?*"

Rillan gave him an odd look. "Do you know that he
didn't?"

"Couldn't have." Col shrugged a shoulder. "We left in too
big a hurry, without the—without them." And he wondered
then why he had been part of the first group. He'd been
doing all right with his sword, hadn't he? Maybe even

scored Feiran a good one—he seemed to recall hitting *something*.

"My father is powerful," said Telomir Renne. "But he also taught Feiran all the Warrior Mage lore he knows. Add to that the tutelage of the Malerrisi. . . ." He shook his head. "In a way, we're fortunate it wasn't Glenin who confronted us. Even Gorsha is wary of her."

"But what *happened?*" Col demanded for the third time. "I remember—"

"—very little, I'd imagine," Renne interrupted. "Battle Globes can do that. It was a brave effort, Collan, and together you and Riddon and—and my brother bought us some time. But steel is useless against magic, unless you're extraordinarily lucky *and* possess one of the Fifty Swords."

An old song stirred in memory, something associated with a large folio and long nights of practice to get the fingering just right. And with the memory came the warning knife in his temple. Frowning into Telomir Renne's eyes, he had the distinct feeling that *Fifty Swords* had been mentioned on purpose to elicit just that reaction, so he'd let the matter drop.

He was damned if he'd—

"Perhaps you've heard the old ballad," Renne went on. "It's said to date back to The Waste War, but the definitive version was written by—"

"F–Falundir," Col said, defiant and paying for it in terrible pain.

"Yes. Go sleep it off, Collan," he said, not without sympathy. "There should be a cot in the next room, if memory serves."

Collan had no choice. His head simply hurt too damned much. He sprawled across a blanketless canvas cot and squeezed his eyes shut, waiting for the surcease of the silent dark.

8

"Did I mention that this was a lousy idea?"

Sarra barely heard Val's shout over the roar of the acid

storm outside. They had galloped into Longriding half an hour before corrosive winds swept down from the Wraithen Mountains and the town locked up tight. Truly told, they were fortunate to have found this livery stable, the only one in the eastern quarter that had four stalls left. For them, there was a hayloft—at a daily fee that would have bought a week at the best hostelry in Roseguard. At least payment in advance was not demanded; Lady Lilen's name, invoked by her son, once again secured their needs.

The distance between the stable they sheltered in and the Ostin residence was no more than a half mile. It might just as well have been half a million for all the hope Sarra had of getting there anytime soon.

Ignoring Val, she wrapped herself in an old and smelly horse blanket and burrowed into the hay. She cast a nervous glance upward at the ceiling. It looked secure enough, but she'd heard plenty of tales about severe scarring from acid burns.

Alin saw the direction of her worry, and smiled. "It won't leak."

"There's not a single leaky roof in all The Waste," Val agreed.

Elomar, plumping up a straw pillow for himself, added, "A family goes hungry first."

Which says a lot for the Council's concern for its citizens' safety, Sarra thought. *There ought to be an allocation of local tax money, and a similar fund for coastal cities victimized by hurricanes—and while I'm at it, dikes on the Bluehair River so half Kenrokeshir doesn't flood every ten years. . . .*

She fell asleep to plans for civil engineering, but her slumber was made restless by dreams of claws and talons plucking away roof tiles and hurling them at fleeing people who screamed under a fiery rain.

Wraithenbeasts, a part of her mind informed her quite calmly. *They're coming. They're inevitable. They've been gathering strength for hundreds of years. They're waiting for the Lords of Malerris to let them out.*

The dream changed. A plain of black glass stretched before her in all directions. Glenin, laughing and beautiful, turned an enormous key in a gigantic lock. She stepped back and with a graceful gesture invited the iron gates to open.

Beyond lurked horror.

Wraithenbeasts, commented the dispassionate voice in her dream. *Millions of them. Hungering, raging, mindless. Created by Mageborns when they created The Waste. Twice now Mageborns have locked them in. Only Mageborns can let them out. And she will be the one to do it. It is the pattern of her thread in the Great Loom. And only Cailet can stop her. Only Cailet.*

A girl appeared—a child, really, not even eighteen years old—slight, thin, her white-blonde hair tangling above fine black eyes, frowning at Sarra and utterly unaware of the Lady of Malerris—

"Sarra, wake up. Sarra!"

She spasmed upright, clutching at Elomar's arms. A single wild glance by the delicate light of his Mage Globe reoriented her at once. A hayloft in Longriding, acid storm howling outside—not a featureless plain and iron gates unlocked to the howling horrors beyond. Elo, Val, and Alin nearby, familiar and real—not her two sisters, the phantom strangers of her dream.

"I'm all right," she muttered, raking sweaty hair back with both hands.

But, Saints, how she hated portentous, pretentious dreams. Why couldn't her Warded magic give her another useful one, like the one about the books? Fear had caused this one, not magic or foresight or a Saint or anything else. Disgusted by her own lurid flair for the dramatic, she lay back down.

Alin and Val were talking quietly nearby; that she could hear them meant the storm was waning. She felt better at the thought. But the dream would not let her be.

"One good thing about this storm," Alin was saying to Val, "*she* can't get through it, either."

"Unless she's already here."

"What a cheering thought."

Positively delightful, Sarra thought.

"Well, how about this? She's stupid enough or arrogant enough to use a Waste Ladder even in an acid storm."

"Much better. But I don't really believe it, do you?"

Neither do I.

"Sounded good, though."

"Nice try, Val."

"Have to admit, though, it warms my heart to think of her trapped by Wild Magic."

"Mmm. But there's only one Ladder in Longriding, and she'd have to go all the way to Ambrai to use it."

Val laughed. "I can just see her popping into Lady Lilen's green house—"

"—right into the loving embrace of a six-foot spiny-sword!"

I must remember to thank Alin for not taking me through that one. . . .

"Why'd your mother name it after Gorsha instead of you? Except for the height, you and that cactus have a lot in common."

"You could use a razor, yourself. It was his idea to train it into a circle like that. Almost as good as one of his Wards."

Wonderful, Sarra told herself as she drifted off. *All I lack is a dream about an affectionate six-foot cactus. . . .*

But this time she was smiling as she went to sleep, and did not dream.

The next morning she woke to silence. On a hay bale rested a bottle, a hard roll, and a wedge of incredibly stinky cheese. She gobbled ravenously, thinking how outraged Grandmother Allynis would be at her manners, even though nobody was there to see her. With that thought came another: *Does Glenin remember our childhood at the Octagon Court?* When she considered what could have happened if Glenin had seen past the Wards to remember, her stomach turned and for a moment she feared she'd lose her breakfast.

Glenin Feiran had no sister. Sarra Ambrai—she gave herself her true Name defiantly—had only one. And it was time to find and claim her.

When Sarra climbed down from the loft, Alin was renegotiating the price of stabling their four mounts another day.

"Why is he bothering?" she whispered to Val. "We're leaving here by Ladder, not on horseback."

"Makes it look good," Val replied softly.

She gave a shrug. What the citizens of Longriding thought or didn't think was of no interest to her. Taig and Cailet: *they* were important. No one else.

As they walked through the main part of town, Val remarked on the new pits in buildings and pavement. Sarra could discern no difference from what she'd seen before the acid storm. Real rain would have washed everything clean. The stains on Longriding were indelible.

She remembered Ostinhold as an ugly jumble of angles, add-ons, and any-color-available. The Ostin house was a complete surprise. The two-story building was all graceful curves, constructed as a series of seven large bays reminiscent of side chapels in an All Saints Temple. Narrow arching windows were shuttered in dark green to complement pale yellow walls; a fan-lighted doorway was sheltered by a semicircle of columned portico; the domed roof was emphasized by curving patterns of tiles; a slim round tower nestled at the side of the house, with a water cistern on top and—Sarra was positive—the Ladder on one of the other three floors.

Almost eighteen years had passed since Gorynel Desse had taken her through the Ladder; she was a grown woman now, not a child of five. Yet as she walked up the stone path toward the portico, she caught herself glancing around for her mother. She'd thought of Lady Agatine as her mother for so long that Maichen Ambrai's features had blurred in her memory.

Does Glenin remember? Does she ever wonder what happened to Mama and me?

And why *am I thinking about her when it's Cailet who's so close now?*

Simple. Glenin might be close, too.

"So we just walk right on in?" she asked Alin.

"Why not? It's his house, too," Val said.

"That's not what she meant, Val. It's been a few years, but I'm known in Longriding. So's Val. It'd be silly to sneak around."

"Some people probably even remember you, Elo," Val pointed out. "Why haven't you been arrested?"

The Healer Mage allowed himself a smug little smile. "Although not in First Sword Desse's class, I am not inept at Wards."

Sarra resisted a shrug. Magic all around her—Elomar, Alin, even Val with his time-sense—and all she had were dreams and gut-jumping.

But she had warning enough, an urgent fire of danger along her nerves. Before she could speak Glenin's name, even before Alin could use the brass knocker shaped like an oak tree, the door swung open.

A girl stood there, a tall man behind her. Taig.

Cailet.

Not the child from Pinderon. The young woman from the dream. Taller than Sarra, not as tall as Glenin. Pale blonde hair cut short, silky bangs drifting into black eyes that dominated an oblong face.

Dangerous?

Sarra's Warded magic screamed *Yes!*

Cailet saw Alin and Val first. Her eyes grew even wider and her lips parted on a cry of joy she never uttered.

Because she saw Sarra then. Recognized her. Not as the girl from Pinderon. As *Sarra.*

Her lips drew into a rictus of agony and she gave a low moan, echoed an instant later by Alin and Elomar. The Healer Mage collapsed to his knees as Alin sagged bonelessly against Val. Even Sarra felt it: magic, exploding against her Wards, power finally freed, running wild, lashing out in mindless fury after its long imprisonment.

The sisters saw nothing but each other: one stricken to the heart, the other stricken by magic.

Taig stepped forward and swung Cailet up into his arms. "Val! The Wards have broken! Get out of here!"

"Where?" Val cried, lifting Alin as easily as Taig had lifted Cailet. "Not by Ladder—Saints, Taig, *look* at him!"

"Yes, by Ladder! Go on, hurry! Once he's away from her, he might—"

Cailet's sudden spasm was exactly matched by Alin's. Elomar had wrapped his arms around his head, groaning.

"No!" Sarra cried. "I won't leave her—"

"Do you want your own Wards to shatter?" Taig demanded.

Maybe she did.

"Sarra—" Cailet's voice, a rasp of pain.

She knows me. She knows my name. She knows everything—

Cailet's eyes—black, luminous, their mother's eyes— Sarra's eyes—a silent shriek of rage and rampaging magic—

"Go, Sarra! Now!" Taig exclaimed, and fled upstairs with Cailet in his arms.

She would have followed. But Val pushed past, carrying Alin into the house. And Elomar's long fingers clasped her wrist hard. He swayed upright, shaking his head as if to rid it of some horrifying vision. His skin was paste-gray, his eyes flinching with bruises to his magic, perhaps to his very soul.

"The Ladder," he mumbled. "Help me, Sarra."

Cailet—

—has Taig. Doesn't need me. Elo does.

He leaned heavily on her shoulder, tall body no more co-ordinated than a string puppet. Somehow she got him walking. Somehow she kept herself on her feet, supporting his awkward weight. Somehow she found her way across the entry hall to a door.

Val stood in the middle of the greenhouse, guarding Alin, who huddled on his knees. Circling them with a multitude of thin green arms studded with dagger-long spikes was an incredibility of a cactus. Six feet high, growing from a capacious stone trough, it uniquely warded the Ladder. Elomar stumbled through the two-foot wide break by himself. Sarra slid in behind him and crouched beside Alin.

"Take us through," she said.

He was shivering, blue eyes huge with the same bruised expression Elomar wore. "Can't," he muttered.

"Do it, Alin," she demanded. "Now."

"Let him be," Val snarled.

"It won't get any better until he's as far from her as he can be. Take us through, Alin. Now!"

Val's stance became almost threatening. Alin shook his head and reached up for his cousin's hand.

"She's right. Has to be now. Hang onto me, all of you."

Sarra took his other hand. Elomar put both hands on Alin's shoulder. The Blanking Ward formed slowly, sluggishly. A long, stomach-lurching time later, Sarra could see again.

Sitting quietly in an armchair before a brazier, was a thin, dark, elegant man of middle years. He regarded them with sad blue eyes.

Alin wilted onto the carpet. Val gathered him up once more and carried him to the nearby bed. Elomar lurched to another chair and folded his long body into it, exhausted.

Sarra eyed the man. "I know this is Ambrai, but where in the city are we?"

He gave an eloquent shrug.

"You mean you don't know? That's impossible. You're a Mage, you must—"

This time he shook his head.

"You're not a Mage? Then how did you get here?"

He said nothing.

"Tell me who you are and why you're here—wherever 'here' is."

Bright blue eyes watched her; amusement quirked the full lips.

"Vow of silence?" Sarra inquired sharply. "If so, I suggest you break it. There are things I must know, and you're going to tell me."

"Leave be, Sarra," said Elomar, very softly. "You don't understand."

Valirion approached the silent man. He bowed with more respect than Sarra had believed him capable of—but his rudeness in introducing her to him rather than the other way around was wholly in character.

"*Domni*, this is Sarra Liwellan."

The blue eyes in the dark face caught and held hers, and she had the oddest feeling that he would once again shake his head—as if he knew Liwellan was not her real Name.

"Sarra," said Val, "you have the rare honor of being in the presence of Bard Falundir."

9

The First Councillor's private chambers were unWarded. Many long corridors away, in the comfort of her own small sunroom, Glenin both saw and heard the conversation perfectly.

Although *conversation* was much too polite a term for the impressive rampage Anniyas now indulged in at Auvry Feiran's expense. Glenin had never feared the woman before. This morning she learned the folly of her contempt.

"*You* had *him!*" Anniyas shouted. "*Right in your hands, you* had *him! How could you let him escape?*"

Glenin had been wondering that very thing. When her father made no answer, only stood with head bowed and hands clasped, the First Councillor seized a magnificent obsidian vase and hurled it at a mirror. The resulting crash and splinter made Glenin wince.

"Our greatest enemy! Leader of the Rising! First Sword of Warrior Mages—and you lost *him! And don't you dare tell me that within the week there'll be no more Mages, Warrior or otherwise!"* Anniyas shook both fists in Auvry Feiran's face, her own features contorted in fury. *"With Desse still alive, and that moron of a Captal with him—thanks to your stupid daughter—"*

His shoulders stiffened. *"That wasn't Glenin's fault. She did all she could to ensure—"*

"Close your mouth, Prentice Mage!" She spun, knocking against a table. Plump fingers closed around a carved jade bowl and flung it into the wall. *"Find him! Find them both! I want their deaths, do you understand me? Or, by the Weaver and the Loom, I'll have* yours!*"*

"I understand, First Councillor."

"Get out of my sight! Don't come back until you bring me their heads! Both of them—not one and an excuse! And don't try to take Glenin with you! She stays as warrant for your success!"

Glenin choked and nearly lost the spell. Anniyas glared up at the Commandant of the Council Guard, whose every physical line proclaimed submission. All but his hands, Glenin realized suddenly. His head was bent and his shoulders were hunched, and his back was a humble curve—but his hands fisted at his sides as if strangling his own rage.

"By your leave, First Councillor."

"Get out!"

Glenin didn't watch her father's humiliating exit. The last lingering bit of magic gave her the sound of yet another priceless artwork smashing into oblivion. Opening her eyes to the sunroom's dreary view of mist-shrouded Council Lake, she composed herself and went to meet her father.

Several minutes later he entered their suite. He flinched at seeing her, and now she sensed what distance had muted: he was injured. Though his body was whole and unhurt, his magic was badly wounded.

In theory, she knew how to help. The technique had been applied to her once. She'd overreached herself during a lesson at Malerris Castle and they'd given her the further lesson of agonizing pain and utter exhaustion before they eased her suffering. But she didn't help her father because she didn't know why Gorynel Desse had escaped.

"There was no time," he muttered, sagging into his favorite chair. "The Ladder was unWarded—never knew it was there until I sensed Gorsha's presence—he's strong, I'd forgotten how strong. . . ."

She settled before him on a footstool and took his hands, relaxed now from their angry clenching. "You should have called for me."

His head tilted back against the cushion and his eyes closed. "I know what he knows—but he knows what *I* know. You're a cypher to him. You might have—"

I would *have,* she corrected internally. Aloud, she said, "How many of them were there? Do you know who it was he took to safety?"

"Agatine Slegin and her husband died. One of their sons. I assume the other three are with him. A pregnant woman, a little girl . . . one other woman, I think, and two or three more young men. None of them Mages."

Then why waste time on them? She frowned, and rose to pour a large cup full of wine. Giving it to her father, she said, "Here, drink this."

He sipped obediently. "One of the men had a lute strapped to his back. That's all I remember. When the Battle Globes met—and we both called up more—the men drew their swords—" He looked down at his arm, as if expecting to see torn cloth and bleeding flesh. "I'd forgotten how powerful he is. It wasn't just the Battle Globes—he spelled their swords at the same time, to make me believe they could. . . ." He shook his head, drank again. "But of course they didn't. Only Gorsha's could, and he only used magic. . . ."

"What about Telomir Renne?"

"He got away, too. I should've known there'd be a Ladder close by those rooms. They were Gorsha's once."

"You did everything you could." It was what he'd said of her to Anniyas. They were the most galling words either Feiran could ever hear.

"I must go. She commands me to—"

"Later. Tonight. You're not recovered."

"If only I knew where. . . ." Gray-green eyes, dulled with weariness and sick with failure, at last met hers square on. "This is the first place we looked, and you were right. Where is the *next* place, Glensha? Where do I find them to bring back their heads as Anniyas orders me to do?"

"First you must go to Malerris Castle. You'll need help.

They won't refuse it—not if it means killing Gorynel Desse." She almost said *"—and the Captal,"* but caught herself in time to keep from revealing that she had listened where she shouldn't have.

Her father nodded. "Yes. I do need their help in this."

"And then—" She drew in a deep breath, for this particular secret, cherished so briefly, was the most important of any she'd misered away in her life. "Father, I know where they must be."

Feiran straightened slightly, a spark returning to his eyes. "Where?"

"Ambrai."

10

Alin woke, more or less refreshed, sometime around Thirteenth. Elomar was waiting for him, considerably healthier in magical terms; he knew his own power and how to protect himself, though the unleashing of Cailet's magic had strained him to his limits.

Sarra, as silent as Bard Falundir for shame of their first meeting, watched Alin and the Healer vanish from the bedchamber. Elomar would do what he could to Ward Cailet while Alin brought her and Taig through the Ladder.

It might even work.

While they were gone, Val paced. Sarra stared at her folded hands. The great Bard watched her, as he had most of the night; she could feel it, and could not meet his gaze.

He knew who she was. Of this she had no doubt. His eyes said more than most voices. But she just couldn't look at him. The real irritation was that if she'd thought about it for just a minute, she would have recognized this place and spared herself the mortification. She and her mother and Gorynel Desse had used this Ladder long ago. Of all the things she'd been compelled to forget, a long walk in the dead of night had not been one of them: the walk from the Octagon Court to Bard Hall.

"They're coming," Val said suddenly. "I can feel it."

An instant before they appeared in the center of the room,

Sarra could feel it, too: Cailet's magic. The girl was imperfectly Warded by Elomar Adennos—who barely made it to a chair before his knees gave out. Alin staggered into Val's strong arms.

Taig cradled Cailet in his arms, her bright head tucked to his shoulder. As he placed her gently onto the bed, Sarra stifled a cry at the sight of her sister's haggard face, scored by lines of suffering that aged her twenty years.

"Don't look so grim," Taig said. "Healer Adennos's Ward will protect other Mageborns until Gorsha can help her."

"You mean he made a prison for her," Sarra corrected, "until she can be fully Warded again."

"Well . . . yes."

"No. No more Wards."

Taig drew up the threadbare quilt and tucked Cailet in. "Sarra, we can't risk it. You saw what happened to Alin and—"

"No!" she repeated. "Taig, she's in *pain*."

He coaxed her to the far side of the room, away from the others. "Gorsha can help."

"Can he? What if the Wards break again, with even worse results? Her magic has to be freed so she can learn to control it. To use it."

Taig shrugged uncomfortably. "Let's let him decide, shall we?"

"She's *my* sister and *my* responsibility!"

"Don't you understand? It was seeing you that collapsed her Wards! If it happens again—"

Glaring up into his quicksilver eyes, she hissed, "I'm her sister! Not you or Desse or anyone can make me leave her!"

"You don't know what's at stake here."

Sarra turned away from him. "*She* is! You've protected her all these years, you and the whole tribe of Ostins, and thank you very much, I'm grateful. But—"

"Gracious of you," Taig snapped.

"But *I'm* here now. And I won't be separated from her again."

"You have no idea what's going on," he insisted. "The Rising may not survive this, Sarra. People are dying all over Lenfell. They've known for years that this might come, and they know to get here if they can, but so many of them simply didn't believe it—"

He didn't understand that none of them mattered. Not

him, not Alin and Val, not even Sarra herself. She knew it
as surely as she now understood the warning of her dream.
Sarra had faced Glenin without magic. Cailet must not. Her
magic must be set free. And she had only Sarra to fight for
her birthright as a Mageborn.

"The Rising be damned," she said flatly. "Cailet *will* have
her magic."

"Because you say so!"

"Yes!"

There was a noise of many people outside the closed door,
and Taig slapped a hand to his sword. "Shit! They're here.
Val, stop hovering over Alin, he'll be fine. Go talk to the
Mages. Find them somewhere to sleep. It'll be tomorrow
night at the earliest before you can take them to the Academy."

"Mages?" Sarra waited for Taig's explanation. None was
forthcoming. So she followed Val out the door. As little as
anyone but Cailet mattered, she must behave as if they did.

The lie at least had the virtue of giving her something to
do.

"—by whatever Ladders are still functioning. Alin Ostin
will take you through," Val was telling a group of exhausted,
frightened Mage Guardians. Six of them, travel-stained and
hollow-eyed, with four children no older than Jeymi. No,
mustn't think about Jeymi.

"But where can we go?" one young man asked, holding
tight to a sleeping toddler. "The Council Decree says we're
outlaws, we'll die if they find us—"

"They won't find you," Sarra told him. Stepping around
Val to stand in front of him, she went on, "My name is Sarra
Liwellan, and I—"

"Liwellan?" An elderly woman stepped forward and
peered at Sarra in the dimness. "That's not a Mageborn
Name."

"Neither's Maurgen," Val said. "Are you going to condemn anyone who doesn't have magic the way Anniyas con-
demns anyone who does?"

"Don't lecture me, boy." The wrinkled old Mage snorted.
"I recognize you—I heard about that little dance you and
your lover led the Council Guard last year in Cantratown.
But Rising or not, in these times I trust no one I can't trade
spells with. And what would the adopted daughter of Lady
Agatine Slegin be doing here?"

"As it happens," Sarra interposed smoothly, "Liwellan isn't my Name. I'm not at liberty to tell you the real one. Suffice it to say I'm the daughter of Mage Guardians." True, in a way. There was magic in both her parents' families. "They were lost with Ambrai." Also true: Maichen's dying had begun the moment she heard what Auvry Feiran had done here—and the man who had been Sarra's father had been lost in the wrecking of this city.

She continued, "My own magic was Warded for my safety. But I am as Mageborn as any of you. So when I tell you that you will not be caught, you may trust me as you would one of your own. I *am* one of your own. So is Valirion Maurgen—and so are all those who oppose Anniyas and the Malerrisi."

"Understood, Lady," said another woman, with a warning look for the others. "In fact, I believe I can guess who your parents were—though I will never speak of it again."

"Huh! Easy enough to say things you don't have to prove!" the old one scoffed.

"Do you doubt Lady Sarra's word?" Val asked quietly.

"I doubt everything and everyone, boy. That's why I'm still alive. And I say the hell with Anniyas and the Malerrisi for tonight. I'm tired and cold and I want a bed to rest my old bones in."

Sarra suspected this was her version of a graceful capitulation. "*Domni* Maurgen, would you escort them? Thank you."

After only a few steps, the venerable Mage paused and turned. "By the way, girl, I suppose you know those Wards of yours are set in stone."

Sarra blinked. She had sensed no probing—not that she'd know what it might feel like, she reminded herself bitterly.

"But something's been chipping at them lately."

Yes—a solid steel chisel named Cailet. "You know about Wards?" Perhaps she could bolster Elomar's work.

"Enough to recognize Gorsha Desse's crafting. My specialty is knives." One wrinkled lid winked, and one gnarled hand twitched her cloak aside to show a low-slung belt laden with a dozen daggers. "Just what you lack, isn't it?" the ancient mocked. "A thousand-year-old Warrior Mage!"

This was pretty much what Sarra was thinking. She couldn't help a blush.

"Feeble is as feeble thinks, girl. My knives have seen

more Malerrisi guts than you have years, just in the last few days."

Quick as summer lightning, a blade carved a silvery path through the air and thunked, quivering, into the floor at Sarra's feet.

"Keep it to remind you," the Warrior Mage said.

When she was gone, Sarra crouched to inspect the knife. Slim, plain, and unadorned, with twenty-two notches carved into the hilt—she gulped when she'd counted them—it was difficult work to pry it from the grouting between flagstones. A Warrior Mage's knife, for a Warded Mageborn. Sarra slid it into her own belt and rose shakily to her feet. This knife alone had as many kills as she had years.

Back inside Falundir's room, Elomar stood by the bed gazing down in mingled worry and awe at the girl who lay there, still as death. He flicked a glance at Sarra and shook his head.

"By Sparrow and Flame, she is a *power*," he murmured. "Her magic feeds only on itself, yet is never consumed. It grows, self-nourished."

"It sounds like nothing so gentle as Miryenne's Flame," Sarra said. "More like Caitiri's Fires. Elo, will she burn you up before Gorynel Desse comes?"

He shrugged. "Perhaps I can show her how to Ward herself—slide a note into her prison, as it were."

Sarra regretted that he'd heard her earlier remark. "Do what you can."

But she knew—and damned her instincts for the knowing—that Gorynel Desse must come soon.

When he did, it was from the Mage Academy—slung like a bean sack between Telomir Renne and that damned Minstrel.

III

"You made three incredibly stupid mistakes."

First Sword Gorynel Desse waved away Tarise and the cup of steaming tea she insisted he swallow, and resettled himself in bed. He'd been lying there for four solid days, sleeping off his battle with Auvry Feiran. This afternoon he felt well enough to sit up, summon Sarra, Alin, and Val to hear their story—and then lecture them on what they'd done wrong.

"First, you didn't question *why* you ended up on the wrong side of that waterfall, let alone *how*. I suppose you can be excused for lack of Magelore, and knowledge of how to sense such things. But that still doesn't excuse the ridiculous manner in which you simply accepted the change of location. Shut up, Valirion, I'm not finished. To answer the questions you didn't bother to ask yourselves, the 'how' of it is that you were led there by the most clever and subtle of spells—not worked on you, I might add, but at a distance on the very rocks of that tunnel. As for the 'why'—they knew you were there and wanted to trap you without a Ladder. Sheer dumb luck that you figured it out, Alin. And absolute imbecility to have made the attempt.

"Which leads me to your second mistake. Did you ever stop to think that there might have been Wards around that chimney Ladder in Captal Bekke's Tower? Or, worse, that it might have been destroyed? Or, worst of all, Alin Ostin, how I could possibly explain the attendant disasters to your Lady Mother?"

Alin cleared his throat. Desse speared him with a glance. He subsided.

"Third, you haven't even begun to wonder how Glenin Feiran got to Combel."

"By carriage, certainly," Val offered, sounding anything but certain.

The old Mage snorted.

"By Ladder?" Alin asked in amazement.

"Not any Ladder that *you* know, boy." Again he hitched himself straighter against the pillows. "I've never seen one, and up until now it's been only rumor and a few lines in the Archives. But there's a means of casting a Ladder onto silk or velvet—hell, onto plain old wool, as long as it's pure cloth—in magic and stitchery. It's pretty, it's portable, and it's just as good as the real thing. And Glenin Feiran has one."

"That's unsupported speculation," Sarra said.

"Then explain how she arrived at Renig one morning by ship, took the *Rose Crown* by force before nightfall, and the next day met you in that whorehouse?"

"Bower," Val corrected under his breath.

"Whorehouse," Desse repeated. "Which is not to say I'm not at least as fond of its charming mistress as you are. The carriage was from Renig, you say? Well, how many such rigs move back and forth around The Waste every year? Care to take a guess? One hundred? Two? She could have chosen it at a stable in Combel *because* of its origin, or it could have been coincidence."

"The Captal said nothing about a Ladder," Sarra pointed out.

"The Captal, may he prosper to a dull dotage, is no more immune to certain spells than you are—or *I* am. A Forgetting is one of the more complex, but recent memories are relatively easy to block. And that's just what was done to him, so Glenin Feiran could use this portable Ladder of hers to take him and my sister's granddaughter to Combel."

A trace of sorrow creased his face for a moment. Sarra had forgotten that Desse was so closely related to the Alvassys.

"I add," he went on severely, "that Glenin Feiran was in Ryka Court not three days ago—and she'd just be boarding a ship at Renig right now if there was no Ladder. I know for a fact—as does Alin—that there's only one Ladder in Combel, and it goes to Neele."

From whorehouse to sewer, Sarra thought. *Whatever ancient Mage created it, she had a dreadful sense of humor.*

"That's three," she told the old man. "I assume you're finished."

"No. The last item isn't a mistake, it's a potential disaster. You failed to bring Captal Adennos here with you."

"I judged it safer for him to remain in Combel."

"Who elected you to Venkelos' Seat last Wraithenday?"

Her face felt scorched by anger, but her voice was coldly controlled. "That will be enough, Guardian Desse. Tarise, if he won't swallow the medicine, stick a funnel down his throat and pour it in. Alin, Valirion, come with me."

She saw—and approved—the apprehensive glance the two young men exchanged. She did not especially like the little grimace of apology Alin directed at the Mage, but it was beneath her to notice it. She led the pair down a corridor crawling with children, most of them Mageborns and all of them intent on catching Tamsa's exhausted kitten. Sarra gave poor Velvet a sympathetic glance; she felt rather the same way, with everyone trying to track her down and make their individual problems her paramount concern.

Some of it she had gratefully shoved onto Tarise and Rillan: finding food, beds, blankets, and bathrooms, mainly—though she knew they did much more, if only to keep busy. More Mages and members of the Rising arrived every day, some by Academy Ladder, some overland from the coast, some from upriver or down. Bard Hall was the least damaged of all the great centers of learning at Ambrai, and even after so many years there were supplies enough to take care of several dozen people. The food was rather monotonous; beds there were aplenty, though the blankets all had holes; the bathrooms, praise be to whichever Saint interested Herself in sanitation, still functioned perfectly.

But they could not stay here forever.

Once Alin discovered Collan Rosvenir's profession (a fact learned from Val, who recognized him from a Cantratown tavern performance), he'd dragged the Minstrel off to wrangle over versions of the Ladder song. Not even Gorynel Desse knew all the Ladders at the Mage Academy—he'd been thunderstruck to learn of the one in Captal Bekke's Tower—and it was just possible that not all of them had burned. When Alin had one or two secure, he'd take the majority of the Mages and their families to safety.

They all wanted to know where of course, and when, and what they would do when they arrived, and what protection there would be, and so inevitably. This was why Sarra kept to Falundir's little suite of rooms near the Ladder; the instant she showed her nose elsewhere, people crowded around with endless unanswerable questions.

Thus her escort this afternoon. Alin and Val could look forbidding enough when they chose: Val had the height and build for it, and no one could match Alin for ice-eyed menace. Sarra's temper had been scraped raw enough by Gorynel Desse. She had little hope of retaining her composure if yet another frightened Mage made yet another demand for information.

Sarra was frightened, too. And she had no knowledge to give anyone, least of all herself.

Some of the Mages, in fact, knew more than she did about what was happening across Lenfell. Every known Ladder was now watched by Council Guards or Lords of Malerris or both. Many Mages had died trying to flee by Ladder from one place to the next; some of those here had gotten through only because their fellows bought time with their lives. Everyone with any connection at all to the Rising had been arrested. Some were being held over for trial. Some had died by "accident" in or on the way to prison.

Though much was known, much remained a mystery. The fates of Imilial Gorrst and Advar Senison, at sea with a cargo of books; of the Mages Alin had taken back from Combel to Neele (the Ladder was reported taken—she had little hope for their survival); of Lusira Garvedian and Lilen Ostin; of Mai Alvassy's sister and brother; of Tamos and Tamosin Wolvar, Ilisa Neffe, and Captal Adennos. Sarra would not think of any of them as dead until she had proof, but neither would she believe they were safe until they stood before her.

One bit of news had given her grim satisfaction: a bounty had been declared on Mai Alvassy. Val was incensed that his name did not appear on the warrant—until Alin, weak with relief that he wasn't mentioned either, pointed out that this might mean their mothers and families would escape notice. For now. What it meant to Sarra was that Glenin had been forced to accept the switch of identities, and "Sarra Liwellan" was officially dead.

Of the other dead she dared not think. It shamed her that she could not bring herself to be with Riddon and Maugir and Jeymi, weep with them, share their grief. Neither could she go into the room where Sela lay, deeply unconscious thanks to something Elomar had brewed up to prevent labor. Sarra had known Verald Jescarin. She had danced at their wedding. She had visited the cottage in Roseguard Grounds—

No. If she remembered Roseguard, and all the people who had lived there, she'd scream. The most horrifying news brought by the Mages was that Roseguard had been put to the torch.

She could not afford to think of that, nor of the dead and imprisoned all over Lenfell, nor of her own dead. She could do nothing about any of it. She could do nothing for Cailet, either, but Cailet was the one concern in her life right now that no amount of emotional or mental discipline could dismiss.

Cailet was, quite simply, losing her mind.

Sarra paused in the doorway and watched Alin enter the room. He was her measure: yesterday he'd taken ten steps before he paled and trembled. Today it was five careful paces, six—

His breath caught and he backed away.

Elomar Adennos unfolded from a chair by the bed. "Yes. It's worse."

"How do you stand being so close to her?" Alin whispered.

"The Wards are of my making." And that was all he would say.

"Wait for me outside," Sarra told her companions, and as Alin gladly closed the door she advanced to the bed. "I can't feel it."

"Your Wards are of Gorsha's making."

"So were hers—and they shattered."

"You are a spark. *She* is a firestorm." He gestured for her to join him in chairs by the cold hearth. "Yesterday I eased the walls a little. Within her—" He shook his head. "Hurt, anger, and most of all fear."

Sarra sat down, tucking half-frozen hands under her thighs. "She's still a child, Elo. She'll lash out at anyone in reach."

"She loves you very much. She sees you as the only person in the world who truly belongs to her."

Warmth seeped into Sarra's bones, and tears into her eyes.

"Yet . . . I regret, Sarra, but she cannot help but hate you for causing her this pain."

Cold again. So cold. She nodded dully. "I'd hate me, too."

"She'll understand that the fault wasn't yours."

"And hate Gorynel Desse instead. We'll have that in common."

A sandy brow arched. "Yours is not a face meant for bitterness."

"Mine was not a life meant to be bitter," she retorted. "Neither was Cailet's. Yet here we are."

"Nor was Glenin's."

"Now, *there's* a topic! What do you think she's doing right now? Gorynel Desse says she has a portable Ladder woven in cloth, a thing of legend that turns out to be real—by his interpretation of her movements, anyway. Where would the Malerrisi go next? And don't tell me to intuit her actions, Elomar, I was wrong about Longriding."

"Perhaps not. Perhaps she was persuaded otherwise. It doesn't matter now."

Sarra got to her feet and started to pace. "*She* doesn't matter. Cailet does. When can she have her magic?"

"Did I hear someone ask for a little music?"

Collan Rosvenir sauntered into the room, lute slung across his back and Tamsa's kitten sleeping on his shoulder. "Don't blame your pets for letting me in, Lady. I sent them off to help clean tonight's dinner."

"Alin and Valirion are not my 'pets'!"

"Whatever. As I was saying, we'll eat fresh fish tonight. Jumped right into Taig's net, or so he says. But I suspect it was innocent trust—long time since anybody's fished this stretch of the Brai. Hope you're in the mood for trout."

What she was in a mood for was to kick his perfect white teeth down his warbling throat. She remembered every nuance of their last encounter.

Elomar, however, had risen to welcome him. "I was hoping you'd find time today. Shall I take Velvet? I'm about to make my rounds."

"Tamsa lent her to me. Purring's nice harmony. Velenne knows, there's nobody else here who can so much as hum in tune." He snorted. "Bard Hall!"

The Minstrel crossed to the bed, carefully unhooking claws from his longvest. Gently, he placed the kitten near the curve of Cailet's neck. Velvet circled several times, burrowed under the quilt, and settled down to her interrupted nap.

"I'll be back in an hour," Elomar said. "You might stay and listen, Sarra."

She did. So—incredibly—did Cailet. The anguished frown smoothed from her face. Her lips softened. After a while she turned her cheek into the kitten's warm tawny fur. Sarra watched and listened and marveled.

Collan Rosvenir's was a voice in a Generation. He sang lullabies mostly, varied with a ballad now and then, but always in a deep, silken voice that soothed the hurt from Cailet's face—and even some of the hurt from Sarra's heart. When he paused at last to retune the lute, she rose from her chair to perch at the foot of her sister's bed.

"That was beautiful. Thank you."

One broad shoulder hunched and lowered dismissively, and a sidelong glance came her way from very blue eyes beneath wild coppery curls. "I'm better at singing *big* girls to sleep."

He waited politely for a retort she was incapable of uttering. At last he grinned.

"You just didn't stay around long enough last time to find out. I must say, I like you better with your mouth shut."

"The next time you open yours, it had damned well better to be sing!"

"Shh! You're disturbing the kittens." He played a ripple of notes like stream water dancing over smooth stones, and began another lullaby to repair the damage.

> *Come and lie you down, little one,*
> *The golden Sun's a-yawning,*
> *Ladymoon's quilt of silver stars*
> *Will wrap you 'round 'til morning. . . .*

His magic worked once more on Cailet. For Sarra, the spell was broken. *". . . true what they say about a Minstrels' hands!"* she heard his insufferable taunting voice say in memory. Well, she'd break his fingers for him some other time. He was doing Cailet too much good right now.

I'm a spark—she's a firestorm. She repeated Elo's characterization to herself, and knew that as desperately as she had sometimes wished for her own magic, she didn't want it if it meant this kind of pain. And it would end only when Gorynel Desse set her magic free. That particular argument was still ahead of her, but he was going to see things her way. Instinct didn't tell her that. Sheer stubbornness did.

Elomar returned, Tamsa at his heels. She reclaimed her kitten with tender hands, whispering, "Did Velvet help? Did she?"

Rosvenir nodded. "Even more than my music, *Domna*. Thank you."

"I'll bring her again tomorrow," Tamsa announced, and with a smile all around left the room.

Elomar murmured, "You have my gratitude, Minstrel."

Rosvenir got to his feet and stretched. He and Elomar were nearly of a height, though the Healer seemed taller for being so much thinner. It occurred to Sarra that Imi Gorrst would find much to admire in Collan Rosvenir, as would Agata Nalle: both of them liked their men big and lean and muscular.

With the thought of two friends—one certainly and the other probably dead—all her troubles descended once more onto her shoulders. Sarra turned her face away so the men would not see how she bit her lips.

Elomar escorted the Minstrel from the bedchamber, asked him to come back again tomorrow if he could, and shut the door firmly behind him. Given the time, Sarra regained control of herself. She wiped her eyes and met Elomar's gaze as he returned to the bed.

"You know, he's not a bad singer."

"He is the finest voice since Falundir." A tiny smile played about his mouth. "And you know it."

"I never heard Falundir—and I never will," she replied. Suddenly that tragedy did to her what the sight of Cailet and the thought of Imi and Agata—and Agatine and Orlin and Elom and Verald and all the others—had not. Maiming the greatest Bard who ever lived was the first of Anniyas's crimes, predating Ambrai's destruction, presaging all the rest. Sarra found to her horror that she was weeping uncontrollably against Elomar's bony chest.

"Past time, too," he murmured, smoothing her hair. "Let it go, Sarra. Let it all go."

Why did people always say that? she wondered furiously. For her, a "good cry" only resulted in a nose so swollen she couldn't breathe, sandpaper eyelids, a hideously mottled complexion, physical exhaustion, and emotional humiliation. Sarra *hated* to cry.

But cry she did. When she was spent, Elomar coaxed her to curl up at the end of the bed with a blanket around her. Trusting him as she trusted only Alin and Val—but glad neither had seen her this way—she fisted cold hands beneath her chin and closed her eyes.

All in all, a rotten way to learn how much other people mattered to her. Cailet must come first; her heart and the Rising demanded it. But as a leader of whatever would be left of the Rising, Sarra must think of others as well. As a leader. Letting them be important to her personally was why she'd cried. Just before she slept, she promised herself it wouldn't happen again.

12

At Half-Third the next morning, the eleventh day of St. Ilsevet's, Alin and Val escorted thirty Mages and their families to the Academy and took them through two previously unknown Ladders. They left well before dawn, and there was much grumbling at the earliness of the hour. Sarra was patient, reasonable, hiding annoyance that the very people who had complained of not leaving sooner now complained that they didn't feel safe leaving at all. She reassured them that Alin knew exactly where they were going and exactly what awaited them—in Gierkenshir and Domburronshir respectively, Ladders he knew were secure because he'd taken Val and Taig through each of them twice in the last two days. When skeptics—particularly the elderly Warrior Mage with the sharp tongue and sharper perceptions—spoke up, Sarra remarked that they were welcome to stay if they felt their personal Wards were good enough. Because precisely at Fifth, Gorynel Desse would begin his work with Cailet.

None stayed. Whether doubting a weary old man's ability to rein in such powerful magic, or merely reluctant to find out, they left the Academy. By Fifth they were in Gierkenshir or Domburronshir, and on their own.

Cailet's powers and predicament had become known last night. Two Prentice Mages, playing cards in a room six doors down the hall from hers, had suddenly been taken with horrific headaches, fits of shaking, and irrational anger that set them at each other's throats before a Scholar Mage could separate them. If Cailet could affect people—admittedly imperfectly trained—at less than two hundred feet while Warded, St. Miryenne defend every Mageborn within a mile if Desse lost hold of her.

And so the population of Bard Hall decreased to seventeen, of whom six were Mageborn. Telomir Renne, Alin, and Sarra had been strongly Warded in childhood by Desse himself. Elomar, who would stand ready to apply what Healing arts he could, spent the night in meditation designed to bolster his personal defenses. The battle would be between

Cailet's raw young power and Desse's seasoned, subtle knowledge, and Elomar's task was to help their bodies survive it.

Desse told Taig to banish everyone, non-Mageborns included, to the farther reaches of Bard Hall. Sarra told Taig to go to hell; she was staying. While they argued, the three Slegins helped Tarise and Rillan move Sela to another bed. Collan, already warned by Taig, had vanished with Tamsa and the kitten.

Thus only Falundir was present in the Ladder chamber at Half-Fifth when Ilisa Neffe and her husband Tamosin Wolvar brought Captal Lusath Adennos and Scholar Tamos Wolvar through the Ostin greenhouse Ladder in Longriding.

The first Sarra knew of it was Ilisa's wild-eyed, frantic arrival in the hallway outside Cailet's bedchamber. Still arguing with Taig, Sarra was nearly run over as Ilisa all but flung herself down the marble corridor.

"Where's Elomar?" the Mage gasped. "We need him, Sarra, where is he?"

"Why? Who's sick?"

"Tamos, the Captal, they—"

"Calm down," Taig advised, taking her arm to steady her. "Catch your breath. Did Geria kick you out?"

Ilisa shook her head, hair straggling around her face. "No, no, it wasn't your sister. In fact, your mother's in Combel."

He relaxed with a smug little smile. "So much for First Daughter."

Breathing more easily, Ilisa continued, "Lady Lilen told us to come here. Tamos never woke up, Taig. Saints know what Malerrisi magic did to him."

Sarra frowned. "But I thought the Captal's help—"

"He did—by getting us to Longriding by a Folding spell—"

"Wait." Taig eased her down onto the floor so she sat with her spine to the cold marble wall. "Another breath. Now. Tell it in order."

"Your mother came to Combel. She said it would be best for us to leave, the Guard had already been to Ostinhold looking for you and Alin. And Tamos needs a Healer Mage. The Captal cast the Folding spell, but halfway there he had some kind of seizure—his heart, maybe, he's an old man and not used to exerting himself either physically or magically." She paused, raked her hair from her eyes, and coughed.

"Sorry, it's just I'm so tired. . . . Anyway, at Longriding we got into the house and rested a night before using the Ladder. The Captal barely got us through. He needs a Healer Mage." She sagged back, looking in dire need of medical attention herself.

Sarra exchanged glances with Taig and said, "Ilisa, I'm sorry. Elomar can't be spared from helping Cailet and Gorsha. The other Mages are gone—Alin took them to safety hours ago. There aren't any other Healers available."

"Gorsha's here?" Ilisa pushed away from the cold marble. "Take me to him."

"I can't." Taig shook his head. "In fact, the sooner you get away from here the better. Cailet's magic keeps escaping. Any Mageborn in reach is in danger."

"What are you talking about? Who's Cailet?"

"That's a long story," Sarra said. "Taig, see what you can do for the Captal. You can tell her along the way."

Having rid herself of her watchdog, Sarra entered her sister's room—and wished she, too, had a wall behind her to prop her up. Cailet was draped like a corpse in a faded blue quilt, only her head free. Her face was ancient with pain and her square jaw was set as if against a scream.

In a cot beside the bed, Elomar's long body was also laid out as if for burning. His eyes were closed and his fingers were laced beneath his chin. Only the slow, controlled rise and fall of his chest indicated life. The rhythm of his breathing exactly matched Cailet's; Sarra felt her heart give a frightened thud as she realized he was breathing for her.

Gorynel Desse hunched at the edge of the bed, one hand buried in Cailet's pale hair and the other cradling his own skull as if it weighed a thousand pounds. He breathed in time with Elomar, too. The implications horrified Sarra.

Never had she felt so utterly useless. She was walled and Warded so thoroughly that she sensed not the slightest glimmer from the three powerful Mageborns, even though Cailet's face, Desse's posture, and Elomar's trancelike withdrawal shrieked of magic.

Silently, her own breathing matched to theirs, she pulled a chair to the other side of the bed. She ached to hold her sister's hand but didn't dare touch Cailet, or make any sound, or otherwise indicate her presence. If pressed to identify what she did during the next hours, she would have grudgingly admitted that she prayed. To Caitiri the Fiery-

Eyed, Sirrala the Virgin; to Telomar the Patient and Gorynel the Compassionate; to Miryenne the Guardian, to Rilla the Guide—even to Chevasto the Weaver as he had first been canonized: he who held all the beautiful, multicolored threads of life in his hands.

Sarra watched, Desse worked, Cailet trembled, and Elomar breathed for them all. Finally the old man's head lifted. The fingers twined in the girl's hair smoothed limp, disordered strands back into a sleek blonde cap.

"Ah, child, child," he murmured. Then, seeing Sarra across the bed, he managed a tiny smile. "She is everything I thought, and even more powerful besides."

"Too powerful?" Her voice felt raw, as if she'd been screaming.

He snorted.

"Be honest, Gorsha." This from Elomar, who was pushing himself upright. Sweat beaded his face and he looked one step from the death his posture had imitated, but there was a sort of weary victory in his eyes. "She almost got away from you a couple of times."

"Perhaps," he acknowledged. "But at least now she understands that she needn't run from me. That I'm trying to help."

"That you're freeing her magic," Sarra said. When Desse slanted a look at Elomar and received a shrug by way of a reply, Sarra sprang to her feet. "You *have* to! This may be the last chance!"

"Spare me the cliché, Sarra, it's unworthy of you."

"Not half as unworthy as jealousy of a power that outstrips your own!"

"You forget yourself!" He straightened as if a sword had been shoved down his throat. "I am First Sword of the Mage Guardians, answerable only to the Mage Captal."

"And *I* am Lady of both Ambrai and Sheve! Moreover," she added viciously, "all women of your own line being dead, by virtue of your sister's marriage to my grandmother's brother—"

"Sarra, don't," Elomar pleaded.

"—you are answerable to *me*," she finished.

"How *dare* you!" Desse roared.

"Spare me the cliché," Sarra retorted acidly. "You will do as I tell you, Guardian Desse."

"You have no right!"

"I have every right. If you have believed nothing else in your life, believe that I mean what I say."

There was the small, hollow sound of wood and strings knocking gently against a solid surface, and then the noise of sarcastic applause. Sarra whirled and nearly spat at the sight of Collan Rosvenir. His lute lay on a table near the door, freeing his palms to slap together over and over again.

"Amazing!" He sauntered in, still applauding. "Best impersonation of a Blooded First Daughter I ever saw!"

Why did this man constantly appear where he was neither wanted nor needed? And how much had he heard? Not the crux of it, or he'd react with astonishment not sarcasm. Sarra drew breath to order him out. He paused in mid-clap, mock terror contorting his features.

"Have I said something amiss? Was the performance meant to be—oh, that's right, you really *are* a Blooded First Daughter!" He leaned close and in a loud whisper said, "If you want some good advice, work on the costume. The attitude is perfect, but you can't do a really convincing job of it in torn trousers and a dirty vest."

Sarra took her desire to strangle him and shoved it into her mental box labeled LATER. "I don't know why you're here," she began furiously.

"No Minstrel ever needs an invitation, Lady. But as it happens, the Healer asked me to come sing again." Turning to Elomar: "How is she?"

"Progressing," Gorynel Desse replied.

The upward quirk of his brows politely doubted it. "Be that as it may, Taig Ostin says you ought to know one or two things. First, the Captal and the Scholar Mage aren't doing well."

"The Captal—?" Elomar looked at Desse in bewilderment.

"A pair of Mages brought them here a while ago," Rosvenir said. "One's unconscious—has been for days, as I understand it—and the other's got some sort of heart trouble."

The Healer swayed to his feet. "I must go to them."

"And I." Desse pushed himself upright. "Minstrel, be so kind as to sing to the girl until we return."

"You haven't heard the rest of it yet," he warned as he collected his lute from the table. "Val Maurgen saw campfire smoke coming from the Octagon Court."

"More refugees?" Elomar guessed.

Desse shook his head. "The only Ladder there leads to Ryka Court. No Mage would be fool enough—"

"*You* were," Rosvenir observed. He seated himself in the chair Sarra had vacated, crossed lean legs, and began tuning up.

"I should have said that it's a very public place at Ryka Court. It might be innocent, a fire lit by squatters."

"No," Sarra said abruptly. The three men looked at her. "They're searching for us."

"Sarra," Elomar began, "this is the last place—"

"Exactly. The very last place. Don't you see? It's the *only* place with Ladders enough to take Mages in and then take them to safety elsewhere. They couldn't get here by Telo Renne's Ladder. But there's one at Ryka that leads to the Octagon Court." She glared at the old man. " 'Last chance,' Guardian Desse!"

"They can't be certain," he replied, more to convince himself than as a statement of fact. "They'll have to move slowly, make sure they're not caught in any remaining Wards—"

"Then somebody had better set some!"

"And *you'd* better settle down," Rosvenir advised by Cailet's bedside. "You're making her restless."

"Go to the Captal," Sarra ordered the Mages. "Do what you can for him and Tamos Wolvar."

"Generosity worthy of a Saint," the Minstrel remarked.

She ignored him. "But you must finish with Cailet soon. Alin was barely able to get her through the Ladder a few days ago. She'd never make it now."

Elomar nodded and hurried from the room. Gorynel Desse paused a long moment. Then, as the first lilting notes were coaxed from the lute, he gave a mighty sigh and nodded.

"It shall be as you wish, Lady," he said.

"Yes," Sarra said. "It shall."

The Minstrel played song after song, seamlessly, without taking his fingers from the strings even once. This time she felt no enchantment in his music or his voice. All she could do was sit on the cot and stare at her sister's young/old face and worry.

An hour passed, perhaps two. Still Collan Rosvenir played and sang, and gradually Cailet relaxed. Sarra couldn't bring herself to express gratitude even with a glance. It had nothing to do with pride. It was as if she now breathed for Cailet, as if the very beat of her heart was linked to Cailet's, and if she took her gaze away for one instant she'd lose her only sister.

They won't find you, she vowed, wondering how Cailet would react when she understood exactly who "they" were. *It won't happen yet. One day you* will *meet them—I know it, I feel it—but when you do, it will be with your magic shining around you like a Ward of Caitiri's own Fire. . . .*

13

"Put out that damned fire!"

Auvry Feiran's order rang in Glenin's mind as well as in her ears. She flinched in every muscle. Her father used magic so seldom around her that she had forgotten how powerful he truly was.

Hurrying around a corner, she saw a young Malerrisi throw his cloak onto a pathetic pile of half-burned wood. Smoke billowing around him, he jumped onto the smothered remains of his fire and did an absurd little dance, stamping on the cloak, off-balance, a gawky teenager growing fast into adult height but not yet into adult grace. Glenin repressed a sudden ache of recognition: if she ignored the awkward movements, Chava Allard was very like his father's brother, Golonet Doriaz. They shared the same tawny coloring and long bones, and though the boy was but fourteen his talent already reminded many of his dead uncle.

His accomplishments did not, however, include Golonet Doriaz's self-command. He cringed before Auvry Feiran, who was twice his size and four times his age. The boy dug his heel into a protruding piece of charred wood, slipped, and went down in a sprawl of clumsy limbs.

"Cold, were you?"

"I—I'm sorry, I—" He coughed smoke from his lungs. "It won't happen again—"

"In this, you are correct." He raised his voice in a shout. "Lord Keviron!"

Darvas Keviron ran across the gravel and presented himself with so sharp a squaring of his shoulders that Glenin almost heard his bones snap. Squat and short like most of his Name, he was here because he was expendable; he had fathered no Mageborns, and indeed had fathered no children at all.

"Young Allard is your responsibility from now on. He doesn't sneeze without your permission, am I understood?"

"Perfectly, Commandant. Come with me, boy."

Chava scrambled to his feet. "I'm sorry!" he said one last time, and hurried in Lord Keviron's wake.

Glenin hid her twinge of annoyance at the lack of a Malerris title. Success here might just convince the First Lord to grant Glenin her coveted "Lady." But Auvry Feiran had once been a Prentice Mage. He would never hear himself called a Lord of Malerris.

He held out his arm to Glenin, and together they left a side hall of the Octagon Court for what had once been Lady Allynis's private garden. Glenin glanced up at the sky. Icily clear, painfully blue, no smoke ought to have stained its chill and crystalline beauty.

The thought took her by surprise; perhaps it was born of her happiness. Not because she had returned home—she cared nothing for that. It was what they would do here that exhilarated her. Victory sang along her nerves. Mage Guardians were dying all over Lenfell, but the real work would be done here by Glenin and Auvry Feiran, fifty Lords of Malerris, and a fourteen-year-old boy whose presence had been ordered by the First Lord himself.

Glenin knew why. Chava's burgeoning prowess had attracted notice, and the First Lord now wanted a child by Saris Allard. This honor done her son was a long step toward her bed. Or so he thought. Glenin thought otherwise. And so, she was sure, did Vassa Doriaz—who had not been included on this venture. While his adolescent offspring participated in the greatest action against Mage Guardians since the destruction of Ambrai, back at Malerris Castle the Fifth Lord's Scissors were snipping at thin air.

The First Lord's interference had enraged Anniyas—not because of Chava Allard, because of Glenin. But the command was binding: both father and daughter would go to Ambrai. So Glenin was here rather than confined at Ryka Court, and Anniyas's fury at the fact exactly matched Glenin's pleasure.

And—a thing she admitted only to herself—relief. Equally
secret was her understanding that one reason she was here was
to make certain Gorynel Desse did not escape again. This was
the final test of Feiran's loyalty to Malerris: the death of his
old teacher. No one had to tell her that. Nor was it necessary
to spell out the punishment for failure . . . or that she was the
one expected to administer it.

The Commandant of the Council Guard prodded an immaculate boot at the last smoldering bits of wood and fabric.
"That idiot boy," he muttered. "Please the Weaver, no one
saw the smoke."

"I can't imagine they'd be looking for it," Glenin said,
taking his arm. "In any case, it was only a few minutes. The
chances of their having a sentry posted are slim enough.
That someone looked exactly this way at exactly the right
time is outside probability."

" 'Chance' and 'probability' are delicate things, Glensha."
They walked the weed-strewn gravel path away from the
shell of the Octagon Court. "Betrayers, like St. Maidil.
There's a chance of failure. It's not probable, but Desse is
wily as well as powerful. If he escapes again, go at once to
Malerris Castle. The First Lord will protect you from
Anniyas."

"I won't need protection. We'll succeed, don't doubt it for
an instant." She picked her way carefully over the blackened
debris that had once been a trellis for climbing roses. "Have
the other Ladders here been inspected?"

"All are dead these many years." A tiny smile quirked his
lips. "When *I* light a fire, it stays lit."

They entered the garden room, where Gerrin Ostin had
long ago coaxed rare orchids into magnificence for his Lady's delight. All the windows were shattered now; bright sun
and a chill breeze washed in over collapsed shelves, broken
pots, and little iron braziers that had kept the sensitive plants
warm.

"We'll move on to the Healers Ward this afternoon,"
Feiran said.

"Healer Mages would go there first, I suppose," Glenin
mused. "The Ladders leading there would be familiar to
them—assuming those Ladders aren't in the same state as
these. But why can't we go directly to the Academy?"

"It's more convenient this way, my dear." He reacted to
her arched brows with another smile. "There was a Ladder

from the Ward to the Academy infirmary. Damage there wa
not as extensive as elsewhere, so I think it may very well b
alive. We can use it instead of climbing over all the rubble.

She nodded, accepting the explanation.

"It's not only that," her father added suddenly, seriousl
as if sensing that he must justify himself. "We need to se
cure all other possibly extant Ladders first. All those leadin
to the Academy are being watched at the other end. Anyon
who tries them will be killed. If Desse is there, Glenin, he'
trapped."

"Except for this one Ladder at the Healers Ward. I se
Father, what about Bard Hall? Surely it had Ladders."

"Only one I know of." He paused, then finished dryly
"To Ryka Court."

Glenin laughed. "And if the one to the Infirmary *is* avai
able, our appearance will be so sudden he won't have tim
to think, let alone escape!"

"Precisely."

"You know, after we're sure of all the other Ladders, w
can take the Academy pretty much at our leisure. No sens
making it look too easy—either to Anniyas or the Firs
Lord."

Gray-green eyes sparked with amusement. "You have
rather good grasp of tactics."

Glenin smiled back, thinking of a saying in the *Code c
Malerris:*

When you know what to do when there is something to
be done—that is tactics. When you know what to do
when there is nothing to be done—that is strategy.

Her father had learned tactics from Gorynel Desse. Unles
the old man was equally good at strategy, he and all th
Mages with him would be dead before the Equinox.

14

"They're dying," Elomar Adennos said wearily.

"You can't know that," Sarra Liwellan protested.

"I'm a Healer Mage. I know."

Collan softened the notes dancing from his lute, hoping to soothe the anguish that had entered with Adennos and Gorynel Desse. But every note he played sounded like a dirge.

True to First Daughter form, Sarra confronted the old Warrior Mage. "Can't you do something?"

"There is nothing to be done." He sank deeper into the chair, chin lowering to his chest. After a moment his head lifted fractionally and he looked at her from beneath bristling white brows. "Were Tamos' magic a thing of skin and flesh, I would say it had been burned to the bone. And just as flesh cannot survive such damage, neither can a Mageborn mind."

Col had heard the story from Taig—how the Scholar had faced Malerris magic, saving a dozen lives and sacrificing his own. Worthy of a ballad in tribute to such bravery; not for the first time since Verald Jescarin died, Col regretted that his brain was not as facile with words as his throat was with melodies, his fingers with strings.

Sarra Liwellan still wasn't finished. "What of the Capital?"

Elomar Adennos stared at his hands, as if in dull loathing at their uselessness. "While I examined him, his heart spasmed again. I *heard* it, Sarra. I heard death take another step into his body."

"He and Tamos have two days, perhaps three—no more," Desse finished.

After the briefest pause, the young woman said, "Very well. It's nearly sunset. If there's nothing you can do, you might as well get some rest."

Collan let his hands play what they would. He watched Sarra, wondering why this walking icicle had wept uncontrollably over the pitiable girl lying in the bed. He hadn't meant to spy, he'd merely come back for a dropped pick. But there she'd been, sobbing in Adennos's arms. He'd been forced to reconsider his judgment of her and this irritated him.

She went on, "Cailet's sleeping now, thanks to the Minstrel—" Though it was obviously acid on her lips to admit it. "—and you both need sleep as much as she. But the work must be finished tomorrow."

Collan stopped in mid-chord. "Anyone but Cailet is a waste of time, is that the way you see it?"

If that stung, she kept it to herself. "They can do nothing for Tamos Wolvar and the Captal. They have to do what they must for Cailet."

"Is she more important than—"

"Yes!"

"Yes," the old Mage whispered. Then, to Sarra: "Tomorrow?"

"Taig was here a little while ago. He's gone with Riddon and Val over to the Octagon Court. They took Ilisa along to spell them Invisible—I insisted. They need her and she needs something to do."

"Hmm. As I recall, she's fairly accomplished," Desse said. "She'll Ward them well enough so the Ward won't be felt."

"Mages can do that?" Collan asked.

"If I gave you a list of everything Mages can do, we'd be here until St. Rilla's Day."

"How about a list of what they *can't?*"

The First Sword ignored the sarcasm. "We know what Taig will find at the Octagon Court, of course."

"You may, but I don't," Col said.

Sarra gave an impatient shrug of one shoulder. "Evidence of a fire, and of a search. They came by Ladder from Ryka Court, by way of the Spiral Stair."

"Exactly who is 'they'?"

"Council Guards, Lords of Malerris—does it matter?"

"Damned right it matters. They'll expect to find us at the Academy, won't they?"

"A thorough search of the ruins and grounds will take perhaps a day. By tomorrow night at the latest they'll know—"

"—where we aren't," he finished. "But they won't stop looking. Y'know, this just keeps getting better and better."

"Sarra. . . ." Desse cleared his throat. "I may not be able to complete the work by tomorrow."

"I thought you said she trusts you now to help her."

"Yes. However, what I have in mind goes beyond your demand to give her her magic." He rolled the cup between his hands, not meeting her gaze. "Lusath Adennos is dying. So is Tamos Wolvar."

"I know, and I'm sorry, but what does this have to do with Cailet?"

He continued as if she hadn't spoken. "One is a Scholar whose prowess with Mage Globes is unequaled. The other is Capital."

"Their loss will be deeply felt, I—"

And then she stopped, as if instantaneously rendered stone: lips parted, black eyes glassy, angry flush still on her cheekbones. It seemed to Collan that she knew what hadn't yet been said, and the concept so appalled her that body and thought simply froze.

"They need not be lost," said Gorynel Desse.

Bewildered, Col asked, "Then there *is* something you can do for them?"

"No."

"Then what in the hell—"

"To rephrase," the old man said, "what they *know* need not be lost."

Elomar Adennos surged to his feet, outrage scrawled all over his lean unhandsome face. "No! You can't! She's seventeen years old!"

Desse shrugged. "Jonna Halvos was but twenty. Finsenn Girre was eighteen."

Collan glanced at the girl in the bed. Seventeen? She looked twelve. "Now, wait a minute," he began. "What are you talking about?"

"You *moron!*" Sarra Liwellan rounded on him with a fierceness that made him wish she'd stayed a statue. "They mean to make her *Capital!*"

15

Halfway to the Healers Ward, Glenin had understood her father's wisdom in seeking its Ladder as an entry to the Mage Academy. Auvry Feiran and the Council Guard had done their work to perfection in 951: the streets of Ambrai were chaos. Stone rubble, ash, and half-burned support pillars blocked progress through side avenues, and even the widest boulevards were clogged with ruined carts and carriages. Horses would have been useless, even if horses could be brought through a Ladder, for each pile of debris must be climbed or skirted on dangerous footing. Neither would horses have tolerated the stifling odor of smoke that clung to the air despite the breeze.

Glenin minded the stink. She minded even more the litter of human bones, picked clean by scavenger animals and bleached pristine white by seventeen summers of merciless sun. She did not look on them and think that perhaps this or that broken skeleton had been someone she had once known; she thought only of what Lady Allynis and Captal Garvedian had forced her father to do here. If not for those two stubborn, haughty women, she would rule now from the Octagon Court as Lady of Ambrai. During the slow progress across the city—waiting at intersections while scouts sought the easiest routes, perilously climbing over rubble, sliding between ash mountains and wobbly walls—she began for the first time to realize how much work would be required to bring Ambrai back to life. *Damn Grandmother, and damn the Captal,* she thought furiously as an unsuspected splinter struck right through her leather glove. *It's too bad they died before I could order them to clean up the wreckage they're responsible for! On their knees, with their own hands!*

At length she and the other Malerrisi reached the naked stone struts of the Healers Ward dome. The world-famous stained glass "Education of St. Feleris" that had once glowed above was now strewn thickly on the floor. At noon, the pieces might yet shimmer; at dusk, they were as dead as the rest of the city. But they were still dangerous to walk on, and Glenin was tempted to conjure a small Globe to see by. Her father's earlier reaction to Chava Allard's little Warming fire caused her to keep her magic to herself.

They could not begin their search until tomorrow's dawn. Any light might be seen, if the Mages were watching. Auvry Feiran had explained that seeking whatever Ladders might still be here and functional might be sensed by the enemy, but this couldn't be helped. Any Ladder not known to and reserved for the exclusive use of the Lords of Malerris must be found and destroyed.

And for this, they would need fire.

The Malerrisi ate on their feet—a cold meal, for even a spell of Warming might be detected, and a hurried one, for it would be dark soon and light was forbidden as well. As they swallowed bread, sausage, cheese, and wine, Auvry Feiran gave his orders. One Lord would stay here for each Ladder found, and when fire was seen at the Academy, they would set fires here. It might be that the Healers Ward had no extant Ladders but the one to the Academy Infirmary, and even that might be dead. But just as Ladders all over Lenfell were being watched for fleeing Mages, any still here must also be taken care of.

Securing the Healers Ward might take a few hours, or it might take all day. But no one would go to the Academy until tomorrow night at the very earliest. Surprise would be all the greater for the Battle Globes blazing in darkness immediately on arrival from the Infirmary Ladder.

There were no comments and no objections. A Lord of Malerris Auvry Feiran would never be, but Commandant of the Council Guard he had been for seventeen years: his handiwork was all around them. Further, friend and student of Gorynel Desse he had been from the age of sixteen to the age of forty; no one knew the old Warrior Mage better.

The Malerrisi dispersed to a series of round antechambers in which the sick had been treated long ago. Glenin and her father stayed apart from the others, on watch, huddled in their cloaks against the cold that replaced the dying sun.

"You must be frozen," he said softly, drawing her against his chest and wrapping his cloak to enfold her. "You don't have to sit up with me, you know."

"I want to." She snuggled close, tucking her head under his chin as she had when she was a little girl. "Pity we couldn't Fold the distance from the Octagon Court."

"No one could have done it. Too much debris on top of the paving. Try to sleep, Glenin."

She shut her eyes, feeling safe and protected, if not quite warm. "Father?"

"Yes, dearest?"

"Anniyas told you to bring back their heads, didn't she?"

"She vowed to have the Captal's and Desse's, or mine."

"Yours is far too handsome—and useful!—where it is."

"My thanks for the compliment, Lady," he replied, amused. "Most women would've stopped at 'handsome'!"

"Most men would've settled for it. But not you. Father, may I ask a favor?"

"Anything you like, Glensha, that's in my power to give you."

"It's not that much. You can have their heads. I want the Liwellan girl's."

"A very pretty head," he mused. "And clever. But not useful?"

"She has no magic, and I find her annoying."

"My darling, you may kill her or keep her for a pet, whatever you like. I'll tell the others that she's yours."

"Thank you, Father," she said, and fell contentedly asleep.

16

"They mean to make her *Capital!*" Sarra cried.

Elomar spoke coldly into the short silence. "I refuse to countenance this. She's only a child."

"She is all we have," Desse replied.

"With no training beyond what you gave her—and that only vague theory, not true knowledge."

"What she receives from the Captal and Tamos Wolvar will remedy that."

"Or drive her mad! I will not see this done to her!" Elomar finally and spectacularly lost his temper, flinging his winecup to the floor. The shatter of cheap pottery made Sarra flinch. Even the Minstrel gave a start of surprise.

Unmoved, Gorynel Desse said, "She is all we have—but

she is also the *best* we have ever had. It is her share to become Captal. It has been so, always."

Sarra's knees buckled. The Minstrel caught her before she fell. Shaking him off, she made it to the bed and gripped the scarred oak post with both hands. Of all she had ever intuited about what she and Cailet and Glenin might symbolize, she had never guessed that power and circumstance and—according to Desse—fate itself would cast Cailet as Mage Captal.

But it was so obvious—wasn't it? Glenin, born to become Lady of Malerris, adept at malign and manipulative magic. Cailet, destined to become Mage Captal, to oppose and counter and check Glenin's power. Sisters by Blood; enemies by ancient design. And Sarra . . . what was her lot? The power that came of land and wealth and position; political influence, surely; First Councillor, perhaps?

She felt sick. She and Glenin had chosen their own paths. But Cailet—

Desse's attention was fixed on the Healer. "I am still First Sword and the only Senior Mage left. I tell you now that this girl will be the next Captal. Mage Guardian, must I remind you of your duty?"

"*Fuck* his duty," Collan Rosvenir snarled. "Why don't you ask those two old men if they'd prefer to die sooner instead of later? But you can't, can you? Safe enough there! Neither one lucid enough to understand! Is it their *duty* to commit suicide? Or yours to murder them?"

"Stay out of this," Desse warned.

"What about the girl?" Rosvenir demanded, and Sarra swung around to stare in amazement. "Can't ask her what she wants, either! So you'll make the decision for her—*just like a Lord of Malerris!*"

"Silence!" the old man thundered.

Minstrel, I may have misjudged you. Sarra put steel into spine and speech. "Truly told," she said to Desse, "if you do this, you are no better than they."

Very blue eyes slanted around, narrow with speculation and then sparking with grim approval. "You tell him, Lady!"

"Do none of you understand?" Desse climbed painfully to his feet, ragged robe trembling with the tremor in his old bones. "If the Captal's Bequest is lost, the Mage Guardians will wither and die. There will be no one to stand against the Malerrisi. No one! Cailet must become Captal—be *made*

Capital, as it has been since the Founding." He turned to Elomar. "You know how."

He turned white to the lips. "I've never—"

"But it's part of the Healer Mage's training. You're the only one who can keep us all alive long enough. I have never begged anything of anyone in my life, but I beg you now, Healer Mage. If you do not do this, all that we are will be lost forever."

Elomar went very still for a long moment. Then his stricken gaze sought Sarra's. "He's right—I despise him for it, but he's right."

"No!" she exclaimed. "You can't do this to her!"

"He's right," he repeated woodenly. "If I refuse, all that we are will—"

"You're out of your mind!" Rosvenir shouted. "You said it yourself—she's nothing more than a *child!*"

Elomar bent his head and said nothing.

"She is all we have." Gorynel Desse let out a quavering sigh. "The Captal will understand. And Tamos—he is my old friend, and I know what he would say. His knowledge, matched to Cailet's power—"

"That's all you care about," the Minstrel said in disbelief. "Power."

The First Sword regarded him levelly. "Do you want to die? Or to live knowing that Agatine and Orlin and Verald died for nothing?"

Rosvenir's eyes closed for an instant in pain. Then he glared at Desse and said expressionlessly, "You motherless, murdering son of a Fifth."

The old Mage nodded. The Minstrel snatched up his lute and strode out, slamming the door behind him.

"You are, you know," Sarra said. "A murderer."

"And no better than a Lord of Malerris. Yes, I know that, too." He sank back down into his chair. "If it affords you any comfort, I don't doubt that my Wraith will spend all eternity in agony because of it. Captal Adennos knew what would happen when it came his time to die. Tamos would not begrudge his lifetime of knowledge living past his death. Of these things I am certain. But that changes nothing. I *am* about to become a murderer."

"Of my own will, I am your accomplice," Elomar said quietly.

Sarra murmured, "And I."

Desse glanced over at her. "You have nothing to do with this."

She gripped the wood tightly. A splinter dug into one palm. "I want Cailet to have such power. She must become Mage Captal."

For her sisters, when they met—as they must—must meet as equals.

17

Collan snapped the case shut on his lute, muttering under his breath. Council Guards or Lords of Malerris or a gathering of misplaced Wraiths could be roaming Ambrai, he didn't care. He was getting out of here. Now. Tonight. He would not be party to killing a couple of harmless old men and making some innocent girl into High and Mighty Captal—probably kill her in the process, too, and that damned old Mage with her.

And then *all* of them would be dead for nothing.

He'd take Jeymi with him. Riddon and Maugir, too. And maybe her Blooded Liwellan Ladyship—she'd turned out to be all right, more or less. Hell, they could all come with him if they wanted.

But ... Sela wasn't going anywhere except to a birthing chair. And there was poor little Tamsa. ...

He gave up stuffing clothes back into his journeypack. Who was he trying to fool? They all left together or nobody left at all. He was trapped. Everyone was. That was what getting mixed up with Mages and the Rising did. Got you trapped. Probably got you killed, one way or another.

He glanced up as the candle flame flickered. All the rooms they inhabited were interior, with no windows to show the searchers precisely where to look. No mistakes of careless fire here. But the lack of a view made Col feel caged.

The gentle draft of the opening door had caused the flame to dance. Sarra Liwellan stood there. She didn't look trapped. She looked shackled by invisible chains.

"They're going to do it, aren't they?" Col asked.

She nodded.

He thought about accusing her of allowing them to do it, then thought better of it. What real power did she have? Desse could simply spell her to sleep or something. What a world.

"Have you eaten?" he asked instead. When black eyes widened beneath delicately drawn brows, implying that she couldn't even think about food at a time like this, he added, "If you're going to watch over her, you'll need your strength. That means dinner and a nap. Come on."

"You're not used to being around people like me, are you?" The tiny smile hovering around her lips did not mock him.

"I'm a Minstrel. I'm around you Bloods all the time."

She took two steps to his one to keep up with him down the hall. "You really don't order women about, you know. You make polite suggestions."

"Oh, I can do that, too." He sketched a bow as he walked. "Lady, might it be of use to your health and comfort to partake of a little nourishment?"

"A bit overdone, but not bad."

"Takes too long. I wanted to know if you'd had dinner, so that's what I asked. Ceremony's for show. It's not practical." His stomach, always practical, rumbled eagerly at the delicious scent wafting down the hall. Someone had gone fishing again today.

"Sometimes ceremony—manners, some people call it—is all that keeps us from each other's throats."

"Maybe," he admitted. "But if I'd minded my manners the first time we met, I'd probably be dead now." He saw the memory flare in her sudden upward glance, and grinned. "If I let you kick me in the ass again, will we be even?"

"Not even close!" But a corner of her mouth quivered. "Did you ever get tracked down on the attempted rape charge?"

Anger stirred even at this late date. "I spent the rest of that year dodging any Council Guards I saw."

"Good." She gave him both dimples—on purpose, he saw in her gleeful eyes.

Deciding that sticky-sweet deserved sticky-sweeter, he smiled his most charming smile and asked, "Did you ever stop wishing I'd taken you with me?"

Any other woman of Collan's vast experience would have

shouted, slapped him, or stormed off. Sarra Liwellan met him look for look and replied, "Did you ever stop wishing you had?"

She swept gracefully in front of him to enter the common room first, as if he'd minded his manners and allowed her to precede him. All he could do was grind his teeth and follow.

Taig had set the room up as a kind of kitchen-dining area, with braziers for cooking and a motley collection of tables and chairs. Bard Hall had escaped the worst of Feiran's Fires; it rose on its own hill in the middle of a quarter mile of open parkland. Long-ago Bards had built their refuge for silence and solitude. Ambrai had gradually spread out all around the Hall, yet it retained much of its isolation— probably due to the eerie quiet of the dead city. This isolation had not spared the newer brick-and-timber buildings, but the main Hall was relatively unscathed.

So here there was comparative comfort, with beds enough and food enough, though the latter was monotonously de-canted from glass jars in the cellar. That cellar also yielded some very good wines, and what the meals lacked in variety was compensated for by vintages that had aged undisturbed here for over seventeen years.

As he looked around for an empty seat, Collan realized that Ambrai had died probably about the time Cailet Rille had been born. He himself had been twelve or thirteen, and . . . and . . .

He stopped before a headache could even threaten.

Taig crouched near a brazier, turning a succulent fish on the grill. He smiled when he saw them, and said, "Saved this one for you. But I thought I'd be taking a tray to Cailet's room. Is she all right?"

"For the moment," Sarra replied. "Send half of that any-way. And while you're there, make sure Elo and Desse get some sleep."

"As my Lady commands," he said. "I've got some news for you. Imilial Gorrst is here."

"Imi? Holy Saints, where?"

"She and her father just finished eating. They're off to bed—and they need it, believe me." Deftly slicing the fish, he forked portions onto two plates and held them up. "Here. Beets and beans on the table over there. Help yourselves."

Col hated beets only slightly less than he hated beans. He found a wine bottle and a glass, juggled them and his plate on the way to a chair, and applied himself wholeheartedly to the meal.

With Sarra and Taig seated just behind him, he had no choice but to listen to their conversation. Who Imilial Gorrst and her father were, he neither knew nor cared. But he was impressed despite himself at the tale of their travels to Ambrai.

". . . missed him at Renig. I don't know how he did it, with Malerrisi crawling all over the place, but he did. He stole a boat and sailed it alone across Blighted Bay—"

"Kanto Solingirt is almost eighty!"

"Tell *him* that!" Taig chuckled. "After he got across, he stole a horse and went overland to the Brai River. Then he stole *another* boat from a village dock and drifted downstream. He saw Imi just outside town yesterday, and they came in together this evening. I tell you, Sarra, he acts as if all he'd done was go for a stroll!"

Col wished he had half the old man's energy.

"Minstrel Rosvenir," asked Tarise Nalle, "can you spare a drop or two from that bottle for a thirsty woman?"

"I'll gift you with a whole glass, Lady," he replied, and poured her cup full to the brim.

"My thanks, but as my husband will tell you, I'm no lady," she said with a smile, and returned to her seat.

Taig was now in the middle of another tale. This one, by the tone of his voice, made for less happy telling.

". . . sailed to Pinderon with no one the wiser. They sent the books by caravan to friends in Cantratown. Imi is almost certain they'll be safe until we can claim them."

"After all we went through to get them, I hope so! But what about Advar? Isn't he here, too?"

"No. I'm sorry, Sarra."

Her voice was small and soft with grief as she said, "Tell me."

"After hearing what happened at Roseguard and why, they knew to come to the Academy. Somewhere between Pinderon and Ambraishir, a sailor fell from the rigging and broke both legs. Healer Senison did what he could without revealing himself—but the injuries were too extensive. He had to use magic, Sarra."

"And they caught him at it," she said quietly.

Another brave man—and a damned fool, like the Scholar Mage, Collan thought. *What is it with these people, anyway?*

"It was a different ship, he wasn't posing as Imi's husband anymore. They pretended they'd only met in Pinderon. But she was suspect just the same. She couldn't save him, Sarra. She had to denounce him. One of them had to survive. Only they knew about the books."

"How did he die?"

"You don't need to—"

"How did he die, Taig?"

Collan, who didn't especially want to hear, gave her full marks for her own kind of courage.

There was the sound of a large and hasty gulp of wine. "By the sword. Quick and clean. Imi demanded it. They wanted to throw him overboard to drown. But she said she'd heard steel was the only sure way to kill a Mage."

"I . . . understand."

Collan was damned if *he* did. Self-sacrifice was expected of parents when their children were endangered; although he couldn't find even the rudiments of such an emotion in himself, he recognized it as simple practicality. But to give your life to save a woman? Moreover, a woman who told your killers how you ought to die?

Well, maybe he could understand that much. Drowning wasn't his idea of an appealing death. Straight through the heart with a sword was marginally less awful; as Taig had observed, it was quick and clean. But as far as Col was concerned, living was the only sane option. Selecting the least objectionable way to die from a list of possibilities wasn't something he'd ever thought about. If the Saints were kind, he wouldn't have to.

Sarra and Taig rose then, dinners only half eaten. Understandable, after that conversation. Col wasn't enthused about finishing his own, but the fish really was too good to waste. He washed a bite down with more wine, emptying the cup, and bent to retrieve the bottle. As he straightened, he heard Tarise gasp and say, "No, don't come in here!"

Wondering who among them might be forbidden a share of the communal meal, Col leaned around to see past Taig and Riddon. It was nobody very impressive, just a thin, dark-skinned, middle-aged man with brilliant blue eyes. He didn't even look like a Mage, until Col met that shining sky-blue gaze.

And agony exploded in his skull.

18

Heavily dosed and hastily reWarded, Collan Rosvenir lay senseless on a cot inches too short for him. Sarra watched as Gorynel Desse pushed himself to his feet and rubbed his eyes.

"Will he be all right?" she asked.

"Elomar does excellent work. Mine is even better." But it sounded forced, and he looked two steps away from collapse.

The Healer Mage stepped forward to tip a little more of the potion down the Minstrel's throat. It had been supplied by Riddon Slegin, of all people—a circumstance not yet explained to Sarra's satisfaction. She opened her mouth to ask, but Desse suddenly swayed on his feet. Elomar caught him, and Val half-carried the old man out the door.

The two Mages were beyond the limits of their strength—and Cailet and Captal Adennos and Tamos Wolvar must still be dealt with. Sarra clamped her teeth together against a formless, useless cry.

Elomar stretched out on the other bed, feet protruding over the edge as the Minstrel's did. "I've got to get some rest," he muttered. His body agreed, it seemed; he shut his eyes and was asleep in one minute flat.

Sarra fixed on Riddon as her only source of information. Taking his arm, she steered him into the hallway. "I want to know what's going on here, Risha." It was an indication of too much time spent with scandalously independent males that she tacked on, "Please." It was an indication of the manner of his raising that the word took him by surprise. And she didn't know *what* it meant that she disliked the reaction.

"Someplace private?" he suggested, glancing up and down the hall.

"My room."

Her suite at Roseguard was—had been—the epitome of elegance and comfort. Her chamber at Sleginhold was—and, she hoped, remained—as comfortable in a charmingly rustic way. Her bedroom at Bard Hall was the size of a closet. Six feet by four, it boasted a cot with two blankets and no sheets, and a wobbly chair. A water basin nestled precariously in a wall niche not quite deep enough to hold it, where a statue of St. Feleris the Healer had probably once stood.

Riddon lowered himself gingerly into the wooden chair, catching his balance as the bad leg tilted him sideways. Sarra sat on the bed and searched his face. This eldest of her little brothers had always presented himself as careless and carefree, a rich and privileged Blood with no more thought in his head than what to wear to the next Saint's Day Ball. There was much more to Riddon than that, though few knew it. Now there could be no more pretense. He had seen his parents die, and one of his brothers; he had battled a squadron of Council Guard and a Malerrisi-trained Mageborn whom swords could not touch; he had lost his home and everything he knew. At twenty-one, he looked forty.

"Tell me," Sarra said, her voice gentle.

"Collan's Mageborn."

"What?"

"Well, I think so, anyhow. I mean, what else could it be? He's Warded, like you. And that girl, Cailet—Sarra, who *is* she? Why is she so important?"

"Later," she said, with no intention of explaining more than the rudiments. "I want to know what you know about Collan Rosvenir."

So he told her how the man had arrived at Roseguard bearing a portentous message, and been an unwilling guest, and been knocked over the head by Verald Jescarin—presumably at Desse's order—before they left through the Ladder.

"Which doesn't make any sense unless he *is* Mageborn," Riddon said. "The rest of us can go through Ladders without any trouble, but an uneducated Mageborn wouldn't know what to do even though he had the magic to do it with, so it'd be more difficult for the Mage working the Ladder."

She couldn't disagree with his analysis—though it revealed that he knew more about Magelore than she, which surprised her. Alin had discovered Sarra's Wards the first time he took her through a Ladder. Desse might have anticipated problems with Rosvenir, and precluded them by a well-timed knock on the head.

"While we were on Ryka," Riddon continued, "Father

gave me a bottle and said keep it handy at all times. He had one, and I think he gave Tarise another. If Col showed any signs of pain or passed out suddenly, I was to give him a swallow of medicine. I don't know what's in it. And I don't know why seeing Bard Falundir did that to him. I'm sorry, Sarra, I'm not much help."

She thought for a while, picking at the frayed edge of a blanket. Then: "I think you're right, and he *is* a Warded Mageborn. I've heard that sometimes the Wards have to be set so strongly that when they're—oh, attacked, I guess, by what they're supposed to Ward against—it causes the person great pain." She'd done more than hear about it; she'd seen it in Cailet's tortured face.

"We're probably not supposed to know any of this."

"Probably not. Risha, how are you doing? And Maugir and Jeymi—there hasn't been any time, I'm sorry I haven't—"

"It's all right. You've got more important things to do. Don't worry about us, Sarra."

"I do, though," she murmured.

"You're not our mother." He grimaced. "I didn't mean that the way it sounded. Besides, in a way you kind of *are,* aren't you? All the Slegin lands are yours now, and governing Sheve." A wan smile touched his lips. "Not to mention governing *us.* I promise the Slegin boys won't be a worry to you, Lady."

"Riddon Slegin, if you *ever* call me that again, I'll—sweet Saints, what was that?"

The high-pitched screech echoed once more through the hallway, closely followed by a long, plaintive howl.

"Tamsa's kitten and Jeymi's puppy," Riddon said. "They're either fighting or somebody stepped on both of them at once."

"That's not what it sounds like. It's—" Sarra gasped as white-hot pain lanced through her skull. She felt Riddon's hands on her shoulders, holding her upright. Then the pain was gone, leaving her with pounding heart and sweat-slicked skin.

"Sarra? What's the matter? Sarra!"

"I'm all right. It's gone." She rested her forehead against his arm, breathing deeply. "I've never felt—if that was even a hint of what Rosvenir felt—"

"Are *your* Wards falling apart?" he asked worriedly.

"No. At least, I don't think so." She straightened up. "But someone's using powerful magic."

"Or Cailet Rille's got loose again. Sarra, who *is* she?"

"The next Mage Captal," she replied grimly. "And if that was any indication, it may be happening right now."

It was not. What the lightning agony indicated had been guessed by Riddon: Cailet's magic had surged dangerously.

"The interior casing is gone," Elomar told Sarra when she arrived outside Cailet's chamber. "Now she fights exterior Wards."

Inside, Desse was struggling once more to contain her enormous power—so potent in that single burst that it had even touched the two terrified animals.

"But she doesn't know how," Sarra said. "So she's lashing out, trying to find a weak spot. And did, a few minutes ago."

"Yes. Neither Gorsha nor I will get the sleep you promised us. We must begin soon."

"Riddon," she said over her shoulder, "find Taig. Bring the Captal and Scholar Wolvar here at once."

He hesitated, frowning. "Sarra, they're both very sick. Wouldn't it be dangerous to move them?"

"Bring them, please." She was now Lady of his Name, though they shared not a single drop of Blood. He obeyed. She thanked Agatine and Orlin for raising dutiful, mannerly sons—and once more was confused by her own annoyance.

"What about the Minstrel?" she asked Elomar.

"Recovering."

"Him, or his Wards?"

Elomar arched a brow. "You guessed?"

"Well, it's obvious," she said, not mentioning that it had taken Riddon's explanation to make her realize it. "He's Mageborn."

"No, he is not."

"Elo, don't story me as if I was still Tamsa's age!"

"Collan Rosvenir is not Mageborn."

"But—the Wards?"

"Ask Gorsha."

At long last she remembered her lengthy list of issues she'd intended to discuss with the First Sword. Trivial things, now. No, she corrected, they *were* important. Would become important to her again. Like other people. It was all in the timing.

"Elo . . . why Bard Falundir? It was sight of him that caused the pain."

"That, Lady, I may not say," he replied formally, and when she frowned and drew breath to protest he held up his hand in the sign that meant Mage-Right.

She might have argued, had not the door eased open to reveal Gorynel Desse. He leaned heavily against the frame, bleary-eyed and nearly spent.

"That was . . . close." His voice was a raw wound. "It must be tonight."

Timing. There was no time left.

"Bring on my victims," he muttered. "And may Venkelos the Judge show mercy to me."

Sarra surprised herself by saying, "And Gorynel the Compassionate watch over us all."

19

". . . rather hasty patch job, but it ought to hold."

Collan figured he ought to wonder who was talking and what she was talking about, but couldn't work up much enthusiasm for it.

"Don't worry. Guardian Desse says he'll recover."

It occurred to Col that it was himself she was talking about, and curiosity roused enough to pose a query: Just what was he expected to recover *from?*

Another voice, deeper but just as female, said, "You'd better leave, old friend. He mustn't see you—and he may wake any minute now."

Got news for you, domna *whoever-you-are,* Col thought, trying to open his eyes so he could see whoever it was he wasn't supposed to see. He heard a door closing just as his eyes were opening, and cursed inwardly.

What he did see dismayed him. Tarise Nalle's was one of those faces that didn't take stress well. Collan found himself resenting events that had marred her tawny-gold prettiness. Neither could he help contrasting her with Sarra: the fatigue-bruised eyes, the strained thinness of the lips, the tension in shoulders and neck, all were identical—but where Tarise was made haggard by exhaustion and sorrow, Sarra had seemed refined by it, as metal is purified by fire. Perhaps "redefined" was a better word, his Minstrel's mind mused, drawing on a thousand songs and finding none of them adequate to Sarra Liwellan.

Which was, he decided, just about the stupidest thought he'd ever had in his life.

Shifting his muscles to judge the feel of sheet, blanket, and what he lay on, he found things pretty much as he expected: he was tucked in bed right and proper as a newborn babe, and just as naked. A rush of anger and humiliation finished waking him up.

"Where the hell is my shirt?"

Tarise let out a little yelp. "Holy Saints! Don't *do* that!"

"So. You're the famous Collan Rosvenir. How do you feel?" The second woman walked into his line of sight. Tall, square-jawed, and wide-browed, though her garments were tattered nearly to rags she carried her impressive strength—and her sword—with a supple feminine grace.

"I'm fine," he told her. "And I'm getting out of here."

"You don't even know where 'here' is," Tarise said.

"Settle down," the other woman advised. "You're not going anywhere."

"Sorry, *domna,* wrong answer. Where's my shirt?"

She folded her arms. Collan didn't bother staring her down. He flung back the blanket, stood up, and looked around.

"You won't find it."

"Then I'll do without."

"Better give it to him, Imilial," Tarise said with a sigh. "He looks all right to me." A sudden sly smile took all the strain and fifteen years from her face. "*Very* all right, in fact."

"I'd noticed." Imilial eyed Collan. "Interesting scenery."

Col grinned back. "Better after a wash."

"Oh, I don't know. The rugged, day-old-beard look has a certain appeal."

"A lady of rare discernment. My shirt, please?"

"Under the bed."

He didn't crouch; he bent from the waist, knowing they watched his bare backside. They watched while he dressed, too. Decently covered—and grateful that neither woman even glanced at Scraller's mark on his shoulder, let alone commented on it—he gave them a low bow and asked, "Which way to breakfast?"

"Lunch. It's past Eighth." Tarise smiled at his reaction. "You needed the sleep. It's been a rough week."

Nothing wrong with me that a good night's sleep didn't cure. The reassurance came smoothly. He accepted it without wondering why his slumber required monitoring by two women who almost certainly had better things to do.

"The famous Collan Rosvenir," the older woman repeated musingly.

He bowed again. "You may believe everything they say about me."

"Taig praises you as the very model of masculine modesty," she said, straight-faced.

"One of you is a liar, and as I never doubt the word of a lady—especially a lady wearing a sword—it must've been Taig."

"Oh, you're all they say, all right," she responded. "Go get fed and watered, Minstrel."

He did, and afterward lolled outside in the surprisingly warm winter sun, enjoying the silence. Rested, relaxed, with other people's problems as remote as the Wraithenwood, he lacked only his lute to make the afternoon perfect. He considered fetching it, but decided too much energy was involved. He lazed away one hour, then two, until Taig intruded with the news that Sela Trayos was in labor, and this time it would stop only when her child was born.

20

She stood in the center of an expanse of flat black glass, like a mirror of obsidian stretching horizon to horizon, reflecting the occasional swirl of grayish mist in the white sky. She looked down and saw her own face in the blackness: a thick cap of white-blonde hair falling forward to frame sharp bones and a wide mouth and eyes as black as the mirrored surface itself—shining eyes, avid with hunger and flashing silver with need.

Need for magic. For knowledge. For power.

Magic was burning in her eyes, demanding knowledge, Magelore, the words and means to burn even more brightly and light this world of black and white and shadow-gray—demanding to transmute itself into power, the ultimate goal of magic and knowledge.

But to fashion that alchemy, she must feed her hungry magic with knowledge.

And she was alone here. Monumentally alone.

Anger was first, easier to admit than fear. She ran from both, bootheels splintering the mirror, a brittle music of flight.

Behind her a woman's voice cried out. She stopped, whirled, and from a fissure in the glass a gout of gray mist roiled Wraithlike, resolving into the figure of a woman.

Small, slender, golden-haired, black-eyed, shouting defiance to someone unseen: *Whatever* you *may call Auvry Feiran,* I *will call him* mine!

The mist obscured her for an instant. When she appeared again, she was older, desperate, head thrown back and cropped silken hair wild around her cheeks, crying out in anguish: *No! I won't let you take Glenin! You can't! She's* my *daughter, my Firstborn—*

Again gray haze surged up from the crevasse; again it parted to reveal the woman. Wrapped in a black cloak, one hand extended down and curled as if around a child's hand, she said: *Hush, Sarra! We must hurry, my darling, Guardian Desse is waiting for us.*

When next the cloud thinned, the woman lay on the black glass. Exhausted, bereft of physical endurance and emotional strength, she turned her head away and shut her eyes and said: *No. I don't want to see her. She can never be my child, my daughter—I don't want to look at her!*

The mist dissipated on a sudden wind; she felt it touch her cheek and chill tears she didn't know she'd wept. With the wind came another voice, a man's voice, familiar to her, both loved and feared.

"No, Cailet. You cannot take living power from the dead."

"She—she was my mother." Words came hard, each one scraping her lips. "She didn't want to look at me—"

"You don't understand."

"She didn't even want to *look* at me!" she screamed, and again began to run. Glass cracked and shattered behind her.

She tried not to hear. She wanted no more of Wraiths and magic and knowledge—

"Cailet!" He called her name, the mad old man who was Rinnel of the cottage in the canyon, who had cared for her— who was also Warrior Mage Gorynel Desse, who had stolen her magic and left her in The Waste and now had trapped her in this black-white-gray emptiness.

She ran faster. Her every step cracked the glass in shivering, chiming lines that rayed out behind her.

She could not escape him.

"There is nowhere you can run. There is no place but this. There are things you must know, Cailet—"

She didn't want to know. Knowledge hurt. Nothing had ever hurt her so much.

"No, Cailet. *Learning* hurts. And so it should—for the knowledge is all the more precious because of the pain."

Precious? The knowledge that her own mother had hated her so deeply she wouldn't even look at her?

"Listen to me, Cailet. Listen! There is no leaving here until you know what you must. If you run, you will run forever. You will be trapped here, forever."

"*You* trapped me!" she cried, slowing to catch breath enough to accuse him of his crimes. "You stole my magic the day I was born."

"I set Wards upon you, to keep you safe. Stop running, Cailet. There's nowhere to go."

Thin, chill wind sobbed in her throat and lungs. She stumbled to a halt, arms wrapped around herself, and tossed the hair from her eyes.

"So you remember what I did to you. I might have known you would. Power like yours occurs once in ten Generations."

"Power? I have no power! You made sure of that!"

"I made sure you had no access to it. Now you do. Can't you feel it, Cailet? It's there inside you."

"I'm *empty!* And it hurts! Does that mean I'm *learning?*" she cried bitterly.

"Not yet. But there are those who can teach you. Find them, Cailet. They're here, waiting."

"Where?"

"Find them," he repeated.

Magic she could feel inside her. Hungering. But it was not

the same as power. Power was the sum of magic and knowledge.

Knowledge was whispering to her, promising incredible things. She cast about for its source, scanning the empty horizon with increasing panic—where? Where?

Ahead, so far away as to be nearly indistinguishable from the gray shadows that stained the sky, stood a man. Tall, dark-haired, garbed in Guardian black with a cloak of Malerris white. She started for him, wary, soft-footed now on the shining obsidian. For a moment she was able to see the contours of his face: handsome, compelling, he looked directly at her with gray-green eyes that knew her no more than she knew him. But the old man had said people were waiting for her, to teach her—

"No. Not him. Turn from him, Cailet. Now!"

The tall man did not react to the words. She didn't think he heard them. But he frowned with fear in his eyes and left her, hastening his long strides into the distant mist.

"No—come back! Don't leave me here alone—" She stumbled again, onto her knees. A gasp of pain escaped her as the black glass broke on impact and splinters sliced her skin. A shudder crossed the mirrored surface. A thin fissure opened before her, jagged and wild. She heard the sound of a single footstep and looked up. The crack ended at the feet of a beautiful young woman in white and bright gold.

"That is quite enough," the woman said, brushing a strand of long blonde hair from eyes the same color as the man's. But these eyes were different. They had never known fear. "I don't know who you're meant to be, girl, but I don't believe in dream images."

She turned in a sweep of heavy silk skirts and walked away.

When she had vanished as the man had done, Gorynel Desse spoke again. "That was sheer luck, Cailet. Knowledge *of* them is something you need, but their *kind* of knowledge is—"

"Who are they?"

"Your father, Auvry Feiran. Your sister, Glenin."

"M-my—" If it was true, then her true Name was—

No, her Name had come from her mother. But what was the Name of the woman who had rejected even the sight of her own daughter? She knew it was not the Name borrowed for her at birth. It was not Rille.

"Tell me my Name!" she cried suddenly. "Tell me who I really am!"

"That is what you're here to discover. But not from them. Your magic called to them as they sleep, a call of power and shared blood. Praise be to St. Miryenne that he fears you and she does not believe in you."

"Afraid of *me?*" She struggled to her feet. "How can she be my sister? I have only one sister, and her name is Sarra—"

Summons enough, it seemed. In the place where Glenin had stood, Sarra now appeared—not a thing of shadow or mist, but real and warm and clear, gazing at her with yearning, loving eyes. Cailet's own eyes, as black and brilliant as the mirror they stood on, in a face both sweeter and stronger and certainly much more lovely.

"Sarra," she breathed. "Help me."

There was no reply. Cailet watched tears form in her eyes.

"She cannot help you here, or even answer you. This is a place of magic, and hers is Warded."

Cailet saw that it was true: power's fire was dim in Sarra's eyes. "What you did for me, you can do for her!"

Her sister shook her head slightly, a brief smile curving her soft mouth.

"No," said Gorynel Desse. "She cannot help you, Cailet. There are others who *can.* I may not guide you to them, but you must trust that they are here."

Now Sarra nodded, and there was urgency in her eyes.

Cailet started for her, hands outstretched. "Stay with me, please—if you can't help me, then at least stay! Sarra!"

"She must not. Let her go, Cailet."

"I can't! Not when I've only just found her again!"

"Let her go. If you cannot find the strength inside yourself to do so, borrow it from her. She has more than enough to spare."

"Sarra?" She took another step forward. "Will you be there when I wake up?"

"Look at her," Desse said ruefully. "Could Wraithenbeasts keep her away? *I* certainly couldn't."

Sarra's smile widened, her eyes sparkling. With a sigh, Cailet nodded and smiled back. "Be there," she whispered.

Sarra vanished. The splintered rent in the glass fused together. Cailet looked back over her shoulder. The black mirror was perfect once more. Healed.

And Gorynel Desse stood before her, as real as Sarra—and more. He was not an old man. He was young and clean-shaven, with hair even darker than his skin. His green eyes blazed with power.

"Find them," he said.

She realized why, then. "You're trapped here, too. Until I free you, as you freed my magic."

"Yes."

Fear assuaged by Sarra's love, anger boiled over. "Why? Why did you do that to me?"

"Forgive me. I never meant for it to be this way."

Forgive him? For robbing her of family and magic and what she was, *who* she was, and then abandoning her to The Waste—only to bring her to this second wasteland neither of them could escape? Forgive him?

"How *did* you mean it, then?" she demanded furiously. "If I hadn't seen Sarra that day—" *What* day? When had it happened?

"Stop wasting time. Find them, Cailet. Call them to you. Free yourself to know your own power."

"*You're* the one who did this to me! You know everything about me, about what's inside me—"

"Only you can know that."

"Damn you, teach me!"

"No."

And she flung herself at him, battering his body with her fists and his mind with her mind. The mirror quaked and heaved underfoot. He fended her off easily, young and strong and with knowledge besides.

"Stop it!" he commanded, grabbing her wrists and shaking her. The ground quivered slightly, then stilled. "You accomplish nothing by behaving like a child thwarted of a toy!"

"*I'm* a child?" she shouted into his face. "Look at *you*—so jealous of your knowledge and power that you won't even tell me my own Name!"

"My knowledge and power are keeping us alive, you little fool!"

Stricken, she backed away.

"Did you think this was real?" He gestured skyward. "This is a place of magic. I told you that. Our minds wear bodies because our minds are *part* of our bodies—but the flesh and bone we truly are lie senseless in a locked room."

"Where?" she asked with no voice at all.

"Ambrai."

Ambrai—

Cailet Ambrai—

She covered her face with her hands. More knowledge, gotten she knew not how. More hurt.

But there was pride, too, for what Ambrai had been. And sorrow for all of Ambrai that had been lost.

After a time she lowered her hands to her sides. Desse was gone. Again she was alone. Her fear and her anger that had been defenses against the loneliness were gone as well. And the hunger leaped, wild and eager.

She tethered it as she would an untamed wolf, recognizing its danger. Because she knew no other way, she began to scan the expanse of obsidian and the vast white sky, gaze lingering on each momentary swirl of gray cloud until one caught and held her attention. It drifted down, coalescing into a small, weary old man. He smiled at her, shook his head for silence when she would have spoken, and lifted both hands.

Sparks flew from his fingertips, dozens and then hundreds, swelling to milky opalescent spheres. They danced toward her one at a time. As she caught them, she saw within images and words and sometimes people, but only for an instant: just as her hands closed around them, they vanished like bursting soap bubbles with a tingle that spread up her arms and into her brain. It was a pleasant sensation, not painful at all, and when the Mage smiled at her once more she smiled back.

But the elderly man was tiring. She took a step closer, then another, so the spheres would not have so far to go. The sparks like stars continued to fly from his hands, faster now even though he began to sway on his feet. She reached for globe after globe, trying to keep up with him. Yet as she extended her hands for the next, it skipped away from her and returned to him, sheltering behind him.

"Your pardon," he said. "That was a mistake, not meant for you."

"But—you're one of my teachers, I need to know what you know."

"Some things are and must remain my own," he chided gently.

Still the spheres were created of his magic, and still she

caught them and felt her own magic respond. But many of them he waved away from her now, his private things, his memories encased in scintillating light, gathering into a single glow behind him.

At last there was nothing left. He nodded to himself, satisfied, and gave her one last smile of benediction and peace.

"Be wise, Cailet Ambrai," he told her. "Fare well."

The sphere of his memories difted forward to enclose him, and he vanished.

She stared in wonderment at the place the Mage had been. A soft touch on her shoulder turned her head.

"His name was Tamos Wolvar. He was a Scholar Mage, and my friend of many long years."

She had to remind herself that this young man standing beside her was in truth a very old man. Did vanity prompt him to wear his youthful body? Or was it a subtler choice, to impress upon her that whereas his physical body might be nearly eighty years old, his powers were still young and strong?

He smiled at her, green eyes alight with sudden mirth. "Really, Cailet—if you had a choice, would *you* keep the wrinkles and white hairs? Not that I didn't earn every one of them, you understand. Yes, you're right, it's vain of me, but we all have our little foibles."

She smiled back. "No doubt you have a list of mine."

"Vanity doesn't number among them," he replied. "Or you would have done something about your clothes and hair."

Before she could catch herself, one hand raked the bangs from her forehead. He laughed down at her and she made a little shrug of wry agreement.

"Oh, Sarra will teach you all that, I daresay. But that's a different sort of magic, and I must admit I've never understood the sweet mysteries of feminine rituals. At any rate, there are lessons to be learned here, first."

"That wasn't so bad," she offered.

"Tamos was a generous man."

She scowled. "Am I taking things these people don't want to give?"

"You haven't a single 'taking' impulse to your name, my dear."

Glancing away, Cailet bit her lip, for she knew the hungering of her magic argued otherwise. At its imperious bidding, she searched the skies to every horizon, looking for another gray cloud. Tamos Wolvar's gifts had sharpened her senses and her awareness of magic; she felt a glimmering behind her, where she had run from. She closed her eyes to concentrate, and for an instant—

No!

The warning was from her own magic that did not like the taste of that other. Even as she pulled away she recognized it: her father, Auvry Feiran. Made vulnerable to her in some way by sleep, his magic stirred. It was not wholly of Malerris, not like what she now felt as Glenin's cool, metallic sharpness. There was warmth still in her father, and the tang of a freshening breeze. She didn't understand that, but she didn't need to right now.

She needed what she perceived in front of her now. She opened her eyes.

An unimpressive old man with narrow, stooped shoulders and a permanent nervous squint. Another Scholar, she thought automatically, tracked down the thought's source, and knew the man's name.

It meant nothing to her. Perhaps the information had been in one of the spheres—Mage Globes—Tamos Wolvar had kept for himself. But the clothing was oddly familiar, and she didn't know why that should be. She'd never seen anyone dressed all in black—shirt, longvest, trousers, and cloak—with a silver sash around his waist and two small silver pins winking from his collar.

She had no need of Scholar Wolvar's memories to identify the man's tense reluctance. But if he would not teach her, how would she learn?

"You must excuse her," said Gorynel Desse's voice—from thin air again, he had disappeared. "She's never seen our regimentals."

"So few have, these bleak days." Lusath Adennos shrugged off his cloak and draped it over one arm. "And mine are rather disreputable."

"Never that. A little ragged, perhaps, but that's to be understood," Desse replied gently. "You were Mage Captal in a time unworthy of you."

Mage Captal—?

"Kind of you to say so, Gorsha." He glanced at Cailet, then sighed. "I suppose this is necessary."

"I'm sorry!" Cailet burst out.

"Hardly your fault, child. I'm only a bit hesitant, that's all. I remember my own learning, and it wasn't easy. I'll try to go more softly with you." He shrugged. "Then again, you're braver than I ever was."

"I'm not brave. I'm scared," she confessed. "I don't know what's happening to me, but I know it has to happen. Does that make any sense?"

"So Gorsha didn't tell you all of it yet? Typical. I suppose he's right, though. He usually is." Straightening, he held out ink-stained hands. "Well, let's get on with it. You're here to learn and I'm here to teach you."

She walked forward, slipping her fingers into his palms. Deftly he changed the positioning so that her hands clasped his.

"Close your eyes, child. That's right. Can you see your magic? No, don't chase it down like a stray puppy, just let it flow through you, and—by Deiket's Snowy Beard! Gorsha, why didn't you *tell* me?"

"Would you have believed me?"

"N–no. No, I don't suppose I would. Still . . . I see now that you *were* right."

"I usually am."

The Captal snorted. "More conceit than Leninor Garvedian! There now, child, it's all right. We'll begin now. . . ."

There was so *much!*

Spells and Wards and conjurations; small witcheries and magnificent sorceries; tricks of hand and eye and word and gesture—

—and the rules a Mage Guardian lived by.

So much, so much, and yet she knew there was more, that esoteric theory and practical knowledge and ancient ethic were not the whole. Something else, something that made a Captal, something—

"Great St. Miryenne, *no!*"

Gorynel Desse's shout shattered her concentration. Her eyes flew open. Her hands were empty. Captal Adennos was gone. His cloak lay like broken, abandoned raven wings on the obsidian mirror, visible atop the matching blackness only because of its thick woolen opacity.

In front of Cailet, just out of reach, hovered a curious thing like a Mage Globe, but completely alien to Tamos Wolvar's all-inclusive knowledge. The hazy sphere glowed ruby-red, webbed with a complex throbbing pattern of silver and gold and blue. There was magic in it and of it. Cailet sensed a power completely unlike her own: smaller. Quieter. Content to rest, to wait.

"No!" echoed once more from the white sky, and Cailet didn't understand Desse's panic. There was no danger here, no threat.

It was only a baby. . . .

21

"All clear," Alin said. "I left Val behind to guard the door, and—"

"His time would be better spent in trimming that damned cactus of Mother's," Taig muttered.

"Just once I wish you'd let me finish a sentence. It so happens that the damned cactus *has* been trimmed. And as there's only one person allowed to touch it. . . ." He grinned up at Taig.

"Mother's at the Longriding house?" He let out a whoop and thwacked Alin on the shoulder, a genial blow that nearly felled his slight brother.

Collan divided a bewildered stare between them. "Cactus?"

"You'll find out soon enough, believe me," Taig replied. "You take Tamsa. Telo and I will carry Sela. Can you handle all of us, little brother?"

"You and the horses you rode in on, big brother—if you'd ridden in on horses, that is, and if any Ladder was of a size for it."

Taig smiled at Col's skeptical raised brow. "Cocky little Blood, isn't he?"

"I just hope you two know what you're doing."

"There's nothing else we *can* do." Taig sobered. "At Longriding we can send for a physician. She needs medical attention."

"Tarise didn't look happy about taking Sela through a Ladder. I'm no doctor, but it seems to me she shouldn't be moved at all."

The brothers exchanged glances, and the elder cleared his

throat. "Probably not. But whatever's going on with Cai is affecting the baby."

"Mageborn?" Col let out a low whistle.

Alin nodded. "Cai's like an exposed nail, ripping at any magic within reach. It's not her fault. She can't help it. People with training—"

"Or really good Wards," Collan interrupted.

"—they can protect themselves. Sela's baby can't. The Ladder's going to be a shock. But there's a good chance of surviving it. If Sela stays here. . . ."

Col didn't care for the ominous way he trailed off. Neither did he like the anguished groan that announced Sela's arrival. Telomir Renne and Rillan Veliaz carried her in a rickety wooden chair. They and the Ostin brothers maneuvered her into the Ladder's circle, trying to pretend they weren't terrified by the expression on her face. *Like someone was tearing her heart out,* Col thought, and shivered inside.

Tamsa and her kitten were in Tarise's arms. Col took the little girl against his chest, wincing as Velvet used needle-fine claws to scramble up on his shoulder. Strange, how she'd yowled loud enough to summon Wraiths yesterday but now was purring. The gentle rumble was pleasant in his ear, the soft vibration soothing against his neck. Col liked cats. He'd had one when he was a little boy, a big gray male with white paws and mane. Cloudy? No, Smoky, that had been the cat's name. . . .

He nearly dropped Tamsa as he realized he'd remembered without hurt. So little of his childhood remained to him—and much of what did had headaches attached—but he could see Smoky as clearly as if the cat padded across the flagstones toward him. And there was no pain.

Velvet was purring, but Tamsa was crying. Col held her closer and smoothed her hair, knowing there was nothing he could say to assuage her fear. Saints, to be four years old and helpless . . . he remembered what that felt like. . . .

He remembered what it felt like—and there was no pain.

"Collan? Col, let's go!"

Blindly, he responded to Taig's voice, stepping into the circle. No one hit him over the head this time. Not that there was anything to be seen or felt or heard: there was nothing at all for the space of five heartbeats. Just as he was telling himself that the sensible thing to do was get scared, and before he could reply that the sensible thing was to shut up about it, a sunlit room snapped into existence around him. A greenhouse: air heavy with moisture, glass panes curving upward to a domed ceiling. He shifted his feet and stifled a curse as something stuck him in the backside.

"Careful!" Taig warned.

"Too late. Your Lady Mother's cactus, I presume?" He turned slowly—and cautiously—to look at the thing. It was gigantic. The spines really were the size of swords. He could've broken one off and used it against half an army.

"Cute, isn't it?" said Valirion Maurgen. He stood by the door, well out of range of the Ladder.

"Adorable," Collan growled.

"Let's get Sela upstairs," said Telomir Renne. "Val, Taig, you—"

He never finished the sentence. Val staggered forward, down onto his knees between tubbed fruit trees as the door slammed into his back. Alin cried out, a sound nearly lost in Sela's scream—not of pain but of terror. For through the wooden door and across Maurgen's sprawled body surged a dozen Council Guards.

Collan knelt swiftly, stashing Tamsa under the cactus's vicious arms. "Stay here. Don't move."

She was too frightened even to call for her mother. He tried to pry the cat loose from his shoulder but Velvet was having none of it; she dug in, hissing. Col gave up—he had no time. He could hear the lethal music of swords.

Drawing his own, he whirled and barely felt a cactus spine slice his shirt. Taig and Telomir were defending Sela, helpless in the chair, against four red uniforms. Alin was keeping another busy and frustrated by dodging his sword with the suppleness of a Wraith, using plants as cover. Val had struggled to his feet and was hacking away at another Guard. Two were already down. *Good,* Collan thought, *enough left to entertain me for a while.*

He grabbed the back of Sela's chair with one hand and dragged her out of the way. With more room to fight now, he chose his opponent and set to work. The first he impaled on his sword; the second he impaled on the cactus. The third was deprived of his weapon when Collan deprived him of his hand. The fourth got lucky, and got inside Col's guard. His luck ran out when one of the twin Rosvenir knives ran through his ribs straight to his heart.

A woman shrieked from somewhere beyond the door. Col

spared a thought for Taig's and Alin's mother as he angled his blade into a Guard's thigh deep enough to cut a chunk out of the bone. He stepped lightly out of the way as the man toppled, and gave him a little push to correct his fall— right onto a smaller but no less vicious cactus.

Collan decided he liked the denizens of Lady Lilen's greenhouse after all.

Yet another walking corpse in a red longvest attacked him, and was dispatched with a slash to his throat. *We used up the original dozen a while ago—but they just keep coming.* He shook his head in disgust. Didn't they know when they were beaten?

Val Maurgen was now defending the weaponless Alin; he looked to be doing all right. Col eyed the door and judged that it needed shutting. He lost count of his kills by the time he got through to the hallway. Taig was right behind him. A woman stood halfway up the stairs, screaming now with barely a pause for breath. A glance told Col she was too young to be mother to anyone past ten years of age. Whoever she might be, her lung capacity was impressive.

More Guards. More blood. He hoped the Ostins kept a lot of servants, and that they weren't squeamish about cleaning up messes. Come to think of it, there ought to be somebody besides Council Guards and the screamer here. A footman wielding a fireplace iron, a groom with a pitchfork, *somebody*. Unless they'd all been killed.

Taig ran past to what Collan assumed was the front door. After a quick look around—nothing on the floor moved but the slowly spreading blood—Col went after him.

He looked up and down the street in disbelief. Not only was it dusk—had he been fighting that long?—but the neighborhood was completely deserted. No horses—the Guards must have come on foot, or been here so long their mounts were in the Ostin stable. No pedestrians, either. No nothing. The houses were set well apart on big parcels, but surely someone had heard the commotion.

"That's all of them," Taig said, panting as he approached Col. "The whole squadron of twenty-five."

"Too bad. I was having a good time."

Taig gave him an odd look, and after a moment said, "Yes, I imagine you were. My sister is famous for her entertainments."

"The lady on the stairs?" he asked as they strode back up the walk.

"Geria, First Daughter of Ostin First Daughters—and 'lady' isn't the word I'd use to describe her."

Something in the grim set of Taig's handsome face alerted Col. "You think she—your own sister?"

"I *know* she did. She probably wined and dined all twenty-five for three days—and slept with half of them. The patriotic sort, my sister Geria," he added bitterly. "I should've guessed."

"At least she stopped screaming," Col observed as they entered the house.

"She'll start again very soon, if I have any say in the matter." He crossed the littered floor to the foot of the stairs. Geria Ostin stared down at him, mercifully mute with shock. Not at his presence, Collan thought critically, but that he was quite unaccountably alive.

"Where's Mother? What have you done with her?" Taig demanded.

His sister shut her mouth tight.

"Geria," Taig said with almost gentle menace, "if she's come to any harm, I'll kill you with my own hands. Where is she?"

When the First Daughter showed no inclination to answer, Collan said, "Probably upstairs, locked in somewhere. I'll go find her."

"Would you? Thanks."

He paused to wipe his sword on a Guard's cloak, but did not sheathe the blade. He'd mounted five steps when Geria came back to life.

"How *dare* you! Get out of my house at once!"

Amazing, Collan marveled. She was even better than Sarra at Blooded Arrogance.

Taig didn't even turn on his way back to the greenhouse. Collan paused, waiting to hear what she'd say next. It was bound to be another astonishment he could add to his collection.

"I'll ruin you, Taig!" she shouted to his retreating back. "You'll never get a brass cutpiece from me!"

Col couldn't help it. He began to laugh.

She rounded on him. "You motherless shit!" Descending one step, then two, she lifted a hand to slap him.

Velvet, forgotten on Collan's shoulder, let out a furious

hiss and leaped for Geria's face. She screamed and flailed, and Col hastily jumped up to rescue the kitten. But Velvet needed no help from him. After scoring Geria brow to cheeks to chin with her claws, she landed daintily and wrapped her front legs around Geria's ankle, adding her teeth for good measure. She had bounded up the stairs before the woman could even try to shake her off.

Collan spent a moment appreciating the cat's handiwork before the screams got to be too much for his sensitive Minstrel's ears. He left Geria clutching her bloodied face, shrieking.

Upstairs in the hallway, he called out, "Lady Ostin? Taig sent me to find you! Give me a yell if you can!"

Nothing. Velvet galloped up and wove herself around his boots. He picked up the kitten and resettled her on his shoulder.

"Nice work back there. But what I need right now is a hunting hound with a good nose."

He set about opening doors. Some were unlocked; those that didn't yield to a twist on the knob he kicked in. It was growing dark rapidly now, and no lanterns had been lit. Finally he found the right room. It contained a big canopied bed, a gorgeously carved wardrobe, various chairs and tables, and a plump, dark-eyed matron whose looks were immediately improved when he tugged the gag from her mouth.

"Thank you," the Lady gasped. "I trust I'm not too late to flay my daughter alive?"

"You'll find the job already begun, courtesy of my little friend here," he replied as he knelt to undo the ropes tying her ankles to the chair. Velvet hopped into her lap, turned a circle, and settled down to clean her paws.

"I hope she scarred Geria for life," said Geria's mother.

"Entirely probable." He tossed the rope to one side and started on her right wrist. "Collan Rosvenir, Lady, and delighted to be of service."

"Lilen Ostin. Damn that whelp of mine, she's had me locked in here for three days! In my own house!"

"While she did the honors of hospitality to the Council Guard?"

"Two of them outside my door day and night. Don't be so tentative about it, Collan, I'm not made of glass. Once I'm free, I'll see to your cuts."

He glanced up, surprised. But at her mention of them, the rents in his skin began to sting. So the Guards had scored him a few times; he must be getting clumsy. "My thanks, Lady, but there's someone else who needs you more." And he explained why they had come.

She moved as quickly as her blood-starved limbs could manage, and more quickly with every step. Geria was no-where to be seen; probably just as well, Collan told himself. The look in her mother's eyes boded worse than bruises.

Velvet purred once again on Col's shoulder. As they neared the greenhouse door, she mewed frantically and bounded down—a long drop for a little cat—and raced in-side. Col and Lady Lilen followed, stepping around the wooden door that hung from a single warped hinge.

Taig and Tamsa were with Sela, and Velvet was back where she belonged in the child's arms. In the dim room, amid the wreckage of plants and pots and overturned shelv-ing, Col didn't see Alin or Val or Telomir.

"Mother—" Taig spun around even before she spoke. His silver-gray eyes were bleak with agony.

She caught her breath. "Alin?"

"Val." He gathered Sela in his arms, lifting her bulk as gently as he could. She was unconscious, her head lolling.

Lady Lilen rallied at once. "Take her to the music room. You'll never get her all the way upstairs. I'll be there shortly. Irien's medical kit is in his bedroom—*damn,* why didn't I bring him with me from Ostinhold? Never mind. Take the child with you when you go up. There's poppy syrup in the kit, give her a spoonful and put her to bed."

Taig nodded and did as told. While he coaxed Tamsa to follow along behind him, Lady Lilen turned to Collan. "Drag all the Guards in here. When you're finished, set the kettle on in the kitchen—the big iron kettle, not the copper. The linen closet is one door down from the kitchen. Take all the sheets and blankets you can find to the music room. It's through the hall, you can't miss it. Then come back here."

Col, too, did as told. He figured it was the usual response to this woman.

As he stacked bodies around the greenhouse perimeter, he could hear voices from behind a pair of toppled fruit trees. The snatches of conversation chilled him to the marrow.

"—your cloak, Telo, I've got to stop the bleeding."

"Here. I'll get Val's, too."

"No. It's soaked through with blood."

Collan heaved a corpse on the pile and went back for another. He got a grip on a pair of ankles and hauled the body through the door.

"—was defending Alin, who had no sword."

"Oh sweet Saints, how am I going to tell his mother?"

He went out again, and came in again with another Guard.

"His sword is still in the body. It must've happened almost simultaneously. And very fast—his wound is through the heart."

"So will Alin's be."

There were so many bodies. The greenhouse floor was three deep in them.

"—will kill Alin. Put your hand here, and press hard. I'll see if I can do something about his leg."

There were so many bodies.

"Val?"

"Hush, sweeting. It's all right, my Alinsha, I'm here."

"Val!"

He went to get the last corpse. Next to last. He pulled the crimson-clothed body away by the shoulders, pausing to pull the sword from the belly. Lady Lilen and Telomir crouched just beyond the last corpse. Val's.

Finished. Kitchen next. But he hesitated, then stripped off his own cloak and longvest and shirt, placing them in Lady Lilen's reach.

Kitchen. He stopped in the doorway, stomach tensing. Saints, how he hated kitchens. Always had. For the first time in his life he wondered why.

Iron kettle on the hob and coals fanned to flames fed with two logs, he made for the linen closet. And then the music room. Sela Trayos lay on an elegant silk sofa. She was still unconscious. Collan stood there helplessly, arms full of sheets and blankets, and told himself it wasn't possible for him to see the rippling muscles of her distended belly move beneath her smock in a powerful contraction.

"Collan? Look alive, young man," said a brisk voice behind him. "Those sheets won't do any good clutched in your arms like that. Make a bed for her near the hearth."

He gulped, relieved that Lady Lilen had come to tell him what to do. Later, perhaps, he might be disgusted with himself for so readily obeying a woman—he who had always prided himself on his independence, his self-reliance, he who treasured his freedom from feminine discipline and who scorned men who did as told like good little boys. Later. Perhaps. But right now he was abjectly relieved that a woman was here to give orders.

So he did as told, and helped Lady Lilen ease Sela down onto the floor. He was ordered to fetch the kettle and on his way yell at Taig to get a move on. These things he did, because he didn't know what else to do.

When he returned, Sela was awake and biting her lips bloody trying not to scream. He set the kettle on the now glowing hearth and knelt beside her.

"It's all right, Sela, nothing to worry about. Lady Lilen will take care of everything." Though his certainty was born of mere minutes' acquaintance with the Lady, he was equally certain she had that effect on everybody.

"C–Collan?" Sela gritted her teeth against another spasm. "Where's Tamsa?"

"Upstairs asleep with her kitten. She's fine. Don't worry."

"Thank you," she breathed, groping for his hand. "For everything. You've been so good to us—"

Squeezing her fingers lightly, he dredged up a grin from somewhere and made his face wear it. "Just don't do anything silly like name the baby after me!"

Sela's smile was a sudden miracle. "I'd love to embarrass you, but I already know his name." She caught her breath, and his hand. "Oh, St. Josselet, it wasn't anything like this with Tamsa!"

But this baby was definitely Mageborn, and affected by whatever they were doing back in Ambrai to make that child the next Captal. Col extracted his fingers from Sela's grip before she could break the bones.

"Be easy, my dear," said Lady Lilen. "Don't worry. You're doing very well. Thank you, Collan, but you'd best go now. They should be about ready for you in the greenhouse."

"Ready for me?" he echoed stupidly. He'd been adding his own incoherent petition to Sela's Name Saint, plus Gelenis First Daughter and Lirance Cloudchaser and obscure Colynna Silverstring, long-forgotten patron of the lute, for good measure.

"Everything's perfectly in order here. I can take care of Sela and her children—both of them. Taig has locked Geria in the cellar until I can get around to her. In a few days," she added maliciously.

"Make it a week."

"I just might. But you'll have to go back to Bard Hall. I can explain Sela, once the neighbors get back from the celebration in town, but I can't explain the rest of you."

So *that* was where everyone was. He'd forgotten that this was the first day of Spring Moon. There would be more festivities on the third, with the Equinox. *I should live so long,* he thought sourly.

"You've all been listed for bounty, you see," Lady Lilen finished.

"Bounty? On *me?*" After all the slightly shady, arguably moral, and downright illegal things he'd ever done—and gotten clean away with—helping his friends had finally made him famous in all the wrong circles.

"I'm surprised I'm not on it, too. Although that's probably attributable to my darling First Daughter." Sela whimpered, and Lady Lilen reached for the box of medicines at her side. "Go on, Collan."

He struggled to think straight, a difficult task when all he could think about was a broadsheet with his name at the top and a woodcut of him in the middle and a substantial price at the bottom. Like the price put on a slave. The mark on his shoulder seemed to burn.

"Alin's wounded," he managed. "He's the only one who can work the Ladder."

"Alin is dying," she corrected softly, not looking up. "Go. Hurry, Collan. Tell Sarra and Cailet I love them. And tell Gorsha there's nothing to forgive."

He fairly stumbled from the music room—knocked into a rack of silver flutes, in fact—and slipped several times on the bloody hall floor. In the greenhouse, Taig and Telomir huddled on their knees beside Alin's still living and Valirion's dead bodies. Collan joined them, crouching at the edge of the circle. Bare to the waist, he shivered slightly, the increasing night chill following him into the greenhouse.

"Now, Alin," said Taig.

Pale blue eyes opened. "Val?"

"Here with us. Alin—please, little brother, you must try."

"Hurts," he muttered, sounding puzzled.

"You need a Healer. Take us through the Ladder."

Col shifted uneasily, wondering if Taig knew that no

Healer could help his brother. The scrape of his boots on the floor drew Alin's attention. His gaze found Collan in the dimness. A smile curved his lips.

"Val," he whispered.

Gently, aware of the soaked cloth at Alin's chest and thigh and abdomen, he reached out a hand to cradle the blond head. There was a warm, matted stickiness at the back of his skull. Expertly pitching his voice to be as much like Valirion Maurgen's as possible, he said, "Let's get out of here, Alin."

There was nothingness for a long, long time. And then there was the room at Bard Hall, and Sarra Liwellan staring at him and at Alin and then at him again, with a look on her face as if her heart had broken.

22

She had barely savored the child's magic—so serene, like a still pool of pure, luminous water—when the sphere vanished.

"Praise all Saints," whispered Gorynel Desse.

"But what happened? Where—?"

"Out of reach. Safe, I think. I hope. How *could* you have called to an unborn?" he accused suddenly, voice like thunder across the black-mirror plain.

"I didn't!"

"Something brought that baby here!"

"Something took the Captal away, too—and it wasn't *me!*" She glared up at the sky, outraged that he had all but convicted her of trying to steal the child's magic. When his voice spoke from beside her, she jumped.

"It was death that claimed Captal Adennos." He was subdued now, sorrowful.

"Death—? Oh, no—not the baby, too!"

"No. The child lives, and will be born." Pointing to the black cloak, he said, "I do not like to think what that means."

"How can it mean anything? It's no more real than you or I."

"It's very real, Cailet."

She bent down to pick it up. She couldn't touch it. There was no tingle of a warning Ward, no invisible Mage Globe surrounding it; her hand did not pass through it; she simply could not bunch her fingers in the cloth.

"You can have mine, if you want."

This was a voice she knew. Walking shyly toward her, golden hair wind-tousled and blue eyes smiling with singular sweetness, Alin proffered his own wool cloak of Ostin gray.

"I won't need it anymore, Cai," he went on. "It's not the Captal's, but at least it's something."

"Alin!" She ran to embrace him joyfully. "What are *you* doing here?"

"This is where you tried to find me—remember?"

She did; the day of St. Agvir's Wood, and her fall and her broken arm.

"You couldn't find me then. But I'm here now." He drew away and shook out the cloak. "Take it, little sister."

"Alin. . . ." Gorynel Desse stepped forward. "Are you sure?"

"Oh, yes. I never much wanted it anyway."

"Forgive me," the Mage said.

"Why? It wasn't you who gave me the knowing and the nightmares." His pale gaze sought Cailet's and he gave her a reassuring smile. "For you, they'll just be dreams. The only thing you were ever afraid of was the dark. Take it, Cai. Val's waiting for me."

She turned her back so he could drape the soft gray wool around her shoulders. "It even fits—we're the same height."

"Of course it fits," Alin chided. "Gorsha, doesn't she know yet?"

"Not yet. Soon."

Cailet looked from one to the other of them. This was the second hint of things she didn't know.

"It'll be all right, Cai." Alin hugged her briefly. "Don't be scared. And don't be sad, either, you or Sarra. Tell her we loved her, as much as we loved you." He touched her cheek, smiled again, and strode into the distance with quick, eager steps.

"But not as much as they loved each other," Desse murmured.

"He's dead," Cailet heard herself say. "They're all dead. Scholar Wolvar, the Captal—now Alin."

"Yes. Tamos gave you all he knew of Mage Globes, and more besides. Alin—"

"Ladders. Alin knew Ladders." Her lips felt numb.

"And now so do you. As for Adennos, I'm afraid he died before the work could be finished."

"Work?" She spun to face him, infuriated. "Is that what this is to you? They *died* doing this 'work'! It killed them—*I* killed them!"

"They were already dying, Cailet. The Captal's heart was failing. Tamos was sorely wounded in other ways. And Alin. . . ." He shook his head. "I can only guess that he chose to follow Val Maurgen into death. But each consciously chose to relinquish knowledge to you. It is always so in these circumstances."

"That's not true! Leninor Garvedian was alive and unhurt when you forced her to make Adennos Captal!" She knew that now. She knew many things—perhaps more than he had guessed. "You could have saved her, taken *her* to safety in Shellinkroth instead of him!"

"She was forced by events, not by me."

"But you did it! You knew that Auvry Feiran was coming, you came to her with Adennos spelled and in tow—and then you made him Captal and she was dead before a single torch was lit in Ambrai!"

"Enough!" he shouted. "Don't you think I know all that? Don't you think it was the hardest thing I've ever done?"

"One question, First Sword," Cailet said heatedly. "Why didn't you make *yourself* Captal?"

That hit, and hard. She saw it in the flinch of his whole body, in the fear and shame—and frustrated hunger—twitching across his face. Oh, she'd learned what "Rinnel" had told her to learn, all right. She knew how to read faces now.

"I—I was too old."

"Liar."

After a moment's hesitation, he whispered, "I was . . . not worthy."

"And I am?"

Cailet dug her fingers into his flawless regimentals, black on black from uncoifed head to dark skin, from powerful shoulders to shining boots, with a red and silver sash circling his lean waist and silver Sword and Candle at his collar, the garb of the First Sword, commander of the Captal's Warders and of all Warrior Mages.

"Why me? Why a seventeen-year-old girl who inherited magic by accident? Whose father's magic came from who knows where? Don't look so surprised, I know how startled they all were when you brought him to the Academy—all that power, all so unexpected!"

"You can't possibly know! Get your hands off me!"

She tightened her grip on his longvest and shirt, staring up at him, glaring him down. "Why not you, Gorynel Desse? Why not the man with at least one Mageborn in every breeding pair of his Blood—right back to The Waste War?"

"Because I *failed!*" He broke away from her with such force that she staggered. "There it is, Cailet Ambrai, the simple truth! I *failed!*"

"At what?"

"I thought you knew everything now!"

"Tell me!"

A glimmer of hope sparked in his eyes. "No," he said, and smoothed his clothing with absolute finality.

"Damn you, *tell* me!"

But within her was no spell, no word, no Warding, no trick of mind or will, that could take from him what he did not want to give.

"No," he said again, when at last her assault ceased. "And don't ever try anything like that again. Especially not on a Malerrisi. You may know, but you don't yet understand, that there are defenses against magic other than that wall I showed you how to build."

Cailet felt all the anger flood from her body, leaving her shaky and afraid. "Oh, damn it, Gorsha, don't you see? I just proved that I'm a mistake. This should never have happened to me."

"You're wrong." Desse pushed the thick black curls from his eyes. "You'll have plenty of time to despise me for this, you know. But one day you'll find out the completeness—and, I might add, the complexity—of the truth. And then you can despise me for all the right reasons. It won't matter anymore."

"But you can't tell me now."

"No. And I'm not sorry for it, either." The fierce green of his eyes gentled to the warmth of sunlight through spring leaves. "You're so young, Cailet. Too young to know so

much, most would say—and *will* say. But *I* know *you*. There
has been no mistake. Not this time."

He approached her, lithe and strong, and took her face between his hands. She tilted her head back, full of questions
but no accusations. First Sword Gorynel Desse had been a
whispered legend; Rinnel had been her fascinating, eccentric
friend. But this was a young man who stood cradling her
face in his fingers now, one hand drifting up to brush her
hair from her wondering eyes.

"For just this moment, Cailet," he murmured, "try not to
hate me."

"I don't—" she began.

And then he kissed her. Not an old man's affectionate
kiss, but a young lover's: long, deep, searching, tender—and
ah, Saints, so sweet. . . .

*I would have loved you this way, Cailet. For the magic of
it, the magic of you and me. Remember this, heartling. Remember that I loved you.*

23

Something had been on Auvry Feiran's mind, something un-
connected to the finding and burning of the Academy Ladders. It had been a disappointment, of course, to discover no
Mage Guardians hiding in the ruins, but this was not what
shadowed his eyes.

At last Glenin asked. They were seated in what had been
a schoolroom in Captal Bekke's Tower, where the Ladder to
Viranka's Breast still lived on the top floor. It was late, and
after the day's exertions few were awake. They'd eaten hot
food that night, cooked over open fires. Smoke had risen
from torched Ladders all day; even if the Mages were somewhere in the city, a few more fires didn't matter. In fact,
Glenin enjoyed the notion that they huddled somewhere in
stark terror that their only means of escape had gone up in
flames—if only she was sure the Mages were here.

"If they're in Ambrai, where?" she said to her father after
casting a Warming onto her coffee mug. Chava Allard made

the worst brew she'd ever tasted, and only stinging heat
made it palatable. "It's been bothering you also, hasn't it?"

"Hmm? Oh—no, Glensha, they *are* here."

"Can you sense them?" She was mildly irked that he
might perceive what she could not. She had been the one to
find the three living Ladders, after all. But perhaps his Mage
training made him more sensitive to the Guardians—and to
his teacher Gorynel Desse in particular.

"Not directly, if that's what you mean. But they're here."
He gulped coffee and leaned back against a concrete wall,
stretching long legs before him. Two days in Ambrai had
scarred his immaculate boots and stained his faultless uniform. "Truly told, what I've been pondering since this morning was a dream I had last night."

Glenin did not voice impatience or scorn. She never
dreamed—or at least did not remember what she dreamed.
She had willed it of herself in childhood. For nearly a year
after arriving at Ryka Court, all her dreams had been of her
mother and sister and Ambrai—not dreams but nightmares.
She feared them, was shamed by them, and did not want to
remember them. So she had decided not to. Her will, reinforced later by a kind of personal Warding, remained intact.

"I know you don't think of dreams as meaningful," her father said, as if he'd followed her thoughts. "This one was
strange, though. I can't forget that girl's face."

"Who? Sarra Liwellan?"

"No. This girl . . . she reminded me a little of your
mother."

Glenin drew her cloak around her, wishing the window
embrasure they sat in had a few pillows. Her back was aching. "You're in Ambrai. It's natural to dream about her."

"But she *wasn't* Maichen, that's just it. Taller, no more
than eighteen or so—and Mageborn. I knew that about her.
She practically shone with power."

"And on the basis of this, you believe the Mage Guardians are here?"

"I didn't say that."

"But you implied it."

"Very well, then—yes. Because it wasn't just the girl I
sensed. I *saw* her. But I *felt* Gorynel Desse."

"In a dream," she said, unable to keep the sharpness from
her voice. "What about now, when you're awake?"

"He's gone," Feiran stated flatly. "Since a little after

Fourteenth. But all day long I could feel him, Glensha. Distant, not very clear, but—"

"Father, I don't mean to belittle your instincts, but the Academy is deserted. The Ladders are all dead. There's no one here but us."

"Yes."

"Do you think they were here, and somehow escaped?"

"I think they were never here at all. Not at the Academy."

"Where else, then?"

Broad shoulders shrugged. "I only wish I knew. We'll search tomorrow, of course. From the top of this tower we can spread a Net of sorts."

"Of sorts?" she echoed.

"It is not a technique I ever mastered fully," he admitted.

"Then let me direct the Net."

"You don't know what to cast for."

"A Mageborn is a Mageborn," Glenin reminded him.

"Only until training defines her magic. I know Mage Guardians, Glensha. You don't. Imperfect as the Net will be, I must be the one to cast it."

She subsided, composing herself for sleep. But as she curled around herself and spelled her cloak to comfortable Warmth, she wondered once more if, on finding Desse again, his former student would not allow him to escape again.

24

Sarra watched in numb grief as Imilial Gorrst closed and locked a door in the farthest corridors of Bard Hall. Within was a Battle Globe that would burst and burn at the Warrior Mage's bidding thought. Until that time, the Globe would shine on the bodies of Alin Ostin and Valirion Maurgen.

Silently, those left alive walked to the next door. This time it was Tamosin Wolvar who entered to set a similar Globe over his uncle's corpse. He lingered a moment, yielding only to Ilisa Neffe's soft murmur of his name. Then he locked the door behind him, and the small procession moved on.

Kanto Solingirt, Scholar and senior Mage present, con-

jured the Globe that would guard and eventually burn Captal
Lusath Adennos. Elomar would have performed this rite for
his kinsman, but Elomar could not be wakened. Neither
could Cailet.

They returned to the small tower where the Ladder was.
Sarra walked between Riddon and Maugir, but the person
she was most aware of was behind her. Collan Rosvenir had
sung for Val and Alin while Tarise helped Sarra wash their
bodies and arrange them side-by-side in the same bed. He
had sung also for the Captal and for Tamos Wolvar while
they were readied, giving the Wraiths music to comfort their
journey. It was traditional, and Sarra had heard the songs at
other funerals, but Collan's was such powerful and beautiful
music that she had to struggle against tears. Yet when she
glanced at him, her fingers smoothing Alin's bright hair, she
saw that he did not sing ease to the dead or consolation to
the living. He sang for himself. Whatever feeling he had for
the dead—all the dead, including those left behind on
Ryka—was submerged somehow in the music. He did not
sing to rid himself of his own sorrow, nor to express that of
voiceless others. The music was a Ward against all emotion,
including his own. Sarra marveled that such beauty and such
feeling could mean so much to her and little if anything to
him.

Yet she could feel his strength as he walked behind her. It
was not what she had known with Orlin or Val or Alin: their
strength had invited her use, been offered to her need, stood
ready always to protect her, hers without even the asking.
Collan's was not of this kind. Not exactly selfish, but never
to be given unless specifically requested. He would never
give anything of himself, she thought resentfully, unless
bludgeoned into it.

Ah, but that was unfair. Had she not seen him cradle
Alin's head in his hand, and reply in a voice almost Val's
when Alin called his lover's name? Perhaps the imposture
had been the only way to get Alin to take them through the
Ladder. Sarra didn't think so. There were generous impulses
in Collan Rosvenir—he needn't have sung to Cailet, after
all—but he would probably deny or explain away every one
of them.

He had not sung for Gorynel Desse.

The Mage's body lay in the room next to Cailet's. But for
the faint movements of her breathing, exactly in time with

Elomar's, she might have been as dead as he. The Healer Mage was the one who twitched and whimpered in his sleep—at least, Sarra hoped it was sleep for both him and Cailet. People woke from sleep. Until Cailet woke, she who was now Mage Captal, Sarra and all the others were trapped in Bard Hall.

She sat with Taig Ostin and Telomir Renne in the noon sunshine, cups of wine untouched in their hands. The inner garden was renewing itself, only one day before the Spring Equinox: herbs and roses grown wild showed new leaves, and the white cherry tree trembled on the verge of blooming. Another week of sun, a little more rain, and the grass would be ankle-deep.

"They're at the Academy," Telomir said into the stillness. "There was smoke all day yesterday, and no reason for it except to burn Ladders. We can go only to Longriding, and only if Cailet learned all that Alin knew."

"Was there time?" Taig asked bitterly. "He lived not even fifteen minutes."

"We must trust that the necessary was accomplished."

Sarra looked down at her wine and said nothing. There was a vine climbing the wall opposite her, untrimmed for not quite eighteen years. She wondered what color the flowers were. Well, blue, of course. Bardic Blue.

"None of the other Mages know this Ladder," Telo went on.

"It was rarely used," said Taig. "The house was a dowry five Generations ago. There were Bards in my ancestor's line, and he was from The Waste, so I suppose that's why the Ladder exists at all. Now it's the only one left in all of Ambrai."

"The only one we can use," Telo corrected. "They won't burn the one at the Octagon Court, or the one to Malerris Castle."

The breeze was chilly, even sitting here in the sun, and brought a distant sting of smoke. There would be nothing left at the Mage Academy now—even less nothing than Auvry Feiran had left not quite eighteen years ago. Sarra wondered dully if anyone had noticed that there were books missing from the cellar vault. She almost said something about searching Bard Hall for folios of songs, then asked herself what was the use: Alin was dead.

But Cailet lived. Cailet—and Alin's knowledge of Ladders, and Tamos Wolvar's of Mage Globes, and Lusath Adennos's of whatever it was that made a Captal worth saving at all costs. Sarra mused on what Gorynel Desse had known that Cailet now knew.

"There must be no magic until we go through the Ladder to Longriding," Telo said. "They'll search for us. They'll use magic first, and when they find nothing they'll come on foot. All of it will take time."

"Enough for Cailet to recover and wake?"

"We must trust so."

"You keep using that word."

"It's a good one, Taig."

"I don't find much comfort in the concept right now."

"Don't you? I learned it from my father, when first he Warded my magic," Telo replied serenely.

"And never unWarded it."

"That will be the Captal's decision."

He was talking about Cailet. *Cailet*—not quite eighteen years old, and the most important and powerful Mageborn in the world. She could hear Collan demanding to know if anybody had asked Cailet whether she wanted this.

"She can get us to Longriding," Taig said. "But where we go from there is problematical. Ostinhold, maybe."

"The Captal will discover if it's safe."

"Damn you!" Sarra flung her winecup down, surging to her feet. "She has a *name!*" She ran indoors, ignoring Taig's stunned "Sarra!" behind her.

If one counted Lusath Adennos as a caretaker—for that was exactly what he'd been, Sarra realized—then the only image she had of a Mage Captal was Leninor Garvedian. Her memories of the fiery Captal belonged to an overawed little girl. Tales she'd heard since had confirmed her impressions: Leninor had been powerful, energetic, reckless, and arrogant. In some ways, truly told, the Captal and Grandmother Allynis had merged in Sarra's mind.

Cailet was Allynis's granddaughter. She was also the Mage Captal. *She's not even eighteen years old!*

Maugir stood guard by the open door of Cailet's room. Sarra went past him without a word and stood gazing down at the frail girl in the bed. This child, Mage Captal? *My sister,* she told herself, ferociously protective. *Cailet is my sister first. The Mage Guardians and the Rising have second claim.*

She turned suddenly as a soft stir in the air announced another visitor. Bard Falundir stepped silently toward the bed,
bare feet and ragged clothes making no more sound than his
voice ever could. Still stinging from their initial encounter,
she looked away. He paused beside the cot on which Elomar
lay, then moved to the other side of Cailet's bed. Sarra could
feel him willing her to meet his gaze; at length, she did.

Never had she seen such loving warmth, such tender compassion, in anyone's eyes. This man knew grief beyond anything Sarra had ever experienced; she had twice lost family
and friends and home, but he had lost the words and music
that were the essence of his being. Yet there was no bitterness, no lingering fury or outrage at what had been done to
him, even though the greatest Bard in ten Generations had
been silenced for as many years as Cailet had been alive.

Sarra drank of his serenity without knowing how she did
so. And it occurred to her that Mageborn or not, this was
magic. To give in silence; to create music with eyes and
heart. Knowing pain and anger, Falundir offered that with
which to bear them. This was the essence of the true Bard.
No matter how magnificent Collan Rosvenir's musicianship,
he would never become a true Bard until he learned such
giving.

She wanted to thank Falundir, and did not know how. He
smiled very slightly and settled at the foot of the bed, useless hands lax in his lap. Sarra took the same position on the
other side.

"I promised her I'd be here," she said.

Falundir nodded. Together they watched over Cailet, and
waited.

25

An inarticulate cry spun Glenin on one heel. "Father?" She
ran in from the balcony surrounding the top of Captal
Bekke's Tower and approached the circle of Malerrisi.
Auvry stood in its exact center, laughing. "Do you have
them? Are you sure?"

The weariness of the day-long search sluiced from him as

if success was a bright waterfall. "It's them." He paused, closed his eyes for a moment, then said, "But you'll never guess where."

The Malerrisi, fifty-one of them shoulder-to-shoulder, shifted as they were released from the Net. They shivered in the evening chill as minds became aware again of bodies. A few slid down to rest with heads lowered to bent knees, and others began to pace off the stiffness of hours of fruitless searching.

"The Council House?" ventured Glenin. "One of the Guildhalls?"

Chava Allard, as fresh-faced and chipper as if he'd just risen from a full night's sleep, gave a snort. "They're in Bard Hall! Even *I* felt it!"

Feiran nodded approvingly. Glenin eyed the boy with concealed annoyance, understanding something of Vassa Doriaz's apprehensions.

"Can we do anything about it tonight?" she asked her father.

"Everyone needs food and sleep. Tomorrow will be soon enough. Believe me, they're not going anywhere."

Chava was practically dancing with gleeful anticipation. "Only one Ladder at Bard Hall—straight to Ryka Court!"

"Yes," she said. "I know."

He was crestfallen at the rebuke, but not long enough to suit her. "I'll go start dinner!" And he bounded out to the balcony and down the exterior stairs.

Someone sighed. "Would that Velireon the Provider would provide us with another cook."

Glenin forced a smile. She wanted to share the mood of triumph. She had done nothing to earn it. All day she'd kept her magic in check, except for one or two stealthy forays that gleaned nothing but a directionless impression of *obstacle* that was almost but not quite a Ward. Evidently her father had run into the same thing until a few minutes ago.

"Let's go downstairs, Glenin," he said, touching her elbow gently.

"I'll be along later," she replied. "I want to watch the stars come out."

"Don't wait till it gets too dark. These stairs—"

"—will be lit very nicely by a Globe. Stop worrying. Do you take me for a Novice Mage?" Because he was her father, she softened the words with a smile.

He nodded, saying nothing more. The comprehending sympathy in his eyes galled her. When she was alone, she went back outside and found the outlines of Bard Hall against the blackening sky. He would be a fool not to discern her resentment at being excluded from the Net, but he would need the abilities of Elinar Longsight, patron of fortune-tellers, to sense the rest.

Once again—*Damn Garon!*—she was pregnant.

26

Sarra had no idea when she'd fallen asleep. She woke when something moved the blanket against her cheek, and sat up groggy-eyed. Falundir was gone. So was Elomar. She and Cailet were alone in a delicate half-darkness.

And Cailet was awake.

"You're here," she said softly, black eyes set in bruises of fatigue, eyes that were huge and unfathomable and utterly calm. "You stayed with me."

Sarra struggled to sit up. "Of course I did."

"The others are gone." Cailet drew her legs up and hugged her knees, looking barely twelve years old—except for those eyes. "Our parents, our sister, the other Mages. They're all gone. Some of them died."

"I know."

"Do you know what I am now?"

Sarra raked her hair back with both hands. Her fingers felt numb. "You're my sister."

A vague surprise, a subtle curiosity, a small gentling of her face. Then: "Do I scare you?"

"No. You're my sister. I love you."

"I—I know," Cailet replied shyly. "I felt that." Then her shoulders tensed. "Gorsha loved me, too. But I frightened him. Do I frighten you, Sarra?"

"No," she said once more. "Oh, Caisha—" She held out her arms to this strange, fey child who was her sister—and the Mage Captal.

Cailet clung to her, trembling just a little. "Sarra—help me," she whimpered. "Stay with me, please—"

"Always, dearest. I promised. I'm here, Caisha, I'll always be here. Hush now, sweeting. It's all right. All over now."

"It hasn't even started. I'm scared, Sarra. There's so much inside me and I'm *dangerous* now, don't you see?"

Sarra held her by the arms, looking into tear-filled eyes. Her own eyes; their mother's eyes. "I see my sister. Cailet Ambrai."

"That's the first time I've ever heard it aloud." She gulped, rested her forehead against Sarra's, and whispered, "Please, say it again. One last time."

"Cailet Ambrai." Sarra held her close once more.

After a time, the girl drew away. "You didn't question that it *was* the last time."

"I'm not entirely ignorant of certain realities," Sarra responded with a smile. "You and I know, and Telomir Renne, and Elomar Adennos—"

"The Healer Mage who kept me alive," Cailet interrupted.

"Yes. Taig knows. And Lady Lilen."

"And Bard Falundir, I think." Bitterly: "Well, *he's* safe enough."

"Cailet! You can't possibly think the others would—"

"—betray us? You don't know me very well yet. I meant that he's safe from the danger of knowing. The others aren't. I told you, Sarra. I'm dangerous. And in this, so are you. To everyone who knows us."

"We'll be careful. Caisha, how do you feel? It's been days since you've had anything but water and a little soup."

Cailet began to laugh silently. "Are you always so practical?"

"Ruthlessly." She laughed and got to her feet. "You've much to learn about me, as well. Stay right here and I'll go find you something to eat. I wonder what time it is?"

"Just past First. Alin had a good time-sense, too," the Captal added.

How often would this happen before anyone got used to it? Other people's knowledge springing from Cailet's lips—if Sarra secretly dreaded the prospect, what must it be doing to Cailet?

"Sarra . . . he said to tell you that he and Val loved you very much."

Nodding slowly, she whispered, "Not half as much as they loved each other."

"Gorsha said the same thing. He told me a lot, but there's so much I want to know about Ambrai and our family and—"

"One thing you should know about me right away. Auvry Feiran is no more my father than Glenin is my sister."

After a moment, Cailet replied steadily, "True enough."

"You know what I'm saying."

"I do. And I think you're wrong. But we'll discuss it some other time."

Sarra went to the door, summoning a smile to reassure Maugir, and before she opened it said over her shoulder, "No, Cailet, we will not."

27

"Sixteen people at once?" Imilial Gorrst shook her head emphatically. "Impossible!"

Collan paused in the doorway to consider. His knowledge of Ladders began and ended with eight versions of that silly children's song—well, maybe not so silly; Alin had seized on a variant verse and declared one of the riddles solved—so he couldn't exactly give an expert's opinion. But Imilial Gorrst was a Mage, and a Warrior at that; he'd take her word for it.

Cailet Rille did not.

"Why impossible?" she asked calmly, then glanced up from the tray on her lap. "You're the Minstrel!" she cried in genuine delight.

"That I am, *domna,* and pleased to see I won't be singing to your deaf ears from now on." He bowed and smiled, pretending not to notice Tarise's frown. He knew Cailet was now Mage Captal and should be addressed as such, but he figured she'd get *Captal*-ed until she was sick of it from now on. Somebody ought to treat her like a human being.

"Oh, but I heard every single song. It was wonderful!" Her smile was almost childlike in its sweetness. "Will you sing for me again sometime?"

"At your slightest whim." Taking a straight chair from

near the brazier, he turned it around and straddled it, arms folded across its back. "I hear we're taking a little trip."

"Just as soon as Healer Adennos reassures everyone that I'm all right."

"Which remains to be seen," Tarise said sharply. "Go away, both of you, and let the Captal finish her breakfast."

Aha—he'd been right. The title might become familiar in time, but right now it still startled her.

Imilial pursed her lips and shook her head. "I'll get everyone ready, as you say. But it might be two trips, Captal: For one thing, the circle simply isn't big enough to hold all of us."

"Then I'll just have to make it bigger, won't I? And please, call me by my name. Unless I have to order that, too?" A prospect that obviously tasted sour; her mouth screwed up and she made a comical little face, but Collan saw the real unhappiness in her eyes. Gorgeous eyes, he thought absently, definitely her best feature. Lovely hair, too, if she'd let it grow out.

Imilial gave her a wry grin. "Cailet, then. But you'd better get used to the other."

"And insist on it from certain people," Tarise added.

Maybe Tarise had a point. A girl this young would never be taken seriously in a position of such importance. Oh, she might begin to look the role in about twenty years. Until then, insistence on the title would remind everyone of Who She Was.

Have to do something about the clothes, though, Col mused. *What* does *the well-dressed Mage Captal wear? I know a shop in Firrense that'd fix her up just fine. Can't beat Firrense for really good tailors. She's a charming little kitten who'll grow into a sleek black-eyed cat, but she'll disappear into those regimentals unless something's done to soften them . . . maybe a jewel or two, earrings at least. . . .*

". . . with Minstrel Rosvenir for a while alone please, Tarise."

He roused at the sound of his name. When Tarise had left them, Cailet set the tray aside and scooted to the middle of the bed. Cross-legged, body inclining toward him, she caught his gaze with those infinitely black eyes.

"I *did* hear your music, you know," she said. "You're very gifted."

"Thank you."

"I'm going to ask something very difficult of you, *Domni* Rosvenir. I want you to trust me."

He arched a brow, but for some reason could not toss back a bantering reply.

"I know more about you than you think," she said, and did not elaborate. "I'm going to say a name, and I want you to tell me what you feel when you hear it. Ready?"

So she knew about the Wards? For an instant he felt a wild urge to ask her to remove them. An instant later he knew he didn't want that. He'd lived all his life with those Wards in place; would he be the same person without them?

"Go on," he said warily.

The Mage Captal looked levelly into his eyes. "Falundir," she said.

He caught his breath. "He's here—he was the one who— sweet St. Velenne, he's *alive!*"

"Yes. Did his name hurt?"

"What? Oh—no, not at all. Why should it?" Then, belatedly: "Oh."

Cailet sat back against the pillows, hands laced loosely in her lap. "Well. Gorsha does do exquisite work, doesn't he?"

"Why?" he blurted. "I mean, the other night I felt—"

She nodded.

"But not now? Not anymore, ever?"

"Evidently not." She regarded him thoughtfully. "I haven't a clue why Falundir's name should mean anything to you besides his greatness as a Bard. But Gorsha knew you'd have to see him again, so he did something to your Wards. Do you remember anything connected to Falundir? Anything at all?"

Col chewed his lip, frowning. "Nothing I can chase down. But as I understand it, that could be a function of the Wards, too, right?"

"Right. Minstrel Rosvenir . . ."

"Collan. Col if you start to like me," he said, smiling a little.

"I'm Cailet—Cai if *you* start to like *me*. Col, doesn't it make you angry? The Wards, I mean."

"Damned right it does," he answered honestly. "Never knowing when I'll hear something that'll give me a headache like the morning after a five-night drunk, and the feeling that St. Kiy Herself siphoned wine into me to make me forget—"

"Me, too," Cailet confided. "Only, with me, there wasn't anything to remember. And there wasn't any pain until I saw Sarra."

"So I'm told. If this is what knocking them down does, I'll pass."

"You're not Mageborn," she replied. "It wouldn't hurt you as much as it did me." After a moment's hesitation, she finished, "I was about to ask if you wanted me to get rid of the Wards."

"No thanks. I guess they've been there so long that they're part of me now. I like my life—or I did until I was fool enough to get mixed up in all this," he added in disgust.

"Truly told, you'd be different without the Wards. I know I am."

"But you're still yourself. Still Cailet Rille."

"Mmm. Yes, I'm myself. *And* Cailet Rille."

He didn't understand that, or the speculative bitterness in her eyes.

"But I'm also the Captal. Or—at least everybody thinks I am."

This time the bewilderment made him blink. Twice.

Leaning forward again, she spoke urgently. "You mustn't tell anyone, Col. Not even Sarra knows. I shouldn't have told you—but I trust you. Maybe you can trust more if I tell you the truth." Her mouth curved at one corner, a sardonic expression much too old for her face. "*There's* a paradox for you. By telling you that you can't trust what they say I am, I'm hoping you'll trust me."

"What, exactly, are you saying?" he asked carefully.

"It wasn't finished. I learned everything Scholar Wolvar knew, everything Alin knew—" Grief thinned her generous mouth for a moment before she went on. "—and everything Gorsha thought I needed to know. But Lusath Adennos died too soon. He gave me so much—more than I'm aware of right now, I'm sure. But not all of it. I'm not the Mage Captal, Collan. I'm . . . incomplete."

He pulled in a breath large enough to sing two verses and the chorus to any song in his folios, and let it out very slowly. "Cailet, whatever you aren't, you're still who you *are*. That's how I've had to live my life. I see that now. Whatever's missing . . . well, there's nothing I can do about it but fill in the gaps as best I can."

"And never let anyone know about the holes. I guess I have to look at it that way, don't I?"

"I guess." He paused. "And if you're asking, I can't think of anybody else I'd trust more than you. All right, yes, it surprises me, too! But it's true enough." Managing a crooked grin, he finished, "Maybe we both have to trust the old man's judgment about all of it, huh?"

"Old m—? Oh, you mean Gorsha. He was very fond of you, you know. I think that's partly why I—"

"Fond of me?" he echoed. "He had me conked over the head!"

"I promise I won't do the same when we go through the Longriding Ladder," she teased.

"Aw, thanks," he retorted. Then: "Cai, can you really expand it?"

She nodded solemnly. "I've always had the magic, you know. Now I have the knowledge. Both together equal power. Yes, I can do it."

"And this is where I'm supposed to start trusting you, right?" He stood, swung his leg over the chair back, and picked up the tray. "I'm crazy to say it, but I do. You'll be all right, kitten. And I won't tell the others."

She drew up her knees and propped her elbows on them, chin in hands. "Kitten?" she echoed with a touch of whimsy.

"Sorry."

"No, I kind of like it. It's nice. Brother-ish." Bright eyes watched him in amusement. "I begin to see what Sarra likes so much about you."

"Sarra?" He couldn't help laughing. "Oh, she likes me fine—as long as I do what she tells me to!"

"Well, there *is* that part of her personality . . ." Cailet grinned up at him.

"Someday I'll tell you what happened when we first met."

"Will you? I never did hear the whole juicy scandal!"

"One of these days I'll give you every detail. There's a tavern in Renig—no, better make that a *different* tavern in Renig, come to think of it. I'll buy you a drink and tell you all about it. But not until you're legal, Cai. All I lack on my charge sheet is corrupting an underage girl. You want to get some rest now or talk to the Healer Mage?"

"Elomar, please, if he's not sleeping." Again she hesitated, then said shyly, "Col? Thank you. I'd like it if we became friends."

"We already are. And I promise never to call you Captal in private."

"I'd rather you promised never to call me that at all," she complained.

"Can't do it, kitten. In public, that's what you are."

"But for me, for myself and my friends, I can be just Cailet?" She nodded. "I guess I can live with that."

He thought it best not to mention that she'd *have* to live with it.

28

Perfectly simple, really.

The Mages didn't think she could do it, of course. A spell of Convincing was available to her that would work even on them. She didn't use it, nor any of the other words and workings that bounded up like startled galazhi at her every thought. She told herself she'd have to do some serious organizational thinking very soon now. All these spells were a distraction and sometimes she found it hard to concentrate on what people were saying.

Collan trusted her. So did Sarra. And Elomar, of course—he had *breathed* for her, he knew the essence of her power. The trio of Slegins were willing to take Sarra's word for it, as were Tarise Nalle and her husband Rillan Veliaz—more or less. She had only to meet Bard Falundir's eyes to see implicit belief that she could do whatever she said she could do.

But Telomir Renne, Tamosin Wolvar, Ilisa Neffe, Imilial Gorrst, and Kanto Solingirt knew too little about her and too much about Magelore. A Ladder was a Ladder was a Ladder, created long ago by Mages far wiser than they with esoteric spells lost in The Waste War, and Ladders could not be altered in any way—except to kill them with fire.

Cailet could have ordered them, of course. She was the Captal. They were compelled to obey her by oaths they had sworn long ago. Even Telomir, whose magic had been Warded on its first appearance, but who knew almost everything there was to know about being a Mage Guardian.

Taig Ostin was missing from the group gathered in the

Ladder chamber. She hadn't seen him since Longriding. He hadn't come to her early this morning the way all the others had, after Elomar pronounced her recovered. The neglect hurt. Was he frightened of her, too? To see doubt in his silver-gray eyes would be more than she could bear.

"It's not necessary," Ilisa Neffe was saying. "Forgive me, Captal, but it truly is not."

Oh, but it was. And not just to prove to all of them that she could do it, to make this one action proof of her true power. But not of the truth. This they must not know.

"I disagree," she said quietly. "Any outpouring of magic, and much is needed to work a Ladder, will attract the Malerrisi."

"It'd take them half a day to get here from the Academy," Ilisa replied. "The streets simply aren't negotiable."

Cailet repressed a sigh. "Shainkroth?"

The Mage stiffened and glanced at her husband. He looked a little sick. Cailet couldn't blame him. It was not something she should have known—except it had been part of his uncle's instruction in Mage Globes. Two years ago in Shainkroth Tamos Wolvar had shown them how to construct near-invisible spheres "tasting" of their magic, and left them as decoys while they escaped the city. The Net closing in on them had been woven by the Fifth Lord himself at a distance of three miles.

"Point taken," whispered Tamosin Wolvar.

Imilial Gorrst hadn't understood a word of this and was about to say so in no uncertain terms. Cailet forestalled her by addressing Kanto Solingirt.

"Your own studies must show that what I propose is possible."

"Your pardon, Captal, but 'possible' is not the same thing as 'probable.' The subtle complexities of Ladders have been speculated over for thirty Generations, but no one has ever been able to—"

"Oh, for—" Collan looked up from stuffing an extra blanket in Jeymi's pack. "If it works, great. If it doesn't, we'll be dead. But if the Malerrisi catch us, we'll be dead, too. What's the difference?"

Cailet tucked a smile away from the corners of her mouth—an action not made any easier by the glance Sarra gave the Minstrel.

"Have you any more pithy comments to make, or does that about sum it up as far as you're concerned?"

"That's it," he affirmed blithely.

"For your enlightenment," Sarra went on coldly, "the difference is that some of us will be alive in Longriding. But I still believe Cailet is right. We must go together, all at once."

"Isn't that what I just said?"

His expression of puzzled innocence—ludicrously overdone, of course—brought a twitch to Cailet's mouth. She disciplined her features and before Sarra could frame a retort said, "When Taig returns, we'll leave."

"Captal," Telomir began.

"Enough." She loathed herself for saying it, and for the way they all bent their heads in submission. All except Sarra and Collan—thank all the Saints, Cailet thought gratefully.

To her intense relief, Taig entered a moment or two later. His jaw was set and the look he gave her was given to the Captal. Cailet felt a painful squeezing around her heart. All her life he had been too old for her, too loftily Blooded for a Third Tier, too richly dowered for an orphaned nobody. He was still all those things: but she had become Mage Captal. If there had been distance before, it was a chasm now.

"They're gathering up in the tower, just like yesterday," he said.

"Another Net," Ilisa remarked. "We evaded the first one. If they weave it before we're out of here, we won't make it through the Ladder."

"Another—?" Cailet faced her, frowning. "Why wasn't I told?"

"Your pardon, Captal. With everything else—but there was no magic for them to sense, I swear it."

"There is now," Sarra stated. "The Mage Globes."

Kanto Solingirt limped to the Ladder circle. "That's it, then. Hurry up, all of you. Captal, we must leave *now*."

They pressed together—sixteen people plus journeypacks, Collan's lute case, and two crates of Bardic books. Jeymi stood on one, Cailet on the other, bringing her eye-to-eye with Taig, Telomir Renne, and Collan. The first two looked grim. The third gave her a wink.

She closed her eyes and drew on Alin's knowledge. *I miss you,* she thought, *but I guess part of you is always with me. . . .* The Blanking Ward came into being around her, but not around those at the perimeter. Momentary panic—*I can't do this, what made me think I could possibly do this?*—vanished as Tamos Wolvar's lifetime of study slid smoothly into her mind. *Oh, of course! Just like pouring magic into the thought-mold of a Mage Globe to expand it. More . . . a little more . . . St. Miryenne be merciful, no wonder nobody's ever tried this before!*

It was taking everything she had to push the boundary of the circle even a few inches. She needed at least a foot, preferably two. And the circle must be a *perfect* circle or the swirling energies of the ancient Ladder spell would angle wildly and crash into each other and—

(That's why Ladders are circular—and so many buildings—magical energy trapped inside whirls around and around, never to escape. How many rooms and temples and closets—and even sewers!—were designed for the possibility of Ladders? But what about the really old shrines, like the one in the hills above Havenport? Triangular, not round—)

The musings vanished, dismissed as irrelevancies by another part of her mind (hers? Alin's? Wolvar's? Adennos's? Gorsha's? How could she possibly tell?). There was something more important to think about: the Ladder at the other end. She had to expand *that* circle as well before they could go anywhere at all, and if she couldn't, those outside the circle would die. Those partially inside . . . she shied away from that idea, stomach clenching.

More. More, *damn it!* She explored the circle and found it flawless. Then, casting her mind to the destination Ladder, she fed its spells with her magic. No one had ever tried this before because no one had ever known how—and no one had had power enough, either. Cailet drained herself nearly dry, not knowing how she did it and not caring, and felt still greater power flow forth from some unsuspected source deep within her.

How did Gorsha manage to Ward this? Where did it come from?

His voice, deep and soft and mildly amused, said, *My dear, you wouldn't believe me if I told you.*

She remembered something then. A promise she'd made him, and forgotten on waking. She cast out with what magic she could spare and found the Mage Globes. None had yet shattered into funeral fire.

You gave them no time, even after Sarra's warning. It's up to you, Caisha. As you and I both feel it should be.

Yes. She centered on the one guarding Alin and Val, lingered a moment to smile at the sight of them lying side by side, and then with a wordless farewell exploded the sphere. She did the same to the Globe hovering over Lusath Adennos. And then, hesitantly, found her own creation that lit Gorynel Desse where he lay in what had been Cailet's own bed.

Do it, love. Don't let them find me.

It wasn't as difficult as she'd dreaded. It was an old man who lay there, white-bearded, spent, in some ways gladly dead. She would always think of him as she had seen him on the black-glass plain. Fire cascaded down onto the body she could not believe was truly him.

Thank you, Cailet. Hurry now. The Malerrisi Net is nearly woven.

Gorsha?

But the voice was gone. The wisp of the feel of him was gone.

So was the Blanking Ward.

And the room in Bard Hall.

"Shit!" exclaimed Collan Rosvenir. "Damned cactus!"

Had the press of bodies around her not been so tight, Cailet would have toppled bonelessly from her perch on the crate. As it was, she was further crushed as people winced away from threatening spiny blades and Collan swore additional vengeance on the cactus. It was almost funny, and if she'd had any strength she would've laughed.

All urge to mirth died as *something* prodded at the hazy remains of the Ladder spell. Tempted to catch at it, for it seemed achingly familiar, in the next instant she flung up an instinctive Ward.

Against Glenin.

It's not time yet. One day—but not yet.

As Taig helped her down, she wondered whose thought it had been.

29

"And so," said the First Councillor, "you tell me it is over."

Neither Glenin nor Auvry had said that. Neither one corrected her statement. Anniyas rose slowly from her desk chair, plump fists sparkling with rings in the lamplight. Garon stood beside her. Father and daughter, mother and son. Glenin met her husband's gaze steadily, thinking what a happy little family they made.

"Gorynel Desse is dead," replied Auvry Feiran. "As is the Captal."

"Yes, I've seen their heads. Thoughtful of you to enclose my little trophies in Globes to preserve them. Pity they're not in better condition."

Feiran said nothing more. Glenin had said not a single word in the hour since they'd come here directly from the Ladder. It was Solstice Night, and all Ryka Court was celebrating at a ball hosted by the Doyannis Blood. The few sentries on watch didn't so much as lift a brow at their dishevelment. Glenin was exhausted and filthy and bruised from climbing over rubble at an alarming pace during the frantic attempt to reach Bard Hall before all the evidence burned. Her father looked even worse, but somehow, through some trick of posture or interior strength, managed to give the impression that his uniform was spotless.

Garon had accompanied his mother from the party. He was overdressed, as usual, in silver velvet—longvest, trousers, and shirt—with rainbow ribbons sewn along the underseam of his sleeves from armpit to wrist. When he first saw Glenin, he flung open his arms and took three running steps toward her before his mother extended a hand to stop him. With her arm braced across his chest, and an agonized expression on his face, he'd looked like a bird shot dead in flight just before it begins to fall.

He'd obeyed Anniyas, not his compulsion to be with Glenin. She didn't let it bother her. Anniyas could do nothing to her now.

"You promised me two heads," the First Councillor went

on. "And delivered." She turned to Glenin. "*You* must be disappointed. The Liwellan girl got away."

"How can that matter?" Garon protested, unable to keep silent any longer. "She's officially dead. She has no power anyway. She's not Mageborn, she—"

"*She is now surrounded with all the Mage Guardians left in this sorry world!*" Anniyas bellowed.

"And how many might that be?" Glenin inquired quietly. "Five? A dozen? Reports list more than five hundred Mage Guardians killed all across Lenfell, another two hundred imprisoned. We know what will happen to *them!*"

"Seven hundred out of a thousand! I want that thousand—every damned one of them!"

"However many survive, they're nothing but a pathetic remnant. Lacking a Captal, the Mage Guardians are as good as dead—and lacking Desse, the Rising *is* dead. They will trouble us no more. We have the future to think of now."

Anniyas glared at her. "You're damned sure of yourself for a woman who just lost the most important game of her life so far!"

"I am damned sure of myself," Glenin replied calmly, "for a woman who will deliver of a Mageborn son this autumn."

Not Wards or Wraiths or the command of St. Chevasto himself could keep Garon pent now. He ran for her, ribbons flying, arms encompassing. Over his shoulder she saw the flare of stunned joy in her father's eyes—and the spurt of terror in Anniyas's.

Garon, realizing his exuberance was half-strangling her, drew back and let her breathe. "My darling! Why didn't you tell me? How long have you known? Mother, isn't this spectacular news?"

"Spectacular," she repeated flatly, then roused herself to a mockery of a smile. "How wonderful, Glenin."

Glenin smiled back with equal sincerity. "I only found out for certain yesterday. I would never have gone on so dangerous a journey if I'd known earlier, Garon."

"I'm going to take *such* good care of you this time," he promised, catching both her hands to his lips and slobbering kisses all over them. "First thing is to get you into a hot bath, poor lamb, and then to bed. Come with me, beloved. I'll see to everything."

"You're so sweet to me, Garon," she purred. Leaning

against him, his arm about her waist to give her support she didn't need now and never would, she smiled at her father. "I forgot to tell you that the First Lord says you still look much too young to be a grandfather!"

Thus did she put the child's grandmother on notice that this pregnancy, unlike the other, was sanctioned.

As Garon assisted her to the door, Anniyas said to Auvry, "You didn't tell me you'd gone to Malerris Castle before coming here."

"We didn't, First Councillor. The First Lord came to us, through the Traitor's Ladder to Captal Bekke's Tower."

What her father didn't know was that Glenin had used that Ladder early this morning before anyone was awake. Then, from the obsidian circle overlooking the waterfall, she'd cast a spell toward the Castle and been answered—at first irritably, for she'd roused the First Lord from sleep. For reasons of his own, the First Lord had chosen not to mention this visit; it made him look so much wiser and cannier if it appeared instinct had led him to the Academy.

"Lots of rest," Garon was saying. "And I'll hire our own special cook to see to your needs."

All the way to their suite he continued in this vein. She stifled a sigh. Twenty weeks of this would surely drive her mad.

But for her son, decreed by the Lords of Malerris and destined to stand at the Great Loom as its Warden and Master, she could endure anything. Even her son's father.

The Rising

Of all the things Lady Lilen had been called on to explain, the presence of twenty-five Council Guard corpses in her greenhouse was not among them.

The day before Cailet woke, Elin and Pier Alvassy had arrived at the Ostin house in Longriding. Elin's was the superior magic, but her brother's devious instincts were such that Cailet suspected his Name Saint, Pierga Cleverhand, of personally blessing him in the cradle. Though his plan made his sister and Lady Lilen rather queasy, they had to admit it was the only thing to be done. So while Elin used her magic to create temporary ruin of the two-acre garden in back of the house—screened from neighboring properties by a ten-foot fence—Pier lived up to his thieving naming by stripping Guard corpses to bare skin. Uniforms, swords, identity disks, personal jewelry—all of it went into a trunk for storage, a pile for washing and mending, or the trash for disposal. As for the bodies. . . .

"Mulch."

Cailet winced. "Sorry I asked."

"Oh, I don't know," Collan remarked. "It's not so bad, really—not when you think that they'll end up as roses or lavender."

"Kind of poetic," Pier agreed.

"What happens when somebody comes looking for them?" Sarra wanted to know.

"Somebody already did." Elin's feral smile was unexpected on an otherwise sweetly delicate face. "The local Justice was here on Solstice Night. I told her the squadron had marched off, following Lady Lilen to Ostinhold."

"And she believed it?" Col asked.

"Oh, yes," Elin assured him, green eyes dancing.

In point of fact, Lilen had indeed gone to Ostinhold. With her were Geria, spelled to selective amnesia by Elin, Sela Trayos's two children, and Sela's body. She had given birth to a son, named him, and died. What that name might be, neither Elin nor Pier knew.

"Lady Lilen says he ought to be anonymous for now," Elin explained. "For his own protection."

Cailet agreed. But she couldn't help wondering if, in fourteen or so years, she would meet up with a boy whose magic she would recognize.

Fourteen years? She could scarcely think ahead fourteen days.

In the last eleven, she had sent small groups deeper into The Waste. First to depart had been Riddon, Maugir, and Jeymi Slegin, with Ilisa Neffe and Tamosin Wolvar. Their destination was Maurgen Hundred, near Ostinhold. Biron Maurgen—tall, dark, and strongly built, but otherwise so little like Val that Sarra had difficulty believing they were twins—had ten days ago offered the refuge of his family's out-country property.

"With my mother's permission, naturally," he said, showing a nice sense of the proprieties. "And, of course, my sister Riena's. She runs the Hundred these days, since Mother's back got so bad."

"Lady Sefana is ill?" Taig asked. "Not seriously, I hope."

"She's all right as long as she stays off a horse—which is like asking her to cut off her legs."

Cailet nodded. Vigorous, impulsive Sefana Maurgen had practically been born in a saddle.

"Actually, Cai—I mean, Captal—I was wondering if your Healer Mage might be willing. . . ."

"Certainly," Elomar responded at once. "Anything I can do will be done."

"Thanks." Biron smiled his gratitude, then sobered. "People don't realize, you know. About Mage Guardians, I mean. Even the last years, with so few of them around—"

Cailet nodded her understanding, and he finished with a relieved sigh. Val had always been most obviously his mother's son: the silver-tongued charmer, the handsome self-described Wastrel. Biron cheerfully described himself as an amiable plodder who rubbed along on thoughtfulness and steady consciousness of duty, with a face that at least didn't frighten babies. He had confessed privately to Cailet that with his twin dead, he felt as if half of himself had been taken away. "The best half," he said, and only shook his head when she protested that this wasn't so.

His problem was the exact opposite of Cailet's. She was still wholly herself, but the addition of other people's memories and knowledge had made her skull a crowded place to live. Every evening for the last eleven days she had spent long hours before bed simply letting her mind run free— listening to those others, as it were, tagging each bit of information, absorbing techniques and memories as parts of herself now. But there was so much. So much. . . .

She'd had to order Imilial Gorrst, Kanto Solingirt, and Telomir Renne to Ostinhold. There were certain advantages to single-minded loyalty (especially when embodied in Imi, sword in talented hand), but much as Cailet appreciated their fierce desire to protect her, there were things she must do that they would not approve. Thus the three had to be safely shunted aside.

The same motivation told Cailet that Taig ought to go with them—their need for a guide was a good enough excuse. Somehow, she couldn't make herself say it. When Sarra did it for her, she was both angry and relieved. Imilial had bristled, asking tartly if Sarra thought her unable to read a map. Cailet had found sudden fascination in a snagged thread on Gorynel Desse's cloak.

She wore it now, even indoors—ostensibly because it was chilly. Only Collan knew it was a substitute for the one Lusath Adennos had not lived long enough to give her. Tarise had mended, washed, and soaked the wool in a vat of black dye to freshen the color. She had also hemmed it a full eight inches and altered seams at the sides and shoulders. Cailet supposed it fit. But she was still trying to get used to it.

And to the look in Taig's eyes sometimes when he thought

her attention elsewhere. She didn't want him to leave. She just wished he'd stop watching her that way—as if aware that it was just Cailet, just the girl he'd known since her birth, and yet not Cailet at all but some strange near-mythical personage wearing Cailet's face. It was confusing him, she knew that all too well. How did he think *she* felt. Especially when he called her *Capital*. . . .

But Captal she was, and as such had ordered Imilial Gorrst, her aged father, and Telomir Renne to Ostinhold. She'd thought about sending Tarise and her husband Rillan with them, but on the day of departure another new arrival appeared: Taguare Veliaz.

He was no more a Veliaz than Sarra was a Liwellan. He was a former slave, Bookmaster at Scraller's Fief, purchased and freed years ago by Orlin Renne. Rillan's family had given him a Name, and Lady Agatine had given him a job as tutor to her sons. Left behind at Roseguard by his own request to accomplish certain unstated Rising goals, the tale of his journey to Longriding was, Cailet surmised, fairly typical of those lucky enough to have avoided arrest.

When she noticed Collan's reaction to Taguare she began to wonder once again about his Wards. Vague recognition was followed by puzzlement, as if he knew that he knew this man but didn't how how. Then he gave a tiny shrug as if resigning himself once more to the holes in his memories. At least, Cailet told herself, the sight of Taguare and the sound of his name brought him no pain.

Perhaps Gorsha had reset Col's Wards on purpose, changing them in subtle ways so perhaps one day he would remember the truth of who he was. Col had said he didn't want to remember, but it just might be that he would have no choice.

Whatever Gorsha had done had impaired his memory for music and lyrics not at all. He knew eight distinct versions of the Ladder song and during one very long afternoon in Lady Lilen's elegant sitting room he sang all of them in order of antiquity, plus the version he'd learned from Alin at Bard Hall. Sarra scribbled frantically whenever she heard a difference from the song she knew.

When Collan finally finished, the debate began. Eloman thought this, Taig thought that, Elin was reminded of something else, and Sarra talked and took notes simultaneously—but Cailet noticed that Collan had nothing to say. Almost as if he was letting them talk themselves to a standstill before presenting his own brilliant solution. Irked, she decided she could wait just as long as he could any day of the week.

Sarra was not possessed of Cailet's patience—either that, or she wasn't quite as stubborn. "Well?" she asked at last. "You haven't contributed your two cutpieces yet. What do you think?"

He shrugged. "I think you're idiots, all of you. You shouldn't be tracking down the oldest version of that silly song—you should find the newest."

All eyes were on him now. Cailet couldn't help but admire, grudgingly, his Minstrel's instinct for gathering an audience.

He grinned, enjoying himself, and ticked off points on his fingers. "How long has that shop had a pink pig sign? Twenty years? Thirty? What was there before the toy shop? Has the Bower of the Mask ever been sold and its name changed? When did the Garvedians buy *Domna* Lusira's house in Cantratown? I know for a fact that the Affe Name hasn't always owned their house there."

Taig was nodding. "So the song has to change to match the changes in what surrounds the Ladders."

"And the Ladders were built before The Waste War," Collan went on, "or so everybody says. Roke Castle Lighthouse has been there half of forever—but if history is anywhere near accurate, a lot of Roke Castle was destroyed in that war. An army or two has trotted through since, and they managed some serious damage. But the song is specific about a lighthouse. It's the only way to read the rhyme." He spread his hands wide. "So either the song changes to keep it up to date on ancient Ladders, or the Ladders aren't so ancient after all."

It was Elomar's turn to nod in agreement. "Centuries later, Captal Caitirin Bekke created two."

"That we know of," Col added.

"Holy Saints, you're right," Sarra said, and whether she was more amazed at the deductions or that Collan had made them, Cailet wasn't about to guess. "The wharf pylon at Roseguard—wood constantly attacked by tides doesn't last Generations. When was it last replaced? That'll tell us one of the latest dates for the creation of a Ladder—"

"Figuring out *when* doesn't solve the other rhymes,"

Cailet said. "I think somebody's been lying about the Ladders for a very long time."

"You made the ones here and at Bard Hall bigger," Taig said. "Could you build one from scratch? If one Captal did it, maybe it's part of the Bequest."

If that knowledge *was* in the Bequest, Lusath Adennos had not been able to give it to her. That she was incomplete, not a true Captal, was not something she would admit in front of people who didn't already know.

Sarra fielded Taig's question for her. "It may be a special talent, like being a Healer Mage."

"And I don't have it," Cailet said, grateful that her sister had provided a workable explanation—which could be correct for all she knew.

"I wonder," Pier ventured, "if the Malerrisi can."

"If they could, they would. Bet on it." Collan took a long swallow of coffee, grimaced, and got up to warm the mug from the pot. "Look at the list. Every Ladder we know of to Malerris Castle is in someplace certifiably ancient. Except Captal Bekke's Tower, of course. I don't think they know how." He sat down again, crossing long legs at the ankles. "Besides, they don't need to."

"The velvet Ladder!" Sarra picked up his thought instantly. "They wouldn't need a permanent one if they could use one of those whenever they pleased."

"But how do they work?" Cailet got to her feet and began to pace the carpet. "I still don't quite believe they can exist. How do you put all the necessary energy and spells and Wards into a piece of cloth?"

Elomar did credit to his upbringing by rising to replenish everyone else's cups. "Most surgical instruments are carved with spells."

"I've seen them on a lot of things," Sarra agreed. "The spines of books, silver goblets—the velvet must be covered in embroidery. Maybe the cloth itself was spelled as it was woven. Their patron is the Weaver, after all."

Cailet held still long enough for Elomar to pour coffee, then went back to wearing a path in Lady Lilen's rug. "You said Glenin used hers to get inside the bower. Near another Ladder. Maybe proximity is necessary. Maybe they can't be used to go just anywhere—there has to be a Ladder someplace nearby."

"Why?" Col challenged.

"How should I know? I've been Captal for—what, a whole week now?"

"Just about," he drawled. "Done a fair job of it so far."

She made a face at him and flopped into a chair. "I'm overwhelmed by your praise, Minstrel. If you ever turn any of this into a song, don't tell the truth or I'll use my magic to turn you into a toad."

"It'd be an improvement." Sarra plied her dimples. "In looks *and* wits."

Unperturbed, Collan replied, "Careful, First Daughter— you know what happens when you kiss a toad."

"I'd sooner step on you to hear you croak. Come to think of it, a toad would be a vocal improvement as well. Anytime you're ready, Minstrel dear."

He gave a languishing sigh. "And to think that in Pinderon you could hardly keep your hands off me."

"That was to keep you *alive!* And I never came *close* to kissing you!"

"Maybe, but you sure were *thinking* about it."

Taig rapped his knuckles on the arm of his chair, grinning. "Now, now! A man never argues with a lady unless he's married to her—or wants to be."

Cailet repressed a giggle. Far from shutting their mouths, Taig's rebuke made their jaws drop open.

"Back to the Ladders, if you please," he went on.

"Uh—yes," Cailet said, responding to the brow he arched in her direction.

"Oh, must we?" Pier pouted, dark eyes dancing.

"Ladders," Elomar said firmly.

"All right, then," Taig resumed. "My brother believed there were three hubs. Let's say for the sake of argument that they were laid out before The Waste War. Ryka Court for the government, the Academy for the Mages, and Malerris Castle for the Lords."

"No," Cailet said, sitting up straighter. "Go back before that—before the Malerrisi. There'd be cooperation between the government and the Guardians, so they wouldn't need Ladders from Ryka to every Shir. Just one or two from Ryka to Ambrai. They'd continue on from there."

Recovering, Sarra said, "So we can safely assume at least fourteen pairs at the Academy. That's twenty-eight Ladders. Cailet, you can sense one when you're near it, can't you?"

She gaped at her sister. "I can't possibly go search every

round building on Lenfell! The temples and shrines alone—not to mention sewer pipes!"

"Will you let me finish? All you really need is a little logic. Where would Ladders be needed?"

"The major population centers, obviously—but that doesn't explain the one in the foothills of Caitiri's Hearth."

"Let's stick with Sarra's logic a while, shall we?" said Taig. "When everyone cooperated, travel was easy. But after the Malerrisi left the Mages, they'd want their own Ladders. And very likely all of them would be secret, but for the one to Ryka Court. They'd need that to be open, just for appearances' sake—and no, Elomar, that was *not* a pun!"

Collan grinned appreciatively, then said, "There had to be Ladders in to Isodir and Firrense to keep them from starving during Veller Ganfallin's wars. Maybe even a ladder between the two cities."

"Let's not go wild with our speculations here," Taig cautioned.

"I'm not," he said at the same time Sarra said, "He's not." They looked at each other in confusion for a moment before she continued. "Alin told me the same thing. He also thought there also had to be one between Domburr Castle and Domburron. Otherwise it's impossible for Anniyas to have won the battle against Grand Duke Whatever-his-name-was and kill that Warrior Mage in the same day."

"That I'll grant you," Taig said, nodding.

"You pretty much have to," Col responded dryly. "I know what the rhymes for those Ladders are."

Cailet gave a start. "You do? Why didn't you say something?"

"Kitten, we've only been discussing this for the last five hours. There hasn't been time yet to bring it up."

She laughed at him. "Is that a hint that you're hungry?"

"If he's not, I am." Sarra stood up and stretched—to the enraptured fascination of every male present. "Which of you otherwise useless men will cook tonight while we women discourse learnedly on more important things? Elo, you are *not* a candidate. Stoves explode when you come near them."

Rillan Veliaz had been doing the honors in the kitchen. Two days ago Cailet had sent him and Tarise and Taguare to a minor Ostin property up the Shainkroth Road—and had regretted it at every meal since. But they would be safer with every mile put between them and Longriding, though doubtless they would be about as inconspicuous as tone-deaf musicians in the Isodir Opera Orchestra. Still, by and large you were what you said you were in The Waste. Its citizens had neither the time nor the desire to pry into other people's business; usually their own was shady at best. The trio would be remarked upon, but few if any questions would be asked.

The days went by, consumed by plans and discussions and simple rest. Then it was the first night of Seeker's Moon, the Festival of St. Alilen—patron of birds, singers, and crazy people. Longriding's residents lingered outdoors under the full moon, serenaded by roving choral groups paid for their performances with feather tokens. The general population handed out the real thing; the prosperous were expected to provide real silver. Caught unprepared, Sarra ordered all the lights extinguished and no fires lit, and hoped aloud that the ruse would work.

"Otherwise it's eggs on the portico and soap on the windows," she said.

"Not in The Waste," Elomar told her, sharing an amused glance with Cailet and Taig.

Cailet explained. "Eggs and soap are too expensive. What you get on the front walk—"

"—is horse shit," Col finished with a grin, revealing himself familiar with local custom.

"Whatever did we do without your Minstrel's elegance?" Sarra observed.

"Your pardon, Lady," he said with one of those elaborate bows—this one with an equally overdone expression of regret—that so irritated Sarra. "Ought I to have said 'the inevitable result of intestinal collaboration between animals of the equine persuasion and certain varieties of nutritional fodder'?"

"Descriptive, if long-winded," Sarra said: the discerning critic. "But perhaps you ought to join the celebrants. Feathers aren't your usual fee, I'm sure, but more than you've earned in the last four weeks. Your purse must be positively hollow."

"Gracious of you to worry about my finances. Rest easy, Lady. I'm promised adequate payment for my expertise in keeping you and the Council Guard unacquainted."

Sarra's dimples were in full play as she replied, "Indeed? And what do you consider 'adequate' for the privilege of participating in circumstances that ensure your continued breathing?"

"Look, Lady," Collan began, his temper getting the better of him.

Cailet held up a hand for silence, simultaneously dimming the four small Mage Globes she'd conjured—and so easily—to ease the back parlor's gloom. "Shh! Someone's coming!" *Praise all Saints,* she added in a glance to Taig. He didn't notice.

The choral group didn't stop outside the Ostin house but continued on across the broad avenue. The music was just audible. Cailet watched the faces around her in the dimness as voices wove the intricate patterns of a dainty Firrensean madrigal. Collan and Falundir listened with Bardic precision; Sarra with subsiding annoyance; Taig and Elin with eyes closed; Pier with one finger tapping the arm of his chair. Elomar alone seemed unimpressed, by which Cailet supposed he was tone deaf. Pity. The song really was lovely. When the singers had moved on, she allowed the Globes to brighten once more.

"If no one has any objections, then on the third we'll leave for Renig."

"Why Renig?" Sarra asked.

"Lady Lilen has a house there, doesn't she?" Elin said.

Taig nodded. "On the cliffs overlooking the sea. It's my favorite."

"And undoubtedly crawling with Council Guards," Sarra reminded them. "Malerrisi, too, for all we know."

Cailet smiled. "Oh, they've come and gone at all the Ostin residences, looking for Taig. Not even Anniyas would order Lady Lilen arrested—"

"Which must be breaking Geria's heart," Taig interrupted.

"If she has one," Cailet added nastily. Cailet's private worry about Geria was put to rest by a few minutes' thought. First Daughter had no idea who Cailet really was. Neither did anyone else in The Waste except Taig and Lady Lilen. Gorsha had seen to it before he took Sarra to Roseguard shortly after Cailet's birth.

"Why won't Anniyas touch Lady Lilen?" Collan wanted to know.

"Because the Ostin Web tangles half Lenfell, and my mother sits at its center." Taig shrugged. "That'll only work just so long, you know. Eventually the Council and the

Guilds will figure out a way to unravel it without fatal damage to their own interests."

"Possibly," Sarra said. "But for now, she's safe. We've seen the bounty sheets. Most of us are listed. Lady Lilen isn't."

"Neither am I," Cailet pointed out. "The Lords of Malerris don't even know I exist."

"So we're going to Renig to put them on notice that you do?" Sarra asked in a sharp voice.

"No. We're going to Renig to join the Council Guard." She grinned at her sister's astonishment, and heard Col give a snort of laughter. "Well, we've got twenty-five complete uniforms, all patched and mended. Besides, I haven't played dress-up since I was eleven."

"Geria's Candleweek gown," Taig said, chuckling. "I remember!"

"Turquoise was never her color," Cailet observed, delighted that she was herself again in his eyes. "But it is mine."

"Mine, too," said Sarra, a smile teasing her mouth.

"I know," Taig said—and it was the Ambrais he spoke to, whose Blood colors were black and turquoise.

"Personally," Col said in a drawling voice, "I've always wondered what I'd look like in uniform. Though the cut of the tunic could use a little work. And I've never approved of that gold sash. Gaudy."

Elin gave him a look that doubted his sanity. Then, to Cailet: "Forgive me, but you don't seriously intend to pass us off as Council Guards?"

"People see their uniforms, not their faces. And like it or not, Col, that gold sash is authorization to go anywhere. But not all of us will be in uniform." She pulled in a deep breath, knowing they weren't going to like this at all. "I'm the only woman tall enough to join you men in impersonating Council Guards . . . who are bringing to justice the renegade Sarra Liwellan, the equally traitorous Elin Alvassy—and the infamous Bard Falundir."

The silence could not have been more deafening if she'd announced she was turning her cloak to become a Lord of Malerris. The explosion that followed the silence actually made her wince.

The only part she'd hesitated about was using Falundir, but when she met his gaze he was nodding, a satisfied smile on his face. Relieved that he agreed with her plan, she waited the others out. It felt like half an hour before she could get a word in edgewise.

"Will you listen to me a minute? Thank you. Who does Glenin Feiran want? The woman who escaped her—and the sister of the woman who caused that to happen. Who does the First Councillor want? The man who condemned her in front of all Ryka Court. Any of you would do—but all three of you together are guaranteed passage to the people we want most to see."

"We?" Collan echoed. "Not on your life, Captal!"

She felt the title as betrayal and warning. But she didn't back down. "You may do as you like," she told him steadily. "I have no claim on you. In fact, the obligation is mine."

He shrugged that off, mouth pulling into a line of disgust. "You can't do this, Cailet. It's insane."

"Tonight I've been inspired," she replied lightly. "The Festival of St. Alilen, who watches over crazy people. Who'd be crazy enough to look for a Minstrel in a Council Guard uniform?"

It applied to them all, of course. All but her. Her father and eldest sister didn't even know she was alive; neither did Anniyas or the Lords of Malerris. Cailet Rille was nothing more than a name in a volume labeled *Year 951: Births* gathering dust at the Ministry of the Census.

They were all going to find out otherwise.

Sarra was regarding her with something closely akin to horror. "Cailet—you can't do this."

"Because it isn't what you'd do?" She rose, and crossed the carpet to take her sister's hands. "You said you and Glenin can more or less anticipate each other. She knows nothing about me. *Nothing.* No guesswork, no instinct, no logic in the world can help her."

"But she does know me," Sarra said slowly. "And that makes me useless to you except as an indicator of what you *shouldn't* do. Oh, don't worry. I don't mind." The smile was a very bad fit on her beautiful face. "I make a good lure, too. Very well. I'm with you. But not as Sarra Liwellan." She reached inside her shirt for the identity disk on its long chain. "She's dead. I'm Mai Alvassy now, Cailet."

"Oh, I'd forgotten that."

"You're *both* crazy!" Collan exclaimed.

"Full moon," Taig growled. "Col's right—it isn't 'we'

who need to confront the Malerrisi. It's you, Captal. I don't like your reasoning."

Speechless, Cailet spun to stare at him. Before she could find words, Sarra rose to stand beside her.

"And I don't like your tone!" Sarra snapped. "Do I need to spell it out for you, Taig? She has Alin's Ladder Lore. How do you think we got here? She has Tamos Wolvar's knowledge of Mage Globes. Where did you think those came from?" She gestured to the four spheres hovering in the corners of the room. "And she has what Lusath Adennos gave her and a goodly dose of Gorynel Desse as well."

"I know!" he cried, and a whimper of pain clogged in Cailet's throat. "Don't you think I see them looking out from her eyes? All of them—Gorsha—and m–my brother—"

Sarra was shaking with rage. Wonder-struck, Cailet realized that here was protection and defense for always, and not because she was the Mage Captal. *"You're my sister, and I love you." She* meant it. . . .

"Cailet isn't Alin! Or any of the others! If you ever doubt it again, Taig, just ask yourself if any of them—if anyone in the entire history of magic on Lenfell!—could have done what she did to those Ladders!"

Silver-gray eyes sought Cailet's, slid away again as if it hurt too much even to look at her. His anguish was a living thing that twisted the muscles of his face and made his lips stiff as he said, "They gave her what they knew. But there's never been magic like hers. Gorsha said it long ago."

"The hell with what he said!" This from Collan, her other staunch defender. *"You* look at her, Taig. Know her for who she is. Holy Saints, man, you've known her all her life!"

It was a long time before Taig lifted his head. He searched her face, sighed quietly, and murmured, "Forgive me, Caisha. I'm sorry."

Her voice was thick, but she forced out the words. "It's all right, Taig. I understand." She made herself walk toward him and take his outstretched hands.

His hands are as cold as mine. We'll find no warmth in each other's touch. . . .

She knew that as if she'd always known it. A memory wafted up, hesitantly offering understanding and comfort: a girl, deeply loved, who had promised to wait. That same girl, a young woman now, shaking her head in slow and sorrowful negation. *"I'm sorry. You're so different now. . . ."*

But Cailet didn't need a memory not her own (whose? Not Alin's.). The endearment from childhood had told her everything. Taig had to see her as the Cailet he had known all her life, or begin seeing the others in her eyes again. He would never see her whole. She could be Cailet or the Capal but not both at the same time. And he would never see that the little girl who had worshiped him was now a young woman who loved him, and needed more from him than a brother's love.

Maybe someday, when all this is over, and we can have a little peace . . . ?

No. Never.

It was her own voice asking, her own voice answering. Forbidding regret or bitterness, she released Taig's icy fingers and glanced around. Elin and Pier and Elomar were staring at their hands. Falundir was watching her and Taig, compassion in his blue eyes. Sarra was looking at Col with speculation arching one brow.

"We leave on the third for Renig, then," Cailet said, a smile curving her mouth unbidden as she caught the Minstrel's eye. "Tomorrow we'll try on the uniforms. *You* can judge the fit."

"If I do, they'll *know* we're faking it," he shot back. "Those tunics have to look sloppy."

She heard the *we,* of course, as he'd meant her to. Odd, how she'd known him little more than a week, yet could no longer imagine life without him.

Or Sarra. Especially Sarra.

She was still thinking about it when she crawled wearily into bed. It was almost as if they had been waiting for her. As if this life had been waiting for her.

It had, for nearly eighteen years.

"Whoever said that," she mumbled aloud, "go away and let me sleep."

2

"What the hell is your mother running here, a shelter for stray Mages?"

Collan had dragged Taig by the elbow to one side of the entry hall, away from the latest refugees—who had very nearly fainted when Lady Lilen's front door was answered by two men in the red regalia of the Council Guard.

Taig grinned. "She's the central contact for all North Lenfell."

"Oh, wonderful. Just wonderful. So all it'd take would be one of them singing to the Guard—"

"Even if they do, which is damned near impossible, it won't matter. We'll be gone tomorrow." Taig slapped his shoulder companionably. "You worry too much, Col. The Council can't and won't touch my mother. One way or another, she owns half Lenfell."

"It's the half Anniyas owns that concerns me," he retorted.

"Relax. We've planned for circumstances just like these." Taig walked off to join the others in the music room. Grinding his teeth, Col followed.

Lusira Garvedian—exhausted but as exquisite as ever—had yet to unstick herself from Elomar Adennos's side. Each looked stunned with joy at finding the other alive. Collan sighed a bit at her unavailability, but didn't wonder, as once he might have, what the gorgeous Garvedian saw in the plain-faced, skinny-limbed Healer Mage. He liked Elo, and considered Lusira a lucky woman with excellent taste in men.

Unlike Cailet, who would probably never understand that the Rising meant more to Taig than she ever could—either as Mage Captal or as herself. Poor little kitten. . . .

Tiron Mossen and Keler Neffe were too numbed with weariness to react to anything except the embrace of deep upholstery; they sank into chairs as if they'd been on their feet for four weeks straight. Which was almost the case.

Fortified by wine and food from Lady Lilen's larder, Lusira told their tale. She'd left Cantratown the same night Tamos Wolvar had battled Glenin Feiran with Mage Globes in Combel. What had happened to Lusira was pretty much what had happened to Lady Agatine: warned by a bouquet—genuine, delivered by a trusted agent of the Rising—she packed and fled on the appointed day. With no Mage to take her through the Ladder, she traveled on horseback to Pinderon. There, learning the extent of the disaster, fearing for her friends, she warily approached the local members of the Rising. The new mistress of the Feathered Fan hid her until passage to The Waste could be arranged.

A few days later Keler Neffe and Tiron Mossen arrived at the bower. Of all the Mages Alin had taken back to Neele that night, they alone survived. Last in line to climb out, they'd leaped back down into the sewer when Tiron's mother, Sirralin, cried out a warning just before she died. After three days in the maze of pipes, they emerged and sneaked aboard a cargo ship bound for Pinderon; the captain was glad enough of extra deckhands, for six of his crew had been arrested as suspected members of the Rising. A ship to Renig was next, and the regular post coach to Longriding, and here they were.

Sarra, first to speak after Lusira finished, directed her remark at Elomar. "If they were going to catch anything from that filth, I suppose they would have by now."

"What? Oh—yes." The besotted Healer dragged his gaze from Lusira's face. "To be safe, I'll give them something."

Tiron winced. "How bad will it taste?"

This, Collan mused, from a boy who—Lusira said—staved off thirst by guzzling lukewarm bathwater as it poured down a sewer spout. Well, better a bath than—no, he didn't want to finish that thought.

"Fairly awful," Elomar said. "You'll survive. Come on."

When they were gone—Lusira as well, tucked into the curve of the Healer Mage's arm—Cailet finally spoke.

"I wonder if there are others."

"I doubt it." Taig rose to check that the curtains were securely drawn. "I can't show my recognizable Ostin face in Longriding, but Pier went out this morning for an hour or so. Want to tell her what you found out?"

The young man, who until now had been impressed with his own adventures, started at hearing his name. "Can you *believe* that? Three days in a sewer!"

"The broadsheet?" Taig prompted.

"Oh, that. I read that the Council reports over six hundred Mage Guardians either dead or imprisoned."

Taig said, "The Lists burned with Ambrai, of course, but the total number of living Mages is officially somewhere around a thousand. Gorsha's count was one thousand one hundred and nine."

Collan glanced at Pier. "What was the header on the broadsheet?"

"Feleson Press, seventh day of Spring Moon."

"Over a week ago. Old news. By now it's probably eight or nine hundred." Col chewed his lip a moment. "They won't stop until they've got their thousand."

Sarra was frowning. "Did the broadsheet say anything about trials?"

"Ryka Court," Pier said. "They'll be tried in two bunches: Mage Guardians first, then Rising. There was an editorial praising the government's economy in sparing the judicial budget."

"What's the schedule?"

"Three weeks. Time to ship 'em all from various jails around Lenfell."

"That's . . . interesting."

Seeing her exchange a glance with Cailet, Collan knew with nauseating certainty what was next. Had he said *wonderful* earlier? This was worse than wonderful. It was bloody damned *perfect*.

"Aw, what the hell," he muttered. "You can stop running mental mazes. I've been in Renig Jail."

3

While others plotted and planned based on information he gave them, Collan climbed the stairs and went to bed. If what little he'd overheard thus far was any indication, he was going to need the extra sleep.

What he couldn't for the life of him figure out was why he was still with these crazy people. Roseguard to Ryka to Ambrai, he'd gone along with it all—and letting other people decide where he went and what he did was so foreign to his nature that he wondered if Gorynel Desse had bespelled him.

And yet . . . and yet. Here he was. And there *they* were downstairs scheming out his future again. Fundamental honesty made him admit that he stayed because he really did want to. First for Verald and Sela and Tamsa; then, maddeningly, Sarra; now Cailet. Poor kitten. . . .

Truly told, she seemed to be doing all right for herself so

far. If he listened to her without looking at her, he could believe she was Mage Captal. It was watching her face, her
very young face, that jostled his perceptions—and reinforced
his determination to give her all the help he could.

Saints help *him*.

As for the rest of them—he'd now met more Mage Guardians than he had fellow Minstrels, and he couldn't say he
was entirely enamored of the breed. They kept arriving at
Lady Lilen's house, and Cailet kept sending them away after
a good meal and a good night's sleep to places she felt were
safer. They didn't like it much, but they went. Captal's orders.

By and large, they were a fairly dull lot, the Warriors
among them notwithstanding. There seemed an excess of
Scholars; three more arrived during the night, and Collan
had the bad luck to be accosted by a very famous one at
breakfast the next morning.

Her name was Lisivet Mikleine. She was sixty-six years
old and Dean of Neele College. Her students had hidden her,
smuggled her to the sewer under Naplian Street, created a
diversion for any interested Malerrisi and Council Guards,
and now here she was with one of her faculty and a grand-
son in tow. Collan was discussing knives with the boy,
Fleran, when Dean Mikleine plumped her considerable self
into a chair and began without preamble to explain her pet
theory. Fleran hastily decamped. Two minutes into the worthy Mage's discourse, Col wished he'd done the same.

"My linguistic studies will interest you, Minstrel," she
said vigorously, iron-gray curls bobbing as she nodded
agreement with herself. "Consider! What do we call the animal we ride? A horse. What does 'horse' mean?"

Laconically: "It means 'horse.' "

"But what connection does the word have to any description of a four-legged beast with split hooves and a mane and
tail, a creature that eats grass and grain and runs fast? Why
not call it a fish? And what about the tree that blooms in
spring with purple-blue flowers? What's it called?"

Verald Jescarin, Master of Roseguard Grounds, would
have known. Collan hadn't a clue, and said so.

"It's a jacaranda, of course. Now, what the hell kind of
word is that?"

He sipped coffee, smiled politely, and wondered why the
hell such thoughts had ever occurred to this woman. Didn't

she have enough to do as Dean of the most exclusive college on Lenfell?

Pier Alvassy came around with a pitcher of coffee. Lisivet Mikleine pointed imperiously to her cup and didn't stop talking for an instant. Pier gave Collan a grin that said *Better you in the lecture hall than me!*

"There's a little bird in Sheve Dark called the blue chitterling. A *descriptive* name, don't you see? One that *means* something. Color and sound. And the rare Stevvin four-horn that roams upper Tillinshir—Stevvin being the village nearest its feeding range, four the number of horns on its ugly little skull—another name that *describes*. But horse? Jacaranda? Dolphin? Where did such words come from? Nobody knows."

Collan didn't see why anyone would want to. He didn't say so. And that was another thing: he'd caught himself minding his manners recently. Disgusting.

"Well? Don't you think it's odd?" demanded the Dean.

"Uh-huh." He ate faster; the end of his meal would mean an end to his martyrdom. But, by St. Velireon the Provider, this was the best coffee that had been provided him all year, and he sincerely hated to rush through his first cup in the morning.

She pointed her egg-laden fork at him. "Why name some things with words that have no meaning, and yet name others with descriptions of what they are?"

"They ran out of funny words?"

"No, no! They already *had* names for those things! Horse, jacaranda, dolphin—they were familiar and were given the familiar names. But things they'd never seen before—*that's* when they used descriptions rather than—"

"Your pardon, Scholar, but who is 'they'?"

"Our ancestors, of course. They came to Lenfell long before The Waste War. It's the only thing that makes sense. Haven't you been listening? I've compiled a list of over a thousand names that mean nothing, and another thousand that mean something. I have it somewhere in my baggage—"

Collan blinked. "Came to Lenfell from where? How?"

"Damned if I know," Scholar Mikleine said mournfully. "But it's all in the language, you know. The clues. What they already had names for, and what was new to them so they had to make up names for it."

He was intrigued in spite of himself. Half a Minstrel's trade was language, after all. Which led him to think of the other half. Perhaps some of the music as well as some of the words came from sources he had never imagined.

"My oath on it," she said, "they came to settle Lenfell the way we settle new areas of Kenrokeshir. Nothing on the face of this whole world dates from much before The Waste War. And *that* couldn't have destroyed *everything*. So obviously there was a time when we were here, and a time before we were here."

"You mean there's somebody else out there somewhere?"

Scholar Mikleine turned into a statue, her fork arrested in midair and dripping butter.

"If they came from somewhere else, then the somewhere else still exists, probably, with people still there, probably."

Her distinctive almond-shaped brown eyes, common in several branches of her Name, were now perfectly round with astonishment.

"And if they came once," Col went on, warming to his theme—and, truly told, shamelessly enjoying his accomplishment, for it wasn't often one so startled a world-renowned Scholar, "it also means they might come back."

Lisivet Mikleine looked positively stricken. Col began to think of more words—like *seizure* and *stroke*. At last she shook herself, buttered eggs flying in all directions, and set her fork on her plate with a clatter.

"Do you know what you've done, young man?" she accused. "You've opened up an entirely new realm of speculation!" She sounded as if he'd dug her a desperately needed new well and struck a gush of liquid pitch instead.

"Sorry," he offered.

"So you should be! Do you realize that now I'll have to consult whole libraries for clues? Whether or not they come back depends on why they came in the first place. Were they explorers, or were they exiles? And what about—"

He tried to be soothing. "There's no sign that they've been back in the last thousand years or so. If they'd wanted to see what happened to us, they would've come back long ago, right?"

"—what they hoped to accomplish, and what they'd think of us now—"

Was he really sitting here discussing visitations from another world? Mages were each uniquely but all completely insane. Collan said, "Well, by now the language has changed so much we couldn't understand each other anyway, so it's all moot."

"There, you see? *Another* bizarre word!"

"Another for your list—but I want credit for it!" He grinned his best grin and left her mumbling in a dark ecstasy of linguistic and philosophical conjecture that would, he surmised, keep her busy for the next twenty years.

Scholars! he thought, and then: *Mages!* with equal exasperation. He was getting just as crazy as they were. The sooner he was quit of them all, the better. He should ride up to Ostinhold and see Tamsa and the new baby, and give Lady Lilen their father's jewelry, which he'd kept forgetting in the whirl of events.

But he didn't leave Longriding. He stayed. Damned if he knew why.

4

A Folding spell cast by the new Mage Captal got them to Renig at dusk on the fifth day of Seeker's Moon. The duty constable at Renig Jail fell all over herself when eight dusty Council Guards marched in with three prisoners for the local collection.

Cailet had chosen Lusira for the role of captain. As her name wasn't on the bounty broadsheets, her value as a "captive" was nonexistent. But her beauty was a vital asset; no one looked elsewhere when Lusira was around. The other "Guards" wouldn't even be noticed and Cailet would be positively anonymous.

Lusira showed a real flair for the role, using a perfect mix of impatience and condescension in her demand for the most secure cells in the building. Nine Mages and eleven suspected members of the Rising (three of them no older than fifteen) were summarily evicted from three tiny, pitch-black basement rooms.

Falundir went meekly into the indicated cell, a smile playing about his lips as if all this was a chaotic dress rehearsal for an opera written, performed, and produced by children.

The door—solid iron but for a plate-sized slot for food—clanged shut behind him. Elin Alvassy was next, glaring at her brother when he prodded her through the doorway. Sarra gave Collan a look that promised strangulation with his own lute strings if he tried for similar authenticity. He grinned down at her with cheerful ferocity that widened the eyes of the Watch constable who held the keys.

With her sister, her cousin, and the great Bard safely locked up, Cailet turned her attention to the other prisoners. Filthy, dull-eyed, hollow-cheeked, not one of the twenty was alert enough to comprehend any but the most obvious hint. She murmured a few words to Elomar, who nodded.

On the way down dark hallways to a larger cell for drunks, thieves, and petty criminals, the Healer Mage delayed the duty constable with questions. By the first turn, they lagged four steps behind; by the second, nearly ten. Taig, Lusira, and Tiron Mossen went ahead of the twenty prisoners while Collan, Pier Alvassy, and Keler Neffe walked shoulder-to-shoulder behind Cailet. Adequately screened, she nudged one of them in the back.

No response. She tried again, more forcefully this time, and bit her lip when he stumbled. The woman next to him steadied him and gave Cailet a look of mute loathing. Frayed and dirty as she was, she still wore Mage insignia: a small silver Sword at one collar point and a Sparrow at the other. Cailet thanked St. Rilla for guiding her to a Mageborn, and a Warrior into the bargain. She pulled the woman's gaze quickly down to her own cupped hands. Between them she kindled a tiny Globe.

There was a brief gasp. Cailet banished the sphere and allowed the woman's gaze to meet hers again. Her own heart lifted as hope sparked and took flame in the woman's weary eyes. For emphasis, Cailet put a hand on her sword. After a moment it was recognized. Pale lips mouthed *Gorynel Desse,* and Cailet nodded.

"Hurry up!" Lusira barked as the twenty shuffled into a large cell already inhabited by the dregs of Renig. "Damned thirsty walk from Longriding! Before St. Lirance's strikes Fourteenth, I want half a barrel of wine down my gullet!"

"With a well-hung lad to follow!" Cailet called out, winning a shocked glance from Taig.

By Half-Twelfth the Council Guards were in conspicuous and obnoxious pursuit of their stated goals. The dockside

Anchor and Chain bower boasted the best vintages and the prettiest boys in Renig. Cailet couldn't judge one way or the other, having been in only one bower in her life—and that in Pinderon. Taig, who knew Renig dockside to farm gates, assured her this was the best place for their purpose: to be perceived as drunken louts who, when they departed sometime around Fifteenth, could barely walk.

At which point they would return in stealth to Renig Jail, liberate the Mages and Rising prisoners—aware now that help had arrived—and get them out of town. Tomorrow morning Lusira would commandeer a ship for the transport of three prize subversives. They'd be sailing for Ryka by noon.

Cailet poured half her wine into a convenient potted orange tree. They sat outside at three tables pushed together, watching the boisterous dockside life of Renig. Their dinner of sausages and potatoes had been tasty and nourishing, if rather blunt and to the point. Now they ordered jug after jug of Cantrashir red, careful to spill or otherwise dispose of twice as much as they drank.

Cailet, Pier, and Tiron were doing so, anyway. She wasn't so sure about the others. Col and Keler in particular seemed to be drinking quite a bit. The things Cailet now knew did not include a spell to banish drunkenness, so she had to trust that they would not exceed their capacities.

Lusira behaved as if she had reached her limit two jugs ago. She pinched every male bottom that came in reach, called out raucous compliments to passing strangers, toasted good-looking sailors liberally, and in general brilliantly portrayed the worst sort of loud, lusty, leering female. Her looks guaranteed many offers of instant cooperation. She fended these off with a close inspection and a rude assessment of her probable satisfaction.

The men of their party were precluded from responding— or protesting, in Elomar's glowering case—because Lusira was their captain. Cailet had the impression Lusira was having a fine time teasing her lover. The others usually caught themselves before reacting to her more outrageous sallies, which had Cailet alternately giggling and aghast. She could never hope to emulate the performance, and so merely sat back to enjoy it while she waited out the hours until they could leave in a drunken stupor.

It was Half-Fourteenth by the leaden bell of St. Lirance's

when a bizarre group rounded a corner, heading for the Anchor and Chain. Five sizable slaves with necks like wine barrels were dwarfed by a tall skeleton wearing a garish crimson cloak and a brown coif from which inky hair sprouted at odd angles.

"Who's the walking corpse in the bad wig?" Keler whispered to Cailet.

"I don't—oh, Saints!" she breathed, catching sight of the golden sigils stitched on either shoulder of his cloak. She had never seen him before, had only heard of him—at length, and furiously, from everyone at Ostinhold unfortunate enough to have dealings with him. "Scraller!"

"Who? Oh, the one who used to own Taguare?"

"There's only one of him, Saints be praised." She drank to get the taste from her tongue. "He's in Renig every Equinox and stays till St. Sirrala's."

"Charming," Keler said, wrinkling his nose. "Especially his escort."

"Oh, he's a legend, is Scraller. He owns half the slaves in The Waste. And when he gets tired of them, he goes to bowers and hires young boys. The youngest and prettiest he can get."

He smiled, amused by what he thought was her country-bred innocence. "I'm not inclined that way myself, but—"

"You don't understand. All he ever does is have them read him bad poetry."

"Poetry?" The young Mage choked on his wine.

She grinned with satisfaction. "*Very* bad poetry."

Keler rallied. "How do you know what a pervert like that does in a bower?"

"Told you—he's a real legend."

"Well, he seems to be making his legendary way to the Anchor and Chain. Do Council Guards bow to him, or he to us?"

The point became moot as the next table overturned, spilling wine and shattering cups onto the pavement. A bellow of insane rage was followed by the hiss of drawn steel and the screams of those Collan Rosvenir trampled on his way to murdering Scraller Pelleris.

The parts of Cailet that were Gorsha and Alin and Adennos and Wolvar instantly flung courses of action into her conscious mind. The part of her that was a seventeen-year-old girl went into paralytic shock.

It lasted long enough for Col to knock over two of Scraller's bodyguards, dig one of his twin knives into a third, and impale Scraller himself to the hilt of his sword. Taig rushed the two slaves left standing. Keler joined him, kicking the struggling pair before spitting each with his sword—and his look of pure joy as he killed terrified Cailet.

But not as much as what she saw in Collan's face. He yanked his blade from Scraller's twitching body only to plunge it in again. And again, and again, each thrust bringing a jerk and a groan from the dying man. The sword rose and fell, point down, dripping blood. Col's blue eyes were fired by madness.

Elomar grabbed him from behind. Snarling, he shook the Healer off. Cailet staggered upright, bracing herself against the table, and parted her lips to speak the Word of a spell. Lusira cried "No!"; concentration broken, realizing the stupidity and danger of magic here, Cailet subsided.

The five slaves were dead. So was Scraller. Collan kept digging his sword into the corpse—more slowly now, panting for breath, exhausted. There was blood everywhere.

A shrill, high-pitched whistle brought a spasm to Cailet's whole body. The mistress of the Anchor and Chain strode into the street, her massively muscled bouncer at her side. She blew another summons from the silver whistle at her lips then glared at Lusira, hatred for the Council Guard seething in her eyes.

Once more, this time with Taig's help, Elo laid hands on Collan to stop him. The violence of the Minstrel's reaction tore buttons off his tunic and ripped a sleeve from his shirt. The three began a wrestling match made all the more dangerous by Col's sword—but he didn't use it against Taig and Elomar. He was too intent on digging it once more into Scraller.

"Stop it!" Taig shouted. "It's over! He's dead!"

Collan froze. Taig pried the sword from his two-handed grip and laid it on the table.

"Dead?" Col's voice was childlike in its bewilderment.

"Very." Elomar guided him to a chair and helped him sit down, keeping one hand on his bared shoulder.

He frowned at his handiwork. "Dead," he repeated.

"Yes. You killed him."

Collan thought this over. "Who was he?"

Cailet had no time to think what this meant. Five soldiers

of the Renig Watch came running—only to skid to a halt at the sight of all that carnage and all those Council Guard uniforms.

"What're you waiting for?" shouted the bower mistress. "Get this vermin off my property! And don't think I won't send the Council a bill for cleaning up all this blood!"

"*Domna,*" said one of the Watch, casting nervous glances at Taig and Collan, "they're Council Guards. They're immune to—"

"They slaughtered six men without provocation!" She glanced around at the cowering patrons. "First they murder Mages, then Rising folk, and now—"

"Scraller Pelleris," someone said with deep appreciation.

"And good riddance," another added.

"Does it matter who he was? What did he do but walk down the street?" cried the woman. "Where will it stop? Who will they kill next?" There were mumbles of anger and agreement, glances of wary resentment—but no moves on the Council Guards. "Cowards!" she spat. "Motherless sons of Fifths! Don't come crying to me when one day soon they come for *you!*"

Cailet supposed she ought to feel heartened; after all, popular loathing was a powerful weapon against the Council and its Guard. But at present *she* was wearing the uniform popularly loathed.

"Am I to understand we're no longer welcome here?" Lusira asked mildly. She stood, donned her cloak with the exaggerated care of the drunk, and faced the apprehensive Watch. "You heard the *domna,* clear away this vermin. Scraller, eh? Don't you Wasters ever say the Council Guard never did anything for you!"

Collecting the others with her eyes, she started for the street. Cailet slung Gorsha's cloak over her arm and hopped two chairs to get to Collan.

"Get this idiot walking," she said loudly.

Taig and Elomar began to pull him to his feet. He slapped them away and stood on his own. Fumbling at shirt and tunic buttons, he growled at finding most of them gone and the material splattered with blood.

"No, don't!" Elomar hissed—too late. Collan stripped off the tunic. Most of the shirt came with it, fully revealing the golden galazhi on his shoulder.

"Look at that!"

"See the mark? He's *Scraller's!*"

"Saints, no wonder he killed him!"

"He's no Council Guard—he's a *slave!*"

Cailet took a step back from him, boots crunching on broken glass. "Seize him!" she ordered Taig and Elomar. "Captain! This man's an imposter!"

The writhing shame in Collan's eyes was superseded by stunned betrayal. Cailet unsheathed Gorsha's sword and pointed it at his throat.

"Take him, I said!" she shouted at Taig and Elomar, who each grabbed an arm. "How'd you manage it, slave? Who did you kill to get that uniform?" The look Col gave her broke her heart.

Lusira strode up, shock all over her lovely face. "What's this you say? By Swordsworn's Gauntlet, look at that abomination on his shoulder!" She spat on the ground. "I had my doubts about you, showing up alone with a tale of your squad being killed! Into Renig Jail, slave, with your fellows of the Rising!"

Cailet caught and held the Minstrel's stunned gaze. Urgently, wordlessly, she tried to make him understand. At last he did, with a blink of comprehension and a brief wry twist of his lips. He struggled as they dragged him into the street, kicked over another table, yelled his innocence. The performance continued all the way to Renig Jail, the Watch trailing along behind them.

"Keys," Lusira snapped at the duty constable. As the clattering collection was duly produced, she went on with a nasty smile for Collan, "Four dangerous prisoners, but only three cells. I think I'll dump you in with the high-and-mighty Lady Sarra."

The constable ventured. "But—surely, Captain, a man in the same cell as a woman—alone with her—even if she is a traitor—"

"That's the whole point, moron! Let's see how a Blooded First Daughter likes spending the night with a slave!"

It had been no part of their plan to put Collan inside. Truly told, it was potential disaster. And got worse—for no sooner was Col locked into Sarra's cell than the Chief Justice of The Waste arrived.

Inara Lunne was closely related to the Fiella Lunne who sat on the Council for The Waste. Cailet knew Justice Lunne's reputation very well. The terror of local Advocates, she had presided over all major and most minor trials in the Shir for thirty-eight years. Her rate of convictions was unequaled on Lenfell. Her code of sentencing was simple: ten years in prison, slavery, or death. The population of Talon Gorge, a jail in the depths of The Waste where iron ore was mined, was relatively small—indication enough of the punishments she preferred. The odd thing was that she was dedicated to The Waste and saw no cruelty in her decisions, only simple logic. Those who could be of use to the Shir were imprisoned, those whose usefulness was strictly financial were sold for the Shir's profit, and those who were no use to anyone were executed.

At the sight of her in the constable's office, Taig faded instantly into the background. So did Elomar. Their faces were on bounty broadsheets, and Guard uniforms might not be enough to fool an officer of the Council Courts.

Justice Lunne spared them not even a glance. They were beneath her notice, true—but Cailet had indeed chosen her Guard Captain wisely. Men salivated over Lusira; women either despised her on sight or wanted as desperately as the men to bed her.

Inara Lunne was for several minutes in the grip of this last emotion. Lusira took advantage of her stupefaction to say rapidly, "I'm glad you're here, Justice. Though it's a pity you were disturbed at this time of night."

"Never mind that," said the Justice, clearing her throat. "So somebody finally had the balls to kill Scraller?"

"A former slave, posing as a Guard whose squadron was killed. He'll be tried at Ryka with the rest of our haul. Would you care to inspect—"

"He'll be tried in *my* court," Justice Lunne snapped.

"My orders are to transport all suspected adherents of the Rising to Ryka."

"He's no more Rising than you! Don't worry your pretty head about it. I'll try him at Seventh, convict him by Eighth, and execute him at Ninth."

Lusira stiffened. "His offense against the Council Guard takes precedence over a local charge of murder. I must protest your usurpation of my authority."

"That nice red uniform of yours don't mean shit around here. Murderers're mine." When Lusira frowned, the Justice quite visibly ceased to find her attractive. "Maybe the

Mages, too. Fair warning, girlie—we don't take kindly to meddlers here in The Waste."

"But they're—"

"They're already dead," said the Justice, flat and final. "You know it, I know it, they know it. Here or Ryka, what's it matter?" She flicked a finger at the constable. "Line 'em all up tomorrow morning at my court, Tereiz. And make sure they've got Advocates. I want it done quick, but I want it done legal."

"Justice Lunne," Lusira said in desperation, "the First Councillor herself will hear about this!"

"Fine," the older woman nodded. "Anniyas owes me a letter—and a rise in salary."

A nervous hour later Cailet and the others huddled in the shadows behind Renig Jail, waiting for the Watch to change.

"I can't help wondering," Taig muttered, "which Saint is laughing at us."

Lusira shook her head. "The Saints send difficulties to teach us our abilities and limitations, not for their own amusement."

"Religious debate won't get those people out of there," Keler observed.

"Surely we can spare a moment," Taig said wryly, "to mourn all our lovely plans."

Cailet sympathized. It had sounded so ... well, not easy, exactly, but it had fallen together very nicely. The idea had been to put their own people inside to open Collan's way out, while at the same time letting the other prisoners know to expect an escape. Taig, Col, Elo, and Cailet would take separate groups to separate gates and see them on their way to safety at Ostinhold or Maurgen Hundred, with—she hoped—Mages in each group who could Fold the long road.

Now Collan himself was in jail—which might not be as bad as she feared, but which made her nervous because it wasn't part of the plan. What business had she in making such plans, anywhow? *I'm just a Waster. Three weeks ago I was at Ostinhold riding the herd!*

And now you are Mage Captal. Stop worrying, Caisha. It will come out all right in the end.

She almost answered him aloud. Hunching into the black wool cloak that still carried his scent of wind and growing things—and an ineffable fragrance of power that she knew was only her imagination—she shut her eyes and thought. *So tell me how. Tell me what to do.*

Silence.

Didn't you hear that Justice? Sarra and Col and all the others are going to die tomorrow!

After a moment: *Everyone dies eventually.*

Everyone but you! You're still alive, here in my head—

Not in your heart? You wound me, Caisha.

Stop it, damn you! It's not funny!

Neither is your proclivity for sighting a goal and drawing yourself a straight line directly to it—and then panicking if some unanticipated difficulty puts a crimp in the path. Recall the Second Rule of Magic.

Do I really deserve this lecture?

Yes, you really do, and don't get sarcastic with me, young woman.

Cailet sighed to herself. *All right, so I have a simplistic mind. I'll work on it. But you have to help me, Gorsha.*

Silence.

Either tell me what to do or go away!

Silence.

Gorsha?

Cursing his Wraith that lived inside her mind—and cursing her own insanity for believing such a thing was possible—she cast a spell of Warming onto his cloak and tried to be subtle. A minute later she swore again. She'd let her anger invade the spell. The wool was so hot she was sweating.

And let that be another lesson to you, chided his voice in her head.

"Oh, leave me alone," she muttered.

"Captal? Anything wrong?"

"Nothing, Lusira."

5

They'd fixed the drain cover.

After his eyes adjusted to the darkness, Collan strode to the middle of the cell and crouched down to pry up the two-foot circle of iron latticework in the floor. His memory of previous hospitality in Renig Jail was a trifle faulty; he'd been pretty drunk at the time and didn't recall which cell he'd been thrown into. He knew how he'd gotten out, though.

Maybe they'd put him in the wrong cell.

"Why are *you* here?" demanded a familiar, annoyed voice in the dark.

He wedged his fingertips into the spaces between the bars and yanked hard enough to wrench his shoulders. The drain cover gave not an inch.

"You're wasting your time."

He tried again, then felt around the grille's edge. It used to be screwed to the iron frame of the vertical drainpipe. Now it was cemented into slots cut into the flagstone around it.

"I could've told you it won't budge."

Definitely they'd put him in the wrong cell.

"Now that we've established that, perhaps you'll tell me what stupidity landed you in here when you should be out there."

Saints knew he was trying, but she was a difficult woman to ignore. Just his luck to be stuck in a cell with Almighty First Daughter Lady Sarra.

"I thought you knew how to get out of Renig Jail. Evidently you're better at getting *in*."

A feeble breath of night air touched his cheek. Prior experience told him that what passed for a window was a narrow slit twelve feet up the outer wall. Hopeless.

"Damn you, *talk* to me!"

"I'm trying to think! Will you shut the hell up?"

She subsided for all of five minutes—long enough for him to ascertain with the tooth of his belt buckle that the cement was pick-proof. Then she said, "Don't you ever speak to me that way again."

Rolling his eyes, he straightened up and by poking around with his boot found a mess of more or less clean straw in the far corner. He stretched out on it. "Command understood. Get some sleep." At least that would shut her up.

To his astonishment, her cloak landed on his bare chest. The fine wool was warm, and smelled of her.

"Put that over you, you'll freeze."

As he sat up to wrap the cloak around him, he suggested, "We could share."

Her silence eloquently expressed her preference: she'd *rather* freeze.

"Thanks, First Daughter," he said wryly.

"What happened to your clothes, anyway?"

For an instant he tensed. But though the lamplight in the hall was faint, in this pitch blackness she'd shied away from it as the cell door opened. And surely if she'd seen the mark on his shoulder she would have said something. He said easily, "Lost 'em in a fight."

"Is that why you're in here?"

"More or less." He lay back and shut his eyes. The world circled gently, like the slow arcs of a hunting hawk riding the wind in search of prey. "Might as well go to sleep, First Daughter."

"Shouldn't we stay awake? Won't they be coming for us soon?"

"Believe me, we'll know when they do."

She was quiet for a moment. Then: "Who'd you have the fight with?"

He couldn't answer because he didn't quite remember. But it had felt good.

"Collan, will you please tell me—"

"Why don't *you* tell *me* something?" he interrupted. "Why do you want to hold this revolution, anyway?"

The nearby straw rustled. "You make it sound like a Saint's Day Ball."

"Both need advance planning," he observed. "How're you going to do it?"

"What do you mean, 'how'?"

"Just that. March on the Council and Assembly?"

"Don't be ridiculous."

"Capture strategic towns, set up your own government, and work on the rest of the world when you've got a power base?"

There was a pause, as if Sarra was thinking this over. Collan repressed a sigh; she really didn't have a clue.

"No," she said at length.

"Then how?"

"First a public identification of the enemy, so that people know what the threat is. The Malerrisi, Anniyas—"

"And Feiran, father and daughter. All of 'em with magic

to burn and then some. What've *you* got but a collection of Mages and a bunch of non-Mageborns and absolutely no idea how to use 'em?"

"We have Cailet."

"A Captal who doesn't know how to be a Captal. Lady, pardon my bluntness, but are you crazy?"

"Things have to change."

"Who says people *want* things changed?"

With supreme confidence: "They will when they understand the danger."

Collan sighed. "So explain it to me."

Another shifting of straw, as if she'd turned to face him. He imagined her lying on her side, propped on one elbow, blonde hair straying into black eyes.

"The Lords of Malerris will run everyone's lives. We'll all be little cogwheels in a great big clock—"

He snorted. "You think that's not true now?"

"People have a choice!" she replied heatedly. "What if somebody told you that you couldn't be a Minstrel, you had to be a miner?"

"Nobody'd tell me any such thing. I'm far too good a Minstrel."

"And modest with it, too."

"No point in lying. Keep on about how awful things would be. Convince me, First Daughter."

"You live your life as you please. Maybe you can't understand what it is to be forced into something you don't want to do."

"Is that how *your* life has been? Seems to me you've had it pretty much your own way so far. Rich, powerful—"

"—and with a bounty on my head!" she exclaimed.

"Mai Alvassy's head," he corrected. "And why shouldn't they want you captured and killed? The government sees you as the enemy. You want the power they now hold. What makes you think you've any more right to it than they?"

"The lawfully elected Assembly and Council don't run the government. Anniyas does, and the Lords of Malerris."

He very nearly laughed. "Elected? Lawful? There's not one of 'em didn't buy her seat one way or another."

"Something else that will change," she stated.

"What makes you think you've got the right to change things? No, don't tell me, let me guess. You're right, the Malerrisi're wrong, and there's an end to it. Just answer the original question: why would people want change? What would be better?"

"Marriage, for a start. Present custom is obscene. Like a slave auction."

He repressed a wince even though she couldn't see him. "Go on."

"Women should give their property to their sons if they please, instead of everything going to the First Daughter. Men should own property in their own names even after marriage, and dispose of it as they see fit." She paused, and her voice grew curiously sad. "Divorced husbands and unmarried fathers should see their children."

Of all his intimate conversations with women in the middle of the night, this was inarguably the strangest. That he was enjoying it gave him a momentary qualm about his sanity.

"Those are changes in society, not the way government works. I'll concede you've got some good ideas. But they've nothing to do with me. And most of Lenfell will say the same thing."

"They have *everything* to do with you. If you got married, who'd take possession of the money you've earned and do with it exactly as she pleased?"

"Married?" Collan laughed. "Not me, Lady!"

"But it's not just social change, it's philosophical change. The right to choose what to do with your life. The Malerrisi would decide for you. We *are* right, Collan, and they *are* wrong. Once the people see that and understand—"

"What do you know about *the people?*" he demanded, more harshly than intended. "You're an innocent and a fool, First Daughter. You want to know what *the people* care about? Keeping children fed and clothed. Keeping wind and rain out in winter. Keeping what they *have*. They grumble at taxes, but they'll put up with any government that doesn't change what they know."

After a long silence, she murmured, "I see. They put up with the destruction of Ambrai. They put up with the loss of Mage Guardians. But I tell you they *won't* put up with the Malerrisi telling them how to live."

"Won't they?"

"Don't you understand? If we don't do something now—"

"Sarra, listen!" He sat up and damned near shouted across the cell toward her voice. "Nobody cares about Ambrai except those who used to live there! Whatever Mages used to do, teachers and doctors and hired swords do it now! You Mageborns keep forgetting what happened the last time you fought it out! You and your kind made The Waste! Why the hell should anybody join your Rising if it means that kind of war again and that kind of misery?"

"Because my life is *mine*, not theirs!"

Her cry from the heart wrung something inside him, squeezing blood from a rock of fear in his guts. It was why he'd killed Scraller, this fear; it was, in the end, why he hadn't seized the first chance to escape these crazy people who would challenge Anniyas and the Malerrisi.

His life belonged to *him*.

And his Wards? To whom did they belong?

He could have been rid of them. Cailet had offered. But he'd chosen to keep them. They were his, part of him.

And this knowledge sprang from places the Wards didn't even touch. There were levels in his mind and awareness now, like stacked song folios on a shelf containing memories from childhood and adulthood, aspects of his personality and character, things he knew and things he was. That his Wards were of his own choosing was at the very bottom of the piled volumes. He *knew* they were his.

And the Malerrisi would take them away to find out who he was without them.

"All right, Sarra. For what it's worth, I'm with you."

"At least until you're out of Renig Jail," she said cynically.

For a time he simply couldn't speak. Then he lunged toward her, snagging one of her shoulders and an elbow in the dimness. "I could've left you a hundred times by now!" he hissed into her unseen face. "If I say I'm with you, then I'm *with* you, First Daughter!"

"Let go of me!" There was real panic in her voice, the fear of a woman who has never dreamed any man would dare to lay rough hands on her.

He released her and drew breath to apologize. Then he saw the faint golden glint of her hair.

He turned to the tiny window high in the wall and squinted. Light. The palest, most elusive hint of dawn. . . .

Cailet should have been here hours ago.

6

"I can't! It won't move!"

Cailet heard the echo of her own words again and again, each repetition stinging her cheeks anew with shame. Collan had described his exit route from Renig Jail and she'd been positive it would be the simplest thing in the world to reverse the process. Find the sewer grate, pry it loose, crawl down the shaft, turn left, turn right, push the flagstone up in the cell—

She couldn't get the grate open. She'd put her magic to it, and failed. The men had put their strength to it, and failed. Application of magic plus brute force yielded nothing but a headache for her and sore muscles for them. The grate was cemented into its iron frame. Why hadn't she anticipated this, planned for it, figured out a way around it—

Because I'm arrogant and unsubtle, and I think I know everything about everything. Gorsha made me Captal, but he couldn't make me smart.

She couldn't loosen the grate from the cement, she couldn't melt the iron to a puddle of molten metal, she couldn't chip away the stone, she couldn't do a damned thing. They'd all been so kind about it. Not her fault, couldn't have known, must be another way. She nearly choked on their generosity.

And now, with the dawn, other words began to repeat inside her head: *"Try him at Seventh, convict him by Eighth, execute him at Ninth."* Only it wouldn't be just Collan. It would be Sarra and Elin and Falundir, and all the other Mages and adherents of the Rising held in Renig Jail.

Taig spent the long hours before daybreak plotting with Keler. Cailet listened to them explain things to the others and felt worse than useless. All her new magic and knowledge and power, and she could only listen. Only follow them to the Council House. Only stand silent guard while the prisoners were brought into the courtroom.

Falundir alone was serene. Somehow his calmly confident

half-smile wounded Cailet more than the worry or fear or betrayal in the eyes of the others.

Lusira strode to Justice Inara Lunne's chambers to lodge another protest. She returned almost immediately, grim-lipped. A moment before the Justice entered the courtroom, a thin little woman who reminded Cailet of nothing so much as a nervous galazhi hurried in. Her red tunic and gold Hollow Circle badge marked her as an Advocate; the Spoked Wheel within the Circle further identified her as an Annison. Justice Lunne frowned down from the carved desk on a raised dais that served as the bench.

"Agva, what are *you* doing here? I thought your sister's First Daughter was about to deliver."

"Last night, Justice—but it was only a boy, so my duties are over. Your pardon for being late. I was only told half an hour ago that my name headed the list of available Advocates for the Defense." She shuffled papers as she talked, her words as fidgety as her fingers. "In the circumstances, I would ask for a delay so I may familiarize myself with the specifics of each case, if the Justice would be so kind—"

"Advocate Annison, there will be no delays." Inara Lunne brought her gavel down on the desktop to make it official, and the bored clerk made a note in his ledger. "The prisoners are as guilty of crimes as the rest of us are of breathing. They'll all be convicted without any of us even working up a sweat."

"I haven't *talked* to any of them!" the Advocate wailed.

"Nothing they say is worth hearing, I'm sure. The clerk will read the charge sheets. For efficiency, I've combined cases as the offenses warrant."

At school, Cailet had learned how trials were conducted, and on a field trip had seen the Courtroom at Combel. Re-nig's was much grander, as befitted the capital of a Shir. All the chairs and the low fences around the witness, prisoner, and condemned boxes were carved of expensive wood. The roof was a fine stained-glass dome. Portraits of Garony the Righteous, Gorynel the Compassionate, and Venkelos the Judge were painted on the walls. Behind the Justice's bench was a gilt-plaster medallion of the Council Eagle clutching the Arrows of the Anniyas Blood.

Though familiar with the proceedings in principle, Cailet had never seen Lenfell's jurisprudence at work. Its swiftness was literally breathtaking. The Mage Guardians were called forward by the clerk, who accused them of sedition. Agva Annison pled them all not guilty. Justice Lunne rattled off the facts of their arrest while attempting to flee Renig. Two officers of the Watch gave verbal evidence of magical assault (there being no physical evidence), then departed without Agva Annison's directing a single question at them. The Mages were asked to speak in their own defense. Not one of them said a word.

"Very well. It is the verdict of this Court that the accused are guilty as charged. The sentence is death, to be carried out at the end of these proceedings." The gavel banged down. "Next."

It had taken fifteen minutes.

Those associated with the Rising were dealt with next. From accusation to sentencing, their trial was half the length of the Mages'. After a squint at the long-case clock by the door, Justice Lunne ordered someone to fetch her a vanilla-cinnamon (extra sugar) from the coffee bar down the street. Elomar volunteered, earning a nasty look from Lusira; fetch-and-carry was beneath the dignity of the Council Guard. Then Falundir was called to the box and accused of composing and disseminating treasonous songs. The coffee had not yet arrived before the Bard joined the ranks of the condemned.

Only three people were left in the box holding the accused. Collan looked bored; Sarra, tense; Elin, determined.

"Mai Alvassy."

Sarra stepped forward. Cailet watched in bewilderment, hearing Lusira catch her breath softly and Taig's muttered curse, as Elin joined her.

"I am Elin Alvassy, and this woman is not my sister."

The Justice set down her coffee. "Don't try to confuse the issue, girl."

"I am attempting to clarify it. She is not Mai Alvassy."

"Clerk, bring me the accused's identity disk."

Grinning, the man reached for Sarra's shirt. She gave him a glare to ignite ice cubes and brought out the disk herself, slipping the chain over her head.

After due examination, the Justice said, "Her identity as Mai Alvassy is confirmed."

"On the evidence of a stolen disk?" Elin cast a scathing glance at Sarra. "I am an Alvassy of Ambrai," she went on, and her Blood haughtiness was such that she could have given lessons to Geria Ostin. "I refuse to allow this woman to pose as one of my ancient Name."

Justice Lunne took a long swallow from her cup. "Nonsense."

"She is no more an Alvassy than you are, and I demand that she not be tried under that Name."

Lunne had been a Fourth Tier Name, and nothing was more calculated to annoy a Fourth Tier than a display of Blood arrogance. Cailet poked a finger into Taig's side and whispered, "What is she doing?"

He shook his head, as mystified as she.

"The charge sheet reads Mai Alvassy," said the Justice with an awful frown. "The identity disk reads Mai Alvassy. She *is* Mai Alvassy. And even if she isn't—"

Elin actually smiled. "The Council might be made extremely unhappy if this woman turned out to be someone even more important than my sister."

Lusira rose and strode down the aisle between spectator seats. "Justice Lunne, the prisoners must be taken to Ryka Court, where the truth of this matter can be ascertained without doubt."

"Siddown and shuddup." Irritation was getting the better of her carefully elegant judicial diction. "I don't give a shit if she's Grand Duchess Veller Ganfallin reborn."

"Nothing so dramatic," Elin said with a sniff. "Only Lady Sarra Liwellan, primary on the bounty sheets and heir to all the Slegin properties in Sheve."

"Impossible!" exclaimed Taig from the spectator seats.

"Huh? Who?" Collan seconded from the box.

"If you'll recall," Elomar fretted loudly, "there *were* two of them. They looked very alike. You commented on it at the time, Captain."

"Don't be an idiot," Lusira snapped over her shoulder. "We killed the Liwellan girl and captured Mai Alvassy."

"Shut the hell up!" roared the Justice.

Advocate Annison half-rose, sat down, then stood. "Your pardon, but if the accused's identity cannot be established—"

"I say she's an Alvassy!"

"And I say she's not!" proclaimed Elin.

"—then she cannot be tried," finished the Advocate in a timorous whisper.

What all this might gain, beyond a delaying confusion,

Cailet had no idea. Sarra was told to state her Name for the record; she dimpled sweetly and refused to open her mouth. The Justice's direct order produced the same result.

The "Council Guards" were called one by one to the witness box, starting with Lusira, to describe the capture. Fully cognizant of the circumstances of Mai's death, Lusira presented a brilliantly revised version that left room for doubt with the very vehemence of her telling. Elomar was next, then Taig, each giving the same basic report and contradicting each other on the details.

The clerk pointed at Cailet. She walked up the aisle and through the little wooden gate in a state of near panic: she couldn't remember the Name of the Guard whose uniform and identity disk she wore. Stepping into the witness box, she pressed her damp palms against her trousers and tried not to tremble.

"Name and rank," said the clerk.

Cailet began to cough. The clerk brought her a glass of water. She drank gratefully, coughed a few more times, and wondered if there was a spell available to her now that would send everyone in the courtroom to sleep for half a minute. Then she could pretend when they woke that she'd already given the information and awaited questioning. No, wouldn't work, there'd be nothing written in the ledger. . . .

Inara Lunne nodded once. And again. And nodded off.

The courtroom waited in breathless silence. Cailet dared a glance at her companions as a faint snore issued from the bench. Elomar's face was so wooden that she knew at once the Healer Mage was responsible. *Of course! The coffee!*

Cailet assessed the room swiftly—something she should have done on entering, she told herself in disgust. The Watch had departed but for a single man beside the Justice's chamber door. The clerk sat with the ledger in his lap, eyes fixed in astonishment on the slumbering Justice. In the condemned box were the twenty Mages and members of the Rising, and the Bard. Standing accused were Elin, Sarra, and Collan. Beyond the short fence were the Council Guards.

We own *this place,* she thought in amazement. *The Justice and the clerk think they're perfectly safe, with us here. Saints and Wraiths, why didn't I realize this before?*

Because she was still thinking like the seventeen-year-old Waster she was, instead of the Mage Captal she had become.

She cleared her throat softly. The clerk's gaze shifted to

her. She reached for a spell and her magic, murmured a
word, and saw his eyes close. The Watch, now—a little
more difficult to gain eye contact, but she managed it and
sent him to sleep as well.

"Quick," she said, vaulting the rails of the witness box.
"Taig, Keler, do something about their chains if you can—"

A terrified squeak stopped her in mid-stride, halfway to
Sarra. The Advocate was huddled in her chair, huge pale
eyes as round as her thin pale mouth.

Damn! Forgot she was even there. Cailet prepared to send
her to sleep too.

"No, please!"

Cailet went to the table behind which the woman cowered.
"Better for you if I do," she said, not without sympathy.
"They'll wonder, otherwise."

"You—you're a Mage, aren't you?" Agva Annison whispered.

Cailet nodded.

"Are you going to k–kill us?"

Lusira answered for her. "Were that her intent, you would
already be dead." She went past, readying her sword to pry
open the chains binding Sarra and Collan and Elin.

"I'll have to make you sleep now," Cailet said. "I'll remember that you tried to help us."

"Please don't spell me!" Tears trickled down sharp cheekbones. "I'll pretend you did, I won't tell anyone—"

"Well. . . ." Cailet knew it was smarter to treat her as she
had the others. But the woman's terror of magic made her
hesitate. Was this what she could look forward to, this
shrinking away from her as if she had sprouted the horns and
fangs and claws of a Wraithenbeast?

"I swear!" The Advocate was almost sobbing.

Cailet nodded. She just couldn't use magic, however be-
nevolent, on the woman. If she was ever to be regarded
without fear, then she'd have to prove herself—and other
Mages—harmless. No time like the present.

"Oh, thank you, thank you! I won't breathe a word of this,
I'll say that you had to overpower me—"

Cailet winced. "Just make it convincing—for your own
sake, not mine."

The Advocate immediately sprawled her arms across the
table and slumped over with her cheek on the scarred wood.

"She looks a bit too comfortable," Collan said critically, rubbing his wrists as he approached.

"Leave her be. Let's get out of here."

"Past time for it, if I may say so."

"You may *not* say so," Sarra told him. "Cailet, we'll need horses. Not even you can Fold the road for so many."

"We're only going as far as the docks." She touched her sister's hand lightly, to reassure herself.

"Not me or mine," said a woman behind her, and she turned. The Warrior Mage she had alerted yesterday stood there, hollow-eyed and angry. "I don't know who you are, and while I thank you for rescuing us, we'll take care of ourselves from now on."

A voice mused in Cailet's mind: *Mages are a singularly independent lot. The only command they'll obey is the Captal's.*

"Done a terrific job of it so far," Collan observed.

"We were betrayed," the woman snapped. "And now we'll be going."

"Where to?" he asked with exaggerated politeness.

"Anywhere!"

"I think not," Sarra said blandly. "Not without the Captal's permission." And she nodded, almost bowing her head, at Cailet.

The Warrior stared. *"What?"*

"Introductions later," Taig interrupted. "Everybody's cut loose from their chains, Cailet, and we ruined six swords doing it. Let's go. However you spelled the others, Elomar says the Justice won't sleep all day."

"Right," Sarra said briskly. "Five groups, I think. No sense in looking like a parade. We'll meet at the docks."

"And get the hell out of here," Col said. "And I *still* say it's past time for it."

Cailet agreed. There was just one problem. None of the doors would open.

The one to the Justice's chambers was stuck tight. The one through which the prisoners had entered seemed cemented shut. The double doors leading to the outer hallway wouldn't budge. Taig and Keler assaulted the brass handles with their sword hilts. Col went to work on the hinges.

"Don't bother." Cailet folded her arms and sat on the fence railing. "They've been Warded."

"What?" Taig spun around. "That's not possible, Cailet,

there aren't any Mages here but our own people, and why would they—"

"Not a Mage. A Mageborn."

Sarra blinked. Cailet glanced at her and nodded. Of the others, Tiron Mossen was the first to figure it out. Summoning him with a glance, she also collected Elomar, Keler, and Elin. Together they returned down the aisle.

"Ward the others," Cailet murmured. "I'll be safe enough."

At the sound of her voice, Agva Annison straightened and turned in her chair: no more the skinny, skittish galazhi but a lean and cunning predator. She smiled at Cailet through the sudden faint shimmer of a protective Mage Globe that ensphered her entire body.

"I'll have to make an offering to Gorynel the Compassionate," she said, "for touching your tender heart regarding my poor, pitiable self."

Cailet kept walking toward her, and made no answer.

"You can't get out until I release the Wards," said the Advocate. "And you'll never get inside this Globe."

Elomar held the gate open. Cailet stepped through, gesturing to him and the other three Mages to remain where they were. A combination of Wards sprang up to protect those behind: Tiron casting his onto the wood itself, the more accomplished Keler building on it into the air, and Elin easily reinforcing all with a floor-to-ceiling Ward just behind theirs. Elomar smoothed out the whole structure with a mastery Cailet envied. She had never yet cast a Ward. She did not do so now.

Agva Annison laughed, the indulgent chuckle of a teacher whose pupil has made a silly mistake. "A Mage Captal who couldn't smell the magic around the doors? This will be easier than the First Lord ever dared dream!"

Tiron growled with all the outraged pride of his fifteen years. Cailet felt strangely aloof, much older than he; the insult didn't even touch her. She said almost humbly, "Truly told, I have much to learn. For example, I don't know how long it will be before the real Council Guard arrives."

The woman shrugged. "They make their rounds every hour when court is in session. I should think you have about five minutes."

"Thank you." Cailet nodded. "That's just time enough." She drew Gorynel Desse's sword.

Agva Annison lost her smile.

"You recognize it?" Cailet asked, genuinely surprised.

"It—it's one of the Fifty," she stammered. "How did you get it?"

"A gift from its last owner," Cailet replied somberly. "If you know what it is, then you know how much it will hurt. Drop the Wards."

The Malerrisi rose to her feet, proudly defiant. "No."

"As you say, I do have much to learn. I don't know how well I can control this sword. Actually, I've never used it before."

"No."

"Please reconsider. I don't want to kill you, and for all I know this sword might do just that."

"No."

Cailet half-turned away, as if she'd changed her mind. She had a glimpse of Sarra down by the double doors: her hair like a wild golden flame amid darker heads and black Mage cloaks; her face as strong and beautiful as white fire. *"You're my sister, and I love you,"* Cailet heard again in memory. *I am also Captal, Sarra. Love this part of me, if you can.*

Later, when they discussed it, Col would tell her that when he fought, time sped up. For Cailet, it slowed. Each command of brain to nerve to muscle seemed a separate stream of light and energy. Each movement lasted hours. She swung Desse's sword, magic flaring along its length unsummoned by her. She saw the contemptuous sneer on Agva Annison's face change to incredulity and then terror as the woman realized Cailet had not changed her mind and the sword was coming at her with lethal force.

The blade connected with the Globe. Languid lightning crawled up the steel, reversing before it reached her hands, directed back at the glistening sphere—which shattered in a million silent shards and vanished.

The Malerrisi's scream went on forever.

So did time, as Cailet strove to check the sword's arc, fighting its hunger. The battle was as unexpected as it was fierce; she'd been unsure of how powerful the sword's magic might prove, but she'd had no inkling it would be like this. *Gorsha, why didn't you tell me this thing feeds on my magic and Malerrisi blood? I can't hold it, it's too strong. I don't want to kill her!*

After an almost audible snap inside Cailet's head, minutes were minutes again. Agva Annison lay crumpled across the back of her chair. Cailet stared at her, expecting blood. But there was none.

Not because you are stronger than the sword, Cailet. Because you truly did not wish her death. If you had. . . .

She lifted the blade, assessing its clean, straight, arrogant rise toward the ceiling. *You mean I can't lie to this sword.*

Truly told, Captal. I know; I tried.

"Cailet!"

She blinked and lowered the sword. "What? Sarra?"

Her sister's hand cupped her cheek, blessedly cool against burning skin. "It's over, Caisha. The Wards are gone."

"Oh," she said inadequately. "That's good."

Collan was there as well, regarding the senseless Advocate. "Just goes to show," he drawled, "never can trust a lawyer."

Cailet managed a wan smile. Was she exhausted from using power or not using it? Was it the shattering of the Globe or the fight with the sword that had drained her so? The blade chattered into the scabbard with the shaking of her hands. Looking over her shoulder, she saw that the others had left through the double doors. With one last glance at the somnolent courtroom, she said, "This was badly done. I apologize."

Sarra alone nodded. "Agreed. Next time, a better plan."

"The difficulty of our position as Mage Guardians," said Elomar, "is that we cannot act until threatened."

"Compunctions and ethics *are* inconvenient." Col's crooked grin appeared. "I've never had much use for them, personally."

"Fancy that," Sarra murmured.

He favored her with an arched sardonic brow, but addressed Cailet. "*Now* can we please get out of here?"

Halfway to the door, her steps dragging with weariness, Cailet heard a creak of wood behind her. At the same time there popped into her head a crazy image: a brick wall in a rugged stony canyon. Then she staggered as Col shoved her into Elomar and reached for his sword. Sarra was quicker. She spun, one hand already at her belt. Cailet's mind and magic fumbled for the meaning of the knife's silvery flight into Agva Annison's chest.

She felt Elomar wrap her in his arms for a moment,

tightly, as if grasping something infinitely precious. Then he set her on her feet and bowed to Sarra.

"You shouldn't have let her live," Sarra said matter-of-factly, and went to retrieve the knife.

Cailet watched, numb with shock. *For me,* she thought, as her sister bent and jerked out the knife and wiped it on the dead Malerrisi's tunic. *Sarra killed for me. She did what I should have done. She just said so. And she's right....*

"Captal!"

Thickened wits responded slowly to Lusira's shout. But the ringing of steel on steel triggered some new and alien reaction: energy, magic, power, whatever she cared to term it, its strength surged into her body and she was running for the outer hall with Gorynel Desse's sword gripped once more in her hand.

7

The twenty-five members of the real Council Guard squadron got the shock of their lives in the courtroom hallway that morning. Their usual boring rounds—Council House, jail, docks, residential districts, markets—turned into a brawl not a hundred yards from their own barracks.

It was to their captain's credit that she instantly recognized the incongruity: so many people, some wearing ragged Mage regimentals, all wearing the pallor of long days in prison, and none wearing chains, should not be freely exiting any courtroom, especially Inara Lunne's.

Taig anticipated the captain and drew his sword almost before her suspicions formed. The twenty former prisoners had since the previous evening gone from hope to despair to stunned joy; now, liberty threatened, they blindly attacked. The Mages held to their ethic, aware that their new Captal was present. No magic assailed the Council Guards. But if steel no longer circled their wrists and hung from their ankles, neither was any steel in their hands. Against well-armed and well-trained soldiery, it was hopeless.

Then the Captal arrived.

Not quite five minutes later, no Council Guard was left standing.

Sarra watched most of it from the double doors. Still shaky from her first Malerrisi kill, with an absurd reminder nattering in her head that she must cut a new notch on the knife, she saw her sister carve into living bodies like a sculptor shaping cold marble. Cailet was no clumsy butcher, cleaving meat with hacking strokes; her movements were efficient, precise, graceful. Almost gentle, some of them. *So must St. Delilah have looked,* Sarra thought absently; *the warrior who dances with no partner but her sword.*

She felt no curiosity or amazement that this should be so. Her instincts, badly bruised by the backlash of what Gorynel Desse had done to Cailet, reaffirmed their recovery by giving her the obvious answer: it was Desse's sword in Cailet's hands, and he who moved in Cailet's body with the lithe elegance of the born swordmaster.

She wondered if Cailet knew it.

When all the Council Guards sprawled bleeding on paving tiles—red, and so highly polished that the blood scarcely showed—Sarra saw Taig sheathe his own sword and approach Cailet with hands outstretched. The Captal eyed him warily.

"Cai," he said softly. "You can stop now."

She glanced around. Drawing a deep breath, she tilted her head back to meet Taig's gray eyes. "They're *not* dead," she told him.

"I know. You're too good with a sword to have killed them."

"They would be, if I'd wanted them dead."

"I know," he repeated quietly. "We have to leave now, Cai."

Sarra would hate herself all her life for being unable to go to her sister. But she couldn't do it. She just couldn't. She could not keep the Wraith of Gorynel Desse from enshrouding that slight, golden-haired girl.

Taig knew her before. He knew Cailet. The person I'll know isn't just my little sister. She's Alin Ostin and Tamos Wolvar and Lusath Adennos and Gorynel Desse. Taig can see the Cailet she was, and still is somewhere inside. He can reach her. But I'll never know her as she was before. There's too much knowledge in the way.

A familiar solid strength grazed her senses: Collan

Rosvenir. "Come on," he said softly. "Pier and Keler have taken the others out. We've got to get Cailet away from here before someone comes."

"Yes," she said mindlessly. "Of course."

Out. The warm sunlight of Renig's central circle, the cool shadows of side streets; the scents of old stone and fresh bread and the sea; the calls of street vendors to indifferent customers, aggravated fathers to wayward children, sailors on deck to their mates high in the riggings. Sarra was remotely aware of all these, but nothing truly touched her senses until she emerged from a darkened alley and saw the sun-sparked ocean.

To sail it as she had sailed with Mai Alvassy—to come to know her sister as she had her cousin. Just to *talk* with Cailet, alone, with no one and nothing demanding their time. Confessing, confiding; sharing their lives and hopes and dreams; learning who and what they had been, were now, and wanted to be. There would be no need for those Others, no need for the Mage Captal to work spells or cast Wards or even so much as make a decision.

Until Ryka.

She understood then a little of what must happen to Collan. *Ryka* was a word that caused her pain.

Sarra gripped Col's wrist. "Where is she? Where's Cailet?"

"Right up there ahead of us. She's all right. Taig's gone to find a ship—"

"No," Sarra managed, her breathing sketchy and her eyes wincing from the brilliant sun flash of the waves. "We mustn't go to Ryka."

She could feel him staring down at her, heard him clear his throat. "The idea doesn't thrill me, either, but—"

"Then help me," she whispered. "She can't go there. She'll die."

"What?" He turned her from the bright sea, taking her shoulders in his hands. "What are you talking about? What do you know?"

"Help me," she repeated. Forcing herself to look at him, she thought distractedly how incredibly blue his eyes were as suspicion and speculation replaced his puzzled frown. "I'm Mageborn, too," she said, trying to steady her voice and nerves under that piercingly blue gaze. "I don't know

any spells, but you have to believe that there *is* magic in
me—"

"And it's telling you not to go to Ryka." A sigh hissed between his teeth. A moment later he muttered, "How did I get
myself involved with you people?"

He let go of her, and without his supporting hands she
swayed, dizzy. The pain inside her stilled. Catching her balance, she started across the cobbles to Cailet, who leaned
against the wooden rails separating boardwalk from beach.
Her sister was staring out to sea: southwest, toward Ryka.

"Cailet—"

The pale golden head turned. Tousled and exhausted, the
Mage Captal looked barely twelve years old. Except for her
eyes—fierce with black fire, terrifying in their hunger. Sarra
stumbled on uneven pavement, falling to her knees as if a
wind had slammed into her back.

And a wind it was—sudden, unnatural, staggering everyone in sight, swinging shop signs full around on creaking
iron hinges and tearing at skirts and cloaks and coifs. Canvas sails ripped from repair frames on the beach. Drooping
pennants snapped to life and tore loose from poles. The
boardwalk fencing groaned as it shook and splintered. Sarra
scrambled to her feet and was blown toward her sister just
as the wood gave way. The two of them fell ten feet onto the
packed rocky sand below.

8

Though the memory lacked details, Collan knew that a
strong wind had saved his life once. He felt its assault as a
warning now. Taig Ostin lurched against him and only luck
kept him upright. He swung around, eyes watering as fine
grains of dust needled his face, and saw Sarra and Cailet
tumble through the shattered railing.

"Get these people to shelter!" he yelled at Lusira
Garvedian, and vaulted the fence. He landed hard, knees
cracking as they flexed to absorb the shock of impact. Protected here from the wind, he ran to the tangle of fair hair
and dark cloaks lying too motionless on the sand.

He separated them carefully and turned them over. Blood seeped from a gash on Cailet's forehead; when he tried to coax her arm from its outflung position, she cried out. Sarra sat up on her own at the sound, biting her lips white as she reached for her ankle.

"Broken?" Col asked, cradling the younger girl's head in one hand while he dabbed at the blood with the edge of her cloak.

"I d–don't think so. Hurts, though. Is she all right?"

"I think you each cushioned the other's fall. Lucky. How're your ribs? Take a breath. Good. Now a deeper one."

She did so, and nodded. "I'm fine. It's just my ankle and my shoulder." She ran gentle fingers along Cailet's ribs, pressing lightly and watching for reaction. "She doesn't seem bruised, either. What's wrong with her arm?"

"Sore shoulder, seems like. Where's that Healer Mage?"

"Probably flat on his face in the street with everyone else. Listen—it's still howling up there. But how could any wind blow in that fast?"

"And you say you're a Mageborn," he retorted. The split on Cailet's brow was clean now—not even an inch long, probably wouldn't scar, but head wounds did bleed like a sieve.

"Then that Advocate wasn't the only Malerrisi in Renig?" She let loose with a few choice phrases that made Collan blink. Were Blooded First Daughters supposed to know words like that? She finished with, "How could I have been so stupid?"

"Not stupid," he soothed. "Just wrong. Happens to the rest of us all the time. Got anything clean to put on this? They gave me a clean coif this morning, but this shirt hasn't seen soap and water in weeks."

"I spent the night in jail, too, remember? My clothes are as filthy as yours." She began tearing the sleeve off Cailet's shirt. "What do you mean, 'wrong'?"

He'd known the instant he said it that he should've kept his mouth shut. How to explain that he knew the wind was not an attack but a warning? *Well, y'see, First Daughter, when I was a little boy. . . .*

Cailet stirred and began to waken, which spared Collan's having to answer. "Easy, kitten," he soothed.

Sarra leaned closer. "Cailet? Does anything hurt?"

Long, pale eyelashes lifted from startlingly black eyes.

"You mean something in particular, not just everything in general?"

Col grinned down at her. "You're all right."

"That's *your* opinion." She used her good arm to push herself up, and gingerly rotated the other shoulder. "It's sore, but nothing cracks. That's good, right?"

"Right." He took off the dark brown coif the Watch had made him put on that morning and drew it down over her head. "This will hold the bandage in place."

"Bandage? Oh," she added, flinching as he eased the material down over the small wad of white shirt on her forehead.

"Hide her hair inside it," Sarra said suddenly.

Col glanced at her. She was looking up toward the invisible boardwalk with an odd expression on her face—like the one when she'd told him they mustn't go to Ryka. He opened his mouth to ask what she was talking about, then realized that they both could sense things that had no rational explanation. Did that make him a Mageborn, too? No, Cailet had said he wasn't. A definite relief. . . .

"They'll look for a blonde girl in a Council Guard uniform," Cailet said.

Sarra nodded. Col figured that if the Mage Captal trusted this woman's instincts, he might as well do the same. He finished tying the laces of the coif at Cailet's chin, and then sat back on his heels.

"But they'll recognize us prisoners immediately," he reminded Sarra. "And nobody with eyes would ever believe *you're* a boy."

He didn't understand why she tensed at the words, as if they'd caused pain. Cailet gave a brief snort, distracting him.

"Thanks, Minstrel," she said wryly.

"Listen!" Sarra sat straighter. "The wind's stopped."

"I've yet to figure out who started it," Cailet responded. "But I wish I knew how. We could get to Ryka in no time with that kind of wind in the sails."

"Nobody's going to Ryka." Col held up a palm to forestall her protest. "Sarra says it's a bad idea and I agree with her. We can go anyplace else you fancy, kitten, but *not* to Ryka."

"But I—"

"He's right," Sarra stated flatly. "Anywhere but Ryka."

Nearly invisible brows drew together over Cailet's sharp, straight little nose. "I'm Mage Captal," she began.

"And do you forget who *I* am?" Sarra retorted.

"That doesn't give you the authority—"

"Doesn't it just!"

The angular, bony jaw acquired a stubborn jut. "We're going to Ryka!"

"We are not!"

Tempted to clap a hand over each mouth, Col interrupted with, "Fascinating as you ladies are, I don't give a damn who *either* of you thinks she is. The only place we're going right now is to find Elomar. The way you're talking, you both got all the sense knocked out of you. Come on."

He stood, helped Cailet up, and when she was secure on her feet reached for Sarra's hand. When she set her right foot to the sand, she would have fallen if he hadn't caught her around the waist.

"Put me down. I can walk."

"Sure you can." Swinging her up into his arms, he started to the boardwalk steps a few hundred feet away. Cailet followed, trying not to limp. "By the way, did you stop to think what people are going to see in that courtroom?"

"What do you mean?" Sarra demanded. "A Justice, a clerk, and a Watch officer, and a dead Malerrisi."

"A dead Advocate," he corrected. "With no evidence of her being Malerrisi. And that's once they get past a whole squadron of bleeding Council Guards."

"I shouldn't have done it," Cailet said at his left shoulder. "There were other ways—"

"You did the best you knew," Collan said firmly. "The mistake was killing the Advocate."

"It was *not* a mistake!" Sarra exclaimed. "She would've killed Cailet!"

"Tactical error, then. Stop wriggling, First Daughter." He bounced her in his embrace to emphasize the point, then asked, "Why do I have to keep telling you that?"

He came to an abrupt halt as Elomar Adennos simply appeared before him. Rationally, Col knew an Invisibility Ward had just been dropped; irrationally, he was so startled he nearly dropped Sarra.

"Hide," was all the Healer said, and they flattened themselves against the rocky wall below the boardwalk.

"Spell us Invisible," Sarra whispered to Cailet. The girl shut her eyes and bit both lips bloodless, but at length shook her head.

"I can't, Sarra, I'm too tired."

"Elo?"

"Only for myself. Hush."

Boot heels thundered a regimented rhythm on the board-walk and came to a smart two-stomp halt. *Geridon gelded!* thought Collan in shock. *Nobody marches like that but the Ryka Legion!* He tried to hollow out a man-sized hole in the stones with his spine, his grip on Sarra tightening.

One set of boots was out of step, drumming furiously to catch up while their owner barked out breathless orders. "—*everyone*, understand? I'll have 'em all on murder charges, every motherless one of 'em! Get the rest of your people off-loaded and to work! And no more shit about the wind keeping you from landing sooner! You'll make up for it now!"

Justice Lunne had evidently woken up in a perfectly foul temper.

Another voice, rigidly controlled, said, "We are here to transport Mage Guardians to Ryka for trial, not to clean up your mess. The Council—"

"—couldn't find their own sorry asses with a mirror! You do as I say or I'll have *your* ass up on charges!"

"The law prohibits interference with the Legion."

"You're lookin' at the law in Renig, girlie! I'll interfere as I damn please! Now, *move!*"

Part of Collan hoped they'd go on arguing so the Mages had more time to escape. Part of him wished they'd go away before they heard the pounding of his heart. And part of him wanted desperately to be a Mageborn so he could Ward the broken section of wooden fence with a Nothing Down There But Sand And Seaweed.

Well, he'd been right about the wind, anyhow. It got Sarra and Cailet out of the way—not exactly subtle, but a cut fore-head and a wrenched ankle healed while a slit throat wouldn't. More importantly, the wind had delayed the land-ing of the Legion's ship. He could just imagine what might have occurred had the soldiers marched up the wharf just as their little group marched down it.

Thing was, where had the wind come from?

After a few more threats, Justice Lunne prevailed. The boots thudded away. Col heard something about searching the beach, and held his breath.

"Justice, the area is obviously deserted, but you're welcome to sift the sand for renegade Mages if you like. Good morning."

More angry footsteps. After what Collan judged to be a sufficient length of time, he whispered, "What now—wait for the tide and then float out to sea?"

"Don't tempt me," Sarra replied, her voice pitched to his ears alone. "Drowning would suit you. We're the problem, you know. Elo can Ward himself Invisible, and Cailet doesn't look like Cailet anymore. They can get away. But you and I are recognizable. And I can't walk."

He thought for a moment, then whispered, "Back me up, Sarra. I can get rid of them."

Cailet was inching her way over. She looked like a pretty adolescent boy in her brown coif and Guard regimentals— young even for the lowest rank, but certainly unidentifiable as Mage Captal, let alone female.

"Get out of here," Collan told her. "You and the Healer are getting in the way of two lovers looking for a little privacy."

Black eyes widened. He felt Sarra twitch a little in his arms, but her voice was cool and steady.

"We'll meet up later. Go on, Cai."

Elomar was nodding. "Meet where?"

Col was ready. "The Shipwrecked Sailor, down the Coast Road to Blighted Bay. Tell the owner I sent you."

With a swift shake of her head, Cailet said, "I can't leave you—and Elo has to look at Sarra's ankle—"

"You have a dozen Mages depending on you, Captal," Sarra said.

"Go on," Col urged. "We'll be fine. I've gotten out of worse than this." Setting Sarra down to balance on her good leg, he said, "I'm about to sweep you off your feet, First Daughter. Strip down to your shirt and trousers."

She opened her mouth, then shut it and did as told. Smart girl.

"I won't leave you!" Cailet caught at Sarra's hand.

"Can you swim?" the older girl demanded.

"What?"

"Swim, damn it! That's the other alternative! Do as I say, Cailet."

"Captal." The Healer Mage tugged Cailet's arm—the sore one; she winced. "We must hurry."

"Stop calling me that!" But she went with him, and even

after he vanished beside her (which ranked right up there with Lady Lilen's cactus as one of the most incredible things Col had ever seen), Cailet kept looking back over her shoulder. At last both were gone up the stairs, and Collan sighed his relief.

Leaning back against the wall, he took off his boots. Then he unbuttoned his pants. "Better hope that if we get caught, the soldiers are women."

Sarra turned her back. "So?"

"Distraction, First Daughter. Distraction."

Her reaction was half choke, half laugh, and all insult. "One look at you in all your glory and they'll forget their own Names, is that it?"

Only one response to that. "Well, have a look for yourself," he invited, kicking sand over their discarded clothing.

"Thank you, no," she replied. "I prefer to remain as optimistic as possible about my chances of surviving this."

One thing about Blooded-First-Daughter Liwellan, Col mused: she was never slow with a reply. "Aw, just one little peek. It'd do wonders for your confidence, I promise." Then, without warning, he caught her up in his arms again. She spluttered; he grinned; she glared.

"I don't like you," she hissed.

"Sure, you do." Striding swiftly down the beach, he stayed close to the wall so the short cliff would hide them from anyone on the boardwalk above.

"No, I don't." Wriggling a little, she added, "This is ludicrous."

"You have a better idea? Dignified can equal dead, First Daughter. And remember, you don't have an identity disk anymore. If we're caught, it has to be in the most improbable circumstances we can think up. That way, the obvious gets overlooked."

"Oh, *now* I understand!" she said sweetly. "No circumstances could be more improbable than me disporting myself with you!"

He told himself he was too preoccupied with finding just the right place to be bothered thinking up an answer; besides, he really ought to let her score at least once. Masculine generosity in such cases allowed women to continue the smug delusion that they were superior. He hurried toward the fishing wharf, a narrow projection of wood with a few benches at its far end. Quick-footing it past the beach steps, he ducked beneath the wharf and waded into sluggish surf.

"What do you think you're doing?"

"Oh, shut up and hold your breath," he said an instant before plunging them both underwater.

She came up coughing. "What exactly did *this* accomplish?"

"If they listened to the Justice, they'll be looking for a blonde woman and a red-haired man. My hair looks brown now, and in a few minutes you won't be a blonde anymore."

"This is your brilliant disguise? What do you mean, I won't be a blonde?" She gasped and clutched her loosened braids. "You're *not* going to cut my hair!"

"Did I say I was going to? Women!"

He walked out of the waves and put her on the damp sand. At the bottom of the nearest pylon he found what he wanted. He sliced his fingers prying loose a few tide-starved mollusks, then added a handful of sticky seaweed. He sat down beside her and cracked open the shells, squeezing dark, viscous fluid onto the seaweed. Then he smeared the whole mess into her hair.

"Undo your braids and rub that in. Don't worry, it's not permanent." He paused to consider. "Would it look more realistic if you ripped my shirt open for me? No, don't bother. They won't be looking at my chest." He tore the material himself, buttons popping.

She sniffed at her fingers. "What's in those shells?"

"They use it to dye leather."

Regarding with horror a handful of formerly golden tresses, she wailed, "It'll never wash out!"

Deploring the ill-timed vanity, and aware that she had no intention of doing as told, he reached over and fingercombed black muck through her long hair. Sarra crabwalked away from him, swearing as her sore ankle protested.

"If you touch me again, I'll kill you!"

"Who'd *want* to touch something that looks like you do right now?" The truth of this made him scoot near—careful of the sand scraping his bare butt—and scrub some of the streaky black from her face.

"I may kill you anyway!"

Suddenly there were footsteps again, on the wharf overhead. By now he knew the sound of government-issue boots—and they were tromping down the wooden stairs to the beach.

"Some other time, First Daughter," he whispered, and kissed her.

9

Council Guard uniforms still provided protection—though Lusira's arrogance had no effect on the Legionnaires except to annoy them. Only belatedly did Cailet recognize Lusira's attitude for a deliberate ploy; they needed to be elsewhere, and being ordered out of the commander's presence was a good start down what she feared would be a long road.

Elin and Bard Falundir had vanished with the other Mages. The seven of them left—Cailet, Lusira, Taig, Elomar, Pier, Keler, and Tiron—marched smartly down the waterfront street and took the first chance to duck down a side alley.

"St. Fielto alone knows if we'll find them all," Pier said. "My sister will know to look for us, but she also has to look for those looking for *her*."

"They're Mages," Keler reminded him. "There are spells and Wardings—"

"—which they're all probably too exhausted to try," Lusira interrupted.

Cailet knew exactly what she meant. She ached all over from the fall, the cut on her brow stung, and her shoulder was stiffening up. And fear wasn't helping. Her inability to cast a Ward of Invisibility a little while ago had shaken her badly—but how was she supposed to know how to do it, when she'd never done it before? Nothing had popped instantly into mind, not the ready-worked Ward nor an instructional guide nor even the surety that she could do such a thing.

Now, however, a dozen possible uses of magic whirled in her head, from Invisibility accomplished in an instant to kindling of directional Mage Globes for each fugitive that would have been the work of five minutes. *I know so much,* she told herself caustically, *so much, in fact, that I know ab-*

solutely nothing. Was it supposed to be this way, Gorsha? Was it?

"Well," said Taig, "twenty-two people to find, Mages and Rising. The seven of us should be able to show ourselves in enough places so most of them will see us, even if they're in hiding."

"Safe houses?" Elomar asked.

"Probably not safe anymore. Let's split up and start looking. Pier, you and Keler take the east end of town, work toward the center circle. Luse, you—"

"No," Cailet heard herself say. They all stared at her. "Pier, Keler, and Tiron will retrieve our journeypacks. Meet us at the St. Tamas Shrine, Stonekettle Street."

"Cailet—"

"I know what I'm doing, Taig," she said shortly. "The shrine was a refuge long before the hatmaker's on Market Circle or the Mikleine coach house."

He swallowed hard, then managed, "How did you—"

"I *know,*" she repeated. "Just as I know that we don't have to go looking for them. They'll come to us."

"Yes, Captal," said Pier, with a crisp nod for Cailet and a warning glance for Taig. He set off with Keler and Tiron for the stables where they'd left everything not in keeping with the accoutrements of the Council Guard. Thank the Saints, she told herself, for properly raised, obedient men.

"May I ask how you intend to accomplish this?" Taig asked, respectfully enough but with an edge to his voice.

It was as odd for her to be giving him orders as it was for him to receive them. Yet part of her automatically expected him to obey her as if she were Gorynel Desse. *I'm not. I'm* not! *I'm me, Cailet—*

Mage Captal.

"The St. Tamas Shrine is shaped like a starfish," she said as she started walking. "The design makes more sense on an island, because you can sail in all directions. But Renig is on the tip of a cape, so the only point of the star that doesn't apply is due north."

"There's a similar shrine in Pinderon," Lusira said. "A pretty little thing, too. But, Captal, I don't quite see—"

She continued as if the woman hadn't spoken. "Pottery starfish tokens are left in the apse that points in the direction you're sailing. It's for luck, to draw the Saint's attention to the voyage. The energy of Tamas's protection, if you will.

The same can be done with the energy of magic. Mageborns will feel it, and come to us there."

"I've never heard of any such thing," Taig said.

Cailet shrugged. "You're not Mageborn. It's part of the Captal's Bequest." She fell silent as they rounded a corner into an arcade of stalls. People leaped warily aside as they marched past. At the end of the block they turned into another empty alleyway, and she continued, "News that all Mage Guardians are required to know is disseminated in this fashion—the approaching death of a Captal, a gathering for defensive action or discussion of policy, a dire threat from the Lords of Malerris—"

"Captal Bekke's Tower!" Elomar exclaimed, then looked embarrassed and lowered his voice. "It's the tallest at the Academy, if that matters."

Cailet nodded. "It doesn't, but you're right. That's one location. Another is the Octagon Court."

Lusira's great dark eyes lit with revelatory joy to match her lover's. "Eight points! All the directions of the compass!"

"Precisely. I intend to use the six points of the shrine's starfish design to the same purpose. Potentially—"

"Cailet, talk like *you*," Taig burst out. "Precincts, disseminated—you never used words like that before in your life!"

She refused to feel the burn of blood in her cheeks. "I've never had to," she replied stiffly. "I don't know any other way to say such things."

Elomar spoke a quiet rebuke. "With the knowledge came the vocabulary of two accomplished Scholars."

Taig's resentment flared, brightly silvering his gray eyes. Then he gave an awkward, pained little smile and said, "Sorry, Cai. I don't mind the Scholarly language, truly told. Just please tell me you don't remember all the profanity my brother learned from Val Maurgen."

"If she did," Lusira contributed lightly, "she's too much of a lady ever to admit it. St. Tamas's is two blocks away now, isn't it? It's been a long time since I was last in Renig, and I don't quite remember."

Four blocks, in fact—four very silent blocks, while Cailet raged internally. She couldn't even open her mouth anymore without hurting Taig. And without Taig's hurt hurting her.

A polished brass plaque at the entrance informed visitors

that the shrine had been founded in 771 by the Eddavar Name in gratitude for the safe return of their First Daughter from a war against Veller Ganfallin. A small wooden sign below announced that the Resident Votary was Fellis Eddavar. Cailet asked Taig to find him and keep him occupied. She stationed Elomar and Lusira just inside the front door. Then she strode to the center of the shrine.

Radiating from a central circle were six long, narrow, triangular apses. One faced due north; in that direction was the rest of The Waste. South, southeast, and southwest was Great Viranka, the ocean that girdled Lenfell. To the northwest was a stretch of sea toward Tillinshir. And to the northeast was Blighted Bay. Cailet expected to find plenty of votive starfish in that apse.

The floor tiles might once have been gorgeous, but only a faint wash of color lingered here and there, mainly sea-blue with touches of gold and white like sun and spray on waves. The walls needed fresh plaster and paint, and the windows set at random in the steeply pitched roofs were pitted and murky after Generations of storms. What light filtered down was softly mysterious: rather appropriate for the magic Cailet was about to work here.

Despite the central circle, no Ladder had ever existed here. But she did sense hints of prior magic—like a whisper spoken just before she entered, or a candle snuffed early this morning. She paced off the circumference, feeling where magic might be strongest. Nothing drew her to one triangle or another. With a shrug, she returned to the center and faced southeast.

Walking straight down the middle to its point, she noted strings of shells and seaweed charms braided of silk or wool hanging here and there. On the floor were a dozen or so pottery starfish. Some were painted in colors never seen in nature; some were plain; a few were real, which surprised her. The creatures were unknown north of Bleynbradden, and rare everyplace else.

Thanks to her benefactors, she knew where the starfish lived. She knew about the good-luck charms. And she knew how to use the point of the apse to direct her magic in a call only Mageborns could sense.

What she didn't know—and, as the others hadn't asked, thought it wiser not to mention—was whether *all* Mageborns would sense it.

A small Mage Globe, white-gold and opaque, appeared at
the triangle's apex when she bid it appear. Power revolved
within, gathering strength. After a minute or two it burst.
The energy it contained pushed against the starfish point and
vanished, arrowing to the southeast.

*My proclivity for drawing a straight line to my goal
again,* she thought, and went to another pointed apse.

Cailet knew what she was doing. One day, she promised
herself grimly, she would know how she was doing it. For
the present, she only hoped she wasn't sending this summons all the way to Seinshir.

She sent the next one south, where beyond Renig lay
thousands of miles of open sea until Roke Castle. Then the
southeast, in the direction of Ryka Court. Northeast; north;
northwest—and she was done.

And exhausted.

Her muscles had been aching ever since the battle with
the real Council Guard. But that magic had been the
sword's, not hers. It had been the same when she shattered
Agva Annison's Globe. Now she was drained of magic to
her marrowbones, her temples throbbing and her eyes sand-
raspy with weariness.

"No wonder they didn't do this very often," she muttered,
dragging herself to the middle of the circle once more. She
sat down, too tired to move any farther, and when Elomar
hurried over to ask if she was all right, said, "Fine. Now we
wait."

"We'll wait. You sleep."

Excellent advice, and if she'd been able to keep her eyes
open she would have told him so.

10

Sarra was positive she'd never get the taste of him out of her
mouth—an unsavory combination of last evening's wine, the
gone-off cheese and moldy bread they'd been given this
morning, and plain old unscrubbed teeth. His was by no
means her first kiss, but if the future couldn't offer anything
better, it would damned well be her last.

Two soldiers of the Ryka Legion—an elite corps that answered not to Auvry Feiran but to the First Councillor—found them at about the same time Sarra was running out of breath. For that reason she was almost glad to see them. They strode across wet sand and ducked under the wharf, careful not to snag their journeypacks on the splintering wood.

"What's this, then?"

Collan yelped and pretended shyness, covering his groin with one hand and his uncovered hair with the other as he rolled off Sarra. The single wild glance he cast in her direction made it clear that talking their way out of this was her responsibility.

Wonderful.

Taking a little gasping breath, she cried, "Don't tell my mother!"

Amusement tinged with scorn twitched the Legionnaires' faces—flavored with intense interest in Col's anatomy, just as he'd boasted. They were tall, strapping women in their late thirties who wore their swords the way wealthy women wore jewels: with easy pride and absolute authority.

"You've more taste than sense, *domna*," the fairer one observed, grinning at Collan's imitation of cringing embarrassment. "Bet he cleans up awful pretty."

"*Please* don't tell my mother," Sarra begged. "She'll kill me!"

"What happened to your clothes?" the Legionnaire asked Collan.

"She—she ordered me to undress," he whimpered, tugging the shirt around him in a fine impersonation of pathetic victim—while making sure, Sarra noticed, that they saw the holes where buttons used to be. "Then she th–threw my clothes into the sea."

"Well, I can't say as I blame her," she said, grinning. Col actually blushed. Sarra was so amazed by it that she vowed to ask him how he managed it.

The second soldier was chuckling. "Wouldn't think to look at her she's so feisty, would you?"

"Poor boy. Shenna, you still have that extra cloak in your pack? He needs something to wear."

Boy? Sarra thought. *He's thirty if he's a day! I ordered him, indeed!*

"Right here. Promise to give it back."

Col nodded, wide-eyed.

A few minutes later, decently wrapped though lacking a coif to hide his tangled, sopping hair—which looked anything but red—Collan scrambled to his feet and bowed humble thanks.

Sarra wanted to slap him.

"Now, you be sure to buy him clothes to replace the ones you took," scolded the fair-haired woman. "That's a nasty trick to play on a nice boy like this."

"Yes, m'lady," Sarra breathed.

"Don't suppose you've seen anybody running away or hiding, have you? Two men, two blonde girls?"

They shook their wet heads, Sarra hoping hers looked anything but blonde.

"Mage Guardians, all of them," came the severe warning. "If you do see them, you come to one of the Legion right quick, understand?"

This time they nodded.

"There's a house-to-house lock going on, so nobody'll be on the streets to see you—" She stopped to laugh. "Not that there's much of him to see now but legs, more's the pity. Anyway, you go on back home. If anyone stops you, show 'em this." She handed Sarra a small, flat brass square with a round hole cut in the middle. "Return it when you bring the cloak back to our ship at dusk. All right? Be on your way, then."

"Yes, Lady," Sarra whispered, amazed at the luck. "Thank you!"

"And remember, girl, that while a woman has a right to any unmarried man who takes her fancy, if he's someone you know your mother wouldn't approve—"

"A lecture from *you?* That's a good one!" Shenna chortled. "*Your* mother caught you with a Fourth Tier stablehand when you were fifteen!"

"Sixteen, and it's not as if I wanted to *marry* him," her companion sniffed. Then, with a wink at Sarra, she finished, "He was almost as hung as your boy here. Get going, and be more careful next time."

With a nod, the two soldiers walked back out into the sunlight and up the creaking wharf steps.

"Do you know what this is?" Sarra murmured to Collan. "It's safe passage not just through town, but out of it."

"Is it, now?" He straightened up, running fingers through limp curls. "Not bad, if I do say it myself."

"I had every confidence you *would* say it yourself," Sarra told him. "Come on. Their invitation to get out of here i one I'm inclined to accept."

Blue eyes, their color made more intense by the black smears of mollusk dye, laughed down at her. "Now, now First Daughter, don't grump. Just because you're disap pointed that they came along so soon—"

If she'd had the use of her magic, she would have blasted him to cinders right where he stood. What she did possess was full command of thirty-three Generations of Blooded ar rogance. Allowing her gaze to descend to his groin, decently hidden now beneath the cloak, she said sweetly, "The disap pointment was obviously hardest on you. Shall we go?"

Renig was all but deserted. Street vendors had abandoned their carts, shops were closed up tight, and even the usua assortment of beggars had fled. Sarra didn't notice this las until Collan remarked on it.

"Beggars?"

He pointed, then hastily gathered the cloak about him again. "See that corner Shrine? St. Maurget Quickfingers It's where they always gather. I guess when the Ryka Legion puts a lock on a town, they mean it."

"Everybody back to their homes, doors and windows barred?"

He nodded. "Don't ask me where the beggars go. It's no a profession I've ever tried."

Limping along beside him, she slanted a startled glance upward. "What do you mean, 'profession'? You make i sound like being a farmer or a shoemaker."

"There's considerable skill involved, for which they re ceive payment. I've never begged, but I've done my share o street performing. Same thing."

"Hardly honest work."

"It's not thievery," he retorted. "But this is." And he ducked down an alleyway, vanishing into the noonday shad ows.

"Collan!" she exclaimed, flinching as if her voice echoed heartbeat speeding up as her gaze darted nervously around the empty street. The next moment, a hideous metallic shriek issued from the alley. "Collan!"

"What're you waiting for? Come on!"

She ran after him, cursing her unsteady ankle. The alley was a dead end. A water pump and a wall-shrine to St. Viranka projected from the twelve-foot stone barricade. Col was applying muscle to the pump, which finally ceased its complaints and gave forth a steady stream of water.

"Wash off," he told her. "It's fresh and this is The Waste, so we're thieves."

She knelt and stuck her head beneath the spigot. Nothing short of lye soap would get the dye out of her hair, but she gave it a good try. She scrubbed her face and neck, soaking her clothes once more, then exchanged places with Collan and wielded the handle with all her strength while he cleaned up.

"I need dry clothes," she said. "You need clothes, period. I have a little money—"

"—and less imagination," he interrupted. "Stay put, First Daughter."

He sprinted back down the alley. Sarra eyed the shuttered windows above, hoping none of the worthy citizens of Renig peered out through the cracks. She wrung out her wet hair and knotted it in a tight bun at her nape, furious at the way her fingers trembled. These days she didn't much like being alone.

Collan returned minus the cloak, wearing a shirt that hung to mid-thigh, and trailing a double armful of clothing. "These won't fit, of course," he said with a resigned sigh at the figure he would cut in someone else's clothes. "And I still need boots."

"You *stole* all this?"

After thrusting the bulk of it at her, he hauled on gray pants, grimacing as the hems came up short of his ankles. "I left the cloak as payment."

"It belongs to a Legionnaire!"

"So? All I did was take her cloak. *You* want to put her out of a job."

"But—but someone will recognize what it is—"

"They can cut it down or dye it. It's good material. Hand me that black thing." She did; the longvest had been made for someone just as tall but much thinner through the chest. It proved impossible to button. "Well? The rest of it's for you. Hurry up."

If she told him to turn his back, he'd laugh at her. Besides, at least some of those windows up there must have

people behind them. And it wasn't as if men hadn't seen her
naked before, she told herself, remembering an afternoon
spent splashing in a stream on Shellinkroth. But two of those
men had been physicians, and the other pair couldn't have
cared less about her feminine charms. Well, neither did
Collan, but not for the same reason.

So she unbuttoned her shirt. And wasn't sure if he was being courteous or mocking when he walked away from her toward the street.

She retrieved five cutpieces, two silver eagles, and the
brass token from her pockets and left the sopped clothes by
the water pump. Hopping one-legged down the alley, she
tugged on one boot and then had to lean against a wall to
rest her ankle as she pulled on the other. Then she hurried to
catch up with Collan, who lounged casually against a building.

"Charming," he drawled, looking her down and up.

The brown trousers were skintight and the lurid yellow
shirt was frayed, collarless, and definitely not her color. She
wouldn't have worn these clothes to a tug-of-war over a
mudpit.

"Likewise," she snapped, giving him the same acidic assessment. "Roll up your pants more—you're a barefoot
farmhand escorting me back from town."

He shuffled his toes against the cobbles and tugged at the
curls cascading down his forehead. "Yes, m'Lady, just as
you say, m'Lady."

"Servitude suits you," she observed, sweeping past him.

And instantly regretted the words. She owed him her life
and probably Cailet's as well; he deserved much better than
this from her. But she didn't know how to say she was sorry
without making thing even worse. So she kept silent, and
swore to be nicer to him—no matter how much he annoyed
her.

The Shipwrecked Sailor was east of Renig on the Coast
Road. But in the event that their altered appearances and the
Legion token didn't prevent someone from eventually asso-
ciating them with the escaped Mages, they left by the Farm
Gate to the north. Collan bowed and mumbled fearfully
when the Watch barked questions at Sarra. She made her
eyes their widest and told them she was scared of
Mageborns and wanted only to go home.

"Why isn't that man's head covered?"

"They—they took his coif and didn't give it back—they wanted to see the color of his hair," Sarra stammered. "They're looking for a blond man and a dark-haired girl—or was it the other way around? Please, I just want to go home to my mother!"

"Get on with you, then."

The token worked, but was confiscated. She regretted that; it might have been useful as a pattern for future forgeries. But she gave it up with every evidence of relief, and set as smart a pace as she could down the road to emphasize her fright.

Once over a low rise, they cut across country to the east. There was no hope of reaching the inn by dark. Collan steered them to a tiny hamlet eight miles outside Renig, saying that at the very least they could shelter with some nice warm horses for the night.

To Sarra's eye, the two swaybacked plow Clydies lived better than the human inhabitants. The scant tillable fields, the four buildings, and all ten people she saw—half the population, according to Collan—were sere and brown. So were the two rounds of flatbread and the hunk of cheese she bought for their dinner.

"This is called 'poverty,' First Daughter," Collan said as they took up residence in the barn. He bit into the cheese, then the bread, and washed both down with a gulp of water from a cup dipped straight into the horses' bucket. "Just so you know," he added.

Sarra wanted to tell him she'd recognized it, thanks very much. But, truly told, she'd never seen this kind of poverty before. During her travels, she'd seen plenty of run-down districts—sometimes against her hosts' wishes. She had even seen the like in Roseguard, though Lady Agatine had tried hard to provide for all her people. But this place of one barn, four stone hovels, and what passed for a tavern was something outside her experience. These people had roofs overhead, clothes on their backs, and food to eat. But if the tiles broke in a storm or their coats wore out or the rains didn't come. . . .

Where were their families? she asked herself, perplexed. Why did the First Daughters of their Names allow them to live this way?

Collan paused in his meal, squinting over at her in the dusk. "What? No sharp answers?" When she remained silent, he gave an unpleasant laugh. "Not pretty, is it? But it's about time you saw what you and your kind have done."

"Me and my kind?" He'd used the phrase last night in jail, and she liked it even less today.

"There are maybe three Names here, at least one an upper Tier. The woman who owns that bay over there—she's a Karellos, to judge by the Circled Square brand. But where's her share of the communal Karellos wealth? Where's the rest of her First Tier Name when she needs boots or more seed in the spring? And there's a million just like her all over Lenfell."

"These are the people the Rising was formed to help."

"So you want them to become freedom fighters." He took another swig of stale water, swallowed, and laughed again, even more harshly. "Freedom from what? Anniyas? What do they care about Anniyas? This is the way they've lived since The Waste was safe to live in again and they'll probably live like this long after you and I are dead. So what's the point, First Daughter? You and your Blooded kind made these people—and now you want to change things for them, or so you say. But you'll do what you want, just like always."

Her temper got the better of her. "I refuse to take responsibility for the way these people live! But I'll tell you something, Collan Rosvenir. I intend to take responsibility for *changing* it!"

"Prove it," he challenged. "Not to me—to them. Convince them that fighting is going to get them something."

"I can't do that until we've won! Then we'll have the power to change things—"

"Dammit, that's what I've been trying to tell you! Ninety-nine out of a hundred people in Lenfell don't *have* any power. And the one in a hundred who does usually cracks some kind of whip with it. Why should anybody think you'll be any different, once you're sitting on the Council?"

Fundamental honesty kept her silent. Because he was right. To use power wisely it was first necessary to possess power—which was rarely if ever used with true wisdom.

"Well?" he snarled.

In a subdued voice, she said, "I suppose that the most we can ask for is acquiescence. To put up with it, as you said last night."

"So you *were* listening. You think people will sit back and watch, and not try to stop you?"

"Yes. Once we've succeeded, Collan, they'll understand."

"If you say so, First Daughter. But in case it's escaped you, I'll tell you two other things about poverty. You feel sorry for these people, don't you?"

"Of course I do! That's why I want to help!"

"What if I told you I pity you for not having access to your magic?" He snorted. "Aw, just look at her bristle like a prickleback poked with a stick! See what I mean? Pride, Sarra. *Domna* Karellos here could probably go to her Name for help. But that really *is* begging. See the difference?"

Gritting her teeth, she nodded.

"The other thing is this. Poverty isn't noble suffering, freedom from the burden of possessions, or a lot of good and decent people struggling honorably to survive. Being poor is dirty, brutal, and murderous. So sleep close to me tonight, and with that knife of yours in your fist."

With that he finished his bread and cheese, downed the last of the water, and settled down on the straw.

She made herself eat her share of the food, knowing she needed it. She then lay down with her spine nearly touching his and her knife ready in her hand.

"Collan?"

"Mmm?"

"You've thought about this a lot, haven't you?"

"Not really."

"Then why . . . ?"

He said nothing for a long moment. "Before you can change the world, Sarra, you've got to see it the way it really is."

"And you think I don't."

"You're learning. Stay with me, and you'll learn a lot more."

She didn't point out that *he* was the one staying with *her* and the Mages and the Rising—and marveled at her restraint.

Suddenly, surprisingly, he added, "I just don't want to see you get yourself broken against walls you didn't suspect were there."

"I'm tougher than that," she said.

"If you say so," he repeated. "Good night, First Daughter."

A few minutes later she whispered, "Stop calling me that."

But he was asleep, and made no reply.

II

"... green salad lightly dressed, braised beefsteak in mild pepper sauce, carrots in a brown-sugar glaze, and for dessert—"

"Chocolate," said Glenin.

The cook pursed his lips and consulted his notes. "With regret, Lady, not until next week, according to the schedule—"

"Chocolate," she repeated.

"The diet drawn up by the First Councillor's personal physician forbids—"

"The First Councillor's personal physician isn't having this baby, *I* am."

Garon pried his adoring attention from Glenin long enough to say, "If chocolate she wants, then chocolate she must have."

"May I point out, with respect, my Lord, that the delicacy of a lady in this condition, with morning sickness and suchlike—"

"She's perfectly well, aren't you, my dearest?"

Glenin smiled. She hadn't had a twinge since Ambrai.

The cook tried again. "I must also point out that there has already been a weight gain of three pounds too many according to the physician, and—"

Glenin interrupted once more, mainly for the satisfaction of consistency: not once in the last ten minutes had the cook been allowed to finish a sentence. "I'll get as fat as I please, and I'll do it on chocolate three times a day if it suits me. Go revise your menus accordingly."

"But, Lady Glenin—"

"Out," said Garon. When they were alone, he brought her fingers to his lips and said, "My darling, he may be right. I've read everything I can find about having a baby, and the more weight a woman gains, the more difficult her labor. I couldn't bear it if you suffered even an instant more than absolutely necessary. I don't know how I'll endure what you *will* go through. The very thought is agony. I'd do it all for you if I could."

Of *course* he would. Men had been making that oh-so-generous offer for centuries, secure in its total impossibility. But she behaved as if he was the first ever to say it—because she knew that he of all men truly meant it.

"I know, Garon. Thank you for being so sweet. But you mustn't worry. I'm very strong. Will you excuse me now, darling? I'm supposed to take a nap every afternoon."

"I'll be within call if you need anything."

She watched him go, her smile gradually falling into a frown. Attention was all well and good, but she'd have to find something for Garon to do or he'd drive her quite mad.

She lounged on a daybed before wide windows, a woven silk rug across her knees, and idly contemplated sailboats racing on the lake. The colors of a dozen Names sped along the course, heeling around buoy markers, polished brass fittings and gold or silver paint flashing in the sun. The Doyannis boat, with Elsvet's husband at the tiller, won as usual. Perhaps she ought to encourage Garon to take up sailing. Anything instead of this habit of hovering over her. Not that she wanted him to renew his former hobbies: gambling with her money, drinking her vintage wines, and seducing her acquaintances. Something harmlessly time-consuming, she thought as the bright sails drifted in to shore. Something at which he could excel so that she could smile modestly when people praised her accomplished husband . . . which would please his mother.

Anniyas wasn't being gracious about giving up first place in her darling boy's heart. She was putting up a fight: demanding his presence at all her various meetings, taking him to dinner at expensive inns, paying for a new spring wardrobe. Glenin wondered when she would begin to suspect that a fight was impossible. Some men did behave strangely during impending fatherhood, and thus far this seemed to explain Garon's blind devotion. But Anniyas didn't like it one little bit.

And after the baby was born . . . Glenin had an alarming vision of Garon *and* Anniyas hovering over the cradle.

You're mine, she told her son, stroking her belly. *I gave up my First Daughter, but I'll never give you up. Never.*

Comforted by her own determination, she relaxed and fell
to dreaming of the time when he would be ready to learn
magic. She'd teach him everything, advance with him
through the pages of the *Code of Malerris,* watch as his
skills were honed to perfection. He would be no Chava
Allard, talented but undisciplined. And his father wouldn't
eye him askance, the way Vassa Doriaz eyed his son.

But Anniyas might. Well, Glenin would just have to keep
her boy's grandmother and father out of the picture as much
as possible. Anniyas had politics to keep her busy, but Garon
would definitely have to find other interests. Glenin had no
intention of letting her husband mold the slightest part of his
personality—and especially not his taste in clothes.

She dreamed of her son the way another woman would
dream of her First Daughter. As time passed and she felt him
grow and change her body, she realized she had never
sensed the other baby this way. She had never planned or
worried or wondered who her daughter would resemble—oh,
sweet Saints, *please* don't let her son take after Anniyas in
looks! He must be tall, handsome, broad-shouldered,
compelling—like Auvry Feiran.

"Do you hear me, little one?" she whispered whimsically
to the child. "No stumpy-dumpy like Anniyas! You'll grow
big and strong like your grandfather."

Suddenly she remembered that there was another
grandfather—and grandmother. For the first time in years
Glenin tried to recall what Maichen Ambrai looked like. She
remembered very dark eyes, very pale hair, and very great
beauty. But the exact form of that beauty escaped her. Still,
her mother *had* been beautiful; songs had been composed in
her praise. Of her son's other grandfather, she knew nothing.
Garon himself was tremendously handsome—everyone
thought so—and Anniyas called him his father's very image,
so perhaps there was nothing to worry about.

"Three good-looking grandparents outweigh a plain one,"
she murmured to the baby. "You'll be beautiful, no doubt
about it. As beautiful as my father said he knew I'd be the
minute I was born."

But beauty meant there would eventually be women. And
one day she would be in the same position Anniyas was in
now.

No. Not my *son. He'd never do that to me. We'll have*

more than Blood and a mother-son bond. We'll have our magic. Anniyas and Garon never had that, never.

Anniyas had been too busy with the Assembly and the Council during Garon's childhood to spare much time for him. She loved him devotedly, to be sure—but she had made him the center of her life without making herself the center of his. Drinking, gambling, and carousing had been his way of filling up his life—and perhaps of gaining her attention. Glenin shifted uncomfortably on the daybed, not wanting either to understand him or feel sorry for him.

Yet there was a useful lesson here and a caution against making the same mistake with her own son.

"You'll be with me all the time, precious," she vowed, stroking her belly. "I'll teach you and love you and we'll be together every day. And one day when you marry, *if* you marry, whoever she is will never replace me. Never. Because we'll be like my father and me, alike in our thoughts and dreams and hopes. More than that: both Malerrisi from the first glint of magic in our eyes."

She allowed her magic to swell within her mind as the child was swelling within her body. The feeling reminded her of the days before Golonet Doriaz had come to teach her: pregnant with potential magic, her entire being focused on making it grow.

Her senses expanded, giving her the carefree shouts of sailors on the lake, the crisp breeze, the scents of sun-spangled water and new grass—and the call of a powerful Mage Guardian.

12

"I don't mind saying that was the *oddest* thing I've ever felt in my life." Elin Alvassy shook her head, short blonde curls bouncing, as she poured more wine for herself and Cailet.

"How so?" Cailet was genuinely curious; she knew what she'd done, but had no idea of its effect. Praise St. Miramili, it had worked; seven Mage Guardians and eight of the Rising faithful from Renig Jail were sleeping in the upstairs rooms and the stables of the Shipwrecked Sailor. They had been two days arriving here, but they had made it.

Five hadn't. Three Mages had been taken when the Legion first marched through the city; two of the Rising struck out on their own from hiding and were seized. Taig mentioned going back for them, but he knew as well as the rest did that the five had already been executed.

Elin glanced around the taproom, a little too obvious in her desire not to be overheard. The place was mildly populated: local farmers and their husbands, the blacksmith and his apprentice from down the Coast Road, and a trio of giggling sisters celebrating an eighteenth Birthingday. Keler Neffe and Tiron Mossen were making themselves agreeable to the honoree while Taig traded stories with the blacksmith and Elomar sat apart with Lusira—both to keep the men present from eyeing her overmuch and to watch the back door unhindered. Cailet herself sat midway down a splintery bench that ran the length of the side wall, with the space between tables in front of her and a clear view of the door to her right. The positioning wasn't something she'd even had to think about; another bit of the Bequest, but she doubted it came from the Scholarly Captal Adennos.

Sand-floored, low-ceilinged, reeking of stale wine, and fitfully illuminated by the fire in the central pit, the Shipwrecked Sailor was as dismal a place as Cailet ever hoped to see. But she couldn't fault either the food—classic country cooking, better even than at Ostinhold—or the hospitality. Mention of Collan Rosvenir was responsible for this last. His name had worked a remarkable change on the owner, whose initial suspicions and justifiable outrage at being awakened past Second were transformed into an effusive welcome. *Domna* Kelia Theims and her four dark-eyed daughters had bustled about until nearly Third, preparing a hot meal, changing the sheets on their own beds to accommodate the travelers, and plying them with questions about their beloved Minstrel. Cailet began by wondering which of them Col slept with on his visits, and ended by concluding he shared his favors with all five.

She—or maybe it was Gorynel Desse—admired his energy.

Inspection completed and voice lowered, Elin said, "It was almost a compulsion. Something inside that demanded I find you. And—this will sound thoroughly bizarre, but—I also felt as if I was a compass needle and you were magnetic south."

"So wherever I went, you'd be drawn to me."

Her unacknowledged cousin nodded. "It did get incredibly frustrating, though. By the time we were able to leave hiding, the focus was changing. Then we had to wait until the gates opened in the morning." She chuckled suddenly, showing a hint of Sarra's deep dimples. "If I never do another Invisibility Ward, it'll be too soon!"

She'd cast the Summons long enough for it to be felt, then stopped. But it was lingering about her person, and whether or not it would fade completely was anyone's guess. She cursed her inability to cancel it. All the words and Wards and workings—but maybe this was how a Captal's Summons was supposed to function. If only she were a *true* Captal, she'd know.

She could never admit her failings. They had to think she knew what she was doing—even when she felt as if she was sleepwalking. Sometimes all this was a kind of waking dream anyway. One thing she knew, however—and, on analytical reflection, realized that this was what had prompted her to use the spell to begin with. Mage Guardians would know it for what it was. Malerrisi would not.

Pier Alvassy had also used the image of a compass when he and Keler and Tiron arrived at the St. Tamas Shrine. They'd already known to come there, naturally, but Pier avowed that even if they hadn't known, they would've *known*. That was why Cailet had felt justified in leaving the shrine and Renig behind her. The Mages would follow. To hear them tell it, they had no choice but to follow. Elin's tale pretty much matched those told by the others. Pulled east, they slipped out when the gates opened to let the morning produce carts in. Some Mages, able to cast a Folding spell, had come quickly; some, like Elin, had to walk the whole way without benefit of magic.

Fifteen former prisoners were safe now. Cailet's own little coterie—Elin, Pier, Taig, Elo, Lusira, Keler, Tiron, and Falundir—was complete.

Except for Sarra and Collan. Neither would have felt the summons. They knew to come here; the tavern had been Col's suggestion. But they wouldn't know where to follow. And that meant Cailet couldn't leave the Shipwrecked Sailor. She'd send the others on their way tomorrow, on foot

and on a couple of the small fishing boats that worked
Blighted Bay. But she could not—would not—leave without
Sarra and Col.

Which presented difficulties. Imilial Gorrst had given her
a taste of how Mage Guardians behaved when they perceived their Capital to be in danger. She had a brief vision of
trailing all of them behind her as she walked into Ryka
Court, and made a face.

"The wine's not *that* bad," Elin smiled. "Unless you're
used to the finest Cantrashir reds, or the shabby they make
in Bleynbradden. Bottled sunlight, my grandfather called it,
despite the silly name."

"It's a slurring of something older," Cailet responded absently. "Like Mikleine and Maklyn—the same Name long
ago, only the original wasn't either."

"Truly told? That's interesting."

"Bards call it language shift, I think." She changed the
subject because she had no idea where—or who—-the information came from. "Will you feel up to traveling again tomorrow? With Folding, it's not that long a trip to Combel."

Elin's pretty face, reminiscent of Sarra's but with the
green Desse eyes, developed a suspicious frown. "Where
you go, I go," she warned. "And that's true of the other
Mages as well."

Cailet gave a sigh and rubbed her shoulder. "I was afraid
you'd say that."

13

The Legion was on the march. Having disposed of five re-
captured Mages and traitors of the Rising, they split into
squadrons and began a thorough search of the surrounding
countryside.

Sarra and Collan were about three miles ahead of them.

Taking the Coast Road to the Shipwrecked Sailor was not
an option. That would lead the soldiers straight to Cailet. So
they turned due north, and for two days and two nights
walked the brown and gray scrub hills toward Combel.

Sarra's boots, chosen with the rest of the Guard uniform

for fit, supported her bad ankle well enough to make a fast pace only mildly painful. Collan made do with a pair of clogs filched from a doorstep back in Renig. His heels were spared blisters, but by the second night his toes were raw and bleeding. From dusk until full dark he immersed his feet in an inch-deep trickle of water muddied by sheep earlier in the day. When Sarra tried to give him her socks, he laughed, asking if she thought the seams would survive his big toes.

What food they had brought with them from Renig was gone by the third morning. Col was fairly sure there was a small holding up the road that cut across to Blighted Bay; after all, somebody close by must own the herd of sheep. But late that afternoon it began to rain, cutting visibility to half a mile. It wasn't an acid storm, Sarra assured Col before it hit; she'd learned what one of those smelled like as it approached. This rain came from a stray cloudbank drifting over St. Deiket's Blessing, the mountains that were Ambraishir's border with and protection from The Waste.

Clean water wouldn't scar them, but they were well on the way to drowning by sunset. The hills were curtained in silver rain beneath a dark gray sky. Gulleys filled, overflowed, flooded, washed away topsoil in rivers of mud. There were no sheltering trees and no sign of human habitation—not even a shepherd's hut. Col would have settled for a sheep to hide under.

Sarra fought her way to the top of another rise and turned to face him. "Is my hair clean yet?" she shouted over the pounding rain.

He gave her a weary grin. "You'll be blonde again by Twelfth!"

"We can't stay out here all night! There's got to be someplace to go!"

"Why do you think they call it The Waste?"

By the time they topped the next hill, after several slips and a spill or two in the rushing mud, the sun was no longer even a pretense in the west. Wordlessly, Sarra took Col's hand. Hers was very small and very cold, and for the first time in his life he felt that his own was too big and too clumsy. He could coax the most delicate music from even a child-sized lute or mandolin, but he was now almost afraid of breaking the slight fingers curled in his palm.

A moronic thought, but he couldn't shake it. What the hell was she doing here, anyhow? A Blooded Lady like her, born to wealth and privilege—she should've been snug and warm before a roaring hearth, wearing a velvet gown, her hair all in loose curls and a book of poetry in her hands.

Ah, but she had a *conscience,* he reminded himself, trying to walk and not slide his way down the hill. She wanted to *change* things. Most women contented themselves with running the lives of their husbands and children. Saints save him from a woman who wanted to run the whole damned world—after she'd changed it to suit her, of course.

"Collan?" she yelled suddenly. "Is that a light?"

He squinted into the dark and driving rain. "Where?"

"That way—no, more to the left—"

"I don't see anyth—wait!" He shook his face clear of water. "There!"

"I thought I was imagining it! Come on!"

Shivering now, drenched to the bone, they slogged along a ravine three feet above flowing mud. The light wavered, vanished, reappeared. All at once Collan felt packed earth underfoot: soaked but distinctly different from the soggy hillside soil. It couldn't remotely be termed a road—sheep track was about the height of its dignity—but it led toward the flickering golden light.

Perhaps a quarter of a mile later he saw a house. The path they were on intersected with another, and tucked to one side of the crossing was a rustic two-story cottage. The light came from an oil lantern on a hook beside the door. White stone walls, narrow dark windows, thickly tiled roof, the dwelling looked old enough to be a relic from before The Waste War. Col experienced a fleeting, wistful vision of the cozy chambers above the taproom of the Shipwrecked Sailor, banished it with a sigh, and resigned himself to straw, icy drafts, and rats.

At least it had a roof. After two nights of dirt beds, straw sounded great. And almost anything—even with rats—was preferable to Renig Jail.

He tugged Sarra's hand and pointed. She nodded numbly, hair plastered to her skull and rain streaming down her face. She freed her fingers and went to open the door, calling out, "Anyone here?"

Silence. Darkness. Col unhooked the lantern and joined Sarra in the tiny hallway, closing the door behind him. "Nobody home. Think they'd mind . . . ?"

"Probably. But *I* mind drowning."

Col raised the lantern to have a look around. A narrow hall ran down the middle of the house. A white iron staircase doglegged at a small landing, then rose to a wooden balcony above the front door. The steps were punctured in a floral pattern to ease their weight, and each bar supporting the banister ended in a little rosebud finial. Flecks of red, yellow, orange, pink, and lavender paint clung to the roses, and various shades of green to the leaves.

To the right through a doorless opening was a huge, cold, empty kitchen with a hearth big enough to roast an elk. *Two* elks. Sarra investigated while Collan stepped across the hall to the opposite room, which was strewn with splintered trestle tables and benches.

"The cupboard," Sarra reported, "is bare."

"Upstairs, then."

They climbed, dripping rain. She opened the right-hand door; he opened the left. The large room was empty but for an impressive array of cobwebs and an ancient iron-strapped chest secured by a formidable lock.

"Col. . . ."

There was an odd note in her voice, as if once again she required a witness to justify what she thought she saw. He followed her voice across the landing. In the doorway he stopped, blinked, and stared.

It was a chamber fit for a Grand Duchess of Domburronshir, if there'd been any such personage after Veller Ganfallin. A gigantic oaken bed dominated, framing a mattress thick enough to sink a rowboat. The swagged hangings were of heavy gold-on-green brocade. The matching spread was quilted in bullion thread, its intricate patterns piercing through the contributions of a whole flock of geese. Thick Cloister rugs covered most of the stone floor in darkly glowing colors. Atop them were a pair of cushioned chairs, a low table, and a second, smaller bed over in a recessed alcove. A similar alcove on the other side of the fireplace was partitioned off by a carved wooden screen. The hearth, mate to the one directly below in the kitchen and using the same chimney, was piled with wood just begging to be lit into a conflagration.

Col fished in a sodden pocket for his matchbox and crouched down to do the honors.

"Do you believe in this?" Sarra asked softly.

"I believe I'm about to get warm for the first time all day."

Slowly, almost as if each word must be forced from her lips, she said, "Somebody lives here, despite the neglect downstairs."

Col smiled satisfaction as the kindling caught. "Do you have any money left?"

"Not much, but it's a nice thought." She peeled open a wet vest pocket and came up with a small handful of coins.

"What I had in mind wasn't paying the owners, but flipping for the bed."

With a grimace, she tossed him a copper. "Why would I have thought differently? Everything else we have is stolen, so why not the bed as well?"

He sighed. "I had two choices. Maybe get arrested for stealing the clothes, or definitely get arrested for outraging the public morals. Walking around town half-naked will do that."

"Yet you're the one who shoved my face in how poor everyone is!"

She must be tired; it was too easy to top her. "You're the one who's going to change it all, and you'd never have made it out of Renig without me, so the people I took this stuff from will come out ahead in the end."

"You have a highly individualized notion of ethics."

"If you're waiting for me to be offended, you've got a long wait." He inspected the coin. "Head or—uh, bottom?"

"I'll never know why they made the new cutpiece so vulgar. Head."

St. Delilah's proud profile turned up; the noble, naked wrestler's backside turned down. As the fire warmed the room, Col stripped, too, and draped his clothes to dry. Sarra's came sailing across the room to land at his feet; he grinned to himself, but didn't swing around to look and embarrass her.

Chores done, caution made him slide home the door's dead bolt before he pulled back the covers and snuggled into his feather-studded alcove nest for the night. He doused the lantern, leaving it near his bed. "Sleep well."

"Mmmm," came the drowsy reply.

He lay back, watching fire-thrown shadows on the beamed ceiling. Straw, drafts, and rats? But for the lack of a real bathroom (there was a chamberpot behind the screen)

and the lack of a dinner, this was all he could ask. Warm,
dry, blissfully comfortable, with a fire to last all night and
not a drop of rain leaking through the roof . . . a splendid
refuge, indeed. . . .

14

Cailet was right about the Mages. They refused to set one
foot down any road whatsoever unless she went with them.

The resistance was led by an old man who'd been a
Captal's Warder for thirty years. Gavirin Bekke, seventy-
four this summer and retired since before Leninor
Garvedian's death, was a Warrior Mage to his arthritic fingertips and knew what was what when it came to protecting
a Captal.

Moreover, he was a collateral descendant of the Caitirin
Bekke who had built the tower at the Academy, he had
served as a Warder under First Sword Gorynel Desse, and
his father's cousin's son had at one time been Desse's
Swordsecond. Cailet, dim recognition teasing at her mind,
knew enough about him to know that he meant what he said
when he announced that where the Captal was, there too
would he be. (She also felt mild shock that he had grown so
old—a reaction based on Gorsha's eternally youthful image
of himself, no doubt.)

So here she was on a rainy spring morning, the fifth day
of Lovers' Moon, on a fishing boat plowing the waves of
Blighted Bay. She was dry enough in the tiny wheelhouse,
but staying out of the way in such cramped quarters was a
problem. Two other boats were similarly packed with refugees, the younger ones ready to help with the catch in return
for passage across to Ambraishir. Cailet had given startled
permission for several of the Mages to cast a Come and Eat!
Ward into the water to attract the fish. She hadn't known
that was possible. Then again, none of her four benefactors
had known the first thing about fish.

Elomar, who fished for sport and not for a living, declined
to be taught the spell lest it spoil future fun.

No magic had been necessary to convince the pilots to

take on passengers. Taig arranged it with known Rising sympathizers. Cailet was heartened by the willingness of the Doyannis Blood to help renegade Mages, especially as one of their Name was on the Council. But mere mention of Veliria Doyannis made her distant cousins spit in absolute unison. Cailet instantly deduced that the woman was not beloved.

The reasons for this were many, but heading the list was the tax on fishing nets she had authored. It had the specific purpose of forcing The Waste's branch of the family toward insolvency, at which point she would graciously lend them money—and eventually absorb the business into the main Doyannis Web.

"When you win," said the cousins' grandmother with a fierce smile as she bid Cailet farewell, "pay us back by sending us Veliria."

Cailet grinned and nodded; so much for Councilmember Doyannis. Besides, from what she'd learned about the woman's tantrum at the inheritance hearing, Sarra would enjoy waving her good-bye when she shipped out for The Waste.

Sarra. . . .

Where was she? That Collan was still with her, Cailet did not doubt for an instant. While this gave her some solace—Col had been on the road most of his life, after all, and would take good care of Sarra—she found herself painfully missing both of them. It wasn't just worry over their safety. It was an emptiness inside her, a diminishing of herself.

Which was ridiculous, she reflected as she stared out at the rainswept gray sea. She of all people could scarcely feel lonely—not with the knowledge and memories of four other people to keep her company.

She'd had time to think some of it through while at the Shipwrecked Sailor. Perhaps if she'd done it earlier, she might have averted a disaster or two, or known to do something different in reacting to danger.

Or traced an appropriately jagged path to her goals, rather than the straight line Gorsha deplored.

In Longriding the Bequest had been too new within her. She'd shied from thoughts and memories not her own, frightened that they would subsume what remained of Cailet. Now she was beginning to understand that what she was, she remained. Other lives did not blend into or blot out hers. Instead, she would think a thing, or remember a lesson from school, and it would connect with other knowledge—like the derivation of Mikleine and Maklyn the other night. She *knew* things without having to go through the trouble of *learning* them.

It was a little like having swallowed a whole library that instantly cross-referenced itself in her head.

The trick would be to learn how to use the knowledge. And that would only come with new experiences.

The knowledge was one thing. The magic was different. Spells, Wards, words, gestures, gradations of power, subtleties of casting and controlling—these she must explore one by one. And all this put her in the curious position of having to learn what she already knew. The whole process would take much more time than she could spare now.

The list of things to learn was as lengthy as the list of discovered power; each grew apace, and pretty much in proportion to the other. With every action she analyzed for possible alternatives, spells popped into mind. If the duty of a Mage Guardian was to protect freedom of choice, the Mage Captal was the living repository of more choices than any one person should ever have to deal with.

A sense of humor, however, gave her no choice at all but to laugh at her predicament. If the humor was tinged with bitterness . . . well, at least that emotion belonged to her alone.

"Your pardon, Captal," said one of the Doyannis pilots as he squeezed past her to the hatch. She smiled, shrugged, and returned to her thoughts.

Emotions continued to frighten her. Some came in response to her own feelings—that glimpse, for instance, of a lovely young woman sadly rejecting a young man who had become a Mage. She understood it now as a compassionate gift, an attempt to ease her hurt by showing her that in this pain she was not alone. But while she could accept knowledge and all the benefits of four lives' experience, she had to *feel* for herself or she would go mad.

The alternative terrified her. If any given person or situation prompted joy, anger, humor, disgust, tenderness, hate—how could she know if the reaction was her own? If she found a man attractive, would it be her own response—or Alin's? If she was similarly attracted to a woman, would it be Gorsha's doing?

And what if all four were still somehow *aware* inside her,

as Gorsha seemed to be? What if she had to live the rest of
her life with them *watching* her?

She needed Sarra and Collan. Not because she had known
them before the Bequest, but because she loved them. She,
Cailet, loved them; not Gorynel Desse or Alin Ostin or
Lusath Adennos or Tamos Wolvar. The latter pair hadn't
even known Sarra and Col. Alin, though fond of both, had
truly loved no one in this world but his mother, his sister
Miram, and Valirion Maurgen. As for Gorsha, he felt proud
and exasperated tenderness for Sarra, and nothing at all for
Collan.

But Cailet loved them.

Saints, how she needed them now. They, at least, were
hers.

15

Collan woke to the aroma of fresh hot bread.

Peering out from under the coverlet—plain red wool on
this smaller bed—he inhaled deeply. His stomach growled.
Bread, strips of sizzling roast duck, and hot something-else
with a fine nip to it—wine? He pushed back the covers,
eager to investigate.

And stared in befuddlement at his right arm. And his left
arm. He'd gone to bed naked. He had no fear of discovery
because she'd amply indicated that she would sooner look at
a Wraithenbeast than at him. Now he wore a snowy silken
nightshirt bunched down around his knees, full sleeves tied
loosely at the wrists with white silk ribbons. Similar ribbons
trailed down his chest from an open collar trimmed with
lace.

As he shifted again, something slid off the bed. He looked
over the side, squinting—the fire was still strong and warm,
but the light didn't reach far into the alcove and the single
window was wrapped in fog. On the rug was a heavy splash
of rich brocade, a green-and-gold robe lined in thick brown
fur.

Magic?

No, someone didn't want him to freeze, was all.

Or starve. Seductive scents were making his empty stomach plead for sustenance. He dragged the robe from the floor, stuck his arms into the sleeves, and discovered leather slippers—also fur-lined—peeking from under the bed.

Just his size, too.

Wriggling blistered toes inside the silky softness, he stood up and stretched until his spine and shoulders cracked. Running both hands back through his hair, he ambled over to the fireplace. Stoked with half a tree that he didn't recall putting there, it blazed merry invitation to sit and partake of the waiting breakfast. He'd been right: duck, big thick slices of it. There were also chunks of some gloriously smelly cheese and two loaves of fresh bread wrapped in a cloth. The plates, utensils, goblets, and pitcher of mulled spiced wine were all made of gold.

He then slid behind the carved screen guarding the other alcove. On a stand below a shaving-size mirror at exactly the right height for him were a basin of warm water, soap and a razor, two combs, and two toothbrushes. He used the chamber pot (which emptied down a lidded hole in the wall, next to which was a fragrant spray of herbs), scraped several days' worth of beard from his cheeks and chin, ran a comb through his tangled coppery curls, and postponed the toothbrush until after breakfast.

He was just about to settle down in one of the chairs when he realized that of the clothing spread out to dry the night before, there was no sign. Nor of their knives, shoes, or even pocket change.

Collan chewed his lip for a moment, then went to the door. The massive iron dead bolt couldn't be opened from the outside. At the window, heavy fog limited visibility to the edge of the outside sill. The lock was still in place. Entry was impossible.

Therefore, so was breakfast.

And this ankle-length Grand Duke of Domburronshir thing he wore.

After a moment's consternation, he shrugged. In a world rife with interruptions by friend, foe, or innocent bystander, only a fool turned his back on offered comforts.

It would be churlish not to share. So he approached the monstrous tapestried bed to invite Sarra to breakfast.

For a moment he wondered if she was still in there. Feather mattress and velvet quilt and silk sheets billowed seven feet wide and seven feet long. Discerning which lump was Sarra proved difficult, for amid it all was no sign of a blonde head. Col poked at random, finally rewarded with an inelegant grunt, a rustling of covers, and a pair of black eyes blinking owlishly at him.

"Morning," he drawled. "Before you look around, be warned. All is not as it was last night."

"Huh?"

Playing lady's maid, he picked up the robe—turquoise brocade lined with black fur—from the foot of the bed. "This is the least of it," he added as Sarra's chin descended toward her chest—also covered in white linen, dangling silk ribbons, and lace. "All our own things are gone—and I do mean *gone*."

"What?"

Not exactly articulate of a morning, he thought, but at least not grumpy. He detested women who woke surly.

She swam to the edge of the bed, and halted as abruptly as Collan had on catching sight of what she wore. She looked up at him, down at her sleeve, and up at him again, comically bewildered.

"Here, put this on," he said. As she slid into the robe and stood, tugging at the nightshirt's sleeves, he added, "Don't forget your slippers."

Sarra wandered the room in silence, kicking hems out of her way with every step. She spent quite a while inspecting the window, then the door—the lintel seemed of special interest—and finally the gigantic stone hearth. Seating himself in one of the chairs, Col drank wine and waited. At length Sarra sat opposite him, picked up a two-tined golden fork, and dug in.

"So?" Col asked after they'd demolished most of the food and he had the energy to be curious again. "I mean, I know what *I* think, but—"

Sarra settled more snugly into her robe—looking vastly fetching in it, and as if she'd been born to such riches, which of course she had—and sat back with a solid gold goblet in hand. "I assume you noticed the sigils, the stitching, and the herb wreaths at the windows."

"The what, where?"

She rolled the cup between dainty palms. "Nobody could have entered this room, Col. Yet all our things are gone and all this is here instead. An obvious impossibility."

Col considered. "What are you not saying?"

Sarra shrugged.

"You're still not saying it." He counted to five. "Sarra. . . ."

"We haven't been harmed. In fact, all has been arranged for our comfort. Fire, food, warm clothing, beds—"

"You can get that at any decent inn."

"—and everything that could possibly be of harm has been taken away."

"Including my pants?"

Sarra drew a long breath. "If you're through being facetious—"

"Go on." He waved generously. "I'm listening."

"Only because you can't explain this, and I can. The carvings, the herbs—"

Col snorted and dug his fork into a cube of cheese—a bit emphatically, to be sure. "You're going all Mageborn on me again."

She held the goblet up. "This is the simplest of the spells in this room. The sigils stamped into the gold are charms for health. Orlin Renne had one something like this, made of silver."

"What about the herbs?"

"Protection against outside dangers."

"So what happened to our clothes?"

"Do you ever sleep without knives at hand—at the very least? Neither do I, not since I left Roseguard. Yet last night we both did. Frankly, I'm surprised we didn't throw our weapons out the window."

"If you say so. What else?"

Her brows arched. "What did you think when you woke?"

"That breakfast smelled delicious." He finished the cheese and washed it down with wine.

"No nervousness? No wondering how this could be?"

"Well, naturally, I wondered about it. But—" He stopped abruptly.

"You see? Your first impulse would be to go charging out of here demanding to know where your clothes are and what's going on—and you didn't." She pointed to his feet. "Look at your slippers."

"Now, that's enough! Next you're going to tell me they're spelled to keep me from walking out the door!"

"No. The embroidery is a pattern commonly woven into

blankets, to conserve warmth. The robes probably have something stitched in them as well, though I don't recognize many of the symbols."

"And I suppose somewhere on the fireplace is a 'perpetual flame' squiggle?"

"No," Sarra said calmly. "It would have been burning when we came in. We had to supply the fire. The hearth simply makes sure there's fuel."

Col filled his winecup to the brim, with the impression he was going to need it. "What you're telling me is we're surrounded by magic."

"Very old magic. The headboard of my bed, the weave of the blankets, the cups—the chair and table, for all I know." She raked back her hair. "There's no other explanation, Col. This room, if not this whole house, has been spelled and Warded by a very powerful Mage."

"That's—"

"—crazy?" she interrupted. "Come on, you're a Minstrel. Surely you know an ancient ballad or two about magic houses."

"Not that I recall offhand—and *don't* tell me St. Kiy Herself spelled the wine for forgetfulness, either!" He got to his feet. "Not to slight your arcane knowledge, but I'm sure there's a logical explanation that doesn't involve magic. And I'll prove it to you."

"How?"

After taking a large gulp of wine, he said, "I'm going to go find whoever's responsible and thank her."

Sarra gestured gracefully to the door. "Go right ahead."

With the strong sensation that she knew something else he didn't, Collan picked his robe up out of the way of his slippers and went to the door. It opened readily enough, iron dead bolt sliding silently aside. The door across the hall was closed, just as he'd left it last night. He started down the stairs, descending carefully due to his unfamiliarity with voluminous garments.

Four steps, eight, a dozen. He fixed his gaze on the landing, feeling chill air waft up between the iron risers. He kept moving—ten more steps, twenty.

And didn't get anywhere at all.

He stopped, frowning. He turned, climbed exactly three steps, and was on the wooden balcony again. He swung around and began the descent once more.

Twenty-five carefully counted steps later, he went back up the three risers and returned to the hearthside.

Sarra had filled his goblet again, whether from thoughtfulness, sympathy, or I-told-you-so, he didn't much care.

Col drank, then accused, "You knew."

"I suspected. Nothing can get in. But we can't get out, either."

He stared down at his companion—who was beginning to resemble a Blooded First Daughter of considerable means taking her ease after a strenuous day's hunt. All she lacked was a Senison hound resting its adoring head on her knee.

"What happened just now?" she asked.

"The stairs multiplied."

"Hmm. Let's go have a look in the other room."

Lacking a fire, the room was cold and their robes were more than welcome. Awkwardly, Col adjusted his, figuring there must be a trick to moving in the thing without tripping. He began to appreciate the work it took for a woman to look graceful in a floor-length gown.

The trunk was Sarra's goal, the only other feature of the room being an intricate tapestry of cobwebs. Besides, the thing practically begged to be opened. Sarra circled it twice, careful not to touch, then crouched to inspect the iron lock—which, after a shine-up, would have looked at home on the gates of Ryka Court.

"Fork," she muttered, stood, and vanished into the bed-chamber.

Somehow, Col didn't feel like touching the thing either. Not that he really believed any of this. *All right, then, how do you explain the stairs?* He went to the fog-misted window and tried to open it. The bolt had rusted shut and wouldn't budge. He supposed he could break the panes—but they were thick, bubbly glass that argued extreme age, and somehow he couldn't bring himself to smash some ancient crafter's work.

Or was the cottage protecting itself by *preventing* him from harming the window glass?

Another few thoughts like that, and he'd—

"Fork," said Sarra again from behind him, and he turned to find the lock being picked. After a moment's fiddling there was a loud click. The golden two-tined fork disappeared into a pocket of the robe, and Sarra folded the brocade more comfortably under her knees before hefting open the trunk's lid.

Revealed was nothing more sinister than a pile of old leather-bound books.

She leafed through one, a smile of delight on her face. "Col! Look at this! Aida Mirre's *Natural History of Lenfell*! Do you know how rare this is? There can't be twenty copies in the whole world!"

Col picked up another volume and blew dust off it. Sarra sneezed and glanced up irritably; he hardly noticed in his sudden fascination. Reverently, he opened a book of Saints' lives that was not just illuminated, but luminous.

"Do you like old books?" Sarra asked.

He turned pages gently. "Songbooks, mainly. But the Minstrel's life doesn't make for keeping a library."

"I had a huge library at Roseguard. History, biography, Magelore—most of them on the forbidden list."

"How'd you find them? And where'd you learn Pierga's Art, anyway?"

She shrugged, unrepentant. "Few people know what's in their collections, if the collection's big enough. And you're right, this isn't the first lock I've picked."

"You *stole* their books?"

"Nobody ever missed them. And I needed them."

"My, what highly individualized ethics," he said sweetly. She pulled a face at him. "Very funny."

They settled down happily to investigate the treasures. Neither knew how long they spent exploring and sharing their finds. At length the trunk was empty but for one volume—a huge, heavy tome practically falling apart. Sarra lifted it gingerly and set it on the floor between them. Another sneeze resulted when she opened it.

Col read easily upside down, though the words were not printed but handwritten in a close and spidery style.

" 'Remove entrails, rinse, and reserve . . . combine with three parts red wine no more than two harvestings old—' " He grinned. "Sarra! It's a cookbook!"

But pleasure had faded from her eyes, and she turned pages quickly, reading no more than a few sentences of each. Finally she placed both hands flat on the aged, yellowing vellum.

"No," she said solemnly. "It's a grimoire. A book of spells."

Col laughed. "Love philters and charms against snake-bite?"

"Miryenne's Holy Candle!" she exclaimed. "What's your problem? You've been Warded forever, you've been taken through Ladders, you know a dozen Mage Guardians—you even know the Captal! And—"

"Sarra," he said patiently, "it's a book of *recipes.*"

"—*and* you're sitting in the middle of a house that positively reeks of magic! How can you deny that magic exists?"

"I don't deny it. I just don't like it. Stop bristling like an old boar sow. It's one of your most unattractive traits."

"One of dozens," she snapped, and turned to the book's first page. "No magic? Listen to this!"

> *You are welcome here, Wayfarer.*
> *Shelter and sleep safe and warm.*
> *Rest within. These Wards protect you*
> *From inner strife and outer harm.*
> *This is the Crossroads of St. Feleris*
> *She of Kindness, She Who Heals.*
> *This house will serve, defend, and shield you*
> *From all but what your heart conceals.*

"What the hell does *that* mean?" Col demanded.

"There's more, if you'll shut up long enough to listen."

He sat back on his heels. "Go ahead. I collect examples of bad poetry."

Pausing for a brief glare, she continued.

> *No copper coin, no silver tribute,*
> *No gold or jewel in payment ply.*
> *No key unlocks the doors below you.*
> *No spell betwixt the stones and sky.*

"So how do we get out?" Col scooted around so he could read, too, tucking the warm robe around his feet. A slim finger pointed to the last verse. The writing was odd and the spelling even odder. He read aloud.

> *The only coin this house will treasure,*
> *The only key to these locked doors,*
> *Is only Truth. You, Mageborn Stranger,*
> *Hold coin and key. The truth is yours.*

"I'm not Mageborn," he said, "so I guess that means I'm stuck here forever. With *you*. How wonderful."

Closing the book gently, she began to replace the other volumes in the trunk. "It's getting cold in here."

"Sarra, tell me what you know!"

She closed the grimoire. "It's rather simple, really. We're in a Mageborn safe house."

He listened in bewildered silence as she explained. Set up long ago, as evidenced by the ancient sigils, it was neutral territory. Nothing that could work harm was permitted within; nothing could harm the inhabitants from without. Food, clothing, warmth, and refuge were provided. The only payment the house would accept, the only key to unlocking the door—and the spells—was the gift of Truth.

"Perhaps it means knowledge to add to the grimoire," Sarra mused. "Or maybe Truth has it own magic, and that replenishes the house. Or maybe once Truth is spoken, the house has some sort of power over you. Or—"

"That's enough," Col said firmly. "I've heard all the 'perhapses' and 'maybes' I care to. Not to mention spells, Wards, powers, and endless stairs." He saw Sarra give him a Look. "I know, I know—what about the food? Where did the clothes and firewood come from? There's a million questions to ask but only one that counts. How do we get out of here?"

She ran a fingertip along the trunk's dusty rim. "The Crossroads of St. Feleris," she said meditatively. "Crossroads are traditionally very powerful."

"How do we get out?" Col repeated.

"As neither of us has any magic to offer, presumably by telling the Truth."

He got up and went to the window. The fog had thinned some, but the view was not promising. The hills seemed more distant than he recalled, more forbidding. Almost threatening. Perhaps the magic here was losing its power against the dark.

He faced Sarra again. "Whatever makes this place work, it's fading. Downstairs it doesn't work at all. Except for the trunk, this room's empty. The one across the hall may be all the magic this house has left."

She was quiet for some time. Then: "You want to break the spells."

"Can it be done?"

"I don't want to try. Weak or not, there's magic here, Col. Do you want to risk a backlash? Have you any idea what might happen if we tamper with it?"

He gave a shrug designed to casually dismiss danger. Not sure he'd succeeded, he said, "Whatever happens, how bad can it be?"

"Do you really want to find out?" Sarra pulled the robe tight around her, as if a sudden draft had swept the room. "Well? Are you going to go first, or shall I?"

Huh? "You don't have to tell *me* your 'truth.' Just the house."

"Oh, by all means," she agreed with a grimace. "We'll stand in opposite corners and whisper to the walls. What is it about this that makes you so angry, Collan?"

He was angry? Sarra was practically shooting sparks with those big black eyes of hers. "I don't like being trapped."

"Neither do I."

"Then why can't we—"

"Because I know enough about magic to know I have no intention of trying to break it. So—you first, or me?"

The truth. "Such as?"

The milk-smooth brow creased slightly. "What do you mean?"

"It can't just be that I hate the smell of roast pork," he said impatiently. "It has to be something big enough to repay this place for the fire, the food, and the shelter. And that means it has to *mean* something so important to me that I've never told anyone before, right?"

"I—I suppose so."

"In other words, a secret."

Sarra gave a little shrug, saying, "I can't imagine you'd have any worse secrets than an underage seduction or two." But her gaze skittered away and she seemed nervous all of a sudden.

"Oh, there's worse." And if he wanted out of here, he'd have to say it. Out loud. For Sarra and the house to hear.

Only one thing it could be. She didn't know about him yet. His right shoulder had been turned away from her the day he'd returned by Ladder from Longriding with Alin Ostin dying in his arms. It had been dark in Renig Jail.

Collan dragged in a breath and jerked loose the belt of his robe. Sarra's eyes went wide as he tugged the nightshirt down to expose his shoulder.

"I was born a slave," he said, and waited for the inevitable recoil of disgust.

She surprised him again. Without pity or even compassion, and without moving, she inspected the mark on his shoulder. At length she replied, "No, you weren't."

Her lack of reaction sliced his nerves to shreds. "You think I got this put on for the fun of it?"

"No, of course not," she said, lips thinning. "But it hasn't been there all your life, you know. You weren't slaveborn, Collan. If you'd had that mark from birth, it would've grown larger as you grew. I'd say you were eleven or twelve when that was done."

The world sideslipped around him. "Maybe—maybe when I was old enough to try to run away—"

"No. Scraller sets his mark on his slaves the day they're born."

"How do you know?"

"Several of them lived at Roseguard. Taguare, Agata Nalle . . . Lady Agatine did a lot of business in The Waste. Over the years, she and Orlin bought and freed as many slaves as Scraller would sell." She shook her head. "Not that he parted with many."

"But I remember—" He stopped. What *did* he remember? And of what he did recall, what could he trust?

A gray cat he'd named Smoky. One or two other things—songs sung by a woman with a beautiful voice, Scraller's face, Taguare Veliaz. . . .

Verald and Sela had remembered *him*. But he had never seen them before in his life.

Or had he?

He remembered the headaches throbbing behind his eyes, pain associated with certain words or bits of melody hummed at odd moments. He remembered how forcing his thoughts to something else made the pain go away.

Had it been cowardice not to face it down? Or self-preservation?

Or a function of the Wards?

He pulled nightshirt and robe back up to cover the mark. "I'm going to try the stairs."

"Collan—" Holding the heavy grimoire to her chest, she followed him onto the balcony. After a moment's hesitation, she walked past to the bedchamber. She barely limped now;

the healing stitched into the slippers must be working. He
realized then that his own feet didn't hurt much.

From the top of the stairs he carefully counted steps to the
landing. Fifteen steps. He started down them, pausing on
each one to plant both feet on the wrought iron, like a tod-
dling child or an elderly man unsure of his strength.

After six steps he stopped, turned. The upper hall was exactly six steps above.

But no matter how many times his slippers whispered
against iron risers, the landing never got any nearer.

He tried jumping two and three and four steps at a time.
He even tried swinging over the banister. All that this maneuver gained him was a sore hip when he fell sideways
on the steps.

The house's magic was not yet satisfied. A truth, but not
the Truth.

Col climbed back upstairs. He said nothing as he closed
the bedchamber door, knowing Sarra would see failure in his
face. But Sarra saw nothing; she was asleep in her chair,
golden head drooping to one side, brocade robe wrapped
warmly around her, the grimoire in her lap.

Col sat down, stretching his legs toward the fire. In their
absence, it had replenished itself and burned as merrily
bright as ever.

Magic.

A cottage spelled to provide rest and refuge.

Had this been a tale told him over tavern wine, he would
have enjoyed the story and not believed a word. He might
even had reworked the simplistic verses in the grimoire and
set them to whatever old tune seemed to fit. But his lute was
far away, hidden in the Ostin house at Longriding. The only
"magic" he could claim was gone.

Not even his truths were real anymore. He wasn't slaveborn. But if not, who had sold him? Why? Not the woman
who sang by the fire; not his own mother. . . .

Was that who she had been?

He stared at the flames as if unWarded truth was written
there. Warmth, solace, songs: a hearthfire had always meant
that to him. In tavern or roadhouse, modest country manor
or grand city residence, give him a fireplace to sit near and
a lute to cradle in his arms, and he was happy. A good-
looking woman to sing to was always appreciated, too. . . .

No woman had ever sung to *him* except his mother. Songs were all he had of her, all he could remember.

> *Some night when you are deep asleep,*
>   *And breezes drift amid the trees,*
> *St. Jenavira's quiet hand*
>   *Will open books of memories.*
> *And you will read what's written there;*
>   *Relive the past, recall the dead;*
> *But, on waking, won't remember*
>   *A single thing you did or said.*
> *St. Jenavira's quiet hand*
>   *Will close the books before you read*
> *With open eyes. The past is past.*
>   *And memories are kin to dreams.*

16

"Where do you *think* I've been?' Auvry Feiran wearily untied his coif, stripped it off, and ran both hands through his graying hair. "Culling Mages everywhere from Neele to Isodir to Kenroke. It's filthy work, Glenin."

She shrugged, uninterested in Mages or the foolish Rising. "I've been waiting forever for you to get home. There's something I have to tell you."

He poured himself a large glass of brandy as she described what had happened five afternoons ago in this very room. He heard her out, taking short gulps of liquor and wincing a little after each one.

"Well?" she demanded when she'd finished and he still said nothing.

"I'm sure it seemed very real."

"I tell you I *felt* it!" She paused. "You mean you didn't?"

"No."

"Why not? You're Mageborn!"

"But not pregnant. Women in your condition are sometimes overly sensitive. I suspect that because you're an accomplished Mageborn, you'd be even more so."

"Thank you for making a dubious virtue of my heritage

and my training," she snapped. She paced her sitting room, heels digging into sun-streaked rugs. "I didn't imagine it and I didn't feel it because I'm pregnant! On the last day of Seeker's Moon I was sitting right there watching the sailboats and I felt someone *calling* to me. It was absolutely unmistakable. It—"

"Were you already using a spell?" he interrupted. "Even something simple, like Warming a cup of tea?"

"What I was doing was planning my son's future!" Then she stopped and swung around to stare at the daybed, picturing herself there. "No, I *was* using magic. In a way. Do you remember when we'd walk by the lake and you'd show me how to open myself, to sense the world with magic? I was thinking how wonderful it'll be to teach my son the same things you taught me and I taught Golonet Doriaz." All at once the loss and regret were sharper than at any time in the last nine years. "They don't teach the joy of using magic, you know. The pleasure of accomplishment, yes, but not the laughter. . . ."

"This must change when it comes time to teach your son," her father said with understanding. "Tell me more about this call you sensed, Glensha."

"It wasn't audible, as if there was an actual voice speaking to me. More of a feeling, a need to be somewhere—"

"As if you were being Summoned?" he asked, sharp-voiced now.

She heard the capital he gave the word, the way one said the name of a spell, and turned to face him. "Do you know what it was?"

"I think so. But it may take awhile to explain *how* I know."

"Tell me."

He drew a long breath, then began. "You know that coming into my magic was painful for me. No one knew what it was. There'd never been a Mageborn Feiran, not in all the Generations since The Waste War. Long ago our Name was common in South Lenfell. The Feiran Web owned dozens of mines in the Endless Mountains. But the Domburs coveted what we had, and set out to destroy us. First the price of copper was driven low. We lost money on every ton. Then silver was taxed so high we had to sell at a loss just to sell it at all. Mining accidents scared off many of our workers. The cost of slaves went up whenever we came to buy. The

Domburs planned over Generations, not just years. They wanted to wipe us out as a Name as well as a Web. Our sons went unmarried. It became almost impossible for our daughters to find eligible men. Soon they couldn't even buy husbands. For proud women of a proud Name . . . Glenin, they had to get children off chance-met strangers or go childless. We dwindled to a few hundred, then to a single line that ends with me."

"No," Glenin corrected. "It continues with *me*."

He smiled. "How proud my mother would've been to know you!"

His gratitude hurt. "You've never told me any of this."

"I'm the only one who knows—besides the Domburs, of course. By the time I was born, the Feirans were nearly nothing. Allynis Ambrai certainly thought so. My mother was the second daughter, and she wanted to start the Feiran Name over in the North. Grandmother wished her luck and handed over her dowry. It wasn't much, but it bought a house on the shores of Maidil's Mirror—remote even for that region. It was just the four of us, she and I and my two older brothers."

Glenin sat very abruptly in a chair. "Brothers?"

"Linnar and Garris," he murmured. "I never knew who my father was, but the magic unquestionably came through his line."

A father's Name wasn't supposed to matter, but not to know his Name at all was a terrible thing to do to a child.

"Mother never married. We three boys never knew who our fathers were and never asked." When she blinked at the plural, he smiled. "We looked nothing like each other. Linnar was as sunlight-fair as you are, and looked so much like Mother it was if he had no father at all. He was two years older than Garris, who was four years older than I—dark and elegant, the handsomest man I ever saw. By the time I turned fifteen, they were grown men. But even so, I was taller than they, and stronger. . . ." He trailed off, his eyes blanking.

"Father?" she whispered to bring him back to her. "What happened?"

"Linnar and I were out on the lake, fishing. I found it . . . soothing. Serene. I'd been struggling more than a year with what I didn't know was magic. We all thought it was just moodiness, the way adolescent boys are when they grow too fast. Linnar used to take me climbing to tire me out so I could sleep, or out fishing for the silence of it. At first it helped, but as I got older—I spared you that, Glenin. You never had to go through that, thank St. Chevasto."

Glenin nodded and said softly, "Tell me the rest."

He sat beside her and she took his hands in her own. "That day out on the lake I felt—it was like an explosion inside. I believe now that I was poised on the edge of Wild Magic. But back then I only knew I had to find what had caused the pain. I wanted to kill it, I think. I grabbed the oars and started rowing. Linnar tried to stop me, but I was a head taller and twenty pounds heavier. He screamed and begged, but I rowed for the river outlet as if Wraithenbeasts were after me."

Glenin caught her breath, knowing what must come next.

"The boat was so small," he said tonelessly. "Strong as I was even then, I couldn't control it. We hit rapids and I remember plunging into a trough, and coming up on the other side. Linnar—Linnar was gone. I never saw him again."

He paused, ran his tongue around dry lips, and met her gaze. "Nor any of my family. Later I tried to find them, but the house was deserted. No one knew where my mother and Garris had gone, or even if they were alive. A Mage at the Academy had a cousin at Census who checked for me in 925 and again in 950, but no Feirans were recorded anywhere." He stared down at their twined hands. "However they died, at least it wasn't magic that killed them."

"I'm so sorry," Glenin murmured, stroking his fingers.

"What I'd felt, what made my magic burst inside me, was word going out that Captal Ferros was dead. But the *way* I felt it was twisted—my magic was turning on itself for lack of training. I learned later that it happens that way to the very powerful." He shrugged. "I made it through the rapids somehow, and drifted down the Brai River for days, curled in the boat like a wounded animal. When Gorynel Desse finally found me, I was half-dead."

"Desse found you?"

"He was looking for me. The new Captal, Leninor Garvedian, was having nightmares that she swore came from the north. So he started upriver, Folding the road and casting scrying Mage Globes periodically, and that's how I came to be trained as a Prentice Mage."

"But not at the Academy. You told me that."

"It was two weeks before I was well enough to travel, and another three before we arrived in Ambrai. Gorsha took it slow, teaching me along the way so I wouldn't unleash something dreadful on the whole Academy. But they wouldn't have me. I still lapsed occasionally into Wild Magic, and they had to protect Novices who didn't know how to defend themselves. So I lived in a cottage the Desse Name owned outside the city. Gorsha came every few days to teach me. No one else would," he added with a shrug. "I can't blame them. For years I blamed myself for killing Linnar."

"But you didn't! It wasn't your fault. You didn't know what was happening to you, and it was Mage Guardian magic that was really to blame."

"I know that now. But back then I didn't trust myself and there was no reason for them to trust me, either. Captal Garvedian rode out occasionally to test me, but I was seventeen before she let me live at the Academy. By then I didn't want to. When I turned eighteen, I was recognized as a Prentice and took to the road."

She'd heard his traveler's tales before, but never the whole story of how he became an itinerant Prentice Mage Guardian. "When did you return to Ambrai?"

"Twelve years later. I was nearly thirty ... and your mother was twenty-two, nearly as beautiful as you are now." He leaned back with a sigh. "You know the rest—how furious Allynis was when her First and only Daughter wanted to marry a copperless Feiran who wasn't even a Listed Mage." After a moment he shook off bitter memory and finished, "I told you this to apologize for doubting you, Glensha. What you felt was a Summons, a variation on what I felt back then."

She nodded. "But who did this Summoning? And why?"

"Where did it come from? Which direction?"

"That way. Northeast." She pointed across the room, then frowned. "No, it's a little farther to the right, now." Startled, she exclaimed, "It *moved!* In the last five days, whoever sent the Summons has moved!"

"So you're still feeling it. Excellent. How strongly?"

"I have to concentrate some," she said critically. "It's not urgent, the way it was at first. It's not an imperative to go find it anymore."

He stood, facing in the direction she'd first pointed. "Renig," he mused.

"But it's moved farther east now—Father!" she gasped. "Toward *Ambrai?*"

17

Col returned to consciousness with the light touch on his shoulder.

"Dinner," Sarra said. "I woke up, and here it was. At least whoever set up this place knew how to cook."

Venison steaks smothered in sour cherry sauce, butter-and-herb noodles, red wine, three kinds of cheese, green-apple tart—exactly what he would have ordered at Fielto's Horn, his favorite of the summer-holiday trade eateries overlooking Tillin Lake. He didn't mention it.

Beyond the foggy window it was very dark. Col didn't remember having fallen asleep in his chair, and that bothered him. Perhaps the cottage had done it, dutiful to its spells of rest and serenity.

Or maybe it just didn't want to get caught providing dinner.

"You know," he remarked as he loaded his plate with more venison, "my brain is still arguing that this is completely unreal. But my stomach disagrees, and for now, it's winning."

"You're incorrigible." But she was smiling as she said it.

"At least I'm past the 'there must be a logical explanation' stage. Does that count?"

After the meal, Sarra delved into the grimoire. Collan fire-gazed for a time, then retrieved an illustrated Wraithen-bestiary he'd seen earlier. It was written in an archaic style he could read with just enough effort to distract his mind, but not enough to frustrate him and make him put it aside.

The drawings would give nightmares to a Warrior Mage. There were monsters that were all teeth, all claws, all hideous eyes, or various combinations of same. There were creatures that looked like the progeny of impossible matings between generations of wild animals—a wolf's head on a boar's body with leathery bat-wings and the split hooves of a horse. Some resembled common farm livestock—goats, sheep, geese, swine—dismembered and reassembled into horrible mismatched lumps of hoof and horn, tooth and tail. Yet somehow the worst were the pets: dogs and cats that retained their forms but whose defenses were all out of proportion. One lurid woodcut featured a hound, jaws agape with sword-length fangs; another, a cat whose four-inch claws gleamed like steel.

What struck him most, however, was the fury in the monsters' eyes. As if they *knew* they were freaks of magic and despised themselves as much as they hated their creators for giving them life. And they wanted revenge.

Whatever their shape, they were universally murderous. But, curiously, there was no mention in the text of instantaneous death on merely beholding a Wraithenbeast. *Which follows,* Collan thought, trying for cynicism. *A book about Wraithenbeasts, complete with illustrations, is hardly possible if nobody survived to describe them.*

This implied that it was possible to survive an encounter. Unless the whole dreadful book was simply the product of someone's overheated imagination.

It might have been Half-Twelfth or nearly Fifteenth when he decided to go to bed. Getting to his feet, he stretched and said, "Let me know if you find anything that works against the Ryka Legion."

"Mmm," Sarra replied absently, turning a page.

The alcove basin had been replenished with hot water. He gave himself a rag-bath, paying special attention to his rapidly healing feet, then donned the white nightshirt again and snuggled beneath the blankets in happy anticipation of another long night of uninterrupted sleep, courtesy of an ensorcelled cottage.

For reasons of its own, the cottage did not oblige.

Col woke very suddenly, chilled. He knew he'd accepted the magic when his first thought was, *Some spell—the fire's gone out.* When he checked the gigantic hearth, sure enough, the flames had burned low.

The magic was fading, even in this room—the only one that still worked. Could truth actually renew the waning power here? He snorted when he caught himself wistfully wishing that it could.

Sarra was in bed asleep. All he could see by the dimming

hearthfire light was a long lock or two of curling blonde hair. Moving nearer, huddling into the fur-lined robe, he twitched the quilt aside so he could watch her face.

The spells *were* almost worn out. Sarra was having a nightmare. Even though the grimoire attested that this place was one of rest and ease, there was fear in the knotted fair brows and the trembling of her lips. Collan sank to his knees in billowing silk and took one small, chill hand between his own. "Shh. It's all right, Sarra. Hush now, little one. Hush."

It took only moments—a few words, a touch, a smoothing of her hair. She settled, sinking deep into the enormous bed, her mouth relaxing into a tender curve, the nightmare gone.

Col got to his feet and tried to warm his hands at the fire, glaring down at the dying light.

"What're you trying to do, frighten it out of her? Her truth is none of your damned business, whatever it is. If you want it bad enough to scare it out of us, try me instead. She's the one who believes in you. She's the one who wants to change things so the kind of people who made you don't have to live in fear anymore. Let her be. Let her rest."

The flames flickered, then dimmed. Cursing, he returned to Sarra's bed, sitting on its edge, taking up protective watch over her slumber.

The softening fireglow softened her features, but revealed none of the childlike innocence he might have expected. How could a woman who'd seen and done and endured what Sarra had retain any innocence? Col knew none was left of his own—if he'd ever had any. Memory provided no evidence. But if there was no innocence in Sarra's face, neither was there any disillusionment.

Saints knew he'd done his best to put it there, he accused himself bitterly. Shoving her face in harsh and dirty realities, haranguing her about the Rising and its goals, practically accusing her of being no better than the Malerrisi she despised—

"But you've got to think it all through, Sarra," he heard himself whisper. "You know where you want to go, but you don't have a clue about how to get there or what's in your way. I don't want to see you break your heart. . . ."

Sarra shifted, pushing the heavy quilt from her shoulders, hands lax and vulnerable on the pillow. Such small, delicate hands. One of them had pulled a knife from her belt and thrown it into the heart of a Malerrisi.

The popular "Ballad of Castle Watch" asserted that you never knew the value of your own life until you killed someone. The song was about soldiers in some long-ago siege, and he'd never liked it much, but now he understood. It wasn't that your own life became more precious when you took the life of another. The point was that you discovered your own life's value in who you were willing to risk it to kill.

Facing immediate threats, Collan had made a judgment— *My life is worth more than yours*—and killed. Quite a few times. He wondered if Sarra's own "highly individualized ethics" could encompass that.

He'd killed Scraller Pelleris in what was commonly and erroneously termed "cold blood." Scraller's life was worth nothing. Nobody would miss him or mourn him. Was Scraller the value of Col's own life?

A truly nauseating thought.

Verald Jescarin had been worth more than the dozens Collan had killed to avenge him. His fury of loss slammed into his abrupt realization that a thousand deaths wouldn't make up for the loss of this one kind, humorous friend. Col had known that when he'd killed them. So why had he killed so many?

The other deaths had happened because instinct told him his own life mattered more than the life of the person trying to kill him. Well, of course his life mattered more to *him*. Verald's had mattered at least as much. But Verald was dead before Collan even unsheathed his sword that night. So why—?

That Warrior Mage—what was her name?—Imilial Gorrst. The Healer Mage she'd traveled with had willingly died to keep her safe. Well, he'd loved her, presumably. Col tried hard, but couldn't imagine loving anyone more than his own life.

Sarra did. As he watched her sleeping face—very young, but not the face of a child—he knew absolutely that if there'd been no other way, she would have leaped between Cailet and the Malerrisi and taken the lethal blast of magic herself. Instead, she had grabbed her knife and killed. But the worth of her life wasn't the Malerrisi: it was *Cailet*.

It had been true of the old man as well. And Scholar

Wolvar, and the old Captal. Even Alin—who'd delayed following Val Maurgen into death long enough to teach Cailet
about Ladders. Col hated to think how she'd react when one
day she realized that so many people considered her life
worth their deaths.

But who decided which lives were valuable? The Lords of
Malerris, to hear the Mage Guardians tell it, with an implied
condemnation of their arrogance in claiming the right to decide. But to the Mage Guardians, the Captal's life mattered
more than anyone's in the world.

That was why Sarra had killed. To protect the Captal.

No, that was wrong. Sarra had killed to protect *Cailet.*

At last he had it. It wasn't who you were willing to risk
your life to kill, but who you'd risk it to kill *for.* No one—
Mage, Malerrisi, Council, no one—had the right to make
that decision for you.

And just that simply, Collan Rosvenir joined the Rising.

He knew it, and gazed down at Sarra with real annoyance.
Yet an instinctive *What the hell has she done to me?* was
quickly answered by *I did it to myself.* The realization was
as true and real as the sudden renewed warmth of the fire
across the room.

Straightening, Col stared at the blaze. Then he went
downstairs. All the way to the bottom. Opening the door, he
stood looking out at the misty night for a long time. Then,
his steps slow and soft, he returned to the bedchamber.

18

Glenin stretched her shoulders, sighed, and glared at the list
on her writing desk. Having finished the first fifty invitations to Garon's Birthingday dinner, there were twice that
many left to do. Most of the guests were neither her friends
nor Garon's, but she wasn't giving this party for the fun of
it. The whole Council and selected influential members of
the Assembly; the full roster of ministers and officials from
the Keeper of the Archives to the Keeper of the Zoo (excepting the Minister of Mines, a position vacant since Telomir
Renne's escape); all the Justices and certain Advocates; and

representatives of the most powerful Names and most cash-
heavy Webs.

Plus everyone's personal guest.

On reflection, she was amazed the guest list was only
three hundred.

The Malachite Hall was bespoken, the musicians hired,
the flowers ordered, the menu planned, the various wines
tagged in the cellars. All that remained were the invitations
to be written and the souvenir tokens to be chosen. Manners
obligated Glenin to pen each letter with her own hand, for
all the guests must receive the impression that it was her
personal pleasure to share this celebration with them. One
could get away with printed invitations for a large ball or casual picnic, but to be a guest at dinner was to be included in
a family ritual. So Glenin had decided against a large ball,
a casual picnic, or anything in between. To sit at a First
Daughter's dinner table was an intimate honor—not that
most of them deserved it, Glenin thought with a sniff. But a
dinner celebrating the Birthingday of a First Daughter's husband was an occasion eclipsed only by her own Birthingday
and those of her female children.

Those she selected to attend would be thrilled. What they
didn't know was that her acceptance of the usual return invitations would be just as selective. She intended this, the
first really grand party she'd ever given, as an ambush.
Many invitees were people she didn't like, had no use for, or
wished to impress—not with the dinner itself, but with her
growing power. This year, a polite refusal from Lady Glenin
Feiran would be tantamount to social ruin. Next year, the disaster would be political as well.

No one would know that on the first night of First Flowers. She'd treat every single odious guest as if she'd waited
all year to dine with each of them particularly. Though there
would be twenty-five tables, each would be as much
Glenin's own as if they'd been crammed into her private
chambers. She would design the pattern of porcelain, silver,
crystal, napkins, and flowers herself, and that evening light
each candle with her own hands.

The planning was all very tedious and time-consuming.
But Glenin had been taught her manners by the last Lady of
Ambrai, and though she would never admit it, she secretly
saluted her grandmother's Wraith every time she entertained.
Because of Lady Allynis, even Glenin's hitherto casual par-

ties were the most elegant and talked-about at Ryka Court, and her invitations the most coveted.

Flexing stiff fingers, she let her gaze fall on another list. This was in Anniyas's writing, and suggested possibilities for the tokens each guest would take home from the dinner. They ranged from silver floral crowns (in honor of St. Sirrala, on whose day Garon had been born) to golden gavels (in honor of Garony the Righteous) to gem-studded scissors (in honor of Niya the Seamstress, from whom the Anniyas Blood took its name). There were other suggestions, but all had one thing in common: they were obscenely expensive.

Costly trinkets were appropriate for a Wise Blood celebration, a marriage, or the birth of a First Daughter. This was nothing more important than Garon's thirty-first Birthingday.

But, truly told, Glenin wasn't even giving this dinner for him. During it she would announce a forthcoming and far more momentous Birthingday. She smiled and sighed and considered her hopes for her son. On reflection, the Scissors were the obvious choice.

"But *not* in gold and jewels," she said aloud, taking a fresh sheet of paper from a drawer. She wrote an order for three hundred pairs of steel scissors—in green velvet pouches with gray drawstrings, to remind everyone of the Name of the woman who gave them. The crafters would be working around the clock to fill the order, but that was their problem. As a concession to the week, and rather neatly giving tribute to another Saint she didn't believe in, she added that the handles be engraved with flowers—Miramili's Bells.

The Summoner, she thought suddenly.

If she concentrated, she could still feel the spell's direction, though with more effort than yesterday; the magic must finally be fading. Yet who would have such power to begin with, to send a Summons from The Waste that Glenin had sensed on Ryka, and moreover could still sense six days after its casting?

Gorynel Desse was dead. So was the old Captal. *Who,* damn it?

In the next room, the frantic voice of Glenin's personal maid lifted in protest. The arched door that mimicked the domed ceiling flew inward before Glenin could send a magical thread outward to discover the intruder's identity.

Anniyas. In full and furious cry.

"Get up and come with me," she snarled.

The maid, quivering with equal parts fear of Anniyas and outrage at the intrusion, babbled at the same time, "My Lady, I'm most terribly sorry but the F–First Councillor insisted—"

"It's all right," Glenin said, with a feather stroke spell of Calm. She deplored domestic disturbances, especially in front of Anniyas. "You may go."

The girl nodded, cast a doubtful glance at the unwelcome guest, and made her opinion known by not *quite* slamming the door behind her. Anniyas paid no heed. She paced the chamber round and round, an agitated whirl of heavy charcoal-gray silk with too much gold lace ruffling the hem. The expression on her face made Glenin worry for the jade chess set and crystal camellia bowl among other breakable treasures. But Anniyas looked readier to smash heads than trinkets. Glenin put down her pen and turned sideways in her chair.

"I *hate* not using magic!" Anniyas spat. "Not even a simple spell on a stupid girl to get me in here—and how dare you forbid me your rooms at any time, let alone the middle of the damned day?"

"Is there something I can do for you?" Glenin inquired with a placidity she knew would further annoy her husband's mother.

"I already told you—come with me."

"Where?"

"Are you questioning a direct order, Malerrisi?"

This, Glenin was well aware, was calculated to infuriate her. Had she indulged, nothing in this world would have parted her from her chair. Damping her urge to snarl back, she stood up and silently faced Anniyas.

"Excellent choice. Wear a cloak." The old woman— suddenly not looking very old at all, Glenin thought with a frown—left at once by the garden door.

Snatching a length of green wool from her bedroom closet, Glenin hurried after her. The private garden enjoyed by the Council and certain elite was a week from full spring display, but enough trees and flowers bloomed to make her nose itch. On three sides of the formal plantings were elegant residences; beyond a rose-covered wall, manicured lawns sloped down to the lake.

She caught up with Anniyas at the summerhouse that was

the garden's centerpiece: a round, domed tracery of slatwork painted white and gold, roofed in green, with an arching open doorway at each cardinal point of the compass. Anniyas went around to the eastern entry rather than the nearer south door.

Once Glenin was inside, Anniyas said curtly, "Ward us." And because silent obedience appeared to be the day's theme, Glenin did so at once, nodding when she was through.

"Sight?" Anniyas demanded. "Sound?"

Again she nodded, resisting the urge to suggest—oh so sweetly—that the exalted Lady of Malerris test the Wards herself. This, of course, she could not do; no one must know that she, who intended to rid Lenfell of magic, was herself Mageborn.

"And against prying magic?"

She cocked a brow. "Only iron can do that."

"Then use the fucking nails!"

After a moment's startlement—Anniyas never allowed her rural upbringing to show in her language—Glenin obeyed.

"All right, then." Anniyas sat on the wooden bench that curved along the south wall. Afternoon sunlight angled in, dappling her gray shoulders and graying head with gold. "Sit down. Rest your back. It's a habit you'll want to get into, believe me. All the weight you're gaining with this baby, you'll hardly be able to walk by your tenth week."

Shrugging off the insult, she went to the bench opposite Anniyas and sat. And said nothing.

"Why wasn't I informed about the Summons?"

"I only learned what it was yesterday."

"And when were you going to tell me? Today? Next week? Some morning when you had nothing else to do?"

"I didn't know it was that important."

"Don't lie to me, Glenin, I've known you since you were eight years old and you've never been able to fool me. Not important? A Summons to all Mage Guardians to attend on the Captal as fast as they can possibly get there?"

"I'm not a Mage Guardian. And I had no idea that's what it was."

"Well, now you know," Anniyas growled.

"How did you?"

"Your father let it slip an hour ago. He of all people should have known at once, and come to me—"

"He didn't feel it. I did. And quite frankly I don't understand why. He's the one they trained."

"But yours was the magic open to it at the moment it was sent. We used to keep someone alert like that at Malerris Castle at all times. The present Fifth Lord being an idiot, however—"

"Do you mean I'm the only one of us who felt it?" she asked, astonished.

"And a lucky thing you did! *My* luck. Because *I'm* the one who knows what to do about a Summons. You don't even know why it was sent, do you? There's a new Captal, made at Ambrai—thanks to the incompetence of you and your father!—and she or he is gathering all surviving Mage Guardians for an attack."

Glenin smiled. "There aren't enough left to attack a half-built barn. What's the body count now? Nine hundred? Nine-fifty? You've nearly got your thousand, First Councillor."

"Nine hundred twenty-three. With a living Captal, ten would be enough—if they did it from Ambrai."

"Why? Their Ladders are all dead—nearly all, anyway. There's no power to be had from them, the way the surviving Ladders at Malerris Castle store magic we can use. And Gorynel Desse is just as dead. Whoever this new Captal is, without Desse to—"

Anniyas heaved herself to her feet and began to pace again. "Desse *made* the new Captal! Just as he *made* Leninor Garvedian!"

"Not to mention Lusath Adennos," Glenin added cuttingly, "the joke of Mageborns all over Lenfell."

The First Councillor snorted. "Don't be a fool. Adennos was a box to hide the Bequest in. Oh, don't look so cow-eyed! The Captal's Bequest! Surely you learned about it somewhere!"

Glenin's brain was reeling now. "But it's just a list of spells and Wards and things—"

"—transferred from Captal to Captal for Weaver only knows how many Generations, probably back to their Founding! 'Just a list'? Don't make me laugh!" Anniyas picked at a silver paint chip on a wooden strut. "Desse tricked me with Adennos, I'll give him that. He made it look as if he had nothing better to work with, and we Malerrisi believed him. By the Great Loom, we made it easier for the old son of a Fifth by killing every Mage at the Academy!"

"But now there's a new Captal," Glenin said, bringing her back to the subject. "Who has Summoned all surviving Mage Guardians. What are we going to do about it?"

Anniyas developed a coldly calculating smile. "*I* am going to do precisely nothing. *You* are going to use that clever little velvet Ladder of yours to take your estimable father to a place I have in mind, where—"

"Ambrai?"

"Don't interrupt! If it was Ambrai, I'd go myself by the Octagon Court Ladder! Which, eventually, I will do," she appended with a deeper smile in her blue eyes.

Glenin's mind worked with frantic speed. Anniyas was the First Lord's most valued thread—but Anniyas was weaving her own way through the Great Loom. Glenin had never trusted her, never, and even less so now that the required son nestled in her belly, the child who would grow up more powerful than Anniyas ever dreamed of being, the child Anniyas feared—

All her half-realized insights braided together and knotted around her heart: her son was the child Anniyas *wanted*.

But she was old, nearly seventy. She'd be close to ninety before the boy was fully trained. Ah, but she didn't have to live that long, for at twelve or thirteen his magic would begin and surely the old woman could survive that long. Long enough to raise him, teach him, mold him, so that when magic was his *he* would be *hers*—

All of which meant that the life-thread that was Glenin would be Scissored from the massive Tapestry as soon as she had borne him.

"I'm pregnant," she heard her own voice say very calmly. "Ladders are dangerous."

A dismissive shrug. "You've got weeks and weeks yet before you have to worry about it."

"He's Mageborn," she said, listening to the quiet voice and marveling at its composure. "I can feel it even now, when he's barely formed. He'll be one of those children who's aware even in the womb."

"Nonsense. A fantasy in books."

"Would you care to touch him with your magic?"

Anniyas glared at her. "You'll go where I tell you and do as I say!"

Glenin rose slowly to her feet and looked down on the First Councillor and said, very clearly, "No."

"Don't defy me, girl. Not now, not ever."

"Take it up with the First Lord," Glenin suggested coolly.

Anniyas gave a harsh, braying laugh. "You shit-witted idiot! Haven't you figured it out yet? I *am* the First Lord!"

19

That morning, behind the alcove screen, a small but adequate hip-bath had appeared. Sarra blinked at this evidence of strengthening magic. Collan only shrugged and dug into breakfast. She bathed in silence, glad enough of getting really clean at last, but fretful with maddening speculations.

Not about what had produced the tub and the hot water, scented with her favorite violet perfume. It was obvious enough that the cottage had heard a Truth that paid for its magic. What bothered her was what Truth of Collan's had bought this—and how much it might have cost him.

He didn't seem any the poorer in resources of wit or humor, responding to her offer of first bath with a quip about violet being neither his color nor his cologne. (She privately considered that color perfect for those coppery curls and very blue eyes.) He looked neither restless nor bored, neither troubled nor out of sorts. In fact, he was more relaxed than she had ever seen him—as if he'd finally gotten a decent night's sleep.

She felt the same. And she knew it ought to bother her. The soreness was gone from her ankle much sooner than it should have been. Two whole nights of ease-spelled slumber had restored her completely. Any other time she would have been eager to set out again, get moving, do something. She had energy for more than lazing in a tub and then beside the fire with the grimoire in her lap. And, Saints witness, she certainly had places to go and things to do. But all morning passed and she did nothing.

There was one small anomaly. Collan served her breakfast as politely and elegantly as any woman could wish, keeping an unobtrusive eye on her plate and winecup lest either go empty before her hunger and thirst were assuaged. It was unsettling, this uncharacteristic gentility.

She felt herself growing drowsy in mid-afternoon, and fought off sleep with conversation. Col was eager to talk. They discussed books they'd read, places they'd been, plays and operas they'd attended. Occasionally his tastes even coincided with hers. At length, hiding a tenth yawn behind his hand, Col smiled and told her it wasn't the company, and he certainly found his own stories fascinating, but they really ought to give in to the magic so it could clear the breakfast dishes and set up dinner.

"Do we have a choice?" she asked, barely able to keep her eyes open now.

"Not that I can tell. Take a nap, First Daughter."

She was asleep before she could remind him to stop calling her that.

She woke to a rowdy drinking song and splashing sounds coming from the alcove. Dinner waited on the low table before her: spicy stew, green salad, and six of the palm-sized honey-walnut tarts she adored. She made a face. The house knew her very well. Ambrai colors in her bedrobe, violet scent in the bathwater, her favorite dessert . . . if it already knew so much, why did she have to tell it a Truth?

She glanced up as Collan rounded the screen, toweling his limp, dripping curls. Cheeks and chin shaved silk-smooth of stubble, hair in a mad wet tangle, he looked no older than she was and perhaps a bit younger as he gave her a crooked little grin.

"Don't tell me you squeezed all six feet of you into that hip-tub," she said, smiling back.

"Six feet two inches, and the tub's my size now." He tossed the towel over the screen and approached the fire. "Looks good. And I'm not even wondering where the lettuce came from this early in the season."

"Yes, you are, or you wouldn't have said it." As he sat down, she smelled not a hint of violets. Instead—winter iris and woodsmoke, and something else very masculine that she couldn't identify. "Did the house provide a bigger tub because you're bigger than I am, or because the magic is getting stronger?"

"You're the Mageborn. You tell me." When she started to speak, he shook his damp head and dipped a ladle into the stew. "Later."

Later arrived after one helping of stew (he had three) and a virtuous two walnut pastries (he ate the other four). Sarra put down her napkin, picked up her winecup, and said, "Whatever was said last night did things to the house."

"Probably."

"Did you try the stairs again?"

"Yes."

"And?"

"Halfway down."

"So it's my turn to tell the Truth."

Raking uncombed curls from his brow, he frowned and said, "Look, Sarra, you don't have to say anything you don't want to."

"I thought you were the one who was so anxious to get out of here."

"Maybe I changed my mind. We've got beds, food, clothes, even baths. The beds are soft, the food's great, the bathwater was clean as well as hot, and we don't even have to stoke the fire."

"And the clothes?" She lifted one turquoise-clad arm.

"Well, a little much—but what the hell. Point is that no inn I know has all that at once. And it's even free."

"Not quite." Eyeing him closely, she asked, "Is this how you'd like to live your life?"

He sprawled back, hooking one leg over the chair arm. "All I lack is my lute, Lady."

"Liar," she accused gently.

"*You* look right at home," he observed. "Just the way I'd picture you if I ever stopped to think about it. Taking your ease, reading old books, and sipping good wine all day long—"

"—with sweet dreams guaranteed every night. I'd be bored brainless. And so would you, Minstrel. We both have places to go, work to do—"

"—songs to sing and women to sing to," he appended, winking at her.

She bit her lip. "Collan . . . did I ever thank you for singing to Cailet?"

"Even if you did, I wouldn't mind hearing it again."

"Once is enough. And don't get any ideas about her," she warned.

He laughed heartily. "Me and the kitten? Don't tell me you're jealous!"

"Don't be absurd." She hid behind her winecup. A long swallow, then another, and she set the gold goblet down with a determined thunk. "Just don't chase after her the way you do every other woman you see."

The very blue eyes widened in outrage. *"They* chase *me!"*

"I haven't," she retorted smugly.

"There hasn't been much time," he drawled.

An unexpected giggle escaped her. "Don't you ever stop?"

"Not until I get what I want. Kind of like this house."

Mirth fled, and she stared down at her folded hands. "It's my turn."

"You don't have to," he mumbled. "I lied about the stairs."

"What?"

Draining the wine down his throat, he put the cup on the table. The forks rattled. "Last night I went all the way down them and opened the front door."

If she'd been capable of speech, she would have cursed him up one side and down the other, and probably should have. All today he'd said nothing when, in fact, they were free to go?

He'd stayed, knowing he could leave?

Sarra grabbed up handfuls of the turquoise robe and ran for the iron staircase. One step, two, three, four—

—and she wasn't even halfway down.

Collan walked soft-footed past her, all the way to the bottom. There, he turned and looked up at her. Light spilled from the bedchamber out to the balcony and down onto his face, solemnly gilding his very blue eyes.

> *The only coin this house will treasure,*
> *The only key to these locked doors*
> *Is only Truth. You, Mageborn Stranger,*
> *Hold coin and key. The Truth is yours.*

Collan was free to go. He'd paid up. She hadn't. And he knew it as well as she did.

Sarra returned to the balcony. "All right, then," she muttered, and drew breath to tell a Truth.

The magic here should have sharpened her instincts. She should have had a warning, a twinge in her heart or a twist in her guts. But she was as thunderstruck as Collan when the outer door slammed open and a deep, sonorous voice said, "So. She was right, and there *is* someone here."

After that instant's stunned shock, Collan behaved as if Sarra didn't exist. He turned to Auvry Feiran, saying, "Come on in. Dinner's over, but I'm sure the wine jug will be filled up again by now."

A cold wind swept through the door, and Sarra felt it as a million icy winged things swarming up the stairs. She didn't dare move for fear shifting shadows below would reveal her presence. She hardly dared breathe, though her heart throbbed a demand for air, more air, she'd faint if she didn't breathe—

"Thank you, but I believe I'll decline your invitation. I know what this house is, and what it wants before it will allow one to leave."

"Oldest platitude in the book," Collan replied easily. "The Truth will always free you."

"A tired old saying, I agree. But in this case, appropriate."

"You won't come in to get me because you're afraid of the truth? Or maybe you've forgotten what it is."

There was a brief pause. Then Feiran said calmly, "My understanding of what is true is not shared by the makers of this house."

"And here I always thought true was true, no matter what."

Now he sounded amused. "It appears we're going to have some interesting philosophical discussions, you and I."

"What?" Col exclaimed, pretending astonishment. "I thought people like you just killed people like me straight off. Snag in the Tapestry, and all that."

"It may be necessary at some point. But not yet."

"Imagine my relief."

Sarra was breathing in short, silent gulps now, no longer in danger of fainting. Still, she felt sick listening to the verbal swordplay.

"You might wish to consider coming outside now," said Auvry Feiran.

"Come along quietly like a good boy?"

"You'd find the alternative most unpleasant."

Sarra heard the velvet menace and bit both lips between her teeth to keep from crying out.

Collan's tone had changed, too. "You can't come in, and

believe me, Commandant, there's no way in hell I'm coming out."

The reply was a low, musical chuckle. Sarra remembered it from childhood. Remembered trying to earn it and the smile that went with it. Her father. . . .

"An accurate summation, as far as you know. What you *don't* know is that fire can destroy this house as easily and completely as it destroys Ladders."

Another brief pause.

"I'm not exactly dressed for travel." Collan gave a casual glance upstairs, as if indicating he was about to go change clothes. For the moment that his gaze caught and held Sarra's, there was a strangely sweet, almost tender smile in his eyes.

Auvry Feiran said, "I rarely travel by the usual methods."

"Oh. One of those portable Ladder things?"

"My daughter is an excellent teacher. She would have come herself, but we had no way of knowing who would be here, disturbing its usually placid magic."

"Do you always waste so much time explaining things?"

"There's nothing urgent waiting for me back at Ryka Court."

"Been there, thanks. Good food, lousy service."

"Is there somewhere you'd rather go?" came the silken question.

"Well, I know a great bar in Isodir. They serve brandy in buckets."

"I imagine you *could* use a drink about now. I have a rather good private cellar. Shall we go sample it while you tell me all about the new Captal?"

"New one? What happened to the old one?"

"Oh, I think you know, Minstrel Rosvenir." Menace slid free of its slithery-soft wrappings.

Sarra could see the muscles of Collan's broad shoulders tense beneath the green robe. Fire-burnished curls shifted fractionally, as if he'd nearly looked up again and restrained the impulse. Then he shrugged and walked forward, out of her sight.

"It'll take you about five minutes to find out that whatever you think I know, you're wrong. But let's go. I've got nothing better to do."

Sarra would never know how long she stood there after the door closed. The cold faded as the hearthfire's warmth reached out from the bedchamber, promising rest and sleep and peace.

"I am an Ambrai," she said suddenly, clearly, in a high, strained tone that frightened her. "I am Sarra Ambrai, and the new Mage Captal, Cailet Ambrai, is my sister—" She heard her voice rise to a shout and couldn't stop it. "—and if that's not enough Truth for you, then take this one! I'm in love with Collan Rosvenir! Does that satisfy you? Does it?"

Almost sobbing now, she dragged up the robe in armfuls and started down the stairs. Five steps, six, seven—she stumbled the last few risers and flung herself at the door, hauling it open to the cold misted night.

The silence of The Waste stretched before her in all directions, as bleak as its name, as dangerous as the war that had birthed it.

Wind froze the tears on her face. She whimpered, despising the sound and the words that shaped her lips, the plea of a tired, whining child:

"I want to go home."

Not to Roseguard. To Ambrai.

Truly told, she had nowhere else to go.

20

For the second time in her not-quite-eighteen years, Cailet stood on land her ancestors had ruled. She'd wondered if she would feel a sense of homecoming this time—for, of course, she'd been unconscious during her first arrival in Ambrai-shir scant weeks ago. There was no soft twinge of nostalgia, no warm sigh of the land welcoming one of her children home. Cailet shrugged, dismissed the absurd disappointment, and turned to wave farewell to the fishing boats that had ferried the Mages and what was left of the Rising across Blighted Bay.

Taig had hoped they'd be set ashore as close as possible to the Brai River, within four days' walk or so. Even had the winds not been contrary, there was no adequate anchorage that met his wishes. They stood instead on a beach guarded by towering bluffs that were the spur end of the Wraithen

Mountains—named Deiket's Blessing for good reason, for
the protection given Ambrai from the acid storms of The
Waste.

"Faster to climb than go around," Elomar said as they finished a meager lunch. He pointed to a dozen or so birds flying north. "Only spindle-shanks can walk the salt marshes."

Cailet spelled her coffee to near-boiling and watched the
long-legged birds on their spring migration to Maidil's Mirror. They looked ridiculous: winged, green-iced puff pastries
dangling broken sticks of chocolate.

"Any hope of Folding a way through?" she asked.

"Captal," he smiled, "not even you could make solid
ground of quicksand."

"Then we've got a problem, Elo. Some of us are old and
others aren't well after being in jail so long. Horses would
make the climb much easier for them. But if we had horses,
I couldn't Fold the road." She squinted up at the cliffs and
the layers of hills rising beyond. "And I'm not sure I *can*
Fold whole mountains for so many people."

Taig swirled grounds in his cup and tossed them in a
murky splotch onto the sand. "All you can do is try, Cai. But
I think there's a farming village somewhere around here. We
might get horses there."

Lusira arched both exquisite brows. "Clydie plow-nags
with backs as wide as double beds?"

He gave a rueful grin, the one that always caught Cailet's
heart. "Sorry. No high-stepping Tillinshir grays here, you're
right."

"I'd settle for a 'Burry pony," said Elin. "Horns and all.
Two and a half days on that boat, and I'm so stiff I barely
made it up the beach! And don't you dare mention the word
'bed' again, Luse!"

"Nothing like exercise," Elomar continued.

Cailet finished her coffee and pushed herself to her feet.
"Then let's get started, if that's the Healer's prescription."

They had to climb the bluff without benefit of Cailet's
magic. Despite the age of some and the exhaustion of most
of the rest, no one fell. There were scrapes and bruises
aplenty, but nothing serious. At the top, Cailet cast the Folding spell, trying to analyze what she did while she did it.

It appeared to consist of two separate maneuvers: surrounding the people with one kind of magic, and penetrating
the ground ahead with another. The former was easy to

maintain once cast. The latter required constant adjustment, pushing ahead and digging down at the same time with every step taken. Working it and experiencing it simultaneously tired her, however, and after a few minutes she stopped observing and simply got on with the job.

It was going to take a long, long time to run through the whole of her new knowledge and find out how and why it all worked.

There were Mages enough to teach her, she told herself as the established spell obligingly Folded without her having to supervise. In fact, her magic was as gleeful in its freedom as a child liberated from classes and chores on a sunny spring day. Scholar Mages, Healer Mages, and Warrior Mages could show her how she knew what she knew, how she did what she did. Yet to judge by the wisps of memory blown up by consideration of magic, she doubted that any Mage now living knew the *why* of magic.

There were ways to go about learning, she mused, without revealing that she was not Captal in the way others had been for Generations before her. *I could ask them to review techniques as if I were testing their knowledge—*

—and competence! How insulting! came an instantaneous protest.

I could ask for help in refining particular spells, and sort of work my way around to all of them eventually.

Can you afford to admit that there are things you don't understand? warned another voice.

Frustrated, she thought, *I could sit in on lectures and demonstrations with the Prentices.*

And make the teachers feel you're judging them, while making the students nervous!

Do you suppose you can wait long enough to set up another Academy before you learn how all this works?

She nearly tripped on a fist-sized stone. After a moment's concentration to spruce up the Folding spell, she returned to the irksome internal dialogue. *I know all that! But what can I do?*

Your magic works. Worry about the mechanics later, advised one voice.

Does it even matter? asked another, a bit wryly.

It'll come to you, soothed a third.

If all else fails, said Gorynel Desse, *you might try a few honest questions to Mages you trust as friends.*

Cailet sighed and felt the road grow steeper underfoot. More magic required; but she had plenty and to spare. *All right, all right!* she thought at all four of them. *Later, then. When I've got the time.*

Wondering all the while if she'd kept completely private her doubts about ever having the time.

21

All things considered, he'd rather be in Renig Jail.

Even in one of the cells he couldn't get out of.

The vintage wine Feiran had promised turned out to be spiked. Col knew it the instant he tasted it. He drank anyway. Might as well get it over with.

He figured he knew five really vital pieces of information. In ascending order of importance, they were: Taig Ostin was alive; Sarra Liwellan was alive; Cailet Rille was the new Mage Captal; the Mage Captal possessed the memories and knowledge of Lusath Adennos, Tamos Wolvar, Alin Ostin, and Gorynel Desse—*and* the girl had the old man's sword, one of the legendary Fifty.

He also knew he was expected to answer one really vital question, the one for which he had no answer: Where was the Mage Captal now?

To his surprise, all the wine did was send him to sleep. He woke in a white box. There was no bed, no blanket, no chair, no toilet, no sink, no door, and no window. The eight-foot cube was perfectly, seamlessly white. The floor was a single slab of white marble. Walls and ceiling were equally featureless, as if the box had been carved from snow turned to stone.

He was stark naked, freezing cold, ravenously hungry, and just plain mad.

And maybe a little scared, because he knew this room was an impossibility. So they must be using magic on him. How did he defend himself against magic?

He couldn't. His Wards might, but he couldn't count on them.

With a long sigh, he stood up. The less of him in contact

with that icy floor, the better. The bare soles of his feet made small slapping sounds as he paced his cage, echoing from each wall and up to the ceiling. He heard his breathing quicken, and consciously slowed it down.

Incessant circuits of the white box warmed his blood and loosened his muscles. He noticed after a time that he cast no shadow. Maybe the marble gave off its own light. Some rocks did that. But maybe that was magic, too.

He heard his footsteps become irregular. Arrhythmia displeased his Minstrel's ear. He began to whistle, then hum, then sing every song he knew. It was quite a list. He spared his voice, holding back on notes he usually sang full-throated. He walked and he sang and it might have been four hours or four years before he started to get tired.

At least in this cage, he *could* stand, and pace. Not like that other one.

WHAT OTHER ONE?

Why, the one he'd been put in after the wind knocked him into the ditch, of course.

He kept walking. And singing. As Wards dissolved like Wraiths in strong sunshine.

There'd been a cat in the cage before he took up residence. There'd been a woman wearing an armband set with blue onyx that had belonged to his mother who'd sat with him near the hearth, singing. There'd been a long time in a stuffy wagon and then Flornat the Slavemaster had bought him and marked him as Scraller's.

He'd killed Scraller. He hadn't really known why at the time. Now he did. And felt renewed energy flush through him, honest pleasure in honest vengeance. He walked faster, and sang another song. The memories flashed past almost too quickly to see, as if someone was changing painted glass slides too fast on a projection wall. Acid storms, The Waste, galazhi, Taguare the Bookmaster and Carlon the Lutenist, and *Scraller* with his turgid pornographic bedtime stories and his greasy-lipped guests—

—and Gorynel Desse appearing one night in a swirl of white beard and dark robes to take him to Lady Lilen's in Combel. No wonder he'd instinctively liked her so much when he met her again. He hadn't even known it really was *again*.

There'd been long weeks on his own, and the old man popping up out of nowhere in Cantratown, and—and—

Falundir.

He stopped pacing and his eyes filled with tears that froze on his cheeks. The house in Sheve Dark. The songs. The lute, his lute—*Bard Falundir's* lute! Evenings by the fire, learning, practicing, striving for his best even though his best would always be mediocre compared to the mastery of the cruelly crippled, tragically silenced Bard. He'd cried over that, remembered how some days he'd run miles into the forest and screamed out his rage at Anniyas—

He screamed it now, a voice-ravaging bellow that ripped his throat raw and sucked all the air from his lungs.

"Is that what you've been waiting to hear?" asked a deep masculine voice somewhere overhead.

"Perhaps," a woman answered. "Let's give him a little while longer."

Col heard them, but couldn't be bothered with trivialities right now. He was remembering. The Wards were gone.

He remembered walking down the hill to Sleginhold, and sneezing beneath the flowery trellis when Verald Jescarin handed him the Miramili's Bells. He laughed with genuine joy to know that somehow he'd recalled this friend despite the Wards. He laughed again when he remembered Sela's pert little face and tasted once again the sticky sweetness of violet candies and his first kiss.

He remembered, laughing with delight—*remembered*—

"*That* is what I was waiting for."

The lid slid off the white stone box.

Leave me alone, damn you! There's more, I know there's more to remember—

An old woman stared down at him. Silken waves of graying hair framed a softly plump face. Her lips were parted and moist, her icy-blue eyes avid as a lover's. The tall, middle-aged man beside her, handsome and thoughtful, wore an expression of concerned intellectual curiosity. Collan glared up at them both, enraged that they had dammed the flood of his remembering.

They didn't expect his anger. His outcry had provoked comment; the old woman had said his laughter was what she waited to hear. He saw in their eyes that his cold fury surprised them. *Aw, for shit's sake!* he thought. *They think this silly white room's made me crazy!*

Swift on this realization followed the surety that he'd better act crazy or they'd find another way to do it.

He'd made a mistake by showing them he was furious. But he could use that, improvise on it the way Falundir had taught him to improvise on a single musical phrase. Col gave them what they wanted: insanity. He roared like an enraged bull elk, beat his fists against the wall like a child in a temper tantrum, shrieked curses like a dockworker when the bar runs out of ale.

They watched, leaning on the topmost of three silver rails spanning their side of the box. Their white clothes matched the white wall behind them so that faces and hands seemed to exist independent of bodies. A gleam of satisfaction sparked in the old woman's eyes as Col elaborated on his theme, and her mouth curved in a uniquely unpleasant smile.

Auvry Feiran was not as easily convinced. He frowned, gray–green eyes shadowed by heavy brows knotted over a long nose. Col recognized him now, with the Wards back in place to hold those other memories away from him again. Auvry Feiran. Former Prentice Mage, Commandant of the Council Guard, Lord of Malerris. Which meant, Col told himself—swearing in genuine pain as he jammed a finger against the wall—that the old woman must be First Councillor Anniyas. To merit this kind of exalted attention, they must think he knew a lot more than he did. He heard his voice crack on another howl, wondering about his chances of pretending to be so crazy that he didn't remember his own name.

"I think he's ready, don't you?" Anniyas glanced briefly at Feiran.

"It seems that way."

"Oh, *look* at him! Nobody lasts in here more than two days."

"It's well into the third, for him."

Col choked in mid-tirade. *Three days?* But he knew they must be lying. Just as the impossible seamlessness of the white stone box was a lie. They were Malerrisi, powerful ones. This whole place must be heavily spelled and Warded. Because if it wasn't, and it really had been three days, it was quite probable that Collan was truly-told crazy.

He sank down onto the floor as if exhausted—not a demanding performance, for even a Minstrel's capacious lungs ran out of breath.

"Get on with it," Anniyas said. "I assume you're ready?"

"Of course."

She faced him then, smiling an even less likable smile. "Are you sure Glenin wouldn't like to watch?"

Feiran stiffened. "Not in her condition."

"Of course, poor darling," Anniyas said in a voice oily with sympathy.

Was she sick? Injured? Saints, he hoped so!

Then a third voice intruded—and that it was indeed an intrusion was evident in the two suddenly stiff faces above.

"I suggest, First Councillor, that you and *Domni* Feiran attend on his daughter while I see to this man."

Anniyas went ashen beneath her cheek-rouge, then so red that the flush clashed with the artificial color. Feiran drew himself up to his full height, white robes rustling.

"What the hell are *you* doing here?" the First Councillor demanded.

"My duty as Fifth Lord, of course." A new face peered down at Collan, who let his jaw drop open in an impersonation of idiocy. If Anniyas's smile was unsavory, this man's whole aspect was downright slimy. "He's nowhere near ready, that's obvious."

"It's been three days," said Feiran.

The Fifth Lord's surprise was also obvious. Collan read his expression easily—and Anniyas's angry scowl confirmed his suspicions. *They* did *lie about the three days. So I can't be crazy. But I still better act like it.* He wreathed his arms around his drawn-up knees and began to rock back and forth, singing under his breath.

"Doriaz, return to Seinshir at once!" Anniyas gave the Fifth Lord a look to castrate a full-grown unbroken Tillinshir stud. "You have no right to this man! He's mine!"

"He's a thread that must be rewoven or cut," came the chill reply. "I'm Fifth Lord. That's what I do." A big, thick hand deliberately fingered the golden badge on his white tunic.

"What's the matter, little man?" she jeered. "Haven't killed anyone in the last two days? Scissors getting a bit dull?"

Collan actively prayed that Anniyas would win the skirmish. If he had to be interrogated, he'd take Auvry Feiran over Doriaz any day of the week. There was something corrupted about the Fifth Lord's eyes, like rotting flesh.

"It is my right," he said again.

Feiran interrupted. "Only with direct authorization from the First Lord."

Doriaz flushed, his lips tightening. "The duties of my position demand my taking charge of this man's torture."

Torture? With a cry not entirely feigned, Col sprang to his feet and leaped for a hold on the lowest rung of the silver railing. He caught it, felt it like a pole of solid ice in his palms. His body slammed into the cold marble wall. He swung one leg up, trying to hook a foot on the corner.

Fifth Lord Doriaz raised a flawless white boot. Before he could smash the heel onto unprotected fingers—*Sweet Colynna Silverstring, not my* hands! *Not my* hands!—Col grabbed the boot and yanked.

Doriaz lurched, his other heel skidding out from under him. He fell hard on his ass on the white stone floor. There was a lovely grunt and an even lovelier crack as his head hit.

Dangling now by one hand, Col looked up into Feiran's gray–green eyes—which glinted with amused approval, surely imagined. Gently, swiftly, Feiran unhooked two of Col's fingers from the rail. He landed on his feet, knees bent, panting for breath.

Anniyas leaned over to regard him with an almost comical mix of irritation and gratitude. "Well, it seems Doriaz was right after all. Our little *albadon* hasn't worked on you yet."

He grinned up at her and began to sing Falundir's "The Long Sun."

Once again painted color was a grotesque mismatch for the natural crimson that rushed into her cheeks. For the first time he witnessed the truth of the phrase "blind with fury." Her eyes actually glazed over, their frozen blue nearly swallowed by blackness. Recovering quickly, she demonstrated an impressive command of the language. She cursed for a full minute without using the same phrase twice. Collan heard her out rather admiringly, still grinning, still singing.

Anniyas swung on Feiran, snarling, "Break him!"

And left.

After a moment, Feiran murmured, "That may not have been wise, you know."

The white lid of the white box slid back into place. He was alone in the marble cube. He sang the song until its end. Then he sat down, wincing a little at the cold against his bare backside, and planned how not to break.

22

Dressed in stolen clothes—the uniform of a dead Council Guard and Collan's purloined cloak—Sarra left the Crossroads of St. Feleris the morning after the father she hated captured the man she loved.

Garments and weapons that had vanished the first night had reappeared, his as well as hers. But there was no shaving gear ready for him in the alcove and breakfast was laid for only one. She bathed, combed her hair and braided it tightly, ate, and stuffed her pockets with all the bread and cheese they would hold. She started to tie the golden goblet to her belt for later use, then changed her mind. The thing would probably disappear with her first step out the front door.

She wanted very much to take the grimoire along for Cailet, and at least one songbook for Collan—a promise to herself that she would see him again to give it to him. But these she also left behind, locked in the trunk.

Taking one last look around at the herbs and carvings and woven spells, Sarra wrapped herself in the cloak. Despite an obvious wash, it still somehow smelled of Collan. She turned her cheek briefly to her shoulder to feel the nubby warmth of it, and then went downstairs.

The house was not only satisfied with the payment but actually seemed the stronger. Wood was piled in the great kitchen hearth; the tables and benches of the common room were set neatly upright, ready for a score of visitors. Yet a search of the cupboards for additional food yielded nothing. There was a limit to Truth's magic, it seemed. She couldn't help but wonder if things would be different had she been brave enough to tell her Truth to Collan himself. She opened the door, went outside, and didn't look back.

A breeze was blowing, scattering the clouds and ground mist with a scent tainted by the marshes on the western shore of Blighted Bay. She turned her face to the wind and started walking to the east, where Ambrai was.

The day she began her journey was the eighth of Lovers'

Moon. She knew the date not because of any time-sense like Val's or because she'd kept track of the days, but because the Ladymoon that night showed a full three-quarters. In four nights it would be full again, on the first of Green Bells, when Lenfell would celebrate the feast of Miramili the Summoner. For now, St. Imili watched over the world and especially over new mothers and those newly wedded; Sarra didn't qualify. Sweet-smiling Imili was also the patron of joy—and never had Sarra felt more a stranger to that emotion.

I could use Rilla the Guide or Fielto the Finder about now—for I'm traveling blind and I'm certainly a lost item who needs finding. St. Maidil would be appropriate, too—not as patron of new lovers, which is my own damned fault, but as protector of fools. Which is also my own damned fault.

And these thoughts were getting her exactly nowhere, she reminded herself. Her feet and her need to go home were all she had. A day to get to Blighted Bay, if she was lucky; another two or three days across it, if she could find a boat willing to take her; another five or six days to the Brai River, if she could find a road over the hills; and then she would drift downriver on a barge, if there was any produce being shipped this early in the spring.

If, if, if. How did such a tiny word produce such huge problems?

Combel was closer. Easier. Surely there would be an Ostin or someone related to the Ostins who would shelter her. She could borrow a horse and ride all the way to Ambrai in half the time it would take her by boat and on foot.

Instinct demanded otherwise. Even if the authorities weren't looking for her in Combel—and it was a dead certainty they were—she simply could not turn west. To the east lay Ambraishir. Home. She had to go home. The need was that powerful within her, defying logic and reason that shook their heads like wise elder sisters at her chances of success.

Magic had nothing to do with logic or reason. And it was magic that called her home.

So on the first day she walked the lonely expanses of The Waste, avoiding each of the few farmhouses except for one, from which in the dead of night she stole a man's oversized shirt off the clothesline. Wool, much-mended, with Collan's cloak it would keep her warm enough. The shirt of the Council Guard uniform she left behind in payment; the tunic she buried the next morning by the side of the road.

On the second day she reached Blighted Bay.

On the third day and the fourth—when the moon rose full—she was on a fishing boat helping sort each day's catch. On the fifth day she ended her stint as deckhand by rolling barrel after barrel of fish from boat to dock. She slept that night in a warehouse, cuddled up to a big furry watchdog more interested in having his belly scratched than in savaging intruders. On the sixth morning she left the village nestled in the northeast corner of Blighted Bay and started due east again toward the Brai River.

As it happened, St. Imili was watching out for her after all, even two days into St. Miramili's week of Green Bells. On the sixth day, about half an hour before she would have entered a deadly mire all unknowing, Imilial Gorrst finally caught up to her.

The Warrior Mage galloped up out of nowhere on a strong bay mare, yelling and waving madly. Sarra gaped at her as if she were a Wraith.

"Great Geridon's Stones, girl, I've been chasing you for six days now!"

"You have?" Sarra asked stupidly.

"I figured you'd feel the Summons like the rest of us did," Imi went on, swinging down from the horse. She untied a waterskin from the saddle and gave it to Sarra, who drank, still dazed. "But Telo was worried about you, Warded and all, so before we left Ostinhold my father did a little scrying with one of his Globes. And couldn't find you!"

"I was—in a Warded house," Sarra managed.

"Where?"

"The Waste."

"Truly told? One of the old shelters, I bet. Well, whatever happened, Telo and Miram and I started out—"

"Miram?"

"Ostin. Not a shred of magic, that girl, but the soul of a Warrior Mage. Anyhow, along the way I tried a Globe or two of my own. You look starved, girl. Want something to eat? I've got plenty in my saddlebags."

Sarra shook her head. "I'm fine."

"Right," Imi said skeptically. "Five days ago I finally caught sight of you. Telo and Miram went on ahead, and I backtracked. Lucky the Maurgens breed fast horses, or I'd never have caught you in time." She squinted at the brownish–green expanse of marshland. "Nobody who goes in there comes out."

"I—I didn't know."

"No reason why you should, I guess. Come on. If you're ready to ride, let's get going. It's a bit of a climb over the hills, but from there it's a straight road to Ambrai."

The Warrior Mage swung up into the saddle as if weariness and she had never been within speaking distance. Sarra clambered up behind her, circling her friend's waist with her arms. The mare broke into a brisk canter.

"So, Sarra, what happened to the Minstrel?"

Her throat closed and her eyes welled with infuriating tears.

"Don't tell me he just *left* you to fend for yourself!" Imi exclaimed.

She thought she'd wept herself dry over Collan back at the magical cottage. Evidently not. Imilial waited her out, slowing the horse to a walk and making awkward soothing noises as she patted Sarra's arms. Finally the storm subsided, and Sarra lifted her head from the Mage's powerful shoulder.

"Imi—"

"Just start at the beginning and tell it in order."

She did. Imilial gave several soft explosive curses, and by the time the tale was finished—lacking certain Truths—she was rigid with fury.

"Feiran!" she spat. "You can bet Anniyas and the Lords of Malerris have Col by now. This happened when?"

"The seventh of last week."

"They've got him. And he'll tell them all he knows—not that he isn't a smart boy, and brave and generous despite himself. He kept you safe, when it's you Feiran and Anniyas want more than him and he could've bargained you away easy. But Wards or no Wards, he'll empty his every thought to them once they bind him with magic to the Pain Stake."

"The what?" Sarra breathed, heart hammering with fear.

"A perversion unique to the Malerrisi," the Warrior Mage answered grimly. "He'll survive it, but not as the man we knew. Saints *damn* Auvry Feiran! And every other piece of Malerrisi shit ever born!"

"But—but what is it? What does it do?"

"Sarra, sweet, you don't want to know."

23

Glenin was neither sick nor injured nor fashioned of feather-
weight porcelain, and resented mightily being treated as if
she was all three. Forbidden to go near the *albadon,* the
Warded white box occupied by Collan Rosvenir. Not allowed to cast any spell more complex than Warmth to her
teacup (coffee had been outlawed by that fool of a cook
Garon hired). Prohibited Ladders, lest the magic upset the
Mageborn son in her womb.

She felt a devouring curiosity about the Minstrel's experience with the Pain Stake. She'd read of it in the *Code of
Malerris* but had never seen it applied. She cared little about
small magics (although every morning she craved a good
strong cup of coffee). These were minor things. It was the
Ladders she really wanted, the strictures against them repeated by her father and Garon and Anniyas until it was
damned near impossible for her to resist using one.

On her way to the Octagon Court Ladder she asked herself a trenchant question: Why flout tedious rules and exert
her independence if the rule she broke was of no importance
and the demonstration of her freedom gained her nothing? If
defiance of prohibitions was her goal, she might as well defy
the most serious one. Thus the Ladder to Ambrai.

Certain texts asserted that a fetus exposed to strong magic
actually had an easier time, recognizing magic instinctively
upon its release at puberty. She would never have dreamed
of using a Ladder during the crucial last five weeks of ges-
tation, but she was probably doing her son a favor by using
one now.

And it was vital to know what was happening at Ambrai.
The Summons was almost impossible to pick up now, and it
gave Glenin a headache even to try. But Ambrai must be the
destination—again, the last place anyone would look for the
Captal, the Mage Guardians, and the Rising.

Vassa Doriaz, obliquely questioned before his unfortunate
experience with the Minstrel (Glenin couldn't help but grin
when she heard of it), seemed to know nothing at all about

the Captal's Summons. Darvas Keviron, who'd accompanie
Doriaz to Ryka Court and ended up carrying him back
Seinshir, was just as ignorant. Anniyas had said no Malerri
had felt it, and Anniyas—*First Lord!*—was under no obliga
tion to say a thing about it unless and until she saw fit to d
so.

Glenin was sure she wouldn't. She now understood wh
Anniyas planned. What better demonstration of her powe
than to defeat the new Captal all by herself?

Glenin nodded to the sentries outside the Ladder chambe
who bowed as if to a Council member before they opene
the doors. She waited until the latch clicked shut before sh
smiled at this indication of her growing influence.

Pleasure did not last long. Anniyas was a formidable er
emy even if, at present, an undeclared one. Glenin and he
unborn son were a threat to her. She must prove tha
Glenin's time had not yet come. For if enough Malerri
agreed that the intricate design that was Avira Anniyas wa
now complete, her thread would be summarily tied off an
snipped from the Great Loom. Not even a First Lord coul
escape a Net woven by dozens bent on her elimination
Vassa Doriaz would be more than happy to stand ready wit
his golden Scissors open wide.

As the Blanking Ward wrapped around Glenin, she vowe
that if anyone defeated the new Captal all by herself, he
Name wouldn't be Anniyas.

It was five hours earlier in Ambrai, a beautiful sprin
noontime of unclouded sunlight and fresh blue skies. Gleni
stepped out of the Ladder within the Double Spiral Stair an
looked upward. The roof of the Octagon Court had co
lapsed, probably during the brutal winter of 964 when sno
buried North Lenfell all the way to Roseguard. Tiles an
rafters littered the marble hall of the Double Spiral, makin
it difficult to climb over the debris. Glenin cursed the extr
weight that was rapidly depriving her of suppleness and a
tering her balance. One wouldn't think twelve pounds woul
make such a difference. Soon she'd be unable to hide he
pregnancy any longer.

At dinner a few nights ago, Elsvet Doyannis had mad
some sweetly poisonous remark about Glenin's newly curva
ceous figure, prompting Garon to state loudly that he *adore*
the way Glenin looked. His stupid blush had nearly give
the secret away. She forgave him only because his Birthing

day offered so perfect an occasion to announce the happy news. Another ten days and she could stop pretending—and start wearing comfortable clothes instead of squeezing into gowns, trousers, shirts, and vests now much too tight.

She was out of breath by the time she climbed the Double Spiral to the balcony where the family had often sat watching the sun set over the river. The wrought iron chairs and benches from Isodir still littered the balcony, paint long since weathered away and cushions rotted to nothingness. Yet she could remember each lavishly embroidered pillow, if not the grandfather and cousin who had worked them. Gerrin Ostin and his namesake, Gerrin Desse, had vied in laughing rivalry to outdo each other in the intricacy of their needlework. Glenin could almost see clever fingers dancing across big, ornate embroidery frames, remembered inspecting each pattern's progress. Grandfather had been working on a new cushion for her just before she left for Ryka Court: Feiran Leaf Crown, Halvos Feathers, Vekke Circled Triangle, and Ostin Oak Tree quartered in the middle of an Ambrai Octagon. She remembered asking why her father's ancestral Name sigils were not included, and the scorn that flickered over Grandmother Allynis's face.

Glenin gave a shrug. The threads had probably been picked out by nesting birds years ago. There was nothing left of the Ambrai she had known as a child.

And this suited her very well. She intended to reweave the fabric of Ambrai into whatever pattern she chose and rule here as Lady Glenin Feiran. But she would rule Lenfell from Ryka Court. She refused to allow the worldwide government to intrude on her personal, private city.

And the Malerrisi? From what place would she rule *them?*

Lightly she clasped the wrought iron banister, imagining the view ten years from now. All wreckage cleared away, broad avenues bustling with traffic again, shiny new buildings of glass and marble replacing those burned to the ground, a bigger concert hall to outdo even the gigantic Ryka Opera House, massive wharves and docks filled with the produce of every Shir—

—and no Mage Academy to blot the hillside across the river.

Bard Hall could stay, and the Healers Ward. She'd be generous, for those establishments would once again make Ambrai the center of musical and medicinal arts. But in

place of the Academy, using all the best design elements and
none of the awkwardnesses that had always displeased her,
she would build a true magnificence to replace Malerris Castle. Her son would learn magic there.

Great graceful towers rose in her mind's eye, obliterating
the remains of the Mage Academy. But imagination could
not obscure the sight of the five small barges drifting under
the half-shattered gray bulk of St. Viranka's Bridge.

Glenin sucked in an astonished breath and watched as
ropes flew out and caught on iron moorings imbedded in
concrete. The barges were laboriously hauled in and many
people jumped to the shingle of rocky bank. One person
snagged her attention: a thin blonde girl, the first to leap
ashore. Too tall to be Sarra Liwellan—but who, then? Why
did Glenin not *quite* recognize her?

The girl scrambled up a slope where stairs had once been
and stood on the paved River Walk surveying the ruins of
Ambrai, clear noon sunlight mirrored in her white-gold hair.
So intent was Glenin on tracking down the familiarity that
long minutes passed before she felt the other thing. As she
narrowed her eyes to stare at the girl, she finally felt it: the
Captal's Summons.

This girl, the new Mage Captal?

Ridiculous. Outrageous. Impossible.

All the same, Glenin fashioned a delicate lancet of magic
and sent it slicing through the half-mile of air between them.
Ladders required little effort; fine work like this demanded
prodigious control. She was more than capable of it—but her
baby had never experienced such concentrated magic. He
quivered within her and for an instant she didn't know if the
cold fear in her heart was his or hers or a combination of the
two. She broke off the spell before it found its target, and
slumped, shaking, against the balcony balustrade.

Forgive me, my darling, forgive me! she pleaded with her
child, frantic for indication that all was well despite her
folly. *Beloved? Sweeting, are you all right?*

Slowly she calmed, realizing that there was none of the
pain she would feel if the shock had convulsed him into separation from her nurturing body. Neither did fear radiate
from him anymore. She stroked the swell of him at her abdomen, soothing them both with the caresses.

He was all right. Perfectly safe. And one day he would
know this for the magic it was. Recognize it—welcome it.

*I didn't mean to frighten you, my heart, I should've been
more careful. But now that you've felt magic, you'll never
be afraid of it again. Not my son!*

She didn't stay to watch the Mages and the Rising and the
new Captal start across the city. She didn't give a damn
about any of them, or about Anniyas's plans for them. *Let
her have them,* she thought as she took her time descending
the stairs. *I don't care. Nothing and no one matters except
my son.*

She rested for the better part of an hour on the steps of the
Double Spiral before using the Ladder back to Ryka Court.
The Guards nodded respectfully when she passed. She didn't
care about that, either. Whatever plots and ploys she'd been
dreaming, all were subsumed in terror for her son.

There should have been finality in that—the decision
made, the scheming ended. But when she reached her suite,
she paced restlessly, undressing in abrupt motions that tore
the buttons and laces of her clothes. *I have to care what
Anniyas does. For whatever she does, it will affect my son.
Unless I outthink her, she'll be the one making his future, not
me.*

Intolerable.

She lay down and shut her eyes. Yet she was unable to
sleep until she sought her husband's bed and the adoring
warmth of his arms. At least he was good for *something.* She
knew he'd be no use to her where his mother was concerned.
Though he worshiped Glenin as her magic compelled him,
Anniyas's claim was the older, the claim of blood. When
forced to choose between them, the spell and the instinct
would collide. Glenin didn't need paralysis; she needed help.
And there was only one person certain to give it.

Early the next morning she sought out her father before he
could leave for the *albadon,* and asked a single question.

"That dream you had at Ambrai—what did the girl look
like?"

24

In the fifteen days since the Captal's Summons, Mages a
over Lenfell had been on the move.

In late 968, Gorynel Desse's private count of Mage Guard
ians, including Prentices, was 1,109. When the Purge—as
was being called—began early the next year, 538 were imme
diately killed or captured by the Council Guard or the Lord
of Malerris. Two weeks later, the tally was 812. By the Fea
of St. Miramili, the number was 965—very nearly the thou
sand it was said Anniyas demanded. Add Cailet, and th
Mage Guardians still free and alive totalled 144.

In 951, the year of her birth, there had been over 10,000

Cailet arrived in Ambrai on the second day of Green Bell
with thirteen other Mages. By the fourth, most of the rest be
gan to show up.

It was uncanny. One minute she was sitting in the ruine
and overgrown garden of a small stone house in the suburb
of Ambrai. The next she was staring at five dusty, road
weary Mage Guardians who bowed low to her while tryin
to hide shock, dismay, and amazement that their new Capta
the person who'd sent so powerful and imperative a Sum
mons, was a teenaged girl whose name they didn't eve
know.

Taig performed introductions. The five young men bowe
once more. Cailet nodded acknowledgment—Sarra's gestur
without, she sighed inwardly, Sarra's grace—and remarke
on the spectacular time they'd made from Tillinshir. One o
them allowed as how his brother commanded a prodigiou
Folding spell. Cailet complimented him while matchin
names and faces to Gorsha's Lists in her head, and sent ther
off for food and rest.

Five hours later, three more had found her: the source o
the Summons, the Mage Captal. By dusk, a total of twelv
new arrivals were sleeping wherever they could find spac
in the six-room dwelling, and Cailet began to understan
what she'd done.

But how had *they* done it? Senn Mikleine—officially Sec

ond Warden of Kenroke Castle, secretly a Warrior Mage—
smiled at Cailet's astonishment that so many could come so
far so fast. By spells, he said; by luck; by ship and by horseback; by Ladders not even Alin, not even Gorsha, had
known existed. As for how they'd escaped notice—well,
dozens of Mage Guardians scattered all over Lenfell were
known only to the local officers of the Rising and to—

"Gorynel Desse," she interrupted with a sigh.

"Exactly, Captal." He grinned again, golden-brown eyes
sparkling in a handsome sun-bronzed face. Thirty-seven
years of age, he was one of the last Warriors trained at the
Academy by the First Sword himself. "Never put anything
past him."

"So I'm discovering," she replied dryly.

Other Mages followed, and many brought members of the
Rising with them. Ilisa Neffe and her husband Tamosin
Wolvar came on the sixth with Biron Maurgen and Riddon
and Maugir Slegin. Jeymi, they told her, had to be almost
forcibly restrained from coming along. The next noon,
Telomir Renne and Miram Ostin arrived, bearing Kanto
Solingirt's abject apologies for being too old and feeble to
obey the Captal's Summons.

Cailet winced at that. Thus far the newcomers were all
under forty-five, strong enough to undertake long journeys
at damned near impossible speed. But would even the older
Mages feel compelled to—to *obey* her? It wasn't a word she
was comfortable with. When a contemporary of Gavirin
Bekke—his cousin Lilias, also a retired Warder—was assisted into the Captal's presence by two Prentices even
younger than Cailet, she decided that *obey* was a truly terrible word.

But she had to admit its uses. The compulsion to obey her
Summons had sent Imilial Gorrst riding out of Ostinhold,
and on the way to Ambrai she'd scried with a Mage Globe
and found Sarra.

The two appeared at dusk on the eighth of Green Bells.
Cailet caught her sister in her arms and they sat in the abandoned garden, weeping together until the Ladymoon set.

They were alone together the whole of the next day. More
Mages arrived and were told the Captal would be pleased to
welcome them tomorrow. On the tenth, however, the sisters
eluded Taig, Elomar, and all the forty-nine Mages and thirty-
six Rising partisans and walked to the Octagon Court.

"I suppose I felt it, too," Sarra mused as they picked their way through rubble-clogged streets. "All I really knew was that I wanted to go home."

Cailet nodded. After a time she said, "I guess I put a little more into it than was strictly necessary. I feel guilty about the old ones."

"Don't. I think the journey invigorated quite a few of them. Enis Girre, for instance—Taig says the old man hasn't looked so well in years."

"That may be true," Cailet conceded. "Just to be who and what they are again instead of hiding must be a relief. But Lilias Bekke can hardly walk, and Elo's worried about Shonner Escovor."

"Strange, isn't it?" Sarra asked as they climbed a fallen stone archway. "That a man of the same Name as a Lord of Malerris should be a Mage Guardian."

"That was centuries ago. And the same could be said of the Ambrais, Sarra."

"She is *not* my sister."

Cailet slanted a look at her.

"Or yours," Sarra added sharply.

A little while later they crossed the river at St. Viranka's Bridge, pausing mid-span to look downstream. Cailet ran her fingers lightly over the wounded gray stone where someone seemed to have taken a pickax to it.

"She *isn't*," Sarra said suddenly.

"I'm not arguing with you."

"Yes, you are. I can hear it. All the little wheels turning and all the little voices—" She broke off and glanced away.

"And here I thought I was the only one who heard them," Cailet said mildly.

"I'm sorry."

"It's all right. Actually, I think I'm getting used to it. Them. Alin and the Captal don't say much, truly told. Neither does Scholar Wolvar. It's Gorsha mostly. Sometimes he won't shut up, and sometimes when I need him most he won't say a single word." She pushed away from the wall with a shrug and a rueful smile. "I'll get it all sorted out once there's time for it."

"When?" Sarra asked bleakly.

After I settle a few things with Glenin-who-isn't-our-sister and Auvry-Feiran-who-isn't-our-father. And with Anniyas.

It'll happen, Sarra. I knew it when you told me they have Collan.

But Collan wasn't a subject to be mentioned again. And Sarra would order every Mage now in Ambrai to set Wards on Cailet to prevent encounters with any of the three. Sarra would be obeyed, simply because she was Sarra. *I wonder what that's like, having people do what you tell them simply because you are who you are, with no title to remind them Who You Are.*

"When?" Cailet echoed. "Soon enough. I've given up worrying about it, so don't you start. How far to the Octagon Court?"

"Another two miles. Which will probably take us several hours, and by then it'll be too late to start back."

"I brought lunch and dinner."

"That's not what I meant."

"I know."

Continuing across Viranka's Bridge, they detoured around a fallen statue of the Saint and started down the main avenue. The buildings here had housed their grandmother's bureaucracy: commissioners of this, ministers of that, secretaries of a dozen other things. They lived on the fourth and fifth floors, had private offices on the third, did public business on the second, and spent hot afternoons in cool marble reception chambers and petition halls on the first. To Cailet's left in successive order were Finance, Forests, Fisheries, Agriculture, Trade, and Harbors. To the right was the huge edifice of the Guilds, flanked by narrower houses belonging to various Webs. After a half-mile the avenue split to accommodate a large circle where a bronze St. Jeymian had once stood in a small ocean of green grass, surrounded by all manner of woodland animals. He and his menagerie were melted slag now, and the ground was cracked and dry.

None of the buildings had actually collapsed, but the roofs had all burned and their downward crash—and that of the wooden beams that braced each tiled floor—had crushed everything within each structure. Glass littered the street ankle-deep from windows blown out by fire. Stone statues had been smashed, bronzes melted down. White marble was everywhere stained with soot that not even seventeen years of winter rain and snow could wash clean.

Past St. Jeymian's Circle were more office buildings. Mining, Education, Public Works, the Watch's main constabulary, and the embassies of all fourteen other Shirs lined the cobbled avenue. Cailet had never considered how complex the daily life of Lenfell's largest and most powerful city must have been. Every class and category of person and every human endeavor was represented one way or another along these streets. She began to understand the gargantuan labors her family had shouldered for Generations—a burden Sarra was eager to assume but which Cailet knew was not for her. The Ambrais had guided the total life of the Shir, from commerce to opera to farming to bookbinding, from architecture to medicine to cattle breeding.

And magic.

But the people were all gone—except for scattered piles of bleached bones. Fewer here than at the Academy, or than she'd see at the Octagon Court.

They stopped to rest at the Council House that curved around the closed end of the street, sprawling its width in an arc of empty windows.

"It will never be what it was," Sarra said as they sat down on the steps.

Cailet leaned her elbows on her knees and sighed as she gazed down the length of the broad avenue to the river. "I keep trying to imagine those three days," she murmured. "That's how long it took to do this. The first day they burned the outlying districts, and that was easy because most of the houses were wood. Everyone fled to the central city. Thousands and thousands crowded into the streets and the Academy and the Octagon Court. That made them easy to slaughter. That was the second day. The third, they torched everything. That was easy, too. Everyone who might have stopped them was dead."

"Could *anything* have stopped them?" Sarra asked bitterly.

"Enough Mages working together under the direction of the Captal could have Warded the whole city."

"Leninor Garvedian was dead by then."

"And Lusath Adennos hadn't recovered from the Making. But that wouldn't've mattered. It's our great weakness, you know. We don't easily give up control of our magic to someone else. We're independent. We don't think in terms of working together to become more than the sum of our parts."

"Mages don't think like Malerrisi, you mean," Sarra replied. "I'd call that a great strength."

"Under most circumstances, yes. There are only two things a Mage Guardian does without question: protect a Captal and obey a Summons. The rest of it is all open to debate and personal choice."

"Whereas the Malerrisi allow no debate and no choice. Do you admire that, Cailet?"

"You have to admit it'd be useful on occasion. Like here, in 951." She gestured to the wreckage around them.

"How many occasions would follow?" Sarra asked softly. "How many excuses for occasions?"

"I'm not advocating it as general practice," Cailet responded with an edge to her voice. "I'm just saying that we may have to learn how to work together under one person's direction—"

"Which is easy enough to say when you're obviously the person who'll be doing the directing. And as it happens, you're wrong about the Mages. They did exactly what you're talking about twice in the past. To Ward up the Wraithenbeasts."

"Of course. I'd forgotten." Climbing to her feet, she brushed off the seat of her trousers and started down the steps.

Sarra followed. "I want you to consider why they never did it again."

"What?" Cailet stopped and turned. Her sister stood two steps above her, and it was suddenly a strange thing to be looking up at tiny, fragile Sarra—who just as suddenly looked like a formidable Saint come to life.

"I haven't forgotten the Wraithenbeasts. I've thought about them every day since I figured out what Anniyas has in mind. I've explained it to you, and I know you don't entirely believe me, but what little magic I have tells me it *will* happen. I want you to consider why Mage Guardians don't work the way the Malerrisi do before you try to do it. I don't want you to find out to your cost right in the middle."

Cailet tilted her head. "I assume you have some thoughts on the matter? Warnings? Speculations?"

Sarra frowned, black eyes narrowing, the Saint's solemn aspect acquiring a sheen of anger. "Don't play Captal with me, Cailet Ambrai. It doesn't impress."

It hovered on her lips to rebuke her sister—who had no

magic and no sure knowledge, only instinct. *Go right ahead—and lose the only person who loves you for* you, *Capital.*

Not Gorsha this time. Her own voice.

"I'm sorry," she blurted out, and Sarra's eyes softened. "It's just—I have my own instincts, Sarra, just as strong as yours, and if they're right, then it won't ever come to that. Not even close."

"Meaning?"

"I'm not sure yet," she lied—and she must be getting better at it, for all Sarra did was nod thoughtfully. "When I have a better idea, I'll let you know."

That, at least was the truth. Part of it, anyhow.

They set off again through the deserted streets of their ancestral city, and by mid-afternoon climbed the garden wall that led into the Octagon Court. For a full hour they simply sat, side by side, on a wrought iron bench beneath a bravely flowering cherry tree. They stared up at what had once been the pride of Ambrai, each silent with her own thoughts. Cailet surmised that Sarra must be remembering. She was wrong.

"A lot of it depends on what you have to work with," Sarra commented after a while.

"To work with?" Cailet echoed.

"The Mages and the Rising. The Healers are a great help, of course, in the usual run of things, but not much use in a fight. The Scholars . . . well, they're resources, I suppose. The general run of Mages is fairly extraordinary, though. It seems Gorsha chose wisely when reviewing candidates for leading double lives. Some were scheduled to be collected by Alin and Val and me on our trip back to Roseguard." She kicked at a tuft of grass. "But it seems to me the ones you really need are the Warrior Mages. I'll have a talk with Taig about the Rising, see who can do what, who's got influence where—"

"Sarra," Cailet said gently, "not one of them has influence enough anymore to buy a cup of coffee on credit. As far as any of their friends and family know, they've vanished—and in these times there's only one reason to disappear without a trace."

Sarra began toying with the end of her braid, tied off this morning with a piece of twine. Cailet remembered the flowers that had crowned her hair in another garden, and the elegant pastel dress, and how much she'd hated this lovely girl who'd been sitting with Taig in the moonlight.

"Caisha . . . this is it for them, isn't it? They've thrown in their lot with us. We're responsible for them now. They have no lives but what we can win for them." She looked up and met Cailet's gaze. "I do mean 'we,' you know."

Bereft of words, Cailet nodded. *This is mine—the love I have for her, the love she offers me. Sarra's mine.*

But Sarra was also Collan's, and it was her misfortune not to have discovered it sooner. Cailet wondered if either of them knew that he was just as much hers. *I guess that's my job,* she told herself. And the smile she smiled inside was as much her own as the one she gave Sarra, though she didn't tell her sister the impetus of her humor. Whatever else happened, whatever else she must do, it simply had to end with two broken vows: Sarra's never to marry one of those loud, pesky, impossible creatures called a *man,* and Collan's never to become that gelded, contemptible beast, a *husband.*

Pushing herself to her feet, Cailet held out a hand to her sister. "Come on. I want to go home, too."

Together they entered the Octagon Court.

25

There was a blister on his right foot.

It was between the big and second toes, and the spellwoven slippers had almost healed it, but rubbing the toes together chafed it raw again. This he did on purpose, time after time, and it kept him both silent and sane.

It was pain he gave himself, as distinguished from pain that was given to him, and he knew that when he was unable to make the distinction between the two he would be lost.

The toe bled hardly at all, so Auvry Feiran didn't notice. There was no other blood competing for attention; the pain was entirely in his mind. This was another reason he kept the wound open. It was physical. The other was not.

Trying to keep count of days would have frustrated him, so he didn't bother. He was given food at irregular intervals, always the same bread and cheese, so there was no possibility of tallying breakfasts or dinners. He was allowed to sleep every now and then, and sometimes woke reasonably rested and sometimes was jarred awake still soggy with exhaustion, so his internal rhythms were off-kilter. He couldn't even keep track of time by body processes, for the food turned his bowels to water. Auvry Feiran came and went, always in white, a disembodied head above a pair of casually clasped hands on the silver railing, and let slip no indication of how many hours or days or weeks might have passed. Whenever he let himself think about it, he didn't think it had been that long. For one thing, the blister would have gone gangrenous; for another, judging by the hollows between his ribs, he hadn't lost more than a few pounds.

But he didn't think about time very much. Why concern himself with an uncertainty that could only gnaw at him? He had more pressing worries.

His Wards, for one.

At their fall, he'd remembered. But now they were back— more or less. He knew about the wind and the cage and the blue onyx bracelet, but everything before that and nearly everything after were mere skitters of thought he couldn't hang onto, like phrases of a melody or lines of a lyric that connected to nothing else he could recall. But he did remember Falundir, and the cottage in Sheve Dark, although how he had come there and why he had left were both mysteries. He remembered Sarra, too, and the magical house, and somehow all this linked up in his mind to form a kind of disjointed ballad around a single theme: a hearthfire's warmth. The image formed a kind of steadily repeated chord holding the three disparate tunes together. The place where his mother had sung to him, the place where Falundir had given him music, the place where Sarra sat reading in her turquoise brocade robe.

The strange song was pleasure, though. And to stay silent and sane, he required pain.

So when his fingers, wrapped with wide swathes of white silk around a smooth silver pole, began to burn and ache and bleed without blood, he forgot the hearth and chafed at the suppurating blister on his toe and said nothing.

The Pain Stake rose to a height of seven feet in the exact center of the white box, imbedded in the marble floor. He had awakened from a drugged sleep to find himself hanging from it by numbed hands. Straightening, he was almost com-

fortable: his hands were level with his chin, and he could
bend his elbows and rotate his shoulders to restore circula-
tion. But his fingers were tightly bound to the pole, and he
couldn't slide them either up or down. Neither could he pick
the silk wrappings loose with his teeth. Another Ward, he
told himself, and didn't bother trying again.

When he slept, he tried to brace his body so he wouldn't
slump and sag again and wake with wrenched shoulders. He
was fed by Auvry Feiran himself, by means of a silver fork
five feet long, its two tines sharpened not only at the tips but
along their length, so he must be careful not to slice open his
lips and tongue when he sank his teeth into the bread and
cheese. Biting down on the fork and jerking it away would
probably break his teeth. So he didn't, and accepted the food
with the delicacy of a cat nibbling proffered meat. The water
came in a steady stream from an expertly wielded skin, in
gouts timed perfectly to his swallowing. Possibly all this
was intended to humiliate him—a concept he found quite
funny. What did he care how he ate, as long as there was
food in his belly?

Neither was he mortified when his bladder and bowels
loosened. He did mind the smell and the mess, but he
learned that while he slept someone came in and cleaned
him up. The floor was always pristinely white when he
woke.

Through it all, he never said a word.

Feiran asked two very simple questions. *What is the name
of the new Capital. Where is the Capital now.* When no answers were forthcoming, the Pain Stake began to burn.
There was no shame in crying out, or in crying. The only
shame would be in answering the questions.

There was no escaping the fiery Pain Stake clasped in his
hands. And though no blood stained the white silk bindings,
and he knew the pain was unreal—the pain he gave himself
confirmed it—he must struggle always against the terror that
when it was all over, his hands would be as useless as
Falundir's.

He didn't count how many times he writhed against the
scorching silver. When it happened, he only wanted it to be
over. And when it ended, he only rested his head against his
hands and waited for the next time.

Curiously enough, he became hungry for color. The white
box was numbing; he actually began to look forward to the

gray–green of Feiran's eyes, the black of his eyelashes, the tanned skin of his face and fingers, the dusky rose of his lips. Recognizing this as both sick and dangerous, he thought instead of Falundir's blue eyes. Sarra's golden hair. The blue onyx bracelet. But these were colors seen in memory. Feiran was real.

The pain was not.

It couldn't be. By now his hands would have burned away from his wrists, leaving only bloody stumps.

A new question began to be asked. *What is the name of the new Captal* was followed by *What is the name of the girl with short blonde hair.* This seemed an urgent matter. It was quite a while before he realized the other question had not been asked. Was he supposed to believe that Feiran now knew where and needed only to find out who?

The two names were identical. He knew that. Feiran didn't. And never would, not from him.

Because although he knew that the name of the new Captal and the name of the girl with short blonde hair were the same, he didn't remember that name any more than he remembered his own.

26

"I left a note," Cailet began, but Taig's frown silenced her as effectively as if she were twelve years old again and he'd caught her stowing away on the ship to Pinderon.

"She left a note. Hear that, Elomar? She left a note." Taig loomed over her in the hollow marble corridor, his sarcasm echoing all the way up the Double Spiral Stairs. "When will you learn—"

Sarra interrupted impatiently. "And when will *you* learn that that sword alone is guarantee of her safety? Truly told, you walk a fine line here, Taig. Don't step over it again."

Cailet cringed.

Taig turned crimson, then white, then pivoted on his heel and stalked away.

Elomar shook his head gently; his only comment. Riddon

Slegin looked deeply embarrassed; Miram Ostin only sighed. Sarra didn't seem to notice their reactions at all.

"As long as you're here," she said, "we might as well use this time to make some plans. It's getting dark. Let's go up to the family balcony. We can eat up there and wait for Taig to stop sulking."

The Ladymoon rose nearly full that evening, shimmering slightly on the Ward Elomar insisted on calling to the balcony.

"The Summons may have been felt by others," he told Cailet. "Please Ward yourself at all times from now on."

She glanced away from the beguiling diffusion of light. "What about the rest of you? Especially the non-Mageborns?"

"Lilias and Gavirin Bekke took care of it," Miram assured her. "She says it gives them something to do."

Riddon blinked as he passed a loaf of flatbread to Cailet. "They're both in their seventies!"

"They take turns," Miram replied dryly. "Actually, I find the family quite interesting. Wine, Sarra?"

"Thank you. Descendants of Captal Bekke, I take it?"

"Collateral. She had no children. But it seems the Mageborn Bekkes are and always have been Warriors. Every last one of them. Besides Lilias and Gavirin, Rennon and Granon are here—cousins of some sort, as most of the Mages are. For instance—"

Cailet hid a grin, knowing that a lengthy genealogical lecture was coming; Miram kept the Ostin Name's official records.

"—the Escovor line is especially convoluted. Except for Gaire, who's Shonner's son, all Mages of that Name still alive are fifth cousins. But no two of them are fifth cousins to a third."

"Huh?" This from Riddon, whose entire Name now consisted of himself and his two brothers.

"Aifalun—she's a retired Scholar—is fifth cousin to Shonner, who's fifth cousin to Tirez, who's fifth cousin to Jeniva, who's fifth cousin to Sollan—he's another Scholar. But Jeniva is Shonner's second cousin, and Tirez—well, you get the idea." She chuckled low in her throat. "The really fun part is that all of them are close kin by various marriages to the Kevirons—who as far as I can tell are hardly related to each other at all!"

Riddon gave her an odd look. "This is your idea of 'fun'?"

"Mother always said she would've had a spectacular career at Census," Taig said, emerging from the darkened chamber behind them out onto the balcony. He paused, asking, "May I come in?"

"Oh. Sorry." Elomar canceled the Ward to let him through, then reinstated it. Cailet was impressed by his easy control; Riddon was nearly slack-jawed.

"How do you *do* that?"

"Smoke and mirrors," Miram said with a wink at the Healer Mage.

When he winked back, Sarra warned playfully, "You two stop flirting or I'll tell Lusira. Worse, I'll tell Lilen Ostin!"

Elo clasped his hands at his chest. "Lusira, if you must—but I beg you, *not* Lady Lilen!" Then, turning to Cailet, he said quite seriously, "We're safe only from prying magic, not from an attack."

Riddon was still curious. "Captal—I mean, Cailet—can you do stronger Wards than this?"

"Probably." She shrugged and passed the wine bottle to Taig. Miram handed him a metal cup, and he sat down to share what remained of dinner. "I'm not really sure what I can do until I have occasion to do it."

"I see. I think." Riddon absently soaked a chunk of hard bread in his wine. "What I meant was that if they *do* figure out where we are, we'll need all the protection you can give us."

"I know. But I've got an idea bout that." She shifted on the cold and uncomfortable iron bench; Sarra had told her there used to be cushions, lovingly embroidered by Gerrin Ostin and Gerrin Desse for each member of the family. Here, of an evening, people Cailet would never know had sat talking while the sun set and the Ladymoon rose. Sarra had memories of Ambrai. Cailet had nothing.

"Every Prentice Mage knows how to Ward herself. What I'd like to do is link those Wards together. As if—" And here she smiled slightly. "—each was a brick in a wall. Elo, you and Elin and Keler and Tiron did it in the Renig courtroom."

"For a few minutes only," he said. "But even Mages have to sleep."

"When they do, others will take their places. I think

you're right, and we can't assume that none but Mages felt the Summons. So we can also assume they know where we are. There's been no move made yet, and that worries me."

"It takes time to transport the Council Guard," Taig observed.

"Soldiers against Mageborns?" Miram shook her head. "Not this time, big brother. They can't risk a single escape. They'll use Malerrisi. But what can they be waiting for?"

"I don't have a clue," Cailet admitted.

"They know where," Sarra said slowly. "But they don't know who."

"Go on, Sarra," Riddon urged. Cailet envied him his long knowledge of his foster-sister's instincts.

"The Malerrisi can get here by Ladder. There's one here that goes straight to Ryka Court." Sarra turned to Cailet, moonlight silvering her golden hair and black eyes. "But they don't know who they'll be facing."

"The new Captal!" Riddon gave Cailet a wide, excited grin. "They don't know who you are!"

Sarra murmured, "And there's nothing a Malerrisi hates more than an unidentified thread in the Great Loom."

They don't know who you are!

Neither Riddon nor Miram have any idea who I really am. Sarra knows. And Elo. And Taig ... see him over there, looking at me and still looking for Alin and probably Gorsha as well.

"Knowing your name," Elo said quietly, "will not help them."

... and thus Collan can do no harm. Cailet saw the unspoken words in his eyes. And the thought that her friend would endure the Pain Stake for nothing suddenly enraged her. She stood, paced to the stone balustrade, braced her fists on it as she stared up at the moon.

"I won't stay anonymous much longer," she said.

"Cailet," Sarra warned, "if you're thinking of doing something insane—"

"What's sane about any of this?" Whirling, she spread both arms wide. "The reason Ambrai died is because the Mages who stayed to defend it held to their ethic. They used magic only to protect, not to attack." And she could see it all in one man's terrible memories, how they tried to make of themselves a wall and failed because the Captal—the mortar

that would hold them all together—was dead, and not even
Gorynel Desse could take Leninor Garvedian's place.

Sarra was on her feet now, trembling with anger. "So you
think ethics are a luxury you can't afford?"

"Once this is over—"

"—then you'll have time to be as ethical as any Captal
who ever lived?"

"You weren't prissy about ethics when you killed the Advocate!"

"Who was about to kill *you!*"

"Where's the difference, Sarra?" she cried. "Where's the
line? If you kill to protect me, how is that different from me
killing to protect you and all the others?"

"Magic," Elomar said.

Cailet swung around to face him, his uplifted face clear
and cool by moonlight. "She killed with a knife and not with
a spell, is that it? She's got no magic to use. I do. And I'll
use it as I need to, and if that means killing with it to preserve what we are—"

"You will destroy what we are." He was serene, and a little sad. "Perhaps worse, you will destroy yourself. There are
reasons for our ethic, Captal. Reasons why we do not weave
Nets as the Malerrisi do. We will build your brick wall for
you, but do not command anything more. It will not be
done."

Outright defiance, delivered in a calm tone that struck a
spark off her temper. "Damn me as you will," she said
through gritted teeth. "But I *am* your Captal, and you'll do
as I say, Mage."

"Cailet." She heard Taig's voice as if from a great distance. "Cai, listen to yourself."

"What's the matter—I'm not being me again? Who would
you prefer, Taig? I do a wonderful impersonation of Gorsha
Desse!"

"And an even better one of a Malerrisi First Lord."

He's got you there, Captal, came an infuriating whisper in
her mind.

"Shut up, all of you! *All* of you!" she cried, and ran from
the balcony, breaking Elomar's Ward with an abruptness that
left him gasping.

She took the steps of the Double Spiral two and three at
a time, to the third floor where earlier Sarra had shown her
the family's vast apartments. She knew who had lived in

each: Grandmother and Grandfather in the eight-room suite to her right; Alvassy and Desse kin scattered along the left; her parents in chambers overlooking the river and the Mage Academy. It was here that Cailet now went, the place where Maichen Ambrai had lived with her husband and conceived three daughters, the place she'd fled one night with Sarra's hand in hers and Cailet barely a quiver in her womb.

She could see them, mother and daughter, through Gorsha's eyes. The memory from the black mirror. And the other memory, of Maichen turning her face away and refusing even to look upon her newborn Mageborn child.

The room had burned, but not as thoroughly as the rest of Ambrai. The beams of the coffered ceiling were intact, if stained by smoke and soot. Cailet felt tears sting her eyes and told herself it was the lingering char of wooden furniture, carpets, draperies, clothes.

She crossed the littered floor to the windows and glared across the river to the moonlit ruin of the Academy. Had Auvry Feiran stood here, gloating that those who had rejected his presence for so long were forced to accept his presence in the Ambrai First Daughter's bed?

How could she know that they'd forbidden him the Academy grounds for a long time, fearful of his magic? How could she know that even after he was acknowledged a Prentice, instead of staying to become a Listed Mage, he'd left Ambrai behind for twelve years?

Only to return and become the husband of Maichen Ambrai. And father her three daughters. Glenin, born on St. Chevasto's Day—and there was portent enough for anyone. Sarra, who would be twenty-three years old next week. And herself. Cailet. Third daughter. Afterthought. Accident. Mistake. Born in Wildfire, conceived in lust but not love—

On the last day of the year, Gorsha murmured. *The Wraithenday. I knew when it happened.*

Did the magic shake inside you? she demanded bitterly, sarcastically. *Did the stars tremble in the skies?*

Nothing so trite. Very simply, my dear, their door was locked and Warded all day. He wanted her to come with him; she wanted him to stay. Neither convinced the other. And you're wrong about how it happened. They made love with the last of their love, Cailet. They made you.

"What a comfort," she said aloud. "How long did it take her to learn to hate him? And me?"

She never hated either of you.

"She wouldn't even look at me!"

Silence.

"Why should she want to?" she said at last, too weary to deny it any longer. "I was an accident and a mistake. I killed her. And look how I turned out. I'm not worth it, Gorsha. . . ."

The Ladymoon was setting, and the angle of silvery light revealed the Mage Academy in all its wreckage. It was the place she would have lived as Captal, the center of Mageborn life on Lenfell. Of *ethical* Mageborn life, she reminded herself. Maybe it was a good thing the Academy lay in ruins. She was unworthy of it, of the hundred Captals and the thousands upon thousands of Mages who had gone before her.

Of the sacrifice of her mother's life. . . .

"Cai. I'm sorry."

She'd been expecting Sarra, not Taig. She didn't face him. Couldn't.

A few hesitant steps; a silence; then: "I don't know that I'll ever get used to this. But I promise I'll try harder from now on."

She shook her head, mute.

"You're still so young," he murmured. "No matter what happened to make you Captal, you're still hardly more than a child." More footsteps, one of them crunching something broken and burned behind her. "You haven't lived very much of your own life yet. You're still learning. And I'm not helping much, am I?"

She choked out his name. "Taig—"

"No, let me finish apologizing." His voice was very near now, just over her shoulder. "Not for what I said, but for how I said it."

"It's all right," she said thickly. "I understand. I deserved it."

"Yes, you did," Taig replied, and he was the elder brother again, scolding her for her own good. Then he spoiled it by saying, "But I shouldn't have said it in front of other people. A Captal deserves more respect."

"But *I* don't." She gathered her courage and turned to look at him. Tall and hawk-nosed and tired and silver-eyed—and all she had ever wanted since she could remember, all the solace she'd ever run to find when she was in need. "I was wrong, Taig. You and Sarra and Elo were right. Keep at me about it. Keep correcting me. Who knows, maybe one day you won't have to. Maybe I'll learn how to be a Captal."

"Just be Cailet," he told her with a tender smile. "You can trust her to know what's right."

"Do you?"

His brows arched as if he'd never given it a second thought. "Of course."

She bit both lips. "Taig?"

"What is it, Caisha?"

"Why does it have to be so cold?"

He gathered her into his arms. She hid her face against his chest. Warmth enough, but borrowed. Not really her own to claim.

After a time she pulled away and tilted her head back, trying to smile. "Has Sarra found us someplace to sleep for the night?"

"One floor down. It's a storeroom for antique Cloister rugs too valuable for even you Ambrais to walk on."

"Iron door?" she guessed.

"Steel, in between layers of cedar. They're unrolling the rugs now." He smiled. "You ought to be very comfortable. I remember waking up quite a few mornings to find you curled up on my carpet, sound asleep."

"Taig! I'm too old to be afraid of the dark anymore!"

"All grown up now, eh?"

Cailet shrugged. "I want to stay up here for a while, Taig."

Taking her shoulders in his hands, he said, "Don't be too long," and leaned down to kiss her brow. "And take Elo's advice, will you? I don't like to think of you walking around unWarded."

"Yes, Papa."

With a grin, he squeezed her shoulders and departed. Before following him, she bid good night to the Ladymoon and the tiny companion that followed her like a coin rolling across the sky. It was the work of a word and a thought to construct a Ward that would keep her safe even while she slept. Wrapped in it, aware of its subtleties but too weary to analyze them, she kindled a tiny Globe to light her way to the Double Spiral.

She had descended only two steps when she saw Taig. He

stood five steps below her, motionless, waiting for her, every muscle of face and body taut and his eyes frantic with warning.

In the silence she heard footsteps above her, coming down the other stair.

Sarra had told her that people on one spiral never knew if anyone was on the other. Not quite believing, Cailet had insisted on testing it out. To her surprise, it worked exactly as Sarra said it did. The intruder would not even see the light from the Mage Globe. But had her footsteps been heard? Marble echoed appallingly. Her heartbeats seemed thunderous. She listened to the rhythm of those other boots, nodding her head in time, then trod softly down to Taig, as if the sounds were prints on sand to which she matched her own feet.

He hugged her protectively close. More than halfway to the third-floor landing, they were hidden from anyone coming up their spiral by the sweeping curve of the inner wall. But the outer wall was less than four feet high, a marble balustrade carved with interlocking openwork octagons. When the intruder left the Double Spiral, she or he would see light. So Cailet let the Globe dissolve. In absolute darkness she listened to the descending footfalls. A hesitation, then a halt. Taig's arm tightened around her.

"I know you're here," a man's voice breathed. "I can feel it."

With a silent curse, Cailet let the Ward drop as well.

Other footsteps—lighter, running up the steps two and three at a time—echoed in the Double Spiral.

"Father!" A loud whisper, the voice of an adolescent boy who came to a panting stop on the landing below. "Nobody downstairs. Everything's open except some storerooms with the doors locked from the outside. No magic anywhere."

"I felt nothing upstairs, either. Hush and let me think."

The boy obeyed for all of a minute. "Father? I felt the Summons back at the Castle after you showed me how, but right now all I sense is the Blanking Ward in the Ladder."

"Perhaps that's confusing the magic," the man fretted. "But you're right, the place is empty but for us."

Suddenly Cailet could see the pattern of octagons. Simultaneously, she felt magic—right through two solid marble walls and the Warded circle of the Ladder they enclosed. *Mage Globe,* supplied the calm, quiet voice she associated with Tamos Wolvar, and she knew as well that its ruddy hue was indicative of angry frustration. *As if you required such confirmation after hearing the tone of his words,* the old man appended with wry apology.

Colors don't lie, but voices can, she replied. *Thank you.*

The boy was speaking again. "Maybe we should go back and get some other Lords to help."

"I didn't spend days tracking down that Summons only to let someone else find the new Captal before I do!"

"Why didn't Auvry Feiran feel it? He was Guardian trained, wasn't he?"

"An excellent point, and one I've been considering myself. He should have felt the Summons. He says he didn't. So either he's much less powerful than he would have us believe, or he's a liar."

"He lived here, didn't he? At the Octagon Court."

"When he was Maichen Ambrai's husband, yes."

"It must've been beautiful here once. Before he destroyed it. But it doesn't look in such bad shape to me. Mother says he spared most of it for Lady Glenin, so one day she could—"

"Do not *ever* refer to that woman as 'Lady.' "

"I'm sorry. I forgot. It's just that Mother calls her that."

"Flattering her to her face is one thing, but referring to her with full Malerrisi honors in private is another. Stop chattering and use your magic. You're young and strong—find me the Captal. Concentrate!"

Cailet sent an incoherent prayer of thanks to St. Miryenne that she'd already canceled both Globe and Ward. But she wondered who had locked the storeroom doors and was now in hiding from the father-and-son Malerrisi.

"I'm sorry, Father, I can't feel anything. Mother might—she says I get my sensitivity to other magic from her, and she's much better at it than I am."

"I don't understand," the man muttered. "It was so strong on the way here from the Academy—"

"What's that?" the boy gasped.

In that instant Cailet felt Taig let her go and heard his boots tramp emphatically down the stairs. In a loud, angry voice he said, "I am the Captal, and you'll follow my orders!"

27

*Don't notice me, don't look this way, I have no magic for you
to feel, my Wards are subtle, you can't feel them, you won't
even know I'm here. . . .*

Sarra kept up the litany for what seemed hours after the
footsteps faded into the darkness. Then she took off boots
and socks and tiptoed to unlock the door and set Elomar
free.

He bent his long form to whisper in her ear. "How
many?"

"I heard two. Stay here. Protect Miram and Riddon.
They're not Mageborn." When she felt him tense up, she
added, "I know the Octagon Court. You don't."

"Sarra—"

"Stay put, Elo! I don't need you and they do!" She hurried away, feet already aching with the cold of the marble
floor. She'd known that unlocking the door would cause a
time-wasting argument, but if things went wrong, nobody
knew where Elo and Riddon and Miram were to set them
free. She ran now, memory guiding her true along the corridor to another set of stairs. She concentrated on breathing as
softly as possible—a formidable accomplishment, considering that the race up two flights of steps set her heart to galloping like a terrified galazhi's. Some part of her *was*
frightened. But mostly she was just plain furious.

At exactly whom, she wasn't quite sure. At the Malerrisi,
for finding them; at Cailet, for wanting to see their ancestral
home; at herself, for agreeing; at Collan, for getting himself
captured and not being here when she needed him. Which
was ludicrously unfair. She couldn't help it. *Damn it all, I
suppose I'll have to marry the stupid fool just to keep him
out of trouble.*

This prize bit of insanity warned her that she was on the
edge of hysteria. So at the second floor she stopped long
enough to catch her breath before she crept down the long
hallway toward the Double Spiral.

She couldn't see a thing. She stayed to the center of the

corridor, knowing that all the statue stands, display tables
and cases, and gigantic flower jars had been arranged along
the walls. There were no windows, thank the Saints, and so
no broken glass, and the ceiling tiles hadn't fallen. But just
the same she kept stubbing her toes on toppled half-burned
furniture, stifling curses and wishing her Ambrai ancestors
hadn't been such avid collectors.

Cailet and Taig would use the Double Spiral to come
downstairs. She knew it with simple logic; they knew of no
other way. There was an even chance that they and the
Malerrisi would use opposite sides. Her instincts, however,
had been silent since the first stomach-lurching alarm that
there were people present who must not find them.

Must not find Cailet.

All at once light sprang to life around the corner just
ahead of her. She flattened herself to a wall, inching forward
to the intersection. The light was reddish, like a miniature
sunset. *Mage Globe,* she thought, *but not Cailet's. Hers are
almost pure white.*

She heard voices: indistinct, still over a hundred feet of
corridor away. Poking her head around the corner, she saw
the glow more clearly but could hear no better.

Then Taig practically yelled his arrogant assertion that *he*
was the Captal.

The next minute or so was a blur of shouts and running
steps. Horrified, Sarra ran down the hallway to one of Great-
Grandmother Sarra's five-foot flower vases, incredibly intact
and providing a convenient shadow. Just her size, too.

She could hear everything now.

"You? Impossible!"

"Try getting through my Wards, and find out!"

So Cailet was working the magic while Taig worked the
bluff.

"There's been no magic in the Ostin Blood since—"

Taig laughed. "Are you stupid Malerrisi still trying to
breed true for magic? Don't you know that was outlawed
Generations ago? Besides, it can't be done. Magic happens
as it pleases. Auvry Feiran is proof enough of that!"

"You cannot be the new Captal. You've never used magic
in any of your missions for the Rising."

"Anniyas isn't all that public about her skills, either."

An outraged gasp; another bark of laughter from Taig.

"Oh, it's not a lucky guess, Malerrisi. The Rising isn't

made up of imbeciles. We found out about her long ago. And as Mage Captal, I know such things without having to be told. Now, unless you want to stand here all night, I suggest you use the Ladder at the bottom of these stairs and go back to Ryka Court—where I'm sure you'll have a wonderful time explaining to Anniyas how you warned the Captal that the Malerrisi know where he is, while at the same time failing to capture or kill him."

"I have another idea. You and I will go to Ryka. I'll let the girl leave unhindered—"

"With your son running around loose? I heard his voice, Malerrisi, even if he ran away when he heard mine. Hunting down a defenseless girl would be about the extent of his courage. Call out to him, tell him to get out of here by the Ladder. Then let the girl go, and I'll come with you."

"Taig, no!"

Sarra flinched at Cailet's anguished cry—the same agony she had been unable to voice until Collan was gone.

"Silence!" Taig ordered. "When you took the Rising Oath, you agreed to obey the Captal as if you, too, were a Mage."

"You're *not* the Captal! *I* am!"

Sarra's heart stopped.

The Malerrisi began to laugh. "A girl barely old enough to have breasts?" he jeered. "Run along and play with your dollies, little girl. Obey your sacred Rising Oath!"

A shadow crossed the hall ahead, and Sarra drew back behind the vase. Belatedly she recalled the "son running around loose." *I'm not here, you don't see me, my Wards are too subtle for you to feel—*

"Father?" High-pitched with fright, quivering with uncertainty.

"Go on—use the Ladder to Ryka Court. Make sure the chamber is empty, then wait for me."

"But—"

"Obey the Fifth Lord!" the Malerrisi shouted.

"Y–yes, Father."

The shadow resolved into a slim young boy at least a head taller than Sarra. He scurried to the Double Spiral and disappeared inside. She heard his clattering descent to the bottom, where the Ladder was.

A few moments later, his father said, "He's gone."

"Yes, he is," said Cailet, to confirm it for Taig.

"And how would *you* know?" he snapped. "You've got

about as much magic as one of my father's Senison hounds!"

"Damn you!" she exclaimed. "*You're* the one who wouldn't feel a spell until it killed him! And this man is going to kill you, Taig, don't you see?"

"Shut up." With the sure knowledge of a Ladder Rat's elder brother, he said to the Malerrisi, "I could have killed him before the Ladder took him, when all other magic is canceled. Take it as a gesture of good faith."

"I take it as indication of idiocy. By the Weaver, but you people are all fools! Send the girl on her way. I've no interest in anyone not Mageborn."

Sarra put a shoulder to the heavy vase and got it rocking.

"I'm not going!" Cailet shouted. "I'm the Captal, and—"

With a grunt and a wordless apology to her great-grandmother's Wraith, she finally toppled the vase. The ensuing crash echoed in a sudden silence. Sarra ran through it, making no sound. She entered the Double Spiral, praying she had chosen the correct stair, with her knife in her hand.

She saw Cailet first, one step above Taig, who stood four steps above the Malerrisi. He was tall and brown, with massive muscles gone fleshy, and he held a Mage Globe between his uplifted hands.

The Globe of a Warrior. She knew that without thinking. She threw her knife at the same time the Globe burst and Cailet flung an intercepting sphere to block the gout of crimson fire on its way to Taig's chest.

She would never know whether the Fifth Lord was more astonished by the knife in his guts or the revelation that this "little girl" was indeed the new Mage Captal. But instinct warned her that Cailet's Wards were down, as they must be for her to attack this way—as the Malerrisi's also were, or the knife would never have penetrated his magic.

"Cailet!" she screamed. "Wards!"

The pure white sphere expanded to catch spewing red flames. Blood-colored lightning crawled over its surface in crazy patterns, colliding in showers of sparks. Awed by so much controlled power that contained and controlled Malerrisi magic, Sarra couldn't take her eyes away.

So she didn't see the white-handled knife until it was on its way to Cailet's heart.

Taig saw. He lunged up into its path, right into the flashing sphere of white and crimson. The Globe bounced off his shoulder and sailed over the balustrade, exploding against the far wall. The glare backlit Taig's body as he fell, the knife embedded in his upper thigh.

The Malerrisi was laughing. With both hands he held Sarra's knife in his belly, every chortling spasm doing more damage. "There's another thread cut!"

Sarra screamed for Elomar. Taig was sprawled across the steps, trying to yank the white-handled knife from his thigh. Cailet supported him from behind, ashen-faced. Then all light was gone. Sarra stumbled on a step and fell to her knees. The laughter went on and on, horrifying now in the darkness.

"A good sharp blade—not my Scissors, but it'll do!"

"Cailet!" Sarra cried, struggling to her feet.

A Mage Globe blossomed behind her. Elomar sidestepped both Sarra and the dying Fifth Lord of Malerris, who lay propped against the wall turning the knife in his own guts. He grinned up at the Healer Mage. "Killed him dead, snippety snip!"

Sarra pushed herself upright and fought the urge to reclaim her knife and slit his throat with it.

"The knife wouldn't have hurt me." Cailet cradled Taig's head against her shoulder. "I was Warded. You didn't have to—"

"I'm supposed to know that?" he answered with an attempt at a smile. "I'm not Mageborn."

"And I'm not a child. You could've trusted me to—"

"Cailet." Elomar's voice was hushed. "The knife...."

"What about it?"

"It's spelled to go through any Ward as easily as a fish through water."

"Then why didn't he use it earlier?" Taig asked, grimacing as Elo put a fingertip to the knife hilt.

"The spell must be renewed after each use."

Sarra tried and failed to catch her sister's gaze. "He only had one chance. He couldn't be sure which of you might be the Captal—or even Mageborn, for that matter."

"Captal? Her?" The Fifth Lord found this hilariously funny. "A thin little thread of a girl?"

Without looking at him, Cailet said, "You begin to annoy me, Malerrisi."

Sarra shivered.

"Get this thing out," Taig said, tugging again at the knife.

Elomar replied softly, "It can't be removed."

He bit his lip, white-faced and sweating. For Cailet's sake, Sarra knew, he said, "Well, then, if you have to cut, at least leave me an interesting scar."

"It cannot be removed," the Healer repeated, looking down into Taig's suddenly wide eyes. "Except by his hand and his magic."

Taig swallowed hard. "You mean if he doesn't take it out himself, I'll walk around the rest of my life with—"

"The rest of your life!" laughed the Fifth Lord.

Sarra sprang for him, realizing at last why he laughed, why he twisted her knife. Cailet was only a moment in joining her. They tried to pry his fingers loose from the hilt without doing any more damage. He struggled, writhing in agony now, but Sarra got one of his hands free and planted her knee on the wrist, cracking bones.

He grinned up at her. "Snip snip!" He finally found his heart with the tip of the blade, and died.

Sarra met Cailet's eyes over the still body. Behind them, Taig said, "So now I bleed to death."

Elomar answered, "The spell is a perversion of one I use on surgical blades to ensure a clean cut."

"What the hell does *that* mean?" Sarra rasped.

"This spell ... corrupts."

Cailet's eyes squeezed shut.

"How fast?" Taig asked in a steady voice.

"Very."

"Can you amputate my leg?"

"No. The artery is severed."

Taig glanced up at Cailet again. Sarra was reminded of another man's eyes glancing up with that same look, and her heart wrenched inside her breast. Thinking only of her, worried for her, trying to spare her—

Elo went on in a wooden tone, "The corruption is spreading through your blood. I can do nothing."

"You don't know that!" Sarra cried. "You can't be sure—"

"It is a White Knife. The signs carved into it—" His voice broke. "Taig, I'm sorry."

"I'd rather go cleanly," the young man responded. "Can you help?"

"If you wish."

"Please. It's starting to hurt in more places than my leg."

Sarra saw Elomar nod. She reached across the Malerrisi's

lifeless body to grasp Cailet's shoulder. Black eyes opened
and tears streamed down her cheeks.

"Cai?"

Taig's soft call seemed to go through Cailet's slight body
in a spasm of anguish. Sarra rose and helped her to stand,
whispering, "Tell him."

Soundlessly: "I can't."

"You must." Wisdom from her own hard lessoning in love
and pride and waiting until it was too late.

Cailet wrenched free and knelt beside Taig. Took one of
his hands. Twined the fingers with her own.

"Take me back to Ostinhold, Cai?"

She nodded mutely.

"Don't cry, little one. You're safe. That's all that matters
to me."

"You always kept me s–safe," she managed.

"Somebody else will have to do it from now on," he said
gently. "Find him, Caisha. Love him even more than you
loved me."

She shook her head fiercely. "Don't tell me that, Taig, I
can't!"

"Of course you can. You'll see. Go on, now."

"No."

Taig's jaw set against pain for a moment. "I don't want
you here, Cai."

She caught his hand to her chest, her voice feverish. "I
can fix it—I can get the knife out—I'm Captal, I know all
the spells—"

"Not this one," Elomar said. "Sarra, take her away from
here."

"Come with me now, dearest," Sarra murmured, stroking
the silky hair.

Cailet jerked away. "No!"

Elomar took her shoulders and lifted her to her feet. She
swayed; Sarra held her close. "Go," he ordered. "*Now*,
Cailet."

Sarra guided her away into the darkness. They walked,
Cailet stumbling, Sarra supporting, through half the Octagon
Court before the younger girl suddenly moaned.

"I didn't tell him!"

"He knew."

Cailet whimpered softly. Sarra gathered her close and

rocked her while she cried, thinking that only two nights ago Cailet had done the same for her.

But Collan was still alive.

Forgive me, she prayed silently, *forgive my selfishness— just please let him still be alive. . . .*

28

The boy was choking on a gulp of Anniyas's best brandy when Glenin arrived in the First Councillor's suite. Her father's terse note had interrupted a frustrating session of floral redesign for Garon's Birthingday party: the keepers of the Ryka Court greenhouses could not promise enough Miramili's Bells for her original plans. Thinking that the Minstrel had finally divulged the new Captal's name, Glenin hurried to Anniyas's chambers. Instead of a prized revelation, she was confronted with the shaking form of Chava Allard cowering in an overstuffed armchair.

"Good," said Anniyas, barely glancing at her. "You're here. Get the boy talking, Auvry."

Glenin sank into a nearby chair as her father crouched before the Fifth Lord's son and said, "Better now, aren't you? Easy breath. That's it. Very good. Look at me, Chava, and start at the beginning."

After a few false starts and several more swallows of brandy, the story came out of him. Vassa Doriaz's determination and days-long search; the Traitor's Ladder to the Academy that morning; the stealthy journey to the Octagon Court; the locked storerooms and empty halls; the sudden appearance of some girl Chava hadn't seen and didn't know, and Taig Ostin, who claimed to be the new Captal.

"Ridiculous." Anniyas pushed herself out of a deep sofa and began to pace. "He's as Mageborn as this table!" She slapped a palm on its jade top for emphasis, rings clacking. "Who was the girl?"

"I—I don't know, First Councillor. I only heard her voice. Father made me hide and then he told me to wait for him here and that was *hours* ago—"

"So we have no idea what happened," Feiran mused, "except that Doriaz was unable to come here as planned."

"Doriaz," said Anniyas, "is dead."

Chava shrank back in the chair with a little cry. Glenin rose and poured him another brandy with her own hands. "Here, you need this," she said kindly.

"Th-thank you, Lady."

"Is there anything else?" Anniyas demanded. "Anything the girl said, anything Doriaz or Taig Ostin said, to indicate who the Captal really is?"

Chava sipped, frowned, and shook his head. "No, First Councillor. It all seemed to happen very fast."

"We're very pleased that you're safe," Feiran began.

"We're pleased by *none* of this!" Anniyas snapped. "Find him somewhere to sleep. He can't go back to Malerris Castle in this state, and I can't spare either of you to take him."

"You can stay with me and my husband," Glenin said. "His valet can share with our new cook."

"Always the heart of generosity, my dear," Anniyas remarked—putting Glenin on notice that Anniyas knew full well she wanted the boy under her own eye. Glenin didn't much care. Not only did she like the boy's mother and owe her a favor, but Chava was Golonet Doriaz's nephew and thus precious to her.

"Come with me, Chava," she said, taking the chill, trembling hand in hers.

"I'm not through with him yet," said Anniyas.

"With respect, First Councillor, he's told us all he knows," Feiran said.

"Which is no more than we knew when he got here! What did Doriaz's stupidity do but warn the new Captal? Oh, get him out of here. He's no use to me or anyone. Tomorrow send him back to his mother."

Glenin put an arm lightly across Chava's dejected shoulders as they went through the halls. She said nothing, concentrating on the bittersweet fantasy that this was *her* son, hers and Golonet's.

When they reached her chambers, she ordered the maid to fetch hot tea and then move Garon's valet in with the cook and change the bedding. Chava stood listlessly in the center of the room until she told him to sit down.

"It'll seem odd going to bed this time of the afternoon," Glenin added, "But in Seinshir it's the middle of the night."

"Is it?" he asked, merely to be polite.

"Mm-hm. Nearly Second tomorrow morning. Ladders certainly do play merry old hell with your body's internal clock." She smiled down at him, but he wouldn't look at her. "Chava, pay no attention to Anniyas."

"But she said my father is dead."

"If he is, then all Malerris will mourn him. But you haven't seen his body, have you? And neither has Anniyas." The maid came in, deposited a tray on a nearby table, and left. Glenin handed the boy a cup of steaming tea. "Here. This will settle your stomach after all that brandy."

He drank, coughed, and drank some more. When the maid reappeared to signal that all was ready, Glenin set down her own cup and said, "Now to bed with you, Chava. Tomorrow you'll be back at Malerris Castle with your mother."

"Can't I—I mean, would it be all right if I stayed here with you? My father said to wait for him."

Privately Glenin thought it would be a *very* long wait, for she agreed with Anniyas: Doriaz must be dead. But the boy's wide eyes—dark green sparked with gold and brown, and undoubtedly the best feature of his bony face—were pathetic with trust and need, and Glenin was touched. She brushed at a few strands of brown hair that had escaped his coif to curl on his forehead.

"Perhaps you can remain a while. We'll have to send word to your mother, though. Lady Saris will be frantic."

"I left word," he confessed. "I told one of the slaves to tell her in the morning where we'd gone."

"I'm glad you did. But you know, don't you, that it was wrong to go anywhere with your father—even if he is Fifth Lord—without first consulting her? Until a man marries, his first duty is always to his mother."

"But she wouldn't've let me go."

Secretly amused by this perfect adolescent logic, Glenin nodded. "I quite understand. Have you finished your tea? Come along, then."

On the way to the valet's small chamber, Chava asked, "When my father comes, you'll tell me, won't you?"

"Of course. It must've been very strange, hearing their voices and feeling their magic but not seeing their faces."

He yawned mightily before replying, "I did see them, for just a second."

"Ah." She indicated the bedgown folded on a chair. "The girl was blonde, wasn't she?"

"Uh-huh." Sleepily, he began to undo the buttons of his longvest. "They both were."

"And dark-eyed," Glenin murmured, every sense alert. "And quite young."

"Not much older than me. Isn't that too young to be Captal?" he asked around another yawn. Then his eyes blinked wide open and he turned to her fearfully. "I forgot about that until just now—I didn't remember to tell the First Councillor—"

"It's all right, Chava. You were upset and it's perfectly understandable that a few things slipped your mind. One blonde girl or two, it doesn't matter that much."

"I only saw the other one in the shadows, my Lady. When I was running for the Ladder—"

"I understand," she soothed. "I'll tell Anniyas for you, shall I? And that you're sorry you forgot."

He nodded gratefully. She smiled, bid him sweet dreaming, and shut the door behind her.

Leaning back against it for a moment, she wondered why he would say the girl was too young to be Captal unless someone else had said she was. Well, she supposed that, and the two blondes—or indeed anything else he'd forgotten—didn't signify. Glenin knew who the girls were. She also knew that Doriaz was certainly dead after an encounter with the new Captal.

And she had no intention of telling Anniyas anything about it at all. She returned to her desk and, after fingering a thick letter, resumed redesigning floral arrangements, smiling.

She went to bed early, slept soundly and alone, and before dawn the next morning left her suite. Her father had spent most of the night at the *albadon,* and would be in his own rooms now, resting. She knew his work well, and was easily able to cancel all the complex series of Wards and spells to get inside the cold white box.

Collan Rosvenir sagged bonelessly against the silver Pain Stake, eyes closed, seemingly asleep. She knew he was awake, though; she could feel it, as if he watched her with the rest of his senses. She smiled at his bent head.

"You're an attractive man, Minstrel, even after a week and a day in here. Beginning to be a trifle scrawny, but that's easily cured. How would you like a bath, a shave, and a good hot meal?"

He said nothing. Her father had told her that his silence—but for the agonized cries inevitable in the circumstances—was unique in the lore of the Pain Stake. But it was axiomatic that no one emerged from the *albadon* the same person who went in.

"I offer these things because Anniyas commanded my father to break you, and you've quite remarkably survived. This being the case, I intend to use you to break someone else."

Still no response, not even a ripple through the naked muscles of his back—not even when she trailed a fingertip down his spine. A very fine back, she mused, and excellent shoulders marred only by the mark of slavery. The report from Renig had stated that he'd murdered the nauseating Scraller Pelleris, thereby doing everyone on Lenfell a favor.

"I'm Glenin Feiran, by the way. Would you like me to undo the bindings? I can, you know. I'm completely familiar with the way my father's magic works. Between you and me," she added, lowering her voice, playfully conspiratorial, "his is just a little bit predictable. But you'll discover that mine is not."

She flicked a polished fingernail against the silver to hear it ring. He didn't flinch. His control was truly amazing.

"Don't you want to know why you've lost your value? It's very simple. I know who the new Captal is. I know *where* she is. And I know that Sarra Liwellan is with her."

He straightened and his head lifted, very slowly. His eyes, set in dark bruises of pain and exhaustion, were disturbingly clear and startlingly blue. Lank, unwashed coppery curls fell over his brow. She brushed them back as she had Chava Allard's clean, soft brown curls. He didn't react. Her touch moved to his hollowed cheeks and sharp chin, nails raking lightly over the dense stubble of beard, lighter than his hair and glistening reddish-gold in the diffused light. Cleaned, combed, and properly dressed, he would be stunningly handsome.

"I know all about Renig, you see," she told him, tracing the curves of muscle in his arm down to the elbow and back up again. "Up until that dimwitted Justice and even stupider clerk fell asleep, anyway. But that was enough. Was it you who killed Agva Annison? No, it would take a Mage to kill someone as powerful as she. But I'll bet you accounted for a few of the Council Guards in the hallway, hmm?"

He went on staring at her in silence. She spoke even more softly as she skimmed a palm down his side, absently admiring the strong lines of him, the taut belly and lean thighs.

"The point is, I know about the little comedy over Mai Alvassy's identity disk. I know who stole it and now wears it. And now I know that she's with the Captal in Ambrai, at the Octagon Court. Once you're presentable, you and I will be going there, too." Taking a step back, she smiled almost fondly. "I'm sure Sarra will be glad to see you again."

He spat in her face.

Blind impulse ruled her magic for the first time in her life. She gestured sharply and the Pain Stake ignited from shining silver to hot glowing flame. He shrieked once, head thrown back, body spasming so violently that his shoulders nearly dislocated.

Furious with herself, she terminated the spell. He slumped, hanging from his bound hands, unconscious.

When she lifted her arm to wipe the spittle with her sleeve, she found that she was shaking. No one had ever made her lose control like that before. She wanted to wake him up and punish him anew for this second crime.

And then she remembered her son. She pressed her hands to her belly, frightened. There was no quiver from him, no instinctive terror; instead, she had the oddest impression that he was smiling in his sleep. A pregnant woman's fanciful imaginings. . . .

She left the *albadon* hurriedly, sealing it with her Wards this time, not her father's, and waited until her heartbeats were steady before starting back up endless flights of stairs. Halfway up, she saw her father.

"Glenin—what have you done?" he demanded.

Shrugging: "I got rid of your Wards and set my own."

"Remove them at once!"

She paused to catch her breath and toss the hair from her eyes. "You didn't even come close to breaking him, you know. He's as sane as the moment you put him in there. You should've let me handle it. But that's beside the point now. The new Captal and the blonde girl you dreamed about are the same, and she's in Ambrai with Sarra Liwellan—whose head is still owed me, by the way."

He went very still, something she hadn't seen him do in

a long time. Then he actually backed up a step, the only clumsy movement she had ever seen him make. She saw it without satisfaction, but without regret, either.

"How do you know this?" he asked, voice almost steady.

"A combination of things—including young Chava's experience tonight and a very interesting letter I received yesterday from Renig. I'll explain later. But *not* to Anniyas."

Gray-green eyes narrowed. "Whatever you know, you can't keep it from her."

"Truly told? Perhaps you'd like to hear the rest of what I know! She plans to destroy the Captal all by herself, did you realize that? She sees it as her right—Warden of the Loom! Don't look so shocked. Didn't you guess? That self-important idiot in Seinshir is no more the First Lord than Garon is! Poor Garon, such a disappointment—"

"Glenin—"

"Oh, there's more." She mounted the stairs, closing in on him. "She sees my son as hers, not mine—the son Garon was supposed to be and wasn't. Who do you think gave the order that killed my First Daughter? She doesn't *want* a daughter, she wants a son to replace Garon! She'll take my son when he's born—and then she'll have no more use for me!"

"No, you must be mistaken, she'd never—"

"By the Weaver, don't you even begin to understand her after all these years? She'll *kill* me, Father! Who's to stop her? You? A Prentice Mage against the First Lord?"

"The bargain," he stammered. "Your safety—your position—"

"If I hadn't turned up so powerful, maybe your bargain would've held. But I'm a threat, and my son will be a threat unless she takes him as her own. They'll let her do it. They won't shed any tears over me, Father—not with my son safely born and my little pattern so successfully woven, so neatly tied off, the threads cut nice and clean! If she kills a Mage Captal with nothing but her own magic, which of the Lords would dare oppose her? She won't just be Warden of the Great Loom—she'll *own* it!"

She was level with him now. She put both hands on his chest to feel his racing heart and said softly, "Guess what, Father? I don't want to die."

"You can't believe this." He was almost pleading.

"Glensha, it's not possible, Anniyas wouldn't—our bargain—"

"How can you still think like a Mage Guardian, with their definition of honor? You did your part, she'll do hers—is that it? You butchered Ambrai for her, found your fellow Mages for her so Vassa Doriaz and his sadistic kind could kill them—" She took the next step and turned to face him. How odd; she should still be looking up slightly to meet his eyes, yet she found she must look down. He seemed to have shrunken in on himself—like an old man, she thought in sudden pain, the dark wings of his brows below the coif's silver edging thickly grayed now. This autumn he would be sixty years old. "You taught me how to find them, too, after I learned the *Code of Malerris*."

"I—I thought it would prove to her—I'm sorry—"

"Father, I love you, but you are such a fool. Do you think I minded? I did it gladly, but not for Anniyas. I did it for you."

"Glensha. . . ."

She put her hands on his shoulders, felt them quiver as if palsied. "You fulfilled your part of the bargain. Once all the Mages are dead, Anniyas won't need you, either. Whatever she said, whatever she promised you, it's not going to happen. With the Mages and the Captal dead, she'll have no enemies left—except those who made bargains like yours, who did most of the killing for her. The Fifth Lord is dead. Doriaz was the only one with any power, we both know that. The others can't and won't oppose her. Why should she honor her promises? Who'll hold her to them? You and I and my son are the only threats remaining in all the world. She'll kill us and take him as Garon's replacement." Digging her fingers into his shaking muscles, she whispered fiercely, "We're *not* going to die and she *won't* have my son!"

Auvry Feiran was silent for a long time, head bent. At last he nodded. "Yes. I understand. What do you want me to do, Glenin? What *can* I do?"

She stroked his cheeks, then framed his face with both hands and coaxed him to look up at her. "We'll do it *together*. As we've always done."

"Yes," he said again. "Together, Glensha."

29

The Ladymoon was on the other side of the world, yet she seemed to gaze upon Cailet in her dream. Unsmiling, unmerciful, the cool pallid face looked down with imperious command.

Now.

She woke with the word on her lips. Elomar had given her something to make her sleep, but she felt unrested, bruised, sick, jittery with tension. Her body ached, her heart bled, her mind too stunned by Taig's death to form coherent thought beyond that one word, springing from the depths of her magic.

Now.

She lay back on a soft, thick Cloister carpet and stared at the blackness of the ceiling. After a time she shut her eyes. The Ladymoon appeared as she had in the dream, her tiny companion cowering nearby. One great full circle of light, one small quivering speck. Cailet knew which one she felt like.

Now.

And then a new word: *Tonight.*

Full moon tonight, Cailet told herself, trying to work it through her tired mind. First night of First Flowers . . . Sarra's Birthingday a few nights after. . . .

Magic whispered inside her. She was too weary to listen. If Gorsha had anything to tell her, he'd make it plain enough. She had no strength to ask.

Now. Tonight.

Taig . . . her heart contracted again, grief distilling from her very blood. It would be so until her heart was dry and she died from the loss of blood.

Now. Tonight.

Full moon. Strong, white-silver light spilling over the world, sharpening the shadows of dark places not even she could reach. The darknesses only magic could reach. Strong magic, white-silver as a Captal's should be, reaching for the knife-edged shadow that was Anniyas. .

Her magic. Hers. She felt it as a slim white candle unlit, silken white wings folded close, white-silver bells unsounded—for the flame and the flight and the chiming would be too powerful and too beautiful to be survived.

Miryenne's Candle. Rilla's Wings. Miramili's Bell.

Caitiri's Fire.

Her fire. *Her* magic.

Now, tonight.

The candle lit with her fire, igniting the silken wings to white flames. As they spread and swept the wind behind them across the sky, she heard the lustrous ringing of the Summoner's bell.

Now, Anniyas. Here. Tonight.

When Elomar touched her shoulder an hour later to waken her, she saw the lit candle he held, and smiled.

30

"Fabulous!" Elsvet Doyannis exclaimed in the doorway of the Malachite Hall, handing her cloak to her husband to be placed with the other ladies' wraps. "Glenin, my pet, you've absolutely outdone yourself! People will talk about this for years!"

"Generations," said Auvry Feiran as he bowed to Elsvet. "You're looking especially lovely this afternoon, Lady."

She simpered and smoothed the folds of her gown. Glenin thought it singularly ugly: every conceivable shade of green and blue swirls with golden ships riding the waves. Her headdress was a confusion of green lace, blue feathers, and gold stars bobbing at the ends of a dozen gold wires, set atop a towering arrangement of braids—the half of which Glenin knew to be false.

Her husband, poor thing, wore a longvest of the same material as Elsvet's dress. His coif was blue patterned with gold stars—like a face floating in an absurd rendering of the night sky.

"Ravishing," Glenin cooed. "I'm glad you're the first ones here so I can relax a few minutes with old friends before the whole herd gallops in!"

"Does Garon suspect?"

"He thinks we're spending the day with just family. But of course you *are* almost family, darling. Quick, before the others arrive, come give me your opinion of the flowers. Too many? Too few?"

She knew the flowers were perfect. Sprigs of Miramili's Bells peeked from sprays of luxuriant ivy and delicate rose-buds, all white and green to match the malachite floor and marble tables. The messages of the flowers—to those versed in the lore—were for her unborn son, not her husband: Bells to celebrate him, ivy to pledge fidelity, white rosebuds for purest love coming into flower.

The tables were perfect, too. Plates of frail white porcelain edged in silver; napkins also white, but rather than boring linen or silk she had chosen squares of lace edged in silver. They sprouted cleverly from the largest of the four glasses at each place. Knives, forks, spoons, and other utensils were, like the dishes and crystal, borrowed from the Council. Instead of one candle, there were twelve at each table, circling the flowers like tall, slender blades of spring grass springing up from white flower-shaped holders. At the bottom of each candle was an intricate silver bow, trailing ribbons that wove across the green tables to frame each plate. The scissors in their green-and-gray pouches rested beneath the candles.

"Why, I've seen this tired old service a hundred times," Elsvet remarked sweetly. "But you've made it look quite fresh. What interesting candles. Have you tested the refraction on the crystal?"

"I can hardly expect rainbows in a room this size!" Glenin laughed. "I contented myself with colors I could control." Thinking that once she was free to use her magic, she'd do what her father sometimes did when they ate alone, and make the candlelight dance. "You're over here," she went on. "Forgive me for putting you with Our Lady of the Manure Pit!"

Elsvet giggled girlishly at the nickname everyone used for the Minister of Agriculture. "Oh, don't worry, darling. We'll do just fine."

"Thank you, pet." Glenin smiled, aware that pregnancy had not kept Elsvet from seducing the Minister's great-nephew, who was the old woman's escort.

Others began to arrive. Glenin greeted each as if she'd

been pining for them all week. After a moment's chat with
Glenin, Auvry Feiran stepped forward to guide each woman
to her table—husband, son, cousin, nephew, or lover trailing
along behind. In the brief intervals between guests, Glenin
sipped ice water from a goblet held ready by a servant. What
she really wanted was a good strong Cantrashir red, but she
would need to be clearheaded tonight.

It was Anniyas's task to bring her son to his surprise
party. As the clock at St. Miramili's rang Half-Ninth, Glenin
could imagine the scene in her chambers. Garon would
choose something plain—for him—as it was only a family
party; Anniyas would beg him to wear one of his gorgeous
new suits. He'd smile, and as he changed clothes would
mention that Glenin especially liked the lime-green longvest
with the overlay of beige lace. And Anniyas would acquire
one of those fixed smiles that came over her these days
when Garon spoke Glenin's name.

Glenin's own clothes were both fashionable and blessedly
comfortable. A thigh-length white silk tunic was loosely
belted in gray over a green velvet underdress, all thinly embroidered in silver. Her hair fell free down her back from a
coronet of twisted silver and green ribbons knotted in back
with white roses. Her only jewels were pearl earrings that
had been her wedding gift from her father: perfect spheres of
dark gray iridescence, like a smoky rainbow.

She counted two hundred guests, then two hundred thirty.
No one had refused her invitation, even though it had come
at scandalously short notice. Two hundred fifty-six ... two
hundred seventy-two ... St. Miramili's rang the quarter during a flurry of late arrivals. At last all seats were filled but
the four she, Garon, her father, and his mother would oc-
cupy. The noise was terrific. Guests chattered like chickens
in a coop, the string orchestra sawed and plucked away, servants raced to fill wine goblets, and light from the afternoon
sun glinted off crystal and silver and jewels.

It was time at last. Glenin signaled to the chief butler of
Ryka Court, who ordered his minions and the musicians to
silence. Auvry took his seat. Excited anticipation flickered
through the hush of the Malachite Hall. Glenin waited by the
main doors, heart fluttering. Not for nervousness; for pleasure at what she would announce this day.

Through the slightest crack in the great doors she heard
Anniyas's voice, loud to warn Glenin that all must be silent

or the surprise would be spoiled. "Sweetest boy, this is the
only place in this beehive likely to be empty, and I do so
want to spend just a little time alone with you on your
Birthingday. It was just us two the day you were born, you
know. Just us, and so happy. . . ."

That was for Glenin, too. She gritted her teeth and nodded
to the chief butler. He flung the doors open, and Glenin
smiled her most brilliant smile, and everyone began to
sing—kept more or less in tune by the musicians.

> *Bright was the hour, glad was the day*
> *When you were born—so we all say!*
> *Happy your mother in birthing a boy*
> *And thankful your Lady for bringing her joy!*

There was a different rhyme for women, of course—
*Blessed was your mother/In birthing a girl/And grateful your
husband/For being his world!* That Glenin was Garon's
world was clear in his eyes. He blinked in shock, laughed in
delight, and embraced her with adoring arms. Anniyas acquired that smile again.

Glenin watched it grow more and more fixed during the
lighting of all three hundred candles, the first three courses
of the meal, and the interval in which each Councilmember's
gift was brought in—pretty, useless trinkets unique to each
Shir. A carved obsidian horse from Brogdenguard; leather
gloves from The Waste; a large bottle of Domburron brandy.
Anniyas's smile positively cemented when Garon un-
abashedly declared his favorite to be a painted miniature
portrait from Gierkenshir—a portrait of Glenin.

The next courses were served. Halfway through, Anniyas
excused herself to go wash a bit of sauce from her gray-and-
white striped satin gown. In the next interval, more gifts
were brought in—most of them insultingly cheap. Nested
boxes, a dreadful vase, wine, books (that was a laugh—
Garon hadn't willingly read anything but the numbers on
cards since leaving school). The couplet of Senison hounds
was more like it, Glenin thought, deciding that hunting
would again take up much of Garon's time from now on.
Elsvet, Saints bless her, gave him a book about sailing.

Anniyas hadn't returned.

Glenin didn't notice it until the round of gift-giving was
over. It was nearly Half-Tenth. After dessert was served

Glenin would make her announcement. She glanced at Auvry Feiran, seated across the table chatting pleasantly with ancient Kanen Ellevit. Before she could catch her father's eye, her husband leaned close to whisper in her ear.

"Beloved, this is the most wonderful day of my life. I adore you. This day is the beginning of everything for us. And for the baby."

His breath smelled awful, and he was at that stage of drunkenness when sentiment overcomes sense. Glenin drew back with a smile. "Darling, I'm so glad you're happy. I'm just waiting for your mother to come back so I can tell everyone the news. Where is she?"

"Shall I go find her?"

"No, this is your party, Garon. My father can go look for her."

"I don't mind, truly." He kissed her cheek and smiled at their guests before departing the Malachite Hall.

It was time she mingled again. On her way to the nearest table, she paused to ask her father, low-voiced, what had become of Anniyas. He shook his head. She was making the rounds of the third table when he casually left his seat and slipped out the doors—as many others had done throughout the evening, to blot off spills or repair makeup or relieve themselves.

"Marvelous evening. . . ."

"Exquisite food, Glenin dear. . . ."

"Such a lovely table. . . ."

"So gracious of you to include us. . . ."

"Delicious dinner. . . ."

"Beautiful flowers. . . ."

It went on and on, two hundred and ninety-six variations on the same compliments. She kept track of who was sincere and who was sucking up. In other words, who she would befriend and who she would ruin. The tally was heavily weighted toward ruination.

When she got back to her table, Anniyas was still absent. So was Garon. But her father had returned. She arched a brow; he shrugged and looked puzzled.

The last course was removed. Carts were wheeled in, laden with dessert plates and eight kinds of cake. She tapped playfully at Granon Isidir's shoulder. "Get me something chocolate!" she commanded with a smile, and went to look for Anniyas herself.

The hallways of Ryka Court were deserted but for a few Guards on duty. Everyone who was anyone was at her party; everyone who was not at the party was in hiding, pretending illness or pressing business. Her high heels clicked a rapid rhythm toward the Octagon Court Ladder. But she changed direction halfway there, a terrible suspicion clenching her guts.

She ran as fast as she could for the *albadon*. Down ten flights of stairs, along a corridor, around a corner where she'd placed the first of her Wards—

Gone.

All her Wards, and the Minstrel with them. The white cube was shorn of all spells, nothing more than a cold, empty marble box.

That her father had betrayed her was unthinkable. Impossible.

So was the undoing of her spells.

But Anniyas was First Lord of Malerris, Warden of the Loom. She could unweave entire lives, not just the spells and Wards of a smug and arrogant young woman who wasn't even acknowledged a Lady of Malerris.

By the time she reached the upper halls again there was a stitch in her side. She waited, cursing silently, until she could breathe without wheezing, then headed for her suite. Chava Allard was there, disconsolately beating himself at chess. He glanced up when she entered, hazel eyes brightening.

"Has my father come?"

"What? Oh—no. But don't worry, Chava."

"How's your party? Is it fun? Thank you for sending the dinner, my Lady. It was nice of you to think of me."

On her way to her sitting room, she threw him an abstracted smile. "I'm glad you liked it. There was plenty to share."

She unWarded and unlocked a drawer of her desk and extracted the velvet Ladder. It was folded small, but she had no pocket to hide it in. She went through to her bedroom, seizing a dark green cloak from the wardrobe. Draping it over her arm to hide the Ladder clutched in her hand, she returned to the main room.

"From what I've heard about it," Chava said, "you really *need* a warm cloak in the Malachite Hall."

"Oh—yes. It's rather chilly, even with all the people

crowded in. I've got to hurry, Chava, but I'll tell you all about it tomorrow."

"Good night, Lady Glenin."

Distantly, St. Miramili's struck the quarter. Glenin should be standing at the head table right now, waiting for the servants to pour celebratory sparkling wine into fresh glasses, waiting for the raising of a toast to Garon that she would turn into a toast to her son. Instead, she was muffled in a heavy cloak, hurrying to a corner of Ryka Court she knew to be empty—Anniyas's own chambers—to claim her prisoner and her rightful place from the First Lord.

31

He knew his hands were undamaged. Unburned. Unbroken. Whole.

But he couldn't move them.

Not so much as a flexing of the fingers or a twitching of the wrists. His hands dangled at the ends of his arms, numb and senseless lumps of flesh and bone. *Useless—like Falundir's.* He bit his lip and refused to believe it.

Anniyas had come for him, unwrapped his hands from the Pain Stake, freed him from the white box. But not from spells. A new one was set with a flick of her fingers, taking what strength was left him and turning his muscles to lead.

A pair of stalwart young men with carefully blank faces carried his limp body to a nearby room. Under the First Councillor's keen-eyed direction, he was swiftly and thoroughly bathed, shaved, dried, brushed, combed, and dressed in clothes that made him look like an overage offering at a cheap whorehouse. Skintight red trousers; blue shirt left half-open and tucked into a low belt; unbuttoned yellow longvest and matching coif heavily embroidered with red and purple roses; blue cloak with stiff shoulder pads. He was then draped into a chair, still unable to command his body to stand or move.

Anniyas surveyed him critically. "My son's clothes," she said, "suit you not at all."

It defied imagination. Somebody actually wore all this on purpose?

"But never mind," she went on. "You have two choices, Minstrel. Obey me, or die. I ask very little, as it happens—only that you stand still while we take the Ladder to the Octagon Court. As this is the place you most wish to be, I doubt you'll try to kill me before we get there. I also assume you know that a Ladder cancels any other magic while it's working, and that you're thinking about the moments after we arrive. Let me assure you that my magic is faster than your fists or your feet."

The sentence echoed in memory, as if she'd almost quoted something he'd heard before. Something true. He believed her.

"So. Two choices. Do you agree to obey me?" She gestured slightly. "You'll find you can nod."

He could, and he did. The spell trickled from his head and face and neck like lightning-charged water. He looked down the length of his sprawled body, lip curling. Her son ought to be executed for sheer bad taste.

"Get him standing," she ordered, and the young men each slung one of his arms over their shoulders. His head lolled for a moment before he straightened his neck.

"Walk ahead of me. I'll tell you where to turn. There's no one about, Minstrel, so don't try calling for help."

Now, that was funny. He couldn't use his voice any more than he could use his hands. His tongue was still in his head and every finger was still intact in bone and sinew, but he was as mute as Falundir, his hands just as useless.

So much for his career as a Minstrel.

He wanted to ask her about Glenin Feiran. He'd thought she'd be the one taking him to Ambrai. As it happened, Anniyas was wrong. The Octagon Court was the last place in the world he wanted to go. Sarra was there. The Captal—whose name he couldn't quite remember—was there. Bait or bargaining chip, he'd cause them nothing but trouble.

Truly told, he'd been hoping Sarra thought him dead.

He was dragged up a million steps and down miles of corridor, body helpless, brain working ferociously. Too bad Anniyas wasn't talkative like the Feirans. She'd told him where they were going, and while he had a good notion of what she planned to do with him, she hadn't supplied any details.

Confrontation was imminent; he'd seen that much in the glittering of her icy-blue eyes. Was she up to facing a Captal who was also a Scholar and another Captal and a Ladder Rat *and* the First Sword?

They reached an antechamber. Anniyas kicked the door shut. He watched her face, trying to judge her mood. Confident, but grim with it, as if she both anticipated coming events and—no, not *feared* them, exactly. Not dread, either. He narrowed his gaze, trying to read hers. As his body was placed in the center of the round room and the young men backed off with a bow to Anniyas, he finally had it: she considered this whole matter a vast inconvenience.

Now, that really *was* funny. He wished he had air enough in his lungs for the belly laugh this deserved. As it was, he could manage only a throaty chuckle. The wooden-faced porters backed off as if they thought him insane. Anniyas stood over him, hands on plump hips, scowling.

"Enjoying yourself, Minstrel?"

More laughter escaped in a snort, and he grinned up at her. Oh, how he wanted to sing "The Long Sun" again, just to see her prickle up and growl like an old boar sow.

"Get out," she told the guards, who finally wore expressions—of abject relief—as they fled. She waited until the door slammed before continuing, "Cooperate, and I won't kill you. More, I'll even let you live. I trust you comprehend the difference."

Again he nodded, no longer grinning.

"Good."

She mumbled something under her breath. The spell sluiced down his whole body and he pushed himself shakily to his feet. He teetered a bit on the red leather boots; the heels were two and a half inches high. Evidently Anniyas's son was as sensitive about his height as he was about his shoulders.

She stepped into the Ladder Circle. "Now," he heard her whisper. "Tonight."

The Blanking Ward began to gather around him. Saints, how he wanted the use of his hands—but his arms still worked, and the weakening spell was gone. He slipped around behind her, he flung one arm around her just beneath the ribs, trapping her left elbow against her body and forcing the breath from her lungs in a whoosh. With the other arm, he circled her neck and yanked back.

She tried to suck in air, crying out incoherently, almost voicelessly. He jerked again at her head, furious because this move usually produced swift unconsciousness—and sometimes, if he was really angry, a broken neck. But he hadn't even half his usual strength, and all he could do was struggle to cut off her wind.

She was tougher than her softness indicated. He sensed the Blanking Ward gather inside the Ladder. She did it slowly, but she was doing it. He wrenched again, desperately, trying to take her head from her body.

The door opened. A glance over his shoulder showed him a handsome, hideously dressed man. Her son, he told himself distractedly. Had to be. No two people could have such consistently execrable taste in clothes.

Anniyas was gasping, her physical struggle weakening even as the Blanking Ward grew in strength. Another instant and she'd work the Ladder, and they'd be in Ambrai.

"Mother!" the man screamed, and rushed forward.

Most of him came to Ambrai with them.

Parts of him did not.

32

"—but I thought Taig would've told you what the latest arrivals said about the Rising—"

"—four cities and twenty-two towns—"

"—Neele, Isodir, and Domburr Castle in various stages of rebellion—"

"—hundreds dead, probably thousands by now—"

"—all the Council Guard either killed or driven out of Neele—"

"—Ryka Legion marching to Combel or perhaps Longriding—"

"—spread from Isodir to Firrense soon, or so they think—"

"—damned near spontaneous, and not really our doing—"

"—planned for years, of course, but this is out of anyone's control—"

"—must stop before the Council can send Feiran with the Guard—"

"—and the Malerrisi!"

"Yes," Cailet murmured to the remembered voices of that morning and afternoon. "Yes, it will stop. Now. Tonight."

She'd heard them out, this delegation of Mages, *her* Mages, nodding every so often, saying little. Then she sent them away with a single order: *Construct a Ward as Elomar Adennos will show you. I'll follow you soon.*

It was Eleventh of a fine spring afternoon now. At dusk the Ladymoon would rise, full and strong, white-silver and beautiful, and gaze sternly down on Cailet once more. But until that time, she could sit and think.

The place she chose for it had been shown her yesterday by Sarra. It had a grandiose name—Octonary or Octohedral or some such—but Sarra said Grandmother Allynis thought the emphasis on "eight" was a little too coy, so everyone had simply referred to it as the Hall. Audience chamber, banqueting facility, and reception room, its eight white walls— each corner a point of the compass—rose twenty-five feet high. A line of tiny inlaid turquoise octagons marched at eye-level all the way around the chamber. The floor tiles were solid black octagons, grayed by years of dirt and littered with broken glass. Cailet was reminded of the black mirror. Perhaps this was why she had come here.

She sat on a small step where Generations of Ambrai First Daughters had stood on a splendid Cloister carpet of black and turquoise octagons long since burned to ashes and blown away. Here her ancestors in direct line had governed, feasted, laughed, danced, celebrated victories, heard news of failures. Cailet sat with elbows on her knees, hands loosely clasped, and heard only silence.

She had taken off the red tunic of the Council Guard, and wore now only the uniform's black trousers, white shirt, and high black boots. Gorynel Desse's cloak lay beside her, his sword atop it. The hilt gleamed in the sunshine. Gorsha himself was silent within her, as were the others. She was alone, and curiously at peace with it.

At peace, when parts of Lenfell were at war. In the search for Mages and the Rising, thousands had been killed. Somehow, for whatever reason—Sarra would come up with one, she was sure—this had finally sparked the Rising. In four cities and twenty-two major towns, citizens either killed or put to flight the Council Guard, Justices, and every other official of Lenfell's government.

This frantic lack of organization fretted Sarra. To her mind, word should have gone out as planned, and an orderly, efficient Rising taken place. Cailet had hidden her amusement. So the Rising had a structure for rebellion, did it? As if there could be anything tidy about overthrowing a government. Far better for people to decide on their own: their choice, their timing, their fight. What they did, they did for their own reasons. If these coincided with Rising and Mage Guardian reasons, all well and good. If not ... well, Sarra would just have to get used to it. Cailet found it bothered her not at all. The main thing was to get it done. Worry about the whys of it later.

But it must be done very soon. Every defiance—successful or not—was a threat to the Malerrisi. They were in roughly the same position as the Mage Guardians: there weren't enough to spread around putting out brushfires. There weren't enough to mass an attack. There would be no war pitting Mageborn thousands against each other. Not this time.

It would be just Cailet and Anniyas.

Now. Tonight. Here in the Octagon Court.

She felt the crawl of the sun along her arms, the heat fading as afternoon drew slowly toward night. The Mages—*her* Mages—believed she would join them soon. With luck, they wouldn't realize what she was doing until she'd done it.

She'd told Elomar what she meant by a brick wall. She'd shown him how it worked in her own head by having him bounce a gentle probing spell off it. All Mages knew how to do this, he told her, surprised she hadn't known. But this concept of each Mage sealing a Ward atop or beside another Mage's. . . .

"A faulty image," he decided. "Not a brick wall. The stones of the oldest shrines are cut to fit perfectly with the next."

"You can call it a tongue-and-groove or a dovetailed joint for all I care. Just get it done. You did it in Renig with Elin, Keler, and Tiron. Show the others how. Anyone who balks can leave. And make sure everyone understands that once they're in, that's it."

"Meaning?"

"What do you think?" she asked impatiently. "The one admirable thing I've found about the Malerrisi amid everything I now know about them is that by and large they're disciplined. I don't plan to use the Mages or steal their magic or any other damned thing. I'm trying to save their lives. But it's their choice, Elomar. If they're in, they're in. If they choose otherwise, they have my best wishes for continued survival."

"It's yours that concerns us."

"You'll just have to trust me. Elo, you of all people understand what I am. You watched it happen. If you can't believe in Cailet, surely you can believe in at least one of the others. You knew Alin. You knew Tamos Wolvar. Captal Adennos was your cousin. As for Gorsha—you can't say you don't trust *him!*"

"It is *you* I trust," he said quietly, and she had to turn her head away. It echoed what Taig had said. He had trusted her. And died.

Elomar and Riddon Slegin had taken the corpse of the Fifth Lord and thrown it in the river. Cailet hoped it washed up someday on the shore below Malerris Castle—though she would have enjoyed rending it into a great many small pieces with her own bare hands.

Taig would burn tonight. Lusira had told her that in private, acting almost as if Taig had been Cailet's husband and she was now a widow. Cailet wondered what people had been saying. She supposed she was public property now, gossip fodder, and it would only get worse with time.

The moonlight was direct now, lighting the walls of the Octagon Court. The turquoise edging the audience chamber retreated into shadow. She tilted her head back to stare at the sky. Even after she won—she would not allow herself to consider loss—people would go on dying, perhaps for weeks before word reached Neele and Domburr Castle and Isodir and all those twenty-two towns and uncounted villages where people were busily slaughtering each other.

Ladders could probably get Mages to most places fairly soon. But who was to say that they would be believed—or that Anniyas's fall would even matter? Most people knew little about Anniyas and cared even less. She did not directly touch their daily lives. But the local minions of the Council did, and were dying for it: Guards, Justices, Advocates, deputies of all the ministries and bureaucracies that webbed Lenfell almost as extensively as the Ostin Blood.

Cailet shut her eyes. As hard as she tried to think of other things, it all kept coming back to Taig. Lady Lilen had lost three children now, starting with Margit, who'd been Mageborn, dead years ago in an accident that was no accident. Then gentle, fierce Alin. Now Taig.

Soldiers of the Ryka Legion were marching to Combel, or perhaps Longriding. Or perhaps both. Ostinhold was very near Longriding. First Daughter Geria would be in a frenzy. Cailet wondered if her scratches had healed yet.

She also wondered about the infant boy. Elomar told her that Sela Trayos would have died in the birthing no matter what happened. Ladder or no Ladder, magic or no magic, she simply had been worn out by worry and grief and pain. But the baby might have been damaged. When this was over, Cailet would have to find him and discover what harm she'd done. No, it wouldn't show up until his magic did. Time enough then to apologize for almost having stolen it before he was even born.

Magic tingled at the edges of her senses now. She blinked and realized the sky was dark—night had long since fallen. It might be as late as Fourteenth or thereabouts, and she could feel the Ladymoon readying herself for an appearance, like a beautiful woman at her dressing table. Cool, remote, compellingly powerful, and so silent.

Cailet should be getting ready, too. Not that there was anything to be done. She'd sent her Summons on wings of white fire. Anniyas would be here. *Was* here, if the quiver of magic was any indication.

How odd to feel so calm. So ready.

"Gorsha," she murmured as she got to her feet, "I'll need you."

Here, Captal. All of us.

In the silence she heard footsteps—

—and felt every kind of pretentious idiot, for eventually it was Sarra who strode calmly into the Hall, saying in the most everyday voice imaginable: "Oh, *here* you are!"

"You were looking for me?" Not just an idiot, but an imbecile.

Sarra stepped around a scattering of shards on the black tiles. "No, actually I've been searching all Ambrai for someone else who'll fit these, just like the princess with the silver coif." She pushed a pile of clothes into Cailet's arms. "Get dressed. A Captal doesn't meet a Malerrisi in the remains of a Council Guard uniform."

"Sarra, I don't want you here."

"Too bad. The others cobbled these together for you. Telo is handy with a needle, he altered them to fit—more or less. If you hadn't been so damned silent and forbidding earlier, they would've given these to you then and you could've said a proper thanks." She reached into a pocket and came up with two small silver objects. "Gavirin Bekke started it off by giving Telo his Candle for you. The Sparrow is Imilial Gorrst's."

As Cailet stroked the material of the tunic, from the folds of the shirt slithered a length of shiny gray silk. She caught it before it hit the floor.

Sarra was picking at the clasp of the Sparrow with her fingernails. "The sash ought to be cloth-of-silver, of course, but Miram's scarf was the closest they could come to it. Well? What are you waiting for? Put it on so I can fasten the collar pins."

She took off her white Council Guard shirt. The breeze was chilly on her bare breasts. "Then will you go?"

"Not until I have Collan back safe."

Damn Sarra's instincts. Damn her Warded magic that allowed her to feel things without being able to do anything about them.

"I can't protect you." Cailet thrust her arms into black sleeves. The shirt was raw silk, dull and soft, with a texture nearly that of thin suede. "I don't have power enough or magic enough to protect us and him, too."

"Never mind about that. Just take me with you to Ryka Court."

So her instincts weren't infallible after all. Which did Cailet precisely no good at all. If going to Ryka Court had still been her aim, she could simply have walked into the Ladder and left Sarra behind. But Anniyas would be coming here, to the Octagon Court, and for all Cailet knew she'd already arrived.

"Go. Please." Pulling the tunic over her head, she buttoned it at either side, hipbones to upper ribs.

"Don't forget the sword."

"I won't be needing it."

"Of course you will. Put it on."

"No." Miram's pale gray scarf wrapped twice around her waist, six inches of fringe hanging to mid-thigh.

"Then I'll carry it for you." One dimple flashed in a

mocking little smile. "Just like the brave knight and her faithful squire."

"Damn it, Sarra, this isn't a bedtime story or a Bardic ballad!"

"But you know very well someone will write one someday. If we're lucky, it'll sound much better than it lived." She bent to heft the sword. "Good thing we're both stronger than we look. This thing must weigh fifteen pounds."

Cursing under her breath, Cailet watched Sarra buckle Gorsha's belt around her hips. "Sarra, *leave!* I'm begging you!"

Shaking her head, she approached with the two pins in hand. The Sparrow went on the right collar-point, the Candle on the left. "An Ambrai never begs," she said as she worked. "Nor does a Captal. I'm coming with you, and that's the end of it. You need me." Black eyes glittered almost feverishly in a pallid face, but the hand that reached to smooth Cailet's hair was absolutely steady.

She batted the caress away. "You're a Mageborn who can't work magic. You're a liability. I can't protect you. I can't do what I must if I'm worrying about you."

"You don't have to worry about me *or* protect me. They can't sense me. They won't even know I'm there. That makes me an asset, not a liability." She picked up Gorsha's black cloak. "If you don't mind, I'll wear this. It's night where we're going."

Cailet grabbed her sister's shoulders and shook her. "We're not going anywhere! Anniyas is coming *here!* I used the Bequest to find her and I Summoned her! She's coming with the moonrise—*here*, Sarra, to Ambrai!"

Sarra broke her hold, tossed her hair from her eyes, and smiled. *Smiled.* "So much the better. No one alive knows the Octagon Court better than I."

"Don't you understand? She's coming for *me!*"

"And you'll let her find you." She nodded slowly, no longer smiling. "Do what you must. I'll see to Collan. She'll bring him with her, you know."

"And if she does? You're *nothing* to Anniyas—but you're *everything* to me. She'll use you and Col against me—"

"Do you think I can stand by and do nothing? Especially when it's you and Collan? He means even less to her than I do. It's you she wants. The Captal. You're right, I'm a Mageborn without magic, and I'll curse Gorynel Desse until

I die for the Wards that make me no use to you that way. But I can watch for a chance to get Collan free."

"Sarra—"

"And then it'll be just you and Anniyas. Believe me, Cailet, I'd stop you if I could. But I can't. So let me do this one thing that I *can* do."

Serenity was gone. Resignation took its place—a very different feeling, and one she didn't like. "I hope stupidity doesn't run in the family," Cailet muttered, and Sarra smiled again.

"No, just possessiveness. You're mine, and Collan's mine. We Ambrais defend what's ours."

"The way Lady Allynis did?" Cailet asked bleakly, gesturing to the ruin around them. "To the death, if necessary?"

"The way Glenin will," Sarra replied somberly. "It's not Anniyas who's the real danger, Cai."

Cailet made herself shrug. "One Malerrisi at a time. All right, find a place to hide. Wait as long as you have to for your best chance. She won't kill him while she can still bargain with him, or hurt me with him." She regretted the flinch in her sister's eyes, but continued adamantly, "Whatever happens, don't interfere. When you have Col, get out of here as fast as you can. Promise, Sarra, or I swear I'll spell you to sleep right here and now."

"No, you won't."

"Try me."

After a moment, Sarra nodded. "I promise."

Cailet checked the sword at Sarra's hip, making sure it would pull smoothly free of the scabbard, and felt a subtle tingling of magic on her fingertips. One day she'd have to get Collan to sing her every ballad he knew about the Fifty Swords. St. Caitiri was rumored to have made them in consultation with St. Delilah—and, some said, Steen Swordsworn—

Sarra grabbed her arm as a horrible keening echoed through the Octagon Court, one long shriek piercing enough to shiver the glass on the floor.

"Cailet—?" Sarra whispered. "It sounds like—"

Like a madwoman, like a mortally wounded animal, like a Wraithenbeast.

Cailet glanced up at the sky. Deepest starlit black, Ladymoon ascending but not yet in sight. But she knew who it must be.

Anniyas.

The screams ended. The sisters stared at each other, too stunned even to breathe.

"MAGE CAPTAL!" cried a woman's voice, shredded with grief. *"I HAVE THE MINSTREL! SHOW YOURSELF, OR HE DIES!"*

Cailet touched Sarra's cheek, murmuring, "Miryenne protect you," before she ran the length of the audience chamber. In the corridor she slowed, calming breath and heartbeat and magic as best she could. She was Mage Captal. She would meet the Malerrisi with outward calm and inward power.

And after she had dealt with Anniyas, she would deal with Glenin. Now. Tonight. She knew it, not the way Sarra knew things by instinct, but the way Mage knew Malerrisi.

And perhaps the way Blood knew Blood.

33

The air was thick and vile, making him want to spit out its taste. He shoved Anniyas aside, gaze darting wildly. Whiteness—cold snowy marble closing in on him—for a sickening instant he thought he was back in the white box. But these walls curved. It was a cylinder he stood in, eight feet wide and stretching up, up, all the way to the clear night sky.

He turned. Blood stained the bright white walls. Sprawled on the floor nearly at his feet was what used to be a man. The heart still beat weakly, pumping red liquid to parts no longer attached.

He backed away. Out. He wanted out. Now.

He stumbled over Anniyas, who had collapsed on the floor, gasping, clutching at her bruised throat. He figured he had about a minute before she caught her breath and discovered her son, another minute or two while she reacted. In that time he could be long gone—if only his legs would work. The sore on his foot throbbed hotly, toes crammed together in the red leather boots, and for all the use that leg was to him he might have lost it at mid-thigh, like the man on the floor. Hobbling from the whiteness, he found himself in a broad, smoke-stained hall just as Anniyas began to scream.

Eight corridors met here. The cylinder was the well of a double staircase. *Damn—she got us to Ambrai after all.* Which way should he go to escape her? He could hear nothing but her savage grief, see nothing but vast expanses of marble and burned debris and soot. The stairs—? But the palace was gigantic, and while he could probably hide in its rooms and halls for days, he wanted *out.* He chose a direction at random and started limping.

He'd gone only ten steps before his foot seemed to catch on fire. A groan strangled him, his knees buckled, and behind him Anniyas shouted her challenge to the Mage Captal.

He'd failed. He hadn't kept her from coming to Ambrai, and he was still in her spellbound clutches, and he couldn't even cry warning. He went down hard on the floor, feeble hands unable to break his fall. The madness the white box had been unable to accomplish, despair and failure nearly did.

"Mage Captal! Come to me now or he dies!"

He smelled her, smelled the blood of her son. He couldn't move. Couldn't speak. Could only grovel on his useless hands and bruised knees like a child. His head hung and it took everything he had to raise it and watch for the blonde girl, the Captal, whose name he couldn't remember. Watch her come here, come for him, come to die.

Rage ignited his blood with futile strength. The spell was too powerful; his muscles trembled with need, but he couldn't move. He heard Anniyas's short breaths, his own panting gasps. Then footsteps, calm and unhurried. Yet beneath the other sounds, Minstrel's hearing gave him the quick whisper of other feet, bare and nearly silent on the cold marble.

"Mage Captal!"

"Here," said a quiet, proud voice.

From the corner of his eye he glimpsed a tall, slim girl with a cap of shining white-blonde hair, clad in black with silvery silk around her narrow waist. He knew her. But he didn't know her name.

"Free him," she commanded.

Anniyas walked by, shaking her head. "*You* do it. Prove that you're Captal."

"And while I'm busy unraveling your spell, you'll weave another over me? I don't think so, First Councillor."

"First *Lord*," Anniyas corrected coldly.

A brow quivered. She nodded. "Of course. I should have guessed long ago."

Anniyas gave a snort of amusement. "How long is 'long ago' to someone your age, girl? A year or two?"

"You will address me as Captal. And you of all people should know that a Captal's remembrances extend far beyond her own lifetime. Don't yours?"

He scarcely noticed the mockery. An exquisite coolness began to seep through him—no, not exactly *through,* like wine in his blood, but across his skin beneath the ugly clothes—a second skin between the angry heat of Anniyas's Ward and the impotent fury of his own straining muscles.

"My heritage as First Lord surpasses your own, *Captal*," said Anniyas, matching the scorn. "Where you rule a few Mages—how many now, twenty?—*I* rule all Lenfell."

"Ah. And how *are* things in Neele, First Lord? Domburr Castle? Renig?"

Slowly, subtly, the clean coolness spread, soothing his hurts. He felt Anniyas's magic like a suffocating cloak that he could now throw off anytime he pleased. Beneath, the Captal's spell slid as soft as garments of silk.

"Those places should have taken their lesson from Ambrai long ago. This morning an example was made of Ostinhold."

"You're lying."

"Am I? You won't live long enough to find out one way or the other. Talking of lies and Ostins, I understand Taig tried to pass himself off as Captal. Did the late unlamented Fifth Lord chastise him properly before you killed him?"

"You're misinformed. Doriaz was his own executioner." She hesitated. "And Taig's," she added softly, sorrowfully.

Taig? Dead? Ah, poor kitten. . . . He raised his head and tried to catch the girl's eye. She paid him no attention. Once more he heard the nearly inaudible murmur of bare feet on marble, and shifted his body under the heat of the Ward. No more pain, not even in his foot. But his hands, his fingers . . . useless still, braced flat on the floor and not even feeling it.

"Doriaz always did enjoy a good murder," Anniyas remarked. "I hope his own was the best he ever committed."

A fat sphere like a dying red sun coalesced at her left elbow. Its bloody glow was instantly countered by a matching sphere, this one purest white shot through with silvered rainbows. "We can be civilized or barbaric about this, Captal. Strict rules of magic, or anything goes. Myself, I prefer the latter. I haven't used my magic in years—not even in secret. The last time I killed with it was ... oh, yes. That fool of a Grand Duke of Domburron. I'd forgotten how much I missed it. But no one will know about me until only Malerrisi exist in this world, and I lead them against the Wraithenbeasts."

So she was right about that, he thought, not sure who "she" was.

"*I* will lead them," Anniyas went on. "Not that toad of a First Lord squatting on his ass at Malerris Castle."

"How difficult for you," the girl said with elaborate sympathy. "Knowing they bow to him and not you."

"Oh, *he* knows who wields the real power. Not much longer, of course. This year I'll release and then destroy those disgusting creatures, then take my rightful place as who I truly am. During Rosebloom, I think. My Birthingday gift to myself. But first you're going to give me a little practice in magic that kills. Hardly a fair contest. You're bound by that tiresome Mage Guardian ethic, aren't you? Magic only to defend, never to attack."

"That's the theory."

He gritted his teeth. *So make an exception!*

As if in answer, the silver rainbows sparkling within the white Mage Globe began to pulse like a heartbeat, with just a tinge of scarlet.

"Come now," Anniyas said. "You're supposed to be the Capital. Impress me."

"Let him go," she insisted. "This is between us, no one else."

"My son was a beautiful young man," Anniyas murmured. "I loved him deeply, and he loved me. I'm in no mood to be civilized."

The blood-colored sphere throbbed faster and faster, an almost hypnotic rhythm that caught and sped his own heartbeat before he dragged his gaze away and fixed it on Anniyas. She was rocking lightly back and forth, heel to toe in her white velvet shoes, forefingers rapidly rubbing thumbs at her sides. He waited until he had the timing right—and when she rocked back he surged to his feet, intending to use her own forward motion to propel her off balance and into the vibrating crimson Globe.

"Collan! *No!*"

He heard Sarra's voice at the very instant he slammed into the solid stone wall of Anniyas's personal Ward and fell back in an awkward heap. She stumbled a step, but neither fell nor lost control of the sphere.

"Don't try that again," she said without looking at him.

He felt like laughing aloud. He knew his name again. Collan. The patchwork Wards blew away like cobwebs, and he remembered. Sarra had given him back his name, and his memories with it. And there she was, the fool girl, running from the shadows toward him—clad in an ill-fitting motley of stolen clothes. Once this was all over he'd have to teach her how to dress. He'd refuse to be seen with her otherwise, husband or no husband—

Anniyas began to turn toward her. The Captal—Cailet—gestured frantically and the white Globe collided with the crimson in a shower of rainbow sparks.

Eyes bruised by the light, Collan brought his hands up to rub tears away.

His hands.

The red sphere was intact. The white sphere had vanished. Cailet was crying out in agony.

But Anniyas's magic no longer touched him.

"Collan! Catch!"

Instinct brought his hands up—hands that moved and worked and grasped the cool steel of a sword. Gorynel Desse's sword. One of the Fifty, with magic all its own—even in hands not Mageborn. *His* hands, strong fingers instantly reversing his grip so the blade lifted, shining bright red. His name, his memory, now his hands and a sword—and he found as he raised it that she had also given him back his voice.

"Sarra! Cailet! *Down!*"

He went for the Mage Globe. He knew he wasn't supposed to feel anything from the sword; there was no magic in him. But when the blade smote and shattered the shimmering crimson sphere, he felt the shock of the explosion all the way to his spine. Eyes dazzled half-blind, he cursed as fire licked up the steel, up his hands, his arms, his shoulders, his face—a million pinpricks of searing heat that he was sure burned the clothes off his body and the hair off his scalp. It was the Pain Stake multiplied a thousandfold.

But it was magic, only magic, not real—

Hell if it wasn't! A bellow of pain left his throat as flames raced through him, igniting every nerve. For somebody who hadn't used magic in years, she hadn't forgotten a thing. The sword trembled in scorched hands, but he hung on, determined to drive it first through Anniyas's Wards and then through Anniyas.

Yet as suddenly as the burning began, it ceased. He blinked his eyes free of stinging tears in time to see the sword flicker redly a moment more, then reflect only the misted star-strewn sky and the pure silver of the Ladymoon.

Anniyas was still on her feet, staring skyward. Paralyzed.

Collan started for her. Cailet, half-risen from her defensive huddle on the stones, called out, "No! Don't touch her!"

He wanted blood. So did the sword. But the Captal commanded and he obeyed. Sarra was suddenly at his side, pressing herself against him. He held her close with his free arm and bent his head, burying his lips in her hair. Cailet joined them, clutching Sarra's hand. Together they watched Anniyas.

She worked no magic. She was protected by no Wards. She stood transfixed, head thrown back, gray hair loose of its pins and cascading down her back. From the cool white sphere of the moon floated tendrils of mist. Delicate, descending, spreading across the sky like an opalescent veil, drifting down to hover above the Octagon Court, gathering into a fine silk curtain that rippled gently with a chiming of silvery bells.

"Wraiths. . . ."

Collan heard Cailet's awed whisper and nodded. Sarra slipped an arm around his waist; he held her closer still, wishing he could do the same for Cailet. Especially when she let go of Sarra's hand and took a step forward, then another.

Anniyas screamed as the Wraiths drew nearer. Trembling, Cailet backed away.

"Th–they've come for her," she breathed.

"Those she killed?" Sarra spoke so softly that Collan barely heard.

"Those who . . . who did her killing for her."

Unquiet spirits, Col thought; vengeful souls. Perhaps Scraller was among them. He rather hoped so.

Suddenly the First Lord fisted her upraised hands in defiance. "How *dare* you presume to judge the Warden of the Loom! Go back to the Dead White Forest and be damned! The Capital is mine—"

She broke off with a shriek as part of the filmy, undulating curtain slipped free of the rest: "*Garon—!*" As the name left her lips, a spasm wracked her body and she crumpled to the stones of the Octagon Court.

Cailet was the first to approach her, warily at first, then moving with quiet confidence. She knelt, fingered the pulse at the neck, and sighed. Her silver-gilt hair glinted with the fragile rainbows of the Wraithen assemblage as she glanced up.

"She's yours now."

The mists withdrew, back to the moonlight, and vanished.

34

Behind her, Cailet heard Collan say, "That's it, then." For him and Sarra, this was true. Convincing them might take a bit of doing, though.

Turning, she wondered if they looked as changed to each other as they did to her. Sarra was still Sarra, only more so: more beautiful, more powerful, more vigorously alive than ever. As for Collan—Saints, he looked like a brass trinket buffed and polished in hopes that someone would mistake him for gold. But never had the true gold of him shone more brightly. No one would ever mistake him for a mere Minstrel again. Pure and untarnishable, he was; surely Sarra could see it too, as surely as he could see the love in her eyes.

Cailet watched, smiling, as the sword clattered to the floor and he took Sarra's face in his hands. *Maybe I won't have to write the truth in five-foot letters and shove it under their noses after all.*

"Collan—"

"Shut up," he said roughly. "If I don't say this now, I may never get the chance again. I can put more feeling into other people's love songs than any Minstrel alive. And it's all faked. That's the way I wanted it. I swore I'd never let any woman make those songs real for me. But you have. I don't know how, but you did."

Not bad, Cailet thought, nodding approval. *Come on, Sarra. Your turn.*

Both dimples appeared. "And when do I get to hear these songs, then?"

Oh now really*! You can do better than that!*

But Col seemed to find nothing wrong with this as a declaration. He grinned down at Sarra. "With or without lute? I add—modestly—that I do my best work without."

"Frees up the Minstrel's famous hands," Sarra agreed, almost purring.

"Lady," he murmured, "I'm going to make a song out of *you.*"

Cailet began to count. She marveled at their stamina—then worried about asphyxiation. Who stopped kissing whom was a matter of conjecture, but Col was the first to find his voice. Glancing over at Cailet, he drawled, "Y'know, I seem to say this a lot, but—can we *please* get the hell out of here now?"

Sarra blinked, needing a moment to remember where "here" was. Then she blushed to the roots of her hair. Cailet laughed at her.

"Get out of here. I'll follow in a little while."

"Not a chance! We all go now, or we all stay!"

"Stay?" Col echoed. "Forget it. Leave the bodies for the carrion crows."

"That's not what I meant!" Sarra shook herself free of his embrace. "Glenin's coming and Cailet means to face her alone!"

The flash in his blue eyes was of anger, but the flinch in his body was of fear. To hide it, he bent and picked up the sword. But Cailet had seen. Rage shook her. Collan, afraid? Glenin had done things to him—things she'd pay for. Now. Tonight.

Straightening up, he slid the naked blade through his belt. "If she's coming, we're leaving."

With a sigh, Cailet nodded. And so relieved were they— and so stunned still by each other—that neither thought to question the ease of her acquiescence.

Col slung a companionable arm around her shoulders, keeping Sarra close on his other side, as they walked the empty halls to the garden doors. Cailet smiled at the subtle human magic of their happiness. Though whatever spell love might cast, it hadn't dulled her sister's wits any.

"We've got over fifty Mages here, Caisha, and if the Bard Hall Ladder still works I think some of them should use it to Longriding, and then go see if anything's wrong at Ostinhold."

"Warrior Mages, if you've got any to hand," Collan said at once.

"Several. Imi Gorrst can take charge of them."

"Nobody better for it," he agreed. "But make sure a few have good strong Folding spells, so they'll get to Ostinhold fast."

"Hmm. I hadn't thought of that, but you're right."

Cailet wondered if they heard how they sparked ideas off each other, how well they worked together. Even their steps were matched, boots crunching the gravel path in perfect time as Sarra lengthened her strides and Col shortened his. She banished the smile from her face when Collan glanced at her.

"I think she was lying to goad you, Cai."

She nodded. "So do I. It's twenty-five days' hard march from Renig to Ostinhold, over some rough country."

"There was a bad storm, too," Sarra added. "We got caught in it. That would slow them down. But Lady Lilen will need help, and soon."

"She'll have it. We should try to get people to Neele and Isodir as well, and the bigger towns where there's been fighting."

They angled across the weed-wild lawn toward the wallside copse where they'd climbed trees to get in—when? Yesterday? Day before? She couldn't quite recall, and it didn't really matter. What counted was now. Tonight. She glanced involuntarily up at the bright white Ladymoon.

"Of course," Sarra said. "But first something ought to be done about all these damned Malerrisi. There aren't enough Mages to find them, and frankly I wouldn't know how to begin looking."

"Without a First Lord," Collan pointed out, "they have no one to tell them what to do."

"Of course!" She smiled dazzlingly. "If we're lucky, they'll head back to Seinshir, whimpering the whole way!"

Cailet almost laughed. So much for love blinding a person to all else.

"That's more luck than I've had in quite a while," Collan observed dryly.

"You're free, aren't you?" Sarra retorted.

They reached the copse, and it was as perfect for Cailet's purposes as she remembered. "Can we rest a minute? I don't know about you, but I'm exhausted. And it's a long walk back." She sat on a grassy hillock under a tree.

"Back where? The Academy? Bard Hall?" Col pulled the sword from his belt, put his spine against the same tree, and slid down it, swordtip digging into the earth between the ridiculous red leather boots.

Sarra knelt beside him. "No, some houses downriver. Crowded," she added with a grimace half-lost in the dusk, with the trees shadowing the moonlight.

"Cozy," Cailet amended. "Just like Ostinhold when everyone comes for Lady Lilen's Birthingday. Oh, look—Saint's Spark! Quick, make a wish!"

Their faces tilted upward as she pointed to the sky. Collan got as far as "Where? I don't—" before sliding the rest of the way down the smooth tree trunk, fast asleep. Cailet snatched up the sword before he could endanger anything vital to her sister's future happiness and progeny.

Sarra tipped sideways a moment later; Cailet caught her and eased her down so she wouldn't bruise herself. Pulling her sister closer to the Minstrel, she arranged them side-by-side with Sarra's golden head on Collan's shoulder. Then she tugged Desse's black cloak free and draped it over them both.

Standing, stretching, sighing for the furious scold she'd receive later for her trick, she gazed for a time at Gorsha's sword. No, better not. She'd been telling herself that she didn't intend to kill—but the sword, spelled to work the will of the Mageborn who wielded it, would know if she lied.

Still, she couldn't help but touch it. Hold it. Feel it resonate with power ready to do her bidding. Too much temptation. She left it within Col's reach, and paused to smile at the sleepers.

"I'm sorry," she murmured. "But I love you both, so much."

Boots silent in the tall, thick grass, she ran back to the Octagon Court to meet her other sister and finish it.

35

From Anniyas's empty office at Ryka Court, Glenin used the velvet Ladder to what had been her own room when a child. The Double Spiral was too obvious. Besides, she would wait while Anniyas wore the new Captal down, tiring her out. Glenin's own task would be that much easier. How to get Anniyas out of the way presented a problem, but doubtless something would occur to her.

As she tested the depths of night for magic, her wary senses were buffeted by things she had never felt before. Wild, frightened, ferocious things, not magic but some sort of energy that mimicked magic. Her hands went protectively to her belly. Her son was serenely undisturbed, sleeping in her dark warmth.

He ought to be born in this palace, she thought as she picked her way to the outer corridor. A Lord of Ambrai, scion of a family that scandalized Lenfell by the favors lavished on its sons. Easy enough to see why: the Ambrai women were not great breeders. Three children was the most any had managed in the last fifteen Generations. Some had none at all. Yet somehow the line had survived, each First Daughter producing a First Daughter all the way back to the Fifth Census. Glenin had sacrificed her own to the dictates of the Lords of Malerris—to Anniyas, with her tender, hypocritical words of comfort—but she was still young. A daughter next time, she promised herself. Though she couldn't imagine loving any child as passionately as she loved this son.

She took a back stair to the ground floor. It was deepest night, the Ladymoon high over the Octagon Court, and so quiet she fancied she could hear the baby's heartbeat. Imagination also whispered how dreamlike this was, how much the stuff of mysterious magic. This idiocy she scornfully dismissed. Dreams and undisciplined imaginings were for fools and cowards who didn't know how to make life do what they wanted it to.

She made her way through the palace, intent on keeping

her magic under tight control. Surprise was one of her most
potent weapons. Neither Anniyas nor the new Captal knew
she was coming. She was, in effect, a walking secret. Nothing more powerful, nothing more lovely, than a secret, she
told herself as she passed silently along the mostly roofless
halls toward the Double Spiral—where she sensed magic as
a veteran sailor senses dangerous rocks through fog.

Moonlight washed Anniyas with curious kindness, smoothing the marks of age on her face, turning to carved silver the
waving lengths of her unbound hair. But nothing could soften
the horror in her staring, dead blue eyes.

Glenin gazed down at the corpse for a long time, puzzled
by what she felt. Certainly not sorrow or pity. Neither was
there satisfaction, nor the sense of rightness and completion
that justice done engendered. Sorting emotions, she decided
that what she really felt was cheated.

Tradition demanded trial by magical combat, the First
Lord answering the challenge of a younger Malerrisi—
perhaps stronger, perhaps not. Anniyas claimed she'd dealt
with several in her youth, so thoroughly that no one had
sought her place in over thirty years. Glenin had planned to
wait until her son was born and she had her full strength
back. But there would be no challenge to combat now. The
Captal had cheated her of Anniyas's death.

Still, she supposed she ought to be grateful: her son was
safe from his grandmother. But the Captal had meddled for
the last time in Malerrisi affairs. Glenin would prove herself
worthy of succeeding Anniyas as First Lord by killing the
Captal instead.

Strange, though—the blood on Anniyas's hands, but not a
single wound on her body. Glenin knew better than to hope
it was the Captal's blood. Perhaps it was the Minstrel's? She
moved silently to the Double Spiral, folding the velvet Ladder over her arm.

The smell of blood was strong. Patterns of dark smoke
stained the white marble interior—but even as she peered
within they changed. Not smoke. Smoke didn't smell like
this, or trickle slowly down a wall.

Glenin backed away from what was on the floor. Garon
had often asked to be taken through a Ladder. It seemed his
mother had finally granted his wish.

"I know you're here, Glenin."

She whirled. A girl's voice, light and calm, echoed

through deserted moonlit corridors with an easy authority that astonished her.

"Must you be guided, or is your magic strong enough to find me?"

Had there been any mockery in the words, she would have shouted back in defiance. But it was a simple question, and she decided to answer it just as simply. She walked with unerring steps to the Hall and swung open heavy oaken doors only slightly charred by long-ago fires.

Light poured through the empty ceiling, white rivers of it banked by empty stone traceries. The girl stood in Glenin's place at the top of the Hall, fair hair and silvery sash gleaming. At two hundred feet, Glenin could not see her face clearly. She paced forward, thin shoes crunching bits of fallen windows.

Blonde hair shifted and shimmered with her nod. "You found me."

"And your handiwork," Glenin replied.

"Not mine." She hesitated. "I regret the death of your husband."

"I'm sure you will." Halting halfway across the room, she ordered, "Come down from there. This place is mine by right of inheritance. Only Ambrais stand where you're standing now."

The girl smiled slightly, but said nothing. And didn't move.

"I told you to—"

"I heard you."

She lit a Mage Globe: opalescent as her smoke–pearl earrings, though paler and tinged with green. The color pleased her. Reddish hues would mean anger barely controlled; blues were the shades of intense emotion. Green meant power.

No sphere answered her unspoken challenge.

"I'm unWarded," the girl said. "I'm not afraid of you, Glenin."

"Don't you know who I am?"

"Yes. I know. But I should introduce myself," she said quite seriously. "We almost met once. Glenin Ambrai—"

"Feiran."

"Ambrai. First Daughter of Maichen."

"Feiran," she said again, "First Daughter of Auvry."

A slight sigh. "Is that truly how you name yourself in

your deepest heart? Don't you remember who you were when you lived here?"

"Is there some point to this?" Glenin asked impatiently.

"Not that you're willing to see—not yet, anyhow. My name is Cailet."

"Are you slaveborn, then, to have no family Name?"

"If I told you, you wouldn't believe it."

"No more than I believe you're the new Captal."

"Anniyas asked for proof, too."

"Which you'll now claim you provided by killing her."

"No. She was her own death. Glenin, please listen to me. I don't want the same to happen to you."

Taking another step, Glenin cried out softly and bent as if a shard pierced her shoe. In that moment she sent the thinnest stab of magic at the girl, and had the satisfaction of hearing her gasp. Wards coalesced, too late to deflect the probe entirely, yet strong and subtle enough to transform its original crippling strength into relative harmlessness.

Impressed in spite of herself, Glenin quickly absorbed the backlash and sorted its meanings as Golonet Doriaz had taught her. What she gleaned came not in words, but in emotions—a thing she'd never encountered before. This Cailet might have a control of her thoughts and her magic uncommon in someone twice her age, but her feelings were close to the surface and as vulnerable as any adolescent girl's. Even as Glenin cataloged emotions and the images attached to them, she began to alter her strategy in light of new information.

Grief: Taig Ostin sprawled on the stairs, dying.

Joy: Sarra Liwellan and—the Minstrel? Holy Saints, what a pairing!

Loss: a whole gallery of dead; Glenin recognized only Gorynel Desse.

Pity: for Anniyas? And Garon? And—Glenin herself?

Fear: Ostinhold.

Pain—

Glenin caught her breath. "How do you know my mother's face?"

The girl backed up a pace. "Your mother?" she said, and her voice shook slightly with her rapid heartbeats.

"She was dead before you were born—but you hold her face in your mind—" She advanced, careless of the splintered black floor. "Who *are* you?"

"Mage Captal."

"Tell me your Name!"

Nearer now—and all at once the black eyes in a slender face crowned by cropped gold hair belonged to another face, one of heart-catching beauty and terrible pride. Beauty had been lost to sharper angles, longer bones; pride remained. She knew this face, last seen over eighteen years ago.

Glenin struggled to breathe. "You *can't* be an Ambrai!"

The girl—Cailet—Mage Captal—said quietly, "I am our mother's daughter. I have as much right here as you do."

Glenin stopped twenty feet from her. *Then—she didn't die here, the way Father said she did. He lied—no, he couldn't have lied—but if* she *survived—*

"Sarra!"

36

"Sarra," Cailet confirmed.

"How?" Glenin cried. "I saw Sarra more than once—I never—"

"Wards. Gorynel Desse. But I had none set on me." She shrugged. "Not the same type, anyway."

"Impossible. You can't be—"

"I am. Perhaps I wanted you to know. Don't you see, Glenin, it changes everything." *Doesn't it?*

"It changes nothing!"

"It's why we're here, why this had to happen! You and Sarra and I—Glenin, think what we could be together! Mage and Malerrisi, working for Lenfell, not against each other, with Sarra to show us where and how we're needed—she knows those things, she's brilliant—with her to help us, we could—"

Glenin laughed aloud. Cailet flinched. But the words kept tumbling out, without order or caution, with only a desperate need to make her understand.

"Listen to me, Glenin, please! What we could be, we three together—all the power Lenfell needs—the kind of power you've been taught to want, it's what killed Anniyas!

Wraiths came, people she'd used, whose souls she'd killed long before their bodies died—"

"Oh, dear. Next you're going to tell me she shuddered in terror before them, and dread of their vengeance—what, stopped her heart? Believe me, little sister, she didn't have one."

"She called one of them by name. She called out 'Garon' and died."

A brow arched in genuine surprise. "So he came for her, too? Well, well."

"Glenin! Don't you understand? What you want to be will kill you!"

"We all die eventually."

Cailet stepped down to the black floor, boot heels echoing. Had Glenin been barefoot, they would have been of a height. "Do you want to wait for 'eventually' while every Malerrisi with pretensions to power sharpens her magic like a knife to stick in your back? It doesn't have to be that way! You and Sarra and I together—"

"—will form a happy little family of Mageborns, and right all the wrongs in the world?"

She barely heard the jeering voice. She understood Gorsha now. The vague intimations of schemes within schemes came clear. *Yes!* she wanted to tell Glenin. *We three, Mageborn Ambrais, we could heal the magic—with me leading the Mages and you the Malerrisi, it would all be over and there'd be no more threat of war or Wraithenbeasts or anything to harm Lenfell ever again!*

"Do you expect me to experience a revelation? Grovel before you with the shame of my mistakes, and beg you to make a proper little Mage Guardian of me?" Glenin smiled kindly. "Little sister, you know nothing about real power."

"You could do so much—"

"I intend to. And so will you. You're right about one thing—knowing who you and Sarra are changes my plans."

"H–how do you mean?"

"You're very young—almost eighteen, I take it? The Ambrai women have few children, as a rule, but if we take very good care of you we'll probably get at least two out of you. And the same from Sarra."

Horrified, Cailet retreated. Glenin calmly mounted the step and turned. They watched each other across the black tiled floor patterned in octagons, the Blood Sigil of the Name that had birthed them.

"There, that's better. Mind your manners, Cailet. Even a Captal bows to the First Daughter of her Name."

Gorsha, you were wrong.

Are you giving up so soon?

Look at her, damn you! She's theirs, she'll never—

"Well?" Glenin prompted. "Ambrai to Ambrai, little sister."

Woodenly, without hope, Cailet replied, "You said your Name is Feiran."

"I could call myself anything I liked, and the Octagon Court would still be mine." She pushed her cloak over one shoulder, thin white silk tunic rippling in the night breeze. "I'll let your and Sarra's brats have Grandmother's holy Name, how's that for graciousness? By the way, how *is* Sarra? Delirious with joy at having her Minstrel back, and dreaming of Miramili's Bells? Well, probably not. The Saintly Virgin must save herself for a loftier bed—though not exactly the way she always planned it. I wish I could tell her she'll be missing something truly extraordinary by missing Collan Rosvenir, but honesty compels me to admit that he wasn't much."

"He never touched you!"

"Can you be sure? And how would you know anything about it, anyway? Or did Taig Ostin fulfill your girlish dreams before he died?"

"You—" She choked back the rest.

"Ah. I thought not."

"You can't hurt me, Glenin, not with Collan or Sarra or Taig." But she set her Wards in stone all the same.

"Pain doesn't particularly interest me. At best, it's only a corollary of fear. Besides, I wouldn't damage you now, dear, you're far too valuable."

"You can't frighten me, either."

"Truly told?"

The Mage Globe glistened, greenish light smearing the floor and the shadows and Glenin's beautiful smiling face. It grew, expanding from fist-size to a six-foot sphere. Cailet felt tiny lances of magic spring from it, hurled against her Wards. Pinpricks. But her skin began to crawl as if the points had pierced through to her body—for within the Globe shadows took on human form.

Collan, hands bound by white silk to a silver pole, long body writhing in agony.

Sarra, wrists and ankles bound by white silk, swollen body writhing in childbirth.

Herself, unbound, naked body writhing in ecstasy under some faceless man who thrust into her again and again and again—

Revulsion welled like acid in her throat.

"Hmm," Glenin said musingly. "Perhaps a few variations—"

Collan, gelded, his tongue cut out, his fingers sliced open, every bone shattered. Cailet held the bloody knife.

Sarra, repeatedly raped. Cailet stood watching, smiling as her breasts were fondled by a man standing behind her.

He looked like Taig.

Gorsha! Help me!

Silence.

Glenin was smiling. "So. That's where it starts. I should've guessed. You're very young."

Memories and knowledge, spells and Wards, all those things were of their bequeathing—but her feelings were her own. And they betrayed her. The starry sky throbbed with the power of her hate and the silver moonlight receded into green shadows, chased there by terror. A hollow opened and was filled, only to empty again and overflow again. Over and over the images and the feelings poured into her and drained away until she began to fear the hollowness more than she feared the horror of what she saw and what she felt and what she did.

At length, she was left empty just long enough to make her crave to be filled. Then slender, elegant fingers of magic began to fondle her mind.

37

"Glenin! What are you *doing* to her?"

"Stay out of this, Father. I won't kill her. She's far too valuable. But I *will* break her, the way you should've broken Rosvenir."

Respite. An end. Until it began again.

"Not her, Glenin. Not your own sister!"

"So. You heard it all—or enough, anyway. This old place does echo."

Blind. Mute. Spasms skittering through every muscle. Pain. Pleasure?

"I won't allow you to do this. It's wrong."

"You must've seen Anniyas, too—and what's left of poor Garon. Don't look at me that way, Father. I'm not insane. They're dead, and we're alive—and the Mage Captal is mine."

Pain/pleasure—was there any difference?

"She's an Ambrai. Your own Blood! You can't break her and then use her—"

"I'll do as I please with her, and Sarra, too!"

Pleasure was gone. She wanted it never to come back, never. Pain lingered. This she welcomed, knowing it was sick, clutching it anyway, filling her emptiness and desolation with the fire-flashes along every nerve.

"No! I won't let you destroy a life of my making!"

"But *I'm* the one you love—I'm the one you took with you—it could've been Sarra, but you chose *me!* I'm a Feiran, I'm more yours than I ever was Mother's, you've said it yourself—"

Still blind. Magic groped out in the dark. She recognized him. In the landscape of the black mirror and gray sky she'd sensed his magic, tasted the chill bitterness she would always call Malerrisi in her mind. But . . . different now. She felt him looking down at her from his great height, at a great distance. Her father. His daughter.

"I do love you, Glenin. And because I love you, I can't let you do this to your own sister. I came to warn you—"

"Against what? Using the magic you gave me, doing what I was meant to do? Admit it, Father, you'd spare her only for your own pride! You sired a Mage Captal! *You,* the one they wouldn't even let into the Academy for fear of Wild Magic! And what a vengeance on Allynis Ambrai, for scorning you as her First Daughter's husband, father of her granddaughters!"

His magical image was overlaid with a subtle mist now. It hovered between them, and wispy tendrils of magic reached for her, and she opened her eyes.

"Go back to Malerris Castle, Glenin. Become First Lord, if that's your wish. But leave Cailet here."

"I want them both—but I really only need one of them. Don't make me do it, Father. Don't make me kill her."

Cailet pushed her hands against the cold tiled floor. Levered herself to her knees. Huddled there, vision hazed with sparks of gold and silver and blue and green. It was as if she saw now with both her physical eyes and her magical sight. The Wraith—for Wraith it surely must be—drifted in front of Auvry Feiran. Could Glenin not see it? No, she watched with her eyes, not her magic.

"You don't know what's happening in Ryka. The Legion is anywhere from Neele to The Waste. Most of the Council Guards are gone as well. Tonight almost all the government was in a single room. Flera Firennos, Granon Isidir, and Irien Dombur replaced the servants and Guards with their own people. After you left, they sealed the Malachite Hall and declared the Rising."

"That doddering old lackwit? Think up a better story, Father!"

"Glenin, *listen!* I Warded myself and escaped here, where I knew you'd be, to warn you. They're frantic to find Anniyas. And you. Your Ladder will take you to Seinshir. Use it, quickly!"

"You're lying!"

The Wraith poised protectively between Glenin and their father, taking on the vague shape of someone wearing a black cloak.

"On the love I bore your mother, I swear it's true."

"If anyone's with the Rising, it's you—Prentice Mage!"

"You can think that of me after, Glenin, if I were with the Rising, I'd tell you to go back to Ryka Court! Not even you could withstand so many Mages, so many spells!"

"Mages? What do you mean?"

Tall, black cloak, wink of silver at the collar—Gorsha? But he'd left her. Failed her. Or she had failed him. She was too tired to understand anymore. She was empty again, this time of magic.

"The Mages awaiting trial will be set free, and at least one will know how to use the Ladder. They all felt the Captal's Summons. Glensha, you must believe me! The Rising saw their best chance tonight and prepared for it—"

"And now all I can do is run away to Malerris Castle? I won't leave without Cailet and Sarra!"

"They're your sisters, not breeding stock!"

Sarra ... Collan ... images ... the gaping hollow filled.... Pleasure? Pain?

Glenin took something from under her cloak, gripped it in both hands, then flung it onto the floor. It opened into a circle of velvet all crusted with complex embroidery, large enough for two people to stand close together.

"Cailet's coming with me," Glenin said. "Find Sarra, and take her to the Traitor's Ladder at the Academy."

Auvry Feiran advanced one pace. The Wraith moved with him. "No."

"Do it! Prove to me that you're not still a Mage somewhere deep inside! Prove that you love me best!"

"No."

Glenin choked and her Mage Globe flared crimson and blue and dark seething purple. "You lied—my whole life, you *lied*—you took me with you instead of Sarra—but you would've chosen *her* if you'd known about her! Magic enough to become Mage Captal! Greatest jewel of your begetting! What a First Lord *she* would've made!"

"You're wrong, Glensha."

"Liar! *She's* the one you want—go on, look at her cowering there on the floor! But I swear to *you* that she's as dead as if she'd never been born!"

He lunged through the Wraith. Power lashed from the Globe in scarlet bursts that dazzled Cailet's eyes and magic.

"Your precious daughter the Captal will mother no Mageborns! Tell Sarra that my son and I will be waiting for *hers!*"

His Wards swelled like a blood blister, then collapsed. Cailet screamed, seeing Taig again, seeing him fall mortally wounded in her defense—

The Wraith coalesced, tall and black and terrible: Gorynel Desse. Glenin fell back, one foot on the velvet Ladder. No Blanking Ward sprang up around her, canceling all other magic; the furious crimson sphere erupted in yet more flashes toward her father's sprawled body.

"You can't have him back!" she cried. "Not him, not Cailet—they're *mine!*"

The Globe attenuated to a spear of flung magic, slicing through Gorynel Desse's Wraith and Auvry Feiran's upraised arm toward Cailet. The tip of it touched her, and she screamed.

So did Glenin, holding her belly as if the magic had pierced her womb. She swayed, gasping, both feet on the Ladder now. The Ward gathered. She vanished.

Cailet felt a hideous burning in her side. Her black tunic and shirt were rent open along the ribs, edges smoldering. Half her breast was gone.

Gorsha's Wraith hovered beside her. She looked up at him, then down at the bloody charred mess on her hand. "Should've included . . . a Healer . . . in your Making," she managed. She took a breath, whimpering as her ribs caught fire, and forced herself to sit up. Painfully she tugged Miram's scarf from her waist and pressed it to the blackened, suppurating burn.

A hand—a real one, not Wraithen—touched her knee. "Cailet. Forgive me." He crawled a little nearer. His right arm was a twisted ruin, hanging by a few white sinews just below the shoulder. There was little blood, the wound cauterized by incandescent magic.

"Lied to Glenin," he said. "If I'd known. . . ."

"Would you—" Breath caught in her side like a knife, and she bit her tongue against the pain. New tears sprang to her eyes. "Would you have made *me* the Malerrisi?" she whispered.

"No." He very nearly smiled. "Would've . . . *stayed.*"

The anguish of that merged in her chest with the physical agony. She locked her left arm over the bandage, pressing it to her wound, and freed her right hand so she could touch her father's face. "I believe you," she murmured. Not looking up, she said, "Gorsha. Find Sarra. I need her."

He hesitated, green eyes ablaze, then shook his head.

"Go!" she ordered, Captal to Mage.

His head bent in submission, and he disappeared. Surely she only imagined the words, *Auvry forgive me,* drifting on the moonlight.

"Cailet . . . take my hand. Tighter. Close your eyes . . . that's it . . . yes. . . ."

She felt a tingle of magic flow smooth as water up her arm to the shoulder and across her chest to center on the wound.

"Father, what are you doing?" The pain was already halved.

"Never much of a Healer . . . can't restore . . . but at least I can—"

She tried to snatch her hand away, frightened. But his grip on her fingers was like iron.

"Let me, Cailet, please—"

She would have fought, yet even as she tensed to pull away again, his hand went lax and he sank down onto his side. It was the last of his magic, and they both knew it. Cailet breathed deep with scarcely a twinge. When she took the scarf away, there was no more blood.

"Glenin," her father whispered.

Cailet knelt, took his head onto her knees, stroked his face. "I'm sorry. I should have found a way to make her see—"

"Someday . . . perhaps. But *you* must see the . . . the shadow, Cailet. *She* is your shadow . . . the only dark that can touch you. . . ."

And I am the only light that can touch her.

As if she had spoken aloud, he nodded.

And died.

38

The first thing he heard was a voice like the rustling of the wind. But it was a bizarre thing, because while he heard the wind with his ears, he heard the voice inside his head.

Silly girl, sleep-spelling them almost into a coma—! "First Rule of Magic" indeed! Collan! Wake up!

He was much too comfortable to follow orders. A warm, sweet armful snuggled at his side with her head on his shoulder, and the grass was soft beneath him, and sleep had always been his second-favorite activity when lying down.

The voice wouldn't let him. *Collan! Open your eyes!*

He cracked an eyelid and saw nothing. "Go 'way," he muttered, and buried his lips in silky hair.

Collan!

He knew that voice. He jerked upright, hand instinctively groping for knife or sword—closing around a fierce example of the latter—while Sarra, tumbled from her cozy nest, began to swear.

Col hardly noticed. Just out of reach in the moonlight was another of those things that had come for Anniyas. But when he squinted, this one took on the hazy shape of Gorynel Desse. But the voice hadn't sounded anything like his.

"What the hell—?"

The voice spoke again, from just to the other side of Sarra.

Wake up and polish your wits, boy, said Falundir inside his head. *Cailet needs you.*

"Collan?" Sarra raked her hair back with both hands. "What's—oh, *shit!* I'll wring Cai's neck for this!"

Falundir sat back on his heels. The Wraith faded away. Collan shook his head to clear it.

"Did you—damn it, I *heard* you!" he told the Bard.

A smile teased the dark face, and the blue eyes danced with merriment.

"What are you talking about?" Sarra demanded. "Col, wake up. We've got to find Cailet." Turning to the Bard, she said, "If you know where she is, lead us to her. Hurry!"

The old man helped her up and they ran hand-in-hand for the Octagon Court. Cursing, Collan snatched up the sword and followed. By the angle of moonlight, less than an hour had passed since he'd last come this way. How much trouble could the kitten get into in so short a time? Plenty, if Glenin Feiran had shown up as Sarra believed she would.

He felt the wind on his face and tore off the disgusting coif to let it rinse his hair clean of sweat. Where the hell had Falundir come from? And the Wraith of Gorynel Desse? And how had he heard the Bard's voice—and *known* it was his voice?

Cailet was perfectly well and perfectly calm when she met them at the garden doors. Tired, Col thought critically, but unharmed. Sarra flung her arms around her and alternated epithets with endearments, threats of retaliation with anxious questions about her safety. Collan looked around suspiciously. No Glenin. No Desse. No nothing, just the empty Octagon Court beyond the doors.

"All right, that's enough," he said at last. "Are you going to tell us what happened, or make us guess?"

"I'll tell you everything later," Cailet promised. "Right

now there's too much to be done. Bard Falundir, I'm very glad you've come. You and Sarra and Collan please go to the Double Spiral, there'll be Mages arriving from Ryka any minute now. Go meet them, and—"

"*Mages?*" Sarra echoed, thunderstruck.

"From *Ryka?*" Collan added.

"Didn't I mention that?" Cailet smiled. "We won."

"How?" Sarra demanded.

"They'll tell you. For now, I've got to call the other Mages here, and—" She glanced over her shoulder. "They're here, and in a minute they'll find Anniyas. Take care of them for me, Sarra, I don't have time right now."

"Cai, wait—what about Glenin?"

"She's gone. We won't hear from her again for—oh, years and years, I expect. I'll explain everything later," she repeated. "Take the Mages out to the front courtyard. Leave Anniyas's body, I'll deal with it. Go on, hurry. I'll be with you as soon as I can."

And with that she ran back inside.

"When I catch up with her again," Sarra muttered, "I'm going to—"

"What?" Collan asked mildly.

"Something will occur to me, I'm sure. She may be Mage Captal, but she's still my little sister, and—"

"*What?*" he said again in a totally different voice.

Falundir did something remarkable then. He began to laugh.

Sarra cast him a calculating look, then grinned. "I'll tell you later. Come on, Col. They'll have found Garon Anniyas and—"

"You'll tell me *now!*" He turned a glare on the Bard. "And what's so damned funny?"

Falundir gestured gracefully at Collan himself, still chuckling.

Sarra tugged Col's hand. "There's no time right now. Don't you hear them in there?" But then she paused, looking up at him with limitless black eyes. "Col . . . it's a secret. About me and Cailet, I mean. I swear I'll—"

"—tell me later," he finished in disgust. "Why am I surprised? You two *sound* exactly alike, truly told. Come on, First Daughter. After you."

He bowed her through the door, and for the sheer revenge of adding to her astonishment, walked the prescribed two paces behind her all the way to the Double Spiral Stairs.

Falundir followed them, silent as a Wraith, but Col knew he was still laughing.

39

Cailet stood over her father's body, wondering why she couldn't weep for him. She ought to; she felt that; but she couldn't.

"You will. I daresay you'll cry for him more than for me."

She rounded on Gorynel Desse. He was not as he'd been in the landscape of black glass, but not the Wraithen wisp of before, either. Insubstantial, yes, and beyond her physical touching; she could see the line of turquoise octagons on the white wall behind him. But he was nearly as he had been in life, in youth, the vibrant, black-haired, green-eyed Warrior Mage. First Sword of the Captal's Warders. Her protector, her defender, her teacher.

"You damned son of a Fifth!" Cailet clenched her fists, wishing she could pummel him as she had during the Making. "You let him die!"

"There was nothing I could have done. And he *wanted* to die, Cailet. Glenin saw his defense of you as betrayal of the Malerrisi, and most especially of her. I say it was a return to the man he once was. But . . . others will decide."

She didn't understand and didn't want to. "You let him die and you let her do that to me. Why? Because I didn't do what you always meant me to?"

"That was your own interpretation. Glenin is Malerrisi to her fingertips. The only person who thought she could be convinced otherwise is you."

"Then *why?*"

A quiet sigh. "It was never meant to happen like this."

"Why didn't you help me? I needed you—"

"Everything we are was there for you to use."

"So what happened is *my* fault?"

"No. Mine. Caisha, I couldn't stop her. Am I a living Mage Guardian, to counter Malerrisi magic? It's my fault and my shame that I thought the Bequest would be enough to protect you. I never believed Glenin could do such things to her own Blood."

"Neither did he." She gestured to her father's corpse. "You were both wrong. And I'm the one who paid for it."

"Forgive me."

"Never." Cailet turned her back on him, shaking. She rubbed at the ache in her ribs, avoiding the place where a Ward concealed the damage from prying eyes. "Why are you here?" she demanded. "I don't need you anymore."

"One day you will. I promise I'll be there."

"Don't do me any favors."

"No," he said, and his voice was wry. "I would never presume, Captal."

After a moment she asked, "What about the others? Or are they gone?"

"Their knowledge and experience are yours. But they took their Wraiths with them when they died. For my own part . . . what I knew, you know. But what I *was,* you will no longer be, not even in small part. I'll miss you, though I doubt you'll miss me."

"You're right. I won't."

"Just the same, Caisha. . . ."

She flinched as *something* brushed her shoulders and her hair, like hands and lips bestowing a final caress.

"Remember how much I love you," the Wraithen voice whispered. And then he·was gone, fading into a brief whispering wind.

She half-turned, speaking his name. How could he say he loved her, and let Glenin do what she had done?

Her gaze fell on her father's body. *He* had stopped it. *He* had protected her. Died for her. She felt tears begin in her eyes—no time, not now. She could hear voices nearby. She had already disposed of Anniyas. She had to get her father's body out of here before they found him.

She had no strength left for the burden. But from deep in her mind came a spell, and for the first time it felt only of her own magic: certain, capable, calmly knowing. She cast it onto the body and watched—surprised, unsurprised—a thin, nearly transparent film of white-silver magic appear. It hovered above the body for a moment before wrapping it like a shroud.

With a simple Ward that made her Invisible, and an even simpler Folding, she carried her father through deserted corridors to the gardens and then to the riverbank as easily as if his tall body weighed no more than a child's.

Part Three

Part Three

Dreams

1

It took half the night, but every Mage in Ambrai finally arrived at the great circle outside the Octagon Court. There were freed Mages from Ryka, too, and an amazing number of people avowing they'd been with the Rising all along. Flera Firennos, looking nothing like the senile ancient Sarra had met last year, greeted her with a sparkle in her eyes and a grin on her lips.

"So many years, such a good joke—I'm almost sorry it's come to an end! How I wish I could've seen Anniyas's face. What happened to her, by the way?"

"The Captal is taking care of things," Collan interposed smoothly. "Lady, may I offer you a chair? Some wine?"

They'd found a few sticks of furniture in the same storerooms where last night Sarra had slept on a Cloister rug. Pier Alvassy had brought the wine—great oaken casks from some cellar out in the suburbs, brought here in rickety carts drawn by highly offended riding horses belonging to Tiomarin Garvedian—Lusira's cousin, and nearly her equal in beauty—and Tio's fifteen-year-old son, Viko.

As Collan went to fetch the required items, Councillor Firennos said to Sarra, "Charming boy. But do choose his clothes yourself from now on. Those scarlet trousers! Most regrettable. He needs something fashionable, but not quite so. . . ."

"Flashy?" Sarra suggested, feeling a trifle giddy. "Flamboyant? Florid?"

The old lady giggled. "Flagrant!"

Sarra laughed for the first time in what seemed years at the thought of telling Collan how to dress. "I'll have a word with him," she promised.

"There's a good girl. And one day when we've time, you must tell me where you found him."

"In a whorehouse," she replied. "Excuse me, please, Lady Flera. I need to talk to Healer Adennos."

Who wasn't easy to find in the middle of the celebrations. Someone had kindled a bonfire in the circle center, and Sarra wondered if the older Mages were reminded as painfully as she of other fires at Ambrai. At last she saw Elo dancing with Lusira to the lutes and mandolins and improvised drums of a spontaneous orchestra.

Before she could approach him, however, she was spun around and clasped in Collan's arms. "This is my dance, believe," he drawled. "This one, and all the others for as long as we're both still able to walk."

"But—Cailet—"

"She said she'd be here, and she will. Sarra, we've won. Enjoy it."

Yes, it seemed they'd won. But she hadn't been part of it, hadn't even *known* of it until she and Col met the three Councillors who had been part of the Rising almost since its inception. They had a lot of explaining to do, and though she knew it was childish, she deeply resented her lack of participation in the pivotal event of the age.

"Pay attention," Col admonished. "That's the second time you've stepped on my feet."

"Third."

Truly told, she *had* been in the thick of things. Gathering Mages with Alin and Val; provoking the first real change in inheritance laws in a dozen Generations; helping Mages escape; and, most importantly, arguing Gorynel Desse into giving Cailet her magic. It wasn't lack of participation, she decided. It was lack of perspective. Of planning. Of making moves she understood to be strategic advances toward a defined goal. She'd done all sorts of things without a clue as to what they'd get her—besides another day or week of life.

It was a hell of a way to run a revolution.

All the others had done was wait for the right moment

Tonight had been perfect. Over a hundred Mage Guardians in custody at Ryka Court; the Legion absent; the Council Guard diminished; everyone who was anyone celebrating Garon Anniyas's Birthingday in the Malachite Hall. They would have been fools to pass it up. And so here many of them were—leaving selected powerful Mages and officials back in Ryka, of course, to secure the government—dancing, singing, drinking, and in general behaving as if the night just passed were Kiy's, not Sirrala's.

"Stop thinking so loud—you're ruining the music. And why are you thinking at all? What happened to romance? You should be—"

"—simpering like an idiot with the thrill of dancing in your arms?"

"Something like that," he replied, chuckling.

"Oh, go gallop Imi Gorrst around the bonfire a while. I'm thirsty, anyhow."

"Good. Maybe a few drinks will get you in the mood." Steering her to the carts where wine casks were rapidly emptying, he left her with a bow and, "With your permission, First Daughter—or without it!"

Granon Isidir sidled up a moment later, proffering a filled crystal goblet. "Will you honor me, Lady, by sharing?"

The frothy bubbles should have been chilled, but they went down with a smooth, expensive tingle. "Thank you. Not enough cups to go around?"

"Not nearly. I brought this with me from Ryka Court."

"Admirable foresight, *Domni* Isidir."

"As I have begged before, please call me Granon." He gestured away from the happy jostle around the carts. She walked with him toward a carved stone trough and sat on its edge. "You don't quite believe all this, do you, Lady Sarra?"

"Not in the least," she admitted frankly. "Enlighten me."

"With pleasure." He smiled down at her. "It's a long tale, and for its duration I'll have your attention all to myself."

"Shorten it," she advised, handing him back the cup.

"As you wish. There has been great outrage over the capture and execution of Mage Guardians—so, too, with those of the Rising, many of whom were beloved citizens of their Shirs. This was the spark. The kindling was long suspicion of Anniyas's power, and the Feirans'. Resentments, grievances—"

"And thwarted schemes? *Domni* Isidir, why·are you with the Rising?"

"Because my great-grandmother told me to be, of course! Truly told, Lady Sarra, you're right about the scheming. It is, I believe, Dombur's motive."

"And what might yours be?"

"Besides the esteemed First Isidir Daughter's commands—" And here his expression changed into honest contempt. "I personally had no desire to be ruled in any way by Garon Anniyas. Decision on your Slegin inheritance opened certain doors a crack, one of which the late First Councillor would have kicked down at her first opportunity."

"Giving her son her chair at the Council Table," Sarra said, nodding. "I thought something like that at the time."

"Then you are even more perspicacious than you are beautiful—and your beauty is unsurpassed."

"Do you honestly think Garon Anniyas could have taken what Glenin Feiran desired—or held it long, even if he did?"

"I should've remembered the impossibility of flattery around you. In my view, there wasn't much to choose between them. And whereas a woman's rule is traditionally preferable to man's, a woman like that. . . ." He ended with an eloquent shrug.

"Tell me more about how you became involved."

He sat on the trough beside her and gave her the wineglass. "I am, to be brutally blunt, the most promising of all my hundreds of cousins. I prepared from childhood for the Assembly and Council. Telomir Renne approached me some years ago. Obliquely, of course. After a time, I approached our redoubtable First Daughter—and found that Renne had spoken to her even before he spoke to me. With her approval, I became part of the Rising." He laughed suddenly. "And only a week ago did I learn the Rising leader at Ryka was Flera Firennos!"

"Certainly a shock," Sarra agreed. "Go on."

"Here tonight is but a fraction of the whole. We three of the Council—I brought in Irien Dombur after his election—are the most visible. There are dozens of Assembly members, dozens more government officials of varying ranks. Each is at the center of a wheel—"

"—with spokes reaching to four or five others, and connected to another wheel by an axle," she finished.

"Why, yes. But, naturally, you are at the center of your own wheel."

Sarra nodded and stood. "Just so long as we're all rolling along in the same direction, *Domni* Isidir."

"Granon. Please."

"And at the same speed," she added. "Thank you for the information, and the confirmation. Oh, and the wine." Before he could say anything else, she smiled, set the glass on the stone, and walked off.

Claiming the next available cup—a huge pewter tankard meant for ale—she began to drink in earnest, hoping it would cool her anger. She'd been kept in ignorance all her life. About Cailet, about the Rising, about *everything* that was important. Knowledge was power; she'd seen that demonstrated by both her sisters. From now on, Sarra and ignorance were going to be total strangers.

But she had a few things to attend to first. Skirting the bonfire, she found Flera Firennos and crouched beside her chair. "May I ask a favor, Lady?"

Feet tapping in time to the music, the old woman glanced down. "Hmm? Oh, of course, my dear."

"There's a young woman of your Name who lives in Cantratown with her little boy. He's three or four."

She frowned, trying to sort through innumerable relations. "Firennos, Cantratown . . . oh, do you mean Rina? Is she a friend of yours? I must confess I don't like her much. And her mother is a harridan. My great grandmother's cousin's granddaughter—or was she great grandmother's sister?"

"Rina Firennos, that must be her. Unmarried."

"And not likely to be. She's one of those girls who takes to her bed anything she happens to fancy, and if a child comes of it—well, who cares who fathered the poor mite? I *don't* approve of loose living and no husband and no two children with the same father. After all, who's going to raise the babies if there's no husband around the house?"

"I agree," Sarra said. "And she's no friend of mine. But the father of her son was very dear to me. Valirion Maurgen."

"You don't mean that highly attractive boy who was with you at Ryka Court? Dark, with a roving eye? The build of a wrestler and the look of a pirate?"

Sarra laughed at the description, and how much Val would

have appreciated it. "That's him, head to toe. He was the father of Rina's little boy."

"Was? Oh, yes, I heard about that business at Lilen's in Longriding. You've sent someone there and on to Ostinhold, haven't you?"

Sarra wondered in amazement how the old lady had ever maintained her pose of senility. "At the Captal's order. But Val's son—"

"*You* want to raise him?"

"I think the Maurgens would. I talked with Biron—Val's twin brother, he's over there dancing with Elin Alvassy. I know it's scandalous even to think of giving custody to the father's family, but he's only a son—and he's all the Maurgens have left of Val."

The Lady took a swig of wine, then said flatly, "She'll want compensation."

"She'll get it." But not from the Maurgens; Sarra owned a goodly portion of Sheve now, and what was money for if not to use to good purpose?

"Well, seeing as how I loathe that whole branch of the family, and Rina has two daughters and is pregnant yet again—no morals at all, that girl—I'll look into it." She eyed Sarra narrowly. "And what about you, then? You're not the type to spread wide for anything you're not married to. That Minstrel of yours seems a likely husband to me—especially if you found him in a whorehouse."

Sarra blushed, but couldn't help laughing again. Had Allynis Ambrai and Flera Firennos ever met, they would either have gotten on famously or murdered each other. Strong wills of the same Generation found no middle ground. Sarra, two Generations younger than Councillor Firennos, could simultaneously deplore the old lady's indelicate reference and grin at her blunt honesty.

"He's not 'my' Minstrel—" Remembering the last time she'd said that, she appended, "—*yet.*"

"Then what are you standing around for? I met my first and best husband at a St. Sirrala's Ball!" She gave Sarra a push. "Off with you, girl!"

And just in time, too. Tiomarin Garvedian was eyeing Col with profound interest—*She's absolutely* scrutinizing *him,* Sarra thought indignantly, marching down the steps to claim what was hers.

2

Collan behaved himself. He really did. When that good-looking Blood coaxed Sarra away for private conversation, he went on dancing with Imi Gorrst and only glanced over at them twice.

Well, three times. Maybe four.

He wasn't jealous. Isidir wasn't even Sarra's type. Over-pretty, overmannered, overdressed—*Nervy,* he thought in disgust, *griping about what* he's *got on when I'm tarted up like a cheap bower cockie.* But at least he hadn't chosen what he wore. He wasn't responsible.

A woman's astonished voice saying, *"That's* Collan?" turned his head. The gorgeous Garvedians were watching him: Lusira with a smile, her cousin Tiomarin with startled fascination. He gave them a grin but not the wink that usually went with it—and when he realized he was already adapting his normal responses to beautiful women, he ground his teeth.

Dancing was starting to hurt his foot. Liberal application of alcohol—down his throat, not down his boot—helped some. When next he saw Sarra, she was accepting the hand of Riddon Slegin to begin a new dance. *Fine,* Col nodded to himself. *Stick with the ones she thinks of as brothers or cousins.* Miram Ostin approached to ask when Cailet would join them. He told her what he'd told Sarra: that she'd be here soon. By then Sarra was dancing with Telomir Renne. Desse's son—that was weird enough, but that Sarra and Cailet were sisters—! He tried to work out how, and whether they were Liwellans or Rilles. After all, he deserved to know; whatever their Name was, it would be his children's.

Children: the word waltzed dreamily around in his mind as he whirled Miram around the bonfire in three-quarter time. A daughter, of course—a First Daughter to carry on the Name (whatever it was) ... a little girl with Sarra's black eyes ... Sarra's golden hair ... Sarra's smile—and his own talent for music. He could just see her, frowning over complex fingering and then laughing when she got it right and the lute sang in her hands. . . .

And a son, too, but *not* with his looks, which had gotten him into all sorts of trouble with women. Often quite delectable trouble, to be sure, but whereas such adventures were barely acceptable in a practically Nameless traveling Minstrel, they were frowned on by the upper reaches of society.

Not that any of *his* offspring would turn out perfect little Bloods—like that oh-so-charming Isidir over there, bowing to Sarra at the completion of their dance. Collan scowled, not noticing when Miram's surprise gave way to a sudden impish grin of understanding.

Well, he'd just have to make Sarra marry him. Husbands raised the children. That was how things were done, and they'd damned well be done that way for *his* children. No battalion of nurses and tutors and high-nosed flunkies would turn *his* daughters and sons into—

Sarra floated past, clasped much too closely in the arms of the other Council Blood, Dombur. *Mine,* snarled something that thirty Generations had not bred out of the male animal, and Collan stalked forward, prepared to do battle.

A hand touched his elbow. He turned. Bard Falundir's blue eyes, brighter for wine, held a deeper gleam of amusement. Collan laughed and put an arm around the bony shoulders.

"Damn that old man for not letting me remember you. I hope I've done right by your songs all these years—and your lute."

Falundir smiled, humming low in his throat like a cat purring. A crippled hand lifted, the back of the palm bumping Col's cheek in gentle affection.

"One thing. How come I heard you earlier? Are you Mageborn? Did I only dream your voice?" He sighed in exasperation. "If I guess, will you let me know I'm right?"

A brow arched playfully. Then Falundir drew back, pointing first to the impromptu orchestra and then at Col.

"Now? Here?" When the Bard nodded, Collan flexed his fingers nervously and admitted, "For a while there, I never thought I would again."

Falundir nodded solemnly. He knew; *how* he knew was as much of a mystery as how Collan had heard his voice, but that was something to puzzle out later.

Riddon caught sight of Col holding a lute and yelled for

quiet. Eventually he got it. Retuning the borrowed instrument as he mounted the first few steps leading up to the Octagon Court, Collan faced the murmuring crowd, remembering the first time he'd faced a large gathering. It seemed, he told himself ironically, that although then he had been a slave and now he was free, he was condemned to other men's dreadful clothing.

Gazing out at the eager faces around the snapping bonfire, he wondered what he could possibly play for them. For himself. For Sarra and Cailet and Taig and Verald and even old Gorynel Desse.

His gaze met Falundir's and suddenly his fingers quivered like tuning forks. Slowly, reverently, he began the opening chords of "The Long Sun."

3

Brushing sweat from her forehead, Cailet backed away to evaluate her work. River rocks and stones broken from the walkway formed a hollow circle almost seven feet across. Within, she'd piled kindling—what half-charred wood she'd been able to find—and chopped planks and railings of two of the barges they'd come to Ambrai in. Soon the body of Auvry Feiran would lie there. Flames and wood smoke would rise. By tomorrow there would only be ashes.

Perhaps sometime between now and then she'd be able to cry.

A splash turned her head. The river rippled with the plunge of talons and the sweep of wings. The bird called success to its mate as it flew nestward clutching a silvery slithering fish. A moment later the water stilled, a smoothly perfect black mirror for a billion newborn stars.

Cailet turned aching eyes to the sky. The Ladymoon had set. The stars reigned supreme—companions of solitary nights in The Waste, a vast sparkling painting that changed with the seasons. It was spring now. Fielto rode Her horse low in the sky and Velenne's Lute was below the horizon, though Colynna's coiled strings were still visible. The long knotted rope Tamas had left on the stellar deck straggled down to the spill of dense stars that was Mittru's River, where Ilsevet's hand held a fish. Stories in the stars, written long ago in light. But no new story would ever shine there. What people did mattered even less to the stars than the bird's dinner mattered to the river.

She found solace in that. It put triumph into perspective, eased the sting of failure.

Stripping naked, she slid into the shallows. Chill and clear, the water seemed to wash through her skin to her bones—even where crusty scabs tingled, where half her breast was gone. Gingerly she touched the mutilated part, then what remained: the nipple's aureole, the firm flesh that curved to the center of her breastbone. Had her father not absorbed the worst and deflected the rest, Glenin's magic would have charred the heart from her chest.

She stretched her arm and felt only a twinge of pain, a tug at abused muscles. The loss could be disguised. Not Warded, as she had done earlier; some sort of undergarment could hide—

No. She would cast this Ward the instant she woke every morning of her life. As a reminder.

She dove deep, then surfaced to float on her back in the shallows. She was no longer the girl who'd loved those stars. So much lost, so much forced into a mind unprepared to receive it. She could no longer gaze up at the night sky with a lifting heart, feeling its magic. The Mage Captal could never be free of her own magic again. From now on she would be set apart. Her life was precious: not for who she was, but for what she had become. The river's current tightened like a trap around her body. She fought back panic. She had duties, obligations, responsibilities—all those solid, worthy words that wrapped a life in prison bars of solid gold.

Coward.

She emerged silently from the water, shaking out her wet hair, and dressed, binding herself into her regimentals. Less than a day hers, these clothes, yet she felt she'd worn them for a lifetime. Telo Renne's clever needle had mended old scars in the material, reweaving holes and taking minuscule stitches no one but Cailet would ever know were there. She was scarred now, too. But the Ward would hide the wound as seamlessly as Telo's work, and no one would ever know.

She returned to the stone circle and built a small fire in

sandy soil. Trees stood watch, bird song stilled now, cries
and calls of the river creatures gone. A mile away, with the
bulk of the Octagon Court between, came the muted music
and laughter of celebration. Triumph. Patiently she coaxed
the fire alight, wondering what she'd won.

Was there such a thing as a "clean" victory? Everything
was paid for, one way or another. Was it all just a balance
of wins against losses, hoping that the tilt went toward the
former?

When the flames caught, Cailet got to her feet and looked
to where the tall, still body lay. Was Auvry Feiran's death a
victory? Was she the only one who would feel her father's
loss?

Half-closing her eyes, she spoke a soft word.

Nothing happened. Nothing. No stirring in the night air,
no whisper of magic. She felt, heard, sensed only the throbbing of her weariness.

The corpse was heavy now, as if the deeds of a lifetime
had settled on him. She hooked her elbows beneath his
shoulders, dragging him toward the pyre. She stumbled, fell
to her knees. Her hands slipped from around wide-arching
ribs—and then she felt it. A small pouch, hidden in a pocket
of his longvest, concealed by the cloak. She rocked back on
her heels, loosening the drawstrings.

Into her hand fell two tiny silver pins. Sword and Candle.
Auvry Feiran had never been acknowledged as more than a
Prentice. He had forsworn his allegiance to the Guardians.
But here, secretly with him always, were the honored sym-
bols of a Warrior Mage. More: a Captal's Warder.

She rubbed her fingers over the silver tokens. Polishing
them. Feeling their shape and meaning. The Guide and the
Guardian.

He had guided Glenin to the Malerrisi. But he had been
Cailet's guardian at the end. She closed her fist over the tokens and watched firelight dance warm over the cold dead
face of her father.

Sliding the insignia into her tunic pocket, she hooked her
elbows once more beneath the mighty shoulders. The body
was paradoxically lighter, and not just by the insignificant
weight of two small silver pins. She caught her breath, wondering if she'd been guided to finding them, wondering if
she dared attempt magic again. But now she was strangely
unwilling.

When the corpse rested within the circle, Cailet knelt before the fire, searching for a long twig to carry to the kindling. She tried to dismiss the burning in her eyes as fatigue. She knew better. She could give Auvry Feiran a pyre the size of a temple with flames halfway to the stars, and it wouldn't change a damned thing. Ambrai, Roseguard, even Malerris Castle—all the lives maimed and destroyed, all the magic used for evil—there was no mercy in the whole starry sky that could encompass this man. And his daughter knew it.

He had done what he had done, and now he was dead. Betrayer of both Mageborn factions, taking what the Guardians taught and using it in the service of the Malerrisi—and then denying them the Captal's death. She wanted to believe that he had done it for love of her, of the last of his daughters; certainly he had used the last of his strength and magic to heal her as best he could. He had been a Mage Guardian at the last, protecting the Captal. His daughter. Had he known about her years ago, he would have stayed. . . .

But what had sent him to the Malerrisi instead?

Pleasure/pain—

She stared into the flames. Glenin had shown her what real power was. Chance, not choice, stood between Cailet and what had become of her father.

He was dead. There was no victory here. Only loss. When it came her own time to stand before St. Veneklos. . . .

The Judge was nothing more than a bookkeeper, entering debits in one column and credits in another, while Flerna the Weary added it all up on her Abacus.

Cailet plucked a long, thin branch from the fire and flung it at her father's corpse. Flames caught on the cloak, sputtered, found fuel, ignited.

4

Across the river, just within a little stand of fire-scarred trees, they gathered. Individual mists drifted from water to shore; hazy, insubstantial lights glowed faintly above trees before descending. They came together in silence while the latest—and possibly the last—of their kind built her father's pyre.

"Here assembled," said a woman's voice, low and musical, "in final evaluation of—" She paused, her tone losing its formality. "And there we have the real question, don't we? The title we give him judges him. Captal Garvedian, you knew him best of us all."

"Excepting yourself, First Captal. You know *all* Mageborns. But I'll speak after everyone else, if this is acceptable."

"Very well. Captal Rengirt?"

"I don't see that there's any question. For seeding the destruction of the Wild Magic that was Anniyas, I absolve. Let him be known as Auvry Feiran, Mage Guardian."

A small quiver of tension: they had been approaching this moment for many years, waiting, watching, weighing motive and action and consequence. That the first judgment was to absolve startled some and intrigued others. A few were speechless with outrage.

"Captal Shellin."

"For sparing the life of Bard Falundir, I absolve."

"Captal Bertolin."

"For hunting down and butchering Mage Guardians, I condemn. May he be known as a Malerrisi, and wander forever in the Dead White Forest."

And so the Names were spoken, some of them not heard on Lenfell in many Generations, and the judgments were given, and the reasons. For begetting Sarra and Cailet, absolved. For begetting and perverting Glenin, condemned. For causing countless deaths, condemned. For embracing the ways of the ancient enemy . . . for sparing Gorynel Desse . . . for sparing the Minstrel . . . for Ambrai . . . the Bards . . . the Healers . . . Roseguard . . . for deceit . . . for dishonor . . . for arrogance . . . for vilest ambition. . . .

"Captal Adennos."

"First Captal, we all have reasons for condemnation. Valid reasons. But there is the girl."

Across the river, a slim, pale figure dove through dark shallows and surfaced to gaze up at the stars.

"Exactly." A woman's serene agreement slid through the mist. "Cailet Ambrai, the new Captal, through whom our work will continue."

"Leninor, my dear, that's just it. What of this new Captal?

Her magic is unmatched by anyone now living. She was of my Making, who should know this better than I? But the legacy of her father—"

"With respect," said Bertolin, "do you seriously suggest that we spare Feiran for the girl's sake alone? Do you ask us to forget his crimes?"

"Will Cailet?" retorted Leninor Garvedian.

"Tonight we deal with the father," Stene reminded them. "The daughter's time will come, as it came for us all."

Lusath Adennos said vigorously, "If we condemn the one, we equally sentence the other. Lifelong doubts could destroy her. She will have no faith in mercy if we show none."

The uneasy stirring among the Wraiths caused a few leaves to rustle as the girl emerged from the water and knelt beside her fire.

"And justice?" Trevarin asked. "After all that he wrought—"

Stene broke in. "Could she possibly have *loved* that monster who sired her?"

"Not a monster," Captal Bekke retorted. "A Mage Guardian."

"Now, *really,* Caitirin!"

"Peace," said the First Captal, and they were all silent for a moment. "Leninor, you had something else to say?"

"Always does," someone muttered.

"Damned right I do! You think me a fool, I know, for keeping watch over Collan all these years. But through him in the past weeks I've come to know Cailet. She's a lonely child, sensitive, desperate for love—and sacrificing himself was a demonstration of a father's love, pure and simple."

" 'Pure'?" Channe snorted. "*Nothing* about Auvry Feiran is 'pure.' "

"Except his love for his daughters," Rengirt murmured.

"All three of them," Trevarin reminded them acidly.

The First Captal sighed. "Go on, Leninor. Finish."

"Thank you. I was going to say that if we condemn her father, we'll be turning her inside out. How could she feel that to love him is right? For she does love him, and not just for saving her life. He's her father. That's a relationship deeply discounted since the War, but we must deal with it here."

"Especially considering what she believes about her mother," Bekke reminded them. "And I have a few choice words regarding that for your impossible Gorynel Desse, Leninor!"

"Not hers, Caitirin," Rengirt said slyly. "Her mother's."

"As much as he was ever any woman's," Garvedian replied in kind.

"We judged *his* uniquely difficult case weeks ago," Stene said. "If you're through gossiping, I suggest we return to the matter at hand. It appears to me that the major argument in favor is that Cailet Ambrai's existence as Captal of Mage Guardians caused Auvry Feiran to exist *as* a Mage Guardian again."

"That's how I see it," Adennos agreed. "If we condemn the father she loves, what would it do to her ability to function as Captal?"

"Of which mercy must be a component," added Rengirt. "But mercy is not of the mind, but of the heart. And we would surely break her heart if we condemn."

Garroldin, who had spoken only to give her verdict, now said, "So for the sake of the daughter, you ask us to absolve the father. This is hard, First Captal. Very hard."

A long silence spun among them while they watched the girl fling a burning brand onto the pyre. At last there was a whispering in the air, almost a sigh, and the First Captal spoke once more.

"Never in all the Generations have we been faced with such deeds committed by one who was once one of our own. I, who have witnessed it all, attest to this. Each of you has a valid point to make. Those of you who condemn, the most valid of all. So many crimes! So much magic used to destroy! We Captals have judged many Mages who were guilty of betrayal, murder, dishonor, arrogance, ambition, lies, willful use of magic for wickedness—and a hundred other things our ethic has condemned from the moment of our Founding. But this one man surpasses all. He was ours, yet he became Malerrisi. To many of you, I know, this is the most unforgivable crime of all. It betrays all that we are."

Those who had chosen to absolve drew closer together as if to unite in silent protest against a judgment they would never question aloud. The grasses rippled as if a breeze had bent their tips.

"Yet we *are* met to judge, and that in itself is significant. Had Auvry Feiran remained as he made himself, we would not be here. He all but destroyed the Mage Guardians, yet by siring and then saving Cailet, the Mage Guardians will live and become more powerful than ever. This is heavily in his favor."

The First Captal paused. "Still, it *is* the father we consider, not the daughter. Does the single act of self-sacrifice counter all the self-serving crimes? Is this one thing enough to justify mercy?"

Across the water, the girl's black eyes and white-gold hair were lit in crimson by the flames of her father's pyre.

"If it is not," said the First Captal, "then we have no right to call ourselves Mage Guardians, much less Captals."

She was silent then, measuring the effect of her words on them all. When she judged the time to be correct—keeping before them the image of the girl trudging round-shouldered through the empty gardens—she spoke.

"Malerrisi sacrifice their lives when ordered. This is the fundamental difference between us: that they are compelled, and we *choose*. Out of love, out of duty, out of anger and hate, yes, at times—but for reasons of our own. We will not have those reasons dictated to us.

"I will not do so now, giving reasons why you must choose to absolve Auvry Feiran. Our horror of him and the Malerrisi First Lord he served unbalanced Lenfell's magic as surely as did their use of magic for their own dread purposes all these years. We have feared them and hated them—and thereby contributed to the unbalance. I suggest to you now that we can no longer afford to hate. The power Cailet feels must be as clean as Viranka's Rain, as pure as Caitiri's Fire, as strong as Lirance's Wind. Only we can do this for her. Only we can choose not to condemn him. Not just for her sake, but for our own. Yet, most importantly, because in the end Auvry Feiran *is* deserving."

At length, and after much resistance gradually overcome, the Wraiths gathered as one. And with one voice they spoke: "We are agreed, First Captal."

She spread their offered magic to embrace them all—not just the Captals, but the Generations of Mage Guardians. Including the one they accepted again as one of their own.

"For the life and heart of Cailet Ambrai. For the sake of his turning from the paths of our ancient enemy. For the sake of ourselves, Mage Captals, in mercy and in humility—we absolve. Let Auvry Feiran join with us at last, not as Prentice, but as Mage Guardian, Warrior Mage, Captal's Warder."

5

"Cai!"

Collan turned as Sarra cried out joyfully, and watched her fling herself into her sister's arms. *Sisters,* he thought again in amazement. Why hadn't anybody seen it before? They looked so much alike—

He snorted. They looked nothing at all alike. Dainty, curvaceous Sarra; lanky, long-legged Cailet. Both were blondes, but Sarra's hair was a cascade of bright gold and Cailet's was short, straight, and sun-bleached almost white. One face was all harmonious curves; the other, all angles. The proud grace of a Lady of Blood was completely different from a Waster's lithe suppleness—or a Mage's self-possession.

The only real resemblance was in the eyes, he decided: large, luminous, beautiful black eyes.

But not so luminous in Cailet's weary face, Collan noted with a frown. The elder sister's radiance only emphasized the younger's exhaustion. The smile Cailet gave Sarra held little of the sweetness Col cherished. She hadn't looked this bad even when acknowledging that Taig Ostin was dead. It was the difference between a child whose heart had been broken and a woman whose spirit had been crushed. As she accepted a cup of wine from Riddon Slegin, Collan saw in her eyes a grim determination to devote herself to St. Kiy the Forgetful and get very, very drunk.

Which was probably for the best, he thought, and rejoined the party. But he kept an eye on her and before an hour had gone by was more worried than ever.

She had settled on a lower step with her back to a charred column, a large cup in her hand regularly refilled by whoever happened to be making the rounds with the bucket. She was pleasant enough to those who approached her, smiling and jesting, even laughing. But while others danced, she sat alone. While others sang, she stayed quiet. At last, incapable of enduring the look in her eyes any longer, Collan paused

to refill his own cup—figuring he was going to need it—and
turned to where Cailet sat.

She was gone. And when he turned again, Sarra, too, had
vanished.

6

They left the courtyard bonfire far behind. Though it had
been Sarra's choice to seek privacy, it was Cailet who chose
their path through the gardens, a roundabout tour of tangled
glades and wild-growing meadows that would eventually
lead to the river.

"Wait a minute, Cai. Let's sit for a while."

She turned, and the little Mage Globe at her shoulder
paused with her. The small dark flashes of blue-violet disturbed her and should have warned Sarra. No pure white
light here, no glowing sphere worthy of a true Captal.

They found a stone bench and sat side by side. Sarra
alighted gracefully as a bird; Cailet sprawled long legs and
stared at her boots. Sarra had not sensed the Ward, nor felt
anything physically wrong; her work had passed its first test.
She reminded herself she'd have to be careful to avoid em-
braces until she was fully healed and the pain was gone. And
when she walked arm-in-arm with Sarra or Collan—no one
else must or would get close enough—they would have to be
on her right. Little things, just for a week or so until the last
twinges had passed. Small cautions to hide the greater
illusion—which, from Sarra's lack of reaction, felt solid
enough. Real enough.

Undeniably real were the worry and determination in her
sister's eyes. All the details, everything that was said and
done and felt: Sarra would demand to know it all. Now. Tonight. . . .

Forestalling the inevitable a bit longer, Cailet said, "I
heard Collan singing a little while ago."

"Probably the first time 'The Long Sun' has ever been
sung all the way through. Cailet—"

"He played some of it on board ship to Pinderon that
time, before Lady Lilen stopped him." She thought of

Ostinhold then, and the Ryka Legion, and shunted images aside. It was Sarra she must deal with right now. Sarra who had to understand, before life could keep going.

Sarra had pulled a disgusted face. "Yes, that was one of his more spectacular stupidities. I'm going to have a lovely time of it, I can tell." She paused, then took Cailet's hand. "If you want to talk, I'll listen."

She didn't, but it had to be said. "Simple, really. Glenin came. So did Father. She left. He died."

"D–died?" Sarra breathed.

"I'm sorry—I forgot you didn't know. He died saving me from her magic." When Sarra bit both lips between her teeth and looked away, Cailet tried to keep the challenge from her voice as she said, "Don't you believe me?"

"I'm sure it must have seemed that way to you."

"That's how it happened."

"But why would he do such a thing? He was a Lord of Malerris."

"And *my* father, too, not just Glenin's. Father of the Mage Captal. Mark it up to early training if you like. He was one of us before he was one of them."

Sarra said nothing for a long minute. Then: "I didn't steal this time for us just to cause you more pain."

"I know."

Slender fingers raked back shimmering hair. "Maybe we should've waited until tomorrow."

"It's probably best spoken in darkness."

"Was it that bad? Is that why you sound so bitter?"

"Mostly I'm just tired, Sarra. Sad. I never knew him, except for those few minutes. You never wanted to talk about him or—or Mother."

"You didn't ask. You didn't say you wanted to hear about them."

"It would've hurt you. But I have to ask now. You have memories I need. I saw something of what he must've been once. I need to know about him."

"Now that he's dead." A little shiver ran through her. "I can't believe it, Caisha. Since I was five years old I've been afraid of him—and now he's gone. Why did it have to happen this way? Why did we have to lose him?"

"I think ... I think he lost himself," she replied slowly. "But he came back. He was a Mage Guardian again, Sarra, he came back."

"As you say," she replied, unable to hide the doubt in her eyes.

Glenin is still lost, even though she's been theirs all her life. Does she think of me as her *shadow, all empty and dark and hollow—no, I won't remember, I* won't—*but if she ever does that to me again I'll die—*

"Caisha? What's wrong, love?"

She groped her way from the threatening emptiness and clung to her other sister's hand. "I just feel that I should've done something—"

"Don't be ridiculous. None of it was your fault."

Cailet made herself smile and say, "Yes, big sister."

"That's better. Which reminds me, I still owe you an hour or two of yelling for sending Col and me to sleep like that."

"Why? You looked perfect together. Sorry I couldn't provide a real bed, but—" She laughed as Sarra blushed. "Oh, thank all the Saints that you're exactly like I thought you'd be!"

"What? You didn't even know me until a few weeks ago!"

"Oh, I've had you figured out for a long time," she teased. "Last year when you went to Ryka Court for the vote on your inheritance, the teacher talked about you in school. We sat there making faces behind our hands. So *young,* so *beautiful,* such *manners,* such *elegance,* so much the *model* of dedication and service, *everything* a Blooded Lady ought to be."

Sarra grinned. "Oh, and I'm like that, am I?"

"Not in the least. I'd met you in Pinderon, remember! And I made sure everybody knew what a scheming, arrogant little Blood you were, how you tried to have that poor Minstrel arrested—why are you laughing?"

" 'Poor Minstrel,' my ass! The next day he insulted me, kidnapped me, *hit* me, and left me in the middle of the road thirty miles from nowhere! And what do you mean, arrogant and scheming?"

"Would you prefer 'prideful' and 'clever'?"

"Much! Let's have a little more respect for your elder sister, please!" she laughed. "Caisha, you don't know what it means to have my own little sister—"

"Don't I? You're *my* sister, *my* family, not somebody I borrowed."

"But you still need what I remember."

"Please."

Sarra said nothing for a long time. Then, almost defiantly: "I loved him. He was the strongest, handsomest, most wonderful man in the world. Mother adored him. Grandfather was fond of him, I think—he was prepared to like any man who made Mother so happy. The rest of the family were . . . oh, polite, I suppose, and pleasant enough. But Grandmother hated him."

Cailet nodded.

"When I was very little, I was afraid of the dark, and he'd use his magic to bring the stars down from the sky and make them dance around my room. . . ."

Cailet had feared the dark, too. She tried to imagine having a tall, strong father banish her fear in a dazzle of magical stars.

Sarra's tone changed. "The first time I saw him after I was grown up was at the reception after the vote. Elo had said he wouldn't recognize me, that I was Warded. I was afraid anyhow. But he didn't even *look* the same. He wasn't just older, Cai. He wasn't my father anymore. Part of me was a little girl, wanting to run to him and have him swing me up in his arms the way he used to. But mostly I wanted to run away."

Her grip on Cailet's hand tightened. "There'd be no place *to* run if anyone ever found out who we really are, what our true Name is. We can't tell anyone. You know what they'd say, what they'd suspect. Daughters of a traitor Mage. We'd never be able to convince them otherwise. No one must know."

"Sasha. . . ." She swallowed hard, hating what she had to say. "Can you keep it from Collan?"

"Collan?" Sarra echoed blankly.

"I know we can't let on who we really are. Your position and your work are too important, and I'd never be allowed to continue as Captal. But if we keep our Name secret, we'll have to keep being sisters secret as well."

"We could use the Mage parents I invented for myself."

Cailet shook her head. "A lie wouldn't survive much speculation. There aren't many of the old Mages left, but among them they must've known most of the others." She tried to smile. "Besides, people would expect you to turn into a Mage and me into a Blooded Lady!"

"The first is impossible. As for the second—" She cast a critical eye over Cailet's dishevelment. "—I'll work on it."

Her laughter was genuine. "Sarra! That would be the project of a lifetime! You've better things to do."

"I'll work on it," she repeated in dire tones belied by a wink.

"I'd better add 'dictatorial' to the list."

"Why pretty it up? I'm bossy and we all know it." She hesitated, then shook her head. "I'll admit my faults and failings, Cai, but I won't admit to Collan who I really am. Every time he looked at me, he'd remember. I can't do that to him or to myself."

"Sarra—"

"And don't tell me he deserves to know, either. He doesn't deserve to have a reminder in front of him every day of his life of what he suffered at Auvry Feiran's hands! He may have become a Mage again for you, but when he tortured Col he was a Lord of Malerris. Don't ask me to accept that man as my father. Or Glenin as my sister, either. Not after what they did to him—and to you."

"To me?"

"I don't need my magic to sense that you're hiding something. Glenin hurt you, Caisha. I don't know how, but I'll never forgive her for it any more than I'll ever forgive *him* for what he did to Collan."

At length, Cailet nodded slowly. "It'll be our secret, then." *And Glenin's.* But she didn't say it.

"Actually, I already told Col we're sisters. It kind of slipped out. I'll use the Mage Guardians story to explain us, he won't look into it very hard."

"Are we Liwellans, then?"

"No, but I think we'll leave the Name unsaid. One more lie wouldn't matter, but one less lie is that much easier to—"

"—justify?"

"If you want to see it that way," she replied levelly, "yes."

After a moment Cailet said, "One thing. Promise you'll send me your children when they come into their magic. Let me teach them."

Sarra's brows arched in surprise. "Well, of course—if they're Mageborns."

"They will be."

"Col isn't."

"No. But your children by him will be."

Black eyes—their mother's eyes—searched her face. "You're that certain?"

"Oh, yes."

Recovering from this unsuspected revelation of the future, Sarra told her, "You'll have a fine family zoo in about twenty years, then, what with my children and yours—"

Cailet met her gaze squarely. "I won't have any children."

Glenin had made sure of it. The ravening hollow had been most deeply filled with horror. She had seen herself do unspeakable things—a death-black spider spinning elaborate magical webs, trapping the victim lover, feasting afterward on his blood. She would never risk it. Never. *"She'll mother no Mageborns—but tell Sarra that my son and I will be waiting for* hers!" That Glenin was pregnant with a son was something else she wasn't going to tell Sarra. Not yet.

"What do you mean? Of course you'll have children—"

"No. Don't make me talk about it, Sarra. It's just something I know."

"You're wrong. You'll find someone, Cai. Someone to love, who'll love you. You promised Taig."

Had she? She didn't remember. Sarra didn't understand, she thought it was because of how she'd felt about Taig. If the Saints were merciful, Sarra would never understand.

Arm-in-arm, the sisters walked through the gardens, Cailet subtly steering them to the riverbank where the pyre still burned within the circle of stones.

Sarra stumbled back from the flames, the curling smoke. "You brought me here to show me *that?*"

"And to give you this." From her pocket she took one of the silver pins, the Sword, and pressed it into Sarra's palm. "I'm keeping the other. He had them, all these years—even though he wasn't a Listed Mage, he—"

She flung the pin to the ground. "No!"

"But don't you see? They prove he wasn't the monster everyone said he was!"

"They're probably souvenirs of some Mage Guardian he murdered!"

"No. They were his." Plucking the tiny silver pin from the ground, she held it out to her sister. "You're his daughter, too. Take it. Think of it as belonging to the father you knew as a child, the Prentice Mage."

After what seemed half of eternity, Sarra accepted the pin and tucked it in her pocket. "If it means so much to you. . . ." Then, with a last glance at the pyre: "I'm going back. Are you coming?"

"In a little while."

With a brief nod and an even briefer embrace, Sarra left her alone.

For a long time Cailet gazed at the flames, clutching the tiny silver Candle in her fist. "I was right, wasn't I?" she whispered. "Or is it the child in me that thinks there was still something in you of what you once were?"

A wisp of smoke rose from the pyre. Rather than dissipating on the night breeze, it broadened, grew taller, became more substantial. And drifted slowly toward where Cailet stood rooted to the ground, trembling. The mist resolved into the shape of a man: tall, wide-shouldered, wearing the proud regimentals and the gleaming silver insignia of a Mage Guardian. More: the red and black sash of a Captal's Warder.

"Thank you, Daughter," whispered a deep, warm voice on the wind. The Wraithen face was young and handsome, suffused with vast tenderness and vaster sorrow. "I robbed myself of you before you were even born. Forgive me."

"You saved my life."

"You are the Captal. My daughter."

She filled herself with the love in his gray-green eyes— and the respectful duty, too, owed to a Captal—and the pride.

"Cailet, help Sarra to her magic. She'll need everything she is to do the work she's set herself."

"I'll try. But she's stubborn."

"I remember." And they shared a smile.

"She told me you made the stars dance for her."

"Then she doesn't think of me entirely with pain. I'm glad." His expression changed. "Glenin. . . ."

Cailet kept herself from flinching. Glenin, the daughter he had loved more than Sarra, loved so much he took her with him to the Malerrisi.

"Gorsha saw in you a Mage Captal with power to counter Glenin's. But your heart is more generous, your vision wider. Even after what she did to you, you still wonder how to reach her. How to make her understand."

"I don't know what to do, Father."

"No more do I." Broad shoulders cloaked in Mage Guardian black lifted and fell as he sighed. "We choose our paths as we are led to them. She never saw another path. That was

my doing. But if you could show her, Cailet—help her—and
mend the fabric I tore apart—"

She stiffened instinctively. "Those are Malerrisi words."

"So they are. But the pattern of life is a true image,
Caisha. I thought I saw better order and greater safety in
the rigid weaving of the Great Loom. Glenin still sees it. She
doesn't understand why it's wrong to put the threads in the
hands of the privileged, self-appointed few." He began to
fade with the smoke of his pyre into the night.

"No, don't go, not yet! What am I supposed to do?
Gorynel Desse made me Captal and now—"

"You were Captal from the moment of your birth. That is
why I couldn't know that you existed. Peace, Cailet. Be patient. Soon enough you'll know your true work." He hesitated, almost invisible. "I do love you, Daughter."

"Father—"

But he was gone.

She was crying, and wondered why. For herself, certainly;
for Sarra, who had not seen this proof; for Glenin—perhaps.
But not for Auvry Feiran. How could she weep for a man
whose Wraith, despite all the horrors and betrayals and
deaths and lies, had somehow against all logic not been condemned to endless, aimless wandering in the Dead White
Forest?

7

Still angry with her sister, Sarra arrived back at the courtyard bonfire in time to see a difference of opinion between
Keler Neffe and Sevat Semalson escalate into a shouting
match. Telomir Renne was pleading with them; Granon
Isidir stood by with folded arms and an expression that proclaimed annoyance at not getting a word in edgewise.
Threading her way through the crowd, Sarra heard enough
bits and snatches of commentary to piece together the problem: identity disks. Keler was against them. Semalson, an
assistant at Census, was for them. As Sarra emerged from
the surrounding circle of onlookers, the two young men were
yelling at point-blank range.

"Enough!"

To their mothers' credit, both shut up when a woman ordered them to. The assembly hushed too, anticipating a good show. Sarra gritted her teeth and cursed herself for interfering. Now she'd have to prove her ability to lead—right now, or not at all.

"Couldn't you have waited a few days?" she demanded.

"Lady Sarra, tonight makes an ending and a beginning," Keler said. "The disks are offensive and useless, and—"

"They weren't Anniyas's idea!" exclaimed Semalson. "The disks originated thirty-three Generations ago—"

"And finished serving their purpose long since!"

"I said *enough!*" Sarra eyed the pair of them. "As you seem bent on having this out here and now, you may present your thoughts on the matter. Calmly, rationally, and without screaming. *Domni* Semalson, you first."

"The viewpoint at Census is simply stated, Lady Sarra. The government must accurately identify citizens. How else are contracts to be held legal? Births, marriages, divorces, trade agreements, wills, Dower Funds—all these depend on absolute certainty that every woman, man, and child is—"

"You forgot taxes!" someone yelled from near the bonfire.

"Yes, all right, and taxes!" Semalson's thin dark face flushed with more than wine. "But don't *you* forget that possession of a disk is the right and privilege of freeborns! Without one, you're classified as a slave!"

"An interesting point," Sarra said. "But valid only if slavery continued to exist. Which it won't."

Pandemonium.

She judged that the uproar was mostly in favor. But plenty of Webs dependent on slave labor would howl themselves hoarse over abolition. Let them, she thought impatiently. There was enough in the Council treasury for fair compensation. Emphasis on *fair*. She'd have to find someone who knew the trade and could say when estimations of market value were attempts at extortion.

The argument over slavery would be only the first conflict in the changing of governmental policy. She already knew that everyone in the Rising had distinct ideas about what the Rising was meant to accomplish. *So,* she mused as the tumult died down, *Tarise was right about me years ago. I'm a Warrior after all. I'll have to fight for every single thing I believe to be right. But I'll have to learn how to be Healer, too. And how I'm going to stitch all these wants and needs into a working government is anybody's guess. Even Cailet and her Mages will have demands. Gorsha, if you were here, I'd wrap your beard around your throat and strangle you with it.*

Keler Neffe was grinning ear to ear as he shouted, "There you have it! No more reason for identity disks!"

"I don't agree," said Telomir Renne, frowning worriedly. "Forgive me, Sarra, but while I do agree that slavery should be outlawed, I still think the disks are important. They provide identification in legal matters, of course, but they also prevent anyone's pretending to be someone she isn't. Imposture is not a weapon I'd care to put in the hands of the Lords of Malerris."

"Besides," a woman called out derisively, "the Renne Blood owns the right to mint the damned things. Isn't that right, Minister?"

Keler cut into the burst of laughter before Telomir could do more than turn rigid with outrage. "Bloods, Firsts, Seconds—what better reason to do away with the disks? The whole system became meaningless twenty Generations ago!"

"Do you mean to say," Semalson snarled, "that you Second Tier Neffes are no different from—"

"—the Semalson Bloods? Damned right, that's what I'm saying!"

"No difference?" Jenet Adennos, a cousin of Elomar's and the late Captal's, stepped forward. She was just forty, but the weeks spent in a jail in Kenroke had aged her at least ten years. "What about the fact that you're a Mage Guardian, Keler? Do you still say you're the same as *Domni* Semalson?"

Sarra answered for him. "Yes. He does." And she gave Keler a look that said if he didn't, he'd better rearrange his thinking immediately. She turned the same expression on every Mage Guardian she could find in the crowd.

Suddenly a familiar drawling voice remarked, "Keler may have the advantage in magic, but I know for a fact he can't add two and two. He'd make a hell of a Census taker."

This ridiculous observation didn't strike Sarra as funny at all. But everyone laughed—or almost everyone—as Collan edged out of the tangle and stood with the bonfire behind him. He'd gotten rid of the longvest, and in the plain red and white of trousers and shirt looked nearly presentable.

"You're all missing the point," he went on. "The only people who care about Bloods and Tiers are people who want to keep the system even though they don't have the guts to call it what it is. As for impostors—hell, I'm not wearing a disk, I could be anybody. And look at Lady Sarra. The one *she's* wearing belonged to Mai Alvassy!"

And then he slid a thumb beneath the chain at Sarra's neck and pulled it off over her head and threw it into the bonfire.

Into the deathly silence he said calmly, "Who she is is who *she* says she is. And the same goes for me, and every single person on Lenfell."

Dizzy with pride, Sarra couldn't take her eyes off him. Vaguely she was aware of a few, a dozen, then almost everyone present tossing their disks into the blaze to melt into meaningless bits of silver. In the race to tear off and dispose of the disks, Sevat Semalson was jostled back. He gave Sarra a dire glance as she bumped into her.

"We'll still know. Birth records, marriages, divorces—" His mouth curled unpleasantly. "—*and* tax rolls."

"Fine," she replied, nodding. "A government has a perfect right to know who its citizens are. But not to label them for its own convenience. Not to categorize them. We are who we say we are, not what anyone tells us to be."

She felt a hand tug at her elbow, and turned. Collan. She wanted to throw her arms around him—until she got a good look at his face. He drew her over to the wine carts and rounded on her furiously.

"What the hell was that look for?"

"What look?"

"Little Lady Innocence!" He shook her by the arm; she jerked herself free. "It was as plain as if you'd branded me the way Scraller did!"

"Branded—?"

"Your *property!*" he hissed. "And if you think I'll husband you, First Daughter, think again! I don't belong to *anybody*, least of all you!"

Her temper exploded in his face. "Who says I *want* you? Obviously you're not the kind of man to *be* a husband! I wouldn't have you as mine if you got down on your knees and begged!"

"Oh, you'd like that, wouldn't you?" Then, with the illogic that was the birthright of even the most rational men and the despair of countless Generations of women, he did an incomprehensible about-face and accused, "You need a husband, Lady—and it's going to be me!"

"You!"

"Me," he repeated grimly. "And if you don't say 'yes,' I can change your mind in about five seconds!"

"You might as well agree, Sarra," said a voice from the nearby darkness—and Cailet appeared out of the ragged shadows, grinning. "You will eventually. No sense arguing with a man whose mind's made up. Spare yourself the trouble."

"*He's* the trouble," she snapped. "He'd be nothing but trouble from the day I married him!"

"You're not such a bargain yourself, First Daughter!"

Cailet held up a hand for quiet. "Let us take our lesson from the blue-beak hawk," she intoned like a votary at evening liturgy, black eyes dancing. "It is the male's duty to construct the nest. He exhausts himself gathering twigs and moss. He tears his very down-feathers to build a warm, snug, attractive—"

"Is there a point to this?" Sarra demanded.

"Yes. It's not *domni* blue-beak with the prettiest nest who wins the notice of all the lady blue-beaks. He's too tired to chirp, let alone sing, and he looks just awful with all those feathers plucked out. It's the handsome, noisy, lazy one who didn't pick up so much as a pine needle who gets the girls."

Collan was shaking with repressed laughter. Sarra wanted to slap him. "Lesson being," she said frostily, "that a woman who chooses a man without first inspecting his nest deserves what she gets."

Cailet nodded gleefully. "Of course—because his diligent brothers are too tired to defend what they built, and so he can walk right on into the finest nest! Sarra, you *deserve* Collan. Handsome, noisy—and no nest in sight! No, really, if all you want is a husband to keep house and raise your children—"

"*That* sounds *perfect.*" But she was beginning to see the humor in spite of herself. "Handsome and noisy, eh? Well, a good-looking man is usually self-confident, and you're right about that—I can't see myself with a mouse. As for noisy, he doesn't say anything seriously stupid more than a few times a day. The rest of his noise is actually pleasant, with the lute to back it up. Besides, I've got my own nest—or will, once everything's settled down."

"Excellent!" Cailet turned to Collan. "So how do you feel about beautiful, noisy, rich women?"

He grinned and shook his head. "Nice try, kitten, but she's going to have to ask me right and proper."

"Well?" Cailet prompted. "Sarra?"

"Go away, little sister." She gave Cailet a playful shove.

"Aw, can't I watch?"

"No."

Laughing, Cailet obeyed. When Sarra and Collan were alone and she was gazing up into his eyes, the music and the singing seemed to fade away. In a book, she would have dismissed it as romantic drivel. But it really did happen. She felt as if no one else in the world existed but the two of them.

Which was not the proper attitude for a woman who was about to make substantial changes in that world. But she knew suddenly that this feeling of sweet isolation would become essential to her: contrary and conniving as he was, noisy and nestless and arrogant with no good reason to be, yet when she was with him all else meant nothing. The world would have much of her—but *she* would have *him*.

"I'm waiting," he said.

Suddenly she started to laugh.

"What's so damned funny?"

"Us! We'll drive each other insane. We'll fight and call each other names and be the scandal of all Lenfell."

"Is *that* your 'right and proper' proposal?"

"No, this is." She twined her arms around his neck, fingers toying with coppery curls as she gazed up into very blue eyes. "Minstrel, dear, will you husband me?"

"What do *you* think, First Daughter?"

"I think you'd better say yes or I'll get my sister the Mage Captal to magic it out of you!"

"Magic enough right here," he said, and kissed her.

It occurred to her to think—before she stopped thinking entirely—that there was a definite charm to a noisy man who knew when to shut up.

8

Shamelessly eavesdropping from the shadows, Cailet sighed her satisfaction. *One* thing taken care of, anyway.

There were a thousand others awaiting her, and—aside from her personal delight in their happiness—she knew she'd need both Sarra and Collan at their full powers, undistracted by emotional conflict. She trusted them to keep the sweeter distractions of new love to a minimum. Neither would be able to hide what they felt, but she knew both well enough to know they'd save its more eloquent expression for when there was time enough to enjoy it.

Yet instead of the few days or a week Cailet had anticipated and hoped for, she was allowed only a few hours. At scarcely Seventh of a beautiful spring morning, after very little sleep, and with a throbbing wine-head and an endless dull ache in her side, she learned that Ostinhold had been burned and Malerris Castle had vanished.

Warrior Mage Senn Mikleine brought the first news. Last night he and ten others had gone to Bard Hall, and thence to Longriding. From Lady Lilen's house there he had Folded their path to within five miles of Ostinhold: billowing smoke told all.

Numb and dry-eyed, Cailet had barely heard him out before Aifalun Escovor and Enis Girre begged a moment of her time. The elderly Scholars had separately attempted to contact various Mages through a difficult and esoteric spell that sometimes worked and sometimes didn't. But they had managed to reach old friends in Neele, Domburr Castle, Dinn, and Havenport.

Girre had received an image in return from a fellow Scholar outside Dinn: Malerris Castle—or, rather, its absence from Seinshir.

Cailet frowned. "Destroyed? Down to the foundations, not just a few buildings wrecked for show?"

"No, Captal, *gone.* Vanished." He spread his gnarled old hands wide. "The waterfall is there, but the Castle above it is gone as if it had never been."

"Warded," Cailet said softly.

The old man nodded. "My thought precisely."

If not Glenin's work, then at Glenin's order. Cailet went down to the river where she could see the ruined Academy, marveling at the power it must take to make an entire castle seem to disappear. Lords of Malerris did such things, acting together in the kind of Net that Mage Guardians resisted. If she wanted to break those Wards, she would have to do it alone.

It took an hour of steady thought and thorough review of the Bequest to decide she would not squander her strength. All she need do was set her own trap Wards on all the known Ladders to Malerris Castle. Any Malerrisi attempting to use one of those Ladders would be kept immobile until Cailet or another Mage arrived.

Boats would still bring in supplies, but that was acceptable; she didn't want her sister to starve to death. As for leaving the island to advance new schemes . . . no, not for a long while yet. Last night Flera Firennos said that one reason the Rising had waited so long was for a list of all Malerrisi and their whereabouts. This had been provided only a few days ago by a Rising agent within the Castle itself, and would be given to the Captal as soon as possible.

Many if not most of the Malerrisi had come into the open early this year to assist in the location, capture, and very often the killing of Mage Guardians. They were known now. They might infiltrate in small ways henceforth, but they would never again seat their own as high officials, Ministers, Justices—or First Councillor.

Cailet knew, in the way of Sarra's knowing, that every Lord who was able would return to the Castle as surely as if Summoned. She also knew that the Invisibility was Glenin's way of taunting her. All that was really necessary was to prevent anyone from entering; the additional flourish was mockery meant to grate on the Captal's nerves.

The Captal was unmoved. She stared unseeing at the wreckage across the river, thinking of something Glenin had said: she and her son would be waiting. The Malerrisi might make small forays, but would not emerge in strength until the boy was old enough to lead them at his mother's side.

Cailet hadn't told Sarra about their nephew. She would not, until he made his presence felt. She had no doubt that he would.

Ironic that her work and Glenin's would be identical: training Mageborns. This led to the realization that this if nothing else would bring the Malerrisi out into the larger world. Cailet would have to find such children before Glenin did.

How many were already at Malerris Castle? A few hundred? Close to a thousand? In twenty years, a new Generation could be bred—as Glenin had planned to breed Cailet and Sarra.

She could do nothing about children born at Malerris Castle. But she'd find the others all across Lenfell, damned if she wouldn't.

One she knew about and had hoped to teach was dead now at Ostinhold. It was called unlucky to be born during Equinox or Solstice, with no Saint to watch over the birthing, and worst of all to be born on the very days of the Quarters, like Sela's son. Cailet wondered bitterly if any folklore applied to a child conceived on the Wraithenday.

Glenin had a son of her own. Cailet wrestled with terrible envy. In a curious way, she had thought of Sela Trayos's boy as her own son, linked to her by magic if not by blood.

She told herself there would be other children. None hers, but . . . there were at least a dozen right now, young Prentice Mages who had learned their craft from their elders but who would never be Listed Guardians unless an Academy was reestablished.

Only the Captal could do that. She understood now what her father had told her, that she would soon discover what her work must be.

But she would not accomplish it here in Ambrai. She needed a new place, safely remote, where every stranger would be remarked upon. There she would educate Mageborns—while her sister did the same.

If only Glenin had listened. . . .

9

It was the best possible luck for a woman to take a husband on her own Birthingday. So, on the third day of First Flow-

ers, when Sarra Ambrai turned twenty-three years old, she
married Collan Rosvenir.

Cailet stood witness for the Mage Guardians, for she
could not stand with Sarra as family. That position was filled
by Riddon and Maugir Slegin. Biron Maurgen and Miram
Ostin were there not only because Sarra valued them for
themselves, but in memory of their brothers.

Falundir and—of all people—Imilial Gorrst gave Collan
in marriage. He asked the Bard first, and then, because
Falundir could not speak the proper responses, approached
Imi with an eloquent plea ruined by a wink. She told him he
was hideously cruel to break her heart by husbanding another woman and then asking her not only to watch but to
help officiate, but agreed because at least she'd be giving
him to the one woman—other than herself—who'd appreciate him.

Elin and Pier Alvassy, Elomar Adennos and Lusira Garvedian, and Telomir Renne formed the rest of the company.
They gathered in the little shrine of Imili and Miramili at the
far end of the gardens, where Generations of Ambrai women
had taken husbands. The altar furnishings—Miramili's ceremonial golden bell and Imili's flower basket woven of gold
wire—were long gone. But the altar was strewn with wildflowers, and Miram provided a little silver bell she wore as
a charm around her neck, so the Saints were adequately represented.

Sarra's hastily assembled bridal array was a slim and simple bright green gown provided by Telomir—who, with
Riddon and Miram, sewed frantically all night to get it
ready. She was crowned with flowers as was appropriate to
her name, her Saint, the week, and the ceremony.

Collan sneezed the instant he walked into the shrine, and
throughout the ceremony his nose twitched alarmingly. Otherwise he looked magnificent. His Bardic blue trousers,
longvest, and coif were Falundir's gift. As they walked to
the shrine, Cailet had murmured wryly to the Bard how
amazing it was that such fine new clothes had been available
at such short notice—and such a perfect fit, too. Falundir
smiled, nodded, and looked smug.

The others wore what finery they could borrow. Cailet
was in her makeshift Captal's regimentals, Miram's clean
silvery scarf once more around her waist. The severe black
was enlivened by a garland of woven flowers draped about

her shoulders, like those worn by everyone except Sarra and Col.

All the proper words were spoken, all the hallowed phrases that promised enduring love, constant honor, faithful duty, absolute fidelity, and complete obedience. (Col almost succeeded in hiding annoyance at this last—no marriage was legal without it—but Cailet saw yet another law being re-written in Sarra's eyes.) Sarra then vowed to care for, cherish, and provide for her husband.

Collan took from the altar a chain of flowers he'd woven last night: white roses for love, twining ivy for marriage, lemon blossoms for faithfulness. This he placed around Sarra's shoulders before bending his head so she could gift him with her own flowers.

She reached up suddenly and snatched off his coif. "Your first duty is to obey me, husband—and I order you *never* to wear one of these again!" And she placed her crown of flowers on his bare head.

His reply was lost in an explosive sneeze. Everyone burst out laughing as the crown slipped sideways. Grinning like a fool, the crown at a rakish angle, he stomped a boot on the hated coif as if to nail it to the floor.

Thus were they wed. Later, after many toasts and much kissing and embracing and laughter, they went alone to the riverbank and with silent whispered wishes threw the flower chain and the flower crown into the water.

He drew her into the shelter of his arm as they watched the river. "What did you ask for?"

"Nothing very grand," she confessed. "Just a chance to be happy."

"Saints, what a relief! I thought for sure you'd wish peace and plenty for all Lenfell, a new government, and a hundred other things that're nothing to do with us."

"They *are* to do with us—but not right this moment. What did you wish?"

"I'm ambitious," he told her wryly. "I want one whole uninterrupted night alone with you. Oh, and a good lute."

She laughed. "You're right, the first does seem pretty impossible! But I can do something about the second."

"What?"

"Senn Mikleine came back from Longriding with your lute." She snuggled closer. "I'd like to spend at least a few minutes of our uninterrupted night alone hearing you sing to me. You never have, you know."

"My lute," he said, stunned. Then he wrapped his arms around her. "All the songs—they're all for you, the rest of my life."

"Did you find that in a song somewhere, or make it up just for me?"

"How can I make love to a woman who doesn't trust a single word I say?"

"Keep talking, Minstrel. Convince me."

He did.

10

The next day, Cailet went to Ostinhold. She took Miram with her, and Biron Maurgen, and those Mages who had started to form her unofficial Captal's Warders: Elo, Lusira, Imi, Senn Mikleine, and Granon Bekke. Though she needed no protection now, she did need their experience and their counsel. And their silently offered comfort as they approached the smoldering debris of Ostinhold.

A search was pointless. Nothing could have lived through such fires. There was no telling whether or not anyone had escaped. Cailet cast a single glance at Miram, who shook her head and muttered, "I've seen enough."

Biron led them up the North Road to Maurgen Hundred. They arrived just after dark. The lights of the five domed houses blazed defiantly beyond a perimeter fence sentried by armed ranch hands. One of them recognized Biron and signaled the others to lower their swords—but not to open the gates.

"Y'r pardon, *Domni,* but who'd be these others with you?"

Cailet squinted into the torchlit night. "Kellos Wentrin, isn't it? I thought I recognized that Tillinshir accent."

He squinted back and caught his breath. "*Domna* Cailet?"

"Mage Captal," said Biron. "Let us in, Kellos. Is Lady Sefana here?"

"Mage—?" Wentrin shook himself and gestured for his

fellows to unlock and open the gates. "Aye, *Domni*, not just Lady Sefana but Lady Lilen as well."

Miram gave an incoherent cry and ran through the gates.

Cailet and the others hung back. "What about the rest of Ostinhold?" Biron asked. "We were just there, we saw what the Legion did. Anyone else escape?"

"Nigh on three thousand—which's to say everyone'd already scattered. Some few, they did linger, for Lady Lilen wouldn't leave, and some of *them* died helping her own escaping."

"What about their visitors?" Imilial asked. "There was an elderly Mage—"

"I wouldn't be knowing, *Domna*. But I do know for a certain fact that Geria Ostin's is the fault of it. You go on up to the main house, they can tell you."

Imi burst into tears at the sight of her father. He hugged her close with the arm that wasn't in a sling and told her not to be such a lackwit, he was far too crotchety to die. Miram stood in the middle of a knot comprised of her mother, her sisters Tevis and Lindren, and Terrill, her only remaining brother. All but Lady Lilen were weeping. On seeing Cailet, she eased away and held out her arms. Cailet accepted the embrace in silence. Lilen drew back to search her eyes, then nodded quiet understanding.

"You are now who you were meant to be," she whispered for Cailet's ears alone. "But I hope you'll always be my Cailet, too."

"Lilen—" For the first time she spoke her foster-mother's name without *Lady* in front of it. "I'm so sorry. Taig—"

"Hush. Miram told me. We'll speak of him later, we two. And of Gorsha, and my Alin and his Val."

Sefana Maurgen—not yet fifty, without a single gray strand in her raven hair, and widowed in the same accident that had killed Lilen's husband—limped into the entry hall to herd everyone to a dining room lit by a score of blue candles. Her twin daughters, Riena and Jennis, brought in laden plates and huge pitchers of scalding coffee sweetened with cinnamon sugar. Cailet had often guested at Lady Sefana's table, but never more gratefully than now; she'd eaten nothing since breakfast that morning and it had been a weary journey from Longriding—even for a Mage Captal who could spell twenty-five miles into walking as if they were only one.

When all were settled around the great trestle table, Cailet turned to Lilen. "Kellos Wentrin said Geria was to blame for Ostinhold."

"Are you surprised?" Tevis snapped. "She betrayed us."

"Hush," said her mother. "I'll tell it."

Geria had fled Ostinhold, hiding among a few hundred Ostins heading for Tillinshir. She'd found the Ryka Legion and made a bargain: her life, the lives of her husband and children, and possession of the intact Ostin Web in exchange for specifics about Ostinhold's defenses.

"She expected me to die, of course," Lilen said calmly. "I wasn't disposed to oblige her."

Tevis, unable to stay silent, added acidly, "Geria stood there outside the gates like she was posing for a statue of Gelenis First Daughter, *bragging* that she'd saved Ostinhold and the Web!"

"She told us to surrender," Lilen went on. "She knew full well I never would." Her lips curved in a fierce little smile. "But she didn't expect that I'd set fire to Ostinhold myself before I'd let her set foot in it again."

"Then—*you*—" Cailet could hardly speak.

"Yes. Oh, they finished the job, the Ryka Legion. They're very thorough. But I began it. I thought I wouldn't survive, you see. Little did I know that this old fool had stayed behind with a Ward ready and waiting to whisk me out as invisible as a Wraith!"

Kanto Solingirt cleared his throat. "One hardly 'whisks' a woman who kicks you every step of the way. Don't think I got this—" He lifted his injured arm. "—from anything the Legion did!"

"A hero's wounding all the same," Imilial told him, with a wry look.

"Where's the Legion gone?" Cailet asked.

"Back to Renig." Lady Sefana grinned. "They're in for a hell of a shock."

"Did—did the Trayos children escape?"

Lilen nodded. "North to the mountains. Once things are safe again, everyone will come back. Venkelos the Provider have mercy on me, I don't know where I'm going to put them all."

Tevis shrugged slender shoulders. "They can make themselves useful for a change and help rebuild Ostinhold."

"Well, I suppose so. As for Geria—she's at the Combel

house, I should think. Which reminds me, I must go in to Longriding and file some documents soon. I can't disinherit her completely, but I *can* give most of it to my other daughters while I live. Lenna will have the Renig house. She's the only really civilized Ostin I know of—and a lawyer. She'll do herself and us the most good in the capital. I hope Geria *does* take me to court, actually."

Cailet bit back a smile. Lilen Ostin was in her element; one would think that with Sarra's like talent for taking charge, she and not Cailet had been raised by this Lady.

"Tevis, the house in Longriding will be yours."

"Thank you, Mother. But I won't go near that cactus of yours."

"Oh, I'll take care of it, dear, don't worry. I intend to make a frequent burden of myself at *all* my daughters' homes. Miram—"

"Ostinhold."

"Are you sure?" Lilen frowned. "It'll be years before we break even there, let alone turn a profit."

"Ostinhold. Please, Mother."

"Better you than me, Mirri," Lindren said frankly. "If you've nothing else in mind for me, Mother, then may I have the Renig office block? I can turn some of it into living space and run the merchant fleet from there."

"If that's your wish, of course. This brings me to the Web. Now, Miram, I know how it bores you, but find a husband who enjoys business. All these places come with trade contracts attached. Things may be difficult for a while, but—"

"Lady Lilen," said Kanto Solingirt, "forgive the intrusion, but I may have a useful word. *Domna* Lindren mentioned offices. Within offices are papers—records that presumably are also within the houses mentioned. Would your First Daughter be able to run the parts of the Web you cannot by law take from her without access to records of the rest?"

Granon Bekke let out an involuntary whoop. "Oh, that's *luscious!*"

Sefana regarded Imi across the table. "My dear, although I only met your charming father recently, would you consider my suit for his hand?"

"Mother!" scolded Riena. "Lady Lilen saw him first!"

The old Scholar was blushing. Interestingly, so was Lady Lilen.

"Additionally," he soldiered bravely on, "such records will enable you to . . . adjust . . . the larger Web."

Lindren gave a sharp laugh. "I'll 'adjust' Geria right out of business!"

"Enjoy yourself, dear," said her mother. "I must have a long, legal talk with Lenna very soon. If only I could divert some money to Terrill's dowry. . . ."

"You can, if Sarra Liwellan has her way," Lusira observed, "and I've noted that she usually does. She's already abolished slavery—or at least started us down that road. Marriage and dower customs are high on her list."

"Are they? How very subversive of her!" Lady Sefana pushed herself to her feet. "But it's getting late. Cailet— forgive me, Captal—"

"Cailet. I'm having a law of my own passed. Any of my friends who call me 'Captal' to my face must pay a fine!"

They were escorted upstairs by Riena and Jennis. Elomar stayed behind to inquire about the back trouble Sefana had consulted him about in Longriding—several weeks ago, or maybe several years. Cailet had lost track.

First Daughter Riena was more than a year Cailet's senior; they'd known each other slightly at school. Now, solemn and sincere, Riena termed it a privilege to give her own room to the Captal. Cailet had thought she'd made her point a few minutes ago; evidently not. She almost asked if this meant she and Riena weren't friends, but kept her mouth shut. Her duty as a guest was to accept graciously—and hide a wince.

She had barely looked around the cheerful little room with its blue walls and brown-and-blue plaid bedspread when a knock sounded on the half-open door. Lilen stepped over the threshold, then hesitated.

"Please come in," Cailet said. "Truly told, I'm too tired to sleep." She tried a smile and almost succeeded. "There's something about working a lot of magic in one day. . . ."

"Gorsha used to say the same thing."

They sat on Riena's little couch, Cailet hugging a plaid pillow to her stomach. "I don't know where to begin."

"You needn't tell me everything now, darling. I only want to know if you're all right."

She pretended startlement. "Do I look that awful?"

"Are you trying to fool me, Cailet Ambrai?"

This time the surprise was real, but over in an instant. Of course Lilen knew who she really was. "I'm sorry."

"One day, sweeting, when it's not so new and painful, I'll tell you all about your dear mother." Sliding a comforting arm around Cailet's shoulders, Lilen went on, "I learned about Alin and Val—and Gorsha—from Kanto. But I need to hear about Taig . . . almost as much as you need to tell me."

Haltingly, Cailet did. Trying not to relive it. Failing.

"He saved my life," she finished at last. "If not for him, I'd be dead."

"He loved you very much."

Wordlessly, Cailet rose and went to the foot of the bed, where her journeypack leaned against the iron rails. Taking from it a small wooden box, she returned to Lilen.

"I promised Taig I'd take him back to Ostinhold. But I can't go back there, Lilen, I just can't."

Pressing the box to her breast, Taig's mother replied, "I understand, dear. Ostinhold is the past. Come back when Miram and I have built it anew, and there are no memories."

"There are always memories." *Mine, Gorsha's, Alin's—*

Lilen sighed briefly and stood. "Thank you for telling me about Taig."

Cailet knew she ought to say something. Lilen was the only mother she'd ever known, who loved her as if Cailet was her own child. If she didn't speak now, she never would; she was vulnerable now. By tomorrow duties and obligations and responsibilities would crust the wounds once more. The isolation of being Captal would wrap that much more securely around her.

And it would be her own fault.

She knew it. She couldn't speak. And the moment was lost. Lilen kissed her cheek before silently leaving the room.

Cailet paced to the window, then to the bed, then to the nightstand to wash her face with cool water from the basin. Drops cascading down her cheeks and clinging to her lashes, she met her own eyes in the mirror.

"Coward."

She needed these people, these friends who'd always known her. She didn't want her title to get in the way. Yet her pleas to be called by her name all made reference to her authority. A law she wanted passed, an order—

Captal would keep most people at a distance; making her name a privilege guaranteed that everyone so privileged would recognize it as such every time they spoke it. That was distance, too.

And she craved it. Wanted space and words—and Wards, too—between her and other people. She pressed her left arm against her injured side. In the mirror, the black tunic slid along the natural contour of a breast. She let the Ward dissolve, and saw the ugly difference.

"So that's what you've been hiding."

She spun at the sound of Elomar's stern voice. Part of her wanted to rework the magic, a child frantic to hide evidence of a misdeed.

"Did you think I wouldn't feel the Ward?" he went on, not quite slamming the door behind him. "You're good, I'll give you that. At first I thought it was a personal Ward, and congratulated myself that you'd followed my advice to be cautious. But there was something odd about it, something not quite right."

More words in a row than she'd ever heard him speak; anger and worry spurred him out of taciturn silence. And Cailet herself couldn't think of a single word to say.

"Why didn't you come to me with this? How could you be so foolish? Take that shirt off and let me see."

She stood there, frozen. No one must see the ugliness, the maiming. No one must know how it was physical evidence of—of mental rape.

"Damn it, Cailet, do as I say!"

Moving woodenly, she unbuttoned tunic and shirt with clumsy fingers. His lips thinned as the injury was revealed, but he said nothing as he examined it. She fixed her gaze on the middle distance and tried not to shiver at his careful, impersonal touch.

He asked her to rotate her shoulder, bend to each side, circle her arm. At last he handed her Riena's lace-trimmed nightgown. She yanked it down over her head while he paced angrily, shucked off trousers and boots while he muttered to himself. Then he swung around.

"Someone attempted to Heal this. Amateurishly. You?"

The nightgown fit well; she and Riena were much of a size, and the blue silk clung to her body. "My father," she said.

"Your—" He choked on it.

"My father! Auvry Feiran!" In defiance, as Elomar watched, she called up the Ward. "With the last bit of his magic he tried to heal what Glenin did to me with her magic!"

A spasm of pain crossed his long face. Then he bent his head humbly. "Please forgive me," he murmured. "I had not expected—*generosity*—of him."

"You'll just have to rethink your opinion of the Butcher of Ambrai, then, won't you?"

"Forgive me," he repeated.

"If he hadn't tried, I might have bled to death."

"No. But you would have been crippled for life, the use of the muscles forever impaired. His ... work ... prevented that."

She half-turned from him, hiding relief. Without looking at him again, she said, "Not a word of this to anyone, Elo. Especially not Sarra. Your promise, Healer Mage."

"My promise," he said colorlessly.

"I'm going to bed. Close the door behind you." She said it coolly, knowing that here was another friend being driven away. Distanced.

He left, and she was alone.

And that was the way she wanted it. Didn't she?

11

Cailet woke before dawn, fully rested for the first time in weeks. Most of Maurgen Hundred was still abed. The kitchen was the usual controlled chaos of preparations for breakfast; Cailet was able to sneak a cup of coffee and a plate of cooling apple fritters before walking out to the stables.

She relaxed on a hay bale, listening to the drowsy snufflings of the horses. The Maurgens had always made the most beautiful and comfortable saddles in North Lenfell; six Generations ago they'd diversified and started to breed the animals the gear was meant for. Between 803 and 837, eight Maurgen women took Tillinshir Wentrins to husband. The dowry was horses. Rejected as too dark to breed back into the famous line of Tillinshir grays, the mares and studs were the ancestors of the Maurgen dapple-backs. There were two basic types: night and coal (Cailet could never tell the difference—something to do with skin color), but all bore distinctive white markings from withers to tail. Over the years, the bloodlines had been fixed in several varieties, among them Salty, Flyspeck, and Cutpiece. Lady Sefana's favorites were the Lace coals, with tiny irregular patches of snowy hairs spreading like shawls. Maurgen dapple-backs were beautiful horses: tall, long-limbed, smooth of gait, placid of character. Margit and Taig had taught Cailet to ride on a venerable Starry Sky mare that had looked as if she wore a blanket of stars across her back.

When she finished her breakfast, she meandered around to each of the stalls, counting new foals and greeting a few old friends. She'd last been at Maurgen Hundred back in Neversun for Lady Sefana's Birthingday. Then Taig had taken her to Longriding. . . .

"*You're* up early! Either you slept well enough not to need more, or you didn't sleep at all."

Cailet turned to smile at Jennis Maurgen. Whereas Biron and Val had looked like twins despite their differences, Jennis and Riena hardly seemed to belong to the same family. Some ancestral quirk of fair skin and light eyes had come out in Jennis, along with a small frame that made her look the changeling in Sefana's long-boned, black-haired, dark-eyed brood. But she had the Maurgen chin, square and stubborn.

"I slept very well indeed. What're you doing up?"

"I've got a little lady who just foaled." Jennis hooked her elbow loosely with Cailet's and drew her down the aisle of stalls. "Looks like a new variation, too. Her second by the same stud, and they both came out solid white from withers to tailbone." She opened the upper half of a door and said, "What d'you think of him?"

"Beautiful! Like a cloud settled on his back!"

"That's what we'll call 'em—Cloudbank coals. If we can get a few more and breed true, it'll be the first new type in fifty years."

They leaned on the stall door and admired the mare and foal. The little one tottered around on the longest legs Cailet had ever seen on a horse, seeking breakfast. He nursed enthusiastically, then emerged with his forelock scrunched and crinkled.

Cailet laughed; Jennis moaned. "Geridon help us, I hope

hat silly forelock doesn't breed down the line. His sister's
s just the same. Look at it, sticking straight up in the air!
Like Biron when he gets up in the morning."

"Once it grows longer, it'll droop of its own weight."

"Damn well better. I don't fancy slathering pomade on it
very time he's seen in public!"

After a time, Cai became aware that fingers were stroking
er wrist. Light, soft, the caress demanded nothing but asked
much. Embarrassed, she thought about pulling her arm away,
lecided that would be even more embarrassing, and stayed
s she was. But her body began to tense, and something be-
;an to tremble deep inside her. Something she feared.

Jennis said, "Come on, I'm starving. And Mother's strict
.bout being on time for meals. She says it's the only time
he ever gets to see any of us anymore." She slung an arm
.round Cailet's shoulders.

Cailet pulled away blindly. The *something* caught at her
vith a fire-flash in her breasts and between her thighs that
vas painful and pleasurable and terrified her with its hollow
.ching need to be filled—

"Cai?"

"I—I left my plate and cup back there—you go ahead—"
she was babbling and couldn't stop herself. "Lady Sefana
vill be angry if you're late—"

"Cai, what's the matter?"

"Nothing, nothing at all, I just—"

"Come sit down. Come on."

She moved awkwardly to a hay bale, perched on its edge
vith her clasped hands pressed between her knees. She felt
:old all over, as if her skin was sheened in ice—but the
something inside was a knot of fire. When Jennis stepped
:loser as if to sit beside her, she flinched.

"All right," the other girl soothed, and kept a careful dis-
:ance. "It's all right. I asked, you turned me down. That's all
"here is to it, as far as I'm concerned. No problem. But the
look on your face—Cai, I know you're a virgin, and I figured you'd be scared or nervous, or worried about offending
me when you refused. But that isn't it at all, is it?"

She shook her head, mute and ashamed.

"Want to tell me?"

"I—I can't."

"Well, I'll tell you about me for a minute, then," Jennis
said with a frank smile. "I'm as much a puzzle as my

brother Val. He loved making love to women—I'm surprised there aren't more of his get scattered across Lenfell. He was an energetic lad! And too handsome for his own good."

Startled out of her misery, Cailet asked, "Val fathered children?"

"Only one that I know of. I know what you're thinking: what about Alin Ostin? Val fell in love with him, so he learned to love making love to a man. At least, that's how he explained it to me." Jennis dragged a stool a little nearer Cailet, and sat. "Now, me, I love making love to men. They're good clean fun, and I want lots of children, so in a few years I'll start picking out likely fathers and indulge myself shamelessly! But I fall *in* love with women—on the order of twice a year, usually. Oh, not with you," she added. "You're very pretty, Cai—those big eyes and all that blonde hair—and I've always liked you a lot. But I've never yet been lucky enough to fall in love with a woman I *like!*" She laughed again. "Point is, I'm not in the least bit offended, so don't worry about hurting my feelings. I'm made the way I am, and you're made the way you are, and we love whom we love, and that's that. All right?"

"Yes." Cailet stared down at her hands. *But I'll never love anyone. And I can't let anyone love me.* "I'm just—I don't have those feelings for women. Or men, either."

"If any of this is about Taig. . . ."

She shook her head again. "It's about me."

"You're in shock still from all that's happened. Damn, I should've realized. I'm sorry, Cailet, that was a rotten thing for me to do."

"No, Jen, it wasn't anything you did." She glanced up. "It's me. I think there's something missing inside me." Innocence. Clean desire. Honest joy. And to think she'd worried about being at the mercy of Alin's attraction to men, Gorsha's to women—what she wouldn't give for either of them to take over that part of her life. Then she wouldn't have to be Cailet, maimed and mutilated in spirit as well as body.

"You've been through some rough times," Jennis was saying. "Let yourself heal, Cai. You'll find someone, I know you will."

Sarra had said much the same thing. Cailet would live in terror the rest of her life that she *would* find someone she could love, who would love her.

Someone she could not love, or allow to love her, for she
would inevitably destroy him.

12

Miram and Biron stayed at Maurgen Hundred. Cailet and the
others borrowed horses from Lady Sefana and rode to
Combel. The Bower of the Mask had been closed for weeks,
its mistress killed by Council Guards, all the young men
scattered. Walking down the main avenue, Cailet almost
hoped she'd run into Geria Ostin. A judicious spell would
do First Daughter a world of good.

Mage Guardian regimentals had not been forgotten.
Glances and hesitant nods were respectful, sometimes
awed, often wary. Cailet accepted the first, deplored the
second, and vowed to cure the third. No one should fear
magic.

At an inn recommended by Sefana Maurgen, Cailet was
forced to insist on paying full price for their rooms and
meals. This, too, would have to change, she told herself. No
favors, just because they were Mage Guardians. After dinner, the owner approached shyly and asked if it was true that
the Captal would soon be schooling people in magic again.
It seemed she had a little sister just past her first Wise
Blood. . . .

Cailet agreed to speak to the girl the next day, and, with
Elo's help, ascertained that she was indeed Mageborn.

Young Lira Trevarin was the first. Cailet's work had begun. There were hundreds of such children all over Lenfell.
In the nearly eighteen years since Ambrai, hundreds more
must have been lost. To insanity, some of them, those whose
magic was particularly strong; to use of magic as magic
withered for lack of education. Some Mageborns had been
found during those years, of course, and trained in secret.
But most had been captured and killed with the thousand
Mages Anniyas had set as her goal.

Inquiries must be made. Mages must go to every corner of
Lenfell. But Cailet must be first to search. People must see
her as she was: a young girl, a nothing and a nobody, raised

to Capital by virtue of extraordinary magic, but not a threat. Never a threat.

Which was why she went to Combel instead of Renig. Her three Warrior Mages were all for rounding up the Ryka Legion themselves. Cailet forbade it.

"It's government business. Mage Guardians cannot and will not interfere. No matter what happens, we will not participate in the capture and punishment of anyone indicted by the new Council and Assembly. We must remain independent."

"Sarra won't like that very much," Lusira remarked.

"I know."

The six of them—Cailet, Lusira, Elomar, Imilial, Granon, and Senn—went by ship and by Ladder and by horseback to most of Lenfell's major cities. Cailet visited places she'd only read about and never thought she'd see: Isodir with its fantasies in wrought iron, painted Firrense, the spindle towers of Dinn, the snowy peaks of Caitiri's Hearth above the rooftops of Neele, the Dombur Blood's lavish residence in Domburron. She went to the small towns, too, prosperous places with pretty names like Cascade Springs, Silver Fir, Summer Haven, Rockmere, Shepherd's Rest. But it was in the frontier villages of Kenrokeshir and Tillinshir and Sheve that she felt most at home, for they were much like their rough-and-tumble counterparts in The Waste, even to the names: Thorny Hole, Misery Mines, Rocky Flat, Broken Chimney. She was welcomed everywhere—sometimes warily, to be sure, but when it was discovered that the awesome Mage Captal was but a shyly smiling girl with no pretensions about her, even the stiffest and most suspicious warmed to her.

She found adolescent Mageborns in most places—and a round dozen of them, all Maklyns, at Wyte Lynn Castle, a circumstance no one could explain.

Once they sailed past Seinshir, and saw for themselves that Malerris Castle had indeed vanished. They also sensed the Wards, which even at a distance gave Senn a hideous headache none of Elomar's concoctions could ease.

From First Flowers until Drygrass she traveled: a hundred and twenty-four days, never more than four in the same place. Some days were good: traveling days with the wind or salt spray in her face, when she was free to laugh at the boastful tales traded by the three Warrior Mages. Some days were tense and strained: formal days when she must be Captal every instant. Some of the nights were very bad.

Never more than four days in the same place, never more than five nights without dreams. She grew to recognize danger signals in weariness and a short temper. She became picky about wine, not because her tastes were being educated but because certain varietals better disguised the flavor of the drops she sneaked into her cup when she suspected oncoming nightmares. Elo knew nothing about the sleeping potion. She had bought it from an apothecary in Firrense. Sometimes it worked.

One morning, in the finest bedroom of Pinderon's finest inn, Cailet's breakfast tray included the very first edition of the new *Press,* compliments of the management. Curious, she applied herself to coffee, corn fritters, and the front-page editorial. This informed her that whereas Feleson broadsheets had been printed every week, by the time the paper reached even the major cities the news was old indeed. The *Press* intended to keep the populace informed with timely coverage delivered on the fifth day of every week. Whereas Cailet had no objections to an informed populace, she objected strenuously to the timely method of delivery. The *Press,* it seemed, had struck a deal with Lady Sarra Liwellan on behalf of the Captal. Mage Guardians would hereafter pop through Ladders with bound stacks of broadsheets on a regular basis.

" 'On behalf of the Captal,' " the Captal muttered, resolving to have a little chat with her sister.

Somebody already had. Page two featured intrepid reporter Amili Mirre's "intimate, revealing" interview with the Lady herself (Cailet reflected that attempting to make Sarra reveal anything intimate wasn't intrepid; it was idiotic). The accompanying woodcut portrait made Sarra look sixteen years old and Collan resemble a used-carriage salesman. Cailet read, snickered, choked on her coffee, and finally laughed herself entirely out of her annoyance.

MIRRE: We've discussed many of your ideas for reform, Lady Sarra. But our readers are also interested in you as a woman. For instance, several times you've said that you talk things over with your husband and value his advice. Now, Lord Collan is an extremely attractive man—

LIWELLAN: Oh, he's more than just decorative.

MIRRE: It's rare to find a man with whom one can discuss one's work, especially such important work as yours.

LIWELLAN: I don't think such men are rare at all. I've met and worked with quite a few, in fact. Most women just don't give men credit for having brains.

MIRRE: The roving life of a Minstrel is one of great freedom. Does Lord Collan feel constrained by marriage?

LIWELLAN: It's true that most unmarried men have more freedom. But when a husband vows to obey, he shouldn't be expected to *disobey* his own good sense and intelligence. I rely on my husband for both.

MIRRE: But you still control the purse strings.

LIWELLAN: Not at all. I have my inheritance from Lady Agatine Slegin, and he has his earnings from his years as a Minstrel. I see no reason why I should confiscate his money just because he's now my husband.

MIRRE: "Confiscate" is a rather strong term.

LIWELLAN: But accurate.

MIRRE: So in terms of his financial freedom, marriage hasn't changed a thing. That's an unusual attitude. But I suppose it saves him from worrying that you married him for his dowry!

LIWELLAN: Quite.

Cailet decided to go easy on Sarra about using Mages as a delivery service. The article put her in a splendid humor—not only for its amusement value but because it was Sarra being scrutinized and not herself. She was still chuckling as she got dressed: she could just hear the frozen tone of her sister's voice on that last quelling word.

What she did not hear (it would have sent her into paroxysms of laughter if she had) was what Collan said when he read the piece. He didn't find it funny at all.

13

" 'Decorative'?"

"Well, would you rather I'd thanked her for saying you're handsome, as if I was responsible for it and took all the credit?"

"That's another thing. We go to these stupid dinners and you've got this look on your face that says, 'Hands off, eyes down, he's mine!' Like I'm *your* property and no woman can even look at me but you!"

"If you want me to, I can sit there purring, all smug and satisfied that other women can look but can't touch!"

"Who says they don't?"

"*What?* Who dared—"

"See? There it is again—your property! As if you have to protect me! As if I haven't spent *years* sidestepping hands going for my crotch—"

"Saints and Wraiths, I'm beginning to understand why some women keep their men in robes and coifs everywhere but the bedroom! Col, I don't want to fight about this. I love the way you look, I love showing you off, I love it that other women envy me. That's how a woman is supposed to feel about her husband. But I don't think it's unreasonable that I hate watching them eye-rape you!"

"If you don't like it, don't watch."

"It wouldn't bother me so much if you didn't look back at them that way!"

"What way?"

"You know very well what way!"

"Oh, you mean the way I smile and make nice with all those old cows who run the Webs? All the women *you* complain about? The ones who say you're too young, too radical, too uppity, and too damned rich?"

"Don't do me any favors! All you're doing is getting a reputation for a bold eye—and I can't afford that!"

"Reflects badly on you that you can't control your husband?"

"Yes—no! The things I want to do *are* radical. To get

them done, I have to show that in other things I'm as traditional as the next woman. Don't you see, I can't have you behaving just as you did before I married you!"

"You married me for who I am. Now you want me to be somebody different?"

"No, of course not! Stop twisting my words!"

"Yes, First Daughter. I hear and obey, First Daughter. From now on I'll be meek and modest in dress and demeanor, and make sure everyone knows that my only real value is stud service!"

"Don't be ridiculous. I told her how much I rely on you, and—"

"Oh, right. My 'good sense' and 'intelligence.' How flattering. How kind. How *fucking* condescending!"

"What in hell is your problem? I gave you credit for being my adviser as well as my husband. That's shock enough for people who think men should be rarely seen and *never* heard. I even told her about our financial agreement—"

"You mean the part about letting me keep my own money? You know what that sounded like? How proud you are that I was clever enough to earn it all by my silly little male self!"

"I never said—"

"Look, Sarra, I won't stand around like a bower cockie waiting for you to decide when you need me to help make babies."

"I didn't marry you to keep you for a pet!"

"No? I get trotted out at social occasions, I sing, I cozy up to all those old farts—"

"Collan, it's all part of the game! It won't always be like this. Just until things are settled, and the new government is elected, and I've got what I want. It's important enough to make a few sacrifices. Once we're at home in Roseguard, things will be different."

"They damned well better be, First Daughter."

14

She lost track of time, not really caring what day it was as long as the weather stayed fine. Messages from Sarra awaited her at several locations, asking and then demanding Cailet's presence on Ryka. Deciding to begin as she meant to continue, Cailet ignored the letters. She loved her sister devotedly, trusted her instincts implicitly, and believed her to be the best hope of making Lenfell what it ought to be—but Cailet was Mage Captal and no one, especially not the probable next First Councillor, gave her orders.

But the dessicated ancient who ruled the Garvedians was expected to make an appearance at Ryka Court soon; as Elomar had finally agreed to marriage, Lusira pleaded with Cailet to return there so she could wheedle permission from the old Lady. There was even a convenient Ladder at Wyte Lynn Castle.

It was inside an obscure and neglected little shrine to Eskanto, a Saint removed from the official calendar years ago. The slate floor was its punning reference to the rhyme: "Night or day, day or night/Ladder's blackest inside white." The Ladder led to a print shop at Ryka Court: "Mage or Lord, Lord or Mage/Ladder of the scattered page"—the sigil of Eskanto Cut-Thumb, patron of bookbinders. They arrived at the printer's at Second—the journey carefully timed to avoid shocking the workers—and Cailet said, "You know, some of that song even makes sense if you listen to it right."

Thus Cailet entered Ryka Court for the first time in her life. Chambers had been prepared for her—Telomir Renne's old rooms, which had been Gorsha's long ago. In them was a Ladder to Ambrai, one of those not included in the song.

The unconventional hour of arrival ensured there would be no fuss. But not five minutes after she'd seen the others settled in nearby chambers and was unpacking her few belongings, Sarra and Collan came in. Without knocking—not because they were rude, but because their arms were full of gifts.

"Wha—?" was all Cailet could manage.

"I thought you'd *never* get here!" Sarra dumped packages on the wide couch and threw her arms around Cailet. "Didn't my messages reach you?"

"Umm, well. . . ."

Col grinned. He was resplendent in a dark turquoise robe that matched Sarra's but for the froth of lace. "You'll never make a diplomat, kitten. Somebody find a bottle, it's getting thirsty in here."

"What *is* all this?" Cailet stared in amazement.

"Your Birthingday, idiot," Sarra replied.

"She forgot," Col said. "She forgot her own Birthingday."

"Well, she has a family who remembered for her—and Lusira Garvedian to get her here in time for it!" Sarra pushed her toward the couch. "Hurry up. If you don't start ripping ribbons soon, it'll take all night. The turquoise are from Col and me. Orange is from the Ostins, of course, blue from the Maurgens, silver from your Mages, yellow from Riddon and Maugir and Jeymi—oh, that reminds me! Riddon and Miram are getting married! He's been at Maurgen Hundred since Midsummer Moon—"

"Busy work, falling in love," Col put in.

"—and they'll marry at Harvest and move into the new cottage at Ostinhold to supervise the reconstruction."

Cailet blinked. "Miram and Riddon?"

"News broadsheets later," Col ordered. "Open your loot, kitten!"

Eighteenth Birthingday; eighteen presents. From Sarra and Collan, complete new silk regimentals, including a Silver Sparrow pin—Sarra being well aware that Cailet would always wear Gorsha's black cloak and Auvry Feiran's Candle. There was also a black-and-silver formal gown, with dainty embroidered slippers, that took her breath away. Col's special gift to her, and his design. From her Mages were the silver Captal's sash and a delicate necklace of silver links with a flameflower pendant, sigil of her Name Saint. She fingered the sash reverently—she was still using Miram's gray scarf—before folding it carefully atop the regimentals.

There were three thin boxes from the Maurgens, each containing a slip of paper. One informed her that a saddle made especially for her was ready at the Hundred anytime she cared to come pick it up; the second, that a bridle went with the saddle; and the third, that she had her choice of any three-year-old Maurgen dapple-back that caught her fancy.

"She still hasn't said anything," Col commented to Sarra.

"In shock, I suppose," she replied.

Cailet nodded helplessly and opened her gifts from the Ostins: a tooled black leather scabbard meant for Gorynel Desse's sword, and onyx earrings and an onyx necklace set in silver. Sarra told her Gorsha had given them to Lady Lilen in their youth.

"That's seventeen presents," Sarra went on. "More or less, but there's a lot of Birthingdays to make up for! This last one, though, this is from me alone." She slid an envelope from the pocket of her bedrobe.

"Sarra—it's too much," Cailet said.

"She speaks!" Collan laughed. "Just this one more and a toast to your Name Saint, and then we'll let you get some sleep."

"I'm not tired," she said absently, turning the envelope over. The sealing wax was Liwellan blue, imprinted with that Name's spread-wing Hawk—but the bird flew inside an octagon. "It's not even Seventh in Bleynbradden. We got up early to use the Ladder."

"Well, it's damned near Third here. Open it."

She did. The legal language made no sense to her. She turned a puzzled frown on Sarra, who smiled.

"It's a deed, Caisha. To a house."

"A house?"

"Your house. You own it. It's not big enough for a new Academy, but wherever you end up building, I wanted you to have a place of your very own."

"Near us," Col added. "In Roseguard."

"My house." She shook her head, not quite believing.

"The Slegin properties are mine now," Sarra said. "Six weeks ago the law was changed so a woman may give what she owns to whom she pleases—even a son."

"She tried to give Sleginhold to Riddon," Col interrupted, "but he said it's too far from The Waste. That was our first clue about him and Miram."

Sarra nodded. "I gave it to Maugir instead. Jeymi will have the farm on the Cantrashir border when he's old enough. I'll tell you all about it tomorrow. Happy Birthingday, love!"

Collan found a bottle on the sideboard and poured three glasses. They drank to St. Caitiri the Fiery-Eyed—

appropriately enough, the brandy set Cailet's insides ablaze. She coughed, and Collan clapped her on the back.

"We'll postpone the serious drinking for tomorrow night. You're coming to dinner, by the way. Don't panic, it'll just be the three of us." And he gave Sarra a wink that Cailet didn't understand.

She searched her sister's black eyes and warned, "If you've planned a surprise party, I'll leave."

"Would I do that to you?"

"If you thought you could get away with it, yes!"

"Well, I know I can't, so I didn't."

"*My* doing, kitten," said Col. "You may thank me profusely at your leisure. I threatened to make her life so miserable she'd be compelled to divorce me."

They left after Sarra promised to catch her up on all the latest tomorrow. Cailet suspected there was a whole day's worth of news, with a thousand or so digressions into her sister's projects. She had every faith that there wasn't a single section of the legal code Sarra didn't have a critical eye on or a dainty finger already in.

Cailet sat in the middle of her gifts, touching one and then another—stunned, as Sarra had observed. Eighteen years old today. She'd been born as Ambrai was dying. She'd heard the city was to be rebuilt. But Col had said he and Sarra would live at Roseguard. How could Ambrai be brought back to life without an Ambrai to supervise? But Sarra had no official rights there. No one did, except possibly Glenin.

She'd forgotten the Alvassys. The next day Sarra told her, in the course of the anticipated long, intricate conversation, that through their mutual great-grandmother—another Sarra Ambrai—Elin had the best claim.

"And it's fine with me. I don't want it. I couldn't live there again, Cai."

"I feel the same about Ostinhold. Are you sure about Roseguard, though?"

"Oh, yes. Col and I are agreed. We looked it all over before we came here. The Slegin residence is pretty much a wreck and the Ladder burned, so we'll just level it all and build everything new. As for the city itself . . . the main damage was portside. Your house is good solid brick—gutted, but structurally sound. Just tell me what you like by way of furniture and so on."

Cailet protested; Sarra laughed.

"Dear heart, in case you hadn't noticed, you're a pauper. The Rilles haven't a cutpiece to their Name. There's only about a hundred of them left in the wilds of Tillinshir. And they're as unimpressed that one of their Name is now Mage Captal as they were when Piergan Rille exalted himself by marrying Elinar Alvassy. Rather insulting, but very convenient. You won't have a herd of 'relations' to deal with."

"But do they accept that I'm one of them?"

"They've no objections. Census has all the right records—put there by Gorsha Desse just after you were born." She smiled cynically. "The Liwellans and Rosvenirs are equally accommodating—and the records are equally reliable."

Sarra and Collan would rebuild Roseguard. Elin and Pier would do the same for Ambrai. Miram and Riddon would restore Ostinhold. In the midst of this flurry of construction—which would give the economies of three Shirs a healthy kick—Cailet would look for a place to build something brand new. She wouldn't call it the Academy; she needed another name as well as another location. Sarra had ideas about that; Sarra had ideas about everything.

"It'll have to be the north coast of Brogdenguard, Cantrashir, or Tillin Lake. Oh, really, Cai, think about it! How did the Malerrisi keep prying magic out? A tower with iron all through it. What's the biggest deposit of iron on Lenfell? Caitiri's Hearth! With it between you and Seinshir, they'll never get so much as a glimpse of what you're doing."

Yes, Sarra had ideas about everything, and had thought them through with impressive thoroughness. Intellect and instinct, Cailet told herself; there was no one to match her sister for either.

But when Sarra started in about voting public funds soon for purchasing the land and construction costs, Cailet balked. The ensuing argument lasted all afternoon and only Collan's determination to ignore it made that evening's family dinner bearable. Things were frosty between the sisters for days.

"What you must understand," Telomir Renne said to Cailet one morning, "is that she doesn't think like a Mage Guardian. She thinks like an Ambrai, which is to say she's ruthlessly practical, frighteningly efficient, and completely dedicated to getting her own way."

"What a surprise," Cailet said dryly. "And you? What do you think like?"

"You mean is my father's influence in opposition to my government career? I'm only a Prentice, remember, and Warded. I know basic magic, but nothing fancy."

"That's not what I asked."

He lost his smile. "My loyalties lie with Lenfell." When Cailet nodded acceptance, he relaxed and went on, "My advice regarding Sarra is to wait and let Collan solve your problem for you. He's one of the few people she really listens to. But don't let it get around. Much of her authority here depends on how she's perceived. Ryka Court can be extremely conservative that way."

Cailet didn't understand, and said so. Telo enlightened her. Collan never attended meetings, proclaiming himself bored witless by the politics and legal wranglings that so fascinated Sarra. He busied himself with personal matters, earning a reputation as the ideal husband: conscientious, dutiful, solicitous of his Lady's private peace. In other words, thoroughly domesticated.

Cailet laughed so hard she choked. But she understood perfectly. Whatever ridiculously subservient pose Col had adopted, it was for the benefit of Ryka Court. No social fault must be found in Sarra or her husband—though it was deplored that he refused to wear a decent, modest coif over his coppery curls.

"The very color of his hair is an offense," Telo grinned. "But the only one he's committed so far. And to avoid further offending the offendable before Sarra accomplishes the better part of her goals—"

"—Col's killing himself with his imitation of perfection. I'm glad I came back in time to watch! But Saints help us when he's had enough, because he'll do something *really* outrageous to make up for it all!"

"Oh, yes, he's about as happy as a frog in fruit basket." Telo grinned at Cailet's blank look. "He's got no use for it, doesn't *want* to be there, and on the whole wishes he was *any*place else."

Collan kept in the background, but he was busy all the same. He dickered with artisans over contracts for the reconstruction of Roseguard. He went through every registered deed and account book of the Slegin Web. Declaring himself unable to live in a museum, he had Sarra's assigned chambers at Ryka Court emptied of all furniture, rugs, tapestries, and decorations, and replaced the fuss with a few simple pieces both functional and beautiful. He met with some of the surviving Bards, Minstrels, and Musicians who had scattered across Lenfell like the Mages and Healers after Ambrai's destruction, and started a fund with sums from his own illegal bank accounts for rebuilding Bard Hall.

He also had a little book made, stuffed with words. A slim silver pointer was attached to it by a chain. With this, Falundir could communicate again. A second book, in Col's own hand, was of all the major and minor scales. With it, Falundir could compose again.

So it was that Ryka Court's celebration of the Equinox featured a new song cycle by the finest Bard in ten Generations, performed by ten of Falundir's old comrades led by Collan Rosvenir. Reaction was spectacular—and every woman present that evening cursed Sarra Liwellan for having seen him first.

Collan also spent much time and quite a bit of his own money trying to find Tamsa Trayos and her little brother. They had been traced to a town in the foothills of the Wraithen Mountains where some of the Ostinhold refugees had fled. There the trail ended. In the confusion of nearly a thousand homeless, frightened people, a little girl and a newborn baby were easily lost.

Collan offered a reward and hired people to search. Weeks passed. Then news came, the worst possible news. The woman caring for Tamsa had died of a fever. Taken in by a childless woman in a village near Maidil's Mirror, Tamsa died a few weeks later of the same illness. Her identity was certain only because Velvet had still been with her—fully grown now, with a litter of lion-maned kittens.

Of the infant boy, no trace was found.

Sharing Collan's grief—and his guilt—Cailet reminded him that if the boy lived, they'd find out eventually. He would be found one day during the regular tours by Mage Guardians in search of children coming into their magic. Col nodded and tried to smile, but he was as little comforted by this as she. He owed the duty of friendship to Verald Jescarin, to take care of his children; she, the duty of a Captal. Tamsa was lost to them. Perhaps her brother was not. They could only wait. Col would administer Sela's Roseguard property in trust; Cailet would keep careful watch in a dozen years for Sela's Mageborn son.

The matter of Valirion Maurgen's son ended much more

happily. Rina Firennos, having no husband's dower to ease the burden of providing for her ever-growing brood, gladly traded Val's son for Sarra's cash. When Lady Sefana officially adopted him, she petitioned successfully to change his Name from Firennos to Maurgen. Aidan had been at the Hundred since Allflower, and his doting grandmother avowed him the very image of her dead son.

Of yet another son, Cailet thought much and said nothing. If her guess was correct—taking into account a prior miscarriage and possible dates of conception—he should be autumn-born. If she had expected to sense the birth, she was disappointed; Applefall, Harvest, and Wolfkill passed without a quiver. Cailet only shrugged. Eventually she'd learn the truth about this boy, too.

From Applefall to Snow Sparrow she traveled again, mainly to set Wards on several known Ladders to Malerris Castle. Other Mages were sent to do likewise, until at last Cailet felt reasonably assured of security. She paid no attention to the broadsheets, and even though her position required attendance at countless meetings and dinners, she listened to no gossip. The government's doings were the government's business. She had enough to do being Captal.

Then it was Candleweek, the Feast of Miryenne the Guardian, who with Rilla the Guide was the Mages' patron Saint. Cailet, back at Ryka Court, had intended to keep the holiday privately with the Mages. Politics dictated otherwise.

That afternoon, election results were announced. Campaigns for Assembly and Council had occurred in all Shirs that autumn. All seats were fiercely contested. Balloting was the second day of Diamond Mirror, the week of Maurget Quickfingers—patron of politicians and tax collectors, among others. It was the traditional polling day for every office from Council to Shir to village, for yearly taxes were due then and everyone had to be in town anyway.

Sarra had been astounded that so many elected officials met in her travels through the years were secretly involved in the Rising. Three Councillors, dozens in the Assembly, Mayors, Justices—and many more had managed to distance themselves from Anniyas. Sarra's own election to the Council for Sheve was a foregone conclusion: people knew her, liked her, and trusted her for herself, not just as Agatine Slegin's chosen heir. As for the rest of the seats, everyone expected entirely new faces in the Assembly and Council. Sarra confided to Cailet that she wasn't so sure. Her doubts proved valid: many who won this time were the very same people who had won last time, in 950. Though many local officials had been killed in the Rising, the new Assembly and Council would look very like the old.

Collan shrugged. "Throw the thieving scoundrels out— except for *my* thieving scoundrel. At least I know how she steals, and how much."

Not even Sarra had anticipated Ryka's reaction to the election results.

On the night Flera Firennos, Granon Isidir, and Irien Dombur declared the Rising in the Malachite Hall, rioting had broken out across the city. As had happened in Renig, Neele, and elsewhere, years of rage simply boiled over. People destroyed the property—and, if they could, the lives—of those known to be tied to Anniyas. Frantic, helpless, and with no armed force to quell the riot, the Rising had been three days calming the city.

The first night of Candleweek, after election results were announced, Ryka marched again. What had the Rising accomplished if so many of the voices heard for years in obedience to Anniyas would be heard again in what was supposed to be a new government?

There was no Council Guard, no Ryka Legion, nothing standing between the lawfully—if unpopularly in Ryka— elected representatives and the enraged mob. There were only the Mages.

An appeal was made to the Captal. She and fifty-six Mages climbed to the top of the bell tower at St. Miramili's. From there they could see the length of the main avenue: a river of bright torches and angry faces.

Suddenly those in front toppled to the ground. In successive groups, one after the other, they stumbled and staggered and fell. Screams turned to cries that they only slept and were not dead. Had anyone bothered to count, they would have learned that exactly fifty-seven collapsed at any one time. After only a minute or two, the fallen shook themselves groggily and asked what happened. And then screams began once more, for they all realized it was magic, wielded against them by Mageborns. They fled. And though later most admitted the Captal's wisdom and the benevolence of her magic—no one affected by the spell suffered more than a few bruises—they learned that night to fear her.

Cailet was furious. For the first time in her life she lost control of her temper entirely, with Sarra as its target.

"You *used* us! We are *not* an arm of your government and we will *not* jump at your beck and call!"

"Cailet, people were dying! We had no choice!"

"No, we were just the *easiest* choice! Get the Mages to do it, so none of you fine Councillors need to dirty your hands!"

"That's not true! You know it isn't! How *dare* you!"

"Don't come over all Blooded Lady with me, Sarra!"

"Then stop behaving like the almighty Mage Captal!"

"I *am* the Mage Captal," she snapped, shaking with rage. "And I'm leaving, with every single Mage! You don't own us! We're not your pet magicians to perform on cue! If you can't win acceptance for the new government, maybe you'd better hire back the Council Guard! They can protect you from the people you *say* you want to help!"

The next morning Collan came alone to Cailet's chambers.

"You're hell on my marriage, you know that? Sarra yelled at me all night."

"If you're here with anything other than a full apology, get out."

"There's a limited version."

"Knowing Sarra, *extremely* limited. I do not accept."

Shrugging as if he'd expected it, he went to the sideboard picked up a twig of fat golden grapes. "Funny thing. Nobody expected last night to happen. But they should have."

Cailet returned her attention to the list of newly found Mageborns on the writing desk before her.

Col went right on talking. "There's all sorts of explanations about some people being genuinely angry, some taking advantage of the situation, and some just getting caught up in it. But in a lot of ways it's good that it happened."

Nineteen people died *before we stopped it!* She bit her lips shut and went on scribbling notes beside each name.

"Everybody talks about changing this and fixing that and doing some other damned thing for the good of all Lenfell. But nobody really knows what Lenfell *is*. To Sarra, it's a legal code. To Irien Dombur, a gigantic market. To you—" He paused.

She turned in her chair to face him. "Yes?" she asked coldly.

He popped another grape into his mouth, chewed it, swallowed, and said, "Lenfell is Mageborns. They're all you really see."

"And I suppose to *you* all the world's a tavern taproom shoulder-deep in wealthy patrons, with the biggest Bard's Cup ever seen!"

If she'd thought to make him angry, she failed. "You're not a fool or a child," he said, "so don't act like either."

"Well, then? What's Lenfell to *you?*"

"Right now it's a tune nobody's listening to, let alone singing together, let alone on key."

"Interesting image. Compose a ballad about it, why don't you?"

"I can't. I'm a Minstrel who'll never be a Bard if I live another thousand years. I hear the music—better than you!—but I'll never contribute a single note. You and Sarra *can.* Not, however, if you're busy screaming at each other."

It was difficult to stay angry with someone who made sense. "Go on," she said sullenly.

"Lenfell *is* laws and trade and magic and music and families and a hundred other things besides. We're all part of it. Those people last night—when the Rising was declared, they realized they could make something different of their lives. But what have the other Shirs sent them? The same people they hated in the old government, and they knew the old government better than anyone. Why did that happen, Cailet?"

"You said it yourself, yesterday afternoon."

"Better the bitch whose bite I know than one whose fangs I've never seen? It's more than that. Sending them to Ryka Court keeps them the hell out of local affairs. If they're here, they can't meddle at home."

"What does this have to do with—"

"Just listen, will you? Turns out Sarra was right. Once people see that things *can* be changed, they start wanting change. And they want it *now.* Which is a sword with about a hundred edges. It's better that she learns—and. learns fast—that what *she* wants, what the Rising wants, and what the people want can be completely different. She can deal with that." He gave a brief laugh. "Great Geridon's Balls, she'll have the time of her life sorting through it all. But it'll tear her heart out if she has to fight you, too."

"Last night was wrong, Collan. They were wrong to ask Mage Guardians to—"

"If she admits that, will you start talking to her again?"

"Not until she *believes* it. Don't you see? Mageborns can't even give the appearance of being connected to the government. Collan, it's why they fought The Waste War!"

"And why Anniyas had to die. I know that. So does Sarra."

"Then why doesn't she understand?"

"If it'd been anyone but you, she probably would have."

"Well, it *was* me. She'll have to get over it." She rose to pace the sunlit confines of her sitting room. "I won't be used and I won't be manipulated. Not by the council, not by anyone. Not even Sarra."

"She needs you, Cai."

"And not by you, either! You said what you came to say. I have work to do."

"That's my point, damn it! Neither of you will accomplish anything—much less anything that lasts—if you're not working together!"

"Where I stand is where Captals have stood since the Mage Guardians were founded. And I'm not moving, Collan."

"Fixed in stone, are you?" he snapped.

"Tell Sarra to back away. Because I won't."

"You're sisters, truly told," he said in disgust, turned on his heel, and strode out.

Very good, Captal. Another person you've driven away.

Her shoulders twitched as if to shrug off that thought—and Collan too, angry and detesting him for compelling her to think beyond her anger. But he'd made too much sense, damn him. *Music. If Sarra and I are working on different songs, the least we can do is try to harmonize. Saints know the rest of them won't even make the effort.*

Sarra never did apologize. They never spoke of the matter of Mage Guardian independence from the government again. But Cailet delayed her departure until the new government was seated. It was too important an occasion for the Mage Captal not to lend her presence. And she began to see what Sarra had been fighting all these weeks. What she would continue to battle for years to come.

The Council Chamber had been scrubbed clean, as if to cleanse it of Anniyas's taint. Tiles glistened. Windows sparkled. New crimson velvet upholstered all the chairs. The white marble wedge of the Council table shone. The banners of all extant Names hung stiff with starching from the walls. Yet the faintest smell of smoke clung to the air. On St. Sirrala's Day with the declaration of the Rising, and again on St. Miryenne's when the elections had been announced, a thin gray shroud had drifted across Ryka like a Wraithen host. Citrus polish, pine-oil soap, ammonia used on glass—neither these nor the airing given the Council chamber could disguise the scent of burning.

Cailet approved. It was grim reminder of the people the government was in theory elected to serve.

She and Sarra—on cordial terms again, more or less—sat together in the front row, twenty feet from the Speakers Circle. Collan was on Sarra's right, inspecting his fingernails in an ostentatious show of genuine boredom. Falundir was at Cailet's left. The other Mages and a great many friends were scattered around the hall. Elomar and Lusira were absent: finally married at Snow Sparrow, ordered by the Captal to vanish for two weeks ("Have fun. There'll be plenty of work for you later!").

It had all been rehearsed. Ministers, members of the Assembly, and officials of the Shirs marched up to denounce Anniyas and move to dissolve the old machinery of government. No speech lasted more than three minutes—brevity had been decreed and there were only so many ways of saying the same thing—although everyone looked as if they wished to state each grievance in precise, long-winded detail. Such recitals had been forbidden, not only because of time but because no one wanted opening rounds in power plays to begin just yet. Currently, power translated into reparations for damages—real or imagined—done to towns, cities, Shirs, or Webs during Anniyas's rule.

"Everyone's after the same thing," Sarra had fumed. "Money! They all seem to think we're drowning in cut-pieces!"

"Well, *you* are, anyway," Col observed blithely, which earned him a scathing lecture that upset him not at all. In fact, he gave back as good as he got. Watching the fireworks, Cailet began to understand that Collan actively courted such tirades. If she yelled at him until her anger was exhausted, she could face everyone else with cool self-possession. Cailet also suspected each reveled in the blunt honesty of the other's temper—and that their apologies were made at night, in bed.

Now, as Cailet listened to the calculated outrage of one of the old Assembly members from Sheve, she shifted restlessly in her seat. The black velvet regimentals—not her beautiful silk gifts from Sarra and Col, but a set more appropriate to the chill of Midwinter Moon—had been a mistake. Hundreds packed the Council Chamber, with next to no ventilation. She surreptitiously wiped sweat from her forehead. Saints, she was tired. She'd been half a year chasing around Lenfell with only a brief break at Wildfire for her Birthingday. The youngest Captal in Guardian history felt older than Flera Firennos.

She knew that her duty for the present was to see and be seen by everyone. But while she was growing more comfortable with the role of Captal, she was no Lady of the Ambrai Blood. All the social graces Sarra possessed in abundance were a bad fit when Cailet tried them on. Ryka Court shredded her nerves. Sarra could sympathize but never really understand. Col, however, had given Cailet an interesting view of things last night.

"She *loves* this stuff. It's in her blood—no pun intended. She's an expert at working people around using every trick in the book and then some. She uses all the sweet-talk to persuade somebody else to shovel the shit out of her way. I guess she figures that anybody fool enough to fall for those big eyes and deep dimples deserves what she gives 'em."

"Including you?"

"Very funny. The really odd thing is she's an idealist. It's not blind ignorant faith anymore. What she's seen at Ryka would make a cynic out of a Saint. But her belief in what's right just keeps getting stronger."

"People see that in her," Cailet mused. "I've watched them while she's busy charming them into doing something they don't necessarily want to do. But she can get people to do what they ought to and *like* it."

Perhaps one day she'd learn how to do the same. But for now, despite all her practice in the arts of polite chat and charming persuasion during the last half-year, maintaining her balance was a strain. Especially today, with Au-

vry Feiran mentioned so often in the long catalog of horrors.

Last to speak was the Mayor of Ryka Court. Finally it was
over. Cailet wondered how her sister had kept the same
grave, attentive expression through it all. She was the quint-
essential Blooded First Daughter and Cailet had serious
doubts that a Waster like herself could possibly be the sister
of so grand and marvelous a person.

But as Granon Isidir moved from the Council table to the
Speakers Circle, Sarra turned her head slightly, caught
Cailet's eye, and proved herself human with a wink and a
subtle elbow in the ribs.

"Here it comes," she whispered.

Assembly representatives and delegations from individual
Shirs being unanimous in calling for an end to the present
form of government, Councillor Isidir now asked for a voice
vote. The answer roared back. When the tumult quieted, his
calm, cool accents rang out once more.

"Let it be recorded. Let it be law."

Cheers, applause; sighs of relief that it was finally over;
murmurs about the food and drink in the Malachite Hall that
would precede the formal swearing-in; the rustle of garments
as people prepared to rise and leave.

"Mage Captal Cailet Rille."

She nearly jumped out of her seat. On one side of her,
Sarra gave a start of surprise; on the other, Falundir tensed.
What do they want me *for?* Cailet thought, dreading the an-
swer, and stood.

"Please come forward, Captal. The final matter concerns
you."

They've found out! was her first panicky reaction, quickly
damped down. *Impossible. Those who know, we trust absolutely. But Glenin—oh, Saints, she told them somehow—they
know about Sarra and me—*

She kept her strides supple and her face neutral as she approached the Circle. All eyes were on her. All attention centered on one unprepossessing girl who wore Captal's
regimentals to which she knew she had no right.

Isidir resumed his seat at the triangular table. "Before the
assembled Shirs, we will hear the details of the deaths of
Avira Anniyas and Auvry Feiran."

Recent lessons in the hard school of public demeanor and
dangerous secrets, supplemented by her sister's example,

kept her from making a complete fool of herself. She smoothed her expression and rested her hands on the railing. She sought Sarra's eyes. *Why didn't you warn me?* she wanted to shout, but her sister was as bewildered as she. All this had been presented in a written report weeks ago. Why bring it up again?

Let them ask. I won't volunteer a damned thing.

Only three people were at the huge table: Flera Firennos, Granon Isidir, and Irien Dombur. As members of the former Council elected to the new, they alone still held their seats. Until the installation of the Assembly and Council this evening, they *were* Lenfell's government.

Councillor Firennos cleared her throat and said, "It was suggested this morning that an official account should be entered into the Archive."

And that, Cailet knew, was all the apology she would ever get.

"Please tell us in your own words what happened."

My heart got torn open. I'm still bleeding, damn you—

"After Summoning the First Councillor, I confronted her."

"In an attempt to do what?" This from Dombur, who had used his Name's massive financial resources to organize the systematic ruination of trade—risking nothing but money, and certainly not his position or his life. Of the three Councillors, Sarra considered him the least likely Rising sympathizer, but there he sat all the same. Cailet felt a warrior's scorn for someone who had let others hazard all the dangers while keeping himself perfectly safe.

A Warrior? Me? And she realized all at once why she had never shared the sense of victory. She had never fought a battle of any kind. She'd sliced into a few Council Guards in Renig. She'd called up a few Mage Globes, worked a few spells. She hadn't pitted herself against Anniyas or the Malerrisi for years on end, with each day a battle simply to maintain secrecy.

I didn't even fight Glenin. Not really. To win, you have to fight. I never have.

Until now . . . ?

She dragged her mind back to Dombur's question. What had she wanted to do? What had she meant by confronting Anniyas?

Damned if she knew anymore.

"My—my purpose was to convince her that it was hopeless, and she should surrender power before more people died."

"Surrender to you?"

First Lord to Mage Captal.

"To the Rising."

"How did she die?" Flera Firennos asked softly.

The Wraiths took her. How do I prove that?

"She was unused to working magic after so many years, and was caught in her own spells."

"How?" Dombur insisted.

"I don't know." *Collan can dress me in all the right clothes and the rest of you can term me Captal, but that doesn't make me a Mage!*

"So you can't say for certain?" His eyes were avid, his lips tight and harsh. "You can't prove she's dead, or Auvry Feiran either?"

"Sarra Liwellan and her husband Collan Rosvenir saw Anniyas die. They've given depositions to this effect. As have I."

"What about Glenin Feiran?"

She and her son are at Malerris Castle—something else I can't prove. And I can't prove what she did to me, either. If she'd clawed out my eyes or done to me what Anniyas did to Falundir, I'd be crippled enough to prove what happened. But I won't show you the wound she did give me. And the other wounds . . . you'll never see those, either.

"I don't know where Glenin Feiran is," Cailet lied.

"Anniyas is dead," Councillor Isidir said impatiently. "And Auvry Feiran. What's your point, Irien?"

Annoyed, Dombur shook his head. "A pity neither survived long enough to face justice. Captal, what did you do with the bodies?"

Now she understood. "I threw Anniyas's body into the river."

"And Feiran's?"

"His, I burned."

Mutters of outrage coursed through the Council Chamber. Auvry Feiran had been given honorable burning—and, of all places, in the city he'd destroyed. Sacred cleansing fire for the Butcher of Ambrai. No one but Sarra had known of the disposition of their father's body. Cailet kept defiance from her voice but knew it shone in her eyes.

"His, I burned," she repeated. "I built a pyre beside the Brai River and watched him burn to ashes."

Dombur said heavily, "I find it difficult to reconcile your great service to Lenfell and your office as Captal with giving honors to a Lord of Malerris, Lenfell's most heinous—"

He didn't finish. Sarra was on her feet, her voice an icy knife. "Is the Mage Captal on trial here?"

Granon Isidir blinked. "Not at all, Lady!"

Dombur scowled at him. "We wish merely to ascertain her reasons for not bringing the corpses before us." He turned to Cailet. "May we hear those reasons now, Captal?"

Because you would've forgotten civilization and humanity and your own souls in order to take your vengeance, even on his hollow bones. I couldn't let that happen—not for his sake, or mine, or Sarra's. Or even yours.

Because he was my father and a Mage Guardian, and whatever he became, he was my father and a Mage·Guardian at the end of his life.

Because ... Glenin showed me what Malerrisi power can be. I know what it is to be empty and crave to be filled— even with that. *I understand why he turned to them. I honored him with burning because ... because it could have been* me.

Cailet assumed the stance of Mage Captals in countless formal portraits: head high, shoulders straight, one thumb hooked into the sash and the other hand lifted in the ancient sign of Mage-Right.

The gesture carried the weight of Generations of magic. What a Mage Captal decided was nobody else's business.

Not quite magic enough, though. Flera Firennos bit her lower lip, deeply troubled. "We understand your reference. But you should have brought the corpse before us, so all could witness that he was dead."

"*I* was witness," Cailet replied, and for the first time she consciously called on her Ambrai Blood, projecting the arrogance Sarra could use to such excellent effect. And none of them, not at the Council table nor in the crowded hall, could meet her gaze.

Only Sarra, with her fierce, proud black eyes: *Show them what an Ambrai is made of, little sister.*

"Is this all the answer we can expect, Captal?" Dombur made one last try.

"It is."

"I see." He paused. "What was done with the ashes?"

He wouldn't give up. Cailet wanted to ask what he'd do if he had them—make a pile of them on the great wedge of the table and burn them all over again?

She'd had enough. More than enough. If they didn't like what she'd done, they could do without her. Their pet magician had had enough.

"The wind took his ashes," she said coldly. "I believe it was a northerly that day, so you might look downriver or out to sea." She nodded slightly, more to indicate this idiocy was at an end than to show respect for those who had instigated it. Then she walked with long, stiff strides from the Council Chamber, making her way with blind instinctive need through the halls toward the scent of fresh air and green, growing things.

Yet once she was in the gardens, she was ashamed of what she'd done. She was no Lady of Ambrai, not the way Sarra was, wise in the uses of Blood privilege for the good of all Lenfell. What Cailet had done was to draw on countless generations of Ambrai arrogance. And she was no Mage Captal, either, to have conjured up legends that way, lending the weight of worthier Captals and their truths to lies that were important only to her.

She couldn't even share in the Rising's victory. The one time she could have fought a battle, *should* have fought, she had been betrayed by her own emotions. Glenin had seized her like a silverback cat pouncing on a galazhi, and the only reason Cailet wasn't dead of it was that her father had fought her battle for her.

And won. *His* was the victory. He had lost his life but saved the Captal, his own daughter; he had lost his life but at the end of his life had been a Mage Guardian again. Auvry Feiran had *won*.

And Cailet? Those she loved whom she had not lost, she had pushed away. Her battle from now on would be with herself: how close was too close? How much distance was too much? How did she reconcile her need for Sarra and Collan and the others with her need to Ward herself from them?

She couldn't find out here, amid all these strangers and all their self-serving noise. She wanted distance between herself and Ryka Court. To find her own place far away, somewhere she could teach and learn and fight her private battle and come to some sort of peace.

Col found her a little while later, seated in the latticed springhouse of the Council's private garden. He had a bottle in one hand, two glasses in the other. Sitting beside her on a bench, he poured and gave her a brimming goblet.

"Sarra's a bad influence on me. I never used to bother with glasses."

They drank the first round in silence. Col poured a refill.

"She said to tell you she's sorry. She understands now—about the Council and the Mage Guardians, I mean."

"Does she?"

"She's not so blind that she can't see things when they're shoved in her face," he replied with a faint smile. "And Dombur did that today."

Cailet nodded and drank.

After a time, Col said, "You have to get out of here, you know."

"Yes. I know."

"No telling what they'll think up next."

She took another long swallow, the brandy burning its way down. "If this was any indication, I don't want to find out."

"I wish you could stay," he went on. "But Sarra and I can't protect you anymore the way we've been doing. More players in the game now."

"What do you mean, 'protect' me?" she demanded.

Col snorted. "Who do you think kept you off Ryka? Who's been arguing since Maiden Moon that you're needed out in the world where you can do some good, not caged up? They were all set to build a shrine around you, did you know that?"

She stared at the brandy. "I'm sorry. I never realized."

His voice softening, he said, "And who, little kitten, just arranged for you to go to a place I know in Sheve Dark, where you can think in peace and quiet and decide what you're going to do next—instead of having the new Council *tell* you?"

"Sheve—?"

"You'll like it, kitten." He smiled. "I used to live there with Falundir. It's a nice, cozy little cottage, no nightmares allowed."

Shocked, she stammered out, "How did you—"

"Falundir saw it first, back around your Birthingday. I told Elo to keep an eye on you. And you've been drinking enough to make Kiy the Forgetful start remembering."

She defiantly gulped down the brandy.

"One for health, one for wealth, but that's all," he said, and took the glass from her hand. "Cai. Sarra and I don't want to lose you—not to some mystical Mageborn whatever, or the nightmares, or to what everybody else says you ought to be. You'd lose *yourself*. You did pretty well today. But toward the end you were going out of tune."

Now she had nothing to stare at but her empty hands. At length, and very carefully, she asked, "Do you understand? About Auvry Feiran, I mean?"

Collan was silent for a long moment, turning his glass around and around in lean, sensitive Minstrel's hands. "I'm not sure. I know what I think, and I know what I feel. They're not the same thing."

"They would've made *him* into a shrine, Col—to hate. I couldn't let things begin that way. And he—he put himself between me and Glenin's magic. She would have killed me if he hadn't."

This was news to him. He gave her a hard, searching look. "Why?"

"He was a Mage Guardian. I'm the Captal."

Collan said nothing for a long time. Then: "I guess he found out what his life was worth. Who he was willing to risk it for." He shrugged uncomfortably. "Well, whatever happened, it's all over and done. Dead's dead. He doesn't matter anymore."

It was as much as she could hope for—and more generous than she might have expected—from a man who had suffered at Feiran's hands the way Collan had. Still, Sarra was right: he must never learn the truth. Never.

After a time, Cailet ventured, "I'll miss you and Sarra."

"I didn't say vanish forever," Col replied testily. "She'll have a fit if you're not here when the baby's born."

"Baby? What baby?"

"*Ours*. Surprise." He acquired a slightly foolish, entirely endearing grin.

"Uh—yes. A baby," she repeated, dazed. "When?"

"By her next Birthingday. She's on notice that we're out of here by Ladymoon. That gives her about seven weeks to fix up the world the way she wants it. Anything she doesn't get done by then, she'll have to do from Roseguard. I'm not sticking around this hothouse any longer than that."

His aggrieved tone didn't fool Cailet. What Sarra wanted to do, he would see that she had the chance to do—even if he had to shove his fist down the throat of anyone who got in her way. Where he loved, he protected. If it meant intentionally igniting Sarra's temper, he would do it. If it meant cracking a few skulls, he'd do that, too. And if it meant standing like a living wall between Cailet and the Council—and even between Cailet and Sarra herself—

"Ride down and talk to Maugir at Sleginhold every so often," Col was saying, "so we'll know how you are. I'll send him word when it's her time."

Caliet gave him a smug grin. "What makes you think I won't know without being told?"

He blinked, then growled, "May all Sarra's children be Mageborn, and all of them just like *her!*"

"Ha! Some vengeance!" she scoffed. "From now on I'll pray every night to every Saint in the Calendar that they don't turn out just like *you!*"

Collan laughed and wrapped an arm around her shoulders. She leaned her head against his shoulder, sighing for this moment of perfect peace.

After a while she stirred. "What'm I going to do in Sheve Dark, anyway?"

"Well, for one thing, clean up the garden. It's probably been solid weeds for ten years and more."

"The joys of rustication," she murmured wryly. "What else?"

"You've got a lot of reading to do, kitten."

She sat up straight. "The books! From the Academy!"

"Crates and crates. Tarise and Rillan escorted them personally all the way from Pinderon to Sleginhold about a week ago. You can take old Kanto Solingirt along to play librarian. All in all, you ought to be pretty busy until spring." He drew her against him again, smiling. "So will Sarra, but at least I've got one of you someplace where she can't get into too much trouble."

"All those books. . . ." Cailet closed her eyes and sighed again.

"I kept some of the ones from Bard Hall. Good stuff, things I'd never run across before. Want to hear one?"

"Please."

Sarra found them there half an hour later: her husband still humming lullabies, her sister sleeping like a child, without nightmares.

Epilogue

The full moon rose, blurred and distorted by many-layered Wards. The Weaver's Moon; her own moon. Her twenty-seventh Birthingday.

She turned from the windows to the cradle by her bed. He never cried, did her son, never fretted or fussed. He watched the world with remarkably clear eyes, their color as yet undetermined. But whether blue or gray or green or a combination of all these, those eyes were so *aware* that he frightened people.

Not her. She knew what he was telling her. He knew magic, even at twelve weeks old. The night he'd been born—the Equinox, just at sunset—she'd told him his name, and he'd looked at her, and known her. He *was* aware, and of more than his surroundings. She knew he was aware of magic. How could he not be? He lived within the most powerful Wards a Malerrisi Net had ever constructed.

He was sleeping now. She gazed down at him for a while, dreaming and proud, then moved to her own bed. Whenever she watched him too long, he woke to watch her. As if concerned that he'd miss something; as if waiting for more magic. She couldn't so much as Warm a teacup without feeling his eyes watching her.

Ah, what he would be in twenty years, when the *Code of Malerris* was his memorized possession!

Smiling, she snuggled down in soft sheets to sleep. She didn't mind this exile, not really. Others did. But she had all she needed right here, and the coming years would be full and joyous as her son grew, and grew into his magic.

She could see the full moon from her bed. Though the chambers were not large, they were beautifully appointed in her own Feiran green and gray. They were the chambers vacated on her arrival by an Escovor, who had taken with him all his garish black and orange. They were the chambers Anniyas had never lived in, even though they'd been rightfully hers.

They were Glenin's chambers now. First Lord, Warden of the Loom.

Bidding silent good night to the Weaver's Moon, her own moon, she turned on her side so she could see her son's cradle, and fell asleep smiling.

GENEALOGY

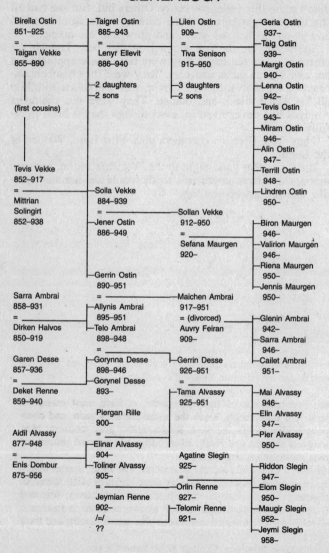

Birella Ostin
851–925
=
Taigan Vekke
855–890

(first cousins)

Tevis Vekke
852–917
=
Mittrian
Solingirt
852–938

Sarra Ambrai
858–931
=
Dirken Halvos
850–919

Garen Desse
857–936
=
Deket Renne
859–940

Aidil Alvassy
877–948
=
Enis Dombur
875–956

Taigrel Ostin
885–943
=
Lenyr Ellevit
886–940

—2 daughters
—2 sons

Solla Vekke
884–939
=
Jener Ostin
886–949

Gerrin Ostin
890–951
=
Allynis Ambrai
895–951
Telo Ambrai
898–948
=
Gorynna Desse
898–946
Gorynel Desse
893–

Piergan Rille
900–
=
Elinar Alvassy
904–
Toliner Alvassy
905–
=
Jeymian Renne
902–
/=/
??

Lilen Ostin
909–
=
Tiva Senison
915–950

—3 daughters
—2 sons

Sollan Vekke
912–950
=
Sefana Maurgen
920–

Maichen Ambrai
917–951
= (divorced)
Auvry Feiran
909–

Gerrin Desse
926–951
=
Tama Alvassy
925–951

Agatine Slegin
925–
=
Orlin Renne
927–
Telomir Renne
921–

Geria Ostin
937–
Taig Ostin
939–
Margit Ostin
940–
Lenna Ostin
942–
Tevis Ostin
943–
Miram Ostin
946–
Alin Ostin
947–
Terrill Ostin
948–
Lindren Ostin
950–

Biron Maurgen
946–
Valirion Maurgen
946–
Riena Maurgen
950–
Jennis Maurgen
950–

Glenin Ambrai
942–
Sarra Ambrai
946–
Cailet Ambrai
951–

Mai Alvassy
946–
Elin Alvassy
947–
Pier Alvassy
950–

Riddon Slegin
947–
Elom Slegin
950–
Maugir Slegin
952–
Jeymi Slegin
958–

SELECTIVE INDEX

Bloods. See *Tiers*

Brogdenguard. Province. Capital: Neele.

Caitiri the Fiery-Eyed, Saint. Patron of Fire, Forge, Ironcrafters. Sigil: Flameflower.

Cantrashir. Province. Capital: Pinderon.

Census. Taken every 25 years. In 950 the population of Lenfell was classed as follows (Tier figures from 125 given for comparison):

Rank	Thirty-Eighth Census Population	Names	Fifth Census Names
Blood	116,516	27	209
First Tier	309,257	29	374
Second Tier	452,944	84	531
Third Tier	687,546	81	688
Fourth Tier	615,172	73	595
Fifth Tier	—	—	572
Slaves	591,874	—	—
TOTAL	2,773,309	294	2,969

Of these:

Mage Guardians	10,000+
Malerrisi	5,000+

Chevasto the Weaver, Saint. Patron of Spinners, Weavers, Basketmakers, Lords of Malerris. Sigil: Loom.

Cloister. Established for 873 girls orphaned in the War of the Tiers. Still a haven for women wishing to withdraw from the world, the Cloister is famous for fine carpets and tapestries.

Colynna Silverstring, Saint. Patron of the Lute. Sigil: Coiled Strings. Removed from official calendar.

Council Guard. Standing army of professional soldiers overseen by a Commandant responsible to the Council. In war, the core of the armed forces; in peace, the Council's worldwide police barracked at Ryka Court and all Council Halls. Regimentals: black trousers and cloak, red tunic, gold badge of eagle clutching a sword. See also *Ryka Legion*

Council Hall. Law court and residence of local Justices and Council Guards.

Council of Lenfell. Executive branch of government. Fifteen members, one from each Shir, chosen by popular vote of enfranchised females. First Councillor chairs the Council. Badge (also worn by personal assistants): gold eagle.

Deiket Snowhair, Saint. Patron of Mountains, Scholars, Teachers. Sigil: Book.

Delilah the Dancer, Saint. Patron of Sword, Soldiers, Dancers, Tailors, Athletes. Sigils: Crossed Swords, Crossed Needles.

Dindenshir. Province. Capital: Dinn.

Domburronshir. Province. Capital: Domburron.

Domburronshir, Grand Duchess of. Born Veller Ganfallin in 721. By 759, the armies of the self-styled Grand Duchess, supported by renegades among both Mage Guardians and Lords of Malerris, controlled most of South Lenfell. In 761, Isodir, Firrense, and Wyte Lynn Castle were beseiged, but never fell due to resupply by Ladder. By 768 she ruled half the world. After her death in 779 her empire fell apart. Her battles directly caused over 100,000 deaths and twice that number of civilians were murdered in seven Shirs. In the late 930s, a purported descendant of Veller Ganfallin attempted to emulate her conquests; he was defeated and killed at the Battle of Domburron.

Dower Fund. Yearly tithe held in trust for dispersal at marriage.

Elinar Longsight, Saint. Patron of Fortune-tellers. Sigil: Owl. Removed from official calendar.

Eskanto Cut-Thumb, Saint. Patron of Bookbinders. Sigil: Scattered Pages. Removed from official calendar.

Falinsen Crystal-Hand, Saint. Patron of Glasscrafters. Sigil: Bottle. Removed from official calendar.

Falundir (916–). Slaveborn eunuch whose gifts as a Bard won him his freedom.

Feleris the Healer, Saint. Patron of Medicine, Physicians, Apothecaries, Perfumers, Beekeepers. Sigils: Mortar and Pestle; Herbal Wreath; Beehive.

Fielto the Finder, Saint. Patron of the Chase, Archers, Hunters, Lost Items. Sigil: Crossed Arrows.

First Daughter. Inherits all money and property; has authority over her sisters for life and her brothers until they marry; responsible for collection and administration of the Dower Fund. The First Daughter of an entire Name is titular head of the family, with (theoretically) dictatorial power over all women and unmarried men of that Name no matter how distantly connected. In practice, each branch's First Daughter wields that power.

Flerna the Weary, Saint. Patron of Accountants. Sigil: Abacus. Removed from official calendar.

Garony the Righteous, Saint. Patron of Advocates, Prisoners. Sigil: Gavel.

Gelenis First Daughter, Saint. Patron of Pregnant Women, Childbirth, First Daughters. Sigil: Carved Chair.

Geridon the Stallion, Saint. Patron of Fathers, Horses, Domestic Animals. Sigil: Horseshoes.

Gierkenshir. Province. Capital: Firrense.

Gorynel the Compassionate, Saint. Patron of Grief, Widows, Cripples, Judges, Printers. Sigil: Thorn Tree.

Healer. Physician, not necessarily Mageborn. Regimentals: green trousers, cloak, and longvest or tunic, gold badge of herb wreath (Healer) or herb sprig (Prentice).

Healers Ward. Medical school in Ambrai.

Identity Disk. Flat, almond-shaped steel disk; Name colors indicated by beads. Obverse: given name, family Name and sigil (if any), birthdate, Blood/Tier status. Reverse: Council Sigil. The Renne Blood has exclusive production rights. Issued at birth and worn until death by everyone but slaves. At death the disk is burned with the corpse. If recovery of the body is impossible, as in battle, the disk is taken instead and returned to the First Daughter.

Ilsevet Waterborn, Saint. Patron of Fish and Fisherfolk. Sigil: Crossed Hooks.

Imili the Joyous, Saint. Patron of Joy, Newlyweds, New Mothers, Old Lovers. Sigil: Flower Basket.

Jenavira Rememberer, Saint. Patron of Memory and Historians. Sigil: Open Book. Removed from official calendar.

Jeymian Gentlehand, Saint. Patron of Wild Animals. Sigil: Open Hand.

Joselet Green-Eyes, Saint. Patron of Gardeners. Sigil: Shovel and Hoe. Removed from official calendar.

Justice. Appointed by Council, ratified by Assembly. Presides over all trials and presents the government's case. Chief Justice of each Shir handles only "federal" law; junior associates take cases of local law.

Kenroke Fever. Two pandemics—one pre-Waste War, the other in 596–601; 20–25% mortality. Cure discovered by Healer Mage Viko Renne.

Kenrokeshir. Province. Capital: Roke Castle.

Kiy the Forgetful, Saint, Patron of Wine, Vintners, Toothaches. Sigil: Spilled Cup.

Lenfell. Corruption of "landfall." Colonized during the Second Great Migration (2458–2493) by 5,876 mainly Catholic settlers after a seven-year voyage on the starship *Stella Alderson.* Their aim was to escape the complications of high technology. Among them were sixteen magicians who became the ancestors of every Mageborn on Lenfell.

Lirance Cloudchaser, Saint. Patron of Wind. Sigil: Tower.

Lords of Malerris. Originated as a splinter group of Mage Guardians advocating Mageborn control of government and society. Approximately 300 years after their founding, the Waste War was fought to a standstill over their philosophical and power dispute with the Guardians.
Organization:

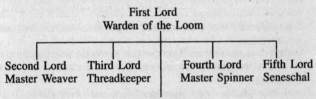

First Lord
Warden of the Loom

Second Lord — Third Lord — Fourth Lord — Fifth Lord
Master Weaver — Threadkeeper — Master Spinner — Seneschal

Lords of Malerris

First Lord (badge: Great Loom) governs all Malerrisi; chosen in trial by fatal magical combat. Second Lord (Shuttle) executes designs. Third Lord (Spool) oversees personnel and placement. Fourth Lord (Spindle) is responsible for planning and training. Fifth Lord (Scissors) renders discipline. The badge of a Lord or Lady is a Threaded Needle. Regimentals are white.

Lusine and *Lusir* the Twins, Saints. Patrons of Innocents, Children, Shepherds. Sigils: Bow (Lusine), Shepherd's Crook (Lusir).

Mage Academy. School for Mage Guardians in Ambrai.

Mageborn. Persons who inherit magic. Except in rare cases, onset of magic comes with puberty and can be dangerous to mental and/or physical health.

Mage Captal. Originally selected in trial by magical combat, in more recent times chosen by Senior Mages; the living repository of all Magelore.

Mage Globe. Controlled fire of varying size according to the power and wishes of the user; the first magic taught Novices to judge strength and teach discipline. Scholars and Healers use Globes for simple illumination and as magical notebooks. Among Warriors, they are a challenge to combat; Mageborns fight with Globes as well as with swords. Color indicates training, sometimes power, and often emotional state. A Senior Mage's Globe is nearly white.

Mage Guardians. Founded by Amaryllis Flynn. Forbidden to hold government office of any kind.

Organization:

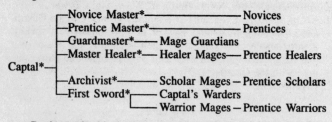

Regimentals: black clothes and cloak, silver collar pins, sash of office.

Captal—emblems are Sparrow (for St. Rilla) and Candle (for St. Miryenne), silver sash; presides over Council of Senior Mages*.

Novice Master—two Sparrows, black-and-silver sash.

Prentice Master—Sparrow and Candle, black-and-silver sash.

Guardmaster—Candle and Sparrow, black-and-silver sash.

Master Healer—Herb Sprig and Candle, green-and-silver sash.

Archivist—Mage Globe and Candle, gray-and-silver sash; responsible for the Library and the Lists (official record of all Mage Guardians).

First Sword—Sword and Candle, red-and-silver sash; commander of Captal's Warders.

Captal's Warders—Sword and Candle, red-and-black sash; elite corps of 50 Warriors whose sole duty is to protect the Captal.

Magic, Rules of. First: Harm nothing. Second (according to Gorynel Desse): Be subtle.

Maidil the Betrayer, Saint. Patron of New Lovers, Fools. Sigil: Mask.

Maurget Quickfingers, Saint. Patron of Jewelers, Gemcutters, Artists, Beggars, Tax Collectors, Politicians. Sigil: Pen and Purse.

Miramili the Summoner, Saint. Patron of Bells, Weddings. Sigil: Miramili's Bells.

Miryenne the Guardian, Saint. Patron of Light, Candles, Magic, Mage Guardians. Sigil: Lighted Candle.

Mittru Bluehair, Saint. Patron of Rivers. Sigil: Sheaf of Reeds.

Money. Decimal coinage system.

    10 copper cutpieces = 1 silver eagle

    100 copper cutpieces = 10 silver eagles = 1 gold eagle

    1000 copper cutpieces = 100 silver eagles = 10 gold eagles

Niya the Seamstress, Saint. Patron of Tailors. Sigil: Scissors. Removed from official calendar.

Pierga Cleverhand, Saint. Patron of Thieves, Condemned Prisoners, Divorced Husbands. Sigil: Broken Lock.

Rilla the Guide, Saint. Patron of Travelers, Coachmen, the Blind, Mage Guardians. Sigil: White Sparrow.

Ryka. Island province.

Ryka Court. Capital of Lenfell.

Ryka Legion. Elite corps of 500 Council Guards under direct command of First Councillor.

Saints. Of the 386 Saints in Lenfell's hagiography—one for each day of the year—34 are celebrated in the Calendar *(q.v.)*. Their origins are more legend than fact, and most of the legends have been forgotten but for a tradition of patronage. Three examples illustrate.

Pierga Cleverhand is a creation of the lightfingered, who, on capture, cried "Pierga protect me!" to warn colleagues. A "life" was invented for her, embroidered as whimsy or inspiration dictated; not the most noble in the Calendar, but certainly among the most colorful. Her sigil is a Broken Lock. The reason for her patronage of divorced husbands is unknown.

Delilah was a Warrior Mage of ca. 375–445 who earned her title "The Dancer" by her grace at swordplay. Her patronage includes athletes, soldiers, and, to the amusement of Mage Guardians, the needle (she never set finger to one in her life). Her feast is celebrated with sword dances and gifts of iron or steel. Her sigils are Crossed Swords or Crossed Needles.

The origin of Lirance Cloudchaser and the symbolism of her Tower have been completely forgotten.

Nine Saints in the Calendar are male: Agvir, Chevasto, Garony, Geridon, Gorynel, Kiy, Lusir, Tamas, and Telomar.

Personal names are always variants on the name of a Saint—as Beth, Lizzy, Bethany, Elise, Ilsa, and Isabel (among dozens) are versions of Elizabeth.

Seinshir. Province of many islands; largest is home to Malerris Castle.

Shellinkroth. Province. Capital: Havenport.

Sheve. Province. Capital: Roseguard.

Sheve Dark. Pine forest stretching across North Lenfell; largely unexplored.

Shonne Dreamdealer, Saint. Patron of Shrines and Pilgrims. Sigil: Triangle. Removed from official calendar.

Sirrala the Virgin, Saint. Patron of Flowers, Gemstones, Virgin Girls. Sigil: Flower Crown.

Steen Swordsworn, Saint. Patron of Male Warriors. Sigil: Leather Gauntlet. Removed from official calendar.

Tamas the Mapmaker, Saint. Patron of Sailors. Sigils: Anchor and Rope; Sextant.

Telomar the Patient, Saint. Patron of Stonemasons and Miners. Sigil: Hammer and Chisel.

Tiers. Categorization of families by incidence of defects (Bloods are "clean") instituted after The Waste War. Names survive only in direct female line. Heraldry designates status: each Name has two colors; Bloods and the First and Second Tiers also use a sigil (in gold for Bloods, silver for Firsts, copper for Seconds).

Tillinshir. Province. Capital: Shainkroth.

Time

Hour: 100 minutes.

Day: 15 hours. Half-Fifth corresponds roughly to 7:30 a.m.; Tenth is about 3:00 p.m.; Thirteenth is around 8:00 p.m.

Week: 10 or 11 days. Begins with each full moon.

Year: 386 days; 36 weeks plus one Wraithenday.

Tirreiz the Canny, Saint. Patron of Merchants, Money, Bankers. Sigil: Coins.

Velenne the Bard, Saint. Patron of Music, Bards, Actors, Poets. Sigil: Lute.

Velireon The Provider, Saint. Patron of the Kitchen, Cooks, Tinkers, Farmers. Sigils: Wheatsheaf, Crossed Spoons.

Venkelos the Judge, Saint. Patron of Death and Dying, the Wraithenday. Sigil: Halved Circle.

Viranka the Gray-Eyed, Saint. Patron of Rain, Water. Sigil: Well.

War, Mageborn. Fought from 481–489 over intentional breeding of Mageborns, ending when it was discovered that in selectively bred children, birth defects appeared at an alarming rate.

War of the Tiers. Planetwide conflict over inequities in societal classifications fought from 306–312. The Tier system remained intact.

War, The Waste. Military and magical conflict between Lords of Malerris and Mage Guardians over establishment of a thaumatocracy. Immediate cause was the near-simultaneous assassinations of Guardmaster and Third Lord of Malerris; the assassins were never identified. Though fought in many Shirs, the final magical onslaught was in The Waste, which gave its name to the whole war. Casualties among the Malerrisi reached 81%; among Mage Guardians, 68%; among the general population, 51%. Worldwide magical pollution spread by wind and water caused high rates of infertility, miscarriage, stillbirth, infant mortality, and birth defects for many Generations. Widespread societal upheaval and near-total anarchy in some areas resulted in the Lost Age (60–70 years) before the First Census.

Waste, The. Province. Capital: Renig.

Web. A family's holdings of property and mercantile interests. In most cases each branch's First Daughter oversees a small Web that may or may not link into her Name's larger Web. Some are planet-wide; most are regional.

Wraith. A dead person's spirit. Some Wraiths keep politely to themselves. Some visit the living for the usual ghostly reasons: assistance, mischief, vengeance, malevolence, or simple yearning to be with those loved in life. They are said to congregate in the Wraithenwood, but have been known to appear wherever they please. Folklore has it that particularly angry Wraiths dwell in the Dead White Forest, a portion of the Wraithen Mountains destroyed in The Waste War.

Wraithenbeast. Magical creature unleashed by the Wild Magic of The Waste War. Although incorporeal, Wraithenbeasts are so terrifying that mere sight of one is lethal. Varieties are limited only by the imagination of their long-dead creators. They are uniformly hideous.

Wraithenbeast Incursion. The first occurred in 448–458, the second in 513–518. Monsters emerged to terrorize North Lenfell and were driven back only by Mageborns—in the former instance, by Mage Guardians and Lords of Malerris working together, but in the latter by Guardians alone.

Wraithen Mountains. Domain of Wraithenbeasts.

Wraithenwood. Domain of Wraiths.

CALENDAR OF SAINTS

Week		
1	First Moon	Lirance Cloudchaser
2	Shepherds Moon	Lusine and Lusir the Twins
3	Lady Moon	Gelenis First Daughter
4	Ilsevet's Moon	Ilsevet Waterborn
5	Spring Moon	*Equinox*
6	Seeker's Moon	Alilen the Seeker
7	Lovers Moon	Imili the Joyous
8	Green Bells	Miramili the Summoner
9	First Flowers	Sirrala the Virgin
10	Thieves Moon	Pierga Cleverhand
11	Hearthfire	Velireon the Provider
12	Maiden Moon	Maidil the Betrayer
13	Ascension	Deiket Snowhair
14	Midsummer Moon	*Solstice*
15	Healers Moon	Feleris the Healer
16	Long Sun	Mittru Bluehair
17	Allflower	Jeymian Gentlehand
18	Sailors Moon	Tamas the Mapmaker
19	Rosebloom	Geridon the Stallion
20	Hunt	Fielto the Finder
21	Drygrass	Garony the Righteous
22	Wildfire	Caitiri the Fiery-Eyed
23	Autumn Moon	*Equinox*
24	Applefall	Agvir the Silent
25	Harvest	Kiy the Forgetful
26	Wolfkill	Delilah the Dancer
27	Water Moon	Viranka the Gray-Eyed
28	First Frost	Tirreiz the Canny
29	Diamond Mirror	Maurget Quickfingers
30	Snow Sparrow	Rilla the Guide
31	Candleweek	Miryenne the Guardian
32	Midwinter Moon	*Solstice*
33	Nettle-and-Thorn	Gorynel the Compassionate
34	Neversun	Velenne the Bard
35	Weavers Moon	Chevasto the Weaver
36	Last Moon	Telomar the Patient
—	Wraithenday	Venkelos the Judge

HOW TO SAY IT
(a guide for purists)

Vowels

<u>a</u>	as in *cat* (Dalakard, Affe)
<u>ai; ay; ei;</u> <u>ey</u>	as in *bay* (Cailet; Trayos; Feiran; Neyos)
<u>au</u>	as in *laurel* (Auvry, Maurgen)
<u>e</u>	as in *seven* (Gelenis); exception is Stene as in *theme*
<u>i</u>	as in *tin* (Ilsevet); sometimes as in *magazine* (Caitiri, Rosvenir, Falundir, Miryenne); sometimes as in *while* (Alilen, Delilah)
<u>ia</u>	as in *median* (Jeymian, Garvedian)
<u>ie</u>	as in *sentries* (Pierga); exceptions are Dalien (Dal-ee-en) and Fielto (Fee-el-toe)
<u>o</u>	usually as in *more* (Gorynel); sometimes as in *bonny* (Garony, Geridon); as an ending is always long (see Fielto above)
<u>u</u>	as in *furnace* (Dombur); sometimes as in *usual* (Mittru)
<u>y</u>	usually as in *tin* (Gorynel); sometimes as in *navy* (Garony, Miryenne)

Further helpful hints

   g is always hard, as in *get*

   shir—as in *shirred* eggs

   Kiy is one syllable, rhymes with *eye*

   All double-consonant names (Affe, Desse, Witte, etc.) are single-syllable except for Bekke, Vedde, and Vekke, which add a final long *e* (Bek-ee).

AUTHOR'S NOTE

The real Double Spiral Stair, designed by Leonardo da Vinci for Francois I, can be found at the remarkable chateau of Chambord in the Loire Valley, France.

Some of you will have noticed that I named a starship after my grandmother. When she was seven years old, her family relocated from Missouri to Colorado—by covered wagon. It seemed appropriate to give her name to a pioneers' starship. . . .

The second volume of *Exiles* is called *The Mageborn Traitor* and will be followed by the concluding book, *The Captal's Tower.*

Melanie Rawn